EVERYMAN'S LIBRARY

EVERYMAN,
I WILL GO WITH THEE,
AND BE THY GUIDE,
IN THY MOST NEED
TO GO BY THY SIDE

CORMAC McCARTHY

The Border Trilogy

All the Pretty Horses
The Crossing
Cities of the Plain

EVERYMAN'S LIBRARY
Alfred A. Knopf New York Toronto
261

THIS IS A BORZOI BOOK

PUBLISHED BY ALFRED A. KNOPF, INC.

The Border Trilogy first published as a single volume in
Everyman's Library, 1999. Individual volumes first published by
Alfred A. Knopf, Inc.

Typography by Peter A. Andersen

Second printing

A portion of *The Crossing* was originally published in *Esquire*.
A limited signed edition of *Cities of the Plain* has been published
by B. E. Trice Publishing, New Orleans

ISBN 0-375-40793-6
LC 99-36551

Library of Congress Cataloging-in-Publication Data
McCarthy, Cormac, 1933–
The border trilogy / Cormac McCarthy,
    p.   cm.—(Everyman's library)
Contents: All the pretty horses – The crossing – Cities of the plain.
ISBN 0-375-40793-6 (alk. paper)
1. Ranch life–New Mexico–Hidalgo County Fiction. 2. Human-animal
relationships–New Mexico–Hidalgo County Fiction. 3. Wilderness
areas–New Mexico–Hidalgo County Fiction. 4. Wolves–New
Mexico–Hidalgo County Fiction. 5. Boys–New Mexico–Hidalgo County
Fiction. 6. Adventure stories, American. 7. Historical fiction, American.
8. Hidalgo County (N.M.) Fiction. 9. Texas Fiction. I. Title.
PS3563.C337B67   1999   99-36551
813'.54–dc21   CIP

Book Design by Barbara de Wilde and Carol Devine Carson

Printed and bound in Germany
by GGP Media, Pössneck

THE BORDER TRILOGY

ALL THE
PRETTY
HORSES

I

THE CANDLEFLAME and the image of the candleflame caught in the pierglass twisted and righted when he entered the hall and again when he shut the door. He took off his hat and came slowly forward. The floorboards creaked under his boots. In his black suit he stood in the dark glass where the lilies leaned so palely from their waisted cutglass vase. Along the cold hallway behind him hung the portraits of forebears only dimly known to him all framed in glass and dimly lit above the narrow wainscotting. He looked down at the guttered candlestub. He pressed his thumbprint in the warm wax pooled on the oak veneer. Lastly he looked at the face so caved and drawn among the folds of funeral cloth, the yellowed moustache, the eyelids paper thin. That was not sleeping. That was not sleeping.

It was dark outside and cold and no wind. In the distance a calf bawled. He stood with his hat in his hand. You never combed your hair that way in your life, he said.

Inside the house there was no sound save the ticking of the mantel clock in the front room. He went out and shut the door.

Dark and cold and no wind and a thin gray reef beginning along the eastern rim of the world. He walked out on the prairie and stood holding his hat like some supplicant to the darkness over them all and he stood there for a long time.

As he turned to go he heard the train. He stopped and waited for it. He could feel it under his feet. It came boring out of the east like some ribald satellite of the coming sun howling and bellowing in the distance and the long light of the headlamp running through the tangled mesquite brakes and creating out of the night the endless fenceline down the dead straight right of way and sucking it back again wire and post mile on mile into the darkness after where the boilersmoke disbanded slowly along the faint new horizon and the sound came lagging and he stood still holding his hat in his hands in the passing ground-shudder watching it till it was gone. Then he turned and went back to the house.

She looked up from the stove when he came in and looked him up and down in his suit. Buenos días, guapo, she said.

He hung the hat on a peg by the door among slickers and blanketcoats and odd pieces of tack and came to the stove and got his coffee and took it to the table. She opened the oven and drew out a pan of sweetrolls she'd made and put one on a plate and brought it over and set it in front of him together with a knife for the butter and she touched the back of his head with her hand before she returned to the stove.

I appreciate you lightin the candle, he said.

Cómo?

La candela. La vela.

No fui yo, she said.

La señora?

Claro.

Ya se levantó?

Antes que yo.

He drank the coffee. It was just grainy light outside and Arturo was coming up toward the house.

HE SAW his father at the funeral. Standing by himself across the little gravel path near the fence. Once he went out to the street to his car. Then he came back. A norther had blown in about midmorning and there were spits of snow in the air with blowing dust and the women sat holding on to their hats. They'd put an awning up over the gravesite but the weather was all sideways and it did no good. The canvas rattled and flapped and the preacher's words were lost in the wind. When it was over and the mourners rose to go the canvas chairs they'd been sitting on raced away tumbling among the tombstones.

In the evening he saddled his horse and rode out west from the house. The wind was much abated and it was very cold and the sun sat blood red and elliptic under the reefs of bloodred cloud before him. He rode where he would always choose to ride, out where the western fork of the old Comanche road coming down out of the Kiowa country to the north passed through the westernmost section of the ranch and you could see the faint trace of it bearing south over the low prairie that lay between the north and middle forks of the Concho River. At the hour he'd always choose when the shadows were long and the ancient road was shaped before him in the rose and canted light like a dream of the past where the painted ponies and the riders of that lost nation came down out of the north with their faces chalked and their long hair plaited and each armed for war which was their life and the women and children and women with children at their breasts all of them pledged in blood and redeemable in blood only. When the wind was in the north you could hear them, the horses and the breath of the horses and the horses' hooves that were shod in rawhide and the rattle of lances and the constant drag of the travois poles in the sand like the passing of some enormous serpent and the young boys naked on wild horses jaunty as circus riders and hazing wild horses before them and the dogs trotting with their tongues aloll and foot-slaves following half naked and sorely burdened and above all the low chant of their traveling song which the riders sang as they rode, nation and ghost of nation passing in a soft chorale across that mineral waste to darkness bearing lost to all history and all remembrance like a grail the sum of their secular and transitory and violent lives.

He rode with the sun coppering his face and the red wind blowing out of the west. He turned south along the old war trail and he rode out to the crest of a low rise and dismounted and dropped the reins and walked out and stood like a man come to the end of something.

There was an old horseskull in the brush and he squatted and picked it up and turned it in his hands. Frail and brittle. Bleached paper white. He squatted in the long light holding it, the comicbook teeth loose in their sockets. The joints in the cranium like a ragged welding of the bone plates. The muted run of sand in the brainbox when he turned it.

What he loved in horses was what he loved in men, the blood and the heat of the blood that ran them. All his reverence and all his fondness and all the leanings of his life were for the ardenthearted and they would always be so and never be otherwise.

He rode back in the dark. The horse quickened its step. The last of the day's light fanned slowly upon the plain behind him and withdrew again down the edges of the world in a cooling blue of shadow and dusk and chill and a few last chitterings of birds sequestered in the dark and wiry brush. He crossed the old trace again and he must turn the pony up onto the plain and homeward but the warriors would ride on in that darkness they'd become, rattling past with their stone-age tools of war in default of all substance and singing softly in blood and longing south across the plains to Mexico.

THE HOUSE was built in eighteen seventy-two. Seventy-seven years later his grandfather was still the first man to die in it. What others had lain in state in that hallway had been carried there on a gate or wrapped in a wagonsheet or delivered crated up in a raw pineboard box with a teamster standing at the door with a bill of lading. The ones that came at all. For the most part they were dead by rumor. A yellowed scrap of newsprint. A letter. A telegram. The original ranch was twenty-three hundred acres out of the old Meusebach survey of the Fisher-Miller grant, the original house a oneroom hovel of sticks and wattle. That was in eighteen sixty-six. In that same year the first cattle were driven through what was still Bexar County and across the north end of the ranch and on to Fort Sumner and Denver. Five years later his great-grandfather sent six hundred steers over that same trail and with the money he built the house and by then the ranch was already eighteen thousand acres. In eighteen eighty-three they ran the first barbed wire. By eighty-six the buffalo were gone. That same winter a bad die-up. In eighty-nine Fort Concho was disbanded.

His grandfather was the oldest of eight boys and the only one to live past the age of twenty-five. They were drowned, shot, kicked by horses. They perished in fires. They seemed to fear only dying in bed. The last two were killed in Puerto Rico in eighteen ninety-eight and in that year he married and brought his bride home to the ranch and he must have walked out and stood looking at his holdings and reflected long upon the ways of God and the laws of primogeniture. Twelve years later when his wife was carried off in the influenza epidemic they still had no children. A year later he married his dead wife's older sister and a year after this the boy's mother was born and that was all the borning that there was. The Grady name was buried with that old man the day the norther blew the lawnchairs over the dead cemetery grass. The boy's name was Cole. John Grady Cole.

He met his father in the lobby of the St Angelus and they walked up Chadbourne Street to the Eagle Cafe and sat in a booth at the back. Some at the tables stopped talking when they came in. A few men nodded to his father and one said his name.

The waitress called everybody doll. She took their order and flirted with him. His father took out his cigarettes and lit one and put the pack on the table and put his Third Infantry Zippo lighter on top of it and leaned back and smoked and looked at him. He told him his uncle Ed Alison had gone up to the preacher after the funeral was said and shook his hand, the two of them standing there holding onto their hats and leaning thirty degrees into the wind like vaudeville comics while the canvas flapped and raged about them and the funeral attendants raced over the grounds after the lawnchairs, and he'd leaned into the preacher's face and screamed at him that it was a good thing they'd held the burial that morning because the way it was making up this thing could turn off into a real blow before the day was out.

His father laughed silently. Then he fell to coughing. He took a drink of water and sat smoking and shaking his head.

Buddy when he come back from up in the panhandle told me one time it quit blowin up there and all the chickens fell over.

The waitress brought their coffee. Here you go, doll, she said. I'll have your all's orders up in just a minute.

She's gone to San Antonio, the boy said.

Dont call her she.

Mama.

I know it.

They drank their coffee.

What do you aim to do?

About what?

About anything.

She can go where she wants to.

The boy watched him. You aint got no business smokin them things, he said.

His father pursed his lips and drummed his fingers on the table and looked up. When I come around askin you what I'm supposed to do you'll know you're big enough to tell me, he said.

Yessir.

You need any money?

No.

He watched the boy. You'll be all right, he said.

The waitress brought their dinner, thick china lunchplates with steak and gravy and potatoes and beans.

I'll get your all's bread.

His father tucked his napkin into his shirt.

It aint me I was worried about, the boy said. Can I say that?

His father took up his knife and cut into the steak. Yeah, he said. You can say that.

The waitress brought the basket of rolls and set it on the table and went away. They ate. His father didn't eat much. After a while he pushed the plate back with his thumb and reached and got another cigarette and tapped it against the lighter and put it in his mouth and lit it.

You can say whatever's on your mind. Hell. You can bitch at me about smokin if you want.

The boy didnt answer.

You know it aint what I wanted dont you?

Yeah. I know that.

You lookin after Rosco good?

He aint been rode.

Why dont we go Saturday.

All right.

You dont have to if you got somethin else to do.

I aint got nothin else to do.

His father smoked, he watched him.

You dont have to if you dont want to, he said.

I want to.

Can you and Arturo load and pick me up in town?

Yeah.

What time?

What time'll you be up?

I'll get up.

We'll be there at eight.

I'll be up.

The boy nodded. He ate. His father looked around. I wonder who you need to see in this place to get some coffee, he said.

HE AND RAWLINS had unsaddled the horses and turned them out in the dark and they were lying on the saddleblankets and using the saddles for pillows. The night was cold and clear and the sparks rising from the fire raced hot and red among the stars. They could hear the trucks out on the highway and they could see the lights of the town reflected off the desert fifteen miles to the north.

What do you aim to do? Rawlins said.

I dont know. Nothin.

I dont know what you expect. Him two years oldern you. Got his own car and everthing.

There aint nothin to him. Never was.

What did she say?

She didnt say nothin. What would she say? There aint nothin to say.

Well I dont know what you expect.

I dont expect nothin.

Are you goin on Saturday?

No.

Rawlins took a cigarette out of his shirtpocket and sat up and took a coal from the fire and lit the cigarette. He sat smoking. I wouldnt let her get the best of me, he said.

He tipped the ash from the end of the cigarette against the heel of his boot.

She aint worth it. None of em are.

He didnt answer for a while. Then he said: Yes they are.

When he got back he rubbed down the horse and put him up and walked up to the house to the kitchen. Luisa had gone to bed and the house was quiet. He put his hand on the coffeepot to test it and he took down a cup and poured it and walked out and up the hallway.

He entered his grandfather's office and went to the desk and turned on the lamp and sat down in the old oak swivelchair. On the desk was a small brass calendar mounted on swivels that changed dates when you tipped it over in its stand. It still said September 13th. An ashtray. A glass paperweight. A blotter that said Palmer Feed and Supply. His mother's highschool graduation picture in a small silver frame.

The room smelled of old cigarsmoke. He leaned and turned

off the little brass lamp and sat in the dark. Through the front window he could see the starlit prairie falling away to the north. The black crosses of the old telegraph poles yoked across the constellations passing east to west. His grandfather said the Comanche would cut the wires and splice them back with horsehair. He leaned back and crossed his boots on the desktop. Dry lightning to the north, forty miles distant. The clock struck eleven in the front room across the hall.

She came down the stairs and stood in the office doorway and turned on the wall switch light. She was in her robe and she stood with her arms cradled against her, her elbows in her palms. He looked at her and looked out the window again.

What are you doing? she said.

Settin.

She stood there in her robe for a long time. Then she turned and went back down the hall and up the stairs again. When he heard her door close he got up and turned off the light.

There were a few last warm days yet and in the afternoon sometimes he and his father would sit in the hotel room in the white wicker furniture with the window open and the thin crocheted curtains blowing into the room and they'd drink coffee and his father would pour a little whiskey in his own cup and sit sipping it and smoking and looking down at the street. There were oilfield scouts' cars parked along the street that looked like they'd been in a warzone.

If you had the money would you buy it? the boy said.

I had the money and I didnt.

You mean your backpay from the army?

No. Since then.

What's the most you ever won?

You dont need to know. Learn bad habits.

Why dont I bring the chessboard up some afternoon?

I aint got the patience to play.

You got the patience to play poker.

That's different.

What's different about it?

Money is what's different about it.

They sat.

There's still a lot of money in the ground out there, his father said. Number one I C Clark that come in last year was a big well.

He sipped his coffee. He reached and got his cigarettes off the table and lit one and looked at the boy and looked down at the street again. After a while he said:

I won twenty-six thousand dollars in twenty-two hours of play. There was four thousand dollars in the last pot, three of us in. Two boys from Houston. I won the hand with three natural queens.

He turned and looked at the boy. The boy sat with the cup in front of him halfway to his mouth. He turned and looked back out the window. I dont have a dime of it, he said.

What do you think I should do?

I dont think there's much you can do.

Will you talk to her?

I caint talk to her.

You could talk to her.

Last conversation we had was in San Diego California in nineteen forty-two. It aint her fault. I aint the same as I was. I'd like to think I am. But I aint.

You are inside. Inside you are.

His father coughed. He drank from his cup. Inside, he said.

They sat for a long time.

She's in a play or somethin over there.

Yeah. I know.

The boy reached and got his hat off the floor and put it on his knee. I better get back, he said.

You know I thought the world of that old man, dont you?

The boy looked out the window. Yeah, he said.

Dont go to cryin on me now.

I aint.

Well dont.

He never give up, the boy said. He was the one told me not

to. He said let's not have a funeral till we got somethin to bury, if it aint nothin but his dogtags. They were fixin to give your clothes away.

His father smiled. They might as well of, he said. Only thing fit me was the boots.

He always thought you all would get back together.

Yeah, I know he did.

The boy stood and put on his hat. I better get on back, he said.

He used to get in fights over her. Even as a old man. Anybody said anything about her. If he heard about it. It wasnt even dignified.

I better get on.

Well.

He unpropped his feet from the windowsill. I'll walk down with you. I need to get the paper.

They stood in the tiled lobby while his father scanned the headlines.

How can Shirley Temple be getting divorced? he said.

He looked up. Early winter twilight in the streets. I might just get a haircut, he said.

He looked at the boy.

I know how you feel. I felt the same way.

The boy nodded. His father looked at the paper again and folded it.

The Good Book says that the meek shall inherit the earth and I expect that's probably the truth. I aint no freethinker, but I'll tell you what. I'm a long way from bein convinced that it's all that good a thing.

He looked at the boy. He took his key out of his coatpocket and handed it to him.

Go on back up there. There's somethin belongs to you in the closet.

The boy took the key. What is it? he said.

Just somethin I got for you. I was goin to give it to you at Christmas but I'm tired of walkin over it.

Yessir.

Anyway you look like you could use some cheerin up. Just leave the key at the desk when you come down.

Yessir.

I'll see you.

All right.

He rode back up in the elevator and walked down the hall and put the key in the door and walked in and went to the closet and opened it. Standing on the floor along with two pairs of boots and a pile of dirty shirts was a brand new Hamley Formfitter saddle. He picked it up by the horn and shut the closet door and carried it to the bed and swung it up and stood looking at it.

Hell fire and damnation, he said.

He left the key at the desk and swung out through the doors into the street with the saddle over his shoulder.

He walked down to South Concho Street and swung the saddle down and stood it in front of him. It was just dark and the streetlights had come on. The first vehicle along was a Model A Ford truck and it came skidding quarterwise to a halt on its mechanical brakes and the driver leaned across and rolled down the window part way and boomed at him in a whiskey voice: Throw that hull up in the bed, cowboy, and get in here.

Yessir, he said.

It rained all the following week and cleared. Then it rained again. It beat down without mercy on the hard flat plains. The water was over the highway bridge at Christoval and the road was closed. Floods in San Antonio. In his grandfather's slicker he rode the Alicia pasture where the south fence was standing in water to the top wire. The cattle stood islanded, staring bleakly at the rider. Redbo stood staring bleakly at the cattle. He pressed the horse's flanks between his bootheels. Come on, he said. I dont like it no bettern you do.

He and Luisa and Arturo ate in the kitchen while she was gone. Sometimes at night after supper he'd walk out to the road and catch a ride into town and walk the streets or he'd stand outside the hotel on Beauregard Street and look up at the room on the fourth floor where his father's shape or father's shadow would pass behind the gauzy window curtains and then turn and pass back again like a sheetiron bear in a shooting-gallery only slower, thinner, more agonized.

When she came back they ate in the diningroom again, the two of them at opposite ends of the long walnut table while Luisa made the service. She carried out the last of the dishes and turned at the door.

Algo más, señora?

No, Luisa. Gracias.

Buenas noches, señora.

Buenas noches.

The door closed. The clock ticked. He looked up.

Why couldnt you lease me the ranch?

Lease you the ranch.

Yes.

I thought I said I didnt want to discuss it.

This is a new subject.

No it's not.

I'd give you all the money. You could do whatever you wanted.

All the money. You dont know what you're talking about. There's not any money. This place has barely paid expenses for twenty years. There hasnt been a white person worked here since before the war. Anyway you're sixteen years old, you cant run a ranch.

Yes I can.

You're being ridiculous. You have to go to school.

She put the napkin on the table and pushed back her chair and rose and went out. He pushed away the coffeecup in front of him. He leaned back in the chair. On the wall opposite above the sideboard was an oilpainting of horses. There were half a dozen of them breaking through a pole corral and their manes were long and blowing and their eyes wild. They'd been copied out of a book. They had the long Andalusian nose and the bones of their faces showed Barb blood. You could see the hindquarters of the foremost few, good hindquarters and heavy enough to make a cuttinghorse. As if maybe they had Steeldust in their blood. But nothing else matched and no such horse ever was that he had seen and he'd once asked his grandfather what kind of horses they were and his grandfather looked up from his plate at the painting as if he'd never seen it before and he said those are picturebook horses and went on eating.

HE WENT UP the stairs to the mezzanine and found Franklin's name lettered in an arc across the pebbled glass of the door and took off his hat and turned the knob and went in. The girl looked up from her desk.

I'm here to see Mr Franklin, he said.

Did you have an appointment?

No mam. He knows me.

What's your name?

John Grady Cole.

Just a minute.

She went into the other room. Then she came out and nodded.

He rose and crossed the room.

Come in son, said Franklin.

He walked in.

Set down.

He sat.

When he'd said what he had to say Franklin leaned back and looked out the window. He shook his head. He turned back and folded his hands on the desk in front of him. In the first place, he said, I'm not really at liberty to advise you. It's called conflict of interest. But I think I can tell you that it is her property and she can do whatever she wants with it.

I dont have any sayso.

You're a minor.

What about my father.

Franklin leaned back again. That's a sticky issue, he said.

They aint divorced.

Yes they are.

The boy looked up.

It's a matter of public record so I dont guess it's out of confidence. It was in the paper.

When?

It was made final three weeks ago.

He looked down. Franklin watched him.

It was final before the old man died.

The boy nodded. I see what you're sayin, he said.

It's a sorry piece of business, son. But I think the way it is is the way it's goin to be.

Couldnt you talk to her?

I did talk to her.

What did she say?

It dont matter what she said. She aint goin to change her mind.

He nodded. He sat looking down into his hat.

Son, not everbody thinks that life on a cattle ranch in west Texas is the second best thing to dyin and goin to heaven. She dont want to live out there, that's all. If it was a payin proposition that'd be one thing. But it aint.

It could be.

Well, I dont aim to get in a discussion about that. Anyway, she's a young woman and my guess is she'd like to have a little more social life than what she's had to get used to.

She's thirty-six years old.

The lawyer leaned back. He swiveled slightly in the chair, he tapped his lower lip with his forefinger. It's his own damned fault. He signed ever paper they put in front of him. Never lifted a hand to save himself. Hell, I couldnt tell him. I told him to get a lawyer. Told? I begged him.

Yeah, I know.

Wayne tells me he's quit goin to the doctor.

He nodded. Yeah. Well, I thank you for your time.

I'm sorry not to have better news for you. You damn sure welcome to talk to somebody else.

That's all right.

What are you doin out of school today?

I laid out.

The lawyer nodded. Well, he said. That would explain it.

The boy rose and put on his hat. Thanks, he said.

The lawyer stood.

Some things in this world cant be helped, he said. And I believe this is probably one of em.

Yeah, the boy said.

AFTER CHRISTMAS she was gone all the time. He and Luisa and Arturo sat in the kitchen. Luisa couldnt talk about it without crying so they didnt talk about it. No one had even told her mother, who'd been on the ranch since before the turn of the century. Finally Arturo had to tell her. She listened and nodded and turned away and that was all.

In the morning he was standing by the side of the road at daybreak with a clean shirt and a pair of socks in a leather satchel together with his toothbrush and razor and shavingbrush. The satchel had belonged to his grandfather and the blanketlined duckingcoat he wore had been his father's. The first car that passed stopped for him. He got in and set the satchel on the floor and rubbed his hands together between his knees. The driver leaned across him and tried the door and then pulled the tall gearlever down into first and they set out.

That door dont shut good. Where are you goin?

San Antonio.

Well I'm goin as far as Brady Texas.

I appreciate it.

You a cattlebuyer?

Sir?

The man nodded at the satchel with its straps and brass catches. I said are you a cattlebuyer.

No sir. That's just my suitcase.

I allowed maybe you was a cattlebuyer. How long you been standin out there?

Just a few minutes.

The man pointed to a plastic knob on the dash that glowed a dull orange color. This thing's got a heater in it but it dont put out much. Can you feel it?

Yessir. Feels pretty good to me.

The man nodded at the gray and malignant dawn. He moved his leveled hand slowly before him. You see that? he said.

Yessir.

He shook his head. I despise the wintertime. I never did see what was the use in there even bein one.

He looked at John Grady.

You dont talk much, do you? he said.

Not a whole lot.

That's a good trait to have.

It was about a two hour drive to Brady.

They drove through the town and the man let him out on the other side.

You stay on Eighty-seven when you get to Fredericksburg. Dont get off on Two-ninety you'll wind up in Austin. You hear?

Yessir. I appreciate it.

He shut the door and the man nodded and lifted one hand and the car turned around in the road and went back. The next car by stopped and he climbed in.

How far you goin? the man said.

Snow was falling in the San Saba when they crossed it and snow was falling on the Edwards Plateau and in the Balcones the limestone was white with snow and he sat watching out while the gray flakes flared over the windshield glass in the sweep of the wipers. A translucent slush had begun to form along the edge of the blacktop and there was ice on the bridge over the Pedernales. The green water sliding slowly away past the dark bankside trees. The mesquites by the road so thick with mistletoe they looked like liveoaks. The driver sat hunched up over the wheel whistling silently to himself. They got into San Antonio at three oclock in the afternoon in a driving snowstorm and he climbed out and thanked the man and walked up the street and into the first cafe he came to and sat at the counter and put the satchel on the stool beside him. He took the little paper menu out of the holder and opened it and looked at it and looked at the clock on the back wall. The waitress set a glass of water in front of him.

Is it the same time here as it is in San Angelo? he said.

I knew you was goin to ask me somethin like that, she said. You had that look.

Do you not know?

I never been in San Angelo Texas in my life.

I'd like a cheeseburger and a chocolate milk.

Are you here for the rodeo?

No.

It's the same time, said a man down the counter.

He thanked him.

Same time, the man said. Same time.

She finished writing on her pad and looked up. I wouldnt go by nothin he said.

He walked around town in the snow. It grew dark early. He stood on the Commerce Street bridge and watched the snow vanish in the river. There was snow on the parked cars and the traffic in the street by dark had slowed to nothing, a few cabs or trucks, headlights making slowly through the falling snow and passing in a soft rumble of tires. He checked into the YMCA on Martin Street and paid two dollars for his room and went upstairs. He took off his boots and stood them on the radiator and took off his socks and draped them over the radiator beside the boots and hung up his coat and stretched out on the bed with his hat over his eyes.

At ten till eight he was standing in front of the boxoffice in his clean shirt with his money in his hand. He bought a seat in the balcony third row and paid a dollar twenty-five for it.

I never been here before, he said.

It's a good seat, the girl said.

He thanked her and went in and tendered his ticket to an usher who led him over to the red carpeted stairs and handed him the ticket back. He went up and found his seat and sat waiting with his hat in his lap. The theatre was half empty. When the lights dimmed some of the people in the balcony about him got up and moved forward to seats in front. Then the curtain rose and his mother came through a door onstage and began talking to a woman in a chair.

At the intermission he rose and put on his hat and went down to the lobby and stood in a gilded alcove and rolled a cigarette and stood smoking it with one boot jacked back against the wall behind him. He was not unaware of the glances that drifted his way from the theatregoers. He'd turned up one leg of his jeans into a small cuff and from time to time he leaned and tipped into this receptacle the soft white ash of his cigarette. He saw a few men in boots and hats and he nodded gravely to them, they to him. After a while the lights in the lobby dimmed again.

He sat leaning forward in the seat with his elbows on the empty seatback in front of him and his chin on his forearms and he watched the play with great intensity. He'd the notion that there would be something in the story itself to tell him about the way the world was or was becoming but there was not. There was nothing in it at all. When the lights came up there was applause and his mother came forward several times and all the cast assembled across the stage and held hands and bowed and then the curtain closed for good and the audience rose and made their way up the aisles. He sat for a long time in the empty theatre and then he stood and put on his hat and went out into the cold.

When he set out in the morning to get his breakfast it was still dark and the temperature stood at zero. There was half a foot of snow on the ground in Travis Park. The only cafe open was a Mexican one and he ordered huevos rancheros and coffee and sat looking through the paper. He thought there'd be something in the paper about his mother but there wasnt. He was the only customer in the cafe. The waitress was a young girl and she watched him. When she set the platter down he put the paper aside and pushed his cup forward.

Más cafe? she said.

Sí por favor.

She brought the coffee. Hace mucho frío, she said.

Bastante.

He walked up Broadway with his hands in his coatpockets and his collar turned up against the wind. He walked into the lobby of the Menger Hotel and sat in one of the lounge chairs and crossed one boot over the other and opened the paper.

She came through the lobby about nine oclock. She was on the arm of a man in a suit and a topcoat and they went out the door and got into a cab.

He sat there for a long time. After a while he got up and folded the paper and went to the desk. The clerk looked up at him.

Have you got a Mrs Cole registered? he said.

Cole?

Yes.

Just a minute.

The clerk turned away and checked the registrations. He shook his head. No, he said. No Cole.

Thanks, he said.

THEY RODE TOGETHER a last time on a day in early March when the weather had already warmed and yellow mexicanhat bloomed by the roadside. They unloaded the horses at McCullough's and rode up through the middle pasture along Grape Creek and into the low hills. The creek was clear and green with trailing moss braided over the gravel bars. They rode slowly up through the open country among scrub mesquite and nopal. They crossed from Tom Green County into Coke County. They crossed the old Schoonover road and they rode up through broken hills dotted with cedar where the ground was cobbled with traprock and they could see snow on the thin blue ranges a hundred miles to the north. They scarcely spoke all day. His father rode sitting forward slightly in the saddle, holding the reins in one hand about two inches above the saddlehorn. So thin and frail, lost in his clothes. Looking over the country with those sunken eyes as if the world out there had been altered or made suspect by what he'd seen of it elsewhere. As if he might never see it right again. Or worse did see it right at last. See it as it had always been, would forever be. The boy who rode on slightly before him sat a horse not only as if he'd been born to it which he was but as if were he begot by malice or mischance into some queer land where horses never were he would have found them anyway. Would have known that there was something missing for the world to be right or he right in it and would have set forth to wander wherever it was needed for as long as it took until he came upon one and he would have known that that was what he sought and it would have been.

In the afternoon they passed through the ruins of an old ranch on that stony mesa where there were crippled fenceposts propped among the rocks that carried remnants of a wire not seen in that country for years. An ancient pickethouse. The wreckage of an old wooden windmill fallen among the rocks. They rode on. They walked ducks up out of potholes and in the evening they descended through low rolling hills and across the red clay floodplain into the town of Robert Lee.

They waited until the road was clear before they walked the horses over the board bridge. The river was red with mud. They rode up Commerce Street and turned up Seventh and rode up Austin Street past the bank and dismounted and tied their horses in front of the cafe and went in.

The proprietor came over to take their order. He called them by name. His father looked up from the menu.

Go ahead and order, he said. He wont be here for a hour.

What are you havin?

I think I'll just have some pie and coffee.

What kind of pie you got? the boy said.

The proprietor looked toward the counter.

Go on and get somethin to eat, his father said. I know you're hungry.

They ordered and the proprietor brought their coffee and went back to the counter. His father took a cigarette out of his shirtpocket.

You thought any more about boardin your horse?

Yeah, the boy said. Thought about it.

Wallace might let you feed and swamp out stalls and such as that. Trade it out thataway.

He aint goin to like it.

Who, Wallace?

No. Redbo.

His father smoked. He watched him.

You still seein that Barnett girl?

He shook his head.

She quit you or did you quit her?

I dont know.

That means she quit you.

Yeah.

His father nodded. He smoked. Two horsemen passed outside in the road and they studied them and the animals they rode. His father stirred his coffee a long time. There was nothing to stir because he drank it black. He took the spoon and laid it smoking on the paper napkin and raised the cup and looked at it and drank. He was still looking out the window although there was nothing there to see.

Your mother and me never agreed on a whole lot. She liked horses. I thought that was enough. That's how dumb I was. She was young and I thought she'd outgrow some of the notions she had but she didnt. Maybe they were just notions to me. It wasnt just the war. We were married ten years before the war come along. She left out of here. She was gone from the time you were six months old till you were about three. I know you know somethin about that and it was a mistake not to of told you. We separated. She was in California. Luisa looked after you. Her and Abuela.

He looked at the boy and he looked out the window again.

She wanted me to go out there, he said.

Why didnt you?

I did. I didnt last long at it.

The boy nodded.

She come back because of you, not me. I guess that's what I wanted to say.

Yessir.

The proprietor brought the boy's dinner and the pie. The boy reached for the salt and pepper. He didnt look up. The proprietor brought the coffeepot and filled their cups and went away. His father stubbed out his cigarette and picked up his fork and stabbed at the pie with it.

She's goin to be around a long longern me. I'd like to see you all make up your differences.

The boy didnt answer.

I wouldnt be here if it wasnt for her. When I was in Goshee I'd talk to her by the hour. I made her out to be like somebody who could do anything. I'd tell her about some of the other old boys that I didnt think was goin to make it and I'd ask her to look after them and to pray for them. Some of them did make it too. I guess I was a little crazy. Part of the time anyway. But if it hadnt of been for her I wouldnt of made it. No way in this world. I never told that to nobody. She dont even know it.

The boy ate. Outside it was growing dark. His father drank coffee. They waited for Arturo to come with the truck. The last thing his father said was that the country would never be the same.

People dont feel safe no more, he said. We're like the Comanches was two hundred years ago. We dont know what's goin to show up here come daylight. We dont even know what color they'll be.

THE NIGHT was almost warm. He and Rawlins lay in the road where they could feel the heat coming off the blacktop against their backs and they watched stars falling down the long black slope of the firmament. In the distance they heard a door slam. A voice called. A coyote that had been yammering somewhere in the hills to the south stopped. Then it began again.

Is that somebody hollerin for you? he said.

Probably, said Rawlins.

They lay spreadeagled on the blacktop like captives waiting some trial at dawn.

You told your old man? said Rawlins.

No.

You goin to?

What would be the point in it?

When do you all have to be out?

Closing's the first of June.

You could wait till then.

What for?

Rawlins propped the heel of one boot atop the toe of the other. As if to pace off the heavens. My daddy run off from home when he was fifteen. Otherwise I'd of been born in Alabama.

You wouldnt of been born at all.

What makes you say that?

Cause your mama's from San Angelo and he never would of met her.

He'd of met somebody.

So would she.

So?

So you wouldnt of been born.

I dont see why you say that. I'd of been born somewheres.

How?

Well why not?

If your mama had a baby with her other husband and your daddy had one with his other wife which one would you be?

I wouldnt be neither of em.

That's right.

Rawlins lay watching the stars. After a while he said: I could still be born. I might look different or somethin. If God wanted me to be born I'd be born.

And if He didnt you wouldnt.

You're makin my goddamn head hurt.

I know it. I'm makin my own.

They lay watching the stars.

So what do you think? he said.

I dont know, said Rawlins.

Well.

I could understand if you was from Alabama you'd have ever reason in the world to run off to Texas. But if you're already in Texas. I don't know. You got a lot more reason for leavin than me.

What the hell reason you got for stayin? You think somebody's goin to die and leave you somethin?

Shit no.

That's good. Cause they aint.

The door slammed. The voice called again.

I better get back, Rawlins said.

He rose and swiped at the seat of his jeans with one hand and put his hat on.

If I dont go will you go anyways?

John Grady sat up and put his hat on. I'm already gone, he said.

HE SAW HER one last time in town. He'd been to Cullen Cole's shop on North Chadbourne to get a broken bridlebit welded and he was coming up Twohig Street when she came out of the

Cactus Drug. He crossed the street but she called to him and he stopped and waited while she came over.

Were you avoiding me? she said.

He looked at her. I guess I didnt have any thoughts about it one way or the other.

She watched him. A person cant help the way they feel, she said.

That's good all the way around, aint it?

I thought we could be friends.

He nodded. It's all right. I aint goin to be around here all that much longer.

Where are you going?

I aint at liberty to say.

Whyever not?

I just aint.

He looked at her. She was studying his face.

What do you think he'd say if he seen you standin here talkin to me?

He's not jealous.

That's good. That's a good trait to have. Save him a lot of aggravation.

What does that mean.

I dont mean nothin. I got to go.

Do you hate me?

No.

You dont like me.

He looked at her. You're wearin me out, girl, he said. What difference does it make? If you got a bad conscience just tell me what you want me to say and I'll say it.

It wouldnt be you saying it. Anyway I dont have a bad conscience. I just thought we could be friends.

He shook his head. It's just talk, Mary Catherine. I got to get on.

What if it is just talk? Everything's talk isnt it?

Not everything.

Are you really leaving San Angelo?

Yeah.

You'll be back.

Maybe.

I dont have any bad feelings against you.

You got no reason to.

She looked off up the street where he was looking but there wasnt much to look at. She turned back and he looked at her eyes but if they were wet it was just the wind. She held out her hand. At first he didnt know what she was doing.

I dont wish you anything but the best, she said.

He took her hand, small in his, familiar. He'd never shaken hands with a woman before. Take care of yourself, she said.

Thank you. I will.

He stood back and touched the brim of his hat and turned and went on up the street. He didnt look back but he could see her in the windows of the Federal Building across the street standing there and she was still standing there when he reached the corner and stepped out of the glass forever.

HE DISMOUNTED and opened the gate and walked the horse through and closed the gate and walked the horse along the fence. He dropped down to see if he could skylight Rawlins but Rawlins wasnt there. He dropped the reins at the fence corner and watched the house. The horse sniffed the air and pushed its nose against his elbow.

That you, bud? Rawlins whispered.

You better hope so.

Rawlins walked the horse down and stood and looked back at the house.

You ready? said John Grady.

Yeah.

They suspect anything?

Naw.

Well let's go.

Hang on a minute. I just piled everthing on top of the horse and walked him out here.

John Grady picked up the reins and swung up into the saddle. Yonder goes a light, he said.

Damn.

You'll be late for your own funeral.

It aint even four yet. You're early.

Well let's go. There goes the barn.

Rawlins was trying to get his soogan tied on behind the saddle. There's a switch in the kitchen, he said. He aint to the barn yet. He might not even be goin out there. He might just be gettin him a glass of milk or somethin.

He might just be loadin a shotgun or somethin.

Rawlins mounted up. You ready? he said.

I been ready.

They rode out along the fenceline and across the open pastureland. The leather creaked in the morning cold. They pushed the horses into a lope. The lights fell away behind them. They rode out on the high prairie where they slowed the horses to a walk and the stars swarmed around them out of the blackness. They heard somewhere in that tenantless night a bell that tolled and ceased where no bell was and they rode out on the round dais of the earth which alone was dark and no light to it and which carried their figures and bore them up into the swarming stars so that they rode not under but among them and they rode at once jaunty and circumspect, like thieves newly loosed in that dark electric, like young thieves in a glowing orchard, loosely jacketed against the cold and ten thousand worlds for the choosing.

BY NOON the day following they'd made some forty miles. Still in country they knew. Crossing the old Mark Fury ranch in the night where they'd dismounted at the crossfences for John Grady to pull the staples with a catspaw and stand on the wires while Rawlins led the horses through and then raise the wires back and beat the staples into the posts and put the catspaw back in his saddlebag and mount up to ride on.

How the hell do they expect a man to ride a horse in this country? said Rawlins.

They dont, said John Grady.

They rode the sun up and ate the sandwiches John Grady had brought from the house and at noon they watered the horses at an old stone stocktank and walked them down a dry creekbed among the tracks of cattle and javelina to a stand of cottonwoods. There were cattle bedded under the trees that rose at their approach and stood looking at them and then moved off.

They lay in the dry chaff under the trees with their coats rolled up under their heads and their hats over their eyes while the horses grazed in the grass along the creekbed.

What did you bring to shoot? said Rawlins.

Just Grandad's old thumb-buster.

Can you hit anything with it?

No.

Rawlins grinned. We done it, didnt we?

Yeah.

You think they'll be huntin us?

What for?

I dont know. Just seems too damn easy in a way.

They could hear the wind and they could hear the sound of the horses cropping.

I'll tell you what, said Rawlins.

Tell me.

I dont give a damn.

John Grady sat up and took his tobacco from his shirtpocket and began making a cigarette. About what? he said.

He wet the cigarette and put it in his mouth and took out his matches and lit the cigarette and blew the match out with the smoke. He turned and looked at Rawlins but Rawlins was asleep.

They rode on again in the late afternoon. By sunset they

could hear trucks on a highway in the distance and in the long cool evening they rode west along a rise from which they could see the headlights on the highway going out and coming back random and periodic in their slow exchange. They came to a ranch road and followed it out to the highway where there was a gate. They sat the horses. They could see no gate on the far side of the highway. They watched the lights of the trucks along the fence both east and west but there was no gate there.

What do you want to do? said Rawlins.

I dont know. I'd like to of got across this thing tonight.

I aint leadin my horse down that highway in the dark.

John Grady leaned and spat. I aint either, he said.

It was growing colder. The wind rattled the gate and the horses stepped uneasily.

What's them lights? said Rawlins.

I'd make it Eldorado.

How far is that do you reckon?

Ten, fifteen miles.

What do you want to do?

They spread their bedrolls in a wash and unsaddled and tied the horses and slept till daybreak. When Rawlins sat up John Grady had already saddled his horse and was strapping on his bedroll. There's a cafe up the road here, he said. Could you eat some breakfast?

Rawlins put on his hat and reached for his boots. You're talkin my language, son.

They led the horses up through a midden of old truckdoors and transmissions and castoff motorparts behind the cafe and they watered them at a metal tank used for locating leaks in innertubes. A Mexican was changing a tire on a truck and John Grady walked over and asked him where the men's room was. He nodded down the side of the building.

He got his shaving things out of his saddlebag and went into the washroom and shaved and washed and brushed his teeth and combed his hair. When he came out the horses were tied to a picnic table under some trees and Rawlins was in the cafe drinking coffee.

He slid into the booth. You ordered? he said.

Waitin on you.

The proprietor came over with another cup of coffee. What'll you boys have? he said.

Go ahead, said Rawlins.

He ordered three eggs with ham and beans and biscuits and Rawlins ordered the same with a sideorder of hotcakes and syrup.

You better load up good.

You watch me, said Rawlins.

They sat with their elbows propped on the table and looked out the window south across the plains to the distant mountains lying folded in their shadows under the morning sun.

That's where we're headed, said Rawlins.

He nodded. They drank their coffee. The man brought their breakfasts on heavy white crockery platters and came back with the coffeepot. Rawlins had peppered his eggs till they were black. He spread butter over the hotcakes.

There's a man likes eggs with his pepper, said the proprietor.

He poured their cups and went back to the kitchen.

You pay attention to your old dad now, Rawlins said. I'll show you how to deal with a unruly breakfast.

Do it, said John Grady.

Might just order the whole thing again.

The store had nothing in the way of feed. They bought a box of dried oatmeal and paid their bill and went out. John Grady cut the paper drum in two with his knife and they poured the oatmeal into a couple of hubcaps and sat on the picnic table and smoked while the horses ate. The Mexican came over to look at the horses. He was not much older than Rawlins.

Where you headed? he said.

Mexico.

What for?

Rawlins looked at John Grady. You think he can be trusted?

Yeah. He looks all right.

We're runnin from the law, Rawlins said.

The Mexican looked them over.

We robbed a bank.

He stood looking at the horses. You aint robbed no bank, he said.

You know that country down there? said Rawlins.

The Mexican shook his head and spat. I never been to Mexico in my life.

When the animals had eaten they saddled them again and led them around to the front of the cafe and down the drive and across the highway. They walked them along the bar ditch to the gate and led them through the gate and closed it. Then they mounted up and rode out the dirt ranch road. They rode it for a mile or so until it veered away to the east and they left it and set out south across the rolling cedar plains.

They reached the Devil's River by midmorning and watered the horses and stretched out in the shade of a stand of black-willow and looked at the map. It was an oilcompany roadmap that Rawlins had picked up at the cafe and he looked at it and he looked south toward the gap in the low hills. There were roads and rivers and towns on the American side of the map as far south as the Rio Grande and beyond that all was white.

It dont show nothin down there, does it? said Rawlins.

No.

You reckon it aint never been mapped?

There's maps. That just aint one of em. I got one in my saddlebag.

Rawlins came back with the map and sat on the ground and traced their route with his finger. He looked up.

What? said John Grady.

There aint shit down there.

They left the river and followed the dry valley to the west. The country was rolling and grassy and the day was cool under the sun.

You'd think there'd be more cattle in this country, Rawlins said.

You'd think so.

They walked doves and quail up out of the grass along the ridges. Now and then a rabbit. Rawlins stepped down and slid his little 25-20 carbine out of the bootleg scabbard he carried it in and walked out along the ridge. John Grady heard him shoot. In a little while he came back with a rabbit and he reholstered the carbine and took out his knife and walked off a ways and squatted and gutted the rabbit. Then he rose and wiped the blade on his trouserleg and folded shut the knife and came over and took his horse and tied the rabbit by its hind legs to his bedroll strap and mounted up again and they went on.

Late afternoon they crossed a road that ran to the south and in the evening they reached Johnson's Run and camped at a pool in the otherwise dry gravel bed of the watercourse and watered the horses and hobbled them and turned them out to graze. They built a fire and skinned out the rabbit and skewered it on a green limb and set it to broil at the edge of the fire. John Grady opened his blackened canvas campbag and took out a small enameled tin coffeepot and went to the creek and filled it. They sat and watched the fire and they watched the thin crescent moon above the black hills to the west.

Rawlins rolled a cigarette and lit it with a coal and lay back against his saddle. I'm goin to tell you somethin.

Tell it.

I could get used to this life.

He drew on the cigarette and held it out to one side and tapped the ash with a delicate motion of his forefinger. It wouldnt take me no time at all.

They rode all day the day following through rolling hill country, the low caprock mesas dotted with cedar, the yuccas in white bloom along the eastfacing slopes. They struck the Pandale road in the evening and turned south and followed the road into town.

Nine buildings including a store and filling station. They

tied their horses in front of the store and went in. They were dusty and Rawlins was unshaven and they smelled of horses and sweat and woodsmoke. Some men sitting in chairs at the back of the store looked up when they entered and then went on talking.

They stood at the meatcase. The woman came from the counter and walked behind the case and took down an apron and pulled a chain that turned on the overhead lightbulb.

You do look like some kind of desperado, John Grady said.

You dont look like no choir director, said Rawlins.

The woman tied the apron behind her and turned to regard them above the white enameled top of the meatcase. What'll you boys have? she said.

They bought baloney and cheese and a loaf of bread and a jar of mayonnaise. They bought a box of crackers and a dozen tins of vienna sausage. They bought a dozen packets of koolaid and a slab end of bacon and some tins of beans and they bought a five pound bag of cornmeal and a bottle of hotsauce. The woman wrapped the meat and cheese separate and she wet a pencil with her tongue and totted up the purchases and then put everything together in a number four grocery bag.

Where you boys from? she said.

From up around San Angelo.

You all ride them horses down here?

Yes mam.

Well I'll declare, she said.

When they woke in the morning they were in plain view of a small adobe house. A woman had come out of the house and slung a pan of dishwater into the yard. She looked at them and went back in again. They'd hung their saddles over a fence to dry and while they were getting them a man came out and stood watching them. They saddled the horses and led them out to the road and mounted up and turned south.

Wonder what all they're doin back home? Rawlins said.

John Grady leaned and spat. Well, he said, probably they're havin the biggest time in the world. Probably struck oil. I'd say they're in town about now pickin out their new cars and all.

Shit, said Rawlins.

They rode.

You ever get ill at ease? said Rawlins.

About what?

I dont know. About anything. Just ill at ease.

Sometimes. If you're someplace you aint supposed to be I guess you'd be ill at ease. Should be anyways.

Well suppose you were ill at ease and didnt know why. Would that mean that you might be someplace you wasnt supposed to be and didnt know it?

What the hell's wrong with you?

I dont know. Nothin. I believe I'll sing.

He did. He sang: Will you miss me, will you miss me. Will you miss me when I'm gone.

You know that Del Rio radio station? he said.

Yeah, I know it.

I've heard it told that at night you can take a fencewire in your teeth and pick it up. Dont even need a radio.

You believe that?

I dont know.

You ever tried it?

Yeah. One time.

They rode on. Rawlins sang. What the hell is a flowery boundary tree? he said.

You got me, cousin.

They passed under a high limestone bluff where a creek ran down and they crossed a broad gravel wash. Upstream were potholes from the recent rains where a pair of herons stood footed to their long shadows. One rose and flew, one stood. An hour later they crossed the Pecos River, putting the horses into the ford, the water swift and clear and partly salt running over the limestone bedrock and the horses studying the water before them and placing their feet with great care on the broad traprock plates and eyeing the shapes of trailing moss in the rips below the ford where they flared and twisted electric green in the morning light. Rawlins leaned from the saddle and wet his hand in the river and tasted it. It's gypwater, he said.

They dismounted among the willows on the far side and made sandwiches with the lunchmeat and cheese and ate and sat smoking and watching the river pass. There's been somebody followin us, John Grady said.

Did you see em?

Not yet.

Somebody horseback?

Yeah.

Rawlins studied the road across the river. Why aint it just somebody ridin?

Cause they'd of showed up at the river by now.

Maybe they turned off.

Where to?

Rawlins smoked. What do you reckon they want?

I dont know.

What do you want to do?

Let's just ride. They'll either show or they wont.

They came up out of the river breaks riding slowly side by side along the dusty road and onto a high plateau where they could see out over the country to the south, rolling country covered with grass and wild daisies. To the west a mile away ran a wire fence strung from pole to pole like a bad suture across the gray grasslands and beyond that a small band of antelope all of whom were watching them. John Grady turned his horse sideways and sat looking back down the road. Rawlins waited.

Is he back there? he said.

Yeah. Somewheres.

They rode till they came to a broad swale or bajada in the plateau. A little off to the right was a stand of closegrown cedar and Rawlins nodded at the cedars and slowed his horse.

Why dont we lay up yonder and wait on him?

John Grady looked back down the road. All right, he said. Let's ride on a ways and then double back. He sees our tracks quit the road here he'll know where we're at.

All right.

They rode on another half mile and then left the road and cut back toward the cedars and dismounted and tied their horses and sat on the ground.

You reckon we got time for a smoke? said Rawlins.

Smoke em if you got em, said John Grady.

They sat smoking and watching the backroad. They waited a long time but nobody came. Rawlins lay back and put his hat over his eyes. I aint sleepin, he said. I'm just restin.

He hadnt been asleep long before John Grady kicked his boot. He sat up and put on his hat and looked. A rider was coming along the road. Even at that distance they both remarked on the horse.

He came along till he was not more than a hundred yards down the road. He had on a broadbrim hat and bib overalls. He slowed the horse and looked down the bajada directly at them. Then he came on again.

It's some kid, Rawlins said.

That's a hell of a horse, said John Grady.

Aint it though.

You think he saw us?

No.

What do you want to do?

Give him a minute and then we'll just ride into the road behind him.

They waited till he was all but out of sight and then they untied the horses and mounted and rode up out of the trees and into the road.

When he heard them he stopped and looked back. He pushed his hat back on his head and sat the horse in the road and watched them. They rode up one at either side.

You huntin us? said Rawlins.

He was a kid about thirteen years old.

No, he said. I aint huntin you.

How come you followin us?

I aint followin you.

Rawlins looked at John Grady. John Grady was watching the kid. He looked off toward the distant mountains and then back at the kid and finally at Rawlins. Rawlins sat with his hands composed upon the pommel of his saddle. You aint been followin us? he said.

I'm goin to Langtry, the kid said. I dont know who you all are.

Rawlins looked at John Grady. John Grady was rolling a smoke and studying the kid and his outfit and his horse.

Where'd you get the horse? he said.

It's my horse.

He put the cigarette in his mouth and took a wooden match from his shirtpocket and popped it with his thumbnail and lit the cigarette. Is that your hat? he said.

The boy looked up at the hatbrim over his eyes. He looked at Rawlins.

How old are you? said John Grady.

Sixteen.

Rawlins spat. You're a lyin sack of green shit.

You dont know everthing.

I know you aint no goddamn sixteen. Where are you comin from?

Pandale.

You seen us in Pandale last night, didnt you?

Yeah.

What'd you do, run off?

He looked from one of them to the other. What if I did?

Rawlins looked at John Grady. What do you want to do?

I dont know.

We could sell that horse in Mexico.

Yeah.

I aint diggin no grave like we done that last one.

Hell, said John Grady, that was your idea. I was the one said just leave him for the buzzards.

You want to flip to see who gets to shoot him?

Yeah. Go ahead.

Call it, said Rawlins.

Heads.

The coin spun in the air. Rawlins caught it and slapped it down on top of his wrist and held his wrist where they could see it and lifted his hand away.

Heads, he said.

Let me have your rifle.

It aint fair, said Rawlins. You shot the last three.

Well go on then. You can owe me.

Well hold his horse. He might not be gunbroke.

You all are just funnin, said the boy.

What makes you so sure?

You aint shot nobody.

What makes you think you wouldnt be somebody good to start with?

You all are just funnin. I knowed you was all along.

Sure you did, said Rawlins.

Who's huntin you? John Grady said.

Nobody.

They're huntin that horse though, aint they?

He didnt answer.

You really headed for Langtry?

Yeah.

You aint ridin with us, said Rawlins. You'll get us thowed in the jailhouse.

It belongs to me, the boy said.

Son, said Rawlins, I dont give a shit who it belongs to. But it damn sure dont belong to you. Let's go bud.

They turned their horses and chucked them up and trotted out along the road south again. They didnt look back.

I thought he'd put up more of a argument, said Rawlins.

John Grady flipped the stub of the cigarette into the road before them. We aint seen the last of his skinny ass.

By noon they'd left the road and were riding southwest through the open grassland. They watered their horses at a steel stocktank under an old F W Axtell windmill that creaked slowly in the wind. To the south there were cattle shaded up in a stand of emory oak. They meant to lay clear of Langtry and they talked about crossing the river at night. The day was warm and they washed out their shirts and put them on wet and mounted up and rode on. They could see the road behind them for several miles back to the northeast but they saw no rider.

That evening they crossed the Southern Pacific tracks just east of Pumpville Texas and made camp a half mile on the far side of the right of way. By the time they had the horses brushed and staked and a fire built it was dark. John Grady stood his saddle upright to the fire and walked out on the prairie and stood listening. He could see the Pumpville watertank against the purple sky. Beside it the horned moon. He could hear the horses cropping grass a hundred yards away. The prairie otherwise lay blue and silent all about.

They crossed highway 90 midmorning of the following day and rode out onto a pastureland dotted with grazing cattle. Far to the south the mountains of Mexico drifted in and out of the uncertain light of a moving cloud-cover like ghosts of mountains. Two hours later they were at the river. They sat on a low bluff and took off their hats and watched it. The water was the color of clay and roily and they could hear it in the rips downstream. The sandbar below them was thickly grown with willow and carrizo cane and the bluffs on the far side were stained and cavepocked and traversed by a constant myriad of swallows. Beyond that the desert rolled as before. They turned and looked at each other and put on their hats.

They rode upriver to where a creek cut in and they rode down the creek and out onto a gravel bar and sat the horses and studied the water and the country about. Rawlins rolled a cigarette and crossed one leg over the pommel of the saddle and sat smoking.

Who is it we're hidin from? he said.

Who aint we?

I dont see where anybody could be hidin over there.

They might say the same thing lookin at this side.

Rawlins sat smoking. He didnt answer.

We can cross right down yonder off of that shoal, John Grady said.

Why dont we do it now?

John Grady leaned and spat into the river. I'll do whatever you want, he said. I thought we agreed to play it safe.

I'd sure like to get it behind me if we're goin to.

I would too pardner. He turned and looked at Rawlins.

Rawlins nodded. All right, he said.

They rode back up the creek and dismounted and unsaddled the horses on the gravel bar and staked them out in the creekside grass. They sat under the shade of the willows and ate vienna sausages and crackers and drank koolaid made from creekwater. You think they got vienna sausages in Mexico? Rawlins said.

Late in the afternoon he walked up the creek and stood on the level prairie with his hat in his hand and looked out across the blowing grass to the northeast. A rider was crossing the plain a mile away. He watched him.

When he got back to the camp he woke up Rawlins.

What is it? said Rawlins.

There's somebody comin. I think it's that gunsel.

Rawlins adjusted his hat and climbed up the bank and stood looking.

Can you make him out? called John Grady.

Rawlins nodded. He leaned and spat.

If I cant make him out I can damn sure make out that horse.

Did he see you?

I dont know.

He's headed this way.

He probably seen me.

I think we ought to run him off.

He looked back at John Grady again. I got a uneasy feelin about that little son of a bitch.

I do too.

He aint as green as he looks, neither.

What's he doin? said John Grady.

Ridin.

Well come on back down. He might not of seen us.

He's stopped, said Rawlins.

What's he doin?

Ridin again.

They waited for him to arrive if he would. It wasnt long before the horses raised their heads and stood staring downstream. They heard the rider come down into the creek bed, a rattling of gravel and a faint chink of metal.

Rawlins got his rifle and they walked out down the creek to the river. The kid was sitting the big bay horse in the shallow water off the gravel bar and looking across the river. When he turned and saw them he pushed his hat back with his thumb.

I knowed you all hadnt crossed, he said. There's two deer feedin along the edge of them mesquite yon side.

Rawlins squatted on the gravel bar and stood the rifle in front of him and held it and rested his chin on the back of his arm. What the hell are we goin to do with you? he said.

The kid looked at him and he looked at John Grady. There wont be nobody huntin me in Mexico.

That all depends on what you done, said Rawlins.

I aint done nothin.

What's your name? said John Grady.

Jimmy Blevins.

Bullshit, said Rawlins. Jimmy Blevins is on the radio.

That's another Jimmy Blevins.

Who's followin you?

Nobody.

How do you know?

Cause there aint.

Rawlins looked at John Grady and he looked at the kid again. You got any grub? he said.

No.

You got any money?

No.

You're just a deadhead.

The kid shrugged. The horse took a step in the water and stopped again.

Rawlins shook his head and spat and looked out across the river. Tell me just one thing.

All right.

What the hell would we want you with us for?

He didnt answer. He sat looking at the sandy water running past them and at the thin wicker shadows of the willows running out over the sandbar in the evening light. He looked out to the blue sierras to the south and he hitched up the shoulder strap of his overalls and sat with his thumb hooked in the bib and turned and looked at them.

Cause I'm an American, he said.

Rawlins turned away and shook his head.

They crossed the river under a white quartermoon naked and pale and thin atop their horses. They'd stuffed their boots upside down into their jeans and stuffed their shirts and jackets after along with their warbags of shaving gear and ammunition and they belted the jeans shut at the waist and tied the legs loosely about their necks and dressed only in their hats they led the horses out onto the gravel spit and loosed the girthstraps and mounted and put the horses into the water with their naked heels.

Midriver the horses were swimming, snorting and stretching their necks out of the water, their tails afloat behind. They quartered downstream with the current, the naked riders leaning forward and talking to the horses, Rawlins holding the rifle aloft in one hand, lined out behind one another and making for the alien shore like a party of marauders.

They rode up out of the river among the willows and rode singlefile upstream through the shallows onto a long gravel beach where they took off their hats and turned and looked back at the country they'd left. No one spoke. Then suddenly they put their horses to a gallop up the beach and turned and came back, fanning with their hats and laughing and pulling up and patting the horses on the shoulder.

Goddamn, said Rawlins. You know where we're at?

They sat the smoking horses in the moonlight and looked at one another. Then quietly they dismounted and unslung their clothes from about their necks and dressed and led the horses up out of the willow breaks and gravel benches and out upon the plain where they mounted and rode south onto the dry scrublands of Coahuila.

They camped at the edge of a mesquite plain and in the morning they cooked bacon and beans and cornbread made from meal and water and they sat eating and looking out at the country.

When'd you eat last? Rawlins said.

The other day, said the Blevins boy.

The other day.

Yeah.

Rawlins studied him. Your name aint Blivet is it?

It's Blevins.

You know what a blivet is?

What.

A blivet is ten pounds of shit in a five pound sack.

Blevins stopped chewing. He was looking out at the country to the west where cattle had come out of the breaks and were standing on the plain in the morning sun. Then he went on chewing again.

You aint said what your all's names was, he said.

You aint never asked.

That aint how I was raised, said Blevins.

Rawlins stared at him bleakly and turned away.

John Grady Cole, said John Grady. This here is Lacey Rawlins.

The kid nodded. He went on chewing.

We're from up around San Angelo, said John Grady.

I aint never been up there.

They waited for him to say where he was from but he didnt say.

Rawlins swabbed out his plate with a crumbly handful of the

cornbread and ate it. Suppose, he said, that we wanted to trade that horse off for one less likely to get us shot.

The kid looked at John Grady and looked back out to where the cattle were standing. I aint tradin horses, he said.

You dont care for us to have to look out for you though, do you?

I can look out for myself.

Sure you can. I guess you got a gun and all.

He didnt answer for a minute. Then he said: I got a gun.

Rawlins looked up. Then he went on spooning up the cornbread. What kind of a gun? he said.

Thirty-two twenty Colt.

Bullshit, said Rawlins. That's a rifle cartridge.

The kid had finished eating and sat swabbing out his plate with a twist of grass.

Let's see it, said Rawlins.

He set the plate down. He looked at Rawlins and then he looked at John Grady. Then he reached into the bib of his overalls and came out with the pistol. He rolled it in his hand with a forward flip and handed it toward Rawlins butt-first upside down.

Rawlins looked at him and looked at the pistol. He set his plate down in the grass and took the gun and turned it in his hand. It was an old Colt Bisley with guttapercha grips worn smooth of their checkering. The metal was a dull gray. He turned it so as to read the script on top of the barrel. It said 32-20. He looked at the kid and flipped open the gate with his thumb and put the hammer at halfcock and turned the cylinder and ran one of the shells into his palm with the ejector rod and looked at it. Then he put it back and closed the gate and let the hammer back down.

Where'd you get a gun like this? he said.

At the gittin place.

You ever shot it?

Yeah, I shot it.

Can you hit anything with it?

The kid held out his hand for the pistol. Rawlins hefted it in his palm and turned it and passed it to him.

You want to throw somethin up I'll hit it, the kid said.

Bullshit.

The kid shrugged and put the pistol back in the bib of his overalls.

Throw what up? said Rawlins.

Anything you want.

Anything I throw you can hit.

Yeah.

Bullshit.

The kid stood up. He wiped the plate back and forth across the leg of his overalls and looked at Rawlins.

You throw your pocketbook up in the air and I'll put a hole in it, he said.

Rawlins stood. He reached in his hip pocket and took out his billfold. The kid leaned and set the plate in the grass and took out the pistol again. John Grady put his spoon in his plate and set the plate on the ground. The three of them walked out onto the plain in the long morning light like duelists.

He stood with his back to the sun and the pistol hanging alongside his leg. Rawlins turned and grinned at John Grady. He held the billfold between his thumb and finger.

You ready, Annie Oakley? he said.

Waitin on you.

He pitched it up underhanded. It rose spinning in the air, very small against the blue. They watched it, waiting for him to shoot. Then he shot. The billfold jerked sideways off across the landscape and opened out and fell twisting to the ground like a broken bird.

The sound of the pistolshot vanished almost instantly in that immense silence. Rawlins walked out across the grass and bent and picked up his billfold and put it in his pocket and came back.

We better get goin, he said.

Let's see it, said John Grady.

Let's go. We need to get away from this river.

They caught their horses and saddled them and the kid kicked out the fire and they mounted up and rode out. They rode side by side spaced out apart upon the broad gravel plain curving away along the edge of the brushland upriver. They rode without speaking and they took in the look of the new country. A hawk in the top of a mesquite dropped down and flew low along the vega and rose again up into a tree a half mile to the east. When they had passed it flew back again.

You had that pistol in your shirt back on the Pecos, didnt you? said Rawlins.

The kid looked at him from under his immense hat. Yeah, he said.

They rode. Rawlins leaned and spat. You'd of shot me with it I guess.

The kid spat also. I didnt aim to get shot, he said.

They rode up through low hills covered with nopal and creosote. Midmorning they struck a trail with horsetracks in it and turned south and at noon they rode into the town of Reforma.

They rode singlefile down the cart track that served as a street. Half a dozen low houses with walls of mud brick slumping into ruin. A few jacales of brush and mud with brush roofs and a pole corral where five scrubby horses with big heads stood looking solemnly at the horses passing in the road.

They dismounted and tied their horses at a little mud tienda and entered. A girl was sitting in a straightback chair by a sheetiron stove in the center of the room reading a comicbook by the light from the doorway and she looked up at them and looked at the comicbook and then looked up again. She got up and glanced toward the back of the store where a green curtain hung across a doorway and she put the book down in the chair and crossed the packed clay floor to the counter and turned and stood. On top of the counter were three clay jars or ollas. Two of them were empty but the third was covered with the tin lid from a lardpail and the lid was notched to accommodate the handle of an enameled tin dipper. Along the wall behind her were three or four board shelves that held canned goods and cloth and thread and candy. Against the far wall was a hand-made pineboard mealbox. Above it a calendar nailed to the mud wall with a stick. Other than the stove and the chair that was all there was in the building.

Rawlins took off his hat and pressed his forearm against his forehead and put the hat back on. He looked at John Grady. She got anything to drink?

Tiene algo que tomar? said John Grady.

Sí, said the girl. She moved to take up her station behind the jars and lifted away the lid. The three riders stood at the counter and looked.

What is that? said Rawlins.

Sidrón, said the girl.

John Grady looked at her. Habla inglés? he said.

Oh no, she said.

What is it? said Rawlins.

Cider.

He looked into the jar. Let's have em, he said. Give us three.

Mande?

Three, said Rawlins. Tres. He held up three fingers.

He got out his billfold. She reached to the shelves behind and got down three tumblers and stood them on the board and took up the dipper and dredged up a thin brown liquid and filled the glasses and Rawlins laid a dollar bill on the counter. It had a hole in it at each end. They reached for the glasses and John Grady nodded at the bill.

He about deadcentered your pocketbook didnt he?

Yeah, said Rawlins.

He lifted up his glass and they drank. Rawlins stood thoughtfully.

I dont know what that shit is, he said. But it tastes pretty good to a cowboy. Let us have three more here.

They set their glasses down and she refilled them. What do we owe? said Rawlins.

She looked at John Grady.

Cuánto, said John Grady.

Para todo?

Sí.

Uno cincuenta.

How much is that? said Rawlins.

It's about three cents a glass.

Rawlins pushed the bill across the counter. You let your old dad buy, he said.

She made change out of a cigar box under the counter and laid the Mexican coins out on the counter and looked up. Rawlins set his empty glass down and gestured at it and paid for three more glasses and took his change and they took their glasses and walked outside.

They sat in the shade of the pole and brush ramada in front of the place and sipped their drinks and looked out at the desolate stillness of the little crossroads at noon. The mud huts. The dusty agave and the barren gravel hills beyond. A thin blue rivulet of drainwater ran down the clay gully in front of the store and a goat stood in the rutted road looking at the horses.

There aint no electricity here, said Rawlins.

He sipped his drink. He looked out down the road.

I doubt there's ever even been a car in here.

I dont know where it would come from, said John Grady.

Rawlins nodded. He held the glass to the light and rolled the cider around and looked at it. You think this here is some sort of cactus juice or what?

I dont know, said John Grady. It's got a little kick to it, dont it?

I think it does.

Better not let that youngn have no more.

I've drunk whiskey, said Blevins. This aint nothin.

Rawlins shook his head. Drinkin cactus juice in old Mexico, he said. What do you reckon they're sayin at home about now?

I reckon they're sayin we're gone, said John Grady.

Rawlins sat with his legs stretched out before him and his boots crossed and his hat over one knee and looked out at the alien land and nodded. We are, aint we? he said.

They watered the horses and loosed the cinches to let them blow and then took the road south such road as it was, riding single file through the dust. In the road were the tracks of cows, javelinas, deer, coyotes. Late afternoon they passed another collection of huts but they rode on. The road was deeply gullied and it was washed out in the draws and in the draws were cattle dead from an old drought, just the bones of them cloven about with the hard dry blackened hide.

How does this country suit you? said John Grady.

Rawlins leaned and spat but he didnt answer.

In the evening they came to a small estancia and sat the horses at the fence. There were several buildings scattered out behind the house and a pole corral with two horses standing in it. Two little girls in white dresses stood in the yard. They looked at the riders and then turned and ran into the house. A man came out.

Buenas tardes, he said.

He walked out the fence to the gate and motioned them through and showed them where to water their horses. Pásale, he said. Pásale.

They ate by oillight at a small painted pine table. The mud walls about them were hung with old calendars and magazine pictures. On one wall was a framed tin retablo of the Virgin. Under it was a board supported by two wedges driven into the wall and on the board was a small green glass with a blackened candlestub in it. The Americans sat shoulder to shoulder along one side of the table and the two little girls sat on the other side and watched them in a state of breathlessness. The woman ate with her head down and the man joked with them and passed the plates. They ate beans and tortillas and a chile of goatmeat ladled up out of a clay pot. They drank coffee from enameled tin cups and the man pushed the bowls toward them and gestured elaborately. Deben comer, he said.

He wanted to know about America, thirty miles to the north. He'd seen it once as a boy, across the river at Acuña. He had brothers who worked there. He had an uncle who'd lived some years in Uvalde Texas but he thought he was dead.

Rawlins finished his plate and thanked the woman and John Grady told her what he'd said and she smiled and nodded demurely. Rawlins was showing the two little girls how he could pull his finger off and put it back on again when Blevins crossed his utensils in the plate before him and wiped his mouth on his sleeve and leaned back from the table. There was no back to the bench and Blevins flailed wildly for a moment and then crashed to the floor behind him, kicking the table underneath and rattling the dishes and almost pulling over the bench with Rawlins and John Grady. The two girls stood instantly and clapped their hands and shrieked with delight. Rawlins had gripped the table to save himself and he looked down at the boy lying in the floor. I'll be goddamned, he said. Excuse me mam.

Blevins struggled up, only the man offering to help him.

Está bien? he said.

He's all right, said Rawlins. You caint hurt a fool.

The woman had leaned forward to right a cup, to quiet the children. She could not laugh for the impropriety of it but the brightness in her eyes did not escape even Blevins. He climbed over the bench and sat down again.

Are you all ready to go? he whispered.

We aint done eatin, said Rawlins.

He looked around uneasily. I caint set here, he said.

He was sitting with his head lowered and was whispering hoarsely.

Why caint you set there? said Rawlins.

I dont like to be laughed at.

Rawlins looked at the girls. They were sitting again and their eyes were wide and serious again. Hell, he said. It's just kids.

I dont like to be laughed at, whispered Blevins.

Both the man and the woman were looking at them with concern.

If you dont like to be laughed at dont fall on your ass, said Rawlins.

You all excuse me, said Blevins.

He climbed out over the bench and picked up his hat and put it on and went out. The man of the house looked worried and he leaned to John Grady and made a whispered inquiry. The two girls sat looking down at their plates.

You think he'll ride on? said Rawlins.

John Grady shrugged. I doubt it.

The householders seemed to be waiting for one of them to get up and go out after him but they did not. They drank their coffee and after a while the woman rose and cleared away the plates.

John Grady found him sitting on the ground like a figure in meditation.

What are you doin? he said.

Nothin.

Why dont you come back inside.

I'm all right.

They've offered us to spend the night.

Go ahead.

What do you aim to do?

I'm all right.

John Grady stood watching him. Well, he said. Suit yourself.

Blevins didnt answer and he left him sitting there.

The room they slept in was at the back of the house and it smelled of hay or straw. It was small and there was no window to it and on the floor were two pallets of straw and sacking with serapes over them. They took the lamp the host handed them and thanked him and he bowed out the low doorway and bid them goodnight. He didnt ask about Blevins.

John Grady set the lamp on the floor and they sat in the straw ticks and took off their boots.

I'm give out, said Rawlins.

I hear you.

What all did the old man say about work in this part of the country?

He says there's some big ranches yon side of the Sierra del Carmen. About three hundred kilometers.

How far's that?

Hundred and sixty, hundred and seventy miles.

You reckon he thinks we're desperados?

I dont know. Pretty nice about it if he does.

I'd say so.

He made that country sound like the Big Rock Candy Mountains. Said there was lakes and runnin water and grass to the stirrups. I cant picture country like that down here from what I've seen so far, can you?

He's probably just tryin to get us to move on.

Could be, said John Grady. He took off his hat and lay back and pulled the serape over him.

What the hell's he goin to do, said Rawlins. Sleep out in the yard?

I reckon.

Maybe he'll be gone in the mornin.

Maybe.

He closed his eyes. Don't let that lamp burn out, he said. It'll black the whole house.

I'll blow it out here in a minute.

He lay listening. There was no sound anywhere. What are you doin? he said.

He opened his eyes. He looked over at Rawlins. Rawlins had his billfold spread out across the blanket.

What are you doin?

I want you to look at my goddamned driver's license.

You wont need em down here.

There's my poolhall card. Got it too.

Go to sleep.

Look at this shit. He shot Betty Ward right between the eyes.

What was she doin in there? I didnt know you liked her.

She give me that picture. That was her schooldays picture.

In the morning they ate a huge breakfast of eggs and beans and tortillas at the same table. No one went out to get Blevins and no one asked about him. The woman packed them a lunch in a cloth and they thanked her and shook hands with the man and walked out in the cool morning. Blevins' horse was not in the corral.

You think we're this lucky? said Rawlins.

John Grady shook his head doubtfully.

They saddled the horses and they offered to pay the man for their feed but he frowned and waved them away and they shook hands again and he wished them a good voyage and they mounted up and rode out down the rutted track south. A dog followed them out a ways and then stood watching after them.

The morning was fresh and cool and there was woodsmoke in the air. When they topped the first rise in the road Rawlins spat in disgust. Look yonder, he said.

Blevins was sitting the big bay horse sideways in the road.

They slowed the horses. What the hell do you reckon is wrong with him? said Rawlins.

He's just a kid.

Shit, said Rawlins.

When they rode up Blevins smiled at them. He was chewing tobacco and he leaned and spat and wiped his mouth with the underside of his wrist.

What are you grinnin at?

Mornin, said Blevins.

Where'd you get the tobacco at? said Rawlins.

Man give it to me.

Man give it to you?

Yeah. Where you all been?

They rode their horses past him either side and he fell in behind.

You all got anything to eat? he said.

Got some lunch she put up for us, said Rawlins.

What have you got?

Dont know. Aint looked.

Well why dont we take a look?

Does it look like lunchtime to you?

Joe, tell him to let me have somethin to eat.

His name aint Joe, said Rawlins. And even if it was Evelyn he aint goin to give you no lunch at no seven oclock in the mornin.

Shit, said Blevins.

They rode till noon and past noon. There was nothing along the road save the country it traversed and there was nothing in the country at all. The only sound was the steady clop of the horses along the road and the periodic spat of Blevins' tobacco juice behind them. Rawlins rode with one leg crossed in front of him, leaning on his knee and smoking pensively as he studied the country.

I believe I see cottonwoods yonder, he said.

I believe I do too, said John Grady.

They ate lunch under the trees at the edge of a small ciénaga. The horses stood in the marshy grass and sucked quietly at the water. She'd tied the food up in a square of muslin and they spread the cloth on the ground and selected from among the quesadillas and tacos and bizcochos like picnickers, leaning back on their elbows in the shade with their boots crossed before them, chewing idly and observing the horses.

Back in the old days, said Blevins, this'd be just the place where Comanches'd lay for you and bushwhack you.

I hope they had some cards or a checkerboard with em while they was waitin, said Rawlins. It dont look to me like there's been nobody down this road in a year.

Back in the old days you had a lot more travelers, said Blevins.

Rawlins eyed balefully that cauterized terrain. What in the putrefied dogshit would you know about the old days? he said.

You all want any more of this? said John Grady.

I'm full as a tick.

He tied up the cloth and stood and began to strip out of his clothes and he walked out naked through the grass past the horses and waded out into the water and sat in it to his waist. He spread his arms and lay backward into the water and disappeared. The horses watched him. He sat up out of the water and pushed his hair back and wiped his eyes. Then he just sat.

They camped that night in the floor of a wash just off the road and built a fire and sat in the sand and stared into the embers.

Blevins are you a cowboy? said Rawlins.

I like it.

Everbody likes it.

I dont claim to be no top hand. I can ride.

Yeah? said Rawlins.

That man yonder can ride, said Blevins. He nodded across the fire toward John Grady.

What makes you say that?

He just can, that's all.

Suppose I was to tell you he just took it up. Suppose I was to tell you he's never been on a horse a girl couldnt ride.

I'd have to say you was pullin my leg.

Suppose I was to tell you he's the best I ever saw.

Blevins spat into the fire.

You doubt that?

No, I dont doubt it. Depends on who you seen ride.

I seen Booger Red ride, said Rawlins.

Yeah? said Blevins.

Yeah.

You think he can outride him?

I know for a fact he can.

Maybe he can and maybe he caint.

You dont know shit from applebutter, said Rawlins. Booger Red's been dead forever.

Dont pay no attention to him, said John Grady.

Rawlins recrossed his boots and nodded toward John Grady. He cant take my part of it without braggin on hisself, can he?

He's full of shit, said John Grady.

You hear that? said Rawlins.

Blevins leaned his chin toward the fire and spat. I dont see how you can say somebody is just flat out the best.

You cant, said John Grady. He's just ignorant, that's all.

There's a lot of good riders, said Blevins.

That's right, said Rawlins. There's a lot of good riders. But there's just one that's the best. And he happens to be settin right yonder.

Leave him alone, said John Grady.

I aint botherin him, said Rawlins. Am I botherin you?

No.

Tell Joe yonder I aint botherin you.

I said you wasnt.

Leave him alone, said John Grady.

DAYS TO COME they rode through the mountains and they crossed at a barren windgap and sat the horses among the rocks and looked out over the country to the south where the last shadows were running over the land before the wind and the sun to the west lay blood red among the shelving clouds and the distant cordilleras ranged down the terminals of the sky to fade from pale to pale of blue and then to nothing at all.

Where do you reckon that paradise is at? said Rawlins.

John Grady had taken off his hat to let the wind cool his head. You cant tell what's in a country like that till you're down there in it, he said.

There's damn sure a bunch of it, aint there.

John Grady nodded. That's what I'm here for.

I hear you, cousin.

They rode down through the cooling blue shadowland of the north slope. Evergreen ash growing in the rocky draws. Persimmon, mountain gum. A hawk set forth below them and circled in the deepening haze and dropped and they kicked their feet out of the stirrups and put the horses forward with care down the shaly rock switchbacks. At just dark they benched out on a gravel shelf and made their camp and that night they heard what they'd none heard before, three long howls to the south-west and all afterwards a silence.

You hear that? said Rawlins.

Yeah.

It's a wolf, aint it?

Yeah.

He lay on his back in his blankets and looked out where the quartermoon lay cocked over the heel of the mountains. In that false blue dawn the Pleiades seemed to be rising up into the darkness above the world and dragging all the stars away, the great diamond of Orion and Cepella and the signature of Cassiopeia all rising up through the phosphorous dark like a sea-net. He lay a long time listening to the others breathing in their sleep while he contemplated the wildness about him, the wildness within.

It was cold in the night and in the dawn before daylight when they woke Blevins was already up and had a fire going on the ground and was huddled over it in his thin clothes. John Grady crawled out and got his boots and jacket on and walked out to study the new country as it shaped itself out of the darkness below them.

They drank the last of the coffee and ate cold tortillas with a thin stripe of bottled hotsauce down the middle.

How far down the road you think this'll get us? said Rawlins.

I aint worried, said John Grady.

Your pardner yonder looks a little misgive.

He aint got a lot of bacon to spare.

You aint neither.

They watched the sun rise below them. The horses standing out on the bench grazing raised their heads and watched it. Rawlins drank the last of his coffee and shook out his cup and reached in his shirtpocket for his tobacco.

You think there'll be a day when the sun wont rise?

Yeah, said John Grady. Judgment day.

When you think that'll be?

Whenever He decides to hold it.

Judgment day, said Rawlins. You believe in all that?

I dont know. Yeah, I reckon. You?

Rawlins put the cigarette in the corner of his mouth and lit it and flipped away the match. I dont know. Maybe.

I knowed you was a infidel, said Blevins.

You dont know a goddamned thing, said Rawlins. Just be quiet and dont make no bigger ass of yourself than what you already are.

John Grady got up and walked over and picked up his saddle by the horn and threw his blanket over his shoulder and turned and looked at them. Let's go, he said.

They were down out of the mountains by midmorning and riding on a great plain grown with sideoats grama and basketgrass and dotted with lechugilla. Here they encountered the first riders they'd seen and they halted and watched while they approached on the plain a mile away, three men on horses leading a train of packanimals carrying empty kiacks.

What do you reckon they are? said Rawlins.

We ought not to be stopped like this, said Blevins. If we can see them they can see us.

What the hell is that supposed to mean? said Rawlins.

What would you think if you seen them stop?

He's right, said John Grady. Let's keep ridin.

They were zacateros headed into the mountains to gather chino grass. If they were surprised to see Americans horseback in that country they gave no sign. They asked them if they'd seen a brother to one of them who was in the mountains with his wife and two grown girls but they'd seen no one. The Mexicans sat their horses and took in their outfits with slow movements of their dark eyes. They themselves were a rough lot, dressed half in rags, their hats marbled with grease and sweat, their boots mended with raw cowhide. They rode old squareskirted saddles with the wood worn through the leather and they rolled cigarettes in strips of cornhusks and lit them with esclarajos of flint and steel and bits of fluff in an empty cartridge case. One of them carried an old worn Colt stuck in his belt with the gate flipped open to keep it from sliding through and they smelled of smoke and tallow and sweat and they looked as wild and strange as the country they were in.

Son de Tejas? they said.

Sí, said John Grady.

They nodded.

John Grady smoked and watched them. For all their shabbiness they were well mounted and he watched those black eyes to see could he tell what they thought but he could tell nothing. They spoke of the country and of the weather in the country and they said that it was yet cold in the mountains. No one offered to dismount. They looked out over the terrain as if it were a problem to them. Something they'd not quite decided about. The little mules entrained behind them had dropped asleep standing almost as soon as they'd halted.

The leader finished his cigarette and let fall the stub of it into the track. Bueno, he said. Vámonos.

He nodded at the Americans. Buena suerte, he said. He put the long rowels of his spurs to the horse and they moved on. The mules passed on behind them eyeing the horses in the road and switching their tails although there seemed to be no flies in that country at all.

In the afternoon they watered the horses at a clear stream running out of the southwest. They walked the creek and drank and filled and stoppered their canteens. There were antelope out on the plain perhaps two miles distant, all standing with their heads up.

They rode on. There was good grass in the level floor of the valley and cattle the color of housecats to tortoiseshell and calico moved off constantly before them up through the buckthorn or stood along the low rise of ancient ground running down to the east to watch them as they passed along the road. That night they camped in the low hills and they cooked a jackrabbit that Blevins had shot with his pistol. He fielddressed it with his pocketknife and buried it in the sandy ground with the skin on and built the fire over it. He said it was the way the indians did.

You ever eat a jackrabbit? said Rawlins.

He shook his head. Not yet, he said.

You better rustle some more wood if you aim to eat thisn. It'll cook.

What's the strangest thing you ever ate?

Strangest thing I ever ate, said Blevins. I guess I'd have to say that would be a oyster.

A mountain oyster or a real oyster?

A real oyster.

How were they cooked?

They wasnt cooked. They just laid there in their shells. You put hotsauce on em.

You ate that?

I did.

How'd it taste?

About like you'd expect.

They sat watching the fire.

Where you from, Blevins? said Rawlins.

Blevins looked at Rawlins and looked back into the fire. Uvalde County, he said. Up on the Sabinal River.

What'd you run off for?

What'd you?

I'm seventeen years old. I can go wherever I want.

So can I.

John Grady was sitting with his legs crossed in front of him leaning against his saddle and smoking a cigarette. You've run off before, aint you? he said.

Yeah.

What'd they do, catch you?

Yeah. I was settin pins in a bowlin alley in Ardmore Oklahoma and I got dogbit by a bulldog took a chunk out of my leg the size of a Sunday roast and it got infected and the man I worked for carried me down to the doctor and they thought I had rabies or somethin and all hell busted loose and I got shipped back to Uvalde County.

What were you doin in Ardmore Oklahoma?

Settin pins in a bowlin alley.

How come you wound up there?

There was a show was supposed to come through Uvalde, town of Uvalde, and I'd saved up to go see it but they never showed up because the man that run the show got thowed in jail in Tyler Texas for havin a dirty show. Had this striptease that was part of the deal. I got down there and it said on the poster they was goin to be in Ardmore Oklahoma in two weeks and that's how come me to be in Ardmore Oklahoma.

You went all the way to Oklahoma to see a show?

That's what I'd saved up to do and I meant to do it.

Did you see the show in Ardmore?

No. They never showed up there neither.

Blevins hauled up one leg of his overalls and turned his leg to the firelight.

Yonder's where that son of a bitch bit me, he said. I'd as soon been bit by a alligator.

What made you set out for Mexico? said Rawlins.

Same reason as you.

What reason is that?

Cause you knowed they'd play hell sowed in oats findin your ass down here.

There aint nobody huntin me.

Blevins rolled down the leg of his overalls and poked at the fire with a stick. I told that son of a bitch I wouldnt take a whippin off of him and I didnt.

Your daddy?

My daddy never come back from the war.

Your stepdaddy?

Yeah.

Rawlins leaned forward and spat into the fire. You didnt shoot him did you?

I would of. He knowed it too.

What was a bulldog doin in a bowlin alley?

I didnt get bit in the bowlin alley. I was workin in the bowlin alley, that's all.

What were you doin that you got dogbit?

Nothin. I wasnt doin nothin.

Rawlins leaned and spat into the fire. Where were you at at the time?

You got a awful lot of goddamned questions. And dont be spittin in the fire where I got supper cookin.

What? said Rawlins.

I said dont be spittin in the fire where I got supper cookin.

Rawlins looked at John Grady. John Grady had started to laugh. He looked at Blevins. Supper? he said. You'll think supper when you try and eat that stringy son of a bitch.

Blevins nodded. You let me know if you dont want your share, he said.

What they dredged smoking out of the ground looked like some desiccated effigy from a tomb. Blevins put it on a flat rock and peeled away the hide and scraped the meat off the bones into their plates and they soaked it down with hotsauce and rolled it in the last of the tortillas. They chewed and watched one another.

Well, said Rawlins. It aint all that bad.

No it aint, said Blevins. Truth is, I didnt know you could eat one at all.

John Grady stopped chewing and looked at them. Then he went on chewing again. You all been out here longer than me, he said. I thought we all started together.

The following day on the track south they began to encounter small ragged caravans of migrant traders headed toward the northern border. Brown and weathered men with burros three or four in tandem atotter with loads of candelilla or furs or goathides or coils of handmade rope fashioned out of lechugilla or the fermented drink called sotol decanted into drums and cans and strapped onto packframes made from treelimbs. They carried water in the skins of hogs or in canvas bags made waterproof with candelilla wax and fitted with cowhorn spigots and some had women and children with them and they would shoulder the packanimals off into the brush and relinquish the road

to the caballeros and the riders would wish them a good day and
they would smile and nod until they passed.

They tried to buy water from the caravans but they had no
coin among them small enough with which to do so. When
Rawlins offered a man fifty centavos for the half pennysworth
of water it would take to fill their canteens the man would have
no part of it. By evening they'd bought a canteenful of sotol and
were passing it back and forth among themselves as they rode
and soon they were quite drunk. Rawlins drank and swung up
the cap by its thong and screwed it down and took the canteen
by its strap and turned to swing it to Blevins. Then he caught
it back. Blevins' horse was plodding along behind with an empty
saddle. Rawlins eyed the animal stupidly and pulled his horse
up and called to John Grady riding ahead.

John Grady turned and sat looking.

Where's he at?

Who knows? Layin back yonder somewheres I reckon.

They rode back, Rawlins leading the riderless horse by the
bridlereins. Blevins was sitting in the middle of the road. He
still had his hat on. Whoo, he said when he saw them. I'm
drunkern shit.

They sat their horses and looked down at him.

Can you ride or not? said Rawlins.

Does a bear shit in the woods? Hell yes I can ride. I was ridin
when I fell off.

He stood uncertainly and peered about. He reeled past them
and felt his way among the horses. Flank and flew, Rawlins'
knee. Thought you all had done rode off and left me, he said.

Next time we will leave your skinny ass.

John Grady reached and took the reins and held the horse
while Blevins lurched aboard. Let me have them reins, said
Blevins. I'm a goddamned buckaroo is what I am.

John Grady shook his head. Blevins dropped the reins and
reached to get them and almost slid off down the horse's shoulder. He saved himself and sat up with the reins and pulled the

horse around sharply. Certified goddamn broncpeeler, what I mean, he said.

He dug his heels in under the horse and it squatted and went forward and Blevins fell backwards into the road. Rawlins spat in disgust. Just leave the son of a bitch lay there, he said.

Get on the goddamned horse, said John Grady, and quit assin around.

By early evening all the sky to the north had darkened and the spare terrain they trod had turned a neuter gray as far as eye could see. They grouped in the road at the top of a rise and looked back. The storm front towered above them and the wind was cool on their sweating faces. They slumped bleary-eyed in their saddles and looked at one another. Shrouded in the black thunderheads the distant lightning glowed mutely like welding seen through foundry smoke. As if repairs were under way at some flawed place in the iron dark of the world.

It's fixin to come a goodn, said Rawlins.

I caint be out in this, said Blevins.

Rawlins laughed and shook his head. Listen at this, he said.

Where do you think you're goin to go? said John Grady.

I dont know. But I got to get somewheres.

Why cant you be out in it?

On account of the lightnin.

Lightnin?

Yeah.

Damn if you dont look about halfway sober all of a sudden, said Rawlins.

You afraid of lightnin? said John Grady.

I'll be struck sure as the world.

Rawlins nodded at the canteen hung by its strap from the pommel of John Grady's saddle. Dont give him no more of that shit. He's comin down with the DT's.

It runs in the family, said Blevins. My grandaddy was killed in a minebucket in West Virginia it run down in the hole a hunnerd and eighty feet to get him it couldnt even wait for him to get to the top. They had to wet down the bucket to cool it fore they could get him out of it, him and two other men. It fried em like bacon. My daddy's older brother was blowed out of a derrick in the Batson Field in the year nineteen and four, cable rig with a wood derrick but the lightnin got him anyways and him not nineteen year old. Great uncle on my mother's side—mother's side, I said—got killed on a horse and it never singed a hair on that horse and it killed him graveyard dead they had to cut his belt off him where it welded the buckle shut and I got a cousin aint but four years oldern me was struck down in his own yard comin from the barn and it paralyzed him all down one side and melted the fillins in his teeth and soldered his jaw shut.

I told you, said Rawlins. He's gone completely dipshit.

They didnt know what was wrong with him. He'd just twitch and mumble and point at his mouth like.

That's a out and out lie or I never heard one, said Rawlins.

Blevins didnt hear. Beads of sweat stood on his forehead. Another cousin on my daddy's side it got him it set his hair on fire. The change in his pocket burned through and fell out on the ground and set the grass alight. I done been struck twice how come me to be deaf in this one ear. I'm double bred for death by fire. You got to get away from anything metal at all. You dont know what'll get you. Brads in your overalls. Nails in your boots.

Well what do you intend to do?

He looked wildly toward the north. Try and outride it, he said. Only chance I got.

Rawlins looked at John Grady. He leaned and spat. Well, he said. If there was any doubt before I guess that ought to clear it up.

You cant outride a thunderstorm, said John Grady. What the hell is wrong with you?

It's the only chance I got.

He'd no sooner said it than the first thin crack of thunder reached them no louder than a dry stick trod on. Blevins took off his hat and passed the sleeve of his shirt across his forehead and doubled the reins in his fist and took one last desperate look behind him and whacked the horse across the rump with the hat.

They watched him go. He tried to get his hat on and then lost it. It rolled in the road. He went on with his elbows flapping and he grew small on the plain before them and more ludicrous yet.

I aint takin no responsibility for him, said Rawlins. He reached and unhooked the canteen from John Grady's saddlehorn and put his horse forward. He'll be a layin in the road down here and where do you reckon that horse'll be?

He rode on, drinking and talking to himself. I'll tell you where that horse'll be, he called back.

John Grady followed. Dust blew from under the tread of the horses and twisted away down the road before them.

Run plumb out of the country, called Rawlins. That's where. Gone to hell come Friday. That's where the goddamn horse'll be.

They rode on. There were spits of rain in the wind. Blevins' hat lay in the road and Rawlins tried to ride his horse over it but the horse stepped around it. John Grady slid one boot out of the stirrup and leaned down and picked up the hat without dismounting. They could hear the rain coming down the road behind them like some phantom migration.

Blevins' horse was standing saddled by the side of the road tied to a clump of willows. Rawlins turned and sat his horse in the rain and looked at John Grady. John Grady rode through the willows and down the arroyo following the occasional bare footprint in the rainspotted loam until he came upon Blevins crouched under the roots of a dead cottonwood in a caveout where the arroyo turned and fanned out onto the plain. He was naked save for an outsized pair of stained undershorts.

What the hell are you doin? said John Grady.

Blevins sat gripping his thin white shoulders in either hand. Just settin here, he said.

John Grady looked out over the plain where the last remnants of sunlight were being driven toward the low hills to the south. He leaned and dropped Blevins' hat at his feet.

Where's your clothes at?

I took em off.

I know that. Where are they?

I left em up yonder. Shirt had brass snaps too.

If this rain hits hard there'll be a river come down through here like a train. You thought about that?

You aint never been struck by lightnin, said Blevins. You dont know what it's like.

You'll get drowned settin there.

That's all right. I aint never been drowned before.

You aim to just set there?

That's what I aim to do.

John Grady put his hands on his knees. Well, he said. I'll say no more.

A long rolling crack of thunder went pealing down the sky to the north. The ground shuddered. Blevins put his arms over his head and John Grady turned the horse and rode back up the arroyo. Great pellets of rain were cratering the wet sand underfoot. He looked back once at Blevins. Blevins sat as before. A thing all but inexplicable in that landscape.

Where's he at? said Rawlins.

He's just settin out there. You better get your slicker.

I knowed when I first seen him the son of a bitch had a loose wingnut, said Rawlins. It was writ all over him.

The rain was coming down in sheets. Blevins' horse stood in the downpour like the ghost of a horse. They left the road and followed the wash up toward a stand of trees and took shelter under the barest overhang of rock, sitting with their knees stuck out into the rain and holding the standing horses by the bridlereins. The horses stepped and shook their heads and the lightning cracked and the wind tore through the acacia and paloverde and the rain went slashing down the country. They heard a horse running somewhere out in the rain and then they just heard the rain.

You know what that was dont you? said Rawlins.

Yeah.

You want a drink of this?

I dont think so. I think it's beginnin to make me feel bad.

Rawlins nodded and drank. I think it is me too, he said.

By dark the storm had slacked and the rain had almost ceased. They pulled the wet saddles off the horses and hobbled them and walked off in separate directions through the chaparral to stand spraddlelegged clutching their knees and vomiting. The browsing horses jerked their heads up. It was no sound they'd ever heard before. In the gray twilight those retchings seemed to echo like the calls of some rude provisional species loosed upon that waste. Something imperfect and malformed lodged in the heart of being. A thing smirking deep in the eyes of grace itself like a gorgon in an autumn pool.

In the morning they caught up the horses and saddled them and tied on the damp bedrolls and led the horses out to the road.

What do you want to do? said Rawlins.

I reckon we better go find his skinny ass.

What if we just went on.

John Grady mounted up and looked down at Rawlins. I dont believe I can leave him out here afoot, he said.

Rawlins nodded. Yeah, he said. I guess not.

He rode down the arroyo and encountered Blevins coming up in the same condition in which he'd left him. He sat the horse. Blevins was picking his way barefoot along the wash, carrying one boot. He looked up at John Grady.

Where's your clothes at? said John Grady.

Washed away.

Your horse is gone.

I know it. I done been out to the road once.

What do you aim to do?

I dont know.

You dont look like the demon rum's dealt kindly with you.

My head feels like a fat lady's sat on it.

John Grady looked out at the morning desert shining in the new sun. He looked at the boy.

You've wore Rawlins completely out. I reckon you know that.

You never know when you'll be in need of them you've despised, said Blevins.

Where the hell'd you hear that at?

I dont know. I just decided to say it.

John Grady shook his head. He reached and unbuckled his saddlebag and took out his spare shirt and pitched it down to Blevins.

Put that on before you get parboiled out here. I'll ride down and see if I can see your clothes anywheres.

I appreciate it, said Blevins.

He rode down the wash and he rode back. Blevins was sitting in the sand in the shirt.

How much water was in this wash last night?

A bunch.

Where'd you find the one boot at?

In a tree.

He rode down the wash and out over the gravel fan and sat looking. He didnt see any boot. When he came back Blevins was sitting as he'd left him.

That boot's gone, he said.

I figured as much.

John Grady reached down a hand. Let's go.

He swung Blevins in his underwear up onto the horse behind him. Rawlins will pitch a pure hissy when he sees you, he said.

Rawlins when he saw him seemed too dismayed to speak.

He's lost his clothes, said John Grady.

Rawlins turned his horse and set off slowly down the road. They followed. No one spoke. After a while John Grady heard something drop into the road and he looked back and saw Blevins' boot lying there. He turned and looked at Blevins but

Blevins was peering steadily ahead from under the brim of his hat and they rode on. The horses stepped archly among the shadows that fell over the road, the bracken steamed. Bye and bye they passed a stand of roadside cholla against which small birds had been driven by the storm and there impaled. Gray nameless birds espaliered in attitudes of stillborn flight or hanging loosely in their feathers. Some of them were still alive and they twisted on their spines as the horses passed and raised their heads and cried out but the horsemen rode on. The sun rose up in the sky and the country took on new color, green fire in the acacia and paloverde and green in the roadside run-off grass and fire in the ocotillo. As if the rain were electric, had grounded circuits that the electric might be.

So mounted they rode at noon into a waxcamp pitched in the broken footlands beneath the low stone mesa running east and west before them. There was a small clearwater branch here and the Mexicans had dug an open firebox and lined it with rock and scotched their boiler into the bank over it. The boiler was made from the lower half of a galvanized watertank and to bring it to this location they'd run a wooden axleshaft through the bottom and made a wooden spider whereby to bed the axle in the open end and with a team of horses rolled the tank across the desert from Zaragoza eighty miles to the east. The track of flattened chaparral was still visible bending away over the floor of the desert. When the Americans rode into their camp there were several burros standing there that had just been brought down from the mesa loaded with the candelilla plant they boiled for wax and the Mexicans had left the animals to stand while they ate their dinner. A dozen men dressed most of them in what looked to be pajamas and all of them in rags squatting under the shade of some willows and eating with tin spoons off of clay plates. They looked up but they did not stop eating.

Buenos días, said John Grady. They responded in a quick dull chorus. He dismounted and they looked at the spot where he stood and looked at each other and then went on eating.

Tienen algo que comer?

One or two of them gestured toward the fire with their spoons. When Blevins slid from the horse they looked at each other again.

The riders got their plates and utensils out of the saddlebags and John Grady got the little enameled pot out of the blackened cookbag and handed it to Blevins together with his old wooden-handled kitchen fork. They went to the fire and filled their plates with beans and chile and took each a couple of blackened corn tortillas from a piece of sheetiron laid over the fire and walked over and sat under the willows a little apart from the workers. Blevins sat with his bare legs stretched out before him but they looked so white and exposed lying there on the ground that he seemed ashamed and he tried to tuck them up under him and to cover his knees with the tails of the borrowed shirt he wore. They ate. The workers had for the most part finished their meal and they were leaning back smoking cigarettes and belching quietly.

You goin to ask em about my horse? said Blevins.

John Grady chewed thoughtfully. Well, he said. If it's here they ought to be able to figure out it belongs to us.

You think they'd steal it?

You aint never goin to get that horse back, said Rawlins. We hit a town down here somewheres you better see if you can trade that pistol for some clothes and a bus ticket back to wherever it is you come from. If there are buses. Your buddy yonder might be willin to haul your ass all over Mexico but I damn sure aint.

I aint got the pistol, said Blevins. It's with the horse.

Shit, said Rawlins.

Blevins ate. After a while he looked up. What'd I ever do to you? he said.

You aint done nothin to me. And you aint goin to. That's the point.

Leave him be, Lacey. It aint goin to hurt us to try and help the boy get his horse back.

I'm just tellin him the facts, said Rawlins.

He knows the facts.

He dont act like it.

John Grady wiped his plate with the last of the tortilla and ate the tortilla and set the plate on the ground and commenced to roll a cigarette.

I'm goddamned starved, said Rawlins. You reckon they'd care if we went back for seconds?

They wont care, said Blevins. Go ahead.

Who asked you? said Rawlins.

John Grady started to reach in his pocket for a match and then he rose and walked over to the workers and squatted and asked for a light. Two of them produced esclarajos from their clothes and one struck him a light and he leaned and lit the cigarette and nodded. He asked about the boiler and the loads of candelilla still tied on the burros and the workers told them about the wax and one of them rose and walked off and came back with a small gray cake of it and handed it to him. It looked like a bar of laundrysoap. He scraped it with his fingernail and sniffed it. He held it up and looked at it.

Qué vale? he said.

They shrugged.

Es mucho trabajo, he said.

Bastante.

A thin man in a stained leather vest with embroidery on the front was watching John Grady with narrowed and speculative eyes. John Grady handed back the wax and this man hissed at him and jerked his head.

John Grady turned.

Es su hermano, el rubio?

He meant Blevins. John Grady shook his head. No, he said.

Quíen es? said the man.

He looked across the clearing. The cook had given Blevins some lard and he sat rubbing it into his sunburned legs.

Un muchacho, no más, he said.

Algún parentesco?

No.

Un amigo.

John Grady drew on the cigarette and tapped the ash against the heel of his boot. Nada, he said.

No one spoke. The man in the vest studied John Grady and he looked across the clearing at Blevins. Then he asked John Grady if he wished to sell the boy.

He didnt answer for a moment. The man may have thought he was weighing the matter. They waited. He looked up. No, he said.

Qué vale? said the man.

John Grady stubbed out the cigarette against the sole of his boot and rose.

Gracias por su hospitalidad, he said.

The man offered that he would trade for him in wax. The others had turned to listen to him. Now they turned and looked at John Grady.

John Grady studied them. They did not look evil but it was no comfort to him. He turned and crossed the clearing toward the standing horses. Blevins and Rawlins rose.

What did they say? said Blevins.

Nothing.

Did you ask them about my horse?

No.

Why not?

They dont have your horse.

What was that guy talkin about?

Nothing. Get the plates. Let's go.

Rawlins looked across the clearing at the seated men. He took up the trailing reins and swung up into the saddle.

What's happened, bud? he said.

John Grady mounted and turned the horse. He looked back at the men and he looked at Blevins. Blevins stood with the plates.

What was he lookin at me for? he said.

Put them in the bag and get your ass up here.

They aint washed.

Do like I told you.

Some of the men had risen. Blevins stuffed the plates into the bag and John Grady reached down and swung him up onto the horse behind him.

He pulled the horse around and they rode out of the camp and into the road south. Rawlins looked back and put his horse into a trot and John Grady came up and they rode side by side down the narrow rutted track. No one spoke. When they were clear of the camp a mile or so Blevins asked what it was that the man in the vest had wanted but John Grady didnt answer. When Blevins asked again Rawlins looked back at him.

He wanted to buy you, he said. That's what he wanted.

John Grady didnt look at Blevins.

They rode on in silence.

What did you go and tell him that for? said John Grady. There wasnt no call to do that.

They camped that night in the low range of hills under the Sierra de la Encantada and the three of them sat about the fire in silence. The boy's bony legs were pale in the firelight and coated with road dust and bits of chaff that had stuck to the lard. The drawers he wore were baggy and dirty and he did indeed look like some sad and ill used serf or worse. John Grady parceled out to him the bottom blanket from his bedroll and he wrapped himself in it and lay by the fire and was soon asleep. Rawlins shook his head and spat.

Goddamn pitiful, he said. You thought any more about what I said?

Yeah, said John Grady. I thought about it.

Rawlins stared long into the red heart of the fire. I'll tell you somethin, he said.

Tell me.

Somethin bad is goin to happen.

John Grady smoked slowly, his arms around his updrawn knees.

This is just a jackpot, said Rawlins. What this is.

At noon the next day they rode into the pueblo of Encantada at the foot of the low range of pollarded mountains they'd been skirting and the first thing they saw was Blevins' pistol sticking out of the back pocket of a man bent over into the engine compartment of a Dodge car. John Grady saw it first and he could have named things he'd rather have seen.

Yonder's my goddamn pistol, sang out Blevins.

John Grady reached behind and grabbed him by the shirt or he'd have slid down from the horse.

Hold on, idjit, he said.

Hold on hell, said Blevins.

What do you think you're goin to do?

Rawlins had put his horse alongside of them. Keep ridin, he hissed. Good God almighty.

Some children were watching from a doorway and Blevins was looking back over his shoulder.

If that horse is here, said Rawlins, they wont have to send for Dick Tracy to figure out who it belongs to.

What do you want to do?

I dont know. Get off the damn street. May be too late anyways. I say we stash him in a safe place somewheres till we can look around.

Does that suit you, Blevins?

It dont make a damn if it suits him or not, said Rawlins. He dont have a say in it. Not if he wants my help he dont.

He rode past them and they turned off down a clay gully that passed for a street. Quit lookin back, damn it, said John Grady.

They left him with a canteen of water in the shade of some cottonwoods and told him to stay out of sight and then they rode slowly back through the town. They were picking their way along one of those rutted gullies of which the town was composed when they saw the horse looking out of the sashless window of an abandoned mud house.

Keep ridin, said Rawlins.

John Grady nodded.

When they got back to the cottonwoods Blevins was gone. Rawlins sat looking over the barren dusty countryside. He reached in his pocket for his tobacco.

I'm goin to tell you somethin, cousin.

John Grady leaned and spat. All right.

Ever dumb thing I ever done in my life there was a decision I made before that got me into it. It was never the dumb thing. It was always some choice I'd made before it. You understand what I'm sayin?

Yeah. I think so. Meanin what?

Meanin this is it. This is our last chance. Right now. This is the time and there wont be another time and I guarantee it.

Meanin just leave him?

Yessir.

What if it was you?

It aint me.

What if it was?

Rawlins twisted the cigarette into the corner of his mouth and plucked a match from his pocket and popped it alight with his thumbnail. He looked at John Grady.

I wouldnt leave you and you wouldnt leave me. That aint no argument.

You realize the fix he's in?

Yeah. I realize it. It's the one he's put hisself in.

They sat. Rawlins smoked. John Grady crossed his hands on the pommel of his saddle and sat looking at them. After a while he raised his head.

I cant do it, he said.

Okay.

What does that mean?

It means okay. If you cant you cant. I think I knew what you'd say anyways.

Yeah, well. I didnt.

They unsaddled and staked out the horses and lay in the dry

leaves under the cottonwoods and after a while they slept. When they woke it was almost dark. The boy was squatting there watching them.

It's a good thing I aint a rogue, he said. I could of slipped up on you all and carried off everthing you own.

Rawlins turned and looked at him from under his hat and turned back. John Grady sat up.

What did you all find out? said Blevins.

Your horse is here.

Did you see him?

Yeah.

What about the saddle?

We didnt see no saddle.

I aint leavin here till I get all my stuff.

There you go, said Rawlins. Listen at that.

What's he say? said Blevins.

Never mind, said John Grady.

If it was his stuff it'd be different I bet. Then he'd be for gettin it back, wouldnt he?

Dont egg it on.

Listen, shit-for-brains, said Rawlins. If it wasnt for this man I wouldnt be here at all. I'd of left your ass back up in that arroyo. No, I take that back. I'd of left you up on the Pecos.

We'll try and get your horse back, said John Grady. If that wont satisfy you then you let me know right now.

Blevins stared at the ground.

He dont give a shit, said Rawlins. I could of wrote it down. Get shot dead for horsestealin it dont mean a damn thing to him. He expects it.

It aint stealin, said Blevins. It's my horse.

A lot of ice that'll cut. You tell this man what you intend to do cause I guarantee you I dont give a big rat's ass.

All right, said Blevins.

John Grady studied him. We get you your horse you'll be ready to ride.

Yeah.

We got your word on that?

Word's ass, said Rawlins.

Yeah, said Blevins.

John Grady looked at Rawlins. Rawlins lay under his hat. He turned back to Blevins. All right, he said.

He got up and got his bedroll and came back and handed Blevins a blanket.

We goin to sleep now? said Blevins.

I am.

Did you all eat?

Yeah, said Rawlins. Sure we ate. Wouldnt you of? We eat a big steak apiece and split a third one.

Damn, said Blevins.

They slept until the moon was down and they sat in the dark and smoked. John Grady watched the stars.

What time you make it to be, bud? said Rawlins.

First quarter moon sets at midnight where I come from.

Rawlins smoked. Hell. I believe I'll go back to bed.

Go ahead. I'll wake you.

All right.

Blevins went to sleep as well. He sat watching the firmament unscroll up from behind the blackened palisades of the mountains to the east. Toward the village all was darkness. Not even a dog barked. He looked at Rawlins rolled asleep in his soogan and he knew that he was right in all he'd said and there was no help for it and the dipper standing at the northern edge of the world turned and the night was a long time passing.

When he called them out it was not much more than an hour till daylight.

You ready? said Rawlins.

Ready as I'm liable to get.

They saddled the horses and John Grady handed his stakerope to Blevins. You can make a hackamore out of that, he said.

All right.

Keep it under your shirt, said Rawlins. Dont let nobody see it.

There aint nobody to see it, said Blevins.

Dont bet on it. I see a light up yonder already.

Let's go, said John Grady.

There were no houselamps lit in the street where they'd seen the horse. They rode along slowly. A dog that had been sleeping in the dirt rose up and commenced barking and Rawlins made a throwing motion at it and it slunk off. When they got to the house where the horse was stabled John Grady got down and walked over and looked in the window and came back.

He aint here, he said.

It was dead quiet in the little mud street. Rawlins leaned and spat. Well, shit, he said.

You all sure this is the place? said Blevins.

It's the place.

The boy slid from the horse and picked his way gingerly with his bare feet across the road to the house and looked in. Then he climbed through the window.

What the hell's he doin? said Rawlins.

You got me.

They waited. He didnt come back.

Yonder comes somebody.

Some dogs started up. John Grady mounted up and turned the horse and went back up the road and sat the horse in the dark. Rawlins followed. Dogs were beginning to bark all back through the town. A light came on.

This is by God it, aint it? said Rawlins.

John Grady looked at him. He was sitting with the carbine upright on his thigh. From beyond the buildings and the din of dogs there came a shout.

You know what these sons of bitches'll do to us? said Rawlins. You thought about that?

John Grady leaned forward and spoke to the horse and put his hand on the horse's shoulder. The horse had begun to step nervously and it was not a nervous horse. He looked toward the houses where they'd seen the light. A horse whinnied in the dark.

That crazy son of a bitch, said Rawlins. That crazy son of a bitch.

All out bedlam had broken across the lot. Rawlins pulled his horse around and the horse stamped and trotted and he whacked it across the rump with the barrel of the gun. The horse squatted and dug in with its hind hooves and Blevins in his underwear atop the big bay horse and attended by a close retinue of howling dogs exploded into the road in a shower of debris from the rotted ocotillo fence he'd put the horse through.

The horse skittered past Rawlins sideways, Blevins clinging to the animal's mane and snatching at his hat. The dogs swarmed wildly over the road and Rawlins' horse stood and twisted and shook its head and the big bay turned a complete circle and there were three pistol shots from somewhere in the dark all evenly spaced that went pop pop pop. John Grady put the heels of his boots to his horse and leaned low in the saddle and he and Rawlins went pounding up the road. Blevins passed them both, his pale knees clutching the horse and his shirttail flying.

Before they reached the turn at the top of the hill there were three more shots from the road behind them. They turned onto the main track south and went pounding through the town. Already there were lamps lit in a few small windows. They passed through at a hard gallop and rode up into the low hills. First light was shaping out the country to the east. A mile south of the town they caught up with Blevins. He'd turned his horse in the road and he was watching them and watching the road behind them.

Hold up, he said. Let's listen.

They tried to quiet the gasping animals. You son of a bitch, said Rawlins.

Blevins didnt answer. He slid from his horse and lay in the road listening. Then he got up and pulled himself back up onto the horse.

Boys, he said, they're a comin.

Horses?

Yeah. I'll tell you right now straight out there aint no way you all can keep up with me. Let me take the road since it's me they're huntin. They'll follow the dust and you all can slip off into the country. I'll see you down the road.

Before they could agree or disagree he'd hauled the horse around by the hackamore and was pounding off up the track.

He's right, said John Grady. We better get off this damned road.

All right.

They rode out through the brush in the dark, taking the lowest country they could keep to, lying along the necks of their mounts that they not be skylighted.

We're fixin to get the horses snakebit sure as the world, said Rawlins.

It'll be daylight soon.

Then we can get shot.

In a little while they heard horses on the road. Then they heard more horses. Then all was quiet.

We better get somewheres, said Rawlins. It's fixin to get daylight sure enough.

Yeah, I know it.

You think when they come back they'll see where we quit the road?

Not if enough of em has rode over it.

What if they catch him?

John Grady didnt answer.

He wouldnt have no qualms about showin em which way we'd headed.

Probably not.

You know not. All they'd have to do would be look at him crossways.

Then we better keep ridin.

Well I dont know about you but I'm about to run out of horse.

Well tell me what you want to do.

Shit, said Rawlins. We aint got no choice. We'll see what daylight brings. Maybe one of these days we might find some grain somewheres in this country.

Maybe.

They slowed the horses and rode to the crest of the ridge. Nothing moved in all that gray landscape. They dismounted and walked out along the ridge. Small birds were beginning to call from the chaparral.

You know how long it's been since we eat? said Rawlins.

I aint even thought about it.

I aint either till just now. Bein shot at will sure enough cause you to lose your appetite, wont it?

Hold up a minute.

What is it?

Hold up.

They stood listening.

I dont hear nothin.

There's riders out there.

On the road?

I dont know.

Can you see anything?

No.

Let's keep movin.

John Grady spat and stood listening. Then they moved on.

At daylight they left the horses standing in a gravel wash and climbed to the top of a rise and sat among the ocotillos and watched the country back to the northeast. Some deer moved out feeding along the ridge opposite. Other than that they saw nothing.

Can you see the road? said Rawlins.

No.

They sat. Rawlins stood the rifle against his knee and took his tobacco from his pocket. I believe I'll smoke, he said.

A long fan of light ran out from the east and the rising sun swelled blood red along the horizon.

Look yonder, said John Grady.

What.

Over yonder.

Two miles away riders had crested a rise. One, two. A third. Then they dropped from sight again.

Which way are they headed?

Well cousin I dont know for sure but I got a pretty good notion.

Rawlins sat holding the cigarette. We're goin to die in this goddamned country, he said.

No we aint.

You think they can track us on this ground?

I dont know. I dont know that they cant.

I'll tell you what, bud. They get us bayed up out here somewheres with the horses give out they're goin to have to come over the barrel of this rifle.

John Grady looked at him and he looked back out where the riders had been. I'd hate to have to shoot my way back to Texas, he said.

Where's your gun at?

In the saddlebag.

Rawlins lit the cigarette. I ever see that little son of a bitch again I'll kill him myself. I'm damned if I wont.

Let's go, said John Grady. They still got a lot of ground to cover. I'd rather to make a good run as a bad stand.

They rode out west with the sun at their back and their shadows horse and rider falling before them tall as trees. The country they found themselves in was old lava country and they kept to the edge of the rolling black gravel plain and kept watch behind them. They saw the riders again, south of where they would have put them. And then once more.

If them horses aint bottomed out I believe they'd be comin harder than that, said Rawlins.

I do too.

Midmorning they rode to the crest of a low volcanic ridge and turned the horses and sat watching.

What do you think? said Rawlins.

Well, they know we aint got the horse. That's for sure. They might not be as anxious to ride this ground as you and me.

You got that right.

They sat for a long time. Nothing moved.

I think they've quit us.

I do too.

Let's keep movin.

By late afternoon the horses were stumbling. They watered them out of their hats and drank the other canteen dry themselves and mounted again and rode on. They saw the riders no more. Toward evening they came upon a band of sheepherders camped on the far side of a deep arroyo that was floored with round white rocks. The sheepherders seemed to have selected the site with an eye to its defense as did the ancients of that country and they watched with great solemnity the riders making their way along the other side.

What do you think? said John Grady.

I think we ought to keep ridin. I'm kindly soured on the citizens in this part of the country.

I think you're right.

They rode on another mile and descended into the arroyo to look for water. They found none. They dismounted and led the horses, the four of them stumbling along into the deepening darkness, Rawlins still carrying the rifle, following the senseless tracks of birds or wild pigs in the sand.

Nightfall found them sitting on their blankets on the ground with the horses staked a few feet away. Just sitting in the dark with no fire, not speaking. After a while Rawlins said: We should of got water from them herders.

We'll find some water in the mornin.

I wish it was mornin.

John Grady didnt answer.

Goddamn Junior is goin to piss and moan and carry on all night. I know how he gets.

They probably think we've gone crazy.

Aint we?

You think they caught him?

I dont know.

I'm goin to turn in.

They lay in their blankets on the ground. The horses shifted uneasily in the dark.

I'll say one thing about him, said Rawlins.

Who?

Blevins.

What's that?

The little son of a bitch wouldnt stand still for nobody high-jackin his horse.

In the morning they left the horses in the arroyo and climbed up to watch the sun rise and see what the country afforded. It had been cold in the night in the sink and when the sun came up they turned and sat with their backs to it. To the north a thin spire of smoke stood in the windless air.

You reckon that's the sheepcamp? said Rawlins.

We better hope it is.

You want to ride back up there and see if they'll give us some water and some grub?

No.

I dont either.

They watched the country.

Rawlins rose and walked off with the rifle. After a while he came back with some nopal fruit in his hat and poured them out on a flat rock and sat peeling them with his knife.

You want some of these? he said.

John Grady walked over and squatted and got out his own knife. The nopal was still cool from the night and it stained their fingers blood red and they sat peeling the fruit and eating it and spitting the small hard seeds and picking the spines out of their fingers. Rawlins gestured at the countryside. There aint much happenin out there, is there?

John Grady nodded. Biggest problem we got is we could run

into them people and not even know it. We never even got a good look at their horses.

Rawlins spat. They got the same problem. They dont know us neither.

They'd know us.

Yeah, said Rawlins. You got a point.

Course we aint got no problem at all next to Blevins. He'd about as well to paint that horse red and go around blowin a horn.

Aint that the truth.

Rawlins wiped the blade of his knife on his trousers and folded it shut. I believe I'm losin ground with these things.

Peculiar thing is, what he says is true. It is his horse.

Well it's somebody's horse.

It damn sure dont belong to them Mexicans.

Yeah. Well he's got no way to prove it.

Rawlins put the knife in his pocket and sat inspecting his hat for nopal stickers. A goodlookin horse is like a good-lookin woman, he said. They're always more trouble than what they're worth. What a man needs is just one that will get the job done.

Where'd you hear that at?

I dont know.

John Grady folded away his knife. Well, he said. There's a lot of country out there.

Yep. Lot of country.

God knows where he's got to.

Rawlins nodded. I'll tell you what you told me.

What's that?

We aint seen the last of his skinny ass.

They rode all day upon the broad plain to the south. It was noon before they found water, a silty residue in the floor of an adobe tank. In the evening passing through a saddle in the low hills they jumped a spikehorn buck out of a stand of juniper and Rawlins shucked the rifle backward out of the bootleg scabbard and raised and cocked it and fired. He'd let go the reins and the horse bowed up and hopped sideways and stood trembling and he stepped down and ran to the spot where he'd seen the little buck and it lay dead in its blood on the ground. John Grady rode up leading Rawlins' horse. The buck was shot through the base of the skull and its eyes were just glazing. Rawlins ejected the spent shell and levered in a fresh round and lowered the hammer with his thumb and looked up.

That was a hell of a shot, said John Grady.

That was blind dumb-ass luck is what that was. I just raised up and shot.

Still a hell of a shot.

Let me have your beltknife. If we dont founder on deermeat I'm a chinaman.

They dressed out the deer and hung it in the junipers to cool and they made a foray on the slope for wood. They built a fire and they cut paloverde poles and cut forked uprights to lay them in and Rawlins skinned the buck out and sliced the meat in strips and draped it over the poles to smoke. When the fire had burned down he skewered the backstraps on two green-wood sticks and propped the sticks with rocks over the coals. Then they sat watching the meat brown and sniffed the smoke where fat dropped hissing in the coals.

John Grady walked out and unsaddled the horses and hobbled them and turned them out and came back with his blanket and saddle.

Here you go, he said.

What's that?

Salt.

I wish we had some bread.

How about some fresh corn and potatoes and apple cobbler?

Dont be a ass.

Aint them things done yet?

No. Set down. They wont never get done with you standin there thataway.

They ate the tenderloins one apiece and turned the strips of meat on the poles and lay back and rolled cigarettes.

I've seen them vaqueros worked for Blair cut a yearling heifer so thin you could see through the meat. They'd bone one out damn near in one long sheet. They'd hang the meat on poles all the way around the fire like laundry and if you come up on it at night you wouldnt know what it was. It was like lookin through somethin and seein its heart. They'd turn the meat and mend the fire in the night and you'd see em movin around inside it. You'd wake up in the night and this thing would be settin out there on the prairie in the wind and it would be glowin like a hot stove. Just red as blood.

This here meat's goin to taste like cedar, said John Grady.

I know it.

Coyotes were yapping along the ridge to the south. Rawlins leaned and tipped the ash from his cigarette into the fire and leaned back.

You ever think about dyin?

Yeah. Some. You?

Yeah. Some. You think there's a heaven?

Yeah. Dont you?

I dont know. Yeah. Maybe. You think you can believe in heaven if you dont believe in hell?

I guess you can believe what you want to.

Rawlins nodded. You think about all the stuff that can happen to you, he said. There aint no end to it.

You fixin to get religion on us?

No. Just sometimes I wonder if I wouldnt be better off if I did.

You aint fixin to quit me are you?

I said I wouldnt.

John Grady nodded.

You think them guts might draw a lion? said Rawlins.

Could.

You ever seen one?

No. You?

Just that one dead that Julius Ramsey killed with the dogs up on Grape Creek. He climbed up in the tree and knocked it out with a stick for the dogs to fight.

You think he really done that?

Yeah. I think probably he did.

John Grady nodded. He might well could of.

The coyotes yammered and ceased and then began again.

You think God looks out for people? said Rawlins.

Yeah. I guess He does. You?

Yeah. I do. Way the world is. Somebody can wake up and sneeze somewhere in Arkansas or some damn place and before you're done there's wars and ruination and all hell. You dont know what's goin to happen. I'd say He's just about got to. I dont believe we'd make it a day otherwise.

John Grady nodded.

You dont think them sons of bitches might of caught him do you?

Blevins?

Yeah.

I dont know. I thought you was glad to get shut of him.

I dont want to see nothin bad happen to him.

I dont either.

You reckon his name is Jimmy Blevins sure enough?

Who knows.

In the night the coyotes woke them and they lay in the dark and listened to them where they convened over the carcass of the deer, fighting and squalling like cats.

I want you to listen to that damned racket, said Rawlins.

He got up and got a stick from the fire and shouted at them and threw the stick. They hushed. He mended the fire and turned the meat on the greenwood racks. By the time he was back in his blankets they were at it again.

They rode all day the day following through the hill country to the west. As they rode they cut strips of the smoked and half dried deermeat and chewed on it and their hands were black and greasy and they wiped them on the withers of the horses and passed the canteen of water back and forth between them and admired the country. There were storms to the south and masses of clouds that moved slowly along the horizon with their long dark tendrils trailing in the rain. That night they camped on a ledge of rock above the plains and watched the lightning all along the horizon provoke from the seamless dark the distant mountain ranges again and again. Crossing the plain the next morning they came upon standing water in the bajadas and they watered the horses and drank rainwater from the rocks and they climbed steadily into the deepening cool of the mountains until in the evening of that day from the crest of the cordilleras they saw below them the country of which they'd been told. The grasslands lay in a deep violet haze and to the west thin flights of waterfowl were moving north before the sunset in the deep red galleries under the cloudbanks like schoolfish in a burning sea and on the foreland plain they saw vaqueros driving cattle before them through a gauze of golden dust.

They made camp on the south slope of the mountain and spread their blankets in the dry dirt under an overhanging ledge of rock. Rawlins took horse and rope and dragged up before their camp an entire dead tree and they built a great bonfire against the cold. Out on the plain in the shoreless night they could see like a reflection of their own fire in a dark lake the fire of the vaqueros five miles away. It rained in the night and the rain hissed in the fire and the horses came in out of the darkness and stood with their red eyes shifting and blinking and in the morning it was cold and gray and the sun a long time coming.

By noon they were on the plain riding through grass of a kind they'd not seen before. The path of the driven cattle lay through the grass like a place where water had run and by midafternoon they could see the herd before them moving west and within an hour they'd caught them up.

The vaqueros knew them by the way they sat their horses and they called them caballero and exchanged smoking material with them and told them about the country. They drove the cattle on to the west fording creeks and a small river and driving pockets of antelope and whitetail deer before them out of the stands of enormous cottonwoods through which they passed and they moved on until late in the day when they came to a fence and began to drift the cattle south. There was a road on the other side of the fence and in the road were the tracks of tires and the tracks of horses from the recent rains and a young girl came riding down the road and passed them and they ceased talking. She wore english riding boots and jodhpurs and a blue twill hacking jacket and she carried a ridingcrop and the horse she rode was a black Arabian saddlehorse. She'd been riding the horse in the river or in the ciénagas because the horse was wet to its belly and the leather fenders of the saddle were dark at their lower edges and her boots as well. She wore a flatcrowned hat of black felt with a wide brim and her black hair was loose under it and fell halfway to her waist and as she rode past she turned and smiled and touched the brim of the hat with her crop and the vaqueros touched their hatbrims one by one down to the last of those who'd pretended not even to see her as she passed. Then she pushed the horse into a gaited rack and disappeared down the road.

Rawlins looked at the caporal of the vaqueros but the caporal put his horse forward and rode up the line. Rawlins fell back among the riders and alongside John Grady.

Did you see that little darlin? he said.

John Grady didnt answer. He was still looking down the road where she'd gone. There was nothing there to see but he was looking anyway.

An hour later in the failing light they were helping the vaqueros drive the cattle into a holdingpen. The gerente had ridden up from the house and he sat his horse and picked his teeth and watched the work without comment. When they were done the caporal and another vaquero took them over and introduced them namelessly and the five of them rode together back down to the gerente's house and there in the kitchen at a metal table under a bare lightbulb the gerente questioned them closely as to their understanding of ranch work while the caporal seconded their every claim and the vaquero nodded and said that it was so and the caporal volunteered testimony on his own concerning the qualifications of the güeros of which they themselves were not even aware, dismissing doubt with a sweep of his hand as if to say that these were things known to everyone. The gerente leaned back in his chair and studied them. In the end they gave their names and spelled them and the gerente put them in his book and then they rose and shook hands and walked out in the early darkness where the moon was rising and the cattle were calling and the yellow squares of windowlight gave warmth and shape to an alien world.

They unsaddled the horses and turned them into the trap and followed the caporal up to the bunkhouse. A long adobe building of two rooms with a tin roof and concrete floors. In one room a dozen bunks of wood or metal. A small sheetiron stove. In the other room a long table with benches for seats and a woodburning cookstove. An old wooden safe that held glasses and tinware. A soapstone sink with a zinc-covered sideboard. The men were already at the table eating when they entered and they went to the sideboard and got cups and plates and stood at the stove and helped themselves to beans and tortillas and a rich stew made from kid and then went to the table where the vaqueros nodded to them and made expansive gestures for them to be seated, eating the while with one hand.

After dinner they sat at the table and smoked and drank coffee and the vaqueros asked them many questions about America and all the questions were about horses and cattle and none about them. Some had friends or relatives who had been there but to most the country to the north was little more than a rumor. A thing for which there seemed no accounting. Someone brought a coal-oil lamp to the table and lit it and shortly thereafter the generator shut down and the lightbulbs hanging by their cords from the ceiling dimmed to a thin orange wire and winked out. They listened with great attention as John Grady answered their questions and they nodded solemnly and they were careful of their demeanor that they not be thought to have opinions on what they heard for like most men skilled at their work they were scornful of any least suggestion of knowing anything not learned at first hand.

They carried their dishes to a galvanized tub full of water and soapcurd and they carried the lamp to their bunks at the farther end of the bunkhouse and unrolled the ticks down over the rusty springs and spread their blankets and undressed and blew out the lamp. Tired as they were they lay a long time in the dark after the vaqueros were asleep. They could hear them breathing deeply in the room that smelled of horses and leather and men and they could hear in the distance the new cattle still not bedded down in the holdingpen.

I believe these are some pretty good old boys, whispered Rawlins.

Yeah, I believe they are too.

You see them old highback centerfire rigs?

Yeah.

You reckon they think we're on the run down here?

Aint we?

Rawlins didnt answer. After a while he said: I like hearin the cattle out there.

Yeah. I do too.

He didnt say much about Rocha, did he?

Not a lot.

You reckon that was his daughter?

I'd say it was.

This is some country, aint it?

Yeah. It is. Go to sleep.

Bud?

Yeah.

This is how it was with the old waddies, aint it?

Yeah.

How long do you think you'd like to stay here?

About a hundred years. Go to sleep.

II

THE HACIENDA de Nuestra Señora de la Purísima Concepción was a ranch of eleven thousand hectares situated along the edge of the Bolsón de Cuatro Ciénagas in the state of Coahuila. The western sections ran into the Sierra de Anteojo to elevations of nine thousand feet but south and east the ranch occupied part of the broad barrial or basin floor of the bolsón and was well watered with natural springs and clear streams and dotted with marshes and shallow lakes or lagunas. In the lakes and in the streams were species of fish not known elsewhere on earth and birds and lizards and other forms of life as well all long relict here for the desert stretched away on every side.

La Purísima was one of very few ranches in that part of Mexico retaining the full complement of six square leagues of land allotted by the colonizing legislation of eighteen twenty-four and the owner Don Héctor Rocha y Villareal was one of the few hacendados who actually lived on the land he claimed, land which had been in his family for one hundred and seventy years. He was forty-seven years old and he was the first male heir in all that new world lineage to attain such an age.

He ran upwards of a thousand head of cattle on this land. He kept a house in Mexico City where his wife lived. He flew his own airplane. He loved horses. When he rode up to the gerente's house that morning he was accompanied by four friends and by a retinue of mozos and two packanimals saddled with hardwood kiacks, one empty, the other carrying their noon provisions. They were attended by a pack of greyhound dogs and the dogs were lean and silver in color and they flowed among the legs of the horses silent and fluid as running mercury and the horses paid them no mind at all. The hacendado halloed the house and the gerente emerged in his shirtsleeves and they spoke briefly and the gerente nodded and the hacendado spoke to his friends and then all rode on. When they passed the bunkhouse and rode through the gate and turned into the road up-country some of the vaqueros were catching their horses in the trap and leading them out to saddle them for the day's work. John Grady and Rawlins stood in the doorway drinking their coffee.

Yonder he is, said Rawlins.

John Grady nodded and slung the dregs of coffee out into the yard.

Where the hell do you reckon they're goin? said Rawlins.

I'd say they're goin to run coyotes.

They aint got no guns.

They got ropes.

Rawlins looked at him. Are you shittin me?

I dont think so.

Well I'd damn sure like to see it.

I would too. You ready?

They worked two days in the holdingpens branding and ear-marking and castrating and dehorning and inoculating. On the third day the vaqueros brought a small herd of wild three year old colts down from the mesa and penned them and in the evening Rawlins and John Grady walked out to look them over. They were bunched against the fence at the far side of the enclosure and they were a mixed lot, roans and duns and bays and a few paints and they were of varied size and conformation. John Grady opened the gate and he and Rawlins walked in and he closed it behind them. The horrified animals began to climb over one another and to break up and move along the fence in both directions.

That's as spooky a bunch of horses as I ever saw, said Rawlins.

They dont know what we are.

Dont know what we are?

I dont think so. I dont think they've ever seen a man afoot.

Rawlins leaned and spat.

You see anything there you'd have?

There's horses there.

Where at?

Look at that dark bay. Right yonder.

I'm lookin.

Look again.

That horse wont weigh eight hundred pounds.

Yeah he will. Look at the hindquarters on him. He'd make a cowhorse. Look at that roan yonder.

That coonfooted son of a bitch?

Well, yeah he is a little. All right. That other roan. That third one to the right.

The one with the white on him?

Yeah.

That's kindly a funny lookin horse to me.

No he aint. He's just colored peculiar.

You dont think that means nothin? He's got white feet.

That's a good horse. Look at his head. Look at the jaw on him. You got to remember their tails are all growed out.

Yeah. Maybe. Rawlins shook his head doubtfully. You used to be awful particular about horses. Maybe you just aint seen any in a long time.

John Grady nodded. Yeah, he said. Well. I aint forgot what they're supposed to look like.

The horses had grouped again at the far end of the pen and stood rolling their eyes and running their heads along each other's necks.

They got one thing goin for em, said Rawlins.

What's that.

They aint had no Mexican to try and break em.

John Grady nodded.

They studied the horses.

How many are there? said John Grady.

Rawlins looked them over. Fifteen. Sixteen.

I make it sixteen.

Sixteen then.

You think you and me could break all of em in four days?

Depends on what you call broke.

Just halfway decent greenbroke horses. Say six saddles. Double and stop and stand still to be saddled.

Rawlins took his tobacco from his pocket and pushed back his hat.

What you got in mind? he said.

Breakin these horses.

Why four days?

You think we could do it?

They intend puttin em in the rough-string? My feelin is that any horse broke in four days is liable to come unbroke in four more.

They're out of horses is how come em to be down here in the first place.

Rawlins dabbed tobacco into the cupped paper. You're tellin me that what we're lookin at here is our own string?

That's my guess.

We're lookin at ridin some coldjawed son of a bitch broke with one of them damned mexican ringbits.

Yeah.

Rawlins nodded. What would you do, sideline em?

Yep.

You think there's that much rope on the place?

I dont know.

You'd be a woreout sumbuck. I'll tell you that.

Think how good you'd sleep.

Rawlins put the cigarette in his mouth and fished about for a match. What else do you know that you aint told me?

Armando says the old man's got horses all over that mountain.

How many horses.

Somethin like four hundred head.

Rawlins looked at him. He popped the match and lit the cigarette and flipped the match away. What in the hell for?

He'd started a breeding program before the war.

What kind of horses?

Media sangres.

What the hell is that.

Quarterhorses, what we'd call em.

Yeah?

That roan yonder, said John Grady, is a flat-out Billy horse if he does have bad feet.

Where do you reckon he come from?

Where they all come from. Out of a horse called José Chiquito.

Little Joe?

Yeah.

The same horse?

The same horse.

Rawlins smoked thoughtfully.

Both of them horses were sold in Mexico, said John Grady. One and Two. What he's got up yonder is a big yeguada of mares out of the old Traveler-Ronda line of horses of Sheeran's.

What else? said Rawlins.

That's it.

Let's go talk to the man.

THEY STOOD in the kitchen with their hats in their hands and the gerente sat at the table and studied them.

Amansadores, he said.

Sí.

Ambos, he said.

Sí. Ambos.

He leaned back. He drummed his fingers on the metal tabletop.

Hay dieciseis caballos en el potrero, said John Grady. Podemos amansarlos en cuatro días.

They walked back across the yard to the bunkhouse to wash up for supper.

What did he say? said Rawlins.

He said we were full of shit. But in a nice way.

Is that a flat-out no do you reckon?

I dont think so. I dont think he can leave it at that.

They went to work on the green colts daybreak Sunday morning, dressing in the half dark in clothes still wet from their washing them the night before and walking out to the potrero before the stars were down, eating a cold tortilla wrapped around a scoop of cold beans and no coffee and carrying their fortyfoot maguey catchropes coiled over their shoulders. They carried saddleblankets and a bosalea or riding hackamore with a metal noseband and John Grady carried a pair of clean gunnysacks he'd slept on and his Hamley saddle with the stirrups already shortened.

They stood looking at the horses. The horses shifted and stood, gray shapes in the gray morning. Stacked on the ground outside the gate were coils of every kind of rope, cotton and manilla and plaited rawhide and maguey and ixtle down to lengths of old woven hair mecates and handplaited piecings of bindertwine. Stacked against the fence were the sixteen rope hackamores they'd spent the evening tying in the bunkhouse.

This bunch has done been culled once up on the mesa, aint it?

I'd say so.

What do they want with the mares?

They ride em down here.

Well, said Rawlins. I can see why they're hard on a horse. Puttin up with them bitches.

He shook his head and stuffed the last of the tortilla in his jaw and wiped his hands on his trousers and undid the wire and opened the gate.

John Grady followed him in and stood the saddle on the ground and went back out and brought in a handful of ropes and hackamores and squatted to sort them. Rawlins stood building his loop.

I take it you dont give a particular damn what order they come in, he said.

You take it correctly, cousin.

You dead set on sackin these varmints out?

Yep.

My old daddy always said that the purpose of breakin a horse was to ride it and if you got one to break you just as well to saddle up and climb aboard and get on with it.

John Grady grinned. Was your old daddy a certified peeler?

I never heard him claim to be. But I damn sure seen him hang and rattle a time or two.

Well you're fixin to see some more of it.

We goin to bust em twice?

What for?

I never saw one that completely believed it the first time or ever doubted it the second.

John Grady smiled. I'll make em believe, he said. You'll see.

I'm goin to tell you right now, cousin. This is a heathenish bunch.

What is it Blair says? No such thing as a mean colt?

No such thing as a mean colt, said Rawlins.

The horses were already moving. He took the first one that broke and rolled his loop and forefooted the colt and it hit the ground with a tremendous thump. The other horses flared and bunched and looked back wildly. Before the colt could struggle up John Grady had squatted on its neck and pulled its head up and to one side and was holding the horse by the muzzle with the long bony head pressed against his chest and the hot sweet breath of it flooding up from the dark wells of its nostrils over his face and neck like news from another world. They did not smell like horses. They smelled like what they were, wild animals. He held the horse's face against his chest and he could feel along his inner thighs the blood pumping through the arteries and he could smell the fear and he cupped his hand over the horse's eyes and stroked them and he did not stop talking to the horse at all, speaking in a low steady voice and telling it all that he intended to do and cupping the animal's eyes and stroking the terror out.

Rawlins took one of the lengths of siderope from around his neck where he'd hung them and made a slipnoose and hitched it around the pastern of the hind leg and drew the leg up and halfhitched it to the horse's forelegs. He freed the catchrope and pitched it away and took the hackamore and they fitted it over the horse's muzzle and ears and John Grady ran his thumb in the animal's mouth and Rawlins fitted the mouthrope and then slipnoosed a second siderope to the other rear leg. Then he tied both sideropes to the hackamore.

You all set? he said.

All set.

He let go the horse's head and rose and stepped away. The horse struggled up and turned and shot out one hind foot and snatched itself around in a half circle and fell over. It got up and kicked again and fell again. When it got up the third time it stood kicking and snatching its head about in a little dance. It stood. It walked away and stood again. Then it shot out a hindleg and fell again.

It lay there for a while thinking things over and when it got up it stood for a minute and then it hopped up and down three times and then it just stood glaring at them. Rawlins had got his catchrope and was building his loop again. The other horses watched with great interest from the far side of the potrero.

These sumbucks are as crazy as a shithouse rat, he said.

You pick out the one you think is craziest, said John Grady, and I'll give you a finished horse this time Sunday week.

Finished for who?

To your satisfaction.

Bullshit, said Rawlins.

By the time they had three of the horses sidelined in the trap blowing and glaring about there were several vaqueros at the gate drinking coffee in a leisurely fashion and watching the proceedings. By midmorning eight of the horses stood tied and the other eight were wilder than deer, scattering along the fence and bunching and running in a rising sea of dust as the day warmed, coming to reckon slowly with the remorselessness of this rendering of their fluid and collective selves into that condition of separate and helpless paralysis which seemed to be among them like a creeping plague. The entire complement of vaqueros had come from the bunkhouse to watch and by noon all sixteen of the mesteños were standing about in the potrero sidehobbled to their own hackamores and faced about in every direction and all communion among them broken. They looked like animals trussed up by children for fun and they stood waiting for they knew not what with the voice of the breaker still running in their brains like the voice of some god come to inhabit them.

When they went down to the bunkhouse for dinner the vaqueros seemed to treat them with a certain deference but whether it was the deference accorded the accomplished or that accorded to mental defectives they were unsure. No one asked them their opinion of the horses or queried them as to their method. When they went back up to the trap in the afternoon there were some twenty people standing about looking at the horses—women, children, young girls and men—and all waiting for them to return.

Where the hell did they come from? said Rawlins.

I dont know.

Word gets around when the circus comes to town, dont it?

They passed nodding through the crowd and entered the trap and fastened the gate.

You picked one out? said John Grady.

Yeah. For pure crazy I nominate that bucketheaded son of a bitch standin right yonder.

The grullo?

Grullo-lookin.

The man's a judge of horseflesh.

He's a judge of craziness.

He watched while John Grady walked up to the animal and tied a twelvefoot length of rope to the hackamore. Then he led it through the gate out of the potrero and into the corral where the horses would be ridden. Rawlins thought the horse would shy or try to rear but it didnt. He got the sack and hobbleropes and came up and while John Grady talked to the horse he hobbled the front legs together and then took the mecate rope and handed John Grady the sack and he held the horse while for the next quarter hour John Grady floated the sack over the animal and under it and rubbed its head with the sack and passed it across the horse's face and ran it up and down and between the animal's legs talking to the horse the while and rubbing against it and leaning against it. Then he got the saddle.

What good do you think it does to waller all over a horse thataway? said Rawlins.

I dont know, said John Grady. I aint a horse.

He lifted the blanket and placed it on the animal's back and smoothed it and stood stroking the animal and talking to it and then he bent and picked up the saddle and lifted it with the cinches strapped up and the off stirrup hung over the horn and sat it on the horse's back and rocked it into place. The horse never moved. He bent and reached under and pulled up the strap and cinched it. The horse's ears went back and he talked to it and then pulled up the cinch again and he leaned against the horse and talked to it just as if it were neither crazy nor lethal. Rawlins looked toward the corral gate. There were fifty or more people watching. Folk were picnicking on the ground. Fathers held up babies. John Grady lifted off the stirrup from the saddlehorn and let it drop. Then he hauled up the cinchstrap again and buckled it. All right, he said.

Hold him, said Rawlins.

He held the mecate while Rawlins undid the sideropes from the hackamore and knelt and tied them to the front hobbles. Then they slipped the hackamore off the horse's head and John Grady raised the bosalea and gently fitted it over the horse's nose and fitted the mouthrope and headstall. He gathered the reins and looped them over the horse's head and nodded and Rawlins knelt and undid the hobbles and pulled the slipnooses until the siderope loops fell to the ground at the horse's rear hooves. Then he stepped away.

John Grady put one foot in the stirrup and pressed himself flat against the horse's shoulder talking to it and then swung up into the saddle.

The horse stood stock still. It shot out one hindfoot to test the air and stood again and then it threw itself sideways and twisted and kicked and stood snorting. John Grady touched it up in the ribs with his bootheels and it stepped forward. He reined it and it turned. Rawlins spat in disgust. John Grady turned the horse again and came back by.

What the hell kind of a bronc is that? said Rawlins. You think that's what these people paid good money to see?

By dark he'd ridden eleven of the sixteen horses. Not all of them so tractable. Someone had built a fire on the ground outside the potrero and there were something like a hundred people gathered, some come from the pueblo of La Vega six miles to the south, some from farther. He rode the last five horses by the light of that fire, the horses dancing, turning in the light, their red eyes flashing. When they were done the horses stood in the potrero or stepped about trailing their hackamore ropes over the ground with such circumspection not to tread upon them and snatch down their sore noses that they moved with an air of great elegance and seemliness. The wild and frantic band of mustangs that had circled the potrero that morning like marbles swirled in a jar could hardly be said to exist and the animals whinnied to one another in the dark and answered back as if some one among their number were missing, or some thing.

When they walked down to the bunkhouse in the dark the bonfire was still burning and someone had brought a guitar and someone else a mouth-harp. Three separate strangers offered them a drink from bottles of mescal before they were clear of the crowd.

The kitchen was empty and they got their dinner from the stove and sat at the table. Rawlins watched John Grady. He was chewing woodenly and half tottering on the bench.

You aint tired are you, bud? he said.

No, said John Grady. I was tired five hours ago.

Rawlins grinned. Dont drink no more of that coffee. It'll keep you awake.

When they walked out in the morning at daybreak the fire was still smoldering and there were four or five men lying asleep on the ground, some with blankets and some without. Every horse in the potrero watched them come through the gate.

You remember how they come? said Rawlins.

Yeah. I remember em. I know you remember your buddy yonder.

Yeah, I know the son of a bitch.

When he walked up to the horse with the sack it turned and went trotting. He walked it down against the fence and picked up the rope and pulled it around and it stood quivering and he walked up to it and began to talk to it and then to stroke it with the sack. Rawlins went to fetch the blankets and the saddle and the bosalea.

By ten that night he'd ridden the entire remuda of sixteen horses and Rawlins had ridden them a second time each. They rode them again Tuesday and on Wednesday morning at day-break with the first horse saddled and the sun not up John Grady rode toward the gate.

Open her up, he said.

Let me saddle a catch-horse.

We aint got time.

If that son of a bitch sets your ass out in the stickers you'll have time.

I guess I'd better stay in the saddle then.

Let me saddle up one of these good horses.

All right.

He rode out of the trap leading Rawlins' horse and waited while Rawlins shut the gate and mounted up beside him. The green horses stepped and sidled nervously.

This is kindly the blind leadin the blind, aint it?

Rawlins nodded. It's sort of like old T-Bone Watts when he

worked for daddy they all fussed about him havin bad breath. He told em it was bettern no breath at all.

John Grady grinned and booted the horse forward into a trot and they set out up the road.

Midafternoon he'd ridden all the horses again and while Rawlins worked with them in the trap he rode the little grullo of Rawlins' choice up into the country. Two miles above the ranch where the road ran by sedge and willow and wild plum along the edge of the laguna she rode past him on the black horse.

He heard the horse behind him and would have turned to look but that he heard it change gaits. He didnt look at her until the Arabian was alongside his horse, stepping with its neck arched and one eye on the mesteño not with wariness but some faint equine disgust. She passed five feet away and turned her fineboned face and looked full at him. She had blue eyes and she nodded or perhaps she only lowered her head slightly to better see what sort of horse he rode, just the slightest tilt of the broad black hat set level on her head, the slightest lifting of the long black hair. She passed and the horse changed gaits again and she sat the horse more than well, riding erect with her broad shoulders and trotting the horse up the road. The mesteño had stopped and sulled in the road with its forefeet spread and he sat looking after her. He'd half meant to speak but those eyes had altered the world forever in the space of a heartbeat. She disappeared beyond the lakeside willows. A flock of small birds rose up and passed back over him with thin calls.

That evening when Antonio and the gerente came up to the trap to inspect the horses he was teaching the grullo to back with Rawlins in the saddle. They watched, the gerente picking his teeth. Antonio rode the two horses that were standing saddled, sawing them back and forth in the corral and pulling them up short. He dismounted and nodded and he and the gerente looked over the horses in the other wing of the corral and then they left. Rawlins and John Grady looked at each other. They unsaddled the horses and turned them in with the remuda and walked back down to the house carrying their saddles and gear and washed up for supper. The vaqueros were at the table and they got their plates and helped themselves at the stove and got their coffee and came to the table and swung a leg over and sat down. There was a clay dish of tortillas in the center of the table with a towel over it and when John Grady pointed and asked that it be passed there came hands from both sides of the table to take up the dish and hand it down in this manner like a ceremonial bowl.

Three days later they were in the mountains. The caporal had sent a mozo with them to cook and see to the horses and he'd sent three young vaqueros not much older than they. The mozo was an old man with a bad leg named Luis who had fought at Torreón and San Pedro and later at Zacatecas and the boys were boys from the country, two of them born on the hacienda. Only one of the three had ever been as far as Monterrey. They rode up into the mountains trailing three horses apiece in their string with packhorses to haul the grub and cooktent and they hunted the wild horses in the upland forests in the pine and madroño and in the arroyos where they'd gone to hide and they drove them pounding over the high mesas and penned them in the stone ravine fitted ten years earlier with fence and gate and there the horses milled and squealed and clambered at the rock slopes and turned upon one another biting and kicking while John Grady walked among them in the sweat and dust and bedlam with his rope as if they were no more than some evil dream of horse. They camped at night on the high headlands where their windtattered fire sawed about in the darkness and Luis told them tales of the country and the people who lived in it and the people who died and how they died. He'd loved horses all his life and he and his father and two brothers had fought in the cavalry and his father and his brothers had died in the cavalry but they'd all despised Victoriano Huerta above all other men and the deeds of Huerta above all other visited evils. He said that compared to Huerta Judas was himself but another Christ and one of the young vaqueros looked away and another blessed himself. He said that war had destroyed the country and that men believe the cure for war is war as the curandero prescribes the serpent's flesh for its bite. He spoke of his campaigns in the deserts of Mexico and he told them of horses killed under him and he said that the souls of horses mirror the souls of men more closely than men suppose and that horses also love war. Men say they only learn this but he said that no creature can learn that which his heart has no shape to hold. His own father said that no man who has not gone to war horseback can ever truly understand the horse and he said that he supposed he wished that this were not so but that it was so.

Lastly he said that he had seen the souls of horses and that it was a terrible thing to see. He said that it could be seen under certain circumstances attending the death of a horse because the horse shares a common soul and its separate life only forms it out of all horses and makes it mortal. He said that if a person understood the soul of the horse then he would understand all horses that ever were.

They sat smoking, watching the deepest embers of the fire where the red coals cracked and broke.

Y de los hombres? said John Grady.

The old man shaped his mouth how to answer. Finally he said that among men there was no such communion as among horses and the notion that men can be understood at all was probably an illusion. Rawlins asked him in his bad spanish if there was a heaven for horses but he shook his head and said that a horse had no need of heaven. Finally John Grady asked him if it were not true that should all horses vanish from the face of the earth the soul of the horse would not also perish for there would be nothing out of which to replenish it but the old man only said that it was pointless to speak of there being no horses in the world for God would not permit such a thing.

They drove the mares down through the draws and arroyos out of the mountains and across the watered grasslands of the bolsón and penned them. They were at this work for three weeks until by the end of April they had over eighty mares in the trap, most of them halterbroke, some already sorted out for saddlehorses. By then the roundup was underway and droves of cattle were moving daily down out of the open country onto the ranch pastures and although some of the vaqueros had no more than two or three horses to their string the new horses stayed in the trap. On the second morning of May the red Cessna plane came in from the south and circled the ranch and banked and dropped and glided from sight beyond the trees.

An hour later John Grady was standing in the ranch house kitchen with his hat in his hands. A woman was washing dishes at the sink and a man was sitting at the table reading a newspaper. The woman wiped her hands on her apron and went off into another part of the house and in a few minutes she returned. Un ratito, she said.

John Grady nodded. Gracias, he said.

The man rose and folded the newspaper and crossed the kitchen and came back with a wooden rack of butcher and boning knives together with an oilstone and set them out on the paper. At the same moment Don Héctor appeared in the doorway and stood looking at John Grady.

He was a spare man with broad shoulders and graying hair and he was tall in the manner of norteños and light of skin. He entered the kitchen and introduced himself and John Grady shifted his hat to his left hand and they shook hands.

María, said the hacendado. Café por favor.

He held out his hand palm upward toward the doorway and John Grady crossed the kitchen and entered the hall. The house was cool and quiet and smelled of wax and flowers. A tallcase clock stood in the hallway to the left. The brass weights stirred behind the casement doors, the pendulum slowly swept. He turned to look back and the hacendado smiled and extended his hand toward the diningroom doorway. Pásale, he said.

They sat at a long table of english walnut. The walls of the room were covered with blue damask and hung with portraits of men and horses. At the end of the room was a walnut sideboard with some chafingdishes and decanters set out upon it and along the windowsill outside taking the sun were four cats. Don Héctor reached behind him and took a china ashtray from the sideboard and placed it before them and took from his shirtpocket a small tin box of english cigarettes and opened them and offered them to John Grady and John Grady took one.

Gracias, he said.

The hacendado placed the tin on the table between them and took a silver lighter from his pocket and lit the boy's cigarette and then his own.

Gracias.

The man blew a thin stream of smoke slowly downtable and smiled.

Bueno, he said. We can speak english.

Como le convenga, said John Grady.

Armando tells me that you understand horses.

I've been around em some.

The hacendado smoked thoughtfully. He seemed to be waiting for more to be said. The man who'd been sitting in the kitchen reading the paper entered the room with a silver tray carrying a coffee service with cups and creampitcher and a sugarbowl together with a plate of bizcochos. He set the tray on the table and stood a moment and the hacendado thanked him and he went out again.

Don Héctor set out the cups himself and poured the coffee and nodded at the tray. Please help yourself, he said.

Thank you. I just take it black.

You are from Texas.

Yessir.

The hacendado nodded again. He sipped his coffee. He was seated sideways to the table with his legs crossed. He flexed his foot in the chocolatecolored veal boot and turned and looked at John Grady and smiled.

Why are you here? he said.

John Grady looked at him. He looked down the table where the shadows of the sunning cats sat in a row like cutout cats all leaning slightly aslant. He looked at the hacendado again.

I just wanted to see the country, I reckon. Or we did.

May I ask how old are you?

Sixteen.

The hacendado raised his eyebrows. Sixteen, he said.

Yessir.

The hacendado smiled again. When I was sixteen I told people I was eighteen.

John Grady sipped his coffee.

Your friend is sixteen also?

Seventeen.

But you are the leader.

We dont have no leaders. We're just buddies.

Of course.

He nudged the plate forward. Please, he said. Help yourself.

Thank you. I just got up from the breakfast table.

The hacendado tipped the ash from his cigarette into the china ashtray and sat back again.

What is your opinion of the mares, he said.

There's some good mares in that bunch.

Yes. Do you know a horse called Three Bars?

That's a thoroughbred horse.

You know the horse?

I know he run in the Brazilian Grand Prix. I think he come out of Kentucky but he's owned by a man named Vail out of Douglas Arizona.

Yes. The horse was foaled at Monterey Farm in Paris Kentucky. The stallion I have bought is a half brother out of the same mare.

Yessir. Where's he at?

He is enroute.

He's where?

Enroute. From Mexico. The hacendado smiled. He has been standing at stud.

You intend to raise racehorses?

No. I intend to raise quarterhorses.

To use here on the ranch?

Yes.

You aim to breed this stallion to your mares.

Yes. What is your opinion?

I dont have a opinion. I've known a few breeders and some with a world of experience but I've noticed they were all pretty short on opinions. I do know there's been some good cowhorses sired out of thoroughbreds.

Yes. How much importance do you give to the mare?

Same as the sire. In my opinion.

Most breeders place more confidence in the horse.

Yessir. They do.

The hacendado smiled. I happen to agree with you.

John Grady leaned and tipped the ash from his cigarette. You dont have to agree with me.

No. Nor you with me.

Yessir.

Tell me about the horses up on the mesa.

There may be a few of them good mares still up there but not many. The rest I'd pretty much call scrubs. Even some of them might make a half decent cowhorse. Just all around using kind of a horse. Spanish ponies, what we used to call em. Chihuahua horses. Old Barb stock. They're small and they're a little on the light side and they dont have the hindquarters you'd want in a cuttinghorse but you can rope off of em . . .

He stopped. He looked at the hat in his lap and ran his fingers along the crease and looked up. I aint tellin you nothin you dont know.

The hacendado took up the coffeepitcher and poured their cups.

Do you know what a criollo is?

Yessir. That's a argentine horse.

Do you know who Sam Jones was?

I do if you're talkin about a horse.

Crawford Sykes?

That's another of Uncle Billy Anson's horses. I heard about that horse all my life.

My father bought horses from Mr Anson.

Uncle Billy and my grandaddy were friends. They were born within three days of each other. He was the seventh son of the Earl of Litchfield. His wife was a actress on the stage.

You are from Christoval?

San Angelo. Or just outside of San Angelo.

The hacendado studied him.

Do you know a book called *The Horse of America*, by Wallace?

Yessir. I've read it front to back.

The hacendado leaned back in his chair. One of the cats rose and stretched.

You rode here from Texas.

Yessir.

You and your friend.

Yessir.

Just the two of you?

John Grady looked at the table. The paper cat stepped thin and slant among the shapes of cats thereon. He looked up again. Yessir, he said. Just me and him.

The hacendado nodded and stubbed out his cigarette and pushed back his chair. Come, he said. I will show you some horses.

THEY SAT opposite on their bunks with their elbows on their knees leaning forward and looking down at their folded hands. After a while Rawlins spoke. He didnt look up.

It's a opportunity for you. Aint no reason for you to turn it down that I can see.

If you dont want me to I wont. I'll stick right here.

It aint like you was goin off someplace.

We'll still be workin together. Bringin in horses and all.

Rawlins nodded. John Grady watched him.

You just say the word and I'll tell him no.

Aint no reason to do that, said Rawlins. Its a opportunity for you.

In the morning they ate breakfast and Rawlins went out to work the pens. When he came in at noon John Grady's tick was rolled up at the head of his bunk and his gear was gone. Rawlins went on to the back to wash up for dinner.

THE BARN was built on the english style and it was sheathed with milled one by fours and painted white and it had a cupola and a weathervane on top of the cupola. His room was at the far end next to the saddleroom. Across the bay was another cubicle where there lived an old groom who'd worked for Rocha's father. When John Grady led his horse through the barn the old man came out and stood and looked at the horse. Then he looked at its feet. Then he looked at John Grady. Then he turned and went back into his room and shut the door.

In the afternoon while he was working one of the new mares in the corral outside the barn the old man came out and watched him. John Grady said him a good afternoon and the old man nodded and said one back. He watched the mare. He said she was stocky. He said rechoncha and John Grady didnt know what it meant and he asked the old man and the old man made a barrel shape with his arms and John Grady thought he meant that she was pregnant and he said no she wasnt and the old man shrugged and went back in.

When he took the mare back to the barn the old man was pulling the cinchstrap on the black Arabian. The girl stood with her back to him. When the shadow of the mare darkened the bay door she turned and looked.

Buenas tardes, he said.

Buenas tardes, she said. She reached and slid her fingers under the strap to check it. He stood at the bay door. She raised up and passed the reins over the horse's head and put her foot in the stirrup and stood up into the saddle and turned the horse and rode down the bay and out the door.

That night as he lay in his cot he could hear music from the house and as he was drifting to sleep his thoughts were of horses and of the open country and of horses. Horses still wild on the mesa who'd never seen a man afoot and who knew nothing of him or his life yet in whose souls he would come to reside forever.

They went up into the mountains a week later with the mozo and two of the vaqueros and after the vaqueros had turned in in their blankets he and Rawlins sat by the fire on the rim of the mesa drinking coffee. Rawlins took out his tobacco and John Grady took out cigarettes and shook the pack at him. Rawlins put his tobacco back.

Where'd you get the readyrolls?

In La Vega.

He nodded. He took a brand from the fire and lit the cigarette and John Grady leaned and lit his own.

You say she goes to school in Mexico City?

Yeah.

How old is she?

Seventeen.

Rawlins nodded. What kind of a school is it she goes to?

I dont know. It's some kind of a prep school or somethin.

Fancy sort of school.

Yeah. Fancy sort of school.

Rawlins smoked. Well, he said. She's a fancy sort of girl.

No she aint.

Rawlins was leaning against his propped saddle, sitting with his legs crossed sideways on to the fire. The sole of his right boot had come loose and he'd fastened it back with hogrings stapled through the welt. He looked at the cigarette.

Well, he said. I've told you before but I dont reckon you'll listen now any more than you done then.

Yeah. I know.

I just figure you must enjoy cryin yourself to sleep at night.

John Grady didnt answer.

This one of course she probably dates guys got their own airplanes let alone cars.

You're probably right.

I'm glad to hear you say it.

It dont help nothin though, does it?

Rawlins sucked on the cigarette. They sat for a long time. Finally he pitched the stub of the cigarette into the fire. I'm goin to bed, he said.

Yeah, said John Grady. I guess that's a good idea.

They spread their soogans and he pulled off his boots and stood them beside him and stretched out in his blankets. The fire had burned to coals and he lay looking up at the stars in their places and the hot belt of matter that ran the chord of the dark vault overhead and he put his hands on the ground at either side of him and pressed them against the earth and in that coldly burning canopy of black he slowly turned dead center to the world, all of it taut and trembling and moving enormous and alive under his hands.

What's her name? said Rawlins in the darkness.

Alejandra. Her name is Alejandra.

Sunday afternoon they rode into the town of La Vega on horses they'd been working out of the new string. They'd had their hair cut with sheepshears by an esquilador at the ranch and the backs of their necks above their collars were white as scars and they wore their hats cocked forward on their heads and they looked from side to side as they jogged along as if to challenge the countryside or anything it might hold. They raced the animals on the road at a fifty-cent bet and John Grady won and they swapped horses and he won on Rawlins' horse. They rode the horses at a gallop and they rode them at a trot and the horses were hot and lathered and squatted and stamped in the road and the campesinos afoot in the road with baskets of garden-stuff or pails covered with cheesecloth would press to the edge of the road or climb through the roadside brush and cactus to watch wide eyed the young horsemen on their horses passing and the horses mouthing froth and champing and the riders calling to one another in their alien tongue and passing in a muted fury that seemed scarcely to be contained in the space allotted them and yet leaving all unchanged where they had been: dust, sunlight, a singing bird.

In the tienda the topmost shirts folded upon the shelves when shaken out retained a square of paler color where dust had settled on the cloth or sun had faded it or both. They sorted through the stacks to find one with sleeves long enough for Rawlins, the woman holding out the sleeve along the out-stretched length of his arm, the pins caught in her mouth like a seamstress where she meant to refold, repin the shirt, shaking her head doubtfully. They carried stiff new canvas pants to the rear of the store and tried them on in a bedroom that had three beds in it and a cold concrete floor that had once been painted green. They sat on one of the beds and counted their money.

How much are these britches if they're fifteen pesos?

Just remember that two pesos is two bits.

You remember it. How much are they?

A dollar and eighty-seven cents.

Hell, said Rawlins. We're in good shape. We get paid in five days.

They bought socks and underwear and they piled everything on the counter while the woman totted up the figures. Then she wrapped the new clothes in two separate parcels and tied them with string.

What have you got left? said John Grady.

Four dollars and somethin.

Get a pair of boots.

I lack some havin enough.

I'll let you have the difference.

You sure?

Yeah.

We got to have some operatin capital for this evenin.

We'll still have a couple of dollars. Go on.

What if you want to buy that sweet thing a soda pop?

It'll set me back about four cents. Go on.

Rawlins handled the boots dubiously. He stood one against
the sole of his own raised boot.

These things are awful small.

Try these.

Black?

Sure. Why not.

Rawlins pulled on the new boots and walked up and down
the floor. The woman nodded approvingly.

What do you think? said John Grady.

They're all right. These underslung heels take some gettin
used to.

Let's see you dance.

Do what?

Dance.

Rawlins looked at the woman and he looked at John Grady.
Shit, he said. You're lookin at a dancin fool.

Hit it there a few steps.

Rawlins executed a nimble ninestep stomp on the old board
floor and stood grinning in the dust he'd raised.

Qué guapo, said the woman.

John Grady grinned and reached in his pocket for his money.

We've forgot to get gloves, said Rawlins.

Gloves?

Gloves. We get done sportin we're goin to have to go back to
work.

You got a point.

Them old hot maggie ropes have eat my hands about up.

John Grady looked at his own hands. He asked the woman
where the gloves were and they bought a pair apiece.

They stood at the counter while she wrapped them. Rawlins
was looking down at his boots.

The old man's got some good silk manilla ropes in the barn,
said John Grady. I'll slip one out to you quick as I get a chance.

Black boots, said Rawlins. Aint that the shits? I always
wanted to be a badman.

* * *

ALTHOUGH THE NIGHT was cool the double doors of the grange stood open and the man selling the tickets was seated in a chair on a raised wooden platform just within the doors so that he must lean down to each in a gesture akin to benevolence and take their coins and hand them down their tickets or pass upon the ticketstubs of those who were only returning from outside. The old adobe hall was buttressed along its outer walls with piers not all of which had been a part of its design and there were no windows and the walls were swagged and cracked. A string of electric bulbs ran the length of the hall at either side and the bulbs were covered with paper bags that had been painted and the brushstrokes showed through in the light and the reds and greens and blues were all muted and much of a piece. The floor was swept but there were pockets of seeds underfoot and drifts of straw and at the far end of the hall a small orchestra labored on a stage of grainpallets under a bandshell rigged from sheeting. Along the foot of the stage were lights set in fruitcans among colored crepe that smoldered throughout the night. The mouths of the cans were lensed with tinted cellophane and they cast upon the sheeting a shadowplay in the lights and smoke of antic demon players and a pair of goathawks arced chittering through the partial darkness overhead.

John Grady and Rawlins and a boy named Roberto from the ranch stood just beyond the reach of light at the door among the cars and wagons and passed among themselves a pint medicine-bottle of mescal. Roberto held the bottle to the light.

A las chicas, he said.

He drank and handed off the bottle. They drank. They poured salt from a paper onto their wrists and licked it off and Roberto pushed the cob stopper into the neck of the bottle and hid the bottle behind the tire of a parked truck and they passed around a pack of chewing gum.

Listos? he said.

Listos.

She was dancing with a tall boy from the San Pablo ranch and she wore a blue dress and her mouth was red. He and Rawlins and Roberto stood with other youths along the wall and watched the dancers and watched beyond the dancers the young girls at the far side of the hall. He moved along past the groups. The air smelled of straw and sweat and a rich spice of colognes. Under the bandshell the accordion player struggled with his instrument and slammed his boot on the boards in countertime and stepped back and the trumpet player came forward. Her eyes above the shoulder of her partner swept across him where he stood. Her black hair done up in a blue ribbon and the nape of her neck pale as porcelain. When she turned again she smiled.

He'd never touched her and her hand was small and her waist so slight and she looked at him with great forthrightness and smiled and put her face against his shoulder. They turned under the lights. A long trumpet note guided the dancers on their separate and collective paths. Moths circled the paper lights aloft and the goathawks passed down the wires and flared and arced upward into the darkness again.

She spoke in an english learned largely from schoolbooks and he tested each phrase for the meanings he wished to hear, repeating them silently to himself and then questioning them anew. She said that she was glad that he'd come.

I told you I would.

Yes.

They turned, the trumpet rapped.

Did you not think I would?

She tossed her head back and looked at him, smiling, her eyes aglint. Al contrario, she said. I knew you would come.

At the band's intermission they made their way to the refreshment stand and he bought two lemonades in paper cones and they went out and walked in the night air. They walked along the road and there were other couples in the road and they passed and wished them a good evening. The air was cool and it smelled of earth and perfume and horses. She took his arm and she laughed and called him a mojado-reverso, so rare a creature and one to be treasured. He told her about his life. How his grandfather was dead and the ranch sold. They sat on a low concrete watertrough and with her shoes in her lap and her naked feet crossed in the dust she drew patterns in the dark water with her finger. She'd been away at school for three years. Her mother lived in Mexico and she went to the house on Sundays for dinner and sometimes she and her mother would dine alone in the city and go to the theatre or the ballet. Her mother thought that life on the hacienda was lonely and yet living in the city she seemed to have few friends.

She becomes angry with me because I always want to come here. She says that I prefer my father to her.

Do you?

She nodded. Yes. But that is not why I come. Anyway, she says I will change my mind.

About coming here?

About everything.

She looked at him and smiled. Shall we go in?

He looked toward the lights. The music had started.

She stood and bent with one hand on his shoulder and slipped on her shoes.

I will introduce you to my friends. I will introduce you to Lucía. She is very pretty. You will see.

I bet she aint as pretty as you.

Oh my. You must be careful what you say. Besides it is not true. She is prettier.

He rode back alone with the smell of her perfume on his shirt. The horses were still tied and standing at the edge of the barn but he could not find Rawlins or Roberto. When he untied his horse the other two tossed their heads and whinnied softly to go. Cars were starting up in the yard and groups of people were moving along the road and he untracted the greenbroke horse out from the lights and into the road before mounting up. A mile from the town a car passed full of young men and they were going fast and he reined the horse to the side of the road and the horse skittered and danced in the glare of the headlights and as they passed they called out at him and someone threw an empty beercan. The horse reared and pitched and kicked out and he held it under him and talked to it as if nothing at all had happened and after a while they went on again. The boil of dust the car had left lay before them down the narrow straight as far as he could see roiling slowly in the starlight like something enormous uncoiling out of the earth. He thought the horse had handled itself well and as he rode he told it so.

THE HACENDADO had bought the horse through an agent sight unseen at the spring sales in Lexington and he'd sent Armando's brother Antonio to get the animal and bring it back. Antonio left the ranch in a 1941 International flatbed truck towing a homemade sheetmetal trailer and he was gone two months. He carried with him letters in both english and spanish signed by Don Héctor stating his business and he carried a brown bank envelope tied with a string in which was a great deal of money in both dollars and pesos together with sight-drafts on banks in Houston and Memphis. He spoke no english and he could neither read nor write. When he got back the envelope was gone together with the spanish letter but he had the english letter and it was separated into three parts along the lines of its folding and it was dogeared and coffeestained and stained with other stains some of which may have been blood. He'd been in jail once in Kentucky, once in Tennessee, and three times in Texas. When he pulled into the yard he got out and walked stiffly to the house and knocked at the kitchen door. María let him in and he stood with his hat in his hand while she went for the hacendado. When the hacendado entered the kitchen they shook hands gravely and the hacendado asked after his health and he said that it was excellent and handed him the pieces of the letter together with a sheaf of bills and receipts from cafes and gas stations and feedstores and jails and he handed him the money he had left including the change in his pockets and he handed him the keys to the truck and lastly he handed him the factura from the Mexican aduana at Piedras Negras together with a long manilla envelope tied with a blue ribbon that contained the papers on the horse and the bill of sale.

Don Héctor piled the money and the receipts and the papers on the sideboard and put the keys in his pocket. He asked if the truck had proved satisfactory.

Sí, said Antonio. Es una troca muy fuerte.

Bueno, said the hacendado. Y el caballo?

Está un poco cansado de su viaje, pero es muy bonito.

So he was. He was a deep chestnut in color and stood sixteen hands high and weighed about fourteen hundred pounds and he was well muscled and heavily boned for his breed. When they brought him back from the Distrito Federal in the same trailer in the third week of May and John Grady and Sr Rocha walked out to the barn to look at him John Grady simply pushed open the door to the stall and entered and walked up to the horse and leaned against it and began to rub it and talk to it softly in spanish. The hacendado offered no advice about the horse at all. John Grady walked all around it talking to it. He lifted up one front hoof and examined it.

Have you ridden him? he said.

But of course.

I'd like to ride him. Con su permiso.

The hacendado nodded. Yes, he said. Of course.

He came out of the stall and shut the door and they stood looking at the stallion.

Le gusta? said the hacendado.

John Grady nodded. That's a hell of a horse, he said.

In the days to follow the hacendado would come up to the corral where they'd shaped the manada and he and John Grady would walk among the mares and John Grady would argue their points and the hacendado would muse and walk away a fixed distance and stand looking back and nod and muse again and walk off with his eyes to the ground to a fresh vantage point and then look up to see the mare anew, willing to see a new mare should one present itself. Where he could find no gifts of either stance or conformation to warrant his young breeder's confidence John Grady would likely defer to his judgment. Yet every mare could be pled for on the basis of what they came to call la única cosa and that one thing—which could absolve them of any but the grossest defect—was an interest in cattle. For he'd broken the more promising mares to ride and he'd take them upcountry through the ciénaga pasture where the cows and calves stood in the lush grass along the edge of the marsh-lands and he would show them the cows and let them move among them. And in the manada were mares who took a great interest in what they saw and some would look back at the cows as they were ridden from the pasture. He claimed that cowsense could be bred for. The hacendado was less sure. But there were two things they agreed upon wholly and that were never spoken and that was that God had put horses on earth to work cattle and that other than cattle there was no wealth proper to a man.

They stabled the stallion away from the mares in a barn up at the gerente's and as the mares came into season he and Antonio bred them. They bred mares almost daily for three weeks and sometimes twice daily and Antonio regarded the stallion with great reverence and great love and he called him caballo padre and like John Grady he would talk to the horse and often make promises to him and he never lied to the horse. The horse would hear him coming and set to walking about in the chaff on its hindlegs and he'd stand talking to the horse and describing to him the mares in his low voice. He never bred the horse at the same hour two days running and he conspired with John Grady in telling the hacendado that the horse needed to be ridden to keep it manageable. Because John Grady loved to ride the horse. In truth he loved to be seen riding it. In truth he loved for her to see him riding it.

He'd go to the kitchen in the dark for his coffee and saddle the horse at daybreak with only the little desert doves waking in the orchard and the air still fresh and cool and he and the stallion would come sideways out of the stable with the animal prancing and pounding the ground and arching its neck. They'd ride out along the ciénaga road and along the verge of the marshes while the sun rose riding up flights of ducks out of the shallows or geese or mergansers that would beat away over the water scattering the haze and rising up would turn to birds of gold in a sun not yet visible from the bolsón floor.

He'd ride sometimes clear to the upper end of the laguna before the horse would even stop trembling and he spoke constantly to it in spanish in phrases almost biblical repeating again and again the strictures of a yet untabled law. Soy comandante de las yeguas, he would say, yo y yo sólo. Sin la caridad de estas manos no tengas nada. Ni comida ni agua ni hijos. Soy yo que traigo las yeguas de las montañas, las yeguas jóvenes, las yeguas salvajes y ardientes. While inside the vaulting of the ribs between his knees the darkly meated heart pumped of who's will and the blood pulsed and the bowels shifted in their massive blue convolutions of who's will and the stout thighbones and knee and cannon and the tendons like flaxen hawsers that drew and flexed and drew and flexed at their articulations and of who's will all sheathed and muffled in the flesh and the hooves that stove wells in the morning groundmist and the head turning side to side and the great slavering keyboard of his teeth and the hot globes of his eyes where the world burned.

There were times in those early mornings in the kitchen when he returned to the house for his breakfast with María stirring about and stoking with wood the great nickelmounted cookstove or rolling out dough on the marble countertop that he would hear her singing somewhere in the house or smell the faintest breath of hyacinth as if she'd passed in the outer hall. On mornings when Carlos was to butcher he'd come up the walkway through a great convocation of cats all sitting about on the tiles under the ramada each in its ordered place and he'd pick one up and stroke it standing there at the patio gate through which he'd once seen her gathering limes and he'd stand for a while holding the cat and then let it slip to the tiles again whereupon it would return at once to the spot from which it had been taken and he would enter the kitchen and take off his hat. And sometimes she would ride in the mornings also and he knew she was in the diningroom across the hall by herself and Carlos would take her breakfast tray to her with coffee and fruit and once riding in the low hills to the north he'd seen her below on the ciénaga road two miles distant and he had seen her riding in the parkland above the marshes and once he came upon her leading the horse through the shallows of the lakeshore among the tules with her skirts caught up above her knees while red-wing blackbirds circled and cried, pausing and bending and gathering white waterlilies with the black horse standing in the lake behind her patient as a dog.

He'd not spoken to her since the night of the dance at La Vega. She went with her father to Mexico and he returned alone. There was no one he could ask about her. By now he'd taken to riding the stallion bareback, kicking off his boots and swinging up while Antonio still stood holding the trembling mare by the twitch, the mare standing with her legs spread and her head down and the breath rifling in and out of her. Coming out of the barn with his bare heels under the horse's barrel and the horse lathered and dripping and half crazed and pounding up the ciénaga road riding with just a rope hackamore and the sweat of the horse and the smell of the mare on him and the veins pulsing under the wet hide and him leaning low along the horse's neck talking to him softly and obscenely. It was in this condition that all unexpectedly one evening he came upon her returning on the black Arabian down the ciénaga road.

He reined in the horse and it stopped and stood trembling and stepped about in the road slinging its head in a froth from side to side. She sat her horse. He took off his hat and passed his shirtsleeve across his forehead and waved her forward and put his hat back on and reined the horse off the road and through the sedge and turned so that he could watch her pass. She put the horse forward and came on and as she came abreast of him he touched the brim of his hat with his forefinger and nodded and he thought she would go past but she did not. She stopped and turned her wide face to him. Skeins of light off the water played upon the black hide of the horse. He sat the sweating stallion like a highwayman under her gaze. She was waiting for him to speak and afterwards he would try to remember what it was he'd said. He only knew it made her smile and that had not been his intent. She turned and looked off across the lake where the late sun glinted and she looked back at him and at the horse.

I want to ride him, she said.

What?

I want to ride him.

She regarded him levelly from under the black hatbrim.

He looked out across the sedge tilting in the wind off the lake as if there might be some help for him in that quarter. He looked at her.

When? he said.

When?

When did you want to ride him?

Now. I want to ride him now.

He looked down at the horse as if surprised to see it there.

He dont have a saddle on.

Yes, she said. I know.

He pressed the horse between his heels and at the same time pulled on the reins of the hackamore to make the horse appear uncertain and difficult but the horse only stood.

I dont know if the patrón would want you to ride him. Your father.

She smiled at him a pitying smile and there was no pity in it. She stepped to the ground and lifted the reins over the black horse's head and turned and stood looking at him with the reins behind her back.

Get down, she said.

Are you sure about this?

Yes. Hurry.

He slid to the ground. The insides of his trouserlegs were hot and wet.

What do you aim to do with your horse?

I want you to take him to the barn for me.

Somebody will see me at the house.

Take him to Armando's.

You're fixin to get me in trouble.

You are in trouble.

She turned and looped the reins over the saddlehorn and came forward and took the hackamore reins from him and put them up and turned and put one hand on his shoulder. He could feel his heart pumping. He bent and made a stirrup of his laced fingers and she put her boot into his hands and he lifted her and she swung up onto the stallion's back and looked down at him and then booted the horse forward and went loping out up the track along the edge of the lake and was lost to view.

He rode back slowly on the Arabian. The sun was a long time descending. He thought she might overtake him that they could change the horses back again but she did not and in the red twilight he led the black horse past Armando's house afoot and took it to the stable behind the house and removed the bridle and loosed the cinches and left it standing in the bay saddled and tied with a rope halter to the hitchingrail. There was no light on at the house and he thought perhaps there was no one home but as he walked back out down the drive past the house the light came on in the kitchen. He walked more quickly. He heard the door open behind him but he didnt turn to look back to see who it was and whoever it was they did not speak or call to him.

The last time that he saw her before she returned to Mexico she was coming down out of the mountains riding very stately and erect out of a rainsquall building to the north and the dark clouds towering above her. She rode with her hat pulled down in the front and fastened under her chin with a drawtie and as she rode her black hair twisted and blew about her shoulders and the lightning fell silently through the black clouds behind her and she rode all seeming unaware down through the low hills while the first spits of rain blew on the wind and onto the upper pasturelands and past the pale and reedy lakes riding erect and stately until the rain caught her up and shrouded her figure away in that wild summer landscape: real horse, real rider, real land and sky and yet a dream withal.

THE DUEÑA ALFONSA was both grandaunt and godmother to the girl and her life at the hacienda invested it with oldworld ties and with antiquity and tradition. Save for the old leatherbound volumes the books in the library were her books and the piano was her piano. The ancient stereopticon in the parlor and the matched pair of Greener guns in the italian wardrobe in Don Héctor's room had been her brother's and it was her brother with whom she stood in the photos taken in front of cathedrals in the capitals of Europe, she and her sister-in-law in white summer clothes, her brother in vested suit and tie and panama hat. His dark moustache. Dark spanish eyes. The stance of a grandee. The most antique of the several oilportraits in the parlor with its dark patina crazed like an old porcelain glazing was of her great-grandfather and dated from Toledo in seventeen ninety-seven. The most recent was she herself full length in formal gown on the occasion of her quinceañera at Rosario in eighteen ninety-two.

John Grady had never seen her. Perhaps a figure glimpsed passing along the hallway. He did not know that she was aware of his existence until a week after the girl returned to Mexico he was invited to come to the house in the evening to play chess. When he showed up at the kitchen dressed in the new shirt and canvas pants María was still washing the supper dishes. She turned and studied him where he stood with his hat in his hands. Bueno, she said. Te espera.

He thanked her and crossed the kitchen and went up the hall and stood in the diningroom door. She rose from the table where she was sitting. She inclined her head very slightly. Good evening, she said. Please come in. I am señorita Alfonsa.

She was dressed in a dark gray skirt and a white pleated

blouse and her gray hair was gathered up behind and she looked like the schoolteacher she in fact had been. She spoke with an english accent. She held out one hand and he almost stepped forward to take it before he realized that she was gesturing toward the chair at her right.

Evenin, mam, he said. I'm John Grady Cole.

Please, she said. Be seated. I am happy that you have come.

Thank you mam.

He pulled back the chair and sat and put his hat in the chair beside him and looked at the board. She set her thumbs against the edge and pushed it slightly towards him. The board was pieced from blocks of circassian walnut and birdseye maple with a border of inlaid pearl and the chessmen were of carved ivory and black horn.

My nephew will not play, she said. I trounce him. Is it trounce?

Yes mam. I believe it is.

Like him she was lefthanded or she played chess with her left hand. The last two fingers were missing and yet he did not notice it until the game was well advanced. Finally when he took her queen she conceded and smiled her compliments and gestured at the board with a certain impatience. They were well into the second game and he had taken both knights and a bishop when she made two moves in succession which gave him pause. He studied the board. It occurred to him that she might be curious to know if he would throw the game and he realized that he had in fact already considered it and he knew she'd thought of it before he had. He sat back and looked at the board. She watched him. He leaned forward and moved his bishop and mated her in four moves.

That was foolish of me, she said. The queen's knight. That was a blunder. You play very well.

Yes mam. You play well yourself.

She pushed back the sleeve of her blouse to look at a small silver wristwatch. John Grady sat. It was two hours past his bedtime.

One more? she said.

Yes mam.

She used an opening he'd not seen before. In the end he lost his queen and conceded. She smiled and looked up at him. Carlos had entered with a tea tray and he set it on the table and she pushed aside the board and pulled the tray forward and set out the cups and saucers. There were slices of cake on a plate and a plate of crackers and several kinds of cheese and a small bowl of brown sauce with a silver spoon in it.

Do you take milk? she said.

No mam.

She nodded. She poured the tea.

I could not use that opening again with such effect, she said. I'd never seen it before.

Yes. It was invented by the Irish champion Pollock. He called it the King's Own opening. I was afraid you might know it.

I'd like to see it again some time.

Yes. Of course.

She pushed the tray forward between them. Please, she said. Help yourself.

I better not. I'll have crazy dreams eatin this late.

She smiled. She unfolded a small linen napkin from off the tray.

I've always had strange dreams. But I'm afraid they are quite independent of my dining habits.

Yes mam.

They have a long life, dreams. I have dreams now which I had as a young girl. They have an odd durability for something not quite real.

Do you think they mean anything?

She looked surprised. Oh yes, she said. Dont you?

Well. I dont know. They're in your head.

She smiled again. I suppose I dont consider that to be the condemnation you do. Where did you learn to play chess?

My father taught me.

He must be a very good player.

He was about the best I ever saw.

Could you not win against him?

Sometimes. He was in the war and after he come back I got to where I could beat him but I dont think his heart was in it. He dont play at all now.

That's a pity.

Yes mam. It is.

She poured their cups again.

I lost my fingers in a shooting accident, she said. Shooting live pigeons. The right barrel burst. I was seventeen. Alejandra's age. There is nothing to be embarrassed about. People are curious. It's only natural. I'm going to guess that the scar on your cheek was put there by a horse.

Yes mam. It was my own fault.

She watched him, not unkindly. She smiled. Scars have the strange power to remind us that our past is real. The events that cause them can never be forgotten, can they?

No mam.

Alejandra will be in Mexico with her mother for two weeks. Then she will be here for the summer.

He swallowed.

Whatever my appearance may suggest, I am not a particularly oldfashioned woman. Here we live in a small world. A close world. Alejandra and I disagree strongly. Quite strongly in fact. She is much like me at that age and I seem at times to be struggling with my own past self. I was unhappy as a child for reasons that are no longer important. But the thing in which we are united, my niece and I . . .

She broke off. She set the cup and saucer to one side. The polished wood of the table held a round shape of breath where they'd stood that diminished from the edges in and vanished. She looked up.

I had no one to advise me, you see. Perhaps I would not have listened anyway. I grew up in a world of men. I thought this would have prepared me to live in a world of men but it did not. I was also rebellious and so I recognize it in others. Yet I think that I had no wish to break things. Or perhaps only those things that wished to break me. The names of the entities that have power to constrain us change with time. Convention and authority are replaced by infirmity. But my attitude toward them has not changed. Has not changed.

You see that I cannot help but be sympathetic to Alejandra. Even at her worst. But I wont have her unhappy. I wont have her spoken ill of. Or gossiped about. I know what that is. She thinks that she can toss her head and dismiss everything. In an ideal world the gossip of the idle would be of no consequence. But I have seen the consequences in the real world and they can be very grave indeed. They can be consequences of a gravity not excluding bloodshed. Not excluding death. I saw this in my own family. What Alejandra dismisses as a matter of mere appearance or outmoded custom . . .

She made a whisking motion with the imperfect hand that was both a dismissal and a summation. She composed her hands again and looked at him.

Even though you are younger than she it is not proper for you to be seen riding in the campo together without supervision. Since this was carried to my ears I considered whether to speak to Alejandra about it and I have decided not to.

She leaned back. He could hear the clock ticking in the hall. There was no sound from the kitchen. She sat watching him.

What do you want me to do? he said.

I want you to be considerate of a young girl's reputation.

I never meant not to be.

She smiled. I believe you, she said. But you must understand. This is another country. Here a woman's reputation is all she has.

Yes mam.

There is no forgiveness, you see.

Mam?

There is no forgiveness. For women. A man may lose his honor and regain it again. But a woman cannot. She cannot.

They sat. She watched him. He tapped the crown of his seated hat with the tips of his four fingers and looked up.

I guess I'd have to say that that dont seem right.

Right? she said. Oh. Yes. Well.

She turned one hand in the air as if reminded of something she'd misplaced. No, she said. No. It's not a matter of right. You must understand. It is a matter of who must say. In this matter I get to say. I am the one who gets to say.

The clock ticked in the hall. She sat watching him. He picked up his hat.

Well. I guess I ought to say that you didnt have to invite me over just to tell me that.

You're quite right, she said. It was because of it that I almost didnt invite you.

ON THE MESA they watched a storm that had made up to the north. At sundown a troubled light. The dark jade shapes of the lagunillas below them lay in the floor of the desert savannah like piercings through to another sky. The laminar bands of color to the west bleeding out under the hammered clouds. A sudden violetcolored hooding of the earth.

They sat tailorwise on ground that shuddered under the thunder and they fed the fire out of the ruins of an old fence. Birds were coming down out of the half darkness upcountry and shearing away off the edge of the mesa and to the north the lightning stood along the rimlands like burning mandrake.

What else did she say? said Rawlins.

That was about it.

You think she was speakin for Rocha?

I dont think she speaks for anybody but her.

She thinks you got eyes for the daughter.

I do have eyes for the daughter.

You got eyes for the spread?

John Grady studied the fire. I dont know, he said. I aint thought about it.

Sure you aint, said Rawlins.

He looked at Rawlins and he looked into the fire again.

When is she comin back?

About a week.

I guess I dont see what evidence you got that she's all that interested in you.

John Grady nodded. I just do. I can talk to her.

The first drops of rain hissed in the fire. He looked at Rawlins.

You aint sorry you come down here are you?

Not yet.

He nodded. Rawlins rose.

You want your fish or you aim to just set there in the rain?

I'll get it.

I got it.

They sat hooded under the slickers. They spoke out of the hoods as if addressing the night.

I know the old man likes you, said Rawlins. But that dont mean he'll set still for you courtin his daughter.

Yeah, I know.

I dont see you holdin no aces.

Yeah.

What I see is you fixin to get us fired and run off the place.

They watched the fire. The wire that had burned out of the fenceposts lay in garbled shapes about the ground and coils of it stood in the fire and coils of it pulsed red hot deep in the coals. The horses had come in out of the darkness and stood at the edge of the firelight in the falling rain dark and sleek with their red eyes burning in the night.

You still aint told me what answer you give her, said Rawlins.

I told her I'd do whatever she asked.

What did she ask?

I aint sure.

They sat watching the fire.

Did you give your word? said Rawlins.

I dont know. I dont know if I did or not.

Well either you did or you didnt.

That's what I'd of thought. But I dont know.

FIVE NIGHTS later asleep in his bunk in the barn there was a tap at the door. He sat up. Someone was standing outside the door. He could see a light through the boardjoinings.

Momento, he said.

He rose and pulled on his trousers in the dark and opened the door. She was standing in the barn bay holding a flashlight in one hand with the light pointed at the ground.

What is it? he whispered.

It's me.

She held the light up as if to verify the truth of this. He couldnt think what to say.

What time is it?

I dont know. Eleven or something.

He looked across the narrow corridor to the groom's door.

We're going to wake Estéban, he said.

Then invite me in.

He stepped back and she came in past him all rustling of clothes and the rich parade of her hair and perfume. He pulled the door to and ran shut the wooden latch with the heel of his hand and turned and looked at her.

I better not turn the light on, he said.

It's all right. The generator's off anyway. What did she say to you?

She must of told you what she said.

Of course she told me. What did she say?

You want to set down?

She turned and sat sideways on the bed and tucked one foot beneath her. She laid the burning flashlight on the bed and then she pushed it under the blanket where it suffused the room with a soft glow.

She didnt want me to be seen with you. Out on the campo.

Armando told her that you rode my horse in.

I know.

I wont be treated in such a manner, she said.

In that light she looked strange and theatrical. She passed one hand across the blanket as if she'd brush something away. She looked up at him and her face was pale and austere in the uplight and her eyes lost in their darkly shadowed hollows save only for the glint of them and he could see her throat move in the light and he saw in her face and in her figure something he'd not seen before and the name of that thing was sorrow.

I thought you were my friend, she said.

Tell me what to do, he said. I'll do anything you say.

The nightdamp laid the dust going up the ciénaga road and they rode the horses side by side at a walk, sitting the animals bareback and riding with hackamores. Leading the horses by hand out through the gate into the road and mounting up and riding the horses side by side up the ciénaga road with the moon in the west and some dogs barking over toward the shearing-sheds and the greyhounds answering back from their pens and him closing the gate and turning and holding his cupped hands for her to step into and lifting her onto the black horse's naked back and then untying the stallion from the gate and stepping once onto the gateslat and mounting up all in one motion and turning the horse and them riding side by side up the ciénaga road with the moon in the west like a moon of white linen hung from wires and some dogs barking.

They'd be gone sometimes till near daybreak and he'd put the stallion up and go to the house for his breakfast and an hour later meet Antonio back at the stable and walk up past the gerente's house to the trap where the mares stood waiting.

They'd ride at night up along the western mesa two hours from the ranch and sometimes he'd build a fire and they could see the gaslights at the hacienda gates far below them floating in a pool of black and sometimes the lights seemed to move as if the world down there turned on some other center and they saw stars fall to earth by the hundreds and she told him stories of her father's family and of Mexico. Going back they'd walk the horses into the lake and the horses would stand and drink with the water at their chests and the stars in the lake bobbed and tilted where they drank and if it rained in the mountains the air would be close and the night more warm and one night he left her and rode down along the edge of the lake through the sedge and willow and slid from the horse's back and pulled off his boots and his clothes and walked out into the lake where the moon slid away before him and ducks gabbled out there in the dark. The water was black and warm and he turned in the lake and spread his arms in the water and the water was so dark and so silky and he watched across the still black surface to where she stood on the shore with the horse and he watched where she stepped from her pooled clothing so pale, so pale, like a chrysalis emerging, and walked into the water.

She paused midway to look back. Standing there trembling in the water and not from the cold for there was none. Do not speak to her. Do not call. When she reached him he held out his hand and she took it. She was so pale in the lake she seemed to be burning. Like foxfire in a darkened wood. That burned cold. Like the moon that burned cold. Her black hair floating on the water about her, falling and floating on the water. She put her other arm about his shoulder and looked toward the moon in the west do not speak to her do not call and then she turned her face up to him. Sweeter for the larceny of time and flesh, sweeter for the betrayal. Nesting cranes that stood singlefooted among the cane on the south shore had pulled their slender beaks from their wingpits to watch. Me quieres? she said. Yes, he said. He said her name. God yes, he said.

HE CAME UP from the barn washed and combed and a clean shirt on and he and Rawlins sat on crates under the ramada of the bunkhouse and smoked while they waited for supper. There was talking and laughing in the bunkhouse and then it ceased. Two of the vaqueros came to the door and stood. Rawlins turned and looked north along the road. Five Mexican rangers were coming down the road riding singlefile. They were dressed in khaki uniforms and they rode good horses and they wore pistols in beltholsters and carried carbines in their saddlescabbards. Rawlins stood. The other vaqueros had come to the door and stood looking out. As the riders passed on the road the leader glanced across at the bunkhouse at the men under the ramada, at the men standing in the door. Then they went on from sight past the gerente's house, five riders riding singlefile down out of the north through the twilight toward the tile-roofed ranchhouse below them.

When he came back down through the dark to the barn the five horses were standing under the pecan trees at the far side of the house. They hadnt been unsaddled and in the morning they were gone. The following night she came to his bed and she came every night for nine nights running, pushing the door shut and latching it and turning in the slatted light at God knew what hour and stepping out of her clothes and sliding cool and naked against him in the narrow bunk all softness and perfume and the lushness of her black hair falling over him and no caution to her at all. Saying I dont care I dont care. Drawing blood with her teeth where he held the heel of his hand against her mouth that she not cry out. Sleeping against his chest where he could not sleep at all and rising when the east was already gray with dawn and going to the kitchen to get her breakfast as if she were only up early.

Then she was gone back to the city. The following evening when he came in he passed Estéban in the barn bay and spoke to the old man and the old man spoke back but did not look at him. He washed up and went to the house and ate his dinner in the kitchen and after he'd eaten he and the hacendado sat at the diningroom table and logged the stud book and the hacendado questioned him and made notes on the mares and then leaned back and sat smoking his cigar and tapping his pencil against the edge of the table. He looked up.

Good, he said. How are you progressing with the Guzmán?

Well, I'm not ready for volume two.

The hacendado smiled. Guzmán is excellent. You dont read french?

No sir.

The bloody French are quite excellent on the subject of horses. Do you play billiards?

Sir?

Do you play billiards?

Yessir. Some. Pool anyways.

Pool. Yes. Would you like to play?

Yessir.

Good.

The hacendado folded shut the books and pushed back his chair and rose and he followed him out down the hall and through the salon and through the library to the paneled double doors at the far end of the room. The hacendado opened these doors and they entered a darkened room that smelled of must and old wood.

He pulled a tasseled chain and lit an ornate tin chandelier suspended from the ceiling. Beneath it an antique table of some dark wood with lions carved into the legs. The table was covered with a drop of yellow oilcloth and the chandelier had been lowered from the twentyfoot ceiling by a length of common tracechain. At the far end of the room was a very old carved and painted wooden altar above which hung a lifesize carved and painted wooden Christ. The hacendado turned.

I play seldom, he said. I hope you are not an expert?

No sir.

I asked Carlos if he could make the table more level. The last time we played it was quite crooked. We will see what has been done. Just take the corner there. I will show you.

They stood on either side of the table and folded the cloth toward the middle and folded it again and then lifted it away and took it past the end of the table and walked toward each other and the hacendado took the cloth and carried it over and laid it on some chairs.

This was the chapel as you see. You are not superstitious?

No sir. I dont think so.

It is supposed to be made unsacred. The priest comes and says some words. Alfonsa knows about these matters. But of course the table has been here for years now and the chapel has yet to be whatever the word is. To have the priest come and make it be no longer a chapel. Personally I question whether such a thing can be done at all. What is sacred is sacred. The powers of the priest are more limited than people suppose. Of course there has been no Mass said here for many years.

How many years?

The hacendado was sorting through the cues where they stood in and out of a mahogany rack in the corner. He turned.

I received my First Communion in this chapel. I suppose that may have been the last Mass said here. I would say about nineteen eleven.

He turned back to the cues. I would not let the priest come to do that thing, he said. To dissolve the sanctity of the chapel. Why should I do that? I like to feel that God is here. In my house.

He racked the balls and handed the cueball to John Grady. It was ivory and yellow with age and the grain of the ivory was visible in it. He broke the balls and they played straight pool and the hacendado beat him easily, walking about the table and chalking his cue with a deft rotary motion and announcing the shots in spanish. He played slowly and studied the shots and the lay of the table and as he studied and as he played he spoke of the revolution and of the history of Mexico and he spoke of the dueña Alfonsa and of Francisco Madero.

He was born in Parras. In this state. Our families at one time were quite close. Alfonsita may have been engaged to be married to Francisco's brother. I'm not sure. In any case my grandfather would never have permitted the marriage. The political views of the family were quite radical. Alfonsita was not a child.

She should have been left to make her own choice and she was not and whatever were the circumstances she seems to have been very unforgiving of her father and it was a great sorrow to him and one that he was buried with. El cuatro.

The hacendado bent and sighted and banked the fourball the length of the table and stood and chalked his cue.

In the end it was all of no consequence of course. The family was ruined. Both brothers assassinated.

He studied the table.

Like Madero she was educated in Europe. Like him she also learned these ideas, these . . .

He moved his hand in a gesture the boy had seen the aunt make also.

She has always had these ideas. Catorce.

He bent and shot and stood and chalked his cue. He shook his head. One country is not another country. Mexico is not Europe. But it is a complicated business. Madero's grandfather was my padrino. My godfather. Don Evaristo. For this and other reasons my grandfather remained loyal to him. Which was not such a difficult thing. He was a wonderful man. Very kind. Loyal to the regime of Díaz. Even that. When Francisco published his book Don Evaristo refused to believe that he had written it. And yet the book contained nothing so terrible. Perhaps it was only that a wealthy young hacendado had written it. Siete.

He bent and shot the sevenball into the sidepocket. He walked around the table.

They went to France for their education. He and Gustavo. And others. All these young people. They all returned full of ideas. Full of ideas, and yet there seemed to be no agreement among them. How do you account for that? Their parents sent them for these ideas, no? And they went there and received them. Yet when they returned and opened their valises, so to speak, no two contained the same thing.

He shook his head gravely. As if the lay of the table were a trouble to him.

They were in agreement on matters of fact. The names of people. Or buildings. The dates of certain events. But ideas . . . People of my generation are more cautious. I think we dont believe that people can be improved in their character by reason. That seems a very french idea.

He chalked, he moved. He bent and shot and then stood surveying the new lay of the table.

Beware gentle knight. There is no greater monster than reason.

He looked at John Grady and smiled and looked at the table.

That of course is the spanish idea. You see. The idea of Quixote. But even Cervantes could not envision such a country as Mexico. Alfonsita tells me I am only being selfish in not wanting to send Alejandra. Perhaps she is right. Perhaps she is right. Diez.

Send her where?

The hacendado had bent to shoot. He raised up again and looked at his guest. To France. To send her to France.

He chalked his cue again. He studied the table.

Why do I bother myself? Eh? She will go. Who am I? A father. A father is nothing.

He bent to shoot and missed his shot and stepped back from the table.

There, he said. You see? You see how this is bad for one's billiard game? This thinking? The French have come into my house to mutilate my billiard game. No evil is beyond them.

HE SAT on his bunk in the dark with his pillow in his two arms and he leaned his face into it and drank in her scent and tried to refashion in his mind her self and voice. He whispered half aloud the words she'd said. Tell me what to do. I'll do anything you say. The selfsame words he'd said to her. She'd wept against his naked chest while he held her but there was nothing to tell her and there was nothing to do and in the morning she was gone.

The following Sunday Antonio invited him to his brother's house for dinner and afterwards they sat in the shade of the ramada off the kitchen and rolled a cigarette and smoked and discussed the horses. Then they discussed other things. John Grady told him of playing billiards with the hacendado and Antonio—sitting in an old Mennonite chair the caning of which had been replaced with canvas, his hat on one knee and his hands together—received this news with the gravity proper to it, looking down at the burning cigarette and nodding his head. John Grady looked off through the trees toward the house, the white walls and the red clay rooftiles.

Digame, he said. Cuál es lo peor: Que soy pobre o que soy americano?

The vaquero shook his head. Una llave de oro abre cualquier puerta, he said.

He looked at the boy. He tipped the ash from the end of the cigarette and he said that the boy wished to know his thought. Wished perhaps his advice. But that no one could advise him.

Tienes razón, said John Grady. He looked at the vaquero. He said that when she returned he intended to speak to her with the greatest seriousness. He said that he intended to know her heart.

The vaquero looked at him. He looked toward the house. He seemed puzzled and he said that she was here. That she was here now.

Cómo?

Sí. Ella está aquí. Desde ayer.

HE LAY AWAKE all night until the dawn. Listening to the silence in the bay. The shifting of the bedded horses. Their breathing. In the morning he walked up to the bunkhouse to take his breakfast. Rawlins stood in the door of the kitchen and studied him.

You look like you been rode hard and put up wet, he said.

They sat at the table and ate. Rawlins leaned back and fished his tobacco out of his shirtpocket.

I keep waitin for you to unload your wagon, he said. I got to go to work here in a few minutes.

I just come up to see you.

What about.

It dont have to be about somethin does it?

No. Dont have to. He popped a match on the underside of the table and lit his cigarette and shook out the match and put it in his plate.

I hope you know what you're doin, he said.

John Grady drained the last of his coffee and put the cup on his plate along with the silver. He got his hat from the bench beside him and put it on and stood up to take his dishes to the sink.

You said you didnt have no hard feelins about me goin down there.

I dont have no hard feelins about you going down there.

John Grady nodded. All right, he said.

Rawlins watched him go to the sink and watched him go to the door. He thought he might turn and say something else but he didnt.

He worked with the mares all day and in the evening he heard the airplane start up. He came out of the barn and watched. The plane came out of the trees and rose into the late sunlight and banked and turned and leveled out headed southwest. He couldnt see who was in the plane but he watched it out of sight anyway.

Two days later he and Rawlins were in the mountains again. They rode hard hazing the wild manadas out of the high valleys and they camped at their old site on the south slope of the Anteojos where they'd camped with Luis and they ate beans and barbecued goatmeat wrapped in tortillas and drank black coffee.

We aint got many more trips up here, have we? said Rawlins.

John Grady shook his head. No, he said. Probably not.

Rawlins sipped his coffee and watched the fire. Suddenly

three greyhounds trotted into the light one behind the other and circled the fire, pale and skeletal shapes with the hide stretched taut over their ribs and their eyes red in the firelight. Rawlins half rose, spilling his coffee.

What in the hell, he said.

John Grady stood and looked out into the darkness. The dogs vanished as suddenly as they had come.

They stood waiting. No one came.

What the hell, said Rawlins.

He walked out a little ways from the fire and stood listening. He looked back at John Grady.

You want to holler?

No.

Them dogs aint up here by themselves, he said.

I know.

You think he's huntin us?

If he wants us he can find us.

Rawlins walked back to the fire. He poured fresh coffee and stood listening.

He's probably up here with a bunch of his buddies.

John Grady didnt answer.

Dont you reckon? said Rawlins.

They rode up to the catchpen in the morning expecting to come upon the hacendado and his friends but they did not come upon him. In the days that followed they saw no sign of him. Three days later they set off down the mountain herding before them eleven young mares and they reached the hacienda at dark and put the mares up and went to the bunkhouse and ate. Some of the vaqueros were still at the table drinking coffee and smoking cigarettes but one by one they drifted away.

The following morning at gray daybreak two men entered his cubicle with drawn pistols and put a flashlight in his eyes and ordered him to get up.

He sat up. He swung his legs over the edge of the bunk. The man holding the light was just a shape behind it but he could see the pistol he held. It was a Colt automatic service pistol. He shaded his eyes. There were men with rifles standing in the bay.

Quién es? he said.

The man swung the light at his feet and ordered him to get his boots and clothes. He stood and got his trousers and pulled them on and sat and pulled on his boots and reached and got his shirt.

Vámonos, said the man.

He stood and buttoned his shirt.

Dónde están sus armas? the man said.

No tengo armas.

He spoke to the man behind him and two men came forward and began to look through his things. They dumped out the wooden coffeebox on the floor and kicked through his clothes and his shaving things and they turned the mattress over in the floor. They were dressed in greasy and blackened khaki uniforms and they smelled of sweat and woodsmoke.

Dónde está su caballo?

En el segundo puesto.

Vámonos, vámonos.

They led him out down the bay to the saddleroom and he got his saddle and his blankets and by then Redbo was standing in the barn bay, stepping nervously. They came back past Estéban's cuarto but there was no sign that the old man was even awake. They held the light while he saddled his horse and then they walked out into the dawn where the other horses were standing. One of the guards was carrying Rawlins' rifle and Rawlins was sitting slumped in the saddle on his horse with his hands cuffed before him and the reins on the ground.

They jabbed him forward with a rifle.

What's this about, pardner? he said.

Rawlins didnt answer. He leaned and spat and looked away.

No hable, said the leader. Vámonos.

He mounted up and they cuffed his wrists and handed him the reins and then all mounted up and they turned their horses and rode two by two out of the lot through the standing gate. When they passed the bunkhouse the lights were on and the vaqueros were standing in the door or squatting along the ramada. They watched the riders pass, the Americans behind the leader and his lieutenant, the others six in number riding in pairs behind in their caps and uniforms with their carbines resting across the pommels of their saddles, all riding out along the ciénaga road and upcountry toward the north.

III

THEY RODE all day, up through the low hills and into the mountains and along the mesa to the north well beyond the horse range and into the country they'd first crossed into some four months before. They nooned at a spring and squatted about the cold and blackened sticks of some former fire and ate cold beans and tortillas out of a newspaper. He thought the tortillas could have come from the hacienda kitchen. The newspaper was from Monclova. He ate slowly with his manacled hands and drank water from a tin cup that could only be partly filled for the water running out through the rivet holding the handle. The brass showed through the nickelplating where it was worn from the inside of the cuffs and his wrists had already turned a pale and poisonous green. He ate and he watched Rawlins who squatted a little ways off but Rawlins would not meet his eyes. They slept briefly on the ground under the cottonwoods and then rose and drank more water and filled the canteens and waterbottles and rode on.

The country they traversed was advanced in season and the acacia was in bloom and there had been rain in the mountains and the grass along the selvedge of the draws was green and blowsy in the long twilight where they rode. Except for remarks concerning the countryside the guards said little among themselves and to the Americans they said nothing at all. They rode through the long red sunset and they rode on in the dark. The guards had long since scabbarded their rifles and they rode easily, half slouched in the saddle. About ten oclock they halted and made camp and built a fire. The prisoners sat in the sand among old rusted tins and bits of charcoal with their hands still manacled before them and the guards set out an old blue granite-ware coffeepot and a stewpot of the same material and they drank coffee and ate a dish containing some kind of pale and fibrous tuber, some kind of meat, some kind of fowl. All of it stringy, all of it sour.

They spent the night with their hands chained through the stirrups of their saddles, trying to keep warm under their single blankets. They were on the trail again before the sun was up an hour and glad to be so.

This was their life for three days. On the afternoon of the third they rode into the town of Encantada of recent memory.

They sat side by side on a bench of iron slats in the little alameda. A pair of the guards stood a little ways off with their rifles and a dozen children of different ages stood in the dust of the street watching them. Two of the children were girls about twelve years of age and when the prisoners looked at them they turned shyly and twisted at their skirts. John Grady called to them to ask if they could get them cigarettes.

The guards glared at him. He made smoking motions at the girls and they turned and ran off down the street. The other children stood as before.

Ladies' man, said Rawlins.

You dont want a cigarette?

Rawlins spat slowly between his boots and looked up again. They aint goin to bring you no damn cigarette, he said.

I'll bet you.

What the hell you goin to bet with?

I'll bet you a cigarette.

How you goin to do that?

I'll bet you a cigarette she brings em. If she brings em I keep yours.

What are you goin to give me if she dont bring em?

If she dont bring em then you get mine.

Rawlins stared out across the alameda.

I aint above whippin your ass, you know.

Dont you think if we're goin to get out of this jackpot we

might better start thinkin about how to get out of it together?

You mean like we got in it?

You dont get to go back and pick some time when the trouble started and then lay everthing off on your friend.

Rawlins didnt answer.

Dont sull up on me. Let's get it aired.

All right. When they arrested you what did you say?

I didnt say nothin. What would of been the use?

That's right. What would of been the use.

What does that mean?

It means you never asked em to go wake the patrón, did you?

No.

I did.

What did they say?

Rawlins leaned and spat and wiped his mouth.

They said he was awake. They said he'd been awake for a long time. Then they laughed.

You think he sold us down the river?

Dont you?

I dont know. If he did it was because of some lie.

Or some truth.

John Grady sat looking down at his hands.

Would it satisfy you, he said, if I was to just go on and admit to bein a fourteen carat gold plated son of a bitch?

I never said that.

They sat. After a while John Grady looked up.

I cant back up and start over. But I dont see the point in slobberin over it. And I cant see where it would make me feel better to be able to point a finger at somebody else.

It dont make me feel better. I tried to reason with you, that's all. Tried any number of times.

I know you did. But some things aint reasonable. Be that as it may I'm the same man you crossed that river with. How I was is how I am and all I know to do is stick. I never even promised you you wouldnt die down here. Never asked your word on it either. I dont believe in signing on just till it quits suitin you.

You either stick or you quit and I wouldnt quit you I dont care what you done. And that's about all I got to say.

I never quit you, Rawlins said.

All right.

After a while the two girls came back. The taller of them held up her hand with two cigarettes in it.

John Grady looked at the guards. They motioned the girls over and looked at the cigarettes and nodded and the girls approached the bench and handed the cigarettes to the prisoners together with several wooden matches.

Muy amable, said John Grady. Muchas gracias.

They lit the cigarettes off one match and John Grady put the other matches in his pocket and looked at the girls. They smiled shyly.

Son americanos ustedes? they said.

Sí.

Son ladrones?

Sí. Ladrones muy famosos. Bandoleros.

They sucked in their breath. Qué precioso, they said. But the guards called to them and waved them away.

They sat leaning forward on their elbows, smoking the cigarettes. John Grady looked at Rawlins' boots.

Where's them new boots at? he said.

Back at the bunkhouse.

He nodded. They smoked. After a while the others returned and called to the guards. The guards gestured at the prisoners and they rose and nodded to the children and walked out to the street.

They rode out through the north end of the town and they halted before an adobe building with a corrugated tin roof and an empty mud bellcot above it. Scales of old painted plaster still clung to the mud brick walls. They dismounted and entered a large room that might once have been a schoolroom. There was a rail along the front wall and a frame that could once have held a blackboard. The floors were of narrow pine boards and the grain was etched by years of sand trod into them and the windows along both walls had missing panes of glass replaced with squares of tin all cut from the same large sign to form a broken mozaic among the windowlights. At a gray metal desk in one corner sat a stout man likewise in khaki uniform who wore about his neck a scarf of yellow silk. He regarded the prisoners without expression. He gestured slightly with his head toward the rear of the building and one of the guards took down a ring of keys from the wall and the prisoners were led out through a dusty weed yard to a small stone building with a heavy wooden door shod in iron.

There was a square judas-hole cut into the door at eye level and fastened across it and welded to the iron framing was a mesh of lightgauge rebar. One of the guards unfastened the old brass padlock and opened the door. He took a separate ring of keys from his belt.

Las esposas, he said.

Rawlins held up his handcuffs. The guard undid them and he entered and John Grady followed. The door groaned and creaked and thudded shut behind them.

There was no light in the room save what fell through the grate in the door and they stood holding their blankets waiting for their eyes to grade the darkness. The floor of the cell was concrete and the air smelled of excrement. After a while someone to the rear of the room spoke.

Cuidado con el bote.

Dont step in the bucket, said John Grady.

Where is it?

I dont know. Just dont step in it.

I caint see a damn thing.

Another voice spoke out of the darkness. It said: Is that you all?

John Grady could see part of Rawlins' face broken into squares in the light from the grid. Turning slowly. The pain in his eyes. Ah God, he said.

Blevins? said John Grady.

Yeah. It's me.

He made his way carefully to the rear. An outstretched leg withdrew along the floor like a serpent recoiling underfoot. He squatted and looked at Blevins. Blevins moved and he could see his teeth in the partial light. As if he were smiling.

What a man wont see when he aint got a gun, said Blevins.

How long have you been here?

I dont know. A long time.

Rawlins made his way toward the back wall and stood looking down at him. You told em to hunt us, didnt you? he said.

Never done no such a thing, said Blevins.

John Grady looked up at Rawlins.

They knew there were three of us, he said.

Yeah, said Blevins.

Bullshit, said Rawlins. They wouldnt of hunted us once they got the horse back. He's done somethin.

It was my goddamn horse, said Blevins.

They could see him now. Scrawny and ragged and filthy.

It was my horse and my saddle and my gun.

They squatted. No one spoke.

What have you done? said John Grady.

Aint done nothin that nobody else wouldnt of.

What have you done.

You know what he's done, said Rawlins.

Did you come back here?

Damn right I come back here.

You dumb shit. What did you do? Tell me the rest of it.

Aint nothin to tell.

Oh hell no, said Rawlins. Aint a damn thing to tell.

John Grady turned. He looked past Rawlins. An old man sat quietly against the wall watching them.

De qué crimen queda acusado el joven? he said.

The man blinked. Asesinato, he said.

El ha matado un hombre?

The man blinked again. He held up three fingers.

What did he say? said Rawlins.

John Grady didnt answer.

What did he say? I know what the son of a bitch said.

He said he's killed three men.

That's a damn lie, said Blevins.

Rawlins sat slowly on the concrete.

We're dead, he said. We're dead men. I knew it'd come to this. From the time I first seen him.

That aint goin to help us, said John Grady.

Aint but one of em died, said Blevins.

Rawlins raised his head and looked at him. Then he got up and stepped to the other side of the room and sat down again.

Cuidado con el bote, said the old man.

John Grady turned to Blevins.

I aint done nothin to him, said Blevins.

Tell me what happened, said John Grady.

He'd worked for a German family in the town of Palau eighty miles to the east and at the end of two months he'd taken the money he'd earned and ridden back across the selfsame desert and staked out the horse at the selfsame spring and dressed in the common clothes of the country he'd walked into town and sat in front of the tienda for two days until he saw the same man go by with the Bisley's worn guttapercha grips sticking out of his belt.

What did you do?

You aint got a cigarette have you?

No. What did you do?

Didnt think you did.

What did you do?

Lord what wouldnt I give for a chew of tobacco.

What did you do?

I walked up behind him and snatched it out of his belt. That's what I done.

And shot him.

He come at me.

Come at you.

Yeah.

So you shot him.

What choice did I have?

What choice, said John Grady.

I didnt want to shoot the dumb son of a bitch. That was never no part of my intention.

What did you do then?

Time I got back to the spring where my horse was at they was on me. That boy I shot off his horse thowed down on me with a shotgun.

What happened then?

I didnt have no more shells. I'd shot em all up. My own damn fault. All I had was what was in the gun.

You shot one of the rurales?

Yeah.

Dead?

Yeah.

They sat quietly in the dark.

I could of bought shells in Muñoz, said Blevins. Fore I even come here. I had the money too.

John Grady looked at him. You got any idea the kind of mess you're in?

Blevins didnt answer.

What did they say they mean to do with you?

Send me to the penitentiary I reckon.

They aint goin to send you to the penitentiary.

Why aint they?

You aint goin to be that lucky, said Rawlins.

I aint old enough to hang.

They'll lie about your age for you.

They dont have capital punishment in this country, said John Grady. Dont listen to him.

You knew they was huntin us, didnt you? said Rawlins.

Yeah, I knew it. What was I supposed to do, send you a telegram?

John Grady waited for Rawlins to answer but he didnt. The shadow of the iron grid over the judas-hole lay skewed upon the far wall like a waiting chalkgame which the space in that dark and stinking cubicle had somehow rendered out of true. He folded his blanket and sat on it and leaned against the wall.

Do they ever let you out? Do you get to walk around?

I dont know.

What do you mean you dont know?

I caint walk.

You cant walk?

That's what I said.

How come you caint walk, said Rawlins.

Cause they busted my feet all to hell is how come.

They sat. No one spoke. Soon it was dark. The old man on the other side of the room had begun to snore. They could hear sounds from the distant village. Dogs. A mother calling. Ranchero music with its falsetto cries almost like an agony played out of a cheap radio somewhere in the nameless night.

THAT NIGHT he dreamt of horses in a field on a high plain where the spring rains had brought up the grass and the wildflowers out of the ground and the flowers ran all blue and yellow far as the eye could see and in the dream he was among the horses running and in the dream he himself could run with the horses and they coursed the young mares and fillies over the plain where their rich bay and their rich chestnut colors shone in the sun and the young colts ran with their dams and trampled down the flowers in a haze of pollen that hung in the sun like powdered gold and they ran he and the horses out along the high mesas where the ground resounded under their running hooves and they flowed and changed and ran and their manes and tails blew off of them like spume and there was nothing else at all in that high world and they moved all of them in a resonance that was like a music among them and they were none of them afraid horse nor colt nor mare and they ran in that resonance which is the world itself and which cannot be spoken but only praised.

In the morning two guards came and opened the door and handcuffed Rawlins and led him away. John Grady stood and asked where they were taking him but they didnt answer. Rawlins didnt even look back.

The captain was sitting at his desk drinking coffee and reading a three day old newspaper from Monterrey. He looked up. Pasaporte, he said.

I dont have no passport, said Rawlins.

The captain looked at him. He raised his eyebrows in mock surprise. Dont have no passport, he said. You have identification?

Rawlins reached around to his left rear pocket with his manacled hands. He could reach the pocket but he couldnt reach into it. The captain nodded and one of the guards stepped forward and took out the billfold and handed it across to the captain. The captain leaned back in the chair. Quite las esposas, he said.

The guard swung his keys forward and took hold of Rawlins' wrists and unlocked the handcuffs and stepped back and put them in his belt. Rawlins stood rubbing his wrists. The captain turned the sweatblackened leather in his hand. He looked at both sides of it and he looked up at Rawlins. Then he opened it and took out the card and he took out the photograph of Betty Ward and he took out the american money and then the mexican peso bills which alone were unmutilated. He spread these things out on the desk and leaned back in his chair and folded his hands together and tapped his chin with his forefingers and looked at Rawlins again. Outside Rawlins could hear a goat. He could hear children. The captain made a little rotary motion with one finger. Turn around, he said.

He did so.

Put down your pants.

Do what?

Put down your pants.

What the hell for?

The captain must have made another gesture because the guard stepped forward and took a leather sap from his rear pocket and struck Rawlins across the back of the head with it. The room Rawlins was in lit up all white and his knees buckled and he reached about him in the air.

He was lying with his face against the splintry wooden floor. He didnt remember falling. The floor smelled of dust and grain. He pushed himself up. They waited. They seemed to have nothing else to do.

He got to his feet and faced the captain. He felt sick to his stomach.

You must co-po-rate, said the captain. Then you dont have no troubles. Turn around. Put down your pants.

He turned around and unbuckled his belt and pushed his trousers down around his knees and then the cheap cotton undershorts he'd bought in the commissary at La Vega.

Lift your shirt, said the captain.

He lifted the shirt.

Turn around, said the captain.

He turned.

Get dressed.

He let the shirt fall and reached and hauled up his trousers and buttoned them and buckled back the belt.

The captain was sitting holding the driver's license from his billfold.

What is your date of birth, he said.

September twenty-sixth nineteen and thirty-two.

What is your address.

Route Four Knickerbocker Texas. United States of America.

How much is your height.

Five foot eleven.

How much is your weight.

A hundred and sixty pounds.

The captain tapped the license on the desk. He looked at Rawlins.

You have a good memory. Where is this man?

What man?

He held up the license. This man. Rawlins.

Rawlins swallowed. He looked at the guard and he looked at the captain again. I'm Rawlins, he said.

The captain smiled sadly. He shook his head.

Rawlins stood with his hands dangling.

Why aint I? he said.

Why you come here? said the captain.

Come where?

Here. To this country.

We come down here to work. Somos vaqueros.

Speak english please. You come to buy cattle?

No sir.

No. You have no permit, correct?

We just come down here to work.

At La Purísima.

Anywhere. That's just where we found work.

How much they pay you?

We was gettin two hundred pesos a month.

In Texas what do they pay for this work.

I dont know. Hundred a month.

Hundred dollars.

Yessir.

Eight hundred pesos.

Yessir. I reckon.

The captain smiled again.

Why you must leave Texas?

We just left. We didnt have to.

What is your true name.

Lacey Rawlins.

He pushed the forearm of his sleeve against his forehead and wished at once he hadnt.

Blevins is your brother.

No. We got nothin to do with him.

What is the number of horses you steal.

We never stole no horses.

These horses have no marca.

They come from the United States.

You have a factura for these horses?

No. We rode down here from San Angelo Texas. We dont have no papers on them. They're just our horses.

Where do you cross the border.

Just out of Langtry Texas.

What is the number of men you kill.

I never killed nobody. I never stole nothin in my life. That's the truth.

Why you have guns for.

To shoot game.

Ghem?

Game. To hunt. Cazador.

Now you are hunters. Where is Rawlins.

Rawlins was close to tears. You're lookin at him, damn it.

What is the true name of the assassin Blevins.

I dont know.

How long since you know him.

I dont know him. I dont know nothin about him.

The captain pushed back the chair and stood. He pulled down the hem of his coat to correct the wrinkles and he looked at Rawlins. You are very foolish, he said. Why do you want to have these troubles?

They let Rawlins go just inside the door and he slid to the floor and sat for a moment and then bent slowly forward and to one side and lay holding himself. The guard crooked his finger at John Grady who sat squinting up at them in the sudden light. He rose. He looked down at Rawlins.

You sons of bitches, he said.

Tell em whatever they want to hear, bud, whispered Rawlins. It dont make a damn.

Vámonos, said the guard.

What did you tell them?

Told em we was horsethieves and murderers. You will too.

But by then the guard had come forward and seized his arm and shoved him out the door and the other guard shut the door and pushed the boltshackle home in the padlock.

When they entered the office the captain sat as before. His hair newly slicked. John Grady stood before him. In the room aside from the desk and the chair that the captain sat in there were three folding metal chairs against the far wall that had an uncomfortable emptiness about them. As if people had got up and left. As if people expected were not coming. An old seed-company calendar from Monterrey was nailed to the wall above them and in the corner stood an empty wire birdcage hung from a floorpedestal like some baroque lampstand.

On the captain's desk was a glass oil-lamp with a blackened chimney. An ashtray. A pencil that had been sharpened with a knife. Las esposas, he said.

The guard stepped forward and unlocked the handcuffs. The captain was looking out the window. He'd taken the pencil from the desk and was tapping his lower teeth with it. He turned and tapped the desk twice with the pencil and laid it down. Like a man calling a meeting to order.

Your friend has told us everything, he said.

He looked up.

You will find it is best to tell everything right away. That way you dont have no troubles.

You didnt have no call to beat up on that boy, said John Grady. We dont know nothin about Blevins. He asked to ride with us, that's all. We dont know nothin about the horse. The horse got away from him in a thunderstorm and showed up here and that's when the trouble started. We didnt have nothin to do with it. We been workin for señor Rocha goin on three months down at La Purísima. You went down there and told him a bunch of lies. Lacey Rawlins is as good a boy as ever come out of Tom Green County.

He is the criminal Smith.

His name aint Smith its Rawlins. And he aint a criminal. I've known him all my life. We were raised together. We went to the same school.

The captain sat back. He unbuttoned his shirtpocket and pushed his cigarettes up from the bottom in their package and took one out without removing the pack and buttoned the shirt again. The shirt had been tailored in military fashion and fit tightly and the cigarettes fit tightly in the pocket. He leaned in his chair and took a lighter from his coat and lit the cigarette and put the lighter on the desk beside the pencil and pulled the ashtray to him with one finger and leaned back in the chair and sat with his arm upright and the burning cigarette a few inches from his ear in a posture that seemed alien to him. As if perhaps he'd admired it somewhere in others.

What is your age, he said.

Sixteen. I'll be seventeen in six weeks.

What is the age of the assassin Blevins.

I dont know. I dont know nothin about him. He says he's sixteen. I'd guess fourteen is more like it. Thirteen even.

He dont have no feathers.

He what?

He dont have no feathers.

I wouldnt know about that. It dont interest me.

The captain's face darkened. He puffed on the cigarette. Then he put his hand on the desk palm upward and snapped his fingers.

Deme su billetera.

John Grady took his billfold from his hip pocket and stepped forward and laid it on the desk and stepped back. The captain looked at him. He leaned forward and took the billfold and sat back and opened it and began to take out the money, the cards. The photos. He spread everything out and looked up.

Where is your license of operator.

I dont have one.

You have destroy it.

I dont have one. I never did have one.

The assassin Blevins has no documents.

Probably not.

Why dont he have no documents.

He lost his clothes.

He lose his clothes?

Yes.

Why he come here to steal horses?

It was his horse.

The captain leaned back, smoking.

The horse is not his horse.

Well, you have it your own ignorant way.

Cómo?

As far as I know that horse is his horse. He had it with him in Texas and I know he brought it into Mexico because I seen him ride it across the river.

The captain sat drumming his fingers on the arm of the chair. I dont believe you, he said.

John Grady didnt answer.

These are not the facts.

He half swiveled in his chair to look out the window.

Not the facts, he said. He turned and looked across his shoulder at the prisoner.

You have the opportunity to tell the truth here. Here. In three days you will go to Saltillo and then you will no have this opportunity. It will be gone. Then the truth will be in other hands. You see. We can make the truth here. Or we can lose it. But when you leave here it will be too late. Too late for truth. Then you will be in the hands of other parties. Who can say what the truth will be then? At that time? Then you will blame yourself. You will see.

There aint but one truth, said John Grady. The truth is what happened. It aint what come out of somebody's mouth.

You like this little town? said the captain.

It's all right.

It is very quiet here.

Yes.

The peoples in this town are quiet peoples. Everybody here is quiet all the time.

He leaned forward and stubbed out the cigarette in the ashtray.

Then comes the assassin Blevins to steal horses and kill everybody. Why is this? He was a quiet boy and never do no harm and then he come here and do these things something like that?

He leaned back and shook his head in that same sad way.

No, he said. He wagged one finger. No.

He watched John Grady.

What is the truth is this: He was no a quiet boy. He was this other kind of boy all the time. All the time.

When the guards brought John Grady back they took Blevins away with them. He could walk but not well. When the padlock had clicked shut and rattled and swung to rest John Grady squatted facing Rawlins.

How you doin? he said.

I'm okay. How are you?

I'm all right.

What happened?

Nothin.

What'd you tell him?

I told him you were full of shit.

You didnt get to go to the shower room?

No.

You were gone a long time.

Yeah.

He keeps a white coat back there on a hook. He takes it down and puts it on and ties it around his waist with a string.

John Grady nodded. He looked at the old man. The old man was watching them even if he didnt speak english.

Blevins is sick.

Yeah, I know. I think we're goin to Saltillo.

What's in Saltillo?

I dont know.

Rawlins shifted against the wall. He closed his eyes.

Are you all right? said John Grady.

Yeah, I'm all right.

I think he wants to make some kind of a deal with us.

The captain?

Captain. Whatever he is.

What kind of a deal.

To keep quiet. That kind of a deal.

Like we had some kind of a choice. Keep quiet about what?

About Blevins.

Keep quiet about what about Blevins?

John Grady looked at the little square of light in the door and at the skew of it on the wall above the old man's head where he sat. He looked at Rawlins.

I think they aim to kill him. I think they aim to kill Blevins.

Rawlins sat for a long time. He sat with his head turned away against the wall. When he looked at John Grady again his eyes were wet.

Maybe they wont, he said.

I think they will.

Ah damn, said Rawlins. Just goddamn it all to hell.

When they brought Blevins back he sat in the corner and didnt speak. John Grady talked with the old man. His name was Orlando. He didnt know what crime he was accused of. He'd been told he could go when he signed the papers but he couldnt read the papers and no one would read them to him. He didnt know how long he'd been here. Since sometime in the winter. While they were talking the guards came again and the old man shut up.

They unlocked the door and entered and set two buckets in the floor together with a stack of enameled tin plates. One of them looked into the waterpail and the other took the slop pail from the corner and they went out again. They had about them a perfunctory air, like men accustomed to caring for livestock. When they were gone the prisoners squatted about the buckets and John Grady handed out the plates. Of which there were five. As if some unknown other were expected. There were no utensils and they used the tortillas to spoon the beans from the bucket.

Blevins, said John Grady. You aim to eat?

I aint hungry.

Better get you some of this.

You all go on.

John Grady scooped beans into one of the spare dishes and folded the tortilla along the edge of the dish and got up and carried it to Blevins and came back. Blevins sat holding the dish in his lap.

After a while he said: What'd you tell em about me?

Rawlins stopped chewing and looked at John Grady. John Grady looked at Blevins.

Told em the truth.

Yeah, said Blevins.

You think it would make any difference what we told them? said Rawlins.

You could of tried to help me out.

Rawlins looked at John Grady.

Could of put in a good word for me, said Blevins.

Good word, said Rawlins.

Wouldnt of cost you nothin.

Shut the hell up, said Rawlins. Just shut up. You say anything more I'll come over there and stomp your skinny ass. You hear me? If you say one more goddamn word.

Leave him alone, said John Grady.

Dumb little son of a bitch. You think that man in there dont know what you are? He knew what you were fore he ever set eyes on you. Before you were born. Damn you to hell. Just damn you to hell.

He was almost in tears. John Grady put a hand on his shoulder. Let it go, Lacey, he said. Just let it go.

In the afternoon the guards came and left the slop bucket and took away the plates and pails.

How do you reckon the horses are makin it? said Rawlins.

John Grady shook his head.

Horses, the old man said. Caballos.

Sí. Caballos.

They sat in the hot silence and listened to the sounds in the village. The passing of some horses along the road. John Grady asked the old man if they had mistreated him but the old man waved one hand and passed it off. He said they didnt bother him much. He said there was no sustenance in it for them. An old man's dry moans. He said that pain for the old was no longer a surprise.

Three days later they were led blinking from their cell into the early sunlight and through the yard and the schoolhouse and out into the street. Parked there was a ton-and-a-half flatbed Ford truck. They stood in the street dirty and unshaven holding their blankets in their arms. After a while one of the guards motioned to them to climb up on the truck. Another guard came out of the building and they were handcuffed with the same plateworn cuffs and then chained together with a towchain that lay coiled in the spare tire in the forward bed of the truck. The captain came out and stood in the sunlight rocking on his heels and drinking a cup of coffee. He wore a pipeclayed leather belt and holster, the 45 automatic slung at full cock butt-forward at his left side. He spoke to the guards and they waved their arms and a man standing on the front bumper of the truck raised up out of the engine compartment and gestured and spoke and then bent under the hood again.

What did he say? said Blevins.

No one answered. There were bundles and crates piled forward on the truckbed together with some fivegallon army gascans. People of the town kept arriving with parcels and handing slips of paper to the driver who stuffed them into his shirtpocket without comment.

Yonder stands your gals, said Rawlins.

I see em, said John Grady.

They were standing close together, the one clinging to the arm of the other, both of them crying.

What the hell sense does that make? said Rawlins.

John Grady shook his head.

The girls stood watching while the truck was loaded and while the guards sat smoking with their rifles propped against their shoulders and they were still standing there an hour later when the truck finally started and the hood dropped shut and the truck with the prisoners in their chains jostling slightly pulled away down the narrow dirt street and faded from sight in a rolling wake of dust and motorsmoke.

There were three guards on the truckbed with the prisoners, young boys from the country in illfitting and unpressed uniforms. They must have been ordered not to speak to the prisoners because they took care to avoid their eyes. They nodded or raised one hand gravely to people they knew standing in the doorways as they rolled out down the dusty street. The captain sat in the cab with the driver. Some dogs came out to chase the truck and the driver cut the wheel sharply to try to run them down and the guards on the truckbed grabbed wildly for handholds and the driver looked back at them through the rear window of the cab laughing and they all laughed and punched one another and then sat gravely with their rifles.

They turned down a narrow street and stopped in front of a house that was painted bright blue. The captain leaned across the cab and blew the horn. After a while the door opened and a man came out. He was rather elegantly dressed after the manner of a charro and he walked around the truck and the captain got out and the man got into the cab and the captain climbed in after him and shut the door and they pulled away.

They drove down the street past the last house and the last of the corrals and mud pens and crossed a shallow ford where the slow water shone like oil in its colors and mended itself behind them before the run-off from the trucktires had even finished draining back. The truck labored up out of the ford over the scarred rock of the roadbed and then leveled out and set off across the desert in the flat midmorning light.

The prisoners watched the dust boil from under the truck and hang over the road and drift slowly off across the desert. They slammed about on the rough oak planks of the truckbed and tried to keep their blankets folded under them. Where the road forked they turned out onto the track that would take them to Cuatro Ciénagas and on to Saltillo four hundred kilometers to the south.

Blevins had unfolded his blanket and was stretched out on it with his arms under his head. He lay staring up at the pure blue desert sky where there was no cloud, no bird. When he spoke, his voice shuddered from the hammering of the truckbed against his back.

Boys, he said, this is goin to be a long old trip.

They looked at him, they looked at each other. They didnt say if they thought it would be or not.

The old man said it'd take all day to get there, said Blevins. I asked him. Said all day.

Before noon they struck the main road coming down out of Boquillas on the border and they took the road downcountry. Through the pueblos of San Guillermo, San Miguel, Tanque el Revés. The few vehicles they encountered on that hot and guttered track passed in a storm of dust and flying rock and the riders on the truckbed turned away with their faces in their elbow sleeves. They stopped in Ocampo and offloaded some crates of produce and some mail and drove on toward El Oso. In the early afternoon they pulled in at a small cafe by the roadside and the guards climbed down and went in with their guns. The prisoners sat chained on the truckbed. In the dead mud yard some children who'd been playing stopped to watch them and a thin white dog who seemed to have been awaiting just such an arrival came over and urinated for a long time against the rear tire of the truck and went back.

When the guards came out they were laughing and rolling cigarettes. One of them carried three bottles of orange sodawater and he passed them up to the prisoners and stood waiting for the bottles while they drank. When the captain appeared in the doorway they climbed back onto the truck. The guard who'd taken the bottles back came out and then the man in the charro outfit and then the driver. When they were all in their places the captain stepped from the shade of the doorway and crossed the gravel apron and climbed into the cab and they went on.

At Cuatro Ciénagas they struck the paved road and turned south toward Torreón. One of the guards stood up and holding on to the shoulder of his companion looked back at the roadsign. He sat again and they glanced at the prisoners and then just sat looking out over the countryside as the truck gathered speed. An hour later they left the road altogether, the truck laboring over a dirt track across rolling fields, a great and fallow baldíos such as was common to that country where feral cattle the color of candle-wax come up out of the arroyos to feed at night like alien principals. Summer thunderheads were building to the north and Blevins was studying the horizon and watching the thin wires of lightning and watching the dust to see how the wind blew. They crossed a broad gravel riverbed dry and white in the sun and they climbed into a meadow where the grass was tall as the tires and passed under the truck with a seething sound and they entered a grove of ebony trees and drove out a nesting pair of hawks and pulled up in the yard of an abandoned estancia, a quadrangle of mud buildings and the remains of some sheep-pens.

No one in the truckbed moved. The captain opened the door and stepped out. Vámonos, he said.

They climbed down with their guns. Blevins looked about at the ruined buildings.

What's here? he said.

One of the guards leaned his rifle against the truck and sorted through the ring of keys and reached and unlocked the chain and threw the loose ends up onto the truckbed and picked up the rifle again and gestured for the prisoners to get down. The captain had sent one of the guards to scout the perimeter and they stood waiting for him to come back. The charro stood leaning against the front fender of the truck with one thumb in his carved leather belt smoking a cigarette.

What do we do here? said Blevins.

I dont know, said John Grady.

The driver hadnt gotten out of the truck. He was slumped back in the seat with his hat over his eyes and looked to be sleeping.

I got to take a leak, said Rawlins.

They walked out through the grass, Blevins hobbling after them. No one looked at them. The guard came back and reported to the captain and the captain took the guard's rifle from him and handed it to the charro and the charro hefted it in his hands as if it were a game gun. The prisoners straggled back to the truck. Blevins sat down a little apart and the charro looked at him and then took his cigarette from his mouth and dropped it in the grass and stepped on it. Blevins got up and moved to the rear of the truck where John Grady and Rawlins were standing.

What are they goin to do? he said.

The guard with no rifle came to the rear of the truck.

Vámonos, he said.

Rawlins raised up from where he was leaning on the bed of the truck.

Sólo el chico, said the guard. Vámonos.

Rawlins looked at John Grady.

What are they goin to do? said Blevins.

They aint goin to do nothin, said Rawlins.

He looked at John Grady. John Grady said nothing at all. The guard reached and took Blevins by the arm. Vámonos, he said.

Wait a minute, said Blevins.

Están esperando, said the guard.

Blevins twisted out of his grip and sat on the ground. The guard's face clouded. He looked toward the front of the truck where the captain stood. Blevins had wrenched off one boot and was reaching down inside it. He pulled up the black and sweaty innersole and threw it away and reached in again. The guard bent and got hold of his thin arm. He pulled Blevins up. Blevins was flailing about trying to hand something to John Grady.

Here, he hissed.

John Grady looked at him. What do I want with that? he said.

Take it, said Blevins.

He thrust into his hand a wad of dirty and crumpled peso notes and the guard jerked him around by his arm and pushed him forward. The boot had fallen to the ground.

Wait, said Blevins. I need to get my boot.

But the guard shoved him on past the truck and he limped away, looking back once mute and terrified and then going on with the captain and the charro across the clearing toward the trees. The captain had put one arm around the boy, or he put his hand in the small of his back. Like some kindly advisor. The other man walked behind them carrying the rifle and Blevins disappeared into the ebony trees hobbling on one boot much as they had seen him that morning coming up the arroyo after the rain in that unknown country long ago.

Rawlins looked at John Grady. His mouth was tight. John Grady watched the small ragged figure vanish limping among the trees with his keepers. There seemed insufficient substance to him to be the object of men's wrath. There seemed nothing about him sufficient to fuel any enterprise at all.

Dont you say nothin, said Rawlins.

All right.

Dont you say a damn word.

John Grady turned and looked at him. He looked at the guards and he looked at the place where they were, the strange land, the strange sky.

All right, he said. I wont.

At some time the driver had got out and gone off somewhere to inspect the buildings. The others stood, the two prisoners, the three guards in their rumpled suits. The one guard with no rifle squatting by the tire. They waited a long time. Rawlins leaned and put his fists on the truckbed and laid his forehead down and closed his eyes tightly. After a while he raised up again. He looked at John Grady.

They caint just walk him out there and shoot him, he said. Hell fire. Just walk him out there and shoot him.

John Grady looked at him. As he did so the pistol shot came from beyond the ebony trees. Not loud. Just a flat sort of pop. Then another.

When they came back out of the trees the captain was carrying the handcuffs. Vámonos, he called.

The guards moved. One of them stood on the rear axlehub and reached across the boards of the truckbed for the chain. The driver came from the ruins of the quinta.

We're okay, whispered Rawlins. We're okay.

John Grady didnt answer. He almost reached to pull down the front of his hatbrim but then he remembered that they had no hats anymore and he turned and climbed up on the bed of the truck and sat waiting to be chained. Blevins' boot was still lying in the grass. One of the guards bent and picked it up and pitched it into the weeds.

When they wound back up out of the glade it was already evening and the sun lay long in the grass and across the shallow swales where the land dipped in pockets of darkness. Small birds come to feed in the evening cool of the open country flushed and flared away over the grasstops and the hawks in silhouette against the sunset waited in the upper limbs of a dead tree for them to pass.

They rode into Saltillo at ten oclock at night, the populace out for their paseos, the cafes full. They parked on the square opposite the cathedral and the captain got out and crossed the street. There were old men sitting on benches under the yellow lamplight having their shoes polished and there were little signs warning people off the tended gardens. Vendors were selling paletas of frozen fruitjuices and young girls with powdered faces went hand in hand by pairs and peered across their shoulders with dark uncertain eyes. John Grady and Rawlins sat with their blankets pulled about them. No one paid them any mind. After a while the captain came back and climbed into the truck and they went on again.

They drove through the streets and made stops at little dimlit doorways and small houses and tiendas until nearly all the parcels in the bed of the truck had been dispersed and a few new ones taken aboard. When they pulled up before the massive doors of the old prison on Castelar it was past midnight.

They were led into a stonefloored room that smelled of disinfectant. The guard uncuffed their wrists and left them and they squatted and leaned against the wall with their blankets about their shoulders like mendicants. They squatted there for a long time. When the door opened again the captain came in and stood looking at them in the dead flat glare of the single bulb in the ceiling overhead. He was not wearing his pistol. He gestured with his chin and the guard who'd opened the door withdrew and closed the door behind him.

The captain stood regarding them with his arms crossed and his thumb beneath his chin. The prisoners looked up at him, they looked at his feet, they looked away. He stood watching them for a long time. They all seemed to be waiting for something. Like passengers in a halted train. Yet the captain inhabited another space and it was a space of his own election and outside the common world of men. A space privileged to men of the irreclaimable act which while it contained all lesser worlds within it contained no access to them. For the terms of election were of a piece with its office and once chosen that world could not be quit.

He paced. He stood. He said that the man they called the charro had suffered from a failure of nerve out there among the ebony trees beyond the ruins of the estancia and this a man whose brother was dead at the hand of the assassin Blevins and this a man who had paid money that certain arrangements be made which the captain had been at some pains himself to make.

This man came to me. I dont go to him. He came to me. Speaking of justice. Speaking of the honor of his family. Do you think men truly want these things? I dont think many men want these things.

Even so I was surprise. I was surprise. We have no death here for the criminals. Other arrangements must be made. I tell you this because you will be making arrangements you self.

John Grady looked up.

You are not the first Americans to be here, said the captain. In this place. I have friends in this place and you will be making these arrangements with these peoples. I dont want you to make no mistakes.

We dont have any money, said John Grady. We aint fixin to make any arrangements.

Excuse me but you will be making some arrangements. You dont know nothing.

What did you do with our horses.

We are not talking about horses now. Those horses must wait. The rightful owners must be found of those horses.

Rawlins stared bleakly at John Grady. Just shut the hell up, he said.

He can talk, said the captain. It is better when everybody is understand. You cannot stay here. In this place. You stay here you going to die. Then come other problems. Papers is lost. Peoples cannot be found. Some peoples come here to look for some man but he is no here. No one can find these papers. Something like that. You see. No one wants these troubles. Who can say that some body was here? We dont have this body. Some crazy person, he can say that God is here. But everybody knows that God is no here.

The captain reached out with one hand and rapped with his knuckles against the door.

You didnt have to kill him, said John Grady.

Cómo?

You could of just brought him back. You could of just brought him on back to the truck. You didnt have to kill him.

A keyring rattled outside. The door opened. The captain held up one hand to an unseen figure in the partial dark of the corridor.

Momento, he said.

He turned and stood studying them.

I will tell you a story, he said. Because I like you. I was young man like you. You see. And this time I tell you I was always with these older boys because I want to learn every thing. So on this night at the fiesta of San Pedro in the town of Linares in Nuevo León I was with these boys and they have some mescal and everything—you know what is mescal?—and there was this woman and all these boys is go out to this woman and they is have this woman. And I am the last one. And I go out to the place where is this woman and she is refuse me because she say I am too young or something like that.

What does a man do? You see. I can no go back because they will all see that I dont go with this woman. Because the truth is always plain. You see. A man cannot go out to do some thing and then he go back. Why he go back? Because he change his mind? A man does not change his mind.

The captain made a fist and held it up.

Maybe they tell her to refuse to me. So they can laugh. They give her some money or something like that. But I dont let whores make trouble for me. When I come back there is no laughing. No one is laughing. You see. That has always been my way in this world. I am the one when I go someplace then there is no laughing. When I go there then they stop laughing.

They were led up four flights of stone stairs and through a steel door out onto an iron catwalk. The guard smiled back at them in the light from the bulb over the door. Beyond lay the night sky of the desert mountains. Below them the prison yard.

Se llama la periquera, he said.

They followed him down the catwalk. A sense of some brooding and malignant life slumbering in the darkened cages they passed. Here and there along the tiers of catwalks on the far side of the quadrangle a dull light shaped out the grating of the cells where votive candles burned the night long before some santo. The bell in the cathedral tower three blocks away sounded once with a deep, an oriental solemnity.

They were locked into a cell in the topmost corner of the prison. The ironbarred door clanged shut and the latch rattled home and they listened as the guard went back down the catwalk and they listened as the iron door shut and then all was silence.

They slept in iron bunks chained to the walls on thin trocheros or mattress pads that were greasy, vile, infested. In the morning they climbed down the four flights of steel ladders into the yard and stood among the prisoners for the morning lista. The lista was called by tiers yet it still took over an hour and their names were not called.

I guess we aint here, said Rawlins.

Their breakfast was a thin pozole and nothing more and afterward they were simply turned out into the yard to fend for themselves. They spent the whole of the first day fighting and when they were finally shut up in their cell at night they were bloody and exhausted and Rawlins' nose was broken and badly swollen. The prison was no more than a small walled village and within it occurred a constant seethe of barter and exchange in everything from radios and blankets down to matches and buttons and shoenails and within this bartering ran a constant struggle for status and position. Underpinning all of it like the fiscal standard in commercial societies lay a bedrock of depravity and violence where in an egalitarian absolute every man was judged by a single standard and that was his readiness to kill.

They slept and in the morning it all began again. They fought back to back and picked each other up and fought again. At noon Rawlins could not chew. They're goin to kill us, he said.

John Grady mashed beans in a tin can with water till he'd made a gruel out of it and pushed it at Rawlins.

You listen to me, he said. Dont you let em think they aint goin to have to. You hear me? I intend to make em kill me. I wont take nothin less. They either got to kill us or let us be. There aint no middle ground.

There aint a place on me that dont hurt.

I know it. I know it and I dont care.

Rawlins sucked at the gruel. He looked at John Grady from over the rim of the can. You look like a goddamn racoon, he said.

John Grady grinned crookedly. What the hell you think you look like?

Shit if I know.

You ought to wish you looked as good as a coon.

I caint laugh. I think my jaw's broke.

There aint nothin wrong with you.

Shit, said Rawlins.

John Grady grinned. You see that big old boy standin yonder that's been watchin us?

I see the son of a bitch.

See him lookin over here?

I see him.

What do you think I'm fixin to do?

I got no idea in this world.

I'm goin to get up from here and walk over there and bust him in the mouth.

The hell you are.

You watch me.

What for?

Just to save him the trip.

By the end of the third day it seemed to be pretty much over. There were both half naked and John Grady had been blindsided with a sock full of gravel that took out two teeth in his lower jaw and his left eye was closed completely. The fourth day was Sunday and they bought clothes with Blevins' money and they bought a bar of soap and took showers and they bought a can of tomato soup and heated it in the can over a candlestub and wrapped the sleeve of Rawlins' old shirt around it for a handle and passed it back and forth between them while the sun set over the high western wall of the prison.

You know, we might just make it, said Rawlins.

Dont start gettin comfortable. Let's just take it a day at a time.

How much money you think it would take to get out of here?

I dont know. I'd say a lot.

I would too.

We aint heard from the captain's buddies in here. I guess they're waitin to see if there's goin to be anything left to bail out.

He held out the can toward Rawlins.

Finish it, said Rawlins.

Take it. There aint but a sup.

He took the can and drained it and poured a little water in and swirled it about and drank that and sat looking into the empty can.

If they think we're rich how come they aint looked after us no better? he said.

I dont know. I know they dont run this place. All they run is what comes in and what goes out.

If that, said Rawlins.

The floodlights came on from the upper walls. Figures that had been moving in the yard froze, then they moved again.

The horn's fixin to blow.

We got a couple of minutes.

I never knowed there was such a place as this.

I guess there's probably every kind of place you can think of.

Rawlins nodded. I wouldnt of thought of this one, he said.

It was raining somewhere out in the desert. They could smell the wet creosote on the wind. Lights came on in a makeshift cinderblock house built into one corner of the prison wall where a prisoner of means lived like an exiled satrap complete with cook and bodyguard. There was a screen door to the house and a figure crossed behind it and crossed back. On the roof a clothesline where the prisoner's clothes luffed gently in the night breeze like flags of state. Rawlins nodded toward the lights.

You ever see him?

Yeah. One time. He was standin in the door one evenin smokin him a cigar.

You picked up on any of the lingo in here?

Some.

What's a pucha?

A cigarette butt.

Then what's a tecolata?

Same thing.

How many damn names have they got for a cigarette butt?

I dont know. You know what a papazote is?

No, what?

A big shot.

That's what they call the dude that lives yonder.

Yeah.

And we're a couple of gabachos.

Bolillos.

Pendejos.

Anybody can be a pendejo, said John Grady. That just means asshole.

Yeah? Well, we're the biggest ones in here.

I wont dispute it.

They sat.

What are you thinkin about, said Rawlins.

Thinkin about how much it's goin to hurt to get up from here.

Rawlins nodded. They watched the prisoners moving under the glare of the lights.

All over a goddamned horse, said Rawlins.

John Grady leaned and spat between his boots and leaned back. Horse had nothin to do with it, he said.

That night they lay in their cell on the iron racks like acolytes and listened to the silence and a rattling snore somewhere in the block and a dog barking faintly in the distance and the silence and each other breathing in the silence both still awake.

We think we're a couple of pretty tough cowboys, said Rawlins.

Yeah. Maybe.

They could kill us any time.

Yeah. I know.

Two days later the papazote sent for them. A tall thin man crossed the quadrangle in the evening to where they sat and bent and asked them to come with him and then rose and strode off again. He didnt even look back to see if they'd rise to follow.

What do you want to do? said Rawlins.

John Grady rose stiffly and dusted the seat of his trousers with one hand.

Get your ass up from there, he said.

The man's name was Pérez. His house was a single room in the center of which stood a tin foldingtable and four chairs. Against one wall was a small iron bed and in one corner a cupboard and a shelf with some dishes and a threeburner gasring. Pérez was standing looking out his small window at the yard. When he turned he made an airy gesture with two fingers and the man who'd come to fetch them stepped back out and closed the door.

My name is Emilio Pérez, he said. Please. Sit down.

They pulled out chairs at the table and sat. The floor of the room was made of boards but they were not nailed to anything. The blocks of the walls were not mortared and the unpeeled roofpoles were only dropped loosely into the topmost course and the sheets of roofingtin overhead were held down by blocks stacked along their edges. A few men could have disassembled and stacked the structure in half an hour. Yet there was an electric light and a gasburning heater. A carpet. Pictures from calendars pinned to the walls.

You young boys, he said. You enjoy very much to fight, yes?

Rawlins started to speak but John Grady cut him off. Yes, he said. We like it a lot.

Pérez smiled. He was a man about forty with graying hair and moustache, lithe and trim. He pulled out the third chair and stepped over the back of it with a studied casualness and sat and leaned forward with his elbows on the table. The table had been painted green with a brush and the logo of a brewery was partly visible through the paint. He folded his hands.

All this fighting, he said. How long have you been here?

About a week.

How long do you plan to stay?

We never planned to come here in the first place, Rawlins said. I dont believe our plans has got much to do with it.

Pérez smiled. The Americans dont stay so long with us, he said. Sometimes they come here for some months. Two or three. Then they leave. Life here is not so good for the Americans. They dont like it so much.

Can you get us out of here?

Pérez spaced his hands apart and made a shrugging gesture. Yes, he said. I can do this, of course.

Why dont you get yourself out, said Rawlins.

He leaned back. He smiled again. The gesture he made of throwing his hands suddenly away from him like birds dismissed sorted oddly with his general air of containment. As if he thought it perhaps an american gesture which they would understand.

I have political enemies. What else? Let me be clear with you. I do not live here so very good. I must have money to make my own arrangements and this is a very expensive business. A very expensive business.

You're diggin a dry hole, said John Grady. We dont have no money.

Pérez regarded them gravely.

If you dont have no money how can you be release from your confinement?

You tell us.

But there is nothing to tell. Without money you can do nothing.

Then I dont guess we'll be goin anywheres.

Pérez studied them. He leaned forward and folded his hands again. He seemed to be giving thought how to put things.

This is a serious business, he said. You dont understand the life here. You think this struggle is for these things. Some shoelaces or some cigarettes or something like that. The lucha. This is a naive view. You know what is naive? A naive view. The real facts are always otherwise. You cannot stay in this place and be independent peoples. You dont know what is the situation here. You dont speak the language.

He speaks it, said Rawlins.

Pérez shook his head. No, he said. You dont speak it. Maybe in a year here you might understand. But you dont have no year. You dont have no time. If you dont show faith to me I cannot help you. You understand me? I cannot offer to you my help.

John Grady looked at Rawlins. You ready, bud?

Yeah. I'm ready.

They pushed back their chairs and rose.

Pérez looked up at them. Sit down please, he said.

There's nothin to sit about.

He drummed his fingers on the table. You are very foolish, he said. Very foolish.

John Grady stood with his hand on the door. He turned and looked at Pérez. His face misshapen and his jaw bowed out and his eye still swollen closed and blue as a plum.

Why dont you tell us what's out there? he said. You talk about showin faith. If we dont know then why dont you tell us?

Pérez had not risen from the table. He leaned back and looked at them.

I cannot tell you, he said. That is the truth. I can say certain things about those who come under my protection. But the others?

He made a little gesture of dismissal with the back of his hand.

The others are simply outside. They live in a world of possibility that has no end. Perhaps God can say what is to become of them. But I cannot.

The next morning crossing the yard Rawlins was set upon by a man with a knife. The man he'd never seen before and the knife was no homemade trucha ground out of a trenchspoon but an italian switchblade with black horn handles and nickle bolsters and he held it at waist level and passed it three times across Rawlins' shirt while Rawlins leaped three times backward with his shoulders hunched and his arms outflung like a man refereeing his own bloodletting. At the third pass he turned and ran. He ran with one hand across his stomach and his shirt was wet and sticky.

When John Grady got to him he was sitting with his back to the wall holding his arms crossed over his stomach and rocking back and forth as if he were cold. John Grady knelt and tried to pull his arms away.

Let me see, damn it.

That son of a bitch. That son of a bitch.

Let me see.

Rawlins leaned back. Aw shit, he said.

John Grady lifted the bloodsoaked shirt.

It aint that bad, he said. It aint that bad.

He cupped his hand and ran it across Rawlins' stomach to chase the blood. The lowest cut was the deepest and it had severed the outer fascia but it had not gone through into the stomach wall. Rawlins looked down at the cuts. It aint good, he said. Son of a bitch.

Can you walk?

Yeah, I can walk.

Come on.

Aw shit, said Rawlins. Son of a bitch.

Come on, bud. You cant set here.

He helped Rawlins to his feet.

Come on, he said. I got you.

They crossed the quadrangle to the gateshack. The guard looked out through the sallyport. He looked at John Grady and he looked at Rawlins. Then he opened the gate and John Grady passed Rawlins into the hands of his captors.

They sat him in a chair and sent for the alcaide. Blood dripped slowly onto the stone floor beneath him. He sat holding his stomach with both hands. After a while someone handed him a towel.

In the days that followed John Grady moved about the compound as little as possible. He watched everywhere for the cuchillero who would manifest himself from among the anonymous eyes that watched back. Nothing occurred. He had a few friends among the inmates. An older man from the state of Yucatán who was outside of the factions but was treated with respect. A dark indian from Sierra León. Two brothers named Bautista who had killed a policeman in Monterrey and set fire to the body and were arrested with the older brother wearing the policeman's shoes. All agreed that Pérez was a man whose power could only be guessed at. Some said he was not confined to the prison at all but went abroad at night. That he kept a wife and family in the town. A mistress.

He tried to get some word from the guards concerning Rawlins but they claimed to know nothing. On the morning of the third day after the stabbing he crossed the yard and tapped at Pérez's door. The drone of noise in the yard behind him almost ceased altogether. He could feel the eyes on him and when Pérez's tall chamberlain opened the door he only glanced at him and then looked beyond and raked the compound with his eyes.

Quisiera hablar con el señor Pérez, said John Grady.

Con respecto de que?

Con respecto de mi cuate.

He shut the door. John Grady waited. After a while the door opened again. Pásale, said the chamberlain.

John Grady stepped into the room. Pérez's man shut the door and then stood against it. Pérez sat at his table.

How is the condition of your friend? he said.

That's what I come to ask you.

Pérez smiled.

Sit down. Please.

Is he alive?

Sit down. I insist.

He stepped to the table and pulled back a chair and sat.

Perhaps you like some coffee.

No thank you.

Pérez leaned back.

Tell me what I can do for you, he said.

You can tell me how my friend is.

But if I answer this question then you will go away.

What would you want me to stay for?

Pérez smiled. My goodness, he said. To tell me stories of your life of crime. Of course.

John Grady studied him.

Like all men of means, said Pérez, my only desire is to be entertained.

Me toma el pelo.

Yes. In english you say the leg, I believe.

Yes. Are you a man of means?

No. It is a joke. I enjoy to practice my english. It passes the time. Where did you learn castellano?

At home.

In Texas.

Yes.

You learn it from the servants.

We didnt have no servants. We had people worked on the place.

You have been in some prison before.

No.

You are the oveja negra, no? The black sheep?

You dont know nothin about me.

Perhaps not. Tell me, why do you believe that you can be release from your confinement in some abnormal way?

I told you you're diggin a dry hole. You dont know what I believe.

I know the United States. I have been there many times. You

are like the jews. There is always a rich relative. What prison were you in?

You know I aint been in no prison. Where is Rawlins?

You think I am responsible for the incident to your friend. But that is not the case.

You think I came here to do business. All I want is to know what's happened to him.

Pérez nodded thoughtfully. Even in a place like this where we are concerned with fundamental things the mind of the anglo is closed in this rare way. At one time I thought it was only his life of privilege. But it is not that. It is his mind.

He sat back easily. He tapped his temple. It is not that he is stupid. It is that his picture of the world is incomplete. In this rare way. He looks only where he wishes to see. You understand me?

I understand you.

Good, said Pérez. I can normally tell how intelligent a man is by how stupid he thinks I am.

I dont think you're stupid. I just dont like you.

Ah, said Pérez. Very good. Very good.

John Grady looked at Pérez's man standing against the door. He stood with his eyes caged, looking at nothing.

He doesnt understand what we are saying, said Pérez. Feel free to express yourself.

I've done expressed myself.

Yes.

I got to go.

Do you think you can go if I dont want you to go?

Yes.

Pérez smiled. Are you a cuchillero?

John Grady sat back.

A prison is like a—how do you call it? A salón de belleza. A beauty parlor.

A beauty parlor. It is a big place for gossip. Everybody knows the story of everybody. Because crime is very interesting. Everybody knows that.

We never committed any crimes.

Perhaps not yet.

What does that mean?

Pérez shrugged. They are still looking. Your case is not decided. Did you think your case was decided?

They wont find anything.

My goodness, said Pérez. My goodness. You think there are no crimes without owners? It is not a matter of finding. It is only a matter of choosing. Like picking the proper suit in a store.

They dont seem to be in any hurry.

Even in Mexico they cannot keep you indefinitely. That is why you must act. Once you are charged it will be too late. They will issue what is called the previas. Then there are many difficulties.

He took his cigarettes from his shirtpocket and offered them across the table. John Grady didnt move.

Please, said Pérez. It is all right. It is not the same as breaking bread. It places one under no obligation.

He leaned forward and took a cigarette and put it in his mouth. Pérez took a lighter from his pocket and snapped it open and lit it and held it across the table.

Where did you learn to fight? he said.

John Grady took a deep pull on the cigarette and leaned back.

What do you want to know? he said.

Only what the world wants to know.

What does the world want to know.

The world wants to know if you have cojones. If you are brave.

He lit his own cigarette and laid the lighter on top of the pack of cigarettes on the table and blew a thin stream of smoke.

Then it can decide your price, he said.

Some people dont have a price.

That is true.

What about those people?

Those people die.

I aint afraid to die.

That is good. It will help you to die. It will not help you to live.

Is Rawlins dead?

No. He is not dead.

John Grady pushed back the chair.

Pérez smiled easily. You see? he said. You do just as I say.

I dont think so.

You have to make up your mind. You dont have so much time. We never have so much time as we think.

Time's the one thing I've had enough of since I come here.

I hope you will give some thought to your situation. Americans have ideas sometimes that are not so practical. They think that there are good things and bad things. They are very superstitious, you know.

You dont think there's good and bad things?

Things no. I think it is a superstition. It is the superstition of a godless people.

You think Americans are godless?

Oh yes. Dont you?

No.

I see them attack their own property. I saw a man one time destroy his car. With a big martillo. What do you call it?

Hammer.

Because it would not start. Would a Mexican do that?

I dont know.

A Mexican would not do that. The Mexican does not believe that a car can be good or evil. If there is evil in the car he knows that to destroy the car is to accomplish nothing. Because he knows where good and evil have their home. The anglo thinks in his rare way that the Mexican is superstitious. But who is the one? We know there are qualities to a thing. This car is green. Or it has a certain motor inside. But it cannot be tainted, you see. Or a man. Even a man. There can be in a man some evil. But we dont think it is his own evil. Where did he get it? How did he come to claim it? No. Evil is a true thing in Mexico. It goes about on its own legs. Maybe some day it will come to visit you. Maybe it already has.

Maybe.

Pérez smiled. You are free to go, he said. I can see you dont believe what I tell you. It is the same with money. Americans have this problem always I believe. They talk about tainted money. But money doesnt have this special quality. And the Mexican would never think to make things special or to put them in a special place where money is no use. Why do this? If money is good money is good. He doesnt have bad money. He doesnt have this problem. This abnormal thought.

John Grady leaned and stubbed out the cigarette in the tin ashtray on the table. Cigarettes in that world were money themselves and the one he left broken and smoldering in front of his host had hardly been smoked at all. I'll tell you what, he said.

Tell me.

I'll see you around.

He rose and looked at Pérez's man standing against the door. Pérez's man looked at Pérez.

I thought you wanted to know what would happen out there? said Pérez.

John Grady turned. Would that change it? he said.

Pérez smiled. You do me too much credit. There are three hundred men in this institution. No one can know what is possible.

Somebody runs the show.

Pérez shrugged. Perhaps, he said. But this type of world, you see, this confinement. It gives a false impression. As if things are in control. If these men could be controlled they would not be here. You see the problem.

Yes.

You can go. I will be interested myself to see what becomes to you.

He made a small gesture with his hand. His man stepped from before the door and held it open.

Joven, said Pérez.

John Grady turned. Yes, he said.

Take care with whom you break bread.

All right. I will.

Then he turned and walked out into the yard.

He still had forty-five pesos left from the money Blevins had given him and he tried to buy a knife with it but no one would sell him one. He couldnt be sure if there were none for sale or only none for sale to him. He moved across the courtyard at a studied saunter. He found the Bautistas under the shade of the south wall and he stood until they looked up and gestured to him to come forward.

He squatted in front of them.

Quiero comprar una trucha, he said.

They nodded. The one named Faustino spoke.

Cúanto dinero tienes?

Cuarenta y cinco pesos.

They sat for a long time. The dark indian face ruminating. Reflective. As if the complexities of this piece of business dragged after it every sort of consequence. Faustino shaped his mouth to speak. Bueno, he said. Dámelo.

John Grady looked at them. The lights in their black eyes. If there was guile there it was of no sort he could reckon with and he sat in the dirt and pulled off his left boot and reached down into it and took out the small damp sheaf of bills. They watched him. He pulled the boot back on and sat for a moment with the money palmed between his index and middle finger and then with a deft cardflip shot the folded bills under Faustino's knee. Faustino didnt move.

Bueno, he said. La tendré esta tarde.

He nodded and rose and walked back across the yard.

The smell of diesel smoke drifted across the compound and he could hear the buses in the street outside the gate and he realized that it was Sunday. He sat alone with his back to the wall. He heard a child crying. He saw the indian from Sierra León coming across the yard and he spoke to him.

The indian came over.

Siéntate, he said.

The indian sat. He took from inside his shirt a small paper bag limp with sweat and passed it to him. Inside was a handful of punche and a sheaf of cornhusk papers.

Gracias, he said.

He took a paper and folded it and dabbed the rough stringy tobacco in and rolled it shut and licked it. He handed the tobacco back and the indian rolled a cigarette and put the bag back inside his shirt and produced an esclarajo made from a half-inch waterpipe coupling and struck a light and cupped it in his hands and blew up the fire and held it for John Grady and then lit his own cigarette.

John Grady thanked him. No tienes visitantes? he said.

The indian shook his head. He didnt ask John Grady if he had visitors. John Grady thought he might have something to tell him. Some news that had moved through the prison but bypassed him in his exile. But the indian seemed to have no news at all and they sat leaning against the wall smoking until the cigarettes had burned away to nothing and the indian let the ashes fall between his feet and then rose and moved on across the yard.

He didnt go to eat at noon. He sat and watched the yard and tried to read the air. He thought men crossing were looking at him. Then he thought they were at pains not to. He said half aloud to himself that all this thinking could get a man killed. Then he said that talking to yourself could also get you killed. A little later he jerked awake and put one hand up. He was horrified to have fallen asleep there.

He looked at the width of the shadow of the wall before him. When the yard was half in the shade it would be four oclock. After a while he got up and walked down to where the Bautistas were sitting.

Faustino looked up at him. He gestured for him to come forward. He told him to step slightly to the left. Then he told him he was standing on it.

He almost looked down but he didnt. Faustino nodded. Siéntate, he said.

He sat.

Hay un cordón. He looked down. A small piece of string lay under his boot. When he pulled it up under his hand a knife emerged out of the gravel and he palmed it and slid it inside the waistband of his trousers. Then he got up and walked away.

It was better than what he'd expected. A switchblade with the handles missing, made in Mexico, the brass showing through the plating on the bolsters. He untied the piece of twine from around it and wiped it on his shirt and blew down into the blade channel and tapped it against the heel of his boot and blew again. He pushed the button and it clicked open. He wet a patch of hair on the back of his wrist and tried the edge. He was standing on one foot with his leg crossed over his knee honing the blade against the sole of his boot when he heard someone coming and he folded the knife and slid it into his pocket and turned and went out, passing two men who smirked at him on their way to the vile latrine.

A half hour later the horn sounded across the yard for the evening meal. He waited until the last man had entered the hall and then walked in and got his tray and moved down the line. Because it was Sunday and many of the prisoners had eaten food brought by their wives or family the hall was half empty and he turned and stood with his tray, the beans and tortillas and the anonymous stew, and picked a table in the corner where a boy not much older than he sat alone smoking and drinking water from a cup.

He stood at the end of the table and set his tray down. Con permiso, he said.

The boy looked at him and blew two thin streams of smoke from his nose and nodded and reached for his cup. On the inside of his right forearm was a blue jaguar struggling in the coils of an anaconda. In the web of his left thumb the pachuco cross and the five marks. Nothing out of the ordinary. But as he sat he suddenly knew why this man was eating alone. It was too late to rise again. He picked up the spoon with his left hand and began to eat. He heard the latch click shut on the door across the hall even above the muted scrape and click of spoons on the metal trays. He looked toward the front of the hall. There was no one behind the serving line. The two guards were gone. He continued to eat. His heart was pounding and his mouth was dry and the food was ashes. He took the knife from his pocket and put it in the waist of his trousers.

The boy stubbed out the cigarette and set his cup in the tray. Outside somewhere in the streets beyond the prison walls a dog barked. A tamalera cried out her wares. John Grady realized he could not have heard these things unless every sound in the hall had ceased. He opened the knife quietly against his leg and slid it open longwise under the buckle of his belt. The boy stood and stepped over the bench and took up his tray and turned and started down along the far side of the table. John Grady held the spoon in his left hand and gripped the tray. The boy came opposite him. He passed. John Grady watched him with a lowered gaze. When the boy reached the end of the table he suddenly turned and sliced the tray at his head. John Grady saw it all unfold slowly before him. The tray coming edgewise toward his eyes. The tin cup slightly tilted with the spoon in it slightly upended standing almost motionless in the air and the boy's greasy black hair flung across his wedgeshaped face. He flung his tray up and the corner of the boy's tray printed a deep dent in the bottom of it. He rolled away backward over the bench and scrabbled to his feet. He thought the tray would clatter to the table but the boy had not let go of it and he chopped at him with it again, coming along the edge of the bench. He fell back fending him away and the trays clanged and he saw the knife for the first time pass under the trays like a cold steel newt seeking out the warmth within him. He leaped away sliding in the spilled food on the concrete floor. He pulled the knife from his belt and swung the tray backhanded and caught the cuchillero in the forehead with it. The cuchillero seemed surprised. He was trying to block John Grady's view with his tray. John Grady stepped back. He was against the wall. He stepped to the side and gripped his tray and hacked at the cuchillero's tray, trying to hit his fingers. The cuchillero moved between him and the table. He kicked back the bench behind him. The trays rattled and clanged in the otherwise silence of the hall and the cuchillero's forehead had begun to bleed and the blood was running down alongside his left eye. He feinted with the tray again. John Grady could smell him. He feinted and his knife passed across the front of John Grady's shirt. John Grady dropped the tray to his midsection and moved along the wall looking into those black eyes. The cuchillero spoke no word. His movements were precise and without rancor. John Grady knew that he was hired. He swung the tray at his head and the cuchillero ducked and feinted and came forward. John Grady gripped the tray and moved along the wall. He ran his tongue into the corner of his mouth and tasted blood. He knew his face had been cut but he didnt know how bad. He knew the cuchillero had been hired because he was a man of reputation and it occurred to him that he was going to die in this place. He looked deep into those dark eyes and there were deeps there to look into. A whole malign history burning cold and remote and black. He moved along the wall, slicing back at the cuchillero with the tray. He was cut again across the outside of his upper arm. He was cut across his lower chest. He turned and slashed twice at the cuchillero with his knife. The man sucked himself up away from the blade with the boneless grace of a dervish. The men sitting at the table they were approaching had begun to rise one by one silently from the benches like birds leaving a wire. John Grady turned again and hacked at the cuchillero with his tray and the cuchillero squatted and he saw him there thin and bowlegged under his outflung arm for one frozen moment like some dark and reedy homunculous bent upon inhabiting him. The knife passed across his chest and passed back and the figure moved with incredible speed and again stood before him crouching silently, faintly weaving, watching his eyes. They were watching so that they could see if death were coming. Eyes that had seen it before and knew the colors it traveled under and what it looked like when it got there.

The tray clattered on the tiles. He realized he'd dropped it. He put his hand to his shirt. It came away sticky with blood and he wiped it on the side of his trousers. The cuchillero held the tray to his eyes to blind from him his movements. He looked to be adjuring him to read something writ there but there was nothing to see save the dents and dings occasioned by the ten thousand meals eaten off it. John Grady backed away. He sat slowly on the floor. His legs were bent crookedly under him and he slumped against the wall with his arms at either side of him. The cuchillero lowered the tray. He set it quietly on the table. He leaned and took hold of John Grady by the hair and forced his head back to cut his throat. As he did so John Grady brought his knife up from the floor and sank it into the cuchillero's heart. He sank it into his heart and snapped the handle sideways and broke the blade off in him.

The cuchillero's knife clattered on the floor. From the red boutonniere blossoming on the left pocket of his blue workshirt there spurted a thin fan of bright arterial blood. He dropped to his knees and pitched forward dead into the arms of his enemy. Some of the men in the hall had already stood to leave. Like theatre patrons anxious to avoid the crush. John Grady dropped the knifehandle and pushed at the oiled head lolling against his chest. He rolled to one side and scrabbled about until he found the cuchillero's knife. He pushed the dead man away and got hold of the table and struggled up. His clothes sagged with the weight of the blood. He backed away down the tables and turned and staggered to the door and unlatched it and walked wobbling out into the deep blue twilight.

The light from the hall lay in a paling corridor across the yard. Where the men came to the door to watch him it shifted and darkened in the dusk. No one followed him out. He walked with great care, holding his hand to his abdomen. The floodlights along the upper walls would come on at any moment. He walked very carefully. Blood sloshed in his boots. He looked at the knife in his hand and flung it away. The first horn would sound and the lights would come up along the walls. He felt lightheaded and curiously without pain. His hands were sticky with blood and blood was oozing through his fingers where he held himself. The lights would be coming on and the horn would be sounding.

He was halfway to the first steel ladder when a tall man overtook him and spoke to him. He turned, crouching. In the dying light perhaps they would not see he had no knife. Not see how he stood so bloody in his clothes.

Ven conmigo, said the man. Está bien.

No me moleste.

The dark tiers of the prison walls ran forever down the deep cyanic sky. A dog had begun to bark.

El padrote quiere ayudarle.

Mande?

The man stood before him. Ven conmigo, he said.

It was Pérez's man. He held out his hand. John Grady stepped back. His boots left wet tracks of blood in the dry floor of the yard. The lights would come on. Horn would sound. He turned to go, his knees stammering under him. He fell and got up again. The mayordomo reached to help him and he twisted out of his grip and fell again. The world swam. Kneeling he pushed against the ground to rise. Blood dripped between his outstretched hands. The dark bank of the wall rode up. The deep cyanic sky. He was lying on his side. Pérez's man bent over him. He stooped and gathered him up in his arms and lifted him and carried him across the yard into Pérez's house and kicked the door shut behind him as the lights came on and the horn sounded.

HE WOKE in a stone room in total darkness and a smell of disinfectant. He put his hand out to see what it would touch and felt pain all over him like something that had been crouching there in the silence waiting for him to stir. He put his hand down. He turned his head. A thin rod lay luminescing in the blackness. He listened but there was no sound. Every breath he took was like a razor. After a while he put his hand out and touched the cold block wall.

Hola, he said. His voice was weak and reedy, his face stiff and twisted. He tried again. Hola. There was someone there. He could feel them.

Quién está? he said, but no one spoke back.

There was someone there and they had been there. There was no one there. There was someone there and they had been there and they had not left but there was no one there.

He looked at the floating rod of light. It was light from under a door. He listened. He held his breath and listened because the room was small it seemed to be small and if the room was small he could hear them breathing in the dark if they were breathing but he heard nothing. He half wondered if he were not dead and in his despair he felt well up in him a surge of sorrow like a child beginning to cry but it brought with it such pain that he stopped it cold and began at once his new life and the living of it breath to breath.

He knew he was going to get up and try the door and he took a long time getting ready. First he moved onto his stomach. He pushed himself over all at once to get it done with and he was just amazed at the pain. He lay breathing. He reached down to put his hand on the floor. It swung in empty space. He eased his leg over the edge and pushed himself up and his foot touched the floor and he lay resting on his elbows.

When he reached the door it was locked. He stood, the floor cool under his feet. He was trussed in some sort of wrapping and he'd begun to bleed again. He could feel it. He stood resting with his face against the cool of the metal door. He felt the bandage on his face against the door and he touched it and he was thirsty out of all reason and he rested for a long time before starting back across the floor.

When the door did open it was to blinding light and there stood in it no ministress in white but a demandadero in stained and wrinkled khakis bearing a metal messtray with a double spoonful of pozole spilled over it and a glass of orange sodawater. He was not much older than John Grady and he backed into the room with the tray and turned, his eyes looking everywhere but at the bed. Other than a steel bucket in the floor there was nothing in the room but the bed and nowhere to put the tray but on it.

He approached and stood. He looked at once uncomfortable and menacing. He gestured with the tray. John Grady eased himself onto his side and pushed himself up. Sweat stood on his forehead. He was wearing some sort of rough cotton gown and he'd bled through it and the blood had dried.

Dame el refresco, he said. Nada más.

Nada más?

No.

The demandadero handed him the glass of orangewater and he took it and sat holding it. He looked at the little stone block room. Overhead was a single lightbulb in a wire cage.

La luz, por favor, he said.

The demandadero nodded and went to the door and turned and pulled it shut after him. A click of the latch in the darkness. Then the light came on.

He listened to the steps down the corridor. Then the silence. He raised the glass and slowly drank the soda. It was tepid, only faintly effervescent, delicious.

He lay there three days. He slept and woke and slept again. Someone turned off the light and he woke in the dark. He called out but no one answered. He thought of his father in Goshee. He knew that terrible things had been done to him there and he had always believed that he did not want to know about it but he did want to know. He lay in the dark thinking of all the things he did not know about his father and he realized that the father he knew was all the father he would ever know. He would not think about Alejandra because he didnt know what was coming or how bad it would be and he thought she was something he'd better save. So he thought about horses and they were always the right thing to think about. Later someone turned the light back on again and it did not go off again after

that. He slept and when he woke he'd dreamt of the dead
standing about in their bones and the dark sockets of their eyes
that were indeed without speculation bottomed in the void
wherein lay a terrible intelligence common to all but of which
none would speak. When he woke he knew that men had died
in that room.

When the door opened next it was to admit a man in a blue
suit carrying a leather bag. The man smiled at him and asked
after his health.

Mejor que nunca, he said.

The man smiled again. He set the bag on the bed and opened
it and took out a pair of surgical scissors and pushed the bag to
the foot of the bed and pulled back the bloodstained sheet.

Quién és usted? said John Grady.

The man looked surprised. I am the doctor, he said.

The scissors had a spade end that was cold against his skin
and the doctor slid them under the bloodstained gauze cum-
merbund and began to cut it away. He pulled the dressing from
under him and they looked down at the stitches.

Bien, bien, said the doctor. He pushed at the sutures with
two fingers. Bueno, he said.

He cleaned the sutured wounds with an antiseptic and taped
gauze pads over them and helped him to sit up. He took a large
roll of gauze out of the bag and reached around John Grady's
waist and began to wrap it.

Put you hands on my shoulders, he said.

What?

Put you hands on my shoulders. It is all right.

He put his hands on the doctor's shoulders and the doctor
wrapped the dressing. Bueno, he said. Bueno.

He rose and closed the bag and stood looking down at his
patient.

I will send for you soap and towels, he said. So you can wash
yourself.

All right.

You are a fasthealer.

A what?

A fasthealer. He nodded and smiled and turned and went out. John Grady didnt hear him latch the door but there was no place to go anyway.

His next visitor was a man he'd never seen before. He wore a uniform that looked to be military. He did not introduce himself. The guard who brought him shut the door and stood outside it. The man stood at his bed and took off his hat as though in deference to some wounded hero. Then he took a comb from the breastpocket of his tunic and passed it once along each side of his oiled head and put the hat back on again.

How soon you can walk around, he said.

Where do you want me to walk to?

To your house.

I can walk right now.

The man pursed his lips, studying him.

Show me you walk.

He pushed back the sheets and rolled onto his side and stepped down to the floor. He walked up and back. His feet left cold wet tracks on the polished stones that sucked up and vanished like the tale of the world itself. The sweat stood quivering on his forehead.

You are fortunate boys, he said.

I dont feel so fortunate.

Fortunate boys, he said again, and nodded and left.

He slept and woke. He knew night from day only by the meals. He ate little. Finally they brought him half a roast chicken with rice and two halves of a tinned pear and this he ate slowly, savoring each bite and proposing and rejecting various scenarios that might have occurred in the outer world or be occurring. Or were yet to come. He still thought that he might be taken out into the campo and shot.

He practiced walking up and down. He polished the underside of the messtray with the sleeve of his shift and standing in the center of the room under the lightbulb he studied the face that peered dimly out of the warped steel like some maimed and raging djinn enconjured there. He peeled away the bandage from his face and inspected the stitches there and felt them with his fingers.

When next he woke the demandadero had opened the door and stood with a pile of clothes and with his boots. He let them fall in the floor. Sus prendas, he said, and shut the door.

He stripped out of the shift and washed himself with soap and rag and dried himself with the towel and dressed and pulled on the boots. Someone had washed the blood out of the boots and they were still wet and he tried to take them off again but he could not and he lay on the bunk in his clothes and boots waiting for God knew what.

Two guards came. They stood at the open door and waited for him. He got up and walked out.

They went down a corridor and across a small patio and entered another part of the building. They walked down another corridor and the guards tapped at a door and then opened it and one of them motioned for him to enter.

At a desk sat the commandante who'd been to his cell to see if he could walk.

You be seated, said the commandante.

He sat.

The commandante opened his desk drawer and took out an envelope and handed it across the desk.

This is you, he said.

John Grady took the envelope.

Where's Rawlins? he said.

Excuse me?

Dónde está mi compadre.

You friend.

Yes.

He wait outside.

Where are we going?

You going away. You going away to you house.

When.

Excuse me?

Cuándo.

You going now. I dont want to see you no more.

The commandante waved his hand. John Grady put one hand on the back of the chair and rose and turned and walked out the door and he and the guards went down the hallway and out through the office to the sallygate where Rawlins stood waiting in a costume much like his own. Five minutes later they were standing in the street outside the tall ironshod wooden doors of the portal.

There was a bus standing in the street and they climbed laboriously aboard. Women in the seats with their empty hampers and baskets spoke to them softly as they made their way down the aisle.

I thought you'd died, said Rawlins.

I thought you had.

What happened?

I'll tell you. Let's just sit here. Let's not talk. Let's just sit here real quiet.

Are you all right?

Yeah. I'm all right.

Rawlins turned and looked out the window. All was gray and still. A few drops of rain had begun to fall in the street. They dropped on the roof of the bus solitary as a bell. Down the street he could see the arched buttresses of the cathedral dome and the minaret of the belltower beyond.

All my life I had the feelin that trouble was close at hand. Not that I was about to get into it. Just that it was always there.

Let's just sit here real quiet, said John Grady.

They sat watching the rain in the street. The women sat quietly. Outside it was darkening and there was no sun nor any paler place to the sky where sun might be. Two more women climbed aboard and took their seats and then the driver swung up and closed the door and looked to the rear in the mirror and put the bus in gear and they pulled away. Some of the women wiped at the glass with their hands and peered back at the prison standing in the gray rain of Mexico. So like some site of siege in an older time, in an older country, where the enemies were all from without.

It was only a few blocks to the centro and when they eased themselves down from the bus the gaslamps were already on in the plaza. They crossed slowly to the portales on the north side of the square and stood looking out at the rain. Four men in maroon band uniforms stood along the wall with their instruments. John Grady looked at Rawlins. Rawlins looked lost standing there hatless and afoot in his shrunken clothes.

Let's get somethin to eat.

We dont have no money.

I got money.

Where'd you get any money at? Rawlins said.

I got a whole envelope full.

They walked into a cafe and sat in a booth. A waiter came over and put menus in front of them and went away. Rawlins looked out the window.

Get a steak, said John Grady.

All right.

We'll eat and get a hotel room and get cleaned up and get some sleep.

All right.

He ordered steaks and fried potatoes and coffee for both of them and the waiter nodded and took the menus. John Grady rose and made his way slowly to the counter and bought two packs of cigarettes and a penny box of matches each. People at their tables watched him cross the room.

Rawlins lit a cigarette and looked at him.

Why aint we dead? he said.

She paid us out.

The señora?

The aunt. Yes.

Why?

I dont know.

Is that where you got the money?

Yes.

It's got to do with the girl, dont it?

I expect it does.

Rawlins smoked. He looked out the window. Outside it was already dark. The streets were wet from the rain and the lights from the cafe and from the lamps in the plaza lay bleeding in the black pools of water.

There aint no other explanation, is there?

No.

Rawlins nodded. I could of run off from where they had me. It was just a hospital ward.

Why didnt you?

I dont know. You think I was dumb not to of?

I dont know. Yeah. Maybe.

What would you of done?

I wouldnt of left you.

Yeah. I know you wouldnt.

That dont mean it aint dumb.

Rawlins almost smiled. Then he looked away.

The waiter brought the coffee.

There was another old boy in there, said Rawlins. All cut up. Probably wasnt a bad boy. Set out on Saturday night with a few dollars in his pocket. Pesos. Goddamned pathetic.

What happened to him?

He died. When they carried him out of there I thought how peculiar it would of seemed to him if he could of seen it. It did to me and it wasnt even me. Dying aint in people's plans, is it?

No.

He nodded. They put Mexican blood in me, he said.

He looked up. John Grady was lighting a cigarette. He shook out the match and put it in the ashtray and looked at Rawlins.

So.

So what does that mean? said Rawlins.

Mean about what?

Well does it mean I'm part Mexican?

John Grady drew on the cigarette and leaned back and blew the smoke into the air. Part Mexican? he said.

Yeah.

How much did they put?

They said it was over a litre.

How much over a litre?

I dont know.

Well a litre would make you almost a halfbreed.

Rawlins looked at him. It dont, does it? he said.

No. Hell, it dont mean nothin. Blood's blood. It dont know where it come from.

The waiter brought the steaks. They ate. He watched Rawlins. Rawlins looked up.

What? he said.

Nothin.

You ought to be happier about bein out of that place.

I was thinkin the same thing about you.

Rawlins nodded. Yeah, he said.

What do you want to do?

Go home.

All right.

They ate.

You're goin back down there, aint you? said Rawlins.

Yeah. I guess I am.

On account of the girl?

Yeah.

What about the horses?

The girl and the horses.

Rawlins nodded. You think she's lookin for you to come back?

I dont know.

I'd say the old lady might be surprised to see you.

No she wont. She's a smart woman.

What about Rocha?

He'll have to do whatever he has to do.

Rawlins crossed his silver in the platter beside the bones and took out his cigarettes.

Dont go down there, he said.

I done made up my mind.

Rawlins lit the cigarette and shook out the match. He looked up.

There's only one kind of deal I can see that she could of made with the old woman.

I know. But she's goin to have to tell me herself.

If she does will you come back?

I'll come back.

All right.

I still want the horses.

Rawlins shook his head and looked away.

I aint askin you to go with me, said John Grady.

I know you aint.

You'll be all right.

Yeah. I know.

He tapped the ash from his cigarette and pushed at his eyes with the heel of his hand and looked out the window. Outside it was raining again. There was no traffic in the streets.

Kid over yonder tryin to sell newspapers, he said. Aint a soul in sight and him standin there with his papers up under his shirt just a hollerin.

He wiped his eyes with the back of his hand.

Ah shit, he said.

What?

Nothin. Just shit.

What is it?

I keep thinkin about old Blevins.

John Grady didnt answer. Rawlins turned and looked at him. His eyes were wet and he looked old and sad.

I caint believe they just walked him out there and done him that way.

Yeah.

I keep thinkin about how scared he was.

You'll feel better when you get home.

Rawlins shook his head and looked out the window again. I dont think so, he said.

John Grady smoked. He watched him. After a while he said: I aint Blevins.

Yeah, said Rawlins. I know you aint. But I wonder how much better off you are than him.

John Grady stubbed out his cigarette. Let's go, he said.

They bought toothbrushes and a bar of soap and a safety-razor at a farmacia and they found a room in a hotel two blocks down Aldama. The key was just a common doorkey tied to a wooden fob with the number of the room burned into the wood with a hot wire. They walked out across the tiled courtyard where the rain was falling lightly and found the room and opened the door and turned on the light. A man sat up in the bed and looked at them. They backed out and turned off the light and shut the door and went back to the desk where the man gave them another key.

The room was bright green and there was a shower in one corner with an oilcloth curtain on a ring. John Grady turned on the shower and after a while there was hot water in the pipes. He turned it off again.

Go ahead, he said.

You go ahead.

I got to come out of this tape.

He sat on the bed and peeled away the dressings while Rawlins showered. Rawlins turned off the water and pushed back the curtain and stood drying himself with one of the threadbare towels.

We're a couple of good'ns, aint we? he said.

Yeah.

How you goin to get them stitches out?

I guess I'll have to find a doctor.

It hurts worse takin em out than puttin em in.

Yeah.

Did you know that?

Yeah. I knew that.

Rawlins wrapped the towel around himself and sat on the bed opposite. The envelope with the money was lying on the table.

How much is in there?

John Grady looked up. I dont know, he said. Considerable less than what there was supposed to be, I'll bet. Go ahead and count it.

He took the envelope and counted the bills out on the bed.

Nine hundred and seventy pesos, he said.

John Grady nodded.

How much is that?

About a hundred and twenty dollars.

Rawlins tapped the sheaf of bills together on the glass of the tabletop and put them back in the envelope.

Split it in two piles, said John Grady.

I dont need no money.

Yes you do.

I'm goin home.

Dont make no difference. Half of it's yours.

Rawlins stood and hung the towel over the iron bedstead and pulled back the covers. I think you're goin to need ever dime of it, he said.

When he came out of the shower he thought Rawlins was asleep but he wasnt. He crossed the room and turned off the light and came back and eased himself into the bed. He lay in the dark listening to the sounds in the street, the dripping of rain in the courtyard.

You ever pray? said Rawlins.

Yeah. Sometimes. I guess I got kindly out of the habit.

Rawlins was quiet for a long time. Then he said: What's the worst thing you ever done?

I dont know. I guess if I done anything real bad I'd rather not tell it. Why?

I dont know. I was in the hospital cut I got to thinkin: I wouldnt be here if I wasnt supposed to be here. You ever think like that?

Yeah. Sometimes.

They lay in the dark listening. Someone crossed the patio. A door opened and closed again.

You aint never done nothin bad, said John Grady.

Me and Lamont one time drove a pickup truckload of feed to Sterling City and sold it to some Mexicans and kept the money.

That aint the worst thing I ever heard of.

I done some other stuff too.

If you're goin to talk I'm goin to smoke a cigarette.

I'll shut up.

They lay quietly in the dark.

You know about what happened, dont you? said John Grady.

You mean in the messhall?

Yeah.

Yeah.

John Grady reached and got his cigarettes off the table and lit one and blew out the match.

I never thought I'd do that.

You didnt have no choice.

I still never thought it.

He'd of done it to you.

He drew on the cigarette and blew the smoke unseen into the darkness. You dont need to try and make it right. It is what it is.

Rawlins didnt answer. After a while he said: Where'd you get the knife?

Off the Bautistas. I bought it with the last forty-five pesos we had.

Blevins' money.

Yeah. Blevins' money.

Rawlins was lying on his side in the springshot iron bedstead watching him in the dark. The cigarette glowed a deep red where John Grady drew on it and his face with the sutures in his cheek emerged from the darkness like some dull red theatric mask indifferently repaired and faded back again.

I knew when I bought the knife what I'd bought it for.

I dont see where you were wrong.

The cigarette glowed, it faded. I know, he said. But you didnt do it.

In the morning it was raining again and they stood outside the same cafe with toothpicks in their teeth and looked at the rain in the plaza. Rawlins studied his nose in the glass.

You know what I hate?

What?

Showin up at the house lookin like this.

John Grady looked at him and looked away. I dont blame you, he said.

You dont look so hot yourself.

John Grady grinned. Come on, he said.

They bought new clothes and hats in a Victoria Street haberdashery and wore them out into the street and in the slow falling rain walked down to the bus station and bought Rawlins a ticket for Nuevo Laredo. They sat in the bus station cafe in the stiff new clothes with the new hats turned upside down on the chairs at either side and they drank coffee until the bus was announced over the speaker.

That's you, said John Grady.

They rose and put on their hats and walked out to the gates.

Well, said Rawlins. I reckon I'll see you one of these days.

You take care.

Yeah. You take care.

He turned and handed his ticket to the driver and the driver punched it and handed it back and he climbed stiffly aboard. John Grady stood watching while he passed along the aisle. He thought he'd take a seat at the window but he didnt. He sat on the other side of the bus and John Grady stood for a while and then turned and walked back out through the station to the street and walked slowly back through the rain to the hotel.

He exhausted in the days following the roster of surgeons in that small upland desert metropolis without finding one to do what he asked. He spent his days walking up and down in the narrow streets until he knew every corner and callejón. At the end of a week he had the stitches removed from his face, sitting in a common metal chair, the surgeon humming to himself as he snipped with his scissors and pulled with his clamp. The surgeon said that the scar would improve in its appearance. He said for him not to look at it because it would get better with time. Then he put a bandage over it and charged him fifty pesos and told him to come back in five days and he would remove the stitches from his belly.

A week later he left Saltillo on the back of a flatbed truck heading north. The day was cool and overcast. There was a large diesel engine chained to the bed of the truck. He sat in the truckbed as they jostled out through the streets, trying to brace himself, his hands at either side on the rough boards. After a while he pulled his hat down hard over his eyes and stood and placed his hands outstretched on the roof of the cab and rode in that manner. As if he were some personage bearing news for the countryside. As if he were some newfound evangelical being conveyed down out of the mountains and north across the flat bleak landscape toward Monclova.

IV

AT A CROSSROADS STATION somewhere on the other side of Paredón they picked up five farmworkers who climbed up on the bed of the truck and nodded and spoke to him with great circumspection and courtesy. It was almost dark and it was raining lightly and they were wet and their faces were wet in the yellow light from the station. They huddled forward of the chained engine and he offered them his cigarettes and they thanked him each and took one and they cupped their hands over the small flame against the falling rain and thanked him again.

De dónde viene? they said.

De Tejas.

Tejas, they said. Y dónde va?

He drew on his cigarette. He looked at their faces. One of them older than the rest nodded at his cheap new clothes.

Él va a ver a su novia, he said.

They looked at him earnestly and he nodded and said that it was true.

Ah, they said. Qué bueno. And after and for a long time to come he'd have reason to evoke the recollection of those smiles and to reflect upon the good will which provoked them for it had power to protect and to confer honor and to strengthen resolve and it had power to heal men and to bring them to safety long after all other resources were exhausted.

When the truck finally pulled out and they saw him still standing they offered their bundles for him to sit on and he did so and he nodded and dozed to the hum of the tires on the blacktop and the rain stopped and the night cleared and the moon that was already risen raced among the high wires by the highway side like a single silver music note burning in the constant and lavish dark and the passing fields were rich from the rain with the smell of earth and grain and peppers and the sometime smell of horses. It was midnight when they reached Monclova and he shook hands with each of the workers and walked around the truck and thanked the driver and nodded to the other two men in the cab and then watched the small red taillight recede down the street and out toward the highway leaving him alone in the darkened town.

The night was warm and he slept on a bench in the alameda and woke with the sun already up and the day's commerce begun. Schoolchildren in blue uniforms were passing along the walkway. He rose and crossed the street. Women were washing the sidewalks in front of the shops and vendors were setting up their wares on small stands or tables and surveying the day.

He ate a breakfast of coffee and pan dulce at a cafe counter in a sidestreet off the square and he entered a farmacia and bought a bar of soap and put it in the pocket of his jacket along with his razor and toothbrush and then set out along the road west.

He got a ride to Frontera and another to San Buenaventura. At noon he bathed in an irrigation ditch and he shaved and washed and slept lying on his jacket in the sun while his clothes dried. Downstream was a small wooden cofferdam and when he woke there were naked children splashing in the pool there and he rose and wrapped his jacket about his waist and walked out along the bank where he could sit and watch them. Two girls passed down the bankside path bearing between them a cloth-covered tub and carrying covered pails in their free hand. They were taking dinner to workers in the field and they smiled shyly at him sitting there half naked and so pale of skin with the angry red suture marks laddered across his chest and stomach. Quietly smoking. Watching the children bathe in the silty ditchwater.

He walked all afternoon out the dry hot road toward Cuatro Ciénagas. No one he met passed without speaking. He walked

along past fields where men and women were hoeing the earth
and those at work by the roadside would stop and nod to him
and say how good the day was and he agreed with all they said.
In the evening he took his supper with workers in their camp,
five or six families seated together at a table made of cut poles
bound with hemp twine. The table was pitched under a canvas
fly and the evening sun resolved within the space beneath a deep
orange light where the seams and stitching passed in shadow
over their faces and their clothes as they moved. The girls set
out the dishes on little pallets made from the ends of crates that
nothing overbalance on the uncertain surface of the table and an
old man at the farthest end of the table prayed for them all. He
asked that God remember those who had died and he asked that
the living gathered together here remember that the corn grows
by the will of God and beyond that will there is neither corn nor
growing nor light nor air nor rain nor anything at all save only
darkness. Then they ate.

They'd have made a bed for him but he thanked them and
walked out in the dark along the road until he came to a grove
of trees and there he slept. In the morning there were sheep in
the road. Two trucks carrying fieldhands were coming along
behind the sheep and he walked out to the road and asked the
driver for a ride. The driver nodded him aboard and he dropped
back along the bed of the moving truck and tried to pull himself
up. He could not and when the workers saw his condition they
rose instantly and pulled him aboard. By a series of such rides
and much walking he made his way west through the low mountains beyond Nadadores and down into the barrial and took the
clay road out of La Madrid and in the late afternoon entered
once more the town of La Vega.

He bought a Coca-Cola in the store and stood leaning against
the counter while he drank it. Then he drank another. The girl
at the counter watched him uncertainly. He was studying a
calendar on the wall. He did not know the date within a week
and when he asked her she didnt know either. He set the second
bottle on the counter alongside the first one and walked back out

into the mud street and set off afoot up the road toward La Purísima.

He'd been gone seven weeks and the countryside was changed, the summer past. He saw almost no one on the road and he reached the hacienda just after dark.

When he knocked at the gerente's door he could see the family at dinner through the doorway. The woman came to the door and when she saw him she went back to get Armando. He came to the door and stood picking his teeth. No one invited him in. When Antonio came out they sat under the ramada and smoked.

Quién está en la casa? said John Grady.

La dama.

Y el señor Rocha?

En Mexico.

John Grady nodded.

Se fue él y la hija a Mexico. Por avión. He made an airplane motion with one hand.

Cuándo regresa?

Quién sabe?

They smoked.

Tus cosas quedan aquí.

Sí?

Sí. Tu pistola. Todas tus cosas. Y las de tu compadre.

Gracias.

De nada.

They sat. Antonio looked at him.

Yo no sé nada, joven.

Entiendo.

En serio.

Está bien. Puedo dormir en la cuadra?

Sí. Si no me lo digas.

Cómo están las yeguas?

Antonio smiled. Las yeguas, he said.

He brought him his things. The pistol had been unloaded and the shells were in the mochila along with his shaving things,

his father's old Marble huntingknife. He thanked Antonio and
walked down to the barn in the dark. The mattress on his bed
had been rolled up and there was no pillow and no bedding. He
unrolled the tick and sat and kicked off his boots and stretched
out. Some of the horses that were in the stalls had come up
when he entered the barn and he could hear them snuffling and
stirring and he loved to hear them and he loved to smell them
and then he was asleep.

At daylight the old groom pushed open the door and stood
looking in at him. Then he shut the door again. When he had
gone John Grady got up and took his soap and his razor and
walked out to the tap at the end of the barn.

When he walked up to the house there were cats coming from
the stable and orchard and cats coming along the high wall or
waiting their turn to pass under the worn wood of the gate.
Carlos had slaughtered a sheep and along the dappled floor of
the portal more cats sat basking in the earliest light falling
through the hydrangeas. Carlos in his apron looked out from
the doorway of the keep at the end of the portal. John Grady
wished him a good morning and he nodded gravely and withdrew.

María did not seem surprised to see him. She gave him his
breakfast and he watched her and he listened as she spoke by
rote. The señorita would not be up for another hour. A car was
coming for her at ten. She would be gone all day visiting at the
quinta Margarita. She would return before dark. She did not
like to travel the roads at night. Perhaps she could see him
before he left.

John Grady sat drinking his coffee. He asked her for a cigarette and she brought her pack of El Toros from the window
above the sink and put them on the table for him. She neither
asked where he'd been nor how things had been with him but
when he rose to go she put her hand on his shoulder and poured
more coffee into his cup.

Puedes esperar aquí, she said. Se levantará pronto.

He waited. Carlos came in and put his knives in the sink and went out again. At seven oclock she went out with the breakfast tray and when she returned she told him that he was invited to come to the house at ten that evening, that the señorita would see him then. He rose to go.

Quisiera un caballo, he said.

Caballo.

Sí. Por el día, no más.

Momentito, she said.

When she returned she nodded. Tienes tu caballo. Espérate un momento. Siéntate.

He waited while she fixed him a lunch and wrapped it in a paper and tied it with string and handed it to him.

Gracias, he said.

De nada.

She took the cigarettes and the matches from the table and handed them to him. He tried to read in her countenance any disposition of the mistress so recently visited that might reflect upon his case. In all that he saw he hoped to be wrong. She pushed the cigarettes at him. Ándale pues, she said.

There were new mares in some of the stalls and as he passed through the barn he stopped to look them over. In the saddleroom he pulled on the light and got a blanket and the bridle he'd always used and he pulled down what looked to be the best of the half dozen saddles from the rack and looked it over and blew the dust from it and checked the straps and slung it over his shoulder by the horn and walked out and up to the corral.

The stallion when it saw him coming began to trot. He stood at the gate and watched it. It passed with its head canted and its eyes rolling and its nostrils siphoning the morning air and then it recognized him and turned and came to him and he pushed open the gate and the horse whinnied and tossed its head and snorted and pushed its long sleek nose against his chest.

When he went past the bunkhouse Morales was sitting out under the ramada peeling onions. He waved idly with his knife and called out. John Grady called back his thanks to the old man before he realized that the old man had not said that he was glad to see him but that the horse was. He waved again and touched up the horse and they went stamping and skittering as if the horse could find no gait within its repertoire to suit the day until he rode him through the gate and out of view of house and barn and cook and slapped the polished flank trembling under him and they went on at a hard flat gallop up the ciénaga road.

He rode among the horses on the mesa and he walked them up out of the swales and cedar brakes where they'd gone to hide and he trotted the stallion along the grassy rims for the wind to cool him. He rode up buzzards out of a draw where they'd been feeding on a dead colt and he sat the horse and looked down at the poor form stretched in the tainted grass eyeless and naked.

Noon he sat with his boots dangling over the rimrock and ate the cold chicken and bread she'd fixed for him while the staked horse grazed. The country rolled away to the west through broken light and shadow and the distant summer storms a hundred miles downcountry to where the cordilleras rose and sank in the haze in a frail last shimmering restraint alike of the earth and the eye beholding it. He smoked a cigarette and then pushed in the crown of his hat with his fist and put a rock in it and lay back in the grass and put the weighted hat over his face. He thought what sort of dream might bring him luck. He saw her riding with her back so straight and the black hat set level on her head and her hair loose and the way she turned with her shoulders and the way she smiled and her eyes. He thought of Blevins. He thought of his face and his eyes when he pressed his last effects upon him. He'd dreamt of him one night in Saltillo and Blevins came to sit beside him and they talked of what it was like to be dead and Blevins said it was like nothing at all and he believed him. He thought perhaps if he dreamt of him enough he'd go away forever and be dead among his kind and the grass scissored in the wind at his ear and he fell asleep and dreamt of nothing at all.

As he rode down through the parkland in the evening the cattle kept moving out of the trees before him where they'd gone to shade up in the day. He rode through a grove of apple trees gone wild and brambly and he picked an apple as he rode and bit into it and it was hard and green and bitter. He walked the horse through the grass looking for apples on the ground but the cattle had eaten them all. He rode past the ruins of an old cabin. The lintel was gone from the door and he walked the horse inside. The vigas were partly down and hunters or herdsmen had built fires in the floor. An old calfhide was nailed to one wall and there was no glass to the windows for the frames and sash were long since burned for firewood. There was a strange air to the place. As of some site where life had not succeeded. The horse liked nothing about it and he dabbed the reins against its neck and touched it with the heel of his boot and they turned carefully in the room and went out and rode down through the orchard and out past the marshlands toward the road. Doves called in the winey light. He tacked and quartered the horse to keep it from treading constantly in its own shadow for it seemed uneasy doing so.

He washed at the spigot in the corral and put on his other shirt and wiped the dust from his boots and walked up to the bunkhouse. It was already dark. The vaqueros had finished their meal and were sitting out under the ramada smoking.

Buenas noches, he said.

Eres tú, Juan?

Claro.

There was a moment of silence. Then someone said: Estás bienvenido aquí.

Gracias, he said.

He sat and smoked with them and told them all that had happened. They were concerned about Rawlins, more a friend to them than he. They were saddened that he was not coming back but they said that a man leaves much when he leaves his own country. They said that it was no accident of circumstance that a man be born in a certain country and not some other and they said that the weathers and seasons that form a land form also the inner fortunes of men in their generations and are passed on to their children and are not so easily come by otherwise.

They spoke of the cattle and the horses and the young wild mares in their season and of a wedding in La Vega and a death at Víbora. No one spoke of the patrón or of the dueña. No one spoke of the girl. In the end he wished them a good night and walked back down to the barn and lay on the cot but he had no way to tell the time and he rose and walked up to the house and knocked at the kitchen door.

He waited and knocked again. When María opened the door to let him in he knew that Carlos had just left the room. She looked at the clock on the wall over the sink.

Ya comiste? she said.

No.

Siéntate. Hay tiempo.

He sat at the table and she made a plate for him of roast mutton with adobada sauce and put it to warm in the oven and in a few minutes brought it to him with a cup of coffee. She finished washing the dishes at the sink and a little before ten she dried her hands on her apron and went out. When she came back she stood in the door. He rose.

Está en la sala, she said.

Gracias.

He went out down the hall to the parlor. She was standing almost formally and she was dressed with an elegance chilling to him. She came across the room and sat and nodded at the chair opposite.

Sit down please.

He walked slowly across the patterned carpet and sat. Behind her on the wall hung a large tapestry that portrayed a meeting in some vanished landscape between two horsemen on a road. Above the double doors leading into the library the mounted head of a fighting bull with one ear missing.

Héctor said that you would not come here. I assured him he was wrong.

When is he coming back?

He will not be back for some time. In any event he will not see you.

I think I'm owed an explanation.

I think the accounts have been settled quite in your favor. You have been a great disappointment to my nephew and a considerable expense to me.

No offense, mam, but I've been some inconvenienced myself.

The officers were here once before, you know. My nephew sent them away until he was able to have an investigation performed. He was quite confident that the facts were otherwise. Quite confident.

Why didnt he say something to me.

He'd given his word to the commandante. Otherwise you would have been taken away at once. He wished to have his own investigation performed. I think you can understand that the commandante would be reluctant to notify people prior to arresting them.

I should of been let to tell my side of it.

You had already lied to him twice. Why should he not assume you would do so a third time?

I never lied to him.

The affair of the stolen horse was known here even before you arrived. The thieves were known to be Americans. When he questioned you about this you denied everything. Some months later your friend returned to the town of Encantada and committed murder. The victim an officer of the state. No one can dispute these facts.

When is he comin back?

He wont see you.

You think I'm a criminal.

I'm prepared to believe that certain circumstances must have conspired against you. But what is done cannot be undone.

Why did you buy me out of prison?

I think you know why.

Because of Alejandra.

Yes.

And what did she have to give in return?

I think you know that also.

That she wont see me again.

Yes.

He leaned back in the chair and stared past her at the wall. At the tapestry. At a blue ornamental vase on a sideboard of figured walnut.

I can scarcely count on my two hands the number of women in this family who have suffered disastrous love affairs with men of disreputable character. Of course the times enabled some of these men to style themselves revolutionaries. My sister Matilde was widowed twice by the age of twenty-one, both husbands shot. That sort of thing. Bigamists. One does not like to entertain the notion of tainted blood. A family curse. But no, she will not see you.

You took advantage of her.

I was pleased to be in a bargaining position at all.

Dont ask me to thank you.

I shant.

You didnt have the right. You should of left me there.

You would have died.

Then I'd of died.

They sat in silence. The hall clock ticked.

We're willing that you should have a horse. I'll trust Antonio to supervise the selection. Have you any money?

He looked at her. I'd of thought maybe the disappointments in your own life might of made you more sympathetic to other people.

You would have thought wrongly.

I guess so.

It is not my experience that life's difficulties make people more charitable.

I guess it depends on the people.

You think you know something of my life. An old woman whose past perhaps has left her bitter. Jealous of the happiness of others. It is an ordinary story. But it is not mine. I put forward your cause even in the teeth of the most outrageous tantrums on the part of Alejandra's mother—whom mercifully you have never met. Does that surprise you?

Yes.

Yes. Were she a more civil person perhaps I'd have been less of an advocate. I am not a society person. The societies to which I have been exposed seemed to me largely machines for the suppression of women. Society is very important in Mexico. Where women do not even have the vote. In Mexico they are mad for society and for politics and very bad at both. My family are considered gachupines here, but the madness of the Spaniard is not so different from the madness of the creole. The political tragedy in Spain was rehearsed in full dress twenty years earlier on Mexican soil. For those with eyes to see. Nothing was the same and yet everything. In the Spaniard's heart is a great yearning for freedom, but only his own. A great love of truth and honor in all its forms, but not in its substance. And a deep conviction that nothing can be proven except that it be made to bleed. Virgins, bulls, men. Ultimately God himself. When I look at my grandniece I see a child. And yet I know very well who and what I was at her age. In a different life I could have been a soldadera. Perhaps she too. And I will never know what her life is. If there is a pattern there it will not shape itself to anything these eyes can recognize. Because the question for me was always whether that shape we see in our lives was there from the beginning or whether these random events are only called a pattern after the fact. Because otherwise we are nothing. Do you believe in fate?

Yes mam. I guess I do.

My father had a great sense of the connectedness of things. I'm not sure I share it. He claimed that the responsibility for a decision could never be abandoned to a blind agency but could only be relegated to human decisions more and more remote from their consequences. The example he gave was of a tossed coin that was at one time a slug in a mint and of the coiner who took that slug from the tray and placed it in the die in one of two ways and from whose act all else followed, cara y cruz. No matter through whatever turnings nor how many of them. Till our turn comes at last and our turn passes.

She smiled. Thinly. Briefly.

It's a foolish argument. But that anonymous small person at his workbench has remained with me. I think if it were fate that ruled our houses it could perhaps be flattered or reasoned with. But the coiner cannot. Peering with his poor eyes through dingy glasses at the blind tablets of metal before him. Making his selection. Perhaps hesitating a moment. While the fates of what unknown worlds to come hang in the balance. My father must have seen in this parable the accessibility of the origins of things, but I see nothing of the kind. For me the world has always been more of a puppet show. But when one looks behind the curtain and traces the strings upward he finds they terminate in the hands of yet other puppets, themselves with their own strings which trace upward in turn, and so on. In my own life I saw these strings whose origins were endless enact the deaths of great men in violence and madness. Enact the ruin of a nation. I will tell you how Mexico was. How it was and how it will be again. You will see that those things which disposed me in your favor were the very things which led me to decide against you in the end.

When I was a girl the poverty in this country was very terrible. What you see today cannot even suggest it. And I was very affected by this. In the towns there were tiendas which rented clothes to the peasants when they would come to market. Because they had no clothes of their own and they would rent them for the day and return home at night in their blankets and rags. They had nothing. Every centavo they could scrape together went for funerals. The average family owned nothing machine-made except for a kitchen knife. Nothing. Not a pin or a plate or a pot or a button. Nothing. Ever. In the towns you'd see them trying to sell things which had no value. A bolt fallen from a truck picked up in the road or some wornout part of a machine that no one could even know the use of. Such things as

that. Pathetic things. They believed that someone must be looking for these things and would know how to value these things
if only that person could be found. It was a faith that no disappointment seemed capable of shaking. What else had they?
For what other thing would they abandon it? The industrial
world was to them a thing unimaginable and those who inhabited it wholly alien to them. And yet they were not stupid.
Never stupid. You could see it in the children. Their intelligence was frightening. And they had a freedom which we envied. There were so few restraints upon them. So few
expectations. Then at the age of eleven or twelve they would
cease being children. They lost their childhood overnight and
they had no youth. They became very serious. As if some
terrible truth had been visited upon them. Some terrible vision.
At a certain point in their lives they were sobered in an instant
and I was puzzled by this but of course I could not know what
it was they saw. What it was they knew.

By the time I was sixteen I had read many books and I had
become a freethinker. In all cases I refused to believe in a God
who could permit such injustice as I saw in a world of his own
making. I was very idealistic. Very outspoken. My parents
were horrified. Then in the summer of my seventeenth year my
life changed forever.

In the family of Francisco Madero there were thirteen children and I had many friends among them. Rafaela was my own
age within three days and we were very close. Much more so
than with the daughters of Carranza. Teníamos compadrazgo
con su familia. You understand? There is no translation. The
family had given me my quinceañera at Rosario. In that same
year Don Evaristo took a group of us to California. All young
girls from the haciendas. From Parras and Torreón. He was
quite old even then and I marvel at his courage. But he was a
wonderful man. He had served a term as governor of the state.
He was very wealthy and he was very fond of me and not at all
put off by my philosophizing. I loved going to Rosario. In those
days there was more social life about the haciendas. Very elab-

orate parties were given with orchestras and champagne and often there were European visitors and these affairs would continue until dawn. To my surprise I found myself quite popular and very likely I'd have been cured of my overwrought sensibilities except for two things. The first of these was the return of the two oldest boys, Francisco and Gustavo.

They had been in school in France for five years. Before that they had studied in the United States. In California and in Baltimore. When I was again introduced to them it was to old friends, almost family. Yet my recollection of them was a child's recollection and I must have been to them something wholly unknown.

Francisco as the eldest son enjoyed a special place in the house. There was a table under the portal where he held court with his friends. In the fall of that year I was invited to the house many times and it was in that house that I first heard the full expression of those things closest to my heart. I began to see how the world must become if I were to live in it.

Francisco began to set up schools for the poor children of the district. He dispensed medicines. Later he would feed hundreds of people from his own kitchen. It is not easy to convey the excitement of those times to people today. People were greatly attracted to Francisco. They took pleasure in his company. At that time there was no talk of his entering politics. He was simply trying to implement the ideas he had discovered. To make them work in everyday life. People from Mexico began to come to see him. In every undertaking he was seconded by Gustavo.

I'm not sure you can understand what I am telling you. I was seventeen and this country to me was like a rare vase being carried about by a child. There was an electricity in the air. Everything seemed possible. I thought that there were thousands like us. Like Francisco. Like Gustavo. There were not. Finally in the end it seemed there were none.

Gustavo wore an artificial eye as a result of an accident when he was a young boy. This did not lessen his attractiveness to me. I think perhaps the contrary. Certainly there was no company I preferred to his. He gave me books to read. We talked for hours. He was very practical. Much more so than Francisco. He did not share Francisco's taste for the occult. Always he talked of serious things. Then in the autumn of that year I went with my father and uncle to a hacienda in San Luis Potosí and there I suffered the accident to my hand of which I have spoken.

To a boy this would have been an event of consequence. To a girl it was a devastation. I would not be seen in public. I even imagined I saw a change in my father towards me. That he could not help but view me as something disfigured. I thought it would now be assumed that I could not make a good marriage and perhaps it was so assumed. There was no longer even a finger on which to place the ring. I was treated with great delicacy. Perhaps like a person returned home from an institution. I wished with all my heart that I'd been born among the poor where such things are so much more readily accepted. In this condition I awaited old age and death.

Some months passed. Then one day just before Christmas Gustavo came to call on me. I was terrified. I told my sister to beg him to go away. He would not. When my father returned quite late that night he was rather taken aback to find him seated in the parlor by himself with his hat in his lap. He came to my room to talk to me. I put my hands over my ears. I dont remember what happened. Only that Gustavo continued to sit. He passed the night in the parlor like a mozo. Here. In this house.

The next day my father was very angry with me. I will not entertain you with the scene that followed. I'm sure my howls of rage and anguish reached Gustavo's ears. But of course I could not oppose my father's will and in the end I appeared. Rather elegantly dressed if I remember. I'd learned to affect a handkerchief in my left hand in such a way as to cover my deformity. Gustavo rose and smiled at me. We walked in the garden. In those days rather better tended. He told me of his plans. Of his work. He gave me news of Francisco and of

Rafaela. Of our friends. He treated me no differently than before. He told me how he had lost his eye and of the cruelty of
the children at his school and he told me things he had never
told anyone, not even Francisco. Because he said that I would
understand.

He talked of those things we had spoken of so often at Rosario. So often and so far into the night. He said that those who
have endured some misfortune will always be set apart but that
it is just that misfortune which is their gift and which is their
strength and that they must make their way back into the common enterprise of man for without they do so it cannot go
forward and they themselves will wither in bitterness. He said
these things to me with great earnestness and great gentleness
and in the light from the portal I could see that he was crying
and I knew that it was my soul he wept for. I had never been
esteemed in this way. To have a man place himself in such a
position. I did not know what to say. That night I thought long
and not without despair about what must become of me. I
wanted very much to be a person of value and I had to ask
myself how this could be possible if there were not something
like a soul or like a spirit that is in the life of a person and which
could endure any misfortune or disfigurement and yet be no less
for it. If one were to be a person of value that value could not
be a condition subject to the hazards of fortune. It had to be a
quality that could not change. No matter what. Long before
morning I knew that what I was seeking to discover was a thing
I'd always known. That all courage was a form of constancy.
That it was always himself that the coward abandoned first.
After this all other betrayals came easily.

I knew that courage came with less struggle for some than for
others but I believed that anyone who desired it could have it.
That the desire was the thing itself. The thing itself. I could
think of nothing else of which that was true.

So much depends on luck. It was only in later years that I
understood what determination it must have taken for Gustavo
to speak to me as he did. To come to my father's house in that

way. Undeterred by any thought of rejection or ridicule. Above all I understood that his gift to me was not even in the words. The news he brought he could not speak. But it was from that day that I began to love the man who had brought me that news and though he is dead now close on to forty years those feelings have not changed.

She took a handkerchief from her sleeve and with it touched the underlid of each eye. She looked up.

Well, you see. Anyway you are quite patient. The rest of the story is not so difficult to imagine since the facts are known. In the months that followed my revolutionary spirit was rekindled and the political aspects of Francisco Madero's activities became more manifest. As he came to be taken more seriously enemies arose and his name soon reached the ear of the dictator Díaz. Francisco was forced to sell the property he had acquired at Australia in order to finance his undertakings. Before long he was arrested. Later still he fled to the United States. His determination never wavered, yet in those years few could have foreseen that he would become president of Mexico. When he and Gustavo returned they returned with guns. The revolution had begun.

In the meantime I was sent to Europe and in Europe I remained. My father was outspoken in his views concerning the responsibilities of the landed class. But revolution was another matter altogether. He would not bring me home unless I promised to disassociate myself from the Maderos and this I would not do. Gustavo and I were never engaged. His letters to me became less frequent. Then they stopped. Finally I was told that he had married. I did not blame him then or now. There were months in the revolution when the entire campaign was financed out of his pocket. Every bullet. Every crust of bread. When Díaz was at last made to flee and a free election was held Francisco became the first president of this republic ever to be placed in office by popular vote. And the last.

I will tell you about Mexico. I will tell you what happened to these brave and good and honorable men. By that time I was teaching in London. My sister came to join me and she stayed with me until the summer. She begged me to return with her but I would not. I was very proud. Very stubborn. I could not forgive my father either for his political blindness or for his treatment of me.

Francisco Madero was surrounded by plotters and schemers from his first day in office. His trust in the basic goodness of humankind became his undoing. At one point Gustavo brought General Huerta to him at gunpoint and denounced him as a traitor but Francisco would not hear of it and reinstated him. Huerta. An assassin. An animal. This was in February of nineteen thirteen. There was an armed uprising. Huerta of course was the secret accomplice. When he felt his position secure he capitulated to the rebels and led them against the government. Gustavo was arrested. Then Francisco and Pino Suárez. Gustavo was turned over to the mob in the courtyard of the ciudadela. They crowded about him with torches and lanterns. They abused and tormented him, calling him Ojo Parado. When he asked to be spared for the sake of his wife and children they called him a coward. Him, a coward. They pushed him and struck him. They burned him. When he begged them again to cease one of them came forward with a pick and pried out his good eye and he staggered away moaning in his darkness and spoke no more. Someone came forward with a revolver and put it to his head and fired but the crowd jostled his arm and the shot tore away his jaw. He collapsed at the feet of the statue of Morelos. Finally a volley of rifle shots was fired into him. He was pronounced dead. A drunk in the crowd pushed forward and shot him again anyway. They kicked his dead body and spat upon it. One of them pried out his artificial eye and it was passed among the crowd as a curiosity.

They sat in silence, the clock ticked. After a while she looked up at him.

So. This was the community of which he spoke. This beautiful boy. Who had given everything.

What happened to Francisco?

He and Pino Suárez were driven out behind the penitentiary and shot. It was no test of the cynicism of their murderers to claim that they were shot in attempting to escape. Francisco's mother had sent a telegram to President Taft asking him to intercede to save her son's life. Sara delivered it herself to the ambassador at the American Embassy. Most probably it was never sent. The family went into exile. They went to Cuba. To the United States. To France. There had always been a rumor that they were of jewish extraction. Possibly it's true. They were all very intelligent. Certainly theirs seemed to me at least to be a jewish destiny. A latterday diaspora. Martyrdom. Persecution. Exile. Sara today lives at Colonia Roma. She has her grandchildren. We see one another seldom yet we share an unspoken sisterhood. That night in the garden here at my father's house Gustavo said to me that those who have suffered great pain of injury or loss are joined to one another with bonds of a special authority and so it has proved to be. The closest bonds we will ever know are bonds of grief. The deepest community one of sorrow. I did not return from Europe until my father died. I regret now that I did not know him better. I think in many ways he also was ill suited to the life he chose. Or which chose him. Perhaps we all were. He used to read books on horticulture. In this desert. He'd already begun the cultivation of cotton here and he would have been pleased to see the success it has made. In later years I came to see how alike were he and Gustavo. Who was never meant to be a soldier. I think they did not understand Mexico. Like my father he hated bloodshed and violence. But perhaps he did not hate it enough. Francisco was the most deluded of all. He was never suited to be president of Mexico. He was hardly even suited to be Mexican. In the end we all come to be cured of our sentiments. Those whom life does not cure death will. The world is quite ruthless in selecting between the dream and the reality, even where we will not. Between the wish and the thing the world lies waiting. I've thought a great deal about my life and about my country. I think there is little that can be truly known. My family has been fortunate. Others were less so. As they are often quick to point out.

When I was in school I studied biology. I learned that in making their experiments scientists will take some group—bacteria, mice, people—and subject that group to certain conditions. They compare the results with a second group which has not been disturbed. This second group is called the control group. It is the control group which enables the scientist to gauge the effect of his experiment. To judge the significance of what has occurred. In history there are no control groups. There is no one to tell us what might have been. We weep over the might have been, but there is no might have been. There never was. It is supposed to be true that those who do not know history are condemned to repeat it. I dont believe knowing can save us. What is constant in history is greed and foolishness and a love of blood and this is a thing that even God—who knows all that can be known—seems powerless to change.

My father is buried less than two hundred meters from where we now sit. I walk out there often and I talk to him. I talk to him as I could never do in life. He made me an exile in my own country. It was not his intention to do so. When I was born in this house it was already filled with books in five languages and since I knew that as a woman the world would be largely denied me I seized upon this other world. I was reading by the time I was five and no one ever took a book from my hands. Ever. Then my father sent me to two of the best schools in Europe. For all his strictness and authority he proved to be a libertine of the most dangerous sort. You spoke of my disappointments. If such they are they have only made me reckless. My grandniece is the only future I contemplate and where she is concerned I can only put all my chips forward. It may be that the life I desire for her no longer even exists, yet I know what she does not. That there is nothing to lose. In January I will be seventy-three years old. I have known a great many people in that time and few of them led lives that were satisfactory to them. I would like my grandniece to have the opportunity to make a very different marriage from the one which her society is bent upon demanding of her. I wont accept a conventional marriage for her. Again, I know what she cannot. That there is nothing to lose. I dont know what sort of world she will live in and I have no fixed opinions concerning how she should live in it. I only know that if she does not come to value what is true above what is useful it will make little difference whether she lives at all. And by true I do not mean what is righteous but merely what is so. You think I have rejected your suit because you are young or without education or from another country but that is not the case. I was never remiss in poisoning Alejandra's mind against the conceits of the sorts of suitors available to her and we have both long been willing to entertain the notion of rescue arriving in whatever garb it chose. But I also spoke to you of a certain extravagance in the female blood of this family. Something willful. Improvident. Knowing this in her I should have been more wary where you were concerned. I should have seen you more clearly. Now I do.

You wont let me make my case.

I know your case. Your case is that certain things happened over which you had no control.

It's true.

I'm sure it is. But it's no case. I've no sympathy with people to whom things happen. It may be that their luck is bad, but is that to count in their favor?

I intend to see her.

Am I supposed to be surprised? I'll even give you my permission. Although that seems to be a thing you have never required. She will not break her word to me. You will see.

Yes mam. We will.

She rose and swept her skirt behind her to let it fall and she held out her hand. He rose and took it in his, very briefly, so fineboned and cool.

I'm sorry I shant see you again. I've been at some pains to tell you about myself because among other reasons I think we should know who our enemies are. I've known people to spend their lives nursing a hatred of phantoms and they were not happy people.

I dont hate you.

You shall.

We'll see.

Yes. We'll see what fate has in store for us, wont we?

I thought you didnt believe in fate.

She waved her hand. It's not so much that I dont believe in it. I dont subscribe to its nomination. If fate is the law then is fate also subject to that law? At some point we cannot escape naming responsibility. It's in our nature. Sometimes I think we are all like that myopic coiner at his press, taking the blind slugs one by one from the tray, all of us bent so jealously at our work, determined that not even chaos be outside of our own making.

IN THE MORNING he walked up to the bunkhouse and ate breakfast with the vaqueros and said goodbye to them. Then he walked down to the gerente's and he and Antonio went out to the barn and saddled mounts and rode up through the trap looking at the greenbroke horses. He knew the one he wanted. When it saw them it snorted and turned and went trotting. It was Rawlins' grullo and they got a rope on it and brought it down to the corral and by noon he had the animal in a half manageable condition and he walked it around and left it to cool. The horse had not been ridden in weeks and it had no cinchmarks on it and it barely knew how to eat grain. He walked down to the house and said goodbye to María and she gave him the lunch she had packed for him and handed him a rosecolored envelope with the La Purísima emblem embossed in the upper left corner. When he got outside he opened it and took out the money and folded it and put it into his pocket without counting it and folded the envelope and put it in his shirtpocket. Then he walked out through the pecan trees in front of the house where

Antonio stood waiting with the horses and they stood for a moment in a wordless abrazo and then he mounted up into the saddle and turned the horse into the road.

He rode through La Vega without dismounting, the horse blowing and rolling its eyes at all it saw. When a truck started up in the street and began to come toward them the animal moaned in despair and tried to turn and he sawed it down almost onto its haunches and patted it and talked constantly to it until the vehicle was past and then they went on again. Once outside the town he left the road altogether and set off across the immense and ancient lakebed of the bolsón. He crossed a dry gypsum playa where the salt crust stove under the horse's hooves like trodden isinglass and he rode up through white gypsum hills grown with stunted datil and through a pale bajada crowded with flowers of gypsum like a cavefloor uncovered to the light. In the shimmering distance trees and jacales stood along the slender bights of greenland pale and serried and half fugitive in the clear morning air. The horse had a good natural gait and as he rode he talked to it and told it things about the world that were true in his experience and he told it things he thought could be true to see how they would sound if they were said. He told the horse why he liked it and why he'd chosen it to be his horse and he said that he would allow no harm to come to it.

By noon he was riding a farmland road where the acequias carried the water down along the foot-trodden selvedges of the fields and he stood the horse to water and walked it up and back in the shade of a cottonwood grove to cool it. He shared his lunch with children who came to sit beside him. Some of them had never eaten leavened bread and they looked to an older boy among them for guidance in the matter. They sat in a row along the edge of the path, five of them, and the sandwich halves of cured ham from the hacienda were passed to left and to right and they ate with great solemnity and when the sandwiches were gone he divided with his knife the freshbaked tarts of apple and guava.

Dónde vive? said the oldest boy.

He mused on the question. They waited. I once lived at a great hacienda, he told them, but now I have no place to live.

The children's faces studied him with great concern. Puede vivir con nosotros, they said, and he thanked them and he told them that he had a novia who was in another town and that he was riding to her to ask her to be his wife.

Es bonita, su novia? they asked, and he told them that she was very beautiful and that she had blue eyes which they could scarcely believe but he told them also that her father was a rich hacendado while he himself was very poor and they heard this in silence and were greatly cast down at his prospects. The older of the girls said that if his novia truly loved him she would marry him no matter what but the boy was not so encouraging and he said that even in families of the rich a girl could not go against the wishes of her father. The girl said that the grandmother must be consulted because she was very important in these matters and that he must take her presents and try to win her to his side for without her help little could be expected. She said that all the world knew this to be true.

John Grady nodded at the wisdom of this but he said that he had already given offense where the grandmother was concerned and could not depend upon her assistance and at this several of the children ceased to eat and stared at the earth before them.

Es un problema, said the boy.

De acuerdo.

One of the younger girls leaned forward. Qué ofensa le dio a la abuelita? she said.

Es una historia larga, he said.

Hay tiempo, they said.

He smiled and looked at them and as there was indeed time he told them all that had happened. He told them how they had come from another country, two young horsemen riding their horses, and that they had met with a third who had no money nor food to eat nor scarcely clothes to cover himself and that he had come to ride with them and share with them in all they had. This horseman was very young and he rode a wonderful horse but among his fears was the fear that God would kill him with lightning and because of this fear he lost his horse in the desert. He then told them what had happened concerning the horse and how they had taken the horse from the village of Encantada and he told how the boy had gone back to the village of Encantada and there had killed a man and that the police had come to the hacienda and arrested him and his friend and that the grandmother had paid their fine and then forbidden the novia to see him anymore.

When he was done they sat in silence and finally the girl said that what he must do is bring the boy to the grandmother so that he would tell her that he was the one at fault and John Grady said that this was not possible because the boy was dead. When the children heard this they blessed themselves and kissed their fingers. The older boy said that the situation was a difficult one but that he must find an intercessor to speak on his behalf because if the grandmother could be made to see that he was not to blame then she would change her mind. The older girl said that he was forgetting about the problem that the family was rich and he was poor. The boy said that as he had a horse he could not be so very poor and they looked at John Grady for a decision on this question and he told them that in spite of appearances he was indeed very poor and that the horse had been given to him by the grandmother herself. At this some of them drew in their breath and shook their heads. The girl said that he needed to find some wise man with whom he could discuss his difficulties or perhaps a curandera and the younger girl said that he should pray to God.

It was late night and dark when he rode into Torreón. He haltered the horse and tied it in front of a hotel and went in and asked about a livery stable but the clerk knew nothing of such things. He looked out the front window at the horse and he looked at John Grady.

Puede dejarlo atrás, he said.

Atrás?

Sí. Afuera. He gestured toward the rear.

John Grady looked toward the rear of the building.

Por dónde? he said.

The clerk shrugged. He passed the flat of his hand past the desk toward the hallway. Por aquí.

There was an old man sitting in a sofa in the lobby who'd been watching out the window and he turned to John Grady and told him that it was all right and that far worse things than horses had passed through that hotel lobby and John Grady looked at the clerk and then went out and untied the horse and led it in. The clerk had preceded him down the hallway and he opened the rear doors and stood while John Grady led the horse out into the yard. He'd bought a small sack of grain in Tlahualilo and he watered the horse in a washtrough and broke open the grainsack and poured the grain out into the upturned lid of a trashcan and he unsaddled the horse and wet the empty sack and rubbed the horse down with it and then carried the saddle in and got his key and went up to bed.

When he woke it was noon. He'd slept almost twelve hours. He rose and went to the window and looked out. The window gave onto the little yard behind the hotel and the horse was patiently walking the enclosure with three children astride it and another leading it and yet another hanging on to its tail.

He stood in line most of the morning at the telephone exchange waiting for his turn at one of the four cabinets and when he finally got his call through she could not be reached. He signed up again at the counter and the girl behind the glass read his face and told him that he would have better luck in the afternoon and he did. A woman answered the phone and sent someone to get her. He waited. When she came to the phone she said that she knew it would be him.

I have to see you, he said.

I cant.

You have to. I'm coming down there.

No. You cant.

I'm leaving in the morning. I'm in Torreón.

Did you talk to my aunt?

Yes.

She was quiet. Then she said: I cant see you.

Yes you can.

I wont be here. I go to La Purísima in two days.

I'll meet you at the train.

You cant. Antonio is coming to meet me.

He closed his eyes and held the phone very tightly and he told her that he loved her and that she'd had no right to make the promise that she'd made even if they killed him and that he would not leave without seeing her even if it was the last time he would see her ever and she was quiet for a long time and then she said that she would leave a day early. That she would say her aunt was ill and she would leave tomorrow morning and meet him in Zacatecas. Then she hung up.

He boarded the horse at a stable out beyond the barrios south of the railtracks and told the patrón to be wary of the horse as he was at best half broke and the man nodded and called to the boy but John Grady could tell he had his own ideas about horses and would come to his own conclusions. He lugged the saddle into the saddleroom and hung it up and the boy locked the door behind him and he walked back out to the office.

He offered to pay in advance but the proprietor dismissed him with a small wave of the hand. He walked out into the sun and down the street where he caught the bus back to town.

He bought a small awol bag in a store and he bought two new shirts and a new pair of boots and he walked down to the train station and bought his ticket and went to a cafe and ate. He walked around to break in the boots and then went back to the hotel. He rolled the pistol and knife and his old clothes up in the bedroll and had the clerk put the bedroll in the storage room and he told the clerk to wake him at six in the morning and then went up to bed. It was hardly even dark.

It was cool and gray when he left the hotel in the morning and by the time he got settled into the coach there were spits of rain breaking on the glass. A young boy and his sister sat in the seat opposite and after the train pulled out the boy asked him where he was from and where he was going. They didnt seem surprised to hear he was from Texas. When the porter came through calling breakfast he invited them to eat with him but the boy looked embarrassed and would not. He was embarrassed himself. He sat in the diner and ate a big plate of huevos rancheros and drank coffee and watched the gray fields pass beyond the wet glass and in his new boots and shirt he began to feel better than he'd felt in a long time and the weight on his heart had begun to lift and he repeated what his father had once told him, that scared money cant win and a worried man cant love. The train passed through a dreadful plain grown solely with cholla and entered a vast forest of china palm. He opened the pack of cigarettes he'd bought at the station kiosk and lit one and laid the pack on the tablecloth and blew smoke at the glass and at the country passing in the rain.

The train pulled into Zacatecas in the late afternoon. He walked out of the station and up the street through the high portales of the old stone aqueduct and down into the town. The rain had followed them down from the north and the narrow stone streets were wet and the shops were closed. He walked up Hidalgo past the cathedral to the Plaza de Armas and checked into the Reina Cristina Hotel. It was an old colonial hotel and it was quiet and cool and the stones of the lobby floor were dark and polished and there was a macaw in a cage watching the people go in and out. In the diningroom adjoining the lobby there were people still at lunch. He got his key and went up, a porter carrying his small bag. The room was large and high ceilinged and there was a chenille cover on the bed and a cut-glass decanter of water on the table. The porter swept open the window drapes and went into the bathroom to see that all was in order. John Grady leaned on the window balustrade. In the courtyard below an old man knelt among pots of red and white geraniums, singing softly a single verse from an old corrido as he tended the flowers.

He tipped the porter and put his hat on the bureau and shut the door. He stretched out on the bed and looked up at the carved vigas of the ceiling. Then he got up and got his hat and went down to the diningroom to get a sandwich.

He walked through the narrow twisting streets of the town with its ancient buildings and small sequestered plazas. The people seemed dressed with a certain elegance. It had stopped raining and the air was fresh. Shops had begun to open. He sat on a bench in the plaza and had his boots shined and he looked in the shopwindows trying to find something for her. He finally bought a very plain silver necklace and paid the woman what she asked and the woman tied it in a paper with a ribbon and he put it in the pocket of his shirt and went back to the hotel.

The train from San Luis Potosí and Mexico was due in at eight oclock. He was at the station at seven-thirty. It was almost nine when it arrived. He waited on the platform among others and watched the passengers step down. When she appeared on the steps he almost didnt recognize her. She was wearing a blue dress with a skirt almost to her ankles and a blue hat with a wide brim and she did not look like a schoolgirl either to him or to the other men on the platform. She carried a small leather suitcase and the porter took it from her as she stepped down and then handed it back to her and touched his cap. When she turned and looked at him where he was standing he realized she had seen him from the window of the coach. As she walked toward him her beauty seemed to him a thing altogether improbable. A presence unaccountable in this place or in any place at all. She came toward him and she smiled at him sadly and she touched her fingers to the scar on his cheek and leaned and kissed it and he kissed her and took the suitcase from her.

You are so thin, she said. He looked into those blue eyes like a man seeking some vision of the increate future of the universe. He'd hardly breath to speak at all and he told her that she was very beautiful and she smiled and in her eyes was the sadness he'd first seen the night she came to his room and he knew that while he was contained in that sadness he was not the whole of it.

Are you all right? she said.

Yes. I'm all right.

And Lacey?

He's all right. He's gone home.

They walked out through the small terminal and she took his arm.

I'll get a cab, he said.

Let's walk.

All right.

The streets were filled with people and in the Plaza de Armas there were carpenters nailing up the scaffolding for a crepe-covered podium before the Governor's Palace where in two days' time orators would speak on the occasion of Independence Day. He took her hand and they crossed the street to the hotel. He tried to read her heart in her handclasp but he knew nothing.

They ate dinner in the hotel diningroom. He'd never been in a public place with her and he was not prepared for the open glances from older men at nearby tables nor for the grace with which she accepted them. He'd bought a pack of american cigarettes at the desk and when the waiter brought the coffee he lit one and placed it in the ashtray and said that he had to tell her what had happened.

He told her about Blevins and about the prisión Castelar and he told her about what happened to Rawlins and finally he told her about the cuchillero who had fallen dead in his arms with his knife broken off in his heart. He told her everything. Then they sat in silence. When she looked up she was crying.

Tell me, he said.

I cant.

Tell me.

How do I know who you are? Do I know what sort of man you are? What sort my father is? Do you drink whiskey? Do you go with whores? Does he? What are men?

I told you things I've never told anybody. I told you all there was to tell.

What good is it? What good?

I dont know. I guess I just believe in it.

They sat for a long time. Finally she looked up at him. I told him that we were lovers, she said.

The chill that went through him was so cold. The room so quiet. She'd hardly more than whispered yet he felt the silence all around him and he could scarcely look. When he spoke his voice was lost.

Why?

Because she threatened to tell him. My aunt. She told me I must stop seeing you or she would tell him.

She wouldnt have.

No. I dont know. I couldnt stand for her to have that power. I told him myself.

Why?

I dont know. I dont know.

Is it true? You told him?

Yes. It's true.

He leaned back. He put both hands to his face. He looked at her again.

How did she find out?

I dont know. Different things. Estéban perhaps. She heard me leave the house. Heard me return.

You didnt deny it.

No.

What did your father say?

Nothing. He said nothing.

Why didnt you tell me?

You were on the mesa. I would have. But when you returned you were arrested.

He had me arrested.

Yes.

How could you tell him?

I dont know. I was so foolish. It was her arrogance. I told her I would not be blackmailed. She made me crazy.

Do you hate her?

No. I dont hate her. But she tells me I must be my own person and with every breath she tries to make me her person. I dont hate her. She cant help it. But I broke my father's heart. I broke his heart.

He said nothing at all?

No.

What did he do?

He got up from the table. He went to his room.

You told him at the table?

Yes.

In front of her?

Yes. He went to his room and the next morning he left before daylight. He saddled a horse and left. He took the dogs. He went up into the mountains alone. I think he was going to kill you.

She was crying. People were looking toward their table. She lowered her eyes and sat sobbing silently, just her shoulders moving and the tears running down her face.

Dont cry. Alejandra. Dont cry.

She shook her head. I destroyed everything. I only wanted to die.

Dont cry. I'll make it right.

You cant, she said. She raised her eyes and looked at him. He'd never seen despair before. He thought he had, but he had not.

He came to the mesa. Why didnt he kill me?

I dont know. I think he was afraid that I would take my life.

Would you?

I dont know.

I will make it right. You have to let me.

She shook her head. You dont understand.

What dont I understand?

I didnt know that he would stop loving me. I didnt know he could. Now I know.

She took a handkerchief from her purse. I'm sorry, she said. People are looking at us.

IT RAINED in the night and the curtains kept lifting into the room and he could hear the splash of the rain in the courtyard and he held her pale and naked against him and she cried and she told him that she loved him and he asked her to marry him. He told her that he could make a living and that they could go to live in his country and make their life there and no harm would come to them. She did not sleep and when he woke in the dawn she was standing at the window wearing his shirt.

Viene la madrugada, she said.

Yes.

She came to the bed and sat. I saw you in a dream. I saw you dead in a dream.

Last night?

No. Long ago. Before any of this. Hice una manda.

A promise.

Yes.

For my life.

Yes. They carried you through the streets of a city I'd never seen. It was dawn. The children were praying. Lloraba tu madre. Con más razón tu puta.

He put his hand to her mouth. Dont say that. You cant say that.

She took his hand and held it in hers and touched the veins.

They went out in the dawn in the city and walked in the streets. They spoke to the streetsweepers and to women opening the small shops, washing the steps. They ate in a cafe and walked in the little paseos and callejones where old vendresses of sweets, melcochas and charamuscas, were setting out their wares on the cobbles and he bought strawberries for her from a boy who weighed them in a small brass balance and twisted up a paper alcatraz to pour them into. They walked in the old Jardín Independencia where high above them stood a white stone angel with one broken wing. From her stone wrists dangled the broken chains of the manacles she wore. He counted in his heart the hours until the train would come again from the south which when it pulled out for Torreón would either take her or would not take her and he told her that if she would trust her life into his care he would never fail her or abandon her and that he would love her until he died and she said that she believed him.

In the forenoon as they were returning to the hotel she took his hand and led him across the street.

Come, she said. I will show you something.

She led him down past the cathedral wall and through the vaulted arcade into the street beyond.

What is it? he said.

A place.

They walked up the narrow twisting street. Past a tannery. A tinsmith shop. They entered a small plaza and here she turned.

My grandfather died here, she said. My mother's father.

Where?

Here. In this place. Plazuela de Guadalajarita.

In the revolution.

Yes. In nineteen-fourteen. The twenty-third of June. He was with the Zaragoza Brigade under Raúl Madero. He was twenty-four years old. They came down from north of the city. Cerro de Loreto. Tierra Negra. Beyond here at that time all was campo. He died in this strange place. Esquina de la Calle del Deseo y el Callejón del Pensador Mexicano. There was no mother to cry. As in the corridos. Nor little bird that flew. Just the blood on the stones. I wanted to show you. We can go.

Quién fue el Pensador Mexicano?

Un poeta. Joaquín Fernández de Lizardi. He had a life of great difficulty and died young. As for the Street of Desire it is like the Calle de Noche Triste. They are but names for Mexico. We can go now.

When they got to the room the maid was cleaning and she left and they closed the curtains and made love and slept in each other's arms. When they woke it was evening. She came from the shower wrapped in a towel and she sat on the bed and took his hand and looked down at him. I cannot do what you ask, she said. I love you. But I cannot.

He saw very clearly how all his life led only to this moment and all after led nowhere at all. He felt something cold and soulless enter him like another being and he imagined that it smiled malignly and he had no reason to believe that it would ever leave. When she came out of the bathroom again she was dressed and he made her sit on the bed and he held her hands both of them and talked to her but she only shook her head and she turned away her tearstained face and told him that it was time to go and that she could not miss the train.

They walked through the streets and she held his hand and he carried her bag. They walked through the alameda above the old stone bullring and came down the steps past the carved stone bandstand. A dry wind had come up from the south and in the eucalyptus trees the grackles teetered and screamed. The sun was down and a blue twilight filled the park and the yellow gaslamps came on along the aqueduct walls and down the walkways among the trees.

They stood on the platform and she put her face against his shoulder and he spoke to her but she did not answer. The train came huffing in from the south and stood steaming and shuddering with the coach windows curving away down the track like great dominoes smoldering in the dark and he could not but compare this arrival to that one twenty-four hours ago and she touched the silver chain at her throat and turned away and bent to pick up the suitcase and then leaned and kissed him one last time her face all wet and then she was gone. He watched her go as if he himself were in some dream. All along the platform families and lovers were greeting one another. He saw a man with a little girl in his arms and he whirled her around and she was laughing and when she saw his face she stopped laughing.

He did not see how he could stand there until the train pulled out but stand he did and when it was gone he turned and walked back out into the street.

He paid the bill at the hotel and got his things and left. He went to a bar in a sidestreet where the raucous hybrid beerhall music of the north was blaring from an open door and he got very drunk and got in a fight and woke in the gray dawn on an iron bed in a green room with paper curtains at a window beyond which he could hear roosters calling.

He studied his face in a clouded glass. His jaw was bruised and swollen. If he moved his head in the mirror to a certain place he could restore some symmetry to the two sides of his face and the pain was tolerable if he kept his mouth shut. His shirt was torn and bloody and his bag was gone. He remembered things from the night of whose reality he was uncertain. He remembered a man in silhouette at the end of a street who stood much as Rawlins had stood when last he saw him, half turned in farewell, a coat slung loosely over one shoulder. Who'd come to ruin no man's house. No man's daughter. He saw a light over a doorway in the corrugated iron wall of a warehouse where no one came and no one went. He saw a vacant field in a city in the rain and in the field a wooden crate and he saw a dog emerge from the crate into the slack and sallow lamplight like a carnival dog forlorn and pick its way brokenly across the rubble of the lot to vanish without fanfare among the darkened buildings.

When he walked out the door he did not know where he was. A fine rain was falling. He tried to take his bearings from La Bufa standing above the city to the west but he was easily lost in the winding streets and he asked a woman for the way to the centro and she pointed out the street and then watched him as he went. When he reached Hidalgo a pack of dogs was coming up the street at a high trot and as they crossed in front of him one of their number slipped and scrabbled on the wet stones and went down. The others turned in a snarling mass of teeth and fur but the fallen dog struggled up before he could be set upon and all went on as before. He walked out to the edge of the town along the highway north and put out his thumb. He had almost no money and he'd a long way to go.

He rode all day in an old LaSalle phaeton with the top down driven by a man in a white suit. He said that his was the only car of its type in all of Mexico. He said that he had traveled all over the world when he was young and that he had studied opera in Milan and in Buenos Aires and as they rolled through the countryside he sang arias and gestured with great vigor.

By this and other conveyance he reached Torreón around noon of the following day and went to the hotel and got his bedroll. Then he went to fetch his horse. He'd not shaved nor bathed and he had no other clothes to wear and the hostler when he saw him nodded his head in sympathy and seemed unsurprised at his condition. He rode the horse out into the noon traffic and the horse was fractious and scared and it skittered about in the street and kicked a great dish into the side of a bus to the delight of the passengers who leaned out and called challenges from the safety of the windows.

There was an armería in the calle Degollado and he dismounted in front of it and tied the horse to a lampstandard and went in and bought a box of 45 Long Colt shells. He stopped at a tienda on the outskirts of town and bought some tortillas and some tins of beans and salsa and some cheese and he rolled them up in his blanket and tied the bedroll on behind the saddle again and refilled the canteen and mounted up and turned the horse north. The rain had ripened all the country around and the roadside grass was luminous and green from the run-off and flowers were in bloom across the open country. He slept that night in a field far from any town. He built no fire. He lay listening to the horse crop the grass at his stakerope and he listened to the wind in the emptiness and watched stars trace the arc of the hemisphere and die in the darkness at the edge of the world and as he lay there the agony in his heart was like a stake. He imagined the pain of the world to be like some formless parasitic being seeking out the warmth of human souls wherein to incubate and he thought he knew what made one liable to its visitations. What he had not known was that it was mindless and so had no way to know the limits of those souls and what he feared was that there might be no limits.

By afternoon of the day following he was deep in the bolsón and a day later he was entering the range country and the broken land that entabled the desert mountains to the north. The horse was not in condition for the riding he called upon it to do and he was forced to rest it often. He rode at night that its hooves might benefit from the damp or from what damp there was and as he rode he saw small villages distant on the plain that glowed a faint yellow in that incoordinate dark and he knew that the life there was unimaginable to him. Five days later he rode at night into a small crossroads pueblo nameless to him and he sat the horse in the crossroads and by the light of a full moon read the names of towns burned into crateslats with a hot iron and nailed to a post. San Jerónimo. Los Pintos. La Rosita. At the bottom a board with the arrow pointed the other way that said La Encantada. He sat a long time. He leaned and spat. He looked toward the darkness in west. The hell with it, he said. I aint leavin my horse down here.

He rode all night and in the first gray light with the horse badly drawn down he walked it out upon a rise beneath which he could make out the shape of the town, the yellow windows in the old mud walls where the first lamps were lit, the narrow spires of smoke standing vertically into the windless dawn so still the village seemed to hang by threads from the darkness. He dismounted and unrolled his plunder and opened the box of shells and put half of them in his pocket and checked the pistol that it was loaded all six cylinders and closed the cylinder gate and put the pistol into his belt and rolled his gear back up and retied the roll behind the saddle and mounted the horse again and rode into the town.

There was no one in the streets. He tied the horse in front of the store and walked down to the old school and stood on the porch and looked in. He tried the door. He walked around to the rear and broke out the glass and reached in and unlocked the doorlatch and walked in with the pistol in his hand. He crossed the room and looked out the window at the street. Then he turned and walked back to the captain's desk. He opened the top drawer and took out the handcuffs and laid them on top of the desk. Then he sat down and put his feet up.

An hour later the maid arrived and opened the door with her key. She was startled to see him sitting there and she stood uncertainly.

Pásale, pásale, he said. Está bien.

Gracias, she said.

She'd have crossed the room and gone on to the rear but that he stopped her and made her take a seat in one of the metal folding chairs against the wall. She sat very quietly. She didnt ask him anything at all. They waited.

He saw the captain cross the street. He heard his boots on the boards. He came in with his coffee in one hand and the ring of keys in the other and the mail under his arm and he stood looking at John Grady and at the pistol he was holding with the butt resting on the desktop.

Cierra la puerta, said John Grady.

The captain's eyes darted toward the door. John Grady stood. He cocked the pistol. The click of the sear and the click of the cylinderhand falling into place were sharp and clear in the morning silence. The maid put her hands over her ears and closed her eyes. The captain shut the door slowly with his elbow.

What do you want? he said.

I come to get my horse.

You horse?

Yes.

I dont have you horse.

You better know where he's at.

The captain looked at the maid. She still had her hands over her ears but she had looked up.

Come over here and put that stuff down, said John Grady.

He walked to the desk and put down his coffee and the mail and stood holding the keys.

Put down the keys.

He put the keys on the desk.

Turn around.

You make bad troubles for you self.

I got troubles you never even heard of. Turn around.

He turned around. John Grady leaned forward and unsnapped the flap of the holster he wore and took out the pistol and uncocked it and put it in his belt.

Turn around, he said.

He turned around. He hadnt been told to put his hands up but he'd put them up anyway. John Grady picked up the handcuffs from the desk and stuck them in his belt.

Where do you want to put the criada? he said.

Mande?

Never mind. Let's go.

He picked up the keys and came around from behind the desk and pushed the captain forward. He gestured at the woman with his chin.

Vámonos, he said.

The back door was still open and they walked out and down the path to the jail. John Grady unlocked the padlock and opened the door. Blinking in the pale triangular light sat the old man as before.

Ya estás, viejo?

Sí, cómo no.

Ven aquí.

He was a long time rising. He shuffled forward with one hand on the wall and John Grady told him he was free to go. He motioned for the cleaning woman to enter and he apologized for inconveniencing her and she said not to give it a thought and he closed and locked the door.

When he turned the old man was still standing there. John Grady told him to go home. The old man looked at the captain.

No lo mire a él, said John Grady. Te lo digo yo. Ándale.

The old man seized his hand and was about to kiss it when John Grady snatched it away.

Get the hell out of here, he said. Dont be lookin at him. Go on.

The old man hobbled off toward the gate and unlatched it and stepped out into the street and turned and shut the gate again and was gone.

When he and the captain went up the street John Grady was riding the horse with the pistols stuck in his belt and his jacket over them. His hands were handcuffed before him and the captain was leading the horse. They turned down the street to the blue house where the charro lived and the captain knocked at his door. A woman came to the door and looked at the captain and went back down the zaguán and after a while the charro came to the door and nodded and stood picking his teeth. He looked at John Grady and he looked at the captain. Then he looked at John Grady again.

Tenemos un problema, said the captain.

He sucked on the toothpick. He hadnt seen the pistol in John Grady's belt and he was having trouble understanding the captain's demeanor.

Ven aquí, said John Grady. Cierra la puerta.

When the charro looked up into the pistolbarrel John Grady could see the gears meshing in his head and everything turning and falling into place. He reached behind him and pulled the door shut. He looked up at the rider. The sun was in his eyes and he stepped slightly to one side and looked up again.

Quiero mi caballo, said John Grady.

He looked at the captain. The captain shrugged. He looked up at the rider again and his eyes started to cut away to the right and then he looked down. John Grady looked off across the ocotillo fence where from horseback he could see some mud sheds and the rusted tin roof of a larger building. He swung down from the horse, the handcuffs dangling from one wrist.

Vámonos, he said.

Rawlins' horse was in a mud barn in the lot behind the house. He spoke to it and it lifted its head at his voice and nickered at him. He told the charro to get a bridle and he stood holding the pistol while the charro bridled the horse and then he took the reins from him. He asked him where the other horses were. The charro swallowed and looked at the captain. John Grady reached and got the captain by the collar and put the pistol to the captain's head and he told the charro that if he looked at the captain again he would shoot him. He stood looking down. John Grady told him that he had no more patience and no more time and that the captain was a dead man anyway but that he could still save himself. He told them that Blevins was his brother and he'd taken a bloodoath not to return to his father without the captain's head and he said that if he failed there were more brothers each waiting his turn. The charro lost control of his eyes and looked at the captain anyway and then he closed his eyes and turned away and clutched the top of his thin head with one hand. But John Grady was watching the captain and he saw doubt cloud his face for the first time. The captain started to speak to the charro but he pulled him around by the collar with the pistol against his head and told him that if he spoke again he would shoot him where he stood.

Tú, he said. Dónde están los otros caballos.

The charro stood looking out down the barn bay. He looked like an extra in a stageplay reciting his only lines.

En la hacienda de Don Rafael, he said.

They rode out through the town with the captain and the charro doubled on Rawlins' horse bareback and John Grady riding behind them with his hands manacled as before. He carried a spare bridle slung over one shoulder. They rode dead through the center of town. Old women out sweeping the mud street in the early morning air stood and watched them go.

It was some ten kilometers to the hacienda so spoken and they reached it midmorning and rode through the open gate and on past the house toward the stables at the rear attended by dogs who pranced and barked and ran before the horses.

At the corral John Grady halted and removed the cuffs and put them in his pocket and drew the pistol from his belt. Then he dismounted and opened the gate and waved them through.

He led the grullo through and closed the gate and ordered them off the horse and gestured toward the stable with the pistol.

The building was new and built of adobe brick and had a high tin roof. The doors at the far end were closed and the stalls were shuttered and there was little light in the bay. He pushed the captain and the charro ahead of him at gunpoint. He could hear horses snuffing in the stalls and he could hear pigeons cooing somewhere in the loft overhead.

Redbo, he called.

The horse nickered at him from the far end of the stable.

He motioned them forward. Vámonos, he said.

As he turned a man stepped into the doorway behind them and stood in silhouette.

Quién está? he said.

John Grady moved behind the charro and put the gunbarrel in his ribs. Respóndele, he said.

Luis, said the charro.

Luis?

Sí.

Quién más?

Raúl. El capitán.

The man stood uncertainly. John Grady stepped behind the captain. Tenemos un preso, he said.

Tenemos un preso, called the captain.

Un ladrón, whispered John Grady.

Un ladrón.

Tenemos que ver un caballo.

Tenemos que ver un caballo, said the captain.

Cúal caballo?

El caballo americano.

The man stood. Then he stepped out of the doorway light. No one spoke.

Qúe pasó, hombre? called the man.

No one answered. John Grady watched the sunlit ground beyond the stable door. He could see the shadow of the man where he stood to the side of the door. Then the shadow withdrew. He listened. He pushed the two men toward the rear of the stable. Vámonos, he said.

He called his horse again and located the stall and opened the door and turned the horse out. The horse pushed his nose and forehead against John Grady's chest and John Grady spoke to him and he whinnied and turned and went trotting toward the sunlight in the door without bridle or halter. As they were coming back up the bay two other horses put their heads out over the stall doors. The second one was the big bay horse of Blevins'.

He stopped and looked at the animal. He still had the spare bridle looped over his shoulder and he called the charro by name and shrugged the bridle off his shoulder and handed it to him and told him to bridle the horse and bring it out. He knew that the man who'd come to the stable door had seen the two horses standing in the corral, one saddled and bridled and the other bridled and bareback, and he reckoned he'd gone to the house for a rifle and that he would probably be back before the charro could even get the bridle on Blevins' horse and in all of this he was correct. When the man called from outside the stable again he called for the captain. The captain looked at John Grady. The charro stood with the bridle in one hand and the horse's nose in the crook of his arm.

Ándale, said John Grady.

Raúl, called the man.

The charro pushed the headstall over the horse's ears and stood in the stall door holding the reins.

Vámonos, said John Grady.

There were ropes and rope halters and other bits of tack hanging from the hitchrail in the hall and he took a coil of rope and handed it to the charro and told him to tie one end to the bridle throatlatch of Blevins' horse. He knew he didnt have to check anything that the man did because the charro could not have brought himself to do it wrong. His own horse stood in the doorway looking back. Then it turned and looked at the man standing outside against the wall of the stable.

Quién está contigo? the man called.

John Grady took the handcuffs from his pocket and told the captain to turn around and put his hands behind him. The captain hesitated and looked toward the door. John Grady raised the pistol and cocked it.

Bien, bien, the captain said. John Grady snapped the cuffs onto his wrists and pushed him forward and motioned to the charro to bring the horse. Rawlins' horse had appeared in the stable door and stood nuzzling Redbo. He raised his head and he and Redbo looked at them as they came up the bay leading the other horse.

At the edge of the shadowline where the light fell into the stable John Grady took the lead rope from the charro.

Espera aquí, he said.

Sí.

He pushed the captain forward.

Quiero mis caballos, he called. Nada más.

No one answered.

He dropped the lead rope and slapped the horse on the rump and it went trotting out of the stable holding its head to one side so as not to step on the trailing rope. Outside it turned and nudged Rawlins' horse with its forehead and then stood looking at the man crouching against the wall. The man must have made a hazing motion at it because it jerked its head and blinked but it did not move. John Grady picked up the end of the rope the horse was trailing and passed it between the captain's handcuffed arms and stepped forward and halfhitched it to the stanchion the stable door was hung from. Then he stepped out through the door and put the barrel of the revolver between the eyes of the man crouched there.

The man had been holding the rifle at his waist and he dropped it in the dirt and held his hands up. Almost instantly John Grady's legs were slammed from under him and he went down. He never even heard the crack of the rifle but Blevins' horse did and it reared onto its hind legs above him and sprang and hit the end of the rope and was snatched sideways and fell with a great whump in the dust. A flock of pigeons burst flapping out of the gable end of the loft overhead into the morning sun. The other two horses went trotting and the grullo started to run along the fence. He held onto the pistol and tried to rise. He knew he'd been shot and he was trying to see where the man was hidden. The other man reached to retrieve the rifle lying on the ground but John Grady turned and threw down on him with the pistol and then reached and got hold of the rifle and rolled over and covered the head of the horse that was down and struggling so that it would not rise. Then he raised up cautiously to look.

No tire el caballo, called the man behind him. He saw the man who'd shot him standing in the bed of a truck a hundred feet away across the lot with the barrel of the rifle resting on top of the cab. He pointed the pistol at him and the man crouched down and watched him through the rear window of the cab and out through the windshield. He cocked and leveled the pistol and shot a hole in the windshield and cocked the pistol again and spun and pointed it at the man kneeling behind him. The horse moaned under him. He could feel it breathing slow and steady in the pit of his stomach. The man held out his hands. No me mate, he said. John Grady looked toward the truck. He could see the man's boots below the axle carrier where he stood at the rear of the vehicle and he spread himself over the horse and cocked the pistol and fired at them. The man stepped behind the rear wheel and he fired again and hit a tire. The man ran from behind the truck across the open ground toward a shed. The tire was whistling with a single long steady note in the morning silence and the truck had begun to settle at one corner.

Redbo and Junior stood trembling in the shadow of the stable wall with their legs slightly spread and their eyes rolling. John Grady lay covering the horse and held the pistol on the man behind him and called to the charro. The charro didnt answer and he called to him again and told him to bring a saddle and bridle for the other horse and to bring a rope or he would kill the patrón. Then they all waited. In a few minutes the charro came to the door. He called out his own name before him like a talisman against harm.

Pásale, called John Grady. Nadie le va a molestar.

He talked to Redbo while the charro saddled and bridled him. Blevins' horse was breathing with slow regularity and his stomach was warm and his shirt damp from the horse's breath. He found he was breathing in rhythm with the horse as if some part of the horse were within him breathing and then he descended into some deeper collusion for which he had not even a name. He looked down at his leg. His trousers were dark with blood and there was blood on the ground. He felt numb and strange but he felt no pain. The charro brought Redbo to him saddled and he eased himself up from the horse and looked down at it. Its eye rolled up at him, at the endless and eternal blue beyond. He stood the rifle on the ground and tried to get up. When he put his weight on the gunshot leg a white pain went up his right side and he sucked in all the air he could get. Blevins' horse lurched and scrambled to its feet and snatched the rope taut and there was a cry from the barn and the captain tottered forth bent double with his arms up behind him along the quivering length of rope like something smoked out of a hole. He'd lost his hat and his lank black hair hung down and his face was a gray color and he called out to them to help him. The horse hitting the end of the rope at the first gunfire had snatched him up and had already dislocated his shoulder and he was in great pain. John Grady stood and unfastened the rope from the throatlatch of the bay horse and tied on the rope the charro had brought and handed the rope end off to the charro and told him to dally it to Redbo's saddlehorn and bring him the other two horses. He looked at the captain. He was sitting on the ground bent over slightly sideways with his hands cuffed behind him. The second man was still kneeling a few feet away with his hands up. When John Grady looked down at him he shook his head.

Está loco, he said.

Tiene razón, said John Grady.

He told him to call the carabinero out from the shed and he called to him twice but the man would not come out. He knew he would not ride out of the compound without the man trying to stop him and he knew he had to do something about Blevins' thundercrazed horse. The charro stood holding the horses and he took the rope and handed him back the reins and told him to go get the captain and to mount him on the grullo and he leaned against the side of Blevins' horse and got his breath and looked down at his leg. When he looked at the charro he was standing over the captain holding the horse behind him but the captain wasnt going anywhere. He raised the pistol and was about to shoot into the ground in front of the captain when he remembered about Blevins' horse. He looked at the kneeling man again and then using the rifle for a crutch he swung under the horse's neck and picked up Redbo's bridlereins from the ground and jammed the pistol into his belt and put his foot in the stirrup and stood and swung his bloodied leg over into the saddle. He swung it harder than he needed because he knew that if he failed the first time he wouldnt be able to do it again and he almost cried out with the pain. He unhitched the rope from the sad-dlehorn and backed the horse to where the captain was sitting. He had the rifle under his arm and he was watching the shed where the rifleman was holed up. He almost backed over the captain with the horse and he didnt care if he had. He told the charro to unhitch the rope from the stabledoor stanchion and bring it to him. He'd already figured out that there was bad blood between the two men. When the charro brought the rope end he told him to tie it to the captain's handcuffs and he did so and stepped back.

Gracias, said John Grady. He had coiled the rope and now he dallied it midrope to the horn and put the horse forward. When the captain saw his situation he stood up.

Momento, he called.

John Grady rode forward, watching the shed. The captain when he saw the slack rope running out along the ground called out to him and began to run, his hands behind him. Momento, he called.

When they rode out through the gate the captain was riding Redbo and he was doubled on behind him with his arm around the captain's waist. They led the Blevins horse on the rope and drove the other two horses before them. He was determined to get the four horses out of the stable yard if he died in the road and beyond that he had not thought much. His leg was numb and bleeding and felt heavy as a sack of meal and his boot was filling up with blood. When he passed through the gate the charro was standing there holding his hat and he reached down and took it from him and put it on and nodded.

Adiós, he said.

The charro nodded and stepped back. He put the horse forward and they went down the drive, him holding on to the captain and turned partly sideways with the rifle at his waist, watching back toward the corral. The charro was still at the gate but there was no sign of the other two men. The captain in the saddle before him smelled rank and sweaty. He'd partly unbuttoned the front of his tunic and had put his hand inside to sling the arm. When they passed the house there was no one about but by the time they reached the road there were half a dozen women and young girls from the kitchen all peering past the corner of the house.

In the road he got Junior and the grullo horse looseherded in front of him and with the Blevins horse on the leadrope behind they set out back toward Encantada at a trot. He didnt know if the grullo horse would try and quit them or not and he wished he had the spare saddle on Junior instead but there was nothing to be done about it. The captain complained about his shoulder and tried to take the reins and then he said he needed a doctor and then he said he needed to urinate. John Grady was watching the road behind. Go ahead, he said. You couldnt smell much worse.

It was a good ten minutes before the riders appeared, four of them at a hard gallop, leaning forward, holding their rifles out to one side. John Grady let go the reins and swiveled and cocked the rifle and fired. Blevins' horse stood twisting like a circus horse and the captain must have sawed back on Redbo's reins because he stopped dead in the middle of the road and John Grady fell against him and almost pushed him forward out of the saddle. Behind him the riders were pulling up their mounts and milling in the road and he levered a fresh round into the rifle and fired again and by now Redbo had turned in the road to face the pull of the rope and the Blevins horse was wholly out of control and he swung around and whacked the captain's arm with the barrel of the rifle to make him drop the reins and he took the reins up and hauled Redbo around and whacked him with the rifle and looked back again. The riders had quit the road but he saw the last horse disappear into the brush and he knew which side they'd taken. He leaned down and got hold of the rope and drew the walleyed horse to him and coiled the rope and snubbed the horse up short and whacked Redbo again and trotting side by side they overtook the two horses in the road before them and herded them off into the brush and out onto the rolling country west of the town. The captain half turned to him with some new complaint but he only hugged his loathe-some charge more fondly, the captain tottering woodenly in the saddle before him with his pain like a storedummy carried off for a prank.

They rode down into a broad flat arroyo and he put the horses into a lope, his leg throbbing horribly and the captain crying out to be left. The arroyo bore east by the sun and they followed it for a good distance until it began to narrow and grow rocky and the loose horses before him to step cautiously and look toward the slopes above them. He hazed them on and they clambered up through traprock fallen from the rim country above and they led up onto the northfacing slope and along a barren gravel ridge where he gripped the captain anew and looked back. The riders were fanned over the open country a mile below him and he counted not four but six of them before they dropped from sight into a draw. He loosed the rope from

the saddlehorn in front of the captain and dallied it again with
more slack.

You must owe them sons of bitches money, he said.

He put the horse forward again and caught up to the other
horses standing looking back a hundred feet out along the ridge.
There was no place to go up the draw and no place to hide in the
open country beyond. He needed fifteen minutes and he didnt
have them. He slid down and caught the Purísima horse, hobbling after it on one leg and the horse shifting and eyeing him
nervously. He unhitched the bridlereins from about the saddlehorn and stood into the stirrup and pulled himself painfully
onto the horse and turned and looked at the captain.

I want you to follow me, he said. And I know what you're
thinkin. But if you think I cant ride you down you better think
some more. And if I have to come get you I'm goin to whip you
like a dog. Me entiende?

The captain didnt answer. He managed a sardonic smile and
John Grady nodded. You just keep smilin. When I die you die.

He turned the horse and rode back down into the arroyo. The
captain followed. At the rockslide he dismounted and tied the
horse and took out a cigarette and lit it and hobbled up around
the tumbled rocks and boulders carrying the rifle. In the sheltered lee of the slide he stopped and took the captain's pistol out
of his belt and laid it on the ground and he took out his knife and
cut a long narrow strip from his shirt and twisted it into a string.
Then he cut the string in two and tied the trigger back on the
pistol. He wrapped it tightly so as to depress the grip safety and
he broke off a dead limb and tied the other string to it and tied
the free end to the hammer of the pistol. He put a goodsized
rock on top of the stick to hold it and he stretched the pistol out
until the string cocked the hammer and then laid the pistol
down and rolled a rock over it and when he slowly released it it
held. He took a good draw on the cigarette to get it burning and
then laid it carefully across the string and stepped back and
picked up the rifle and turned and hobbled back out to where
the horses stood.

He took the waterbottles and he slid the bridle down off the grullo's head and caught it and he stroked the grullo under the jaw. I hate to leave you old pardner, he said. You been a goodn.

He handed the waterbottles up to the captain and slung the bridle over his shoulder and reached a hand up and the captain looked down at him and then reached down with his good hand and he struggled up onto the horse behind the captain and reached around and took the reins and turned the horse back up the ridge again.

He caught up the loose horses and drove them down off the ridge and out across the open country. The ground was volcanic gravel and not easy to track a horse over but not impossible either. He pushed the horses hard. There was a low rocky mesa two miles across the floodplain and he could see trees and the promise of broken country. Not half way across he heard the dead flat pop of the pistol he'd been listening for.

Captain, he said. You just fired a shot for the common man.

The trees he'd seen from the distance were the breaks of a dry rivercourse and he pushed the horses through the brush and entered a stand of cottonwoods and turned the horse and sat watching back across the plain they'd traversed. There were no riders in sight. He looked at the sun in the south and he judged it a good four hours till dark. The horse was hot and lathered and he looked back across the open country one more time and then pushed on to where the other two horses were standing upriver in a grove of willows drinking from a riverbed pothole. He rode alongside them and slid to the ground and caught Junior and took the bridle from his shoulder and bridled him with it and with the rifle motioned the captain down off the horse. He unbuckled the girthstraps and pulled the saddle and the blanket down onto the ground and picked up the blanket and threw it over Junior and leaned against him to get his breath. His leg was beginning to hurt horribly. He stood the rifle against the actual horse and picked up the saddle and managed to get it on and he pulled the girthstrap and rested and he and the horse blew and then he pulled the strap again and cinched it.

He picked up the rifle and turned to the captain.

You want a drink of water you better get you one, he said.

The captain walked up past the horses holding his arm and he knelt and drank and laved water over the back of his neck with his good hand. When he rose he looked very serious.

Why you no leave me here? he said.

I aint leavin you here. You're a hostage.

Mande?

Let's go.

The captain stood uncertainly.

Why you come back? he said.

I come back for my horse. Let's go.

The captain nodded at the wound in his leg, still bleeding. The whole trouserleg dark with blood.

You going to die, he said.

We'll let God decide about that. Let's go.

Are you no afraid of God?

I got no reason to be afraid of God. I've even got a bone or two to pick with Him.

You should be afraid of God, the captain said. You are not the officer of the law. You dont have no authority.

John Grady stood leaning on the rifle. He turned and spat dryly and eyed the captain.

Get on that horse, he said. You ride ahead of me. You drift out of my sight and I'll shoot you.

Nightfall found them in the foothills of the Sierra Encantada. They followed a dry watercourse up under a dark rincón in the rocks and picked their way over a flood barricade of boulders tumbled in the floor of the wash and emerged upon a stone tinaja in the center of which lay a shallow basin of water, perfectly round, perfectly black, where the night stars were lensed in perfect stillness. The loose horses walked uncertainly down the shallow rock incline of the basin and blew at the water and drank.

They dismounted and walked around to the far side of the
tinaja and lay on their bellies on the rocks where the day's heat
was still rising and sucked at the water cool and soft and black
as velvet and they laved water over their faces and the backs of
their necks and watched the horses drink and then drank again.

He left the captain at the tank and hobbled with the rifle up
the arroyo and gathered dead floodwash brush and hobbled
back and made a fire at the upper end of the basin. He fanned
the blaze with his hat and piled on more wood. The horses in
the firelight reflected off the water were rimed with drying
sweat and shifted pale and ghostly and blinked their red eyes.
He looked at the captain. The captain was lying on his side on
the smooth rock incline of the basin like something that had not
quite made it to water.

He limped around to the horses and got the rope and sat with
his knife and cut hobbles from it for all the horses and looped
them about their forefeet. Then he levered all the shells out of
the rifle and put them in his pocket and took one of the water
bottles and went back to the fire.

He fanned the fire and he took the pistol out of his belt and
pulled the cylinder pin and put the loaded cylinder and the pin
in his pocket along with the rifle shells. Then he took out his
knife and with the point of it unscrewed the screw from the
grips and put the grips and the screw into his other pocket. He
fanned the coals in the heart of the fire with his hat and with a
stick he raked them into a pile and then he bent and stuck the
barrel of the pistol into the coals.

The captain had sat up to look at him.

They will find you, he said. In this place.

We aint stayin in this place.

I cant ride no more.

You'll be surprised at what you can do.

He took off his shirt and soaked it in the tinaja and came back
to the fire and he fanned the fire again with his hat and then he
pulled off his boots and unbuckled his belt and let down his
trousers.

The rifle bullet had entered his thigh high up on the outside and the exit wound was in a rotation at the rear such that by turning his leg he could see both wounds clearly. He took up the wet shirt and very carefully wiped away the blood until the wounds were clear and stark as two holes in a mask. The area around the wounds was discolored and looked blue in the fire-light and the skin around that was yellow. He leaned and ran a stick through the gripframes of the pistol and swung it up and away from the fire into his shadow and looked at it and then put it back. The captain was sitting holding his arm in his lap and watching him.

It's fixin to get kindly noisy in here, he said. Watch out you dont get run over by a horse.

The captain didnt answer. He watched him while he fanned the fire. When next he dragged the pistol from the coals the end of the barrel glowed at a dull red heat and he laid it on the rocks and picked it up quickly by the grips in the wet shirt and jammed the redhot barrel ash and all down into the hole in his leg.

The captain either did not know what he was going to do or knowing did not believe. He tried to rise to his feet and fell backwards and almost slid into the tinaja. John Grady had be-gun to shout even before the gunmetal hissed in the meat. His shout clapped shut the calls of lesser creatures everywhere about them in the night and the horses all stood swimming up into the darkness beyond the fire and squatting in terror on their great thighs screaming and pawing the stars and he drew breath and howled again and jammed the gunbarrel into the second wound and held it the longer in deference to the cooling of the metal and then he fell over on his side and dropped the revolver on the rocks where it clattered and turned and slid down the basin and vanished hissing into the pool.

He'd seized the fleshy part of his thumb in his teeth, shaking in agony. With the other hand he reached for the waterbottle standing unstoppered on the rocks and poured water over his leg and heard the flesh hiss like something on a spit and he gasped and let the bottle fall and he raised up and called out his horse's name to him softly where he scrabbled and fell on the rocks in his hobbles among the others that he might ease the fright in the horse's heart.

When he turned and reached for the water bottle where it lay draining on the rocks the captain kicked it away with his boot. He looked up. He was standing over him with the rifle. He held it with the stock under his armpit and he gestured upward with it.

Get up, he said.

He pushed himself up on the rocks and looked across the tank toward the horses. He could only see two of them and he thought the third one must have run out down the arroyo and he couldnt tell which one was missing but guessed it was the Blevins horse. He got hold of his belt and managed to get his breeches back on.

Where is the keys? said the captain.

He pushed himself up and rose and turned and took the rifle away from the captain. The hammer dropped with a dull metallic snap.

Get back over there and set down, he said.

The captain hesitated. The man's dark eyes were turned toward the fire and he could see the calculation in them and he was in such a rage of pain he thought he might have killed him had the gun been loaded. He grabbed the chain between the handcuffs and yanked the man past him and the captain gave out a low cry and went tottering off bent over and holding his arm.

He got the shells out and sat and reloaded the rifle. He reloaded it one shell at a time sweating and wheezing and trying to concentrate. He hadnt known how stupid pain could make you and he thought it should be the other way around or what was the good of it. When he'd got the rifle loaded he picked up the wet rag of a shirt and used it to carry a brand from the fire down to the edge of the tank where he stood holding it out over the water. The water was dead clear in the stone pool and he could see the pistol and he waded out and bent and picked it up and stuck it in his belt. He walked out in the tank till the water was to his thigh which was as deep as it got and he stood there soaking the blood out of his trousers and the fire out of his wounds and talking to his horse. The horse limped down to the edge of the water and stood and he stood in the dark tinaja with the rifle over his shoulder holding the brand above him until it burned out and then he stood holding the crooked orange ember of it, still talking to the horse.

They left the fire burning in the tank and rode out down the draw and picked up the Blevins horse and pushed on. The night was overcast to the south the way they'd come and there was rain in the air. He rode Redbo bareback in the fore of their little caravan and he held up from time to time to listen but there was nothing to hear. The fire in the tank behind them was invisible save for the play of it on the rocks of the rincón and as they rode it receded to a faint glow pocketed in the otherwise dark of the desert night and then vanished altogether.

They rode up out of the wash and went on along the south-facing slope of the ridge, the country dark and silent and without boundary and the tall aloes passing blackly along the ridge one by one. He reckoned it to be some time past midnight. He looked back at the captain from time to time but the captain rode slumped in the saddle on Rawlins' horse and seemed much reduced by his adventures. They rode on. He'd knotted his wet rag of a shirt through his belt and he rode naked to the waist and he was very cold and he told the horse that it was going to be a long night and it was. Sometime in the night he fell asleep. The clatter of the rifle dropping on the rocky ground woke him and he pulled up and turned and rode back. He sat looking down at the rifle. The captain sat Rawlins' horse watching him. He wasnt sure he could get back on the horse and he thought about leaving the rifle there. In the end he slid down and picked up the rifle and then led the horse up along Junior's offside and told the captain to shuck his foot out of the stirrup and he used the stirrup to mount up onto his own horse and they rode on again.

Dawn found him sitting alone on the gravel face of the slope with the rifle leaning against his shoulder and the waterbottle at his feet watching the shape of the desert country form itself out of the gray light. Mesa and plain, the dark shape of the mountains to the east beyond which the sun was rising.

He picked up the waterbottle and twisted out the stopper and drank and sat holding the bottle. Then he drank again. The first bars of sunlight broke past the rock buttes of the mountains to the east and fell fifty miles across the plain. Nothing moved. On the facing slope of the valley a mile away seven deer stood watching him.

He sat for a long time. When he climbed back up the ridge to the cedars where he'd left the horses the captain was sitting on the ground and he looked badly used up.

Let's go, he said.

The captain looked up. I can go no farther, he said.

Let's go, he said. Podemos descansar un poco mas adelante. Vámonos.

They rode down off the ridge and up a long narrow valley looking for water but there was no water. They climbed out and crossed into the valley to the east and the sun was well up and felt good on his back and he tied the shirt around his waist so it would dry. By the time they crested out above the valley it was midmorning and the horses were in badly failing plight and it occurred to him that the captain might die.

The water they found was at a stone stocktank and they dismounted and drank from the standpipe and watered the horses and sat in the bands of shade from the dead and twisted oaks at the tank and watched the open country below them. A few cattle stood perhaps a mile away. They were looking to the east, not grazing. He turned to see what they were watching but there was nothing there. He looked at the captain, a gray and shrunken figure. The heel was missing from one boot. There were streaks of black and streaks of ash on his trouserlegs from the fire and his buckled belt hung in a loop from his neck where he'd been using it to sling his arm.

I aint goin to kill you, he said. I'm not like you.

The captain didnt answer.

He pulled himself up and took out the keys from his pocket and using the rifle to steady himself he hobbled over and bent and took hold of the captain's wrists and unmanacled them. The captain looked down at his wrists. They were discolored and raw from the cuffs and he sat rubbing them gently. John Grady stood over him.

Take off your shirt, he said. I'm goin to pull that shoulder.

Mande? said the captain.

Quítese su camisa.

The captain shook his head and held his arm against him like a child.

Dont sull up on me. I aint askin, I'm tellin.

Cómo?

No tiene otra salida.

He got the captain's shirt off and spread it out and made him lie on his back. The shoulder was badly discolored and his whole upper arm was a deep blue. He looked up. The beaded sweat glistened on his forehead. John Grady sat and put his booted foot in the captain's armpit and gripped the captain's arm by the wrist and upper elbow and rotated it slightly. The captain looked at him like a man falling from a cliff.

Dont worry, he said. My family's been practicin medicine on Mexicans a hundred years.

If the captain had made up his mind not to cry out he did not succeed. The horses started and milled and tried to hide behind one another. He reached up and grabbed his arm as if he'd reclaim it but John Grady had felt the coupling pop into place and he gripped the shoulder and rotated the arm again while the captain tossed his head and gasped. Then he let him go and picked up the rifle and rose.

Está compuesto? wheezed the captain.

Yeah. You're all set.

He held his arm and lay blinking.

Put on your shirt and let's go, said John Grady. We aint settin out here in the open till your friends show up.

Ascending into the low hills they passed a small estancia and they dismounted and went afoot through the ruins of a cornfield and found some melons and sat in the stony washedout furrows and ate them. He hobbled down the rows and gathered melons and carried them out through the field to where the horses stood and broke them open on the ground at their feet for them to feed on and he stood leaning on the rifle and looked toward the house. Some turkeys stepped about in the yard and there was a pole corral beyond the house in which stood several horses. He went back and got the captain and they mounted up and rode on. When he looked back from the ridge above the estancia he could see that it was more extensive. There was a cluster of buildings above the house and he could see the quadrangles laid out by the fences and the adobe walls and irrigation ditches. A number of rangy and slatribbed cattle stood about in the scrub. He heard a rooster crow in the noon heat. He heard a steady distant hammering of metal as of someone at a forge.

They plodded on at a poor pace up through the hills. He'd unloaded the rifle to save carrying it and it was tied along the saddleskirt of the captain's horse and he had reassembled the fireblackened revolver and loaded it and put it in his belt. He rode Blevins' horse and the animal had an easy gait and his leg had not stopped hurting but it was the only thing keeping him awake.

In the early evening from the eastern rim of the mesa he sat and studied the country while the horses rested. A hawk and a hawk's shadow that skated like a paper bird crossed the slopes below. He studied the terrain beyond and after a while he saw riders riding. They were perhaps five miles away. He watched them and they dropped from sight into a cut or into a shadow. Then they appeared again.

He mounted up and they rode on. The captain slept tottering in the saddle with his arm slung through his belt. It was cool in the higher country and when the sun set it was going to be cold. He pushed on and before dark they found a deep ravine in the north slope of the ridge they'd crossed and they descended and found standing water among the rocks and the horses clambered and scrabbled their way down and stood drinking.

He unsaddled Junior and cuffed the captain's bracelets through the wooden stirrups and told him he was free to go as far as he thought he could carry the saddle. Then he built a fire in the rocks and kicked out a place in the ground for his hip and lay down and stretched out his aching leg and put the pistol in his belt and closed his eyes.

In his sleep he could hear the horses stepping among the rocks and he could hear them drink from the shallow pools in the dark where the rocks lay smooth and rectilinear as the stones of ancient ruins and the water from their muzzles dripped and rang like water dripping in a well and in his sleep he dreamt of horses and the horses in his dream moved gravely among the tilted stones like horses come upon an antique site where some ordering of the world had failed and if anything had been written on the stones the weathers had taken it away again and the horses were wary and moved with great circumspection carrying in their blood as they did the recollection of this and other places where horses once had been and would be again. Finally what he saw in his dream was that the order in the horse's heart was more durable for it was written in a place where no rain could erase it.

When he woke there were three men standing over him. They wore serapes over their shoulders and one of them was holding the empty rifle and all of them wore pistols. The fire was burning from brush they'd piled on it but he was very cold and he had no way to know how long he'd been sleeping. He sat up. The man with the rifle snapped his fingers and held out his hand.

Deme las llaves, he said.

He reached into his pocket and took out the keys and handed them up. He and one of the other men walked over to where the captain sat chained to the saddle at the far side of the fire. The third man stood by him. They freed the captain and the one carrying the rifle came back.

Cuáles de los caballos son suyos? he said.

Todos son míos.

The man studied his eyes in the firelight. He walked back to the others and they talked. When they came past with the captain the captain's hands were cuffed behind him. The man carrying the rifle levered the action open and when he saw that the gun was empty stood it against a rock. He looked at John Grady.

Dónde está su serape? he said.

No tengo.

The man loosed the blanket from his own shoulders and swung it in a slow veronica and handed it to him. Then he turned and they passed on out of the firelight to where their horses were standing in the dark with other companions, other horses.

Quiénes son ustedes? he called.

The man who'd given him his serape turned at the outer edge of the light and touched the brim of his hat. Hombres del país, he said. Then all went on.

Men of the country. He sat listening as they rode up out of the ravine and then they were gone. He never saw them again. In the morning he saddled Redbo and driving the other two horses before him he rode up from the ravine and turned north along the mesa.

He rode all day and the day clouded before him and a cool wind was coming downcountry. He'd reloaded the rifle and he carried it across the bow of the saddle and rode with the serape over his shoulders and looseherded the riderless horses before him. By evening all the north country was black and the wind was cold and he picked his way across the rim country through the sparse swales of grass and broken volcanic rock and he sat above a highland bajada in the cold blue dusk with the rifle across his knee while the staked horses grazed behind him and at the last hour light enough by which to see the iron sights of the rifle five deer entered the bajada and pricked their ears and stood and then bent to graze.

He picked out the smallest doe among them and shot her. Blevins' horse rose howling where he'd tied it and the deer in the bajada leapt away and vanished in the dusk and the little doe lay kicking.

When he reached her she lay in her blood in the grass and he knelt with the rifle and put his hand on her neck and she looked at him and her eyes were warm and wet and there was no fear in them and then she died. He sat watching her for a long time. He thought about the captain and he wondered if he were alive and he thought about Blevins. He thought about Alejandra and he remembered her the first time he ever saw her passing along the ciénaga road in the evening with the horse still wet from her riding it in the lake and he remembered the birds and the cattle standing in the grass and the horses on the mesa. The sky was dark and a cold wind ran through the bajada and in the dying light a cold blue cast had turned the doe's eyes to but one thing more of things she lay among in that darkening landscape. Grass and blood. Blood and stone. Stone and the dark medallions that the first flat drops of rain caused upon them. He remembered Alejandra and the sadness he'd first seen in the slope of her shoulders which he'd presumed to understand and of which he knew nothing and he felt a loneliness he'd not known since he was a child and he felt wholly alien to the world although he loved it still. He thought that in the beauty of the world were hid a secret. He thought the world's heart beat at some terrible cost and that the world's pain and its beauty moved in a relationship of diverging equity and that in this headlong deficit the blood of multitudes might ultimately be exacted for the vision of a single flower.

In the morning the sky was clear and it was very cold and there was snow on the mountains to the north. When he woke he realized that he knew his father was dead. He raked up the coals and blew the fire to life and roasted strips cut from the

deer's haunch and cowled in his blanket he sat eating and watching the country to the south out of which he'd ridden.

They moved on. By noon the horses were in snow and there
was snow in the pass and the horses trod and broke thin plates
of ice in the trail where the snowmelt ran out over the wet black
ground dark as ink and they toiled up through the patches of
snow glazing over in the sun and rode through a dark corridor
of fir trees and descended along the northern slope through
pockets of sunlight, pockets of shadow, where the air smelled of
rosin and wet stone and no birds sang.

In the evening descending he saw lights in the distance and he
pushed on toward them and did not stop and in the dead of
night in deep exhaustion both he and the horses they reached
the town of Los Picos.

A single mud street rutted from the recent rains. A squalid
alameda where there stood a rotting brushwood gazebo and a
few old iron benches. The trees in the alameda had been freshly
whitewashed and the upper trunks were lost in the dark above
the light of the few lamps yet burning so that they looked like
plaster stagetrees new from the mold. The horses stepped with
great weariness among the dried rails of mud in the street and
dogs barked at them from behind the wooden gates and doors
they passed.

It was cold when he woke in the morning and it was raining
again. He'd bivouacked on the north side of the town and he
rose wet and cold and stinking and saddled the horse and rode
back into the town wrapped in the serape and driving the two
horses before him.

In the alameda a few small tin foldingtables had been set out
and young girls were stringing paper ribbon overhead. They
were wet from the rain and they were laughing and they were
throwing the spools of crepe over the wires and catching them
again and the dye was coming off the paper so that their hands
were red and green and blue. He tied the horses in front of the
tienda he'd passed the night before and went in and bought a sack
of oats for the horses and he borrowed a galvanized bucket with

which to water them and he stood in the alameda leaning on the rifle and watching them drink. He thought he'd be an object of some curiosity but the people he saw only nodded gravely to him and passed on. He carried the bucket back into the store and went down the street to where there was a small cafe and he entered and sat at one of the three small wooden tables. The floor of the cafe was packed mud newly swept and he was the only customer. He stood the rifle against the wall and ordered huevos revueltos and a cup of chocolate and he sat and waited for it to come and then he ate very slowly. The food was rich to his taste and the chocolate was made with canela and he drank it and ordered another and folded a tortilla and ate and watched the horses standing in the square across the street and watched the girls. They'd hung the gazebo with crepe and it looked like a festooned brush-pile. The proprietor showed him great courtesy and brought him fresh tortillas hot from the comal and told him that there was to be a wedding and that it would be a pity if it rained. He inquired where he might be from and showed surprise he'd come so far. He stood at the window of the empty cafe and watched the activities in the square and he said that it was good that God kept the truths of life from the young as they were starting out or else they'd have no heart to start at all.

By midmorning the rain had stopped. Water dripped from the trees in the alameda and the crepe hung in soggy strings. He stood with the horses and watched the wedding party emerge from the church. The groom wore a dull black suit too large for him and he looked not uneasy but half desperate, as if unused to clothes at all. The bride was embarrassed and clung to him and they stood on the steps for their photograph to be taken and in their antique formalwear posed there in front of the church they already had the look of old photos. In the sepia monochrome of a rainy day in that lost village they'd grown old instantly.

In the alameda an old woman in a black rebozo was going about tilting the metal tables and chairs to let the water run off. She and others began to set out food from pails and baskets and a group of three musicians in soiled silver suits stood by with their instruments. The groom took the bride's hand to help her negotiate the water standing in front of the church steps. In the water they were gray figures reflected against a gray sky. A small boy ran out and stamped in the puddle and sprayed a sheet of the muddy gray water over them and ran away with his companions. The bride clutched her husband. He scowled and looked after the boys but there was nothing to be done and she looked down at her dress and she looked at him and then she laughed. Then the husband laughed and others in the party also and they crossed the road laughing and looking from one to the other and entered the alameda among the tables and the musicians began to play.

With the last of his money he bought coffee and tortillas and some tinned fruit and beans. The tins had been on the shelves so long they'd tarnished and the labels faded. When he passed out along the road the wedding party was seated at the tables eating and the musicians had stopped playing and were squatting together drinking from tin cups. A man sitting alone on one of the benches who seemed no part of the wedding looked up at the sound of the slow hooves in the road and raised one hand to the pale rider passing with blanket and rifle and he raised a hand back and then rode on.

He rode out past the last low mudbuilt houses and took the road north, a mud track that wound up through the barren gravel hills and branched and broke and finally terminated in the tailings of an abandoned mine among the rusted shapes of pipe and pumpstanchions and old jacktimbers. He crossed on through the high country and in the evening descended the north slope and rode out onto the foreplain where the creosote deep olive from the rains stood in solemn colonies as it had stood a thousand years and more in that tenantless waste, older than any living thing that was.

He rode on, the two horses following, riding doves up out of the pools of standing water and the sun descending out of the dark discolored overcast to the west where its redness ran down the narrow band of sky above the mountains like blood falling through water and the desert fresh from the rain turning gold in the evening light and then deepening to dark, a slow inkening over of the bajada and the rising hills and the stark stone length of the cordilleras darkening far to the south in Mexico. The floodplain he crossed was walled about with fallen traprock and in the twilight the little desert foxes had come out to sit along the walls silent and regal as icons watching the night come and the doves called from the acacia and then night fell dark as Egypt and there was just the stillness and the silence and the sound of the horses breathing and the sound of their hooves clopping in the dark. He pointed his horse at the polestar and rode on and they rode the round moon up out of the east and coyotes yammered and answered back all across the plain to the south from which they'd come.

He crossed the river just west of Langtry Texas in a softly falling rain. The wind in the north, the day cold. The cattle along the breaks of the river standing gray and still. He followed a cattletrail down into the willows and across the carrizal to where the gray water lay braided over the gravels.

He studied the cold gray rips in the current and dismounted and loosed the girthstraps and undressed and stogged his boots in the legs of his trousers as he'd done before in that long ago and he put his shirt and jacket and the pistol after and doubled the belt in the loops to draw shut the waist. Then he slung the trousers over his shoulder and mounted up naked with the rifle aloft and driving the loose horses before him he pushed Redbo into the river.

He rode up onto Texas soil pale and shivering and he sat the horse briefly and looked out over the plain to the north where cattle were already beginning to appear slouching slowly out of that pale landscape and bawling softly at the horses and he thought about his father who was dead in that country and he sat the horse naked in the falling rain and wept.

When he rode into Langtry it was early in the afternoon and

it was still raining. The first thing he saw was a pickup truck
with the hood up and two men trying to start it. One of them
raised up and looked at him. He must have appeared to them
some apparition out of the vanished past because he jostled the
other with his elbow and they both looked.

Howdy, said John Grady. I wonder if you all could tell me
what day this is?

They looked at each other.

It's Thursday, the first one said.

I mean the date.

The man looked at him. He looked at the horses standing
behind him. The date? he said.

Yessir.

It's Thanksgiving day, the other man said.

He looked at them. He looked out down the street.

Is that cafe yonder open?

Yeah, its open.

He lifted his hand off the pommel and was about to touch up
the horse and then he stopped.

Dont neither of you all want to buy a rifle do you? he said.

They looked at each other.

Earl might buy it off of you, the first man said. He'll generally try and help a feller out.

He the man that runs the cafe?

Yep.

He touched the brim of his hat. Much obliged, he said. Then
he put the horse forward and rode on down the street trailing
the loose horses behind him. They watched him go. Neither
spoke for there was nothing to say. The one holding the socket-
wrench put the wrench on the fender and they both stood
watching until he turned the corner at the cafe and there was
nothing more to see.

He rode the border country for weeks seeking the owner of
the horse. In Ozona just before Christmas three men swore out
papers and the county constable impounded the animal. The

hearing was held in the judge's chambers in the old stone court-house and the clerk read the charges and the names and the judge turned and looked down at John Grady.

Son, he said, are you represented by counsel?

No sir I aint, said John Grady. I dont need a lawyer. I just need to tell you about this horse.

The judge nodded. All right, he said. Go ahead.

Yessir. If you dont care I'd like to tell it from the beginning. From the first time ever I seen the horse.

Well if you'd like to tell it we'd like to hear it so just go ahead.

It took him almost half an hour. When he was done he asked if he could have a glass of water. No one spoke. The judge turned to the clerk.

Emil, get the boy a glass of water.

He looked at his notepad and he turned to John Grady.

Son, I'm fixin to ask you three questions and if you can answer em the horse is yours.

Yessir. I'll try.

Well you'll either know em or you wont. The trouble with a liar is he cant remember what he said.

I aint a liar.

I know you aint. This is just for the record. I dont believe anybody could make up the story you just now got done tellin us.

He put his glasses back on and he asked John Grady the number of hectares in the Nuestra Señora de la Purísima Concepción spread. Then he asked the name of the husband of the hacendado's cook. Lastly he laid down his notes and he asked John Grady if he had on clean shorts.

A subdued laughter went around the courtroom but the judge wasnt laughing nor the bailiff.

Yessir. I do.

Well there aint no women present so if you wouldnt find it to be too much of a embarrassment I'd like for you to show the court them bulletholes in your leg. If you dont want to I'll ask you somethin else.

Yessir, said John Grady. He unbuckled his belt and dropped his trousers to his knees and turned his right leg sideways to the judge.

That's fine son. Thank you. Get your water there.

He pulled up his trousers and buttoned them and buckled his belt and reached and got the glass of water from the table where the clerk had set it and drank.

Them are some nasty lookin holes, said the judge. You didnt have no medical attention?

No sir. There wasnt none to be had.

I guess not. You were lucky not to of got gangrene.

Yessir. I burnt em out pretty good.

Burnt em out?

Yessir.

What did you burn em out with?

A pistolbarrel. I burnt em out with a hot pistolbarrel.

There was absolute silence in the courtroom. The judge leaned back.

The constable is instructed to return the property in question to Mr Cole. Mr Smith, you see that the boy gets his horse. Son, you're free to go and the court thanks you for your testimony. I've sat on the bench in this county since it was a county and in that time I've heard a lot of things that give me grave doubts about the human race but this aint one of em. The three plaintiffs in this case I'd like to see here in my chambers after dinner. That means one oclock.

The lawyer for the plaintiffs stood up. Your honor, this is pretty clearly a case of mistook identity.

The judge closed his notebook and rose. Yes it is, he said. Bad mistook. This hearing is dismissed.

That night he knocked at the judge's door while there were still lights on downstairs in the house. A Mexican girl came to the door and asked him what he wanted and he said he wanted to see the judge. He said it in spanish and she repeated it back to him in english with a certain coldness and told him to wait.

The judge when he appeared at the door was still dressed but he had on an old flannel bathrobe. If he was surprised to find the boy on his porch he didnt show it. He pushed open the screen door.

Come in son, he said. Come in.

I didnt want to bother you.

It's all right.

John Grady gripped his hat.

I aint comin out there, said the judge. So if you want to see me you better come on in.

Yessir.

He entered a long hallway. A balustered staircase rose on his right to the upper floor. The house smelled of cooking and furniture polish. The judge was wearing leather slippers and he went silently down the carpeted hallway and entered an open door on the left. The room was filled with books and there was a fire burning in the fireplace.

We're in here, said the judge. Dixie, this is John Cole.

A grayhaired woman rose as he entered and smiled at him. Then she turned to the judge.

I'm goin up, Charles, she said.

All right, Mama.

He turned to John Grady. Set down, son.

John Grady sat and put his hat in his lap.

They sat.

Well go ahead, said the judge. There aint no time like the present.

Yessir. I guess what I wanted to say first of all was that it kindly bothered me in the court what you said. It was like I was in the right about everthing and I dont feel that way.

What way do you feel?

He sat looking at his hat. He sat for a long time. Finally he looked up. I dont feel justified, he said.

The judge nodded. You didnt misrepresent nothin to me about the horse did you?

No sir. It wasnt that.

What was it?

Well sir. The girl I reckon.

All right.

I worked for that man and I respected him and he never had no complaints about the work I done for him and he was awful good to me. And that man come up on the high range where I was workin and I believe he intended to kill me. And I was the one that brought it about. Nobody but me.

You didnt get the girl in a family way did you?

No sir. I was in love with her.

The judge nodded gravely. Well, he said. You could be in love with her and still knock her up.

Yessir.

The judge watched him. Son, he said, you strike me as somebody that maybe tends to be a little hard on theirselves. I think from what you told me you done real well to get out of there with a whole hide. Maybe the best thing to do might be just to go on and put it behind you. My daddy used to tell me not to chew on somethin that was eatin you.

Yessir.

There's somethin else, aint there?

Yessir.

What is it?

When I was in the penitentiary down there I killed a boy.

The judge sat back in his chair. Well, he said. I'm sorry to hear that.

It keeps botherin me.

You must have had some provocation.

I did. But it dont help. He tried to kill me with a knife. I just happened to get the best of him.

Why does it bother you?

I dont know. I dont know nothin about him. I never even knew his name. He could of been a pretty good old boy. I dont know. I dont know that he's supposed to be dead.

He looked up. His eyes were wet in the firelight. The judge sat watching him.

You know he wasnt a pretty good old boy. Dont you?

Yessir. I guess.

You wouldnt want to be a judge, would you?

No sir. I sure wouldnt.

I didnt either.

Sir?

I didnt want to be a judge. I was a young lawyer practicing in San Antonio and I come back out here when my daddy was sick and I went to work for the county prosecutor. I sure didnt want to be a judge. I think I felt a lot like you do. I still do.

What made you change your mind?

I dont know as I did change it. I just saw a lot of injustice in the court system and I saw people my own age in positions of authority that I had grown up with and knew for a calcified fact didnt have one damn lick of sense. I think I just didnt have any choice. Just didnt have any choice. I sent a boy from this county to the electric chair in Huntsville in nineteen thirty-two. I think about that. I dont think he was a pretty good old boy. But I think about it. Would I do it again? Yes I would.

I almost done it again.

Done what, killed somebody?

Yessir.

The Mexican captain?

Yessir. Captain. Whatever he was. He was what they call a madrina. Not even a real peace officer.

But you didnt.

No sir. I didnt.

They sat. The fire had burned to coals. Outside the wind was blowing and he was going to have to go out in it pretty soon.

I hadnt made up my mind about it though. I told myself that I had. But I hadnt. I dont know what would of happened if they hadnt of come and got him. I expect he's dead anyways.

He looked up from the fire at the judge.

I wasnt even mad at him. Or I didnt feel like I was. That boy he shot, I didnt hardly even know him. I felt bad about it. But he wasnt nothin to me.

Why do you think you wanted to kill him?

I dont know.

Well, said the judge. I guess that's somethin between you and the good Lord. Wouldnt you say?

Yessir. I didnt mean that I expected a answer. Maybe there aint no answer. It just bothered me that you might think I was somethin special. I aint.

Well that aint a bad way to be bothered.

He picked up his hat and held it in both hands. He looked like he was about to get up but he didnt get up.

The reason I wanted to kill him was because I stood there and let him walk that boy out in the trees and shoot him and I never said nothin.

Would it have done any good?

No sir. But that dont make it right.

The judge leaned from his chair and took the poker standing on the hearth and jostled the coals and stood the poker back and folded his hands and looked at the boy.

What would you have done if I'd found against you today?

I dont know.

Well, that's a fair answer I guess.

It wasnt their horse. It would of bothered me.

Yes, said the judge. I expect it would.

I need to find out who the horse belongs to. It's gotten to be like a millstone around my neck.

There's nothin wrong with you son. I think you'll get it sorted out.

Yessir. I guess I will. If I live.

He stood.

I thank you for your time. And for invitin me into your home and all.

The judge stood up. You come back and visit any time, he said.

Yessir. I appreciate it.

It was cold out but the judge stood on the porch in his robe and slippers while he untied the horse and got the other two horses sorted out and then mounted up. He turned the horse and looked at him standing in the doorlight and he raised his hand and the judge raised a hand back and he rode out down the street from pool to pool of lamplight until he had vanished in the dark.

ON THE SUNDAY MORNING following he was sitting in a cafe in Bracketville Texas drinking coffee. There was no one else in the cafe except the counterman and he was sitting on the last stool at the end of the counter smoking a cigarette and reading the paper. There was a radio playing behind the counter and after a while a voice said that it was the Jimmy Blevins Gospel Hour.

John Grady looked up. Where's that radio station comin from? he said.

That's Del Rio, said the counterman.

He got to Del Rio about four-thirty in the afternoon and by the time he found the Blevins house it was getting on toward dark. The reverend lived in a white frame house with a gravel drive and John Grady dismounted at the mailbox and led the horses up the drive to the back of the house and knocked at the kitchen door. A small blonde woman looked out. She opened the door.

Yes? she said. Can I help you?

Yes mam. Is the reverend Blevins at home?

What did you want to see him about?

Well. I guess I wanted to see him about a horse.

A horse?

Yes mam.

She looked past him at the standing animals. Which one is it? she said.

The bay. That biggest one.

He'll bless it, but he wont lay hands on.

Mam?

He wont lay hands on. Not on animals.

Who's out there, darlin? called a man from the kitchen.

A boy here with a horse, she called.

The reverend walked out on the porch. My my, he said. Look at them horses.

I'm sorry to bother you sir, but that aint your horse is it?

My horse? I never owned a horse in my life.

Did you want him to bless the horse or not? said the woman.

Did you know a boy about fourteen years old named Jimmy Blevins?

We had a mule one time when I was growin up. Big mule. Mean rascal too. Boy named Jimmy Blevins? You mean just plain Jimmy Blevins?

Yessir.

No. No. Not that I recollect. There's any number of Jimmy Blevinses out there in the world but its Jimmy Blevins Smith and Jimmy Blevins Jones. There aint a week passes we dont get one or two letters tellin us about a new Jimmy Blevins this or Jimmy Blevins that. Aint that right darlin?

That's right reverend.

We get em from overseas you know. Jimmy Blevins Chang. That was one we had here recent. Little old yeller baby. They send photos you know. Snapshots. What was your name?

Cole. John Grady Cole.

The reverend extended his hand and they shook, the reverend thoughtful. Cole, he said. We may of had a Cole. I'd hate to say we hadnt. Have you had your supper?

No sir.

Darlin maybe Mr Cole would like to take supper with us. You like chicken and dumplins Mr Cole?

Yessir I do. I been partial to em all my life.

Well you're fixin to get more partial cause my wife makes the best you ever ate.

They ate in the kitchen. She said: We just eat in the kitchen now that there's just the two of us.

He didnt ask who was missing. The reverend waited for her to be seated and then he bowed his head and blessed the food and the table and the people sitting at it. He went on at some length and blessed everything all the way up to the country and then he blessed some other countries as well and he spoke about war and famine and the missions and other problems in the world with particular reference to Russia and the jews and cannibalism and he asked it all in Christ's name amen and raised up and reached for the cornbread.

People always want to know how I got started, he said. Well, it was no mystery to me. Whenever I first heard a radio I knew what it was for and it wasnt no questions about it neither. My mother's brother built a crystal set. Bought it through the mail. It come in a box and you put it together. We lived in south Georgia and we'd heard about the radio of course. But we never had actually seen one play with our own eyes. It's a world of difference. Well. I knew what it was for. Because there couldnt be no more excuses, you see. A man might harden his heart to where he could no longer hear the word of God, but you turn the radio up real loud? Well, hardness of heart wont do it no more. He's got to be deaf as a post besides. There's a purpose for everthing in this world, you see. Sometimes it might be hard to see what it is. But the radio? Well my my. You cant make it no plainer than that. The radio was in my plans from the start. It's what brought me to the ministry.

He loaded his plate as he talked and then he stopped talking and ate. He was not a large man but he ate two huge platefuls and then a large helping of peach cobbler and he drank several large glasses of buttermilk.

When he was done he wiped his mouth and pushed back his chair. Well, he said. You all excuse me. I got to go to work. The Lord dont take no holidays.

He rose and disappeared into the house. The woman dished out for John Grady a second helping of the cobbler and he thanked her and she sat back down and watched him eat it.

He was the first one to have you put your hands on the radio you know, she said.

Mam?

He started that. Puttin your hands on the radio. He'd pray

over the radio and heal everbody that was settin there with their hands on the radio.

Yes mam.

Fore that he'd have people send in things and he'd pray over em but there was a lot of problems connected with that. People expect a lot of a minister of God. He cured a lot of people and of course everbody heard about it over the radio and I dont like to say this but it got bad. I thought it did.

He ate. She watched him.

They sent dead people, she said.

Mam?

They sent dead people. Crated em up and shipped em railway express. It got out of hand. You cant do nothin with a dead person. Only Jesus could do that.

Yes mam.

Did you want some more buttermilk?

Yes please mam. This is awful good.

Well I'm glad you're enjoyin it.

She poured his glass and sat again.

He works so hard for his ministry. People have no idea. Did you know his voice reaches all over the world?

Is that right?

We've got letters from China. It's hard to imagine. Them little old people settin around their radios over there. Listenin to Jimmy.

I wouldnt think they'd know what he was sayin.

Letters from France. Letters from Spain. The whole world. His voice is like a instrument, you see. When he has the layin on of the hands? They could be in Timbuctoo. They could be on the south pole. It dont make no difference. His voice is there. There's not anyplace you can go he aint there. In the air. All the time. You just turn on your radio.

Of course they tried to close the station down, but it's over in Mexico. That's why Dr Brinkley come here. To found that radio station. Did you know that they can hear it on Mars?

No mam.

Well they can. When I think about them up there hearin the words of Jesus for the very first time it just makes me want to cry. It does. And Jimmy Blevins done it. He was the one.

From inside the house there sounded a long rattling snore. She smiled. Poor darlin, she said. He's just wore out. People have no idea.

He never found the owner of the horse. Along toward the end of February he drifted north again, trailing the horses in the bar ditches along the edge of the blacktop roads, the big semi's blowing them up against the fences. The first week of March he was back in San Angelo and he cut across the country so familiar to him and reached the Rawlins pasture fence just a little past dark on the first warm night of the year and no wind and everything dead still and clear on the west Texas plains. He rode up to the barn and dismounted and walked up to the house. There was a light on in Rawlins' room and he put two fingers to his teeth and whistled.

Rawlins came to the window and looked out. In a few minutes he came from the kitchen and around the side of the house.

Bud is that you?

Yeah.

Sum buck, he said. Sum buck.

He walked around him to get him in the light and he looked at him as if he were something rare.

I figured you might want your old horse back, said John Grady.

I caint believe it. You got Junior with you?

He's standin down yonder at the barn.

Sum buck, said Rawlins. I caint believe it. Sum buck.

They rode out on the prairie and sat on the ground and let the animals drift with the reins down and he told Rawlins all that had happened. They sat very quietly. The dead moon hung in the west and the long flat shapes of the nightclouds passed before it like a phantom fleet.

Have you been to see your mama? said Rawlins.

No.

You knew your daddy died.

Yeah. I guess I knew that.

She tried to get word to you in Mexico.

Yeah.

Luisa's mother is real sick.

Abuela?

Yeah.

How are they makin it?

I guess all right. I seen Arturo over in town. Thatcher Cole got him a job at the school. Cleanin up and stuff like that.

Is she goin to make it?

I dont know. She's pretty old.

Yeah.

What are you goin to do?

Head out.

Where to?

I dont know.

You could get on out on the rigs. Pays awful good.

Yeah. I know.

You could stay here at the house.

I think I'm goin to move on.

This is still good country.

Yeah. I know it is. But it aint my country.

He rose and turned and looked off toward the north where the lights of the city hung over the desert. Then he walked out and picked up the reins and mounted his horse and rode up and caught the Blevins horse by its halter.

Catch your horse, he said. Or else he'll follow me.

Rawlins walked out and caught the horse and stood holding it.

Where is your country? he said.

I dont know, said John Grady. I dont know where it is. I dont know what happens to country.

Rawlins didnt answer.

I'll see you old pardner, said John Grady.

All right. I'll see you.

He stood holding his horse while the rider turned and rode out and dropped slowly down the skyline. He squatted on his heels so as to watch him a little while longer but after a while he was gone.

THE DAY of the burial out at Knickerbocker it was cool and windy. He'd turned the horses into the pasture on the far side of the road and he sat for a long time watching down the road to the north where the weather was building and the sky was gray and after a while the funeral cortege appeared. An old Packard hearse with a varied assortment of dusty cars and trucks behind. They pulled up along the road in front of the little Mexican cemetery and people got out into the road and the pallbearers in their suits of faded black stood at the rear of the hearse and they carried Abuela's casket up through the gate into the cemetery. He stood across the road holding his hat. No one looked at him. They carried her up into the cemetery followed by a priest and a boy in a white gown ringing a bell and they buried her and they prayed and they wept and they wailed and then they came back down out of the cemetery into the road helping each other along and weeping and got into the cars and turned one by one on the narrow blacktop and went back the way they'd come.

The hearse had already gone. There was a pickup truck parked further down the road and he put on his hat and sat there on the slope of the bar ditch and in a little while two men came down the path out of the cemetery with shovels over their shoulders and they walked down the road and put the shovels in the bed of the truck and got in and turned around and drove away.

He stood and crossed the road and walked up into the cemetery past the old stonework crypt and past the little headstones and their small remembrances, the sunfaded paper flowers, a china vase, a broken celluloid Virgin. The names he knew or had known. Villareal, Sosa, Reyes. Jesusita Holguín. Nació.

Falleció. A china crane. A chipped milkglass vase. The rolling parklands beyond, wind in the cedars. Armendares. Ornelos. Tiodosa Tarín, Salomer Jáquez. Epitacio Villareal Cuéllar.

He stood hat in hand over the unmarked earth. This woman who had worked for his family fifty years. She had cared for his mother as a baby and she had worked for his family long before his mother was born and she had known and cared for the wild Grady boys who were his mother's uncles and who had all died so long ago and he stood holding his hat and he called her his abuela and he said goodbye to her in spanish and then turned and put on his hat and turned his wet face to the wind and for a moment he held out his hands as if to steady himself or as if to bless the ground there or perhaps as if to slow the world that was rushing away and seemed to care nothing for the old or the young or rich or poor or dark or pale or he or she. Nothing for their struggles, nothing for their names. Nothing for the living or the dead.

IN FOUR DAYS' riding he crossed the Pecos at Iraan Texas and rode up out of the river breaks where the pumpjacks in the Yates Field ranged against the skyline rose and dipped like mechanical birds. Like great primitive birds welded up out of iron by hearsay in a land perhaps where such birds once had been. At that time there were still indians camped on the western plains and late in the day he passed in his riding a scattered group of their wickiups propped upon that scoured and trembling waste. They were perhaps a quarter mile to the north, just huts made from poles and brush with a few goathides draped across them. The indians stood watching him. He could see that none of them spoke among themselves or commented on his riding there nor did they raise a hand in greeting or call out to him. They had no curiosity about him at all. As if they knew all that they needed to know. They stood and watched him pass and watched him vanish upon that landscape solely because he was passing. Solely because he would vanish.

The desert he rode was red and red the dust he raised, the small dust that powdered the legs of the horse he rode, the horse he led. In the evening a wind came up and reddened all the sky before him. There were few cattle in that country because it was barren country indeed yet he came at evening upon a solitary bull rolling in the dust against the bloodred sunset like an animal in sacrificial torment. The bloodred dust blew down out of the sun. He touched the horse with his heels and rode on. He rode with the sun coppering his face and the red wind blowing out of the west across the evening land and the small desert birds flew chittering among the dry bracken and horse and rider and horse passed on and their long shadows passed in tandem like the shadow of a single being. Passed and paled into the darkening land, the world to come.

THE
CROSSING

I

WHEN THEY CAME SOUTH out of Grant County Boyd was not much more than a baby and the newly formed county they'd named Hidalgo was itself little older than the child. In the country they'd quit lay the bones of a sister and the bones of his maternal grandmother. The new country was rich and wild. You could ride clear to Mexico and not strike a crossfence. He carried Boyd before him in the bow of the saddle and named to him features of the landscape and birds and animals in both spanish and english. In the new house they slept in the room off the kitchen and he would lie awake at night and listen to his brother's breathing in the dark and he would whisper half aloud to him as he slept his plans for them and the life they would have.

On a winter's night in that first year he woke to hear wolves in the low hills to the west of the house and he knew that they would be coming out onto the plain in the new snow to run the antelope in the moonlight. He pulled his breeches off the footboard of the bed and got his shirt and his blanketlined duckingcoat and got his boots from under the bed and went out to the kitchen and dressed in the dark by the faint warmth of the stove and held the boots to the windowlight to pair them left and right and pulled them on and rose and went to the kitchen door and stepped out and closed the door behind him.

When he passed the barn the horses whimpered softly to him in the cold. The snow creaked under his boots and his breath smoked in the bluish light. An hour later he was crouched in the snow in the dry creekbed where he knew the wolves had been using by their tracks in the sand of the washes, by their tracks in the snow.

They were already out on the plain and when he crossed the gravel fan where the creek ran south into the valley he could see where they'd crossed before him. He went forward on knees and elbows with his hands pulled back into his sleeves to keep them out of the snow and when he reached the last of the small dark juniper trees where the broad valley ran under the Animas Peaks he crouched quietly to steady his breath and then raised himself slowly and looked out.

They were running on the plain harrying the antelope and the antelope moved like phantoms in the snow and circled and wheeled and the dry powder blew about them in the cold moonlight and their breath smoked palely in the cold as if they burned with some inner fire and the wolves twisted and turned and leapt in a silence such that they seemed of another world entire. They moved down the valley and turned and moved far out on the plain until they were the smallest of figures in that dim whiteness and then they disappeared.

He was very cold. He waited. It was very still. He could see by his breath how the wind lay and he watched his breath appear and vanish and appear and vanish constantly before him in the cold and he waited a long time. Then he saw them coming. Loping and twisting. Dancing. Tunneling their noses in the snow. Loping and running and rising by twos in a standing dance and running on again.

There were seven of them and they passed within twenty feet of where he lay. He could see their almond eyes in the moonlight. He could hear their breath. He could feel the presence of their knowing that was electric in the air. They bunched and nuzzled and licked one another. Then they stopped. They stood with their ears cocked. Some with one forefoot raised to their chest. They were looking at him. He did not breathe. They did not breathe. They stood. Then they turned and quietly trotted on. When he got back to the house Boyd was awake but he didnt tell him where he'd been nor what he'd seen. He never told anybody.

The winter that Boyd turned fourteen the trees inhabiting the dry river bed were bare from early on and the sky was gray day after day and the trees were pale against it. A cold wind had come down from the north with the earth running under bare poles toward a reckoning whose ledgers would be drawn up and dated only long after all due claims had passed, such is this history. Among the pale cottonwoods with their limbs like bones and their trunks sloughing off the pale or green or darker bark clustered in the outer bend of the river bed below the house stood trees so massive that in the stand across the river was a sawed stump upon which in winters past herders had pitched a four by six foot canvas supply tent for the wooden floor it gave. Riding out for wood he watched his shadow and the shadow of the horse and travois cross those palings tree by tree. Boyd rode in the travois holding the axe as if he'd keep guard over the wood they'd gathered and he watched to the west with squinted eyes where the sun simmered in a dry red lake under the barren mountains and the antelope stepped and nodded among the cattle in silhouette upon the foreland plain.

They crossed through the dried leaves in the river bed and rode till they came to a tank or pothole in the river and he dismounted and watered the horse while Boyd walked the shore looking for muskrat sign. The indian Boyd passed crouching on his heels did not even raise his eyes so that when he sensed him there and turned the indian was looking at his belt and did not lift his eyes even then until he'd stopped altogether. He could have reached and touched him. The indian squatting under a thin stand of carrizo cane and not even hidden and yet Boyd had not seen him. He was holding across his knees an old singleshot 32 rimfire rifle and he had been waiting in the dusk for something to come to water for him to kill. He looked into the eyes of the boy. The boy into his. Eyes so dark they seemed all pupil. Eyes in which the sun was setting. In which the child stood beside the sun.

He had not known that you could see yourself in others' eyes nor see therein such things as suns. He stood twinned in those dark wells with hair so pale, so thin and strange, the selfsame child. As if it were some cognate child to him that had been lost who now stood windowed away in another world where the red sun sank eternally. As if it were a maze where these orphans of his heart had miswandered in their journey in life and so arrived at last beyond the wall of that antique gaze from whence there could be no way back forever.

From where he stood he could not see his brother or the horse. He could see the slow rings moving out over the water where the horse stood drinking beyond the stand of cane and he could see the slight flex of the muscle beneath the skin of the indian's lean and hairless jaw.

The indian turned and looked at the tank. The only sound was the dripping of water from the horse's raised muzzle. He looked at the boy.

You little son of a bitch, he said.

I aint done nothin.

Who's that with you?

My brother.

How old's he?

Sixteen.

The indian stood up. He stood immediately and without effort and looked across the tank where Billy stood holding the horse and then he looked at Boyd again. He wore an old tattered blanketcoat and an old greasy Stetson with the crown belled out and his boots were mended with wire.

What are you all doin out here?

Gettin wood.

You got anything to eat?

No.

Where you live at?

The boy hesitated.

I asked you where you lived at.

He gestured downriver.

How far?

I dont know.

You little son of a bitch.

He put the rifle over his shoulder and walked out down the shore of the tank and stood looking across at the horse and at Billy.

Howdy, said Billy.

The indian spat. Spooked everthing in the country, aint you? he said.

We didnt know there was anybody here.

You aint got nothin to eat?

No sir.

Where you live at?

About two miles down the river.

You got anything to eat at your house?

Yessir.

I come down there you goin to bring me somethin out?

You can come to the house. Mama'll feed you.

I dont want to come to the house. I want you to bring me somethin out.

All right.

You goin to bring me somethin out?

Yes.

All right then.

The boy stood holding the horse. The horse hadnt taken its eyes from the indian. Boyd, he said. Come on.

You got dogs down there?

Just one.

You goin to put him up?

All right. I'll put him up.

You put him up inside somewheres where he wont be barkin.

All right.

I aint comin down there to get shot.

I'll put him up.

All right then.

Boyd. Come on. Let's go.

Boyd stood on the far side of the tank looking at him.

Come on. It'll be dark here in just a little bit.

Go on and do like your brother says, said the indian.

We wasnt botherin you.

Come on, Boyd. Let's go.

He crossed the gravel bar and climbed into the travois.

Get up here, said Billy.

He climbed out of the pile of limbs they'd gathered and looked back at the indian and then reached and took the hand that Billy held down and swung up behind him onto the horse.

How will we find you? said Billy.

The indian was standing with the rifle across his shoulders, his hands hanging over it. You come out you walk towards the moon, he said.

What if it aint up yet?

The indian spat. You think I'd tell you to walk towards a moon that wasnt there? Go on now.

The boy booted the horse forward and they rode out through the trees. The travois poles dragging up small windrows of dead leaves with a dry whisper. The sun low in the west. The indian watched them go. The younger boy rode with one arm around his brother's waist, his face red in the sun, his near-white hair pink in the sun. His brother must have told him not to look back because he didnt look back. By the time they'd crossed through the dry bed of the river and ridden up onto the plain the sun was already behind the peaks of the Peloncillo Mountains to the west and the western sky was a deep red under the reefs of cloud. They set out south along the dry river breaks and when Billy looked back the indian was coming along a half mile behind them in the dusk carrying the rifle loosely in one hand.

How come you're lookin back? said Boyd.

I just am.

Are we goin to carry him some supper?

Yes. We can do that I reckon.

Everthing you can do it dont mean it's a good idea, said Boyd.

I know it.

HE WATCHED the night sky through the front room window. The earliest stars coined out of the dark coping to the south hanging in the dead wickerwork of the trees along the river. The light of the unrisen moon lying in a sulphur haze over the valley to the east. He watched while the light ran out along the edges of the desert prairie and the dome of the moon rose out of the ground white and fat and membranous. Then he climbed down from the chair where he'd been kneeling and went to get his brother.

Billy had steak and biscuits and a tin cup of beans wrapped in a cloth and hidden behind the crocks on the pantry shelf by the kitchen door. He sent Boyd first and stood listening and then followed him out. The dog whined and scratched at the smokehouse door when they passed it and he told the dog to hush and it did. They went on at a low crouch along the fence and then made their way down to the trees. When they reached the river the moon was well up and the indian was standing there with the rifle yokewise across his neck again. They could see his breath in the cold. He turned and they followed him out across the gravel wash and took the cattletrail on the far side downriver along the edge of the pasture. There was woodsmoke in the air. A quarter mile below the house they reached his campfire among the cottonwoods and he stood the rifle against the bole of one of the trees and turned and looked at them.

Bring it here, he said.

Billy crossed to the fire and took the bundle from the crook of his arm and handed it up. The indian took it and squatted before the fire with that same marionette's effortlessness and set the cloth on the ground before him and opened it and lifted out the beans and set the cup by the coals to warm and then took up one of the biscuits and steak and bit into it.

You'll black that cup, Billy said. I got to take it back to the house.

The indian chewed, his dark eyes half closed in the firelight. Aint you got no coffee at your house, he said.

It aint ground.

You cant grind some?

Not without somebody hearin it I caint.

The indian put the second half of the biscuit in his mouth and leaned slightly forward and produced a beltknife from somewhere about his person and reached and stirred the beans in the cup with it and then looked up at Billy and ran the blade along his tongue one side and then the other in a slow stropping motion and jammed the knife in the end of the log against which the fire was laid.

How long you live here, he said.

Ten years.

Ten years. Your family own this place?

No.

He reached and picked up the second biscuit and severed it with his square white teeth and sat chewing.

Where are you from? said Billy.

From all over.

Where you headed?

The indian leaned and took the knife from the log and stirred the beans again and licked the blade again and then slipped the knife through the handle and lifted the blackened cup from the fire and set it on the ground in front of him and began to eat the beans with the knife.

What else you got in the house?

Sir?

I said what else you got in the house.

He raised his head and regarded them standing there in the firelight, chewing slowly, his eyes half closed.

Such as what?

Such as anything. Somethin maybe I can sell.

We aint got nothin.

You aint got nothin.

No sir.

He chewed.

You live in a empty house?

No.

Then you got somethin.

There's furniture and stuff. Kitchen stuff.

You got any rifleshells?

Yessir. Some.

What caliber?

They wont fit your rifle.

What caliber.

Forty-four forty.

Why dont you bring me some of them.

The boy nodded toward the rifle standing against the tree.
That aint a forty-four caliber.

Dont make no difference. I can trade em.

I caint bring you no rifleshells. The old man'd miss em.

Then what'd you say anything about em for?

We better go, said Boyd.

We got to take the cup back.

What else you got? said the indian.

We aint got nothin, said Boyd.

I wasnt askin you. What else you got?

I dont know. I'll see what I can find.

The indian put the other half of the second biscuit in his
mouth. He reached down and tested the cup with his fingers
and picked it up and drained the remaining beans into his open
mouth and ran one finger around the inside of the cup and licked
his finger clean and set the cup on the ground again.

Bring me some of that coffee, he said.

I caint grind it they'll hear it.

Just bring it. I'll bust it with a rock.

All right.

Let him stay here.

What for?

Keep me company.

Keep you company.

Yeah.

He dont need to stay here.

I aint goin to hurt him.

I know you aint. Cause he aint stayin.

The indian sucked his teeth. You got any traps?

We aint got no traps.

He looked up at them. He sucked his teeth with a hissing sound. Go on then, he said. Bring me some sugar.

All right. Let me have the cup.

You can get it when you come back.

When they reached the cattlepath Billy looked back at Boyd and he looked back at the firelight among the trees. Out on the plain the moon was so bright you could count the cattle by it.

We aint takin him no coffee are we? said Boyd.

No.

What are we goin to do about the cup?

Nothin.

What if Mama asks about it?

Just tell her the truth. Tell her I give it to a indian. Tell her a indian come to the house and I give it to him.

All right.

I can be in trouble along with you.

And I can be in more trouble.

Tell her I done it.

I aim to.

They crossed the open ground toward the fence and the lights from the house.

We ought not to of gone out there to start with, Boyd said.

Billy didnt answer.

Ought we.

No.

Why did we?

I dont know.

It was still dark in the morning when their father came into their room.

Billy, he said.

The boy sat upright in the bed and looked at his father standing framed in the light from the kitchen.

What is the dog doin locked in the smokehouse?

I forgot to let him out.

You forgot to let him out?

Yessir.

What was he doin in there in the first place?

He swung out of the bed onto the cold floor and reached for his clothes. I'll let him out, he said.

His father stood in the door a moment and then went back out through the kitchen and down the hall. In the light from the open door Billy could see Boyd crumpled asleep in the other bed. He pulled on his trousers and picked up his boots off the floor and went out.

By the time he'd fed and watered it was daylight and he saddled Bird and mounted up and rode out of the barn bay and down to the river to look for the indian or to see if he was still there. The dog followed at the horse's heels. They crossed the pasture and rode downriver and crossed through the trees. He pulled up and he sat the horse. The dog stood beside him testing the air with quick lifting motions of its muzzle, sorting and assembling some picture of the prior night's events. The boy put the horse forward again.

When he rode into the indian's camp the fire was cold and black. The horse shifted and stepped nervously and the dog circled the dead ashes with its nose to the ground and the hackles standing along its back.

When he got back to the house his mother had breakfast ready and he hung his hat and pulled up a chair and began to spoon eggs onto his plate. Boyd was already eating.

Where's Pap? he said.

Dont you even breathe the steam and you aint said grace, his mother said.

Yes mam.

He lowered his head and said the words to himself and then reached for a biscuit.

Where's Pap.

He's in the bed. He's done ate.

What time did he get in.

About two hours ago. He rode all night.

How come?

I reckon cause he wanted to get home.

How long is he goin to sleep?

Well I guess till he wakes up. You ask more questions than Boyd.

I aint asked the first one, Boyd said.

They went out to the barn after breakfast. Where do you reckon he's got to? said Boyd.

He's moved on.

Where do you reckon he come from?

I dont know. Them was mexican boots he was wearin. What was left of em. He's just a drifter.

You dont know what a indian's liable to do, said Boyd.

What do you know about indians, said Billy.

Well you dont.

You dont know what anybody's liable to do.

Boyd took an old worn screwdriver from a bucket of tools and brushes hanging from the barn post and he took a rope halter off the hitchrail and opened the stall door where he kept his horse and went in and haltered the horse and led it out. He halfhitched the rope to the rail and ran his hand down the animal's foreleg for it to offer its hoof and he cleaned out the frog of the hoof and examined it and then let it back down.

Let me look at it, said Billy.

There aint nothin wrong with it.

Let me look at it then.

Go ahead then.

Billy pulled the horse's hoof up and cupped it between his knees and studied it. I guess it looks all right, he said.

I said it did.

Walk him around.

Boyd unhitched the rope and led the horse down the barn bay and back.

You goin to get your saddle? said Billy.

Well I guess I will if that's all right with you.

He brought the saddle from the saddleroom and threw the blanket over the horse and labored up with the saddle and rocked it into place and pulled up the latigo and fastened the backcinch and stood waiting.

You've let him get in the habit of that, said Billy. Why dont you just punch the air out of him.

He dont knock the air out of me, I dont knock it out of him, Boyd said.

Billy spat into the dry chaff in the floor of the bay. They waited. The horse breathed out. Boyd pulled the strap and buckled it.

They rode the Ibañez pasture all morning studying the cows. The cows stood their distance and studied them back, a leggy and brocklefaced lot, part mexican, some longhorn, every color. At dinnertime they came back to the house stringing along a yearling heifer on a rope and they put her up in the pole corral above the barn for their father to look at and went in and washed up. Their father was already seated at the table. Boys, he said.

You all set down, their mother said. She set a platter of fried steaks on the table. A bowl of beans. When they'd said grace she handed the platter to their father and he forked one of the steaks onto his plate and passed it on to Billy.

Pap says there's a wolf on the range, she said.

Billy sat holding the platter, his knife aloft.

A wolf? Boyd said.

His father nodded. She pulled down a pretty good sized veal calf up at the head of Foster Draw.

When? said Billy.

Been a week or more probably. The youngest Oliver boy tracked her all up through the mountains. She come up out of Mexico. Crossed through the San Luis Pass and come up along the western slope of the Animas and hit in along about the head of Taylor's Draw and then dropped down and crossed the valley and come up into the Peloncillos. Come all the way up into the snow. There was two inches of snow on the ground where she killed the calf at.

How do you know it was a she? said Boyd.

Well how do you think he knows? said Billy.

You could see where she had done her business, said his father.

Oh, said Boyd.

What do you aim to do? said Billy.

Well, I reckon we better catch her. Dont you?

Yessir.

If old man Echols was here he'd catch her, said Boyd.

Mr Echols.

If Mr Echols was here he'd catch her.

Yes he would. But he aint.

THEY RODE after dinner the three of them the nine miles to the SK Bar ranch and sat their horses and hallooed the house. Mr Sanders' granddaughter looked out and went to get the old man and they all sat on the porch while their father told Mr Sanders about the wolf. Mr Sanders sat with his elbows on his knees and looked hard at the porch floorboards between his boots and nodded and from time to time with his little finger tipped the ash from the end of his cigarette. When their father was done he looked up. His eyes were very blue and very beautiful half hid away in the leathery seams of his face. As if there were something there that the hardness of the country had not been able to touch.

Echols' traps and stuff is still up at the cabin, he said. I dont reckon he'd care for you to use whatever you needed.

He flipped the stub of the cigarette out into the yard and smiled at the two boys and put his hands on his knees and rose.

Let me go get the keys, he said.

The cabin when they opened it was dark and musty and had about it a waxy smell like freshkilled meat. Their father stood in the door a moment and then entered. In the front room was an old sofa, a bed, a desk. They went through the kitchen and then on through to the mudroom at the back of the house. There in the dusty light from the one small window on shelves of roughsawed pine stood a collection of fruitjars and bottles with ground glass stoppers and old apothecary jars all bearing antique octagon labels edged in red upon which in Echols' neat script were listed contents and dates. In the jars dark liquids. Dried viscera. Liver, gall, kidneys. The inward parts of the beast who dreams of man and has so dreamt in running dreams a hundred thousand years and more. Dreams of that malignant lesser god come pale and naked and alien to slaughter all his clan and kin and rout them from their house. A god insatiable whom no ceding could appease nor any measure of blood. The jars stood webbed in dust and the light among them made of the little room with its chemic glass a strange basilica dedicated to a practice as soon to be extinct among the trades of men as the beast to whom it owed its being. Their father took down one of the jars and turned it in his hand and set it back again precisely in its round track of dust. On a lower shelf stood a wooden ammunition box with dovetailed corners and in the box a dozen or so small bottles or vials with no labels to them. Written in red crayon across the top board of the box were the words No. 7 Matrix. Their father held one of the vials to the light and shook it and twisted out the cork and passed the open bottle under his nose.

Good God, he whispered.

Let me smell it, Boyd said.

No, said his father. He put the vial in his pocket and they

went on to search for the traps but they couldnt find them. They looked through the rest of the house and out on the porch and in the smokehouse. They found some old number three longspring coyote traps hanging on the smokehouse wall but those were all the traps they found.

They're here somewheres, said their father.

They began again. After a while Boyd came from the kitchen.

I got em, he said.

They were in two wooden crates and the crates had been piled over with stovewood. They were greased with something that may have been lard and they were packed in the crates like herrings.

What caused you to look in under there? said his father.

You said they was somewheres.

He spread some old newspapers on the linoleum of the kitchen floor and began to lift out the traps. They had the springs turned in to make them more compact and the chains were wrapped around them. He straightened one out. The greaseclogged chain rattled woodenly. It was forked with a ring and had a heavy snap on one end and a drag on the other. They squatted there looking at it. It looked enormous. That thing looks like a bear-trap, Billy said.

It's a wolftrap. Number four and a half Newhouse.

He set out eight of them on the floor and wiped the grease from his hands with newspaper. They put the lid back on the crate and piled the stovewood back over the boxes the way Boyd had found them and their father went back out to the mudroom and returned with a small wooden box with a wirescreen bottom and a paper sack of logwood chips and a packbasket to put the traps in. Then they went out and fastened back the padlock on the front door and untied their horses and mounted up and rode back down to the house.

Mr Sanders came out on the porch but they didnt dismount.

Just stay to supper, he said.

We better get back. I thank you.

Well.

I've got eight of the traps.

All right.

We'll see how it goes.

Well. You probably got your work cut out for you. She aint been in the country long enough to have no regular habits.

Echols said there wasnt none of em did anymore.

He would know. He's about half wolf hisself.

Their father nodded. He turned slightly in the saddle and looked out downcountry. He looked at the old man again.

You ever smell any of that stuff he baits with?

Yessir. I have.

Their father nodded. He raised one hand and turned the horse and they rode out into the road.

After supper they set the galvanized washtub on top of the stove and hand filled it with buckets and poured in a scoop of lye and set the traps to boil. They fed the fire until bedtime and then changed the water and put the traps back with the logwood chips and chunked the stove full and left it. Boyd woke once in the night and lay listening to the silence in the house and in the darkness and the stove ticking or the house creaking in the wind off the plain. When he looked over at Billy's bed it was empty and after a while he got up and walked out to the kitchen. Billy was sitting at the window in one of the kitchen chairs turned backwards. He had his arms crossed over the chairback and he was watching the moon over the river and the river trees and the mountains to the south. He turned and looked at Boyd standing in the door.

What are you doin? said Boyd.

I got up to mend the fire.

What are you lookin at?

Aint lookin at nothin. There aint nothin to look at.

What are you settin there for.

Billy didnt answer. After a while he said: Go on back to bed. I'll be in there directly.

Boyd came on into the kitchen. He stood at the table. Billy turned and looked at him.

What woke you up? he said.

You did.

I didnt make a sound.

I know it.

WHEN BILLY got up the next morning his father was sitting at the kitchen table with a leather apron in his lap and he was wearing a pair of old deerhide gloves and rubbing beeswax into the steel of one of the traps. The other traps were laid out on a calfskin on the floor and they were a deep blueblack in color. He looked up and then took off the gloves and put them in the apron with the trap and set the apron on the calfhide in the floor.

Help me with the washtub, he said. Then you can finish waxin these.

He did. He waxed them carefully, working the wax into the pan and the lettering in the pan and into the slots that the jaws were hinged into and into each link in the heavy fivefoot chains and into the heavy twopronged drag at the end of the chain. Then his father hung them outside in the cold where the house odors would not infect them. The morning following when his father entered their room and called him it was still dark.

Billy.

Yessir.

Breakfast be on the table in five minutes.

Yessir.

When they rode out of the lot it was breaking day, clear and cold. The traps were packed in the splitwillow basket that his father wore with the shoulderstraps loosed so that the bottom of the basket carried on the cantle of the saddle behind him. They rode due south. Above them Black Point was shining with new snow in a sun that had not yet risen over the valley floor. By the time they crossed the old road to Fitzpatrick Wells the sun was up there also and they crossed to the head of the pasture in the sun and began to climb into the Peloncillos.

Midmorning they were sitting their horses at the edge of the upland vega where the calf lay dead. Where they'd come up through the trees there was snow in the tracks his father's horse had made three days ago and under the shadow of the trees where the dead calf lay there were patches of snow that had not yet melted and the snow was bloody and trampled and crossed and recrossed with the tracks of coyotes and the calf was pulled apart and pieces scattered over the bloody snow and over the ground beyond. His father had taken off his gloves to roll a cigarette and he sat smoking with the gloves in one hand resting on the pommel of his saddle.

Dont get down, he said. See if you can see her track.

They rode over the ground. The horses were uneasy at the blood and the riders spoke to them in a sort of scoffing way as if they'd make the horses ashamed. He could see no traces of the wolf.

His father stood down from his horse. Come here, he said.

You aint goin to make a set here?

No. You can get down.

He got down. His father had slipped the packbasket straps and stood the basket in the snow and he knelt and blew the fresh snow out of the crystal print the wolf had made five nights ago.

Is that her?

That's her.

That's her front foot.

Yes.

It's big, aint it?

Yes.

She wont come back here?

No. She wont come back here.

The boy stood up. He looked off up the meadow. There were two ravens sitting in a barren tree. They must have flown as they were riding up. Other than that there was nothing.

Where do you reckon the rest of the cattle have got to?

I dont know.

If they's a cow dead in a pasture will the rest of the cattle stay there?

Depends on what it died of. They wont stay in a pasture with a wolf.

You think she's made another kill somewheres by now?

His father rose from where he'd squatted by the track and picked up the basket. There's a good chance of it, he said. You ready?

Yessir.

They mounted up and crossed the vega and entered the woods on the far side and followed the cattletrail up along the edge of the draw. The boy watched the ravens. After a while they dropped down out of the tree and flew silently back to the dead calf.

His father made the first set below the gap of the mountain where they knew the wolf had crossed. The boy sat his horse and watched while he threw down the calfhide hairside down and stepped down onto it and set down the packbasket.

He took the deerhide gloves out of the basket and pulled them on and with a trowel he dug a hole in the ground and put the drag in the hole and piled the chain in after it and covered it up again. Then he excavated a shallow place in the ground the shape of the trap springs and all. He tried the trap in it and then dug some more. He put the dirt in the screenbox as he dug and then he laid the trowel by and took a pair of c-clamps from the basket and with them screwed down the springs until the jaws fell open. He held the trap up and eyed the notch in the pan while he backed off one screw and adjusted the trigger. Crouched in the broken shadow with the sun at his back and holding the trap at eyelevel against the morning sky he looked to be truing some older, some subtler instrument. Astrolabe or sextant. Like a man bent at fixing himself someway in the world. Bent on trying by arc or chord the space between his being and the world that was. If there be such space. If it be knowable. He put his hand under the open jaws and tilted the pan slightly with his thumb.

You dont want it to where a squirrel can trip it, he said. But damn near.

Then he removed the clamps and set the trap in the hole.

He covered the jaws and pan of the trap with a square of paper soaked in melted beeswax and with the screenbox he carefully sifted the dirt back over it and with the trowel sprinkled humus and wood debris over the dirt and squatted there on his haunches looking at the set. It looked like nothing at all. Lastly he took the bottle of Echols' potion from his coatpocket and pulled the cork and dipped a twig into the bottle and stuck the twig into the ground a foot from the trap and then put the cork back in the bottle and the bottle in his pocket.

He rose and handed up the packbasket to the boy and he bent and folded the calfskin with the dirt in it and then stood into the stirrup of the standing horse and mounted up and pulled the hide up into the bow of the saddle with him and backed the horse away from the set.

You think you can make one? he said.

Yessir. I think so.

His father nodded. Echols used to pull the shoes off his horse. Then he got to where he'd tie these cowhide slippers he'd made over the horse's hooves. Oliver told me he'd make sets and never get down. Set the traps from horseback.

How did he do it?

I dont know.

The boy sat holding the packbasket on his knee.

Put that on, his father said. You'll need it if you're goin to make this next set.

Yessir, he said.

By noon they'd made three more sets and they took their dinner in a grove of blackjack oaktrees at the head of Cloverdale Creek. They reclined on their elbows and ate their sandwiches and looked out across the valley toward the Guadalupes and southeast across the spur of the mountains where they could see the shadows of clouds moving up the broad Animas Valley and beyond in the blue distances the mountains of Mexico.

You think we can catch her? the boy said.

I wouldnt be up here if I didnt.

What if she's been caught before or been around traps before or somethin like that?

Then she'll be hard to catch.

There aint no more wolves but what they come up out of Mexico, I reckon. Are they?

Probably not.

They ate. When his father had finished he folded the paper bag the sandwiches had come in and put it in his pocket.

You ready? he said.

Yessir.

When they rode back through the lot and into the barn they'd been gone thirteen hours and they were bone tired. They'd come the last two hours through the dark and the house was dark save for the kitchen light.

Go on to the house and get your supper, his father said.

I'm all right.

Go on. I'll put the horses up.

THE WOLF had crossed the international boundary line at about the point where it intersected the thirtieth minute of the one hundred and eighth meridian and she had crossed the old Nations road a mile north of the boundary and followed Whitewater Creek west up into the San Luis Mountains and crossed through the gap north to the Animas range and then crossed the Animas Valley and on into the Peloncillos as told. She carried a scabbedover wound on her hip where her mate had bitten her two weeks before somewhere in the mountains of Sonora. He'd bitten her because she would not leave him. Standing with one forefoot in the jaws of a steeltrap and snarling at her to drive her off where she lay just beyond the reach of the chain. She'd flattened her ears and whined and she would not leave. In the morning they came on horses. She watched from a slope a hundred yards away as he stood up to meet them.

She wandered the eastern slopes of the Sierra de la Madera for a week. Her ancestors had hunted camels and primitive toy horses on these grounds. She found little to eat. Most of the game was slaughtered out of the country. Most of the forest cut to feed the boilers of the stampmills at the mines. The wolves in that country had been killing cattle for a long time but the ignorance of the animals was a puzzle to them. The cows bellowing and bleeding and stumbling through the mountain meadows with their shovel feet and their confusion, bawling and floundering through the fences and dragging posts and wires behind. The ranchers said they brutalized the cattle in a way they did not the wild game. As if the cows evoked in them some anger. As if they were offended by some violation of an old order. Old ceremonies. Old protocols.

She crossed the Bavispe River and moved north. She was carrying her first litter and she had no way to know the trouble she was in. She was moving out of the country not because the game was gone but because the wolves were and she needed them. When she pulled down the veal calf in the snow at the head of Foster Draw in the Peloncillo Mountains of New Mexico she had eaten little but carrion for two weeks and she wore a haunted look and she'd found no trace of wolves at all. She ate and rested and ate again. She ate till her belly dragged and she did not go back. She would not return to a kill. She would not cross a road or a rail line in daylight. She would not cross under a wire fence twice in the same place. These were the new protocols. Strictures that had not existed before. Now they did.

She ranged west into Cochise County in the state of Arizona, across the south fork of Skeleton Creek and west to the head of Starvation Canyon and south to Hog Canyon Springs. Then east again to the high country between Clanton and Foster draws. At night she would go down onto the Animas Plains and drive the wild antelope, watching them flow and turn in the dust of their own passage where it rose like smoke off the basin floor, watching the precisely indexed articulation of their limbs and the rocking movements of their heads and the slow bunching and the slow extension of their running, looking for anything at all among them that would name to her her quarry.

At this season the does were already carrying calves and as they commonly aborted long before term the one least favored so twice she found these pale unborn still warm and gawking on the ground, milkblue and near translucent in the dawn like beings miscarried from another world entire. She ate even their bones where they lay blind and dying in the snow. Before sunrise she was off the plain and she would raise her muzzle where she stood on some low promontory or rock overlooking the valley and howl and howl again into that terrible silence. She might have left the country altogether if she had not come upon the scent of a wolf just below the high pass west of Black Point. She stopped as if she'd walked into a wall.

She circled the set for the better part of an hour sorting and indexing the varied scents and ordering their sequences in an effort to reconstruct the events that had taken place here. When she left she went down through the pass south following the tracks of the horses now thirty-six hours old.

By evening she'd found all eight of the sets and she was back at the gap of the mountain again where she circled the trap whining. Then she began to dig. She dug a hole alongside the trap until the caving dirt fell away to reveal the trap's jaw. She stood looking at it. She dug again. When she left the set the trap was sitting naked on the ground with only a handful of dirt over the waxed paper covering the pan and when the boy and his father rode through the gap the following morning that was what they found.

His father stood down from the horse onto the calfhide and surveyed the set while the boy sat watching. He remade the set and rose and shook his head doubtfully. They rode the rest of the line and when they returned the following morning the first set was uncovered again and so were four more. They took up three of the sets and used the traps to make blind sets in the trail.

What's to keep a cow from walkin in em? the boy said.

Not a thing in the world, said his father.

Three days later they found another calf dead. Five days later one of the blind sets in the trail had been dug out and the trap overturned and sprung.

They rode in the evening down to the SK Bar and called on Sanders again. They sat in the kitchen and told the old man all that had occurred and the old man nodded his head.

Echols one time told me that tryin to get the best of a wolf is like tryin to get the best of a kid. It aint that they're smarter. It's just that they aint got all that much else to think about. I went with him a time or two. He'd put down a trap someplace and there wouldnt be the first sign of anything usin there and I'd ask him why he was makin a set there and half the time he couldnt answer it. Couldnt answer it.

They went up to the cabin and got six more of the traps and took them home and boiled them. In the morning when their mother came into the kitchen to fix breakfast Boyd was sitting in the floor waxing the traps.

You think that will get you out of the doghouse? she said.

No.

How long do you intend to stay sulled up?

I aint the one that's sulled up.

He can be just as stubborn as you can.

Then I reckon we're in for it, aint we?

She stood at the stove watching him bent at his work. Then she turned and took the iron skillet from the rack and set it on the stove. She opened the firebox door to put in wood but he'd already done it.

When they'd done eating breakfast his father wiped his mouth and put his napkin on the table and pushed back his chair.

Where's the traps at?

Hangin from the clothesline, said Boyd.

He rose and left the room. Billy drained his cup and set it on the table in front of him.

You want me to say somethin to him?

No.

All right. I wont then. Probably wouldnt do no good noway.

When his father came back from the barn ten minutes later

Boyd was at the woodpile in his shirtsleeves splitting stove chunks.

You want to go with us? his father said.

That's all right, said Boyd.

His father went on in the house. After a while Billy came out.

What the hell's wrong with you? he said.

Aint nothin wrong with me. What's wrong with you?

Dont be a ass. Get your coat and let's go.

It had snowed in the night in the mountains and the snow in the pass to the west of Black Point was a foot deep. Their father led his horse afoot through the snow tracking the wolf and they followed her all morning through the high country until she ran out of snow just above the Cloverdale Creek road. He got down and stood looking out over the open country where she'd gone and then he remounted and they turned and rode back up to check the sets on the other side of the pass.

She's carryin pups, he said.

He made four more blind sets in the trail and then they went in. Boyd was shivering in the saddle and his lips were blue. His father fell back alongside him and took off his coat and handed it to him.

I aint cold, Boyd said.

I didnt ask you if you were cold. Put it on.

Two days later when Billy and his father ran the line again one of the blind sets in the trail below the snowline was pulled out. A hundred feet down the trail was a place where the mud had washed out in the snowmelt and in the mud was the track of a cow. A little further on they found the trap. The prongs of the drag had caught and she'd pulled loose leaving a swag of bloodied hide accordioned up on the underside of the trapjaws.

They spent the rest of the morning looking through the pastures for the lame cow but they couldnt find her.

Be a good job for you and Boyd tomorrow, his father said.

Yessir.

I dont want him leavin the house half naked like he done the other day.

Yessir.

He and Boyd found the cow in the early afternoon of the day following. She was standing at the edge of the cedars watching them. The rest of the cattle were drifting along the lower edge of the vega. She was an old dry cow and she'd probably been alone when she walked in the set up on the mountain. They turned into the woods above her to head her out into the open but when she saw what they were about she turned and went back into the cedars. Boyd booted his horse through the trees and cut her off and got a loop on her and dallied and when she hit the end of the rope the girthstrap broke and the saddle was snatched from under him and disappeared down the slope behind the cow whacking and banging off of the trunks of the trees.

He'd done a somersault backwards off the horse and he sat on the ground and watched the cow racketing down through the cedars and out of sight. When Billy rode up he'd already mounted again bareback and they set off after the cow.

They started finding pieces of the saddle almost immediately and after a while they found the saddle itself or what was left of it, just the wooden tree with pieces of leather hanging off of it. Boyd started to get down.

Hell, just leave it lay, Billy said.

Boyd slid down off the horse. It aint that, he said. I got to come out of some of these clothes. I'm damn near afire.

They brought the cow limping in at the end of a rope and put her up and their father came out and doctored the leg with Corona Salve and then they all went in to get their supper.

She tore up Boyd's saddle, Billy said.

Can it be fixed?

There wasnt nothin left to fix.

The latigo busted?

Yessir.

When was the last time you looked at it?

That old hull never was any account, Boyd said.

That old hull was all the hull you had, said their father.

The next day Billy ran the line by himself. Another of the sets had been walked in but the cow left nothing in the trap save some peels and scrapings of hoof. In the night it snowed.

Them traps are under two feet of snow, said his father. What is the use in goin up there?

I want to see where she's usin.

You might see where she's been. I doubt it will tell you where she's goin to be tomorrow or the next day.

It's got to tell you somethin.

His father sat contemplating his coffee cup. All right, he said. Dont wear your horse out. You can hurt a horse in the snow. You can hurt a horse in the mountains in the snow.

Yessir.

His mother gave him his lunch at the kitchen door.

You be careful, she said.

Yes mam.

You be in by dark.

Yes mam. I'll try.

You try real hard and you wont have any problems.

Yes mam.

As he rode Bird out of the barn his father was coming from the house in his shirtsleeves with the rifle and saddlescabbard. He handed them up.

If by any chance at all she should be in a trap you come and get me. Unless her leg is broke. If her leg is broke shoot her. Otherwise she'll twist out.

Yessir.

And dont be gone late worryin your mama neither.

Yessir. I wont.

He turned the horse and went out through the stockgate and into the road south. The dog had come to the gate and stood looking after him. He rode out a little way on the road and then stopped and dismounted and strapped the scabbard alongside the saddle and levered the breech of the rifle partly open to see that there was shell in the chamber and then slid the rifle into the scabbard and buckled it and mounted up and rode on again. Before him the mountains were blinding white in the sun. They looked new born out of the hand of some improvident god who'd perhaps not even puzzled out a use for them. That kind of new. The rider rode with his heart outsized in his chest and the horse who was also young tossed its head and took a sidestep in the road and shot out one hind heel and then they went on.

The snow in the pass was half way to the horse's belly and the horse trod down the drifts in high elegance and swung its smoking muzzle over the white and crystal reefs and looked out down through the dark mountain woods or cocked its ears at the sudden flight of small winter birds before them. There were no tracks in the pass and there were neither cattle nor tracks of cattle in the upper pasture beyond the pass. It was very cold. A mile south of the pass they crossed a running branch so black in the snow it caused the horse to balk just for any slight movement of the water to tell that it was no bottomless crevice that had split the mountain in the night. A hundred yards farther the track of the wolf entered the trail and went down the mountain before them.

He stood down into the snow and dropped the reins and squatted and thumbed back the brim of his hat. In the floors of the little wells she'd stoven in the snow lay her perfect prints. The broad forefoot. The narrow hind. The sometime dragmark of her dugs or the place where she'd put her nose. He closed his eyes and tried to see her. Her and others of her kind, wolves and ghosts of wolves running in the whiteness of that high world as perfect to their use as if their counsel had been sought in the devising of it. He rose and walked back to where the horse stood waiting. He looked out across the mountain the way she'd come and then mounted and rode on.

A mile further she'd left the trail and gone down through the juniper parklands at a run. He dismounted and led the horse by the bridlereins. She was making ten feet at a jump. At the edge of the woods she turned and continued along the upper edge of the vega at a trot. He mounted up again and rode out down the pasture and he rode up and back but he could see no sign of what it was she'd run after. He picked up her track again and followed it across the open country and down along the southfacing slope and onto the benchland above Cloverdale Draw and here she'd routed a small band of cattle yarded up in the junipers and run them off the bench all crazed and sliding and falling enormously in the snow and here she'd killed a two year old heifer at the edge of the trees.

It was lying on its side in the shadow of the woods with its eyes glazed over and its tongue out and she had begun to feed on it between its rear legs and eaten the liver and dragged the intestines over the snow and eaten several pounds of meat from the inside of the thighs. The heifer was not quite stiff, not quite cold. Where it lay it had melted the snow to the ground in a dark silhouette about it.

The horse wanted no part of it. He arched his neck and rolled his eyes and the bores of his nose smoked like fumaroles. The boy patted his neck and spoke to him and then dismounted and tied the bridlereins to a branch and walked around the dead animal studying it. The one eye that looked up was blue and cast and there was no reflection in it and no world. There were no ravens or any other birds about. All was cold and silence. He walked back to the horse and slid the rifle from the scabbard and checked the chamber again. The action was stiff with the cold. He let the hammer down with his thumb and untied the reins and mounted up and turned the horse down along the edge of the woods, riding with the rifle across his lap.

He followed her all day. He never saw her. Once he rode her up out of a bed in a windbreak thicket on the south slope where she'd slept in the sun. Or thought he rode her up. He knelt and placed his hand in the pressed grass to see if it was warm and he sat watching to see if any blade or stem of grass would right itself but none did and whether the bed was warm from her or from the sun he was in no way sure. He mounted up and rode on. Twice he lost her track in the Cloverdale Creek pasture where the snow had melted and both times picked it up again in the circle he cut for sign. On the far side of the Cloverdale road he saw smoke and rode down and came upon three vaqueros from Pendleton's taking their dinner. They did not know that there was a wolf about. They seemed doubtful. They looked at one another.

They asked him to get down and he did and they gave him a cup of coffee and he took his lunch from his shirt and offered what he had. They were eating beans and tortillas and sucking at some sparelooking goatbones and as there was no fourth plate nor any way to divide what any had with any other they passed through a pantomime of offer and refusal and continued to eat as before. They talked of cattle and of the weather and as they were all workscouts for kin in Mexico they asked if his father needed any hands. They said that the tracks he'd followed were probably of a large dog and even though the tracks could be seen less than a quarter mile from where they were eating they showed no inclination to go and examine them. He didnt tell them about the dead heifer.

When they'd done eating they scraped their plates off into the ashes of the fire and wiped them clean with pieces of tortilla and ate the tortillas and packed the plates away in their mochilas. Then they tightened the latigos on their horses and mounted up. He shook out the grounds from the cup and wiped it out with his shirt and handed it up to the rider who'd given it to him.

Adiós compadrito, they said. Hasta la vista. They touched their hats and turned their horses and rode out and when they were gone he got his horse and mounted up and took the trail back west the way the wolf had gone.

By evening she was back in the mountains. He followed afoot leading the horse. He studied places where she had dug but he could not tell what it was she was digging for. He measured the remaining day with his hand at arm's length under the sun and finally he stood up into the saddle and turned the horse up through the wet snow toward the pass and home.

Because it was already dark he rode the horse past the kitchen window and leaned and tapped at the glass without stopping and then went on to the barn. At the dinner table he told them what he had seen. He told them about the heifer dead on the mountain.

Where she crossed back goin towards Hog Canyon, said his father. Was that a cattletrail?

No sir. It was not much of a trail of no kind.

Could you make a set in it?

Yessir. I would of had it not been gettin on late like it was.

Did you pick up any of the sets?

No sir.

You want to go back up there tomorrow?

Yessir. I'd like to.

All right. Take up a couple of traps and make blind sets with em and I'll run the line with you on Sunday.

I dont know how you think the Lord is goin to bless your efforts and you dont keep the Sabbath, their mother said.

Well Mama we aint got a ox in the ditch but we sure got some heifers in one.

I think it's a poor example for the boys.

His father sat looking at his cup. He looked at the boy. We'll run it on Monday, he said.

Lying in the cold dark of their bedroom they listened to the squalls of coyotes out in the pasture to the west of the house.

You think you can catch her? said Boyd.

I dont know.

What are you goin to do with her if you do?

What do you mean?

I mean what will you do with her.

Collect the bounty, I reckon.

They lay in the dark. The coyotes yammered. After a while Boyd said: I meant how will you kill her.

I guess you shoot em. I dont know no other way.

I'd like to see her alive.

Maybe Pap will bring you with him.

What am I goin to ride?

You could ride bareback.

Yeah, Boyd said. I could ride bareback.

They lay in the dark.

He's goin to give you my saddle, Billy said.

What are you goin to ride?

He's gettin me one from Martel's.

A new one?

No. Hell, not a new one.

Outside the dog had been barking and their father went out to the kitchen door and called the dog's name and it hushed instantly. The coyotes went on yapping.

Billy?

What.

Did Pap write Mr Echols?

Yeah.

He never heard nothin though. Did he?

Not yet he aint.

Billy?

What.

I had this dream.

What dream.

I had it twice.

Well what was it.

There was this big fire out on the dry lake.

There aint nothin to burn on a dry lake.

I know it.

What happened.

These people were burnin. The lake was on fire and they was burnin up.

It's probably somethin you ate.

I had the same dream twice.

Maybe you ate the same thing twice.

I dont think so.

It aint nothin. It's just a bad dream. Go to sleep.

It was real as day. I could see it.

People have dreams all the time. It dont mean nothin.

Then what do they have em for?

I dont know. Go to sleep.

Billy?

What.

I had this feelin that somethin bad was goin to happen.

There aint nothin bad goin to happen. You just had a bad dream is all. It dont mean somethin bad is goin to happen.

What does it mean?

It dont mean nothin. Go to sleep.

IN THE WOODS on the southfacing slopes the snow was partly melted from the prior day's sun and it had frozen back in the night so that there was a thin crust on top. The crust was just hard enough for birds to walk on. Mice. In the trail he saw where the cows had come down. The traps in the mountains lay all undisturbed beneath the snow with their jaws agape like steel trolls silent and mindless and blind. He took up three of the sets, holding the cocked traps in his gloved hands and reaching under the jaw and tripping the pan with his thumb. The traps leapt mightily. The iron clang of the jaws slamming shut echoed in the cold. You could see nothing of their movement. Now the jaws were open. Now they were closed.

He rode with the traps packed under the calfhide in the floor of the packbasket where they would not fall out as he rolled sideways in the saddle to duck low branches. When he came to the fork in the trail he followed the track she'd taken the evening before going west toward Hog Canyon. He made the sets in the trail and cut and placed stepping sticks and returned along a route of his own devising a mile to the south and continued down to the Cloverdale road to visit the last two sets on the line.

There was still snow in the upper stretches of the road and there were tiretracks in the road and horsetracks and the tracks of deer. When he reached the spring he left the road and crossed through the pasture and dismounted and watered his horse. It was near noon by the sun and he intended to ride the four miles into Cloverdale and go back by way of the road.

While the horse was drinking an old man in a Model A pickup truck pulled up out at the fence. Billy pulled the horse's head up and mounted and went back out to the road and sat the horse alongside the truck. The man leaned out the window and looked up at him. He looked at the packbasket.

What are you trappin? he said.

He was a rancher from the lower valley along the border and Billy knew him but didnt say his name. He knew the old man wanted to hear that he was trapping coyotes and he wouldnt lie, or wouldnt exactly lie.

Well, he said. I seen a lot of coyote sign down here.

I aint surprised, the old man said. They done everthing down at our place but come in and set at the table.

He scanned the country with his pale eyes. As if the little jackal wolves might be afoot on the plain in broadest day. He took out a pack of readymade cigarettes and shucked one up and took it in his mouth and held up the pack.

Smoke?

No sir. Thank you.

He put the pack away and took from his pocket a brass lighter that looked like something for soldering pipe, burning off paint. He struck it and a bluish ball of flame whooshed up. He lit the cigarette and snapped the lighter shut but it continued to burn anyway. He blew it out and dandled it in one hand to cool it. He looked at the boy.

I had to quit usin the hightest, he said.

Yessir.

You married?

No sir. I aint but sixteen.

Dont get married. Women are crazy.

Yessir.

You'll think you've found one that aint but guess what?

What?

She will be too.

Yessir.

You got any big traps in there?

Like how big?

Number four, say.

No sir. Truth to tell, I dont have none with me of no kind.

What did you ask me how big for then?

Sir?

The old man nodded at the road. There was a mountain lion crossed about a mile down here yesterday evenin.

They're around, the boy said.

My nephew's got some dogs. Got some blueticks out of the Lee Brothers' line. Pretty good dogs. He dont want em walkin in no steeltraps though.

I'm back up here towards Hog Canyon, the boy said. And up towards Black Point.

The old man smoked. The horse turned its head and sniffed at the truck and looked away again.

You hear about the Texas lion and the New Mexico lion? the old man said.

No sir. I dont believe so.

There was this Texas lion and this New Mexico lion. They split up on the divide and went off to hunt. Agreed to meet up in the spring and see how they'd done and all and whenever they done it why the old lion been over in Texas looked just awful. Lion from New Mexico he looked at him and he said Lord son you look awful. Said what's happened to you. Lion been over in Texas said I dont know. Said I'm about starved out. Other old lion said well, said tell me what all you been doin. Said you might be doin somethin wrong.

Well the Texas lion said I just been usin the old tried and true methods. Said I get up on a limb overlookin the trail and then whenever one of the Texans rides underneath it why I holler real big and then I jump out on top of him. And that's what I been a doin.

Well, the old New Mexico lion looked at him and he said it's a wonder you aint dead. Said that's all wrong for your Texans and I dont see how you got through the winter atall. Said look here. First of all when you holler thataway it scares the shit out of em. Then when you jump on top of em thataway it knocks the wind out of em. Hell, son. You aint got nothin left but buckles and boots.

The old man fell across the steering wheel wheezing. After a while he began to cough. He looked up and wiped his watery eyes with one finger and shook his head and looked up at the boy.

You see the point? he said. Texans?

Billy smiled. Yessir, he said.

You aint from Texas are you?

No sir.

I didnt allow you was. Well. I better get on. You want to catch coyotes you come down to my place.

All right.

He didnt say where his place was. He put the truck in gear and pulled the sparklever down and pulled away down the road.

When they ran the traps on Monday the snow had melted off everywhere save in the northfacing rincons or in the deeper woods below the north slope of the pass. She'd pulled out all the sets save for the ones in the Hog Canyon trail and she had taken to turning the traps over and springing them.

They took the traps up and his father made two new sets with double traps, burying one trap under the other and the bottom trap upside down. Then he made blind sets in the perimeter about. He laid these two new sets and they returned home and when they ran the traps the next morning there was a coyote dead in the first set. They pulled this set entirely and Billy tied the coyote on behind the cantle of his saddle and they went on. The coyote's bladder leaked down the horse's flank and it smelled peculiar.

What did the coyote die of? he said.

I dont know, said his father. Sometimes things just die.

The second set was dug out and all five traps sprung. His father sat looking at it for a long time.

There was no word from Echols. He and Boyd rode the outlying pastures and began bringing the cattle in. They found two more calves dead. Then another heifer.

Dont say nothin about this less he asks, Billy said.

Why not?

They sat their horses side by side, Boyd sitting Billy's old saddle and Billy in the mexican saddle his father had traded for. They studied the carnage in the woods. I wouldnt of thought about her pullin down a heifer that big, Billy said.

Why not say nothin? said Boyd.

What would be the use in worryin him over it?

They turned to go.

He might want to know about it anyways, Boyd said.

When's the last time you heard bad news you were glad to get?

What if he finds it himself?

Then he'll find it.

What are you goin to tell him then? That you didnt want to worry him?

Damn. You're worse than Mama. I'm sorry I raised the question.

He was left to run the traps on his own. He rode up to the SK Bar and got the key from Mr Sanders and went to Echols' cabin and studied the shelves in the little mudroom pharmacy. He found some more bottles in a crate in the floor. Dusty bottles with greasestained labels that said Lion, that said Cat. There were other bottles with curled and yellowed labels that bore only numbers and there were bottles made of purple glass dark near to blackness that had no label at all.

He put some of the nameless bottles in his pocket and went back to the front room of the cabin and looked through Echols' little packingcrate library. He took down a book called *Trapping North American Furbearers* by S Stanley Hawbaker and sat in the floor studying it but Hawbaker was from Pennsylvania and he didnt have all that much to say about wolves. When he ran the traps the next day they were dug out as before.

HE LEFT the next morning on the road to Animas and he was on the road seven hours getting there. He nooned at a spring in a glade of huge old cottonwoods and ate cold steak and biscuits and made a paper boat of the bag his lunch had come in and left it turning and darkening and sinking in the clear still of the spring.

The house was on the plain south of the town and no road to it. There had been a track at one time and you could see where it ran like the trace of an old wagonroad and that was where he rode till he came to the cornerpost of the fence. He tied the horse and walked up to the door and knocked and stood looking out over the plains toward the mountains to the west. Four horses were walking along the final rise out there and they stopped and turned and looked his way. As if they'd heard his rapping at the door two miles distant. He turned to rap again but as he did the door opened and a woman stood looking at him. She was eating an apple but she didnt speak. He took off his hat.

Buenas tardes, he said. El señor está?

She bit crisply into the apple with her big white teeth. She looked at him. El señor? she said.

Don Arnulfo.

She looked past him toward the horse tied to the fencepost and she looked at him again. She chewed. She watched him with her black eyes.

Él está? he said.

I'm thinking it over.

What's there to think about? He's either here or he aint.

Maybe.

I aint got no money.

She bit into the apple again. It made a loud cracking noise. He dont want your money, she said.

He stood holding his hat in his hands. He looked out to where he'd seen the horses but they had disappeared over the rise.

All right, she said.

He looked at her.

He's been sick. Maybe he wont say nothin to you.

Well. He will or he wont.

Maybe you like to come back some other time.

I aint got some other time.

She shrugged. Bueno, she said. Pásale.

She held open the door and he stepped past into the low mud house. Gracias, he said.

She gestured with her chin. Atrás, she said.

Gracias.

The old man was in a dark cell of a room at the back of the house. The room smelled of woodsmoke and kerosene and sour bedding. The boy stood in the doorway and tried to make him out. He turned and looked back but the woman had gone on to the kitchen. He stepped down into the room. There was an iron bedstead in the corner. A figure small and dark prone upon it. The room smelled as well of dust or clay. As if it might be that which the old man smelled of. But then even the floor of the room was mud.

He said the old man's name and the old man shifted in his bedding. Adelante, he wheezed.

He stepped forward, still holding his hat. He passed like an apparition through the banded rhomboid light from the small window in the western wall. The routed dustmotes reeled. It was cold in the room and he could see the pale wisps of the old man's breath rise and vanish in the cold. He could see the black eyes in a weathered face where the old man lay on the bare ticking of his pillow.

Güero, he said. Habla español?

Sí señor.

The old man's hand rose slightly on the bed and fell again. Tell me what you want, he said.

I come to ask you about trappin wolves.

Wolves.

Yessir.

Wolves, the old man said. Help me.

Sir?

Help me.

He was holding up one hand. It hung trembling in the partial light, disembodied, a hand common to all or none. The boy reached and took it. It was cold and hard and bloodless. A thing of leather and bone. The old man struggled up.

La almohada, he wheezed.

The boy almost put his hat on the bed but he caught himself. The old man's grip suddenly tightened and the black eyes hardened but he said nothing. The boy put the hat on and reached behind the old man and got hold of the limp and greasy pillow and stood it against the iron bars of the bedstead and the old man clutched his other hand as well and then leaned back fearfully until he came to rest against the pillow. He looked up at the boy. He'd a strong grip for all his frailty and he seemed loath to release the boy's hands until he'd searched out his eyes.

Gracias, he wheezed.

Por nada.

Bueno, the old man said. Bueno. He slacked his grip and Billy freed one hand and took off his hat again and held it by the brim.

Siéntate, the old man said.

He sat gingerly on the edge of the thin pad that covered the springs of the bed. The old man did not turn loose of his hand.

What is your name?

Parham. Billy Parham.

The old man said the name in silence to himself. Te conozco?

No señor. Estamos a las Charcas.

La Charca.

Sí.

Hay una historia allá.

Historia?

Sí, said the old man. He lay holding the boy's hand and

staring up at the kindlingwood latillas of the ceiling. Una historia desgraciada. De obras desalmadas.

The boy said that he did not know this history and that he would like to hear it but the old man said that it was as well he did not for out of some certain things no good could come and he thought this was one of them. His raspy breath had faded and the sound of it had faded and the faint whiteness of it also that had been briefly visible in the cold of the room. His grip on the boy's hand remained as before.

Mr Sanders said you might have some scent I could buy off of you. He said I ought to ask.

The old man didnt answer.

He give me some that Mr Echols had but the wolf's took to diggin out the traps and springin em.

Dónde está el señor Echols?

No sé. Se fué.

Él murió?

No sir. Not that I've heard.

The old man closed his eyes and opened them again. He lay against the ticking of the pillow with his neck slightly awry. He looked as if he'd been thrown there. In the failing light the eyes betrayed nothing. He seemed to be studying the shadows in the room.

Conocemos por lo largo de las sombras que tardío es el día, he said. He said that men took this to mean that the omens of such an hour were thereby greatly exaggerated but that this was in no way so.

I got one bottle that says Number Seven Matrix, the boy said. And another that dont say nothin.

La matríz, the old man said.

He waited for the old man to continue but the old man did not continue. After a while he asked him what was in the matrix but the old man only pursed his thin mouth in doubt. He continued to hold the boy's hand and they sat that way for some time. The boy was about to put some further query to the old man when the old man spoke again. He said that the matrix was not so easily defined. Each hunter must have his own formula. He said that things were rightly named its attributes which could in no way be counted back into its substance. He said that in his opinion only shewolves in their season were a proper source. The boy said that the wolf of which he spoke was in fact herself a shewolf and he asked if that fact should figure in his strategies against her but the old man only said that there were no more wolves.

Ella vino de Mexico, the boy said.

He seemed not to hear. He said that Echols had caught all the wolves.

El señor Sanders me dice que el señor Echols es medio lobo el mismo. Me dice que él conoce lo que sabe el lobo antes de que lo sepa el lobo. But the old man said that no man knew what the wolf knew.

The sun was low in the west and the shape of the light from the window lay suspended across the room wall to wall. As if something electric had been cored out of that space. Finally the old man repeated his words. El lobo es una cosa incognoscible, he said. Lo que se tiene en la trampa no es mas que dientes y forro. El lobo propio no se puede conocer. Lobo o lo que sabe el lobo. Tan como preguntar lo que saben las piedras. Los arboles. El mundo.

His breath had gone wheezy from his exertions. He coughed quietly and lay still. After a while he spoke again.

Es cazador, el lobo, he said. Cazador. Me entiendes?

The boy didnt know if he understood or not. The old man went on to say that the hunter was a different thing than men supposed. He said that men believe the blood of the slain to be of no consequence but that the wolf knows better. He said that the wolf is a being of great order and that it knows what men do not: that there is no order in the world save that which death has put there. Finally he said that if men drink the blood of God yet they do not understand the seriousness of what they do. He said that men wish to be serious but they do not understand how to be so. Between their acts and their ceremonies lies the world and in this world the storms blow and the trees twist in the wind and all the animals that God has made go to and fro yet this world men do not see. They see the acts of their own hands or they see that which they name and call out to one another but the world between is invisible to them.

You want to catch this wolf, the old man said. Maybe you want the skin so you can get some money. Maybe you can buy some boots or something like that. You can do that. But where is the wolf? The wolf is like the copo de nieve.

Snowflake.

Snowflake. You catch the snowflake but when you look in your hand you dont have it no more. Maybe you see this de-chado. But before you can see it it is gone. If you want to see it you have to see it on its own ground. If you catch it you lose it. And where it goes there is no coming back from. Not even God can bring it back.

The boy looked down at the thin and ropy claws that held his hand. The light from the high window had paled, the sun had set.

Escúchame, joven, the old man wheezed. If you could breathe a breath so strong you could blow out the wolf. Like you blow out the copo. Like you blow out the fire from the candela. The wolf is made the way the world is made. You cannot touch the world. You cannot hold it in your hand for it is made of breath only.

He had pulled himself slightly erect in order to utter these proclamations and now he subsided against the ticking and his eyes seemed to study only the roofpoles overhead. He eased his thin cold grip. Where is the sun? he said.

Se fué.

Ay. Ándale, joven. Ándale pues.

The boy withdrew his hand and he rose. He put on his hat and touched the brim.

Vaya con Dios.

Y tú, joven.

Yet before he reached the door the old man called to him again.

He turned and stood.

Cuántos años tienes? the old man said.

Dieciseis.

The old man lay quietly in the dark. The boy waited.

Escúchame, joven, he said. Yo no sé nada. Esto es la verdad.

Está bien.

The matríz will not help you, the old man said. He said that the boy should find that place where acts of God and those of man are of a piece. Where they cannot be distinguished.

Y qué clase de lugar es éste? the boy said.

Lugares donde el fierro ya está en la tierra, the old man said. Lugares donde ha quemado el fuego.

Y cómo se encuentra?

The old man said that it was not a question of finding such a place but rather of knowing it when it presented itself. He said that it was at such places that God sits and conspires in the destruction of that which he has been at such pains to create.

Y por eso soy hereje, he said. Por eso y nada más.

It was dark in the room. He thanked the old man again but the old man did not answer or if he did he didnt hear him. He turned and went out.

The woman was leaning against the kitchen door. She was silhouetted against the yellow light and he could see her figure through the thin dress she wore. She did not seem troubled that the old man lay alone in the dark at the rear of the house. She asked the boy if the old man had told him how to catch the wolf and he said that he had not.

She touched her temple. He dont remember so good sometimes, she said. He is old.

Yes mam.

No one comes to see him. That's too bad, hey?

Yes mam.

Not even the priest. He came one time maybe two but he dont come no more.

How come?

She shrugged. People say he is brujo. You know what is brujo?

Yes mam.

They say he is brujo. They say God has abandoned this man. He has the sin of Satanás. The sin of orgullo. You know what is orgullo?

Yes mam.

He thinks he knows better than the priest. He thinks he knows better than God.

He told me he didnt know nothin.

Ha, she said. Ha. You believe that? You see this old man? You know what a terrible thing it is to die without God? To be the one that God has cast aside? Think it over.

Yes mam. I got to go.

He touched the brim of his hat and stepped past her to the door and walked out into the evening dark. The lights of the town strewn across the prairie lay in that blue vale like a jeweled serpent incandescing in the evening cool. When he looked back at the house she was standing in the doorway.

Thank you mam, he said.

He is nothing to me, she called. No hay parentesco. You know what is parentesco?

Yes mam.

There is no parentesco. He was tío of the dead wife of my dead husband. What is that? You see? And yet I have him here. Who else would take this man? You see? No one cares.

Yes mam.

Think it over.

He unlooped the bridlereins from the post and untied them. All right, he said. I will.

It could happen to you.

Yes mam.

He mounted up and turned the horse and raised one hand. The mountains to the south stood blackly against a violet sky. The snow on the north slopes so pale. Like spaces left for messages.

La fe, she called. La fe es todo.

He turned the horse out along the rutted track and rode on. When he looked back she was still standing in the open door. Standing in the cold. He looked back one last time and the door was still open but she was not there and he thought perhaps the old man had called her. But then he thought probably that old man didnt call anybody.

TWO DAYS LATER riding down the Cloverdale road he turned off for no reason at all and rode out to where the vaqueros had nooned and sat his horse looking down at the dead black fire. Something had been digging in the ashes.

He dismounted and got a stick and poked through the fire. He mounted up again and walked the horse about the perimeter of the encampment. There was no reason to think that the scavenger had been anything other than a coyote but he rode anyway. He rode slowly and turned the horse nicely. Like a show rider at a judging. On his second circling a little farther from the fire he stopped. In the windshadow of a rock where the sand had drifted lay the perfect print of her forefoot.

He dismounted and knelt holding the reins behind his back and he blew at the loose dirt in the track and pushed at the delicate edges of the track with his thumb. Then he mounted up and went back out to the road and home.

The following day when he ran the traps that he'd reset with the new scent they were pulled out and sprung as before. He set them again and made two blind sets but his heart was not in it. When he rode down through the pass at noon and looked out over the Cloverdale Valley the first thing he saw was the thin spire of smoke in the distance from the vaqueros' cookfire.

He sat the horse a long time. He put his hand on the cantle

and looked back toward the pass and he looked out over the valley again. Then he turned and rode back up the mountain.

By the time he'd pulled the traps and packed them in the basket and ridden down into the valley and crossed the road it was early evening. Once more he checked the sun by the width of his hand on the horizon. He had little more than an hour of daylight.

He dismounted at the fire and took the trowel from the pack-basket and squatted and began to clear a space among the ashes and charcoal and fresh bones. At the heart of the fire there were live coals yet and he raked them aside to cool and dug a hole in the ground beneath the fire and then got a trap from the basket. He didnt even bother to put on the deerskin gloves.

He screwed down the springs with the clamps and opened the jaws and set the trigger in the notch and eyed the clearance while he backed off the clampscrew. Then he removed both clamps and dropped the draghook and chain into the hole and set the trap in the fire.

He placed one of the squares of oiled paper over the jaws that no coals lodge under the pan to keep it from tripping and he drifted ash over the trap with the screenbox and scattered back the charcoal and the charred bits of wood and he put back the bones and rinds of blackened skin and drifted more ashes over the set and then rose and stepped away and stood looking at the cold fire and wiping the trowel on the side of his jeans. Lastly he smoothed a place in the sand before the fire, digging out small clumps of grass and buckbrush, and there he wrote a letter to the vaqueros, etching it deep that the wind not take it. Cuidado, he wrote. Hay una trampa de lobos enterrada en el fuego. Then he flung away the stick and dropped the trowel back into the basket and shouldered the basket and mounted up.

He rode out across the pasture toward the road and in the cold blue twilight he turned and looked a last time toward the set. He leaned and spat. You read my sign, he said. If you can. Then he turned the horse toward home.

It was two hours past dark when he walked into the kitchen

His mother was at the stove. His father was still sitting at the table drinking coffee. The worn blue ledgerbook in which they kept accounts lay on the table to one side.

Where you been? his father said.

He sat down and his father heard him out and when he was done he nodded.

All my life, he said, I been witness to people showin up where they was supposed to be at various times after they'd said they'd be there. I never heard one yet that didnt have a reason for it.

Yessir.

But there aint but one reason.

Yessir.

You know what it is?

No sir.

It's that their word's no good. That's the only reason there ever was or ever will be.

Yessir.

His mother had got his supper from the warmer over the stove and she set it down in front of him and laid down the silver.

Eat your supper, she said.

She left the room. His father sat watching him eat. After a while he rose and took his cup to the sink and rinsed it out and set it upside down on the sideboard. I'll call you in the mornin, he said. You need to get over there fore you catch you one of them Mexicans.

Yessir.

We never would hear the end of it.

Yessir.

Aint no guarantee that a one of em can read.

Yessir.

He finished his supper and went to bed. Boyd was already asleep. He lay awake a long time thinking about the wolf. He tried to see the world the wolf saw. He tried to think about it running in the mountains at night. He wondered if the wolf were so unknowable as the old man said. He wondered at the world it smelled or what it tasted. He wondered had the living blood with which it slaked its throat a different taste to the thick iron tincture of his own. Or to the blood of God. In the morning he was out before daylight saddling the horse in the cold dark of the barn. He rode out the gate before his father was even up and he never saw him again.

Riding along the road south he could smell the cattle out in the fields in the dark beyond the bar ditch and the running fence. When he rode through Cloverdale it was just gray light. He turned up the Cloverdale Creek road and rode on. Behind him the sun was rising in the San Luis Pass and his new shadow riding before him lay long and thin upon the road. He rode past the old dance platform in the woods and two hours later when he left the road and crossed the pasture to the vaqueros' noon fire the wolf stood up to meet him.

The horse stopped and backed and stamped. He held the animal and patted it and spoke to it and watched the wolf. His heart was slamming inside his chest like something that wanted out. She was caught by the right forefoot. The drag had caught in a cholla less than a hundred feet from the fire and there she stood. He patted the horse and spoke to it and reached down and unfastened the buckle on the saddlescabbard and slid the rifle free and stepped down and dropped the reins. The wolf crouched slightly. As if she'd try to hide. Then she stood again and looked at him and looked off toward the mountains.

When he approached she bared her teeth but she did not growl and she kept her yellow eyes from off his person. White bone showed in the bloody wound between the jaws of the trap. He could see her teats through the thin fur of her underbelly and she kept her tail tucked and pulled at the trap and stood.

He walked around her. She turned and backed. The sun was well up and in the sun her fur was a grayish dun with paler tips at the ruff and a black stripe along the back and she turned and backed to the length of the chain and her flanks sucked in and out with the motion of her breathing. He squatted on the ground and stood the rifle before him and held it by the forestock and he squatted there for a long time.

He was in no way prepared for what he beheld. Among other things he'd not considered simply whether he could ride to the ranch and be back with his father before the vaqueros arrived at noon if they would so arrive. He tried to remember what his father had said. If her leg were broke or she were caught by the paw. He looked at the height of the sun and he looked back out toward the road. When he looked at the wolf again she was lying down but when his eyes fell upon her she stood again. The standing horse tossed its head and the bridlebit clinked but she paid no attention to the horse at all. He rose and walked back and scabbarded the rifle and took up the reins and mounted up and turned the horse and headed out to the road. Half way he stopped again and turned and looked back. The wolf was watching him as before. He sat the horse a long time. The sun warm on his back. The world waiting. Then he rode back to the wolf.

She rose and stood with her sides caving in and out. She carried her head low and her tongue hung trembling between the long incisors of her lower jaw. He undid the string from his catchrope and slung it over his shoulder and stepped down. He took some lengths of pigginstring from the mochila behind the saddle and looped them through his belt and unlimbered the catchrope and walked around the wolf. The horse was no use to him because if it leaned back on the rope it would kill the wolf or pull it from the trap or both. He circled the wolf and looked for something to tie to that he could stretch her. There was nothing that his rope would reach and double and finally he took off his coat and blindfolded the horse with it and led it forward upwind of the wolf and dropped the reins that it would stand. Then he paid out the rope and built his loop and dropped it over her. She stepped through it with the trap and looked at it and looked at him. Now he had the rope over the trapchain. He looked at it in disgust and dropped the rope and walked out in the desert until he found a paloverde and he cut from it a pole some seven feet long with a forked branch at the end and came back trimming off the limbs with his knife. She watched him. He snared the loop with the end of the pole and pulled it toward him. He thought she might bite at the pole but she did not. When he got the loop in his hand he had to pay the whole forty feet of rope back through the honda and begin again. She watched the rope make its traverse with great attention and when the end of it had passed over the trapchain and withdrew through the dead grass she lay down again.

He built a smaller loop and came forward. She stood. He swung the loop and she flattened her ears and ducked and bared her teeth at him. He made two more tries and on the third the loop dropped over her neck and he snatched the rope taut.

She stood twisting on her hindlegs holding the heavy trap up at her chest and snapping at the rope and pawing with her free foot. She let out a low whine which was the first sound she had made.

He stepped back and stretched her out till she lay gasping on the ground and he backed toward the horse paying out rope and then looped the rope about the saddlehorn and came back carrying the free end. He winced to see her bloodied foreleg stretched in the trap but there was no help for it. She got her hindquarters up off the ground and scrabbled sideways and she twisted and fought the rope and slung her head from side to side and even once got completely to her feet again before he pulled her down. He squatted holding the rope just a few feet from her and after a while she lay gasping quietly in the dirt. She looked toward him with her yellow eyes and closed them slowly and then looked away.

He stood on the rope with one foot and took out his knife again and reached carefully and got hold of the paloverde pole. He cut a threefoot length from the end of it and put the knife back in his pocket and took a length of the pigginstring from his belt and made a noose with it and took it in his teeth. Then he stepped off the rope and picked up the end of it and moved toward her with the stick. She watched with one almond eye, deep yellow, deepening to amber at the iris. She strained at the rope, her face in the dirt, her mouth open and her teeth so white, so perfectly made. He pulled the rope tighter where it was belayed around the saddlehorn. He pulled until he'd shut off her air and then he jammed the stick between her teeth.

She made no sound. She bowed up and twisted her head and bit at the stick and tried to get quit of it. He hauled on the rope and stretched her out wild and gagging and forced her lower jaw to the ground with the stick and stepped on the rope again with his boot not a foot from those teeth. Then he took the pigginstring from his mouth and dropped the loop of it over her muzzle and jerked it tight and seized her by one ear and made three turns of the cord about her jaws faster than eye could follow and halfhitched it and fell upon her, kneeling with the living wolf gasping between his legs and sucking air and her tongue working within the teeth all stuck with dirt and debris. She looked up at him, the eye delicately aslant, the knowledge of the world it held sufficient to the day if not to the day's evil. Then she closed her eyes and he slacked the rope and stood and stepped away and she lay breathing heavily with her forefoot stretched behind her in the trap and the stick in her mouth. He stood gasping himself. Cold as it was he was wringing wet with sweat. He turned and looked at the horse where it stood with his coat over its head. By damn, he said. By damn. He coiled the loose rope from off the ground and walked back to the horse and lifted the rope up and over the saddlehorn and untied the coatsleeves from under the horse's jaw and unhooded it and laid the coat across the saddle. The horse lifted its head and blew and looked toward the wolf and he patted it on the neck and spoke to it and got the clamps out of the mochila and pulled the coil of rope up over his shoulder and turned back to the wolf.

Before he could reach her she leapt up and lunged against the trapchain twisting and slinging her head and pawing at her mouth with her free foot. He pulled her down with the rope and held her. A white foam seethed between her teeth. He approached slowly and reached and held her by the stick in her jaws and spoke to her but his voice seemed only to make her shudder. He looked at the leg in the trap. It looked bad. He got hold of the trap and put the clamp over the spring and screwed it down and then did the second spring. When the eye of the spring dropped past the hinges in the plate the jaws fell open and her wrecked forefoot spilled out limp and bloody with the white bone shining. He reached to touch it but she snatched it away and stood. He was amazed at her quickness. She stood squared off at him, her eyes level with his where he knelt, still not meeting his gaze. He slid the coil of rope off his shoulder to the ground and picked up the end of it and wrapped it around his fist in a double grip. Then he let go slack the short end of the rope by which he held her. She tested the injured foot on the ground and drew it up again.

Go on, he said. If you think you can.

She turned and wheeled away. So quick. He hardly had time to get one heel in front of him in the dirt before she hit the end of the rope. She did a cartwheel and landed on her back and jerked him forward onto his elbows. He scrambled up but she was already off in another direction and when she hit the end of the rope again she almost snatched him off the ground. He turned and dug both heels in and took a turn of the rope around his wrist. She had swung toward the horse now and the horse snorted and set off toward the road at a trot with the reins trailing. She ran at the end of the rope in a circle until she passed the cholla that had first caught the trapchain drag and here the rope brought her around until she stood snubbed and gasping among the thorns.

He rose and walked up to her. She squatted and flattened her ears. Slobber swung in white strings from her jaw. He took out his knife and reached and got hold of the stick in her mouth and he spoke to her and stroked her head but she only winced and shivered.

It aint no use to fight it, he told her.

He cut the trailing length of the paloverde off short at the side of her mouth and put the knife away and walked the end of the rope around the cholla till it was free and then led her twisting and shaking her head out onto the open ground. He could not believe how strong she was. He stood spraddlelegged with the rope in both hands across his thighs and turned and scanned the country for some sight of his horse. She would not quit struggling and he got hold of the rope end again and sat with it doubled in his fist and dug both heels in and let her go. When she hit the end of the rope this time she flew into the air and landed on her back and lay there. He hauled on the rope and dragged her towards him through the dirt.

Get up, he said. You aint hurt.

He walked down and stood over her where she lay panting. He looked at the injured leg. There was a flap of loose skin pushed down around her ankle like a sock and the wound was dirty and stuck with twigs and leaves. He knelt and touched her. Come on, he said. You've done run my horse off so let's go find him.

By the time he'd dragged her out to the road he was all but exhausted. The horse was standing a hundred yards away grazing in the bar ditch. It raised its head and looked at him and bent to graze again. He halfhitched the catchrope to a fencepost and took the last length of cord from his belt and tied the honda to the rope that the noose could not back off loose and then he rose and walked back across the pasture to pick his coat up off the ground and to get the trap.

When he got back she was snubbed up against the fencepost and half strangling where she'd gone back and forth. He dropped the trap and knelt and unhitched the rope from the post and paid the whole length of it back and forth through the wires until he had her free again. She got up and sat in the dusty grass and looked off wildly up the road toward the mountains with the foam seething between her teeth and dripping from the paloverde stick.

You aint got no damn sense, he told her.

He rose and put on his coat and jammed the clamps into his coatpocket and slung the trap over his shoulder by the chain and then dragged her out into the middle of the road and set off with her behind him sliding stifflegged and raking a trail through the dust and gravel.

The horse raised its head to study them, chewing ruminatively. Then it turned and set off down the road.

He stopped and stood looking after it. He turned and looked back at the wolf. In the distance he could hear the chug of the old rancher's Model A and he realized that she had heard it some time ago. He shortened up the rope a couple of reaches and dragged the wolf through the bar ditch and stood by the fence and watched the truck come over the hill and approach in its attendant dust and clatter.

The old man slowed and leaned and peered. The wolf was jerking and twisting and the boy stood behind her and held her with both hands. By the time the truck had pulled abreast of them he was lying on the ground with his legs scissored about her midriff and his arms around her neck. The old man stopped and sat the idling truck and leaned across and rolled down the window. What in the hell, he said. What in the hell.

You reckon you could turn that thing off? the boy said.

That's a damn wolf.

Yessir it is.

What in the hell.

The truck's scarin her.

Scarin her?

Yessir.

Boy what's wrong with you? That thing comes out of that riggin it'll eat you alive.

Yessir.

What are you doin with him?

It's a she.

It's a what?

A she. It's a she.

Hell fire, it dont make a damn he or she. What are you doin with it?

Fixin to take it home.

Home?

Yessir.

Whatever in the contumacious hell for?

Can you not turn that thing off?

It aint all that easy to start again.

Well could I maybe get you to drive down there and catch my horse for me and bring him back. I'd tie her up but she gets all fuzzled up in the fencewire.

What I'd like to do is to try and save you the trouble of bein eat, the old man said. What are you takin it home for?

It's kindly a long story.

Well I'd sure like to hear it.

The boy looked down the road where the horse stood grazing. He looked at the old man. Well, he said. My daddy wanted me to come and get him if I caught her but I didnt want to leave her cause they's been some vaqueros takin their dinner over yonder and I figured they'd probably shoot her so I just decided to take her on home with me.

Have you always been crazy?

I dont know. I never was much put to the test before today.

How old are you?

Sixteen.

Sixteen.

Yessir.

Well you aint got the sense God give a goose. Did you know that?

You may be right.

How do you expect your horse to tolerate a bunch of nonsense such as this.

If I can get him caught he wont have a whole lot of say about it.

You plan on leadin that thing behind a horse?

Yessir.

How you expect to get her to do that?

She aint got a whole lot of choice either.

The old man sat looking at him. Then he climbed out of the truck and shut the door and adjusted his hat and walked around and stood at the edge of the bar ditch. He had on canvas pants and a blanketlined canvas coat with a corduroy collar and he wore boots with walkingheels and a full beaver John B Stetson hat.

How close can I get? he said.

Close as you want.

He crossed the ditch and came up and stood looking at the wolf. He looked at the boy and he looked at the wolf some more.

She's fixin to have pups.

Yessir.

Damn good thing you caught her.

Yessir.

Can you touch her?

Yessir. You can touch her.

The old man squatted and put his hand on the wolf. The wolf bowed and writhed and he snatched his hand away. Then he touched her again. He looked at the boy. Wolf, he said.

Yessir.

What do you aim to do with her?

I dont know.

I guess you'll collect the bounty. Sell the hide.

Yessir.

She dont much like bein touched, does she?

No sir. Not much.

When we used to bring cattle up the valley from down around Ciénega Springs why first night we'd generally hit in about Government Draw and make camp there. And you could hear em all across the valley. Them first warm nights. You'd nearly always hear em in that part of the valley. I aint heard one in years.

She come up from Mexico.

I dont doubt it. Ever other damn thing does.

He rose and looked off down the road to where the horse was grazing. You want my advice, he said, you'll let me fetch you that rifle I see sticking out of the boot yonder and shoot this son of a bitch right between the eyes and be done with it.

If I can just get my horse caught I'll be all right, the boy said.

Well. You suit yourself.

Yessir. I aim to.

The old man shook his head. All right, he said. Wait here and I'll go get him.

I aint goin nowheres, the boy said.

He went back to the truck and got in and drove down to where the horse was standing. When the horse saw the truck coming it crossed through the bar ditch and stood against the fence and the old man got out and walked the horse down along the fence until he could catch the trailing reins and then he led the horse back up the road. The boy sat holding the wolf. It was very quiet. The only sound along the road was the faint dry clop of the horse's hooves in the gravel and the steady chugging of the truck where the old man had left it idling by the roadside.

When he dragged the wolf out to the road the horse backed and stood facing her.

Maybe you better tie the horse, the old man said.

If you'll just hold him a minute I'll be all right.

I aint sure but what I'd about as soon hold the wolf.

The boy paid out enough slack so that the wolf could get to the bar ditch but not enough for her to reach the fence. He dallied the rope to the saddlehorn and turned the wolf loose and she scampered for the ditch on three legs and hit the rope end and flipped endwise and got up and crouched in the ditch and lay waiting. The boy turned and took the reins from the old man and put one knuckle to his hatbrim.

I'm much obliged, he said.

That's all right. It's been a interestin day.

Yessir. Mine aint over.

No it aint. You mind she dont get that mouth loose, you hear? She'll take a chunk out of you you couldnt put in your hat.

Yessir.

He stood in the stirrup and swung up and checked the dally and nudged his hat back and nodded to the old man. I'm much obliged, he said.

When he put the horse forward the wolf came up out of the ditch at the end of the rope with the game foot to her chest and swung into the road and went dragging after the horse stifflegged and rigid as a piece of taxidermy. He stopped and looked back. The old man was standing in the road watching them.

Sir? he said.

Yes.

Maybe you better go on by and get your truck. So you wont have to pass us.

I think that's a good idea.

He walked down and got into the truck and turned and looked back at them. The boy raised his hand. The old man looked like he might be going to call something to him but he didnt and he lifted his hand and turned and pulled away down the road toward Cloverdale.

He went on. Gusts of wind were blowing dust off the top of the road. When he looked back at her she had her windward eye asquint against the blowing grit and she was hobbling along after the horse with her head lowered. He stopped and she came slightly forward to slack the rope and then turned and went down into the bar ditch again. He was about to put the horse forward when she squatted in the ditch and began to make water. When she was done she turned and sniffed at the spot and checked the wind with her nose and then came up into the road and stood with her tail between her hocks and the wind making little furrows in her hair.

The boy sat the horse a long time watching her. Then he got down and dropped the reins and got his canteen and walked around to where she was standing. She backed along the reach of the rope. He slung the canteen over his shoulder and stepped over the rope and held it between his knee and pulled her to him. She twisted and stood but he got hold of the noose and doubled it in his fist and forced her down into the grass by the side of the road and got astraddle of her. It was all he could do to hold her. He slung the canteen around and unscrewed the cap with his teeth. The horse stamped in the road and he spoke to it and then holding the wolf by the stick in her mouth with her head against his knee he began slowly to pour water into the side of her mouth. She lay still. Her eye stopped moving. Then she began to swallow.

Most of the water ran out on the ground but he continued to trickle it between her teeth along the greenstick bit. When the canteen was empty he let go of the stick and she lay quietly getting her breath. He stood and stepped back but she didnt move. He swung the cap up by its chain and screwed it back onto the canteen and walked back out to the horse and slung the canteen over the mochila and looked back at her. She was standing watching him. He mounted up and nudged the horse forward. When he looked back she was limping along at the end of the rope. When he stopped she stopped. An hour down the road he stopped for a long time. He was at Robertson's crossfence. Ahead an hour's ride lay Cloverdale and the road north. South lay the open country. The yellow grass heeled under the blowing wind and sunlight was running over the country before the moving clouds. The horse shook its head and stamped and stood. Damn all of it, the boy said. Just damn all of it.

He turned the horse and crossed through the ditch and rode up onto the broad plain that stretched away before him south toward the mountains of Mexico.

Midday they crossed through a low pass in the easternmost spur of the Guadalupes and rode out down the open valley. They saw riders on the plain in the distance but the riders rode on. Late afternoon they passed through the last low cones of hills on that volcanic ground and an hour later they came to the last fence in the country.

It was a crossfence running east and west. On the other side was a dirt track. He turned the horse east and followed the fence. There was a cattletrail along the fence but he rode a rope length from it that the wolf not cross under the wires and by and by he came to a ranch house.

He sat the horse on a slight rise of ground and studied the house. He could see no safe place to leave the wolf so he continued on. At the gate he dismounted and unpinned the chain and swung the gate open and led horse and wolf through and closed the gate again and remounted. The wolf was standing bowed up in the road with its hair all wrong like something pulled backwards out of a pipe and when he put the horse forward she came skidding behind with her legs locked. He looked back at her. If I'd been eatin these people's cows, he said, I wouldnt want to come callin neither.

Before he could put the horse forward again there was a great howl from the direction of the house and when he looked three large hounds were coming up the road very low and very fast.

Shit almighty, he said.

He stepped down and snubbed the reins to the top fencewire and snatched the rifle out of the scabbard. Bird's eyes were rolling and he began to stamp about in the road. The wolf stood stock still with her tail up and her hair straight out. The horse turned and backed at the reins, the fencewire bowed. He heard in the melee a staple pop and he suddenly saw as in an evil dream the specter of the horse at full gallop on the plain with the wolf behind at the end of the rope and the dogs in wild pursuit and he snatched the rope from about the saddlehorn just as the reins broke and the horse wheeled and went pounding and he turned with the rifle and the wolf to stand off the dogs suddenly all about him in a bedlam of howling and teeth and whited eyes.

They circled scrabbling in the dirt of the road and he pulled the wolf hard up against his leg and yelled at them and whacked them away with the barrel of the rifle. Two were carrying broken lengths of chain at their collar and the third wore no collar at all. In all that whirling pandemonium he could feel the wolf trembling electrically against him and her heart hammering.

They were working hounds and although they circled and bayed he knew that they would be loath to attack anything a man held in absolute custody even if it was a wolf. He turned with them and caught one of them in the side of the head with the barrel of the rifle. Git, he shouted. Git. By now two men were coming from the house at a trot.

They called the dogs by name and two of the dogs actually stopped and looked back down the road. The third arched its back and came at the wolf with a mincing sidelong step and popped its teeth at her and drew away again and stood howling. One of the men had a dinnernapkin hanging from the neck of his shirt and he was breathing heavily. You Julie, he called. Git. Damnation. Get a stick or somethin, RL. Good God.

The other man unlatched his buckle and whipped his belt out through the loops and began to lay about him with the buckle end. Instantly the dogs were yelping and scurrying. The older man stopped and stood with his hands on his hips catching his breath. He turned to the boy. He saw the napkin in his shirt and pulled it free and wiped his forehead with it and stuck the napkin in his back pocket. You mind tellin me what the hell you're doin? he said.

Tryin to keep these damn dogs off of my wolf.

Dont give me no smart answer.

I aint. I come up on your fence and went to huntin a gate is all. I didnt know all hell was fixin to bust loose.

What the hell did you expect was goin to happen?

I didnt know there was dogs here.

Well hell, you seen the house didnt you?

Yessir.

The man squinted at him. You're Will Parham's boy. Aint you?

Yessir.

What's your name?

Billy Parham.

Well Billy this might sound to you like a ignorant question but what in the hell are you doin with that thing?

I caught it.

Well I reckon you did. It's the one with the stick in its mouth. Where are you started with it?

I was started home.

No you wasnt. You was headed yonway.

I was started home with it when I changed my mind.

What did you change it to?

The boy didnt answer. The dogs were pacing up and down, the hair standing along their backs.

RL, take the dogs on to the house and put em up. Tell Mama I'll be there directly.

He turned to the boy again. How do you aim to get your horse back?

Walk him down, I reckon.

Well it's about two miles to the first cattleguard.

The boy stood holding the wolf. He looked off down the road in the direction the horse had gone.

Will that thing ride in a truck? the man said.

The boy gave him a peculiar look.

Hell, the man said. I want you to listen at me. RL can you take him in the truck to catch his horse?

Yessir. Is his horse hard to catch?

Your horse hard to catch? the man said.

No sir.

He says it aint.

Well unless he just wants to go ridin I reckon I can get his horse for him.

You dont want to ride with that wolf is what it is, the man said.

It aint that I dont want to. It's that I aint goin to.

Well I was fixin to say that since it's liable to jump out of the bed of the truck why dont you take it up front in the cab with you and the boy can ride in the back?

RL had the dogs by their trailing pieces of chain and was fastening the third dog to them with his belt. I got a life sized picture of me ridin up the road with a wolf in the cab of my truck, he said. I can just see it plain as day.

The man stood looking at the wolf. He reached to adjust his hat but he had no hat on so he scratched his head. He looked at the boy. And here I thought I knowed all the lunatics in this valley, he said. Country crowdin up the way it is. You caint hardly keep up with your own neighbors even. Have you had your supper?

No sir.

Well come on to the house.

What do you want me to do with her?

Her?

This here wolf.

Well I guess it'll just have to lay around the kitchen till we get done eatin.

Lay around the kitchen?

It's a joke, son. Hell fire. You brought that thing in the house you could hear my wife in Albuquerque with the wires down.

I dont want to leave her outside. Somethin's liable to jump her.

I know that. Just come on. I wouldnt leave her out for nobody to see noways. They'd come and get me with a butterfly net.

They put the wolf in the smokehouse and left her and walked back to the kitchen. The man looked at the rifle the boy was carrying but he didnt say anything. When they got to the kitchen door the boy stood the rifle against the side of the house and the man held the door for him and they went in.

The woman had put the supper above the oven to warm and she brought everything out again and set a plate for the boy. Outside they heard RL start the truck. They passed the dishes, bowls of mashed potatoes and pinto beans and a platter of fried steaks. When he had his plate loaded with about all it could hold he looked up at the man. The man nodded at his plate.

We done blessed the food once, he said. So unless you got some personal business to conduct just tuck on in.

Yessir.

They began to eat.

Mama, the man said, see if you can get him to tell us where it is he's headed with that lobo.

If he dont want to say he dont have to, the woman said.

I'm takin her to Mexico.

The man reached for the butter. Well, he said. That seems like a good idea.

I'm goin to take her down there and turn her loose.

The man nodded. Turn her loose, he said.

Yessir.

She's got some pups somewheres, aint she?

No sir. Not yet she dont.

You sure about that?

Yessir. She's fixin to have some.

What have you got against the Mexicans?

I dont have nothin against em.

You just figured they might could use another wolf or two.

The boy cut a piece from his steak and forked it up. The man watched him.

How are they fixed for rattlesnakes down there do you reckon?

I aint takin her to give to nobody. I'm just takin her down there and turnin her loose. It's where she come from.

The man troweled butter very methodically along the edge of a biscuit with his knife. He put the top back on the biscuit and looked at the boy.

You a very peculiar kid, he said. Did you know that?

No sir. I was always just like everbody else far as I know.

Well you aint.

Yessir.

Tell me this. You aint plannin on just dumpin that thing across the line are you? Cause if you are I'm goin to follow you out there with a rifle.

I was goin to take her back to the mountains.

Take her back to the mountains, the man said. He looked at the biscuit speculatively and then bit slowly into it.

Where all is your family from? the woman said.

We're up at the Charcas.

She means before that, the man said.

We come out of Grant County. And De Baca fore that.

The man nodded.

We been down here a long time.

What's a long time?

Goin on ten years.

Ten years, the man said. Time just flies, dont it?

Go on and eat your supper, the woman said. Dont pay no attention to him.

They ate. After a while the truck pulled into the yard and passed the house and the woman got up from the table and went to get RL's plate from the warmer over the stove.

When they walked out after supper it was evening and growing cold and the sun was low over the mountains to the west. Bird stood in the yard tied by a rope halter to the gate and the bridle and reins were hung over the saddlehorn. The woman stood in the kitchen door and watched them cross toward the smokehouse.

Let's be careful about openin this door, the man said. If that thing has come out of that muzzletie you'll wish you was in a bathtub with a alligator.

Yessir, the boy said.

The man lifted the open lock from the haspstaple and the boy pushed the door in carefully. She was standing, backed into the corner. There was no window in the little adobe building and she blinked when the light fell across her.

She's all right, the boy said.

He pushed the door open.

That poor thing, the woman said.

The rancher turned patiently. Jane Ellen, he said, what are you doin out here?

That leg looks awful. I'm goin to get Jaime.

You're goin to what?

Just wait here.

She turned and set off across the yard. Half way she pulled off the coat she'd thrown over her shoulders and put it on. The man leaned in the door and shook his head.

Where was she goin? the boy said.

More craziness, the man said. We could be in a epidemic.

He stood in the doorway and rolled a smoke while the boy sat holding the wolf by the rope.

You dont use these do you? the man said.

No sir.

That's good. Dont start.

He smoked. He looked at the boy. What would you take for her cash money? he said.

She aint for sale.

What would you take if she was?

I wouldnt. Cause she aint.

When the woman came back she had with her an old Mexican who carried a small green tin deedbox under his arm. He greeted the rancher and nudged his hat and entered the smokehouse with the woman behind him. The woman was carrying a bundle of clean sheeting. The Mexican nodded to the boy and touched his hat again and knelt in front of the wolf and looked at it.

Puede detenerla? he said.

Sí, said the boy.

Necesitas más luz? the woman said.

Sí, said the Mexican.

The man stepped out into the yard and dropped the cigarette and stepped on it. They moved the wolf toward the door and the boy held her while the Mexican took her by the elbow and studied the damaged foreleg. The woman set the tin box on the floor and opened it and took out a bottle of witch-hazel and doped a piece of the sheeting with it. She handed it to the Mexican and he took it and looked at the boy.

Estás listo, joven?

Listo.

He renewed his grip on the wolf and wrapped his legs around her. The Mexican took hold of the wolf's foreleg and began to clean the wound.

She let out a strangled yelp and reared twisting in the boy's arms and snatched her foot out of the Mexican's grip.

Otra vez, the Mexican said.

They began again.

On the second attempt she slung the boy about the room and the Mexican stepped back quickly. The woman had already backed away. The wolf was standing with the slobber seething in and out between her teeth and the boy was lying on the floor beneath her hanging on to her neck. The rancher out in the yard had started to roll another cigarette but now he put the sack back in his shirtpocket and adjusted his hat.

Hang on a minute, he said. Damnation. Just hold it a minute.

He climbed through the door and reached and got hold of the wolf by the rope and twisted the rope in his fist.

People hear about me givin first aid to a damn wolf I wont be able to live in this county, he said. All right. Do your damndest. Ándale.

They finished their surgery in the last light of the sun. The Mexican had pulled the loose flap of skin into place and he sat patiently sewing it with a small curved needle clamped in a hemostat and when he was done he daubed it with Corona Salve and wrapped it in sheeting and tied it. RL had come out and stood watching them and picking his teeth.

Did you give her some water? the woman said.

Yes mam. It's kindly hard for her to drink.

I guess if you took that thing off of her she'd bite.

The rancher stepped over the wolf and out into the yard. Bite, he said. Good God almighty.

When he rode out thirty minutes later it was all but dark. He'd given the trap to the rancher to keep for him and he had a huge lunch wrapped in a cloth packed away in the mochila along with the rest of the sheeting and the jar of Corona Salve and he had an old Saltillo blanket rolled and tied behind the saddle. Someone had spliced new leather into the broken bridle reins and the wolf was wearing a harnessleather dogcollar with a brass plate that had the rancher's name and RFD number and Cloverdale NM stamped into it. The rancher walked out to the gate with him and undid the gatelatch and swung it open and the boy led the horse through with the wolf behind and mounted up.

You take care, son, the man said.

Yessir, I will. Thank you.

I thought about keepin you here. Send for your daddy.

Yessir, I know you did.

He may want to whip me over it.

No he wont.

Well. Watch out for the bandidos.

Yessir. I will. I thank you and the missus.

The man nodded. The boy raised one hand and reined the horse about and set out across the darkening land with the wolf hobbling behind. The man stood at the gate watching after him. All to the south was the dark of the mountains where they rode and he could not skylight them there and soon they were swallowed up and lost horse and rider in the oncoming night. The last thing he saw on that windblown waste was the white bandaged leg of the wolf moving random and staccato like some pale djinn out there antic in the growing cold and dark. Then it too vanished and he closed the gate and turned toward the house.

THEY CROSSED in that deep twilight a broad volcanic plain bounded within the rim of hills. The hills were a deep blue in the blue dusk and the round feet of the pony clopped flatly on the gravel of the desert floor. The night was falling down from the east and the darkness that passed over them came in a sudden breath of cold and stillness and passed on. As if the darkness had a soul itself that was the sun's assassin hurrying to the west

as once men did believe, as they may believe again. They rode
up off the plain in the final dying light man and wolf and horse
over a terraceland of low hills much eroded by the wind and
they crossed through a fenceline or crossed where a fenceline
once had been, the wires long down and rolled and carried off
and the little naked mesquite posts wandering singlefile away
into the night like an enfilade of bent and twisted pensioners.
They rode through the pass in the dark and there he sat the
horse and watched lightning to the south far over the plains of
Mexico. The wind was thrashing softly through the trees in the
pass and in the wind were spits of sleet. He made his camp in
the lee of an arroyo south of the pass and gathered wood and
made a fire and gave the wolf all the water she would drink.
Then he tied her to the washedout elbow of a cottonwood and
walked back and unsaddled and hobbled the horse. He unrolled
the blanket and threw it over his shoulders and took the mochila
and went and sat before the fire. The wolf sat on her haunches
below him in the draw and watched him with her intractable
eyes so red in the firelight. From time to time she would bend
to try the bindings on her leg with her sideteeth but she could
not grip them for the stick in her jaws.

He took a sandwich of steak and lightbread from the mochila
and unwrapped it and sat eating. The little fire sawed about in
the wind and the fine sleet fell slant upon them out of the
darkness and hissed in the coals. He ate and watched the wolf.
She pricked her ears and turned and looked out at the night but
whatever was passing passed and after a while she stood and
looked bleakly at the ground that was not of her choosing and
circled three times and lay down facing the fire with her tail
over her nose.

He woke all night with the cold. He'd rise and mend back
the fire and she was always watching him. When the flames
came up her eyes burned out there like gatelamps to another
world. A world burning on the shore of an unknowable void.
A world construed out of blood and blood's alcahest and blood
in its core and in its integument because it was that nothing save

blood had power to resonate against that void which threatened hourly to devour it. He wrapped himself in the blanket and watched her. When those eyes and the nation to which they stood witness were gone at last with their dignity back into their origins there would perhaps be other fires and other witnesses and other worlds otherwise beheld. But they would not be this one.

The last few hours before dawn he did sleep, cold or no. He rose in the gray light and pulled the blanket about him and knelt and tried to blow life into the dead ashes of the fire. He walked out to where he could watch the east for the sunrise. A mottled scud of clouds lay across the neutral desert sky. The wind had abated and the dawn was soundless.

When he approached the wolf holding the canteen she did not bridle or arch her back at him. He touched her and she edged away. He held her by the collar and pushed her down and sat trickling the water between her teeth while her tongue worked and her gullet jerked and the cold slant eye watched his hand. He held his hand under her jaw at the far side to save the water running out on the ground and she drank the canteen dry. He sat stroking her. Then he reached down and felt her belly. She struggled and her eye rolled wildly. He spoke to her softly. He put the flat of his hand between her warm and naked teats. He held it there for a long time. Then he felt something move.

When he set out across the valley to the south the grass was golden in the morning sun. Antelope were grazing on the plain a half mile to the east. He looked back to see if she had taken notice of them but she had not. She limped along behind the horse steadfast and doglike and in this fashion they crossed sometime near noon the international boundary line into Mexico, State of Sonora, undifferentiated in its terrain from the country they quit and yet wholly alien and wholly strange. He sat the horse and looked out over the red hills. To the east he could see one of the concrete obelisks that stood for a boundary marker. In that desert waste it had the look of some monument to a lost expedition.

Two hours later they'd left the valley and begun to climb through the low hills. Sparse grass and ocotillo. A few thin cattle trotted off before them. By and by they struck the Cajón Bonita which was the main trail south through the mountains and by the side of this track an hour later they came upon a small rancho.

He sat the horse and pulled the wolf close to him by the rope and he called out and waited to see if dogs would show but none did. He rode slowly. There were three crumbling adobe houses and a man dressed in rags stood in the doorway of one of them. The place had the look of an old waystation fallen into ruin. He rode forward and halted in front of the man and sat with his hands crossed at the wrists and resting on the pommel of his saddle.

Adónde va? the man said.

A las montañas.

The man nodded. He wiped his nose with his sleeve and turned and looked toward the mountains so spoken. As if he had not properly considered them before. He looked at the boy and at the horse and at the wolf and at the boy again.

Es cazador usted?

Sí.

Bueno, said the man. Bueno.

The day was cold for all that the sun shone and yet the man was half naked nor was there any smoke coming from the buildings. He looked at the wolf.

Es buena cazadora su perra?

The boy looked at the wolf. Sí, he said. Mejor no hay.

Es feroz?

A veces.

Bueno, said the man. Bueno. He asked the boy if he had tobacco, if he had coffee, if he had meat. The boy had none of these things and the man seemed to accept the inevitable truth of it. He stood leaning in the doorway, looking at the ground. After a while the boy realized that he was discussing something with himself.

Bueno, the boy said. Hasta luego.

The man flung up one arm. His rags flapped about him. Ándale, he said.

He rode on. When he looked back the man was still in the doorway. He was looking out back down the trail as if perhaps to see who might be coming next.

By late afternoon when he would dismount and advance toward her with the canteen she would dip slowly to the ground like a circus animal and roll onto her side waiting. The yellow eye watching, the ear shifting with little movements within the arc of its rotation. He didnt know how much of the water she was getting or how much she needed. He sat trickling the water between her teeth and looking into her eye. He touched the pleated corner of her mouth. He studied the veined and velvet grotto into which the audible world poured. He began to talk to her. The horse raised its head from its trailside grazing and looked back at him.

They rode on. The country was high rolling desert and the trail ran the crests of the ridges and although it seemed traveled he saw no one. On the slopes were acacia, scrub oak. Open parks of juniper. In the evening a rabbit appeared in the middle of the trail a hundred feet in front of him and he reined the horse up and put two fingers to his teeth and whistled and the rabbit froze and he stepped down and shucked the rifle backward out of the scabbard and cocked it all in a single movement and raised the rifle and fired.

The horse shied wildly and he snatched the reins out of the air and hauled it around and got it calmed. The wolf had vanished into the trailside brush. He held the rifle at his waist and levered the spent shell out of the chamber and caught it and put it in his pocket and levered a fresh shell in and let down the hammer with his thumb and undallied the rope and let the reins drop and walked back to see about the wolf.

She was trembling in the weeds just short of a small twisted juniper where she'd sought to hide. At his approach she sprang against the rope and stood thrashing. He stood the rifle against a tree and walked her down along the rope and held her and talked to her but he could not calm her and she did not stop trembling. After a while he took the rifle and went back out to the horse and shoved the rifle into the scabbard and walked back up the trail to look for the rabbit.

There was a long furrow down the center of the track that the rifle slug had plowed and the rabbit had been slung up into the bushes where it lay with its guts hanging in gray loops. It was all but in two pieces and he pooled it up all warm and downy in his hands with the head lolling and carried it out through the woods till he could find a windfall tree. There he kicked away the loose pinebark with the heel of his boot and brushed and blew it clean and laid the rabbit across the wood and took out his knife and straddling the log he skinned the rabbit out and gutted it and cut off the head and feet. He diced up the liver and heart on the log with his knife and sat looking at it. It didnt look much. He wiped his hand in the dead grass and took the rabbit and began to fillet strips from the back and hindquarters and to dice them as well until what he did have made a handful and then he wrapped them in the skin of the rabbit and folded away the knife.

He walked back and spiked the dead rabbit on a broken pine limb and went to where the wolf lay crouched. He squatted and held his hand out to her but she backed away at the end of the rope. He took a small piece of the rabbit's liver and held it to her. She sniffed it delicately. He watched her eyes and the speculation in them. He watched the leather nostrils. She turned her head to one side and when he offered the piece again she tried to back away.

Maybe you just aint hungry enough yet, he said. But you're fixin to get that way.

He made camp that night in a little swale under the windward side of the ridge and he skewered the rabbit on a paloverde pole and set it to broil in front of the fire before he even went to see about the horse and the wolf. When he approached her she stood and the first thing he saw was that the wrapping was gone from her leg. Then he saw that the stick between her teeth was gone. Then he saw that the cord with which her mouth was tied was gone.

She stood square to him with the hackles standing along her back. The catchrope tied to her collar and looped along the ground was frayed and wet where she'd been chewing it.

He stopped and stood dead still. He backed along the rope until he reached the horse and then untied the rope from the saddlehorn. He didnt take his eyes from her.

Holding the free end of the rope he began to circle the wolf. She turned in place watching him. He put a small pine tree between them. He tried to move in a casual manner but he felt all his motives naked to her. He handed the rope in a loop over the top of a high limb and caught it again and then backed away and pulled the rope taut. The slack came uncoiled out of the weeds and pine needles and tugged at her collar. She lowered her head and followed.

When she was standing under the limb he pulled the rope until her forefeet were all but off the ground and then slacked it just slightly and tied the rope off and stood looking at her. She bared her teeth at him and turned and tried to move away but she could not. She seemed to be at odds what to do. After a while she raised her injured leg and began to lick it.

He went back to the fire and piled on all the wood he'd collected. Then he got the canteen and he took one of the last of the sandwiches from the mochila and shucked it out of its wrapper and carried the canteen and the paper back to the wolf.

She watched while he scooped out a hole in the soft turf and she watched while he beat it smooth with the back of his bootheel. Then he spread the paper in the depression and weighed it with a rock and poured it full from the canteen.

He untied the rope and paid out slack as he backed away. She stood watching him. He stepped back a few more paces and squatted on the ground holding the rope. She looked at the fire and she looked at him. She sat on her haunches and licked her sore chops. He rose and went to the hole and poured in more

water and splashed it about. Then he screwed the cap back on
the canteen and stood it beside the waterhole and backed away
again and sat. They watched each other. It was almost dark.
She stood and tested the air with small nudging motions of her
nose. Then she began to come forward.

When she reached the water she sniffed at it tentatively and
raised her head to look at him. She looked at the fire again and
at the shape of the horse beyond the fire. Her eyes glowed in
the light. She lowered her nose to sniff at the water. Her eyes
did not leave him or cease to burn and as she lowered her head
to drink the reflection of her eyes came up in the dark water like
some other self of wolf that did inhere in the earth or wait in
every secret place even to such false waterholes as this that the
wolf would be always corroborate to herself and never wholly
abandoned in the world.

He squatted there watching her with the rope in both hands.
Like a man entrusted with the keeping of something which he
hardly knew the use of. When she'd drunk the hole dry she
licked her mouth and looked at him and then leaned and sniffed
at the canteen. The canteen fell over and she jerked away from
it and then backed off to her site under the limb and sat again
and began to lick her foot again.

He pulled the rope snug overhead and tied it and then walked
back to the fire. He turned the rabbit on its spit and got the
rabbitskin with the diced pieces and walked back and wafted it
in front of her. Then he spread the skin open on the ground and
untied and slacked the rope and backed away with it.

He watched her.

She leaned and sniffed the air.

It's rabbit, he said. I guess you aint ever eat any rabbit before.

He waited to see if she would come forward but she would
not. He took the wind's direction by the smoke from the fire
and gathered up the skin and carried it around upwind of her
and held it out again in one hand while he held the rope with
the other. He laid the skin down and backed away but still she
made no move.

He walked around and tied off the rope as before and went back to the fire. The rabbit on the spit was half burnt and half raw and he sat and ate it and then with his knife constructed a muzzle out of his belt and out of two long pieces of leather that he cut from the fender of the saddle. He fitted the pieces with slits and latigos, studying the wolf from time to time where she lay curled under the tree with the rope ascending vertically in the firelight.

I reckon you think you'll wait till I'm asleep and then you can see about gettin loose, he said.

She raised her head and looked at him.

Yeah, he said. I'm talkin to you.

When he had the muzzle done he turned it in his hand and tried the buckle. It looked pretty good. He folded the knife away and stuffed the muzzle into his back pocket and got the last lengths of pigginstring from out of the mochila and hung them through his beltloop and took the horse's hobbles and put them in his other back pocket. Then he walked over to where the rope was tied. The wolf rose and stood waiting.

He pulled her slowly up by her collar. She pawed at the rope and tried to get at it with her teeth. He spoke to her and tried to calm her but there seemed no point in it so he just hauled her up and halfhitched the rope with her standing upright and half garrotted and her head almost touching the limb overhead. Then he dropped to the ground and crawled to where she stood twisting and tied her back feet together with one of the hobbles and looped the free end of the catchrope around the hobble and tied it and rolled away from under her and stood and backed away. He pulled the halfhitch free and paying out slack to the collar end of the rope with one hand he began to pull her towards him by the legs with the other. If anybody was to see this, he told her, they'd come and carry me off to the loonybin in a rig just like it.

When he had her stretched out he took out the other hobble and tied her back legs to the little jackpine he'd been using for a snubbingpost and then freed the end of the catchrope from her legs and looped up the slack and slung it over his shoulder. When she felt the rope go slack she wrenched herself up and began to snap at the ropes on her legs. He hauled her down again and then walked in a wide swath around her till he could reach the limb the rope was looped over. He paid the free end of the rope back over the limb and stepped away and stretched her out flat on the ground.

I know you think I'm tryin to kill you, he said. But I aint.

He tied the rope off to another of the little jackpines and took the pigginstring from his beltloop and approached her where she lay taut and quivering and gasping between the ropes. He made a noose of the cord and tried to drop it over her nose. On the second try she grabbed it in her mouth. He stood over her, waiting for her to turn loose of it. The yellow eyes watched him.

Turn loose, he said.

He got hold of the cord and pulled at it.

All right, he said. Dont get stupid on me now. He wasnt talking to the wolf. She gets hold of you, he said, they wont even find a beltbuckle.

When she would not turn loose of the pigginstring he got hold of the rope to her collar and pulled on it until he'd cut off her air. Then he reached and got the pigginstring and still holding the rope taut he slung it loose and slipped it over her mouth and pulled her mouth shut and made three passes with the cord and halfhitched it and let go the rope again. He sat back. The fire was dying and with it the light. All right, he said. Dont quit now. Hell, you still got ten fingers.

He pulled the muzzle from his pocket and fitted it over her nose. It fit pretty well. The nosepiece was too loose and he took it off again and took out his knife and made new slits and redid the latigos and refitted it and then buckled it behind her ears. Then he buckled it a notch tighter. He fastened the two trailing jesses to her collar and then he reached through the side of the muzzle with the knife and cut the pigginstring he'd tied her mouth with.

The first thing she did was to suck in a long drink of air. Then she tried to bite the leather. But he'd used the saddle leather around her nose in a broad bosal and she couldnt get it between her teeth for the stiffness of it. He untied her back legs and stepped away. She got up and began to pitch and toss at the end of the rope. He squatted in the pine needles watching her. When she finally quit he rose and untied the rope and led her to the fire.

He thought she'd be terrifed of it but she was not. He hitched the rope midlength to the horn of the saddle where it stood drying before the fire and he got out the sheeting and the jar of salve and sat astraddle of her and cleaned and dressed the leg and rewrapped it. He thought she'd try to bite him even with the muzzle on but she did not. When he was done he let her up and she rose and walked to the end of the rope and sniffed at the wrapping and lay down watching him.

He slept with the saddle for a pillow. Twice in the night he woke with the saddle moving under his head and he reached and snatched at the rope and spoke to her. He lay with his feet to the fire so that if she circled in the night and dragged the rope through the fire she'd have to drag it over him and so wake him. He already knew that she was smarter than any dog but he didnt know how much smarter. Coyotes were yapping in the hills below them and he turned to see if she paid any mind to them but she appeared to be asleep. Yet as soon as his glance fell on her she opened her eyes. He looked away. He waited and then tried it again with more stealth. The eyes opened as before.

He nodded and slept and the fire drew down to coals and he woke in the cold to find the wolf watching him. When he woke again the moon was down and the fire was all but out. It was bitter cold. The stars stood fixed in their places like stampings in a tin lantern. He got up and fed wood to the fire and coaxed back the flame with his hat. The coyotes had hushed and the night was all darkness and silence. He'd had a dream and in the dream a messenger had come in off the plains from the south with something writ upon a ledgerscrap but he could not read it. He looked at the messenger but that face was obscured in shadow and featureless and he knew that the messenger was messenger alone and could tell him nothing of the news he bore.

In the morning he rose and built back the fire and squatted shivering before it wrapped in the blanket. He ate the last sandwich the rancher's wife had made for him and then he got the rabbitskin from the mochila and walked over to where the wolf was lying. She stood at his approach. He unwrapped the stiffening skin and held it out to her. She sniffed at it and glanced at him and circled two steps and stood looking at it with her ears slightly forward.

I believe you'd almost eat, he said.

He walked off and found a broken section of limb and cut it to length and with his knife carved one end of it into a thin spatula. Then he walked back and sat on the ground and got hold of the wolf by the collar and pulled her down against his leg and held her till she quit struggling. He spread the skin on the ground and scooped up a bit of the dark heartmeat and held that feral head to him and passed the spatula back and forth for her to smell. Then cupping her long nose in his hand he raised with his thumb the strange black leather fold of her upper lip. She opened her mouth and when she did he slid the spatula through the leather straps and between her teeth and turned it over and wiped it clean on her tongue and withdrew it.

He thought she would very likely bite the spatula but she didnt. She closed her mouth. He saw her tongue move. Her gullet jerk. When she opened her mouth again she had swallowed the meat.

When she had eaten all of the small handful of the rabbit he had for her he pitched away the skin and wiped the stick in the grass and put it in his pocket and walked out to where he'd last seen the horse. The horse stood half way down the mountain in a swale of winter grass and he walked it down with the bridle in his hand and led it back up to the camp and saddled it and tied the wolf's rope to the saddlehorn and mounted up and rode out south along the Cajón Bonita deeper into the mountains with the wolf at heel.

He rode all day. The wolf seemed to take an interest in the country and she would raise her head and look out over the rolling meadowlands of yellow grass and standing lechuguilla that fell away to the west of the saddleridges. He'd stop at the crest of a rise to let the horse blow and she would skulk into the trailside weeds and squat and make water and turn to sniff at the spot. The first pilgrims they encountered trekking north with their loaded burros halted a hundred yards out and gave the trail at his approach. They greeted him sparingly. The wolf crouched and pressed herself into the grass with her hackles up. Then the first of the burros caught her scent.

The animal's nostrils opened like two holes in wet mud and its eyes went blind white. It flattened its ears back and bowed up and shot out both hind legs and stove a leg from under the burro behind it. This animal fell down screaming beside the trail and in the space of a heartbeat all bedlam was loosed. The burros snapped their leads on every side and went rocketing off down the side of the mountain like enormous partridges with the arrieros after them and the animals careening off the sides of the trees and falling and rolling and righting again and running and the rude wood kiacks breaking up and the panniers breaking open and trailing down the mountainside behind them the baled pelts and hides and blankets and chattelgoods they contained.

He reined in the horse where it stamped and skittered and reached and untied the rope from the saddlehorn. The wolf had run off down the mountain and wrapped herself around a tree and he rode down to get her. By the time he came back dragging her behind him stifflegged and half crazed the trail was deserted save for an old woman and a young girl who sat in the grass by the trailside passing tobacco and cut cornhusks between them and rolling cigarettes. The girl was a year or two younger than he was and she lit her cigarette with an esclarajo and passed it to the old woman and blew smoke and tossed her head and stared at him boldly.

He coiled the rope and dismounted and dropped the reins and hung the coiled rope over the saddlehorn and touched the brim of his hat with two fingers.

Buenos días, he said.

They nodded, the older woman spoke his greeting back. The girl watched him. He walked the wolf down along the rope to where it crouched in the weeds and knelt and talked to it and led it by the collar back out into the trail.

Es Americano, the woman said.

Sí.

She sucked fiercely on the cigarette and squinted at him through the smoke.

Es feroz la perra, no?

Bastante.

They wore homemade dresses and huaraches cobbled up out of leather scraps and rawhide. The woman had on a black shawl or rebozo about her shoulders but the girl was all but naked in the thin cotton dress. Their skin was dark like an indian's and their eyes coal black and they smoked the way poor people eat which is a form of prayer.

Es una loba, he said.

Cómo? said the woman.

Es una loba.

The woman looked at the wolf. The girl looked at the wolf and at the woman.

De veras? said the woman.

Sí.

The girl looked as if she might be about to rise and back away but the woman laughed at her and told her that the caballero was only having a joke with them. She put the cigarette in the corner of her mouth and called to the wolf. She patted the ground for it to come.

Qué pasó con la pata? she said.

He shrugged. He said that she had caught it in a trap. Far below them on the side of the mountain they could hear the cries of the arrieros.

She offered their tobacco but the boy thanked her no. She shrugged. He said that he was sorry about the burros but the old woman said that the arrieros were inexperienced and had little control over their animals anyway. She said that the revolution had killed off all the real men in the country and left only the tontos. She said moreover that fools beget their own kind and here was the proof of it and that as only foolish women would have aught to do with them their progeny were twice doomed. She sucked again on the cigarette which was now little more than ash and let it fall to the ground and squinted at him.

Me entiende? she said.

Sí, claro.

She studied the wolf. She looked at him again. The eye half closed was probably from some injury but it lent her the air of one demanding candor. Va a parir, she said.

Sí.

Como la jovencita.

He looked at the girl. She didnt look pregnant. She had turned her back on them and sat smoking and looking out over the country where there was nothing to be seen although a few faint cries still drifted up the slope.

Es su hija? he said.

She shook her head. She said that the girl was the wife of her son. She said that they were married but that they had no money to pay the priest so they were not married by the priest.

Los sacerdotes son ladrones, the girl said. It was the first she had spoken. The woman nodded her head at the girl and rolled her eyes. Una revolucionaria, she said. Soldadera. Los que no pueden recordar la sangre de la guerra son siempre los más ardientes para la lucha.

He said that he had to go. She paid no mind. She said that when she was a child she'd seen a priest shot in the village of Ascensión. They'd stood him against the wall of his own church and shot him with rifles and gone away. When they were gone the women of the village came forward and knelt and lifted up the priest but the priest was dead or dying and some of the women dipped their handkerchiefs in the blood of the priest and blessed themselves with the blood as if it were the blood of Christ. She said that when young people see priests shot in the streets it changes their view of religion. She said that the young nowadays cared nothing for religion or priest or family or country or God. She said that she thought the land was under a curse and asked him for his opinion but he said he knew little of the country.

Una maldición, she said. Es cierto.

All sound of the arrieros had died away on the slopes below them. Only the wind blew. The girl finished her cigarette and rose and dropped it in the trail and stomped on it with her huarache and twisted it into the dirt as if it contained some malevolent life. The wind blew her hair and it blew her thin dress against her. She looked at the boy. She said the old woman was always talking about curses and dead priests and that she was half crazy and to pay her no mind.

Sabemos lo que sabemos, the old woman said.

Sí, said the girl. Lo que es nada.

The old woman held out one hand palm up in the direction of the girl. As if to offer her in evidence of all that she claimed. She invited him to observe the one who knew. The girl tossed her head. She said that at least she knew who was the father of her child. The woman threw her hand up. Ay ay, she said.

The boy held the wolf against his leg by the rope. He said that he had to go.

The old woman jutted her chin at the wolf. She said that the wolf's time was very near at hand.

Sí. De acuerdo.

Debe quitar el bosal, said the girl.

The woman looked at the girl. The girl said that if the perra should have her puppies in the night she should lick them. She said that he should not leave her muzzled at night because who could say how near her time was? She said that she would have to lick the pups. She said that all the world knew this.

Es verdad, the woman said.

The boy touched his hat. He wished them a good day.

Es tan feroz la perra? the girl said.

He said that she was. He said that she could not be trusted.

She said that she would like to have a little dog from such a bitch because it would grow up to be a watchdog and it would bite everyone who came around. Todos que vengan de alrededor, she said. She made a sweep with her hand that took in the pines and the wind in the pines and the vanished arrieros and the woman watching her out of the dark rebozo. She said that such a dog would bark in the night if there were thieves about or anyone at all who was not wanted.

Ay ay, said the woman, rolling her eyes.

He said that he had to go. The woman told him to go with God and the jovencita just told him to go if he wished and he walked out the trail with the wolf and caught his horse and tied the rope to the saddlehorn and mounted up. When he looked back the girl was sitting beside the woman. They werent talking but just sitting side by side, waiting for the arrieros to return. He rode out along the ridge to the first turning in the trail and looked back again but they had not moved or changed in attitude and they seemed at that distance much subdued. As if his departure had wrested something from them.

The country itself was changeless. He rode on and the high mountains to the southwest seemed no nearer at the day's end than had they been some image in the eye itself. Toward evening riding up through a stand of dwarf oak he flushed a flock of turkeys.

They'd been feeding in the wood below him and they sailed out over a wash and disappeared into the trees on the far side. He sat the horse and marked them with his eye. Then he rode down off the trail and stepped down and tied the horse and unhitched the rope and tied the wolf to a tree and took the rifle and jacked forward the lever to see that there was a shell chambered and then set off across the little valley with one eye on the sun where it was already backlighting the trees at the head of the draw to the west.

The turkeys were on the ground in a glade, passing back and forth among the slatted treetrunks in the deepening dusk like gallery birds in a carnival booth. He squatted and got his breath and began to advance slowly upon them. When he was still the better part of a hundred yards above them one of the hens stepped clear of the banded shadows and stood in the open and paused and craned her neck and stepped again. He cocked the rifle and took a grip on the trunk of a small ashtree and laid the barrel over his foreknuckle and wedged it against the side of the tree with the back of his thumb and took a sight on the bird. He allowed for drop and he allowed for the way the light lay sidelong in the riflesights and fired.

The heavy rifle bucked and the echo of the shot went caroming out over the country. The turkey lay flopping and twisting on the ground. The other birds came boring out of the trees in every direction, some of them passing almost directly over him. He stood and ran toward the bird that was down.

There was blood everywhere in the leaves. She was lying on her side and her legs were running in the leaves and her neck was doubled back oddly. He grabbed her and pressed her to the ground and held her. The shot had broken her neck low and torn open the shoulder of one wing and he saw that he had very nearly missed her altogether.

He and the wolf between them ate the whole bird and then they sat by the fire side by side. The wolf snubbed up close on the rope and starting and quivering at every small eruption among the coals. When he touched her her skin ran and quivered under his hand like a horse's. He talked to her about his life but it didnt seem to rest her fears. After a while he sang to her.

In the morning riding out he came upon a party of mounted men, the first such he'd seen in the country. They were five in number and they rode good horses and all of them were armed. They reined up in the trail before him and hailed him in a manner half amused while their eyes took inventory of everything about him. Clothes, boots, hat. Horse and rifle. The mutilated saddle. Lastly they studied the wolf. Who'd gone to try to hide herself in the thin highcountry bracken a few feet off the trail.

Qué tienes allá, joven? they called.

He sat with his hands crossed on the pommel of his saddle. He leaned and spat. He studied them from under the brim of his hat. One of them had put his horse forward the better to see the wolf but the horse balked and did not want to go and he leaned forward and slapped its cheek and hauled it about roughly with the reins. The wolf lay flat on the ground with her ears back at the end of the rope.

Cuánto quieres por tu lobo? the man said.

He gathered the small slack out of the rope and rehitched it.

No puedo venderlo, he said.

Por qué no?

He studied the horseman. No es mía, he said.

No? De quién es?

He looked at the wolf where she lay quivering. He looked at the blue mountains to the south. He said that the wolf had been entrusted into his care but that it was not his wolf and he could not sell it.

The man sat holding the reins loosely in one hand, the other hand on his thigh. He turned his head and spat without taking his eyes from the boy.

De quién es? he said again.

The boy looked at him and at the waiting riders in the trail. He said that the wolf was the property of a great hacendado and that it had been put in his care that no harm come to it.

Y este hacendado, said the rider, él vive en la colonia Morales?

The boy said that he did indeed live there and in other places as well. The man studied him for a long time. Then he put his horse forward and the other riders put their horses forward with him. As if they were joined together by some unseen cord or unseen principle. They rode past. They rode according to seniority and the last to pass was much the youngest and as he passed he looked at the boy and put his forefinger to the brim of his hat. Suerte, muchacho, he said. Then all rode on and none looked back.

It was cold in the mountains and there was yet snow in the high passes and snow on the Sierra de la Cabellera. Above the Cabellera Canyon snow lay in the trail for the better part of a mile. The snow in the trail was new snow and he was surprised to see the number of travelers who had been upon it and it occurred to him to wonder if there might not be in that country pilgrims so fearful as to quit the track entirely at the approach of any horseman. He studied the ground more closely. Tracks of men and burros. Tracks of women. A few bootprints but mostly the flat heelless prints of huaraches leaving the improbable imprint of tiretracks in that high wilderness. He saw the tracks of children and the tracks of the horses of the riders he had passed that morning. He saw the tracks of people barefoot in the snow. He rode on and as he rode he watched the wolf to see if she might betray the proximity of any travelers crouched in hiding by the wayside but she only trotted on behind the horse swinging her nose to test the air and leaving her own big tracks in the snow for the serranos to wonder at themselves.

They camped that night in the floor of a stone ravine and he led the wolf to a pool of standing water in the rocks below them and held the rope while she stepped down into the water and lowered her mouth into the pool to drink. She raised her head and he could see her gullet moving and the water running from her jaws. He sat in the rocks and held the rope and watched her. The water was black among the rocks in the deepening blue dusk and her breath smoked over the surface of it. She lowered and raised her head, drinking in the manner of birds.

For his supper he had a couple of tortillas with beans wrapped in them given to him by the sole other party he'd passed that day. They were Mennonites making their way north with a young girl to seek medical help. They looked like rustics out of a painting from the century before and they spoke little. They did not say what the girl's trouble was. The tortillas were leathery and the beans were beginning to sour but he ate them. The wolf watched. It aint nothin a wolf would eat, he told her. So dont be lookin.

He finished eating and took a long drink from the new cold water in the canteen and then he built up the fire and circled the perimeter of its light for all the wood he could collect. He'd pitched his little camp a good way below the trail but the glow of it could be seen at some distance in that country and he half expected late travelers might make their way to him in the night. None did. He sat wrapped in the blanket while the night grew cold and the stars ran burning down the sky to the south over the black shapes of the mountains where it must be that the wolves lived and had their home.

The day following in a southfacing valley he saw small blue flowers among the rocks and toward noon he passed through a broad gap in the mountains and stood looking out over the Bavispe River Valley. A faint blue haze hung over the trail in the switchback below. He was very hungry and he sat the horse and he and the wolf tested the air with their noses and then they rode on more cautiously.

The smoke was coming from a draw below the trail where a party of indians had nooned for their meal. They were laborers from the mines in western Chihuahua and they bore the mark of the tumpline across their narrow brows. There were six of them journeying overland to their village in Sonora bearing with them the body of one of their number killed under a scaffolding. They had been three days enroute and three days more lay before them and they had been fortunate in the weather. The dead body lay apart from them in the leaves upon a rude bier of poles and cowhide. It was wrapped in canvas and tied with bindings of grass and rope and the canvas of the shroud was worked with red and green ribbons and laid over with branches of the mountain ilex and one of the indians sat by it to guard it or perhaps to keep the dead man company. They spoke some spanish and they invited him to eat with little ceremony, such was the custom of the country. To the wolf they paid no attention whatever. They squatted in their thin homemade clothing eating pozole out of painted tin bowls with their fingers and passing from hand to hand a common pail that held tea made from some herb they favored. They sucked their fingers and dried them on the backs of their arms and rolled in cornhusks their punche cigarettes. None asked his business. Where he was from or where bound. They told him of uncles and fathers who'd fled to Arizona to escape the wars visited upon them by the Mexicans and one of them had been in that country himself just to see it, walking nine days through mountain and desert till he got there and nine days back. He asked the boy if he were from Arizona and the boy said that he was not and the indian nodded and said that it was customary among men to overstate the virtues of their own country.

That night from the edge of the meadow where he made his camp he could see the yellow windowlights of houses in a colonia on the Bavispe ten miles distant. The meadow was filled with flowers that shrank in the dusk and came forth again at the moon's rising. He made no fire. He and the wolf sat side by side in the dark and watched the shadows of things emerge on the meadow and step and trot and vanish and return. The wolf sat watching with her ears forward and her nose making constant small correction in the air. As if to make acts of abetment to the life in the world. He sat with the blanket over his shoulders and watched the moving shadows while the moon rose over the mountains behind him and the distant lights on the Bavispe winked out one by one till there were none.

In the morning he sat the horse on a gravel bar and studied the moving water where the broad clear river ran down and he studied the light on the riffles downriver where it bowed in the river's bend. He loosed the wolf's rope from the saddlehorn and dismounted. He led horse and wolf into the shallows and all three drank from the river and the water was cold and slatey to the taste. He rose and wiped his mouth and looked out across the country to the south where the high wild ranges of the Pilares Teras stood in the morning sun.

He could find no ford shallow enough for the wolf to cross

without swimming. Still he thought he could keep her afloat and he rode back upriver to the gravel bar and here he put the horse into the river.

He'd not gone far before the wolf was swimming and he'd not gone far before he saw that she was in trouble. Perhaps she could not breathe for the muzzle. She began to chop the water with rising desperation and the wrapping on her foreleg came loose and was flailing about in the water and this seemed to terrify her and she was trying to turn back against the rope. He halted the horse and the horse turned and stood with the water in flumes about its legs and faced the pull of the rope on the horn but by then he had dropped the reins in the river and stood down into water half way up his thigh.

He caught her by the collar and held her up and it was all he could do to stand. He got his other hand under her brisket to lift her up, his hand under the cold leather nipples that were almost naked of hair. He tried to calm her but she was trudging the water wildly. The catchrope lay in a long loop downriver and it was tugging at her collar and he held her up and worked his way back to the horse with the stones on the bottom of the river shifting under his boots and the water surging about his legs and he unhitched the rope and let the end of it float free. It uncoiled itself down the river and straightened and lay swaying in the current. The wrap of sheeting about the wolf's leg had come loose and floated off. He looked back toward the river bank. As he did so the horse surged past him and went clambering and half trotting across the shallows and up onto the gravel bar where it turned and stood smoking in the morning cold and then walked on downriver shaking its head.

He struggled back with the wolf, talking to her and keeping her head up. When they reached the shallows where she could get her footing he let go of her and walked up out of the river and stood on the bar and coiled the trailing rope out of the water while the wolf shook herself. When he had the rope coiled and hung over his shoulder he turned and looked for his horse.

Downriver on the gravel bar side by side were two horsemen watching him.

There was nothing about them that he liked. He looked past them to where his horse stood browsing in the willows with the stock of the rifle sticking out of the bootscabbard. He looked at the wolf. She was watching the riders.

They were dressed in dirty chino workclothes and they wore hats and boots and they had U S Government 45 automatic pistols in black leather holsters hanging from their belts. They had already put their horses forward and they rode at an insolent slouch. They rode up on his left side and one halted his horse and the other rode past and halted behind him. He turned, watching them. The first rider nodded to him. Then he looked back downriver at his horse and he looked at the wolf and he looked at him again.

De dónde viene? he said.

America.

He nodded. He looked out across the river. He leaned and spat. Sus documentos, he said.

Documentos?

Sí. Documentos.

No tengo ningunos documentos.

The man watched him for a while.

Qué es su nombre, he said.

Billy Parham.

The man gestured downriver with a slight jerk of his chin. Es su caballo?

Sí. Claro.

La factura por favor.

The boy looked at the other rider but the sun was behind him and his features were darkened. He looked to his inquisitor again. Yo no tengo esos papeles, he said.

Pasaporte?

Nada.

The rider sat his horse, his hands crossed loosely at the wrist.

He nodded to the other rider and the other rider detached himself and rode off down the gravel bar and caught the boy's horse and brought it back. The boy sat down in the gravel and pulled off his boots, one, the other, and poured the river water out of them and pulled them on again. He sat there with his elbows over his knees and he looked at the wolf and he looked across the river to the high Pilares rising in the sun. He knew that this day at least he would not be going there.

They took the path downriver, the leader riding with the boy's rifle across the bow of his saddle and the boy riding behind with the wolf close at the horse's heels and the third rider bringing up the rear a hundred feet behind. The path diverged from the river and ran out through a broad meadow where cattle were grazing. The cattle raised their heads with their slow jaws milling sideways and studied the riders and then bent to graze again. The riders rode on through the meadow until they struck a road and then turned south along the road and went on until they entered a settlement consisting of a handful of mud houses decomposing by the roadside.

They passed along the rutted street looking neither left nor right. A few dogs rose from their particular places in the sun and fell in behind the horses and sniffed after them. At an adobe building at the end of the street the riders halted and dismounted and the boy tied the wolf to the hounds of a wagon standing there and all entered.

The room had a musty odor to it. On the walls were faded frescoes and faded traces of a painted dado. The ruins of a linen ceiling hung in rags from the high vigas overhead. The floor was of large unglazed clay tiles and like the walls was badly out of true and the tiles were broken in many places where horses had walked upon them. The windows ran only along the south and east walls and contained no glass and they were shuttered that still had shutters while through the others the wind and dust blew and swallows passed in and out. At the far end of the room stood an old refectory table and a carved and ornate chair with a high back and against the wall behind it stood a steel filing cabinet whose top drawer had at one time been opened with an axe. There were tracks everywhere over the dusty tiles of birds and mice and lizards and dogs and cats. As if the room were a constant enigma to all things living in its vicinity. The riders stood under the mosslike hangings of the ceiling and the leader crossed to the double doors at the side of the room with the rifle cradled in one arm and tapped at the door and called out and then removed his hat and stood waiting.

In a few minutes the door opened and a young mozo stood there and he and the rider spoke and the man nodded toward the outside and the mozo looked toward the outer door and at the other rider and at the boy and then withdrew and shut the door. They waited. Outside in the street dogs had begun to assemble in front of the building. Some of them were visible through the open door. They sat looking at the tethered wolf and looking at each other while a rangy cur the color of ashes paced up and back before them with its tail up and the hair roached along its back.

It was a young and halelooking alguacil appeared in the door. He glanced briefly at the boy and turned to the man standing with the boy's rifle.

Dónde está la loba? he said.

Afuera.

He nodded.

They donned their hats and crossed the room. The man holding the rifle pushed the boy forward and the alguacil looked at him again.

Cuántos años tiene? he said.

Dieciseis.

Es su rifle?

Es de mi padre.

No es ladrón usted? Asesino?

No.

He jerked his chin at the man and told him to give the boy his rifle and then stepped out through the open door.

In the road in front of the house were upward of two dozen

dogs and almost as many children. The wolf had crawled up under the wagon and was backed against the wall of the building. Through the webs of the homemade muzzle you could see every tooth in its mouth. The alguacil crouched and pushed back his hat and set his hands palm down on his thighs and studied her. He looked at the boy. He asked if she were vicious and the boy said that she was. He asked him where he'd caught her and he said in the mountains. The man nodded. He rose and spoke to his deputies and then turned and went back into the building. The deputies stood uneasily and looked at the wolf.

Finally they untied the rope and dragged her from under the wagon. The dogs had begun to howl and to pace back and forth and the big gray dog darted in and snapped at the wolf's hindquarters. The wolf spun and bowed up in the road. The deputies pulled her away. The gray dog circled in for another sally and one of the deputies turned and fetched it a kick with his boot that caught it underneath the jaw and clapped its mouth shut with a slap of a sound that set the children to laughing.

By now the mozo had come from the house with a key and they dragged the wolf across the street and unlocked and unchained the doors to an adobe shed and put the wolf inside and locked the doors again. The boy asked them what they intended to do with the wolf but they only shrugged and they got their horses and mounted up and trotted back down the road, curbing the horses' heads this way and that and setting them to prancing as if there were women about. The mozo shook his head and went back inside with the key.

He sat by the door of the house all through the noon. He'd levered the shells out of the rifle and dried them and dried the rifle and reloaded it and put it back in the scabbard and he drank from the canteen and poured the rest of the water into the crown of his hat and watered the horse out of the hat and drove the pack of dogs away from the shed door. The streets were empty, the day cool and sunny. In the afternoon the mozo appeared at the door and said that he'd been sent to ask what he wanted. He said that he wanted his wolf. The mozo nodded and went back in again. When he came out again he said that he'd been sent to say that the wolf was seized as contraband but that he was free to go thanks to the clemency of the alguacil who had considered his youth. The boy said that the wolf was not contraband but was property entrusted into his care and that he must have it back. The mozo heard him out and then turned and went back into the house.

He sat. No one came. Late in the afternoon one of the pair of deputies returned at the head of a small and illsorted procession. Immediately behind came a small dark mule of the type used in the mines of that country and behind the mule an oldfashioned carreta with patched wooden wheels. Behind the cart a motley of people of the country all afoot, women and children, young boys, many of them bearing parcels or carrying baskets or pails.

They halted in front of the shed and the deputy stepped down and the cartdriver climbed down from the rude wood box of the carreta. They stood in the road drinking from a bottle of mescal and after a while the mozo came from the house and unlocked the shed doors and the deputy drew the chains rattling through the wooden barslots and flung the doors open and stood.

The wolf was in the farthest corner and she rose and stood blinking. The carretero stepped back and divested himself of his coat and put it over the mule's head and tied the sleeves under its jaws and stood holding the animal by the cheekstrap. The deputy entered the shed and picked up the rope and dragged the wolf into the doorway. The crowd fell back. Made bold by drink and by the awe of the onlookers the deputy seized the wolf by the collar and dragged her out into the road and then picked her up by the collar and by the tail and hefted her into the bed of the cart with one knee beneath her in the manner of men accustomed to loading sacks. He passed the rope along the side of the cart and halfhitched it through the boards at the front. The people in the road watched every movement. They watched with the attention of those who might be called upon to tell what they had seen. The deputy nodded to the carretero and the carretero loosed the knotted sleeves from under the mule's jaw and drew away the coat. He gathered the drivingreins together up under the mule's throat and stood holding the animal to see how it would do. The mule raised its head slightly to test the air. Then it jacked itself up onto its forelegs and kicked through the leather strap and stove in the bottom board of the carreta where the wolf was tied. The wolf came sliding and scrambling out of the open back of the cart dragging the broken board after it and the people cried out and turned to run. The mule screamed and flung itself sideways in the harness and broke away the offside cartshaft and fell into the road and lay kicking.

The carretero was strong and nimble and he managed to leap astride the little mule's neck and seize the mule's ear in his teeth till he could cover its head with the coat again. He looked about, gasping. The deputy who had been in the act of remounting his horse now stepped into the road again and seized the trailing rope and snatched the wolf up short. He untied the rope where it was hitched about the broken board and flung the board away and dragged the wolf back into the shed and shut the doors. Mire, called the carretero, lying in the road holding his coat over the mule's head, waving a hand at the wreckage. Mire. The deputy spat into the dust and walked across the road and into the house.

By the time they'd sent for someone to repair the cartshaft with lath and rawhide and by the time he'd done these repairs the day was well advanced. The pilgrims who had followed the cart into the town had deployed themselves under the shade of the buildings on the west side of the road and were eating their lunches and drinking lemonade. By late afternoon the cart was ready but the deputy was nowhere to be found. A boy was sent to the house to inquire. Another hour passed before he made his appearance and he adjusted his hat and eyed the sun and bent to examine the repair to the cartshaft as if he were deputized also to inspect such work and then he went back into the house. When he came out again he was accompanied by the mozo and they crossed the road to the shed and unlocked and unchained the doors and the deputy brought out the wolf again.

The carretero stood with the mule's blindfold head against his chest. The deputy studied him and then called for a mozo de cuadra. A young boy stepped forward. He instructed the boy to take charge of the mule and told the carretero to get in the wagon. The carretero relinquished the mule with some misgiving. He gave the muzzled shewolf a wide berth and climbed into the cart and unwrapped the reins from the stanchion and stood at the ready. The deputy once more lifted the wolf into the carreta and tied it close against the boards at the rear. The carretero looked back at the animal and looked at the deputy. His eyes moved over the waiting pilgrims now reassembled until he met the eyes of the young extranjero from whom the wolf had been appropriated. The deputy nodded to the mozo de cuadra and the mozo pulled away the carretero's coat from the mule's head and stepped away. The mule sprang forward wildly in the traces. The carretero fell back clutching at the topmost boards of the cart and trying not to fall on the wolf and the wolf lunged at her lead and let out a wild sad cry. The deputy laughed and booted his horse forward and snatched the coat from the mozo and swung it overhead like a lariat and threw it after the carretero and then reined up again in the road laughing while mule and cart and wolf and driver went bowling out through the settlement in a great clatter of wood and creation of dust.

The people were already gathering up their parcels. The boy went and got his saddle from the side of the house and saddled the horse and buckled up the saddlescabbard and mounted up and turned the horse into the rutted track. Those afoot pressed to the side of the road when the horse's shadow fell upon them. He nodded down to them. Adónde vamos? he said.

They looked up at him. Old women in rebozos. Young girls carrying baskets between them. A la feria, they said.

La feria?

Sí señor.

Adónde?

En el pueblo de Morelos.

Es lejos? he said.

They said that it was not far by horseback. Unas pocas leguas, they said.

He walked the horse beside them. Y adónde va con la loba? he said.

A la feria, sin duda.

He asked what was the purpose in taking the wolf to the fair but they seemed not to know. They shrugged, they tramped beside the horse. An old woman said that the wolf had been brought from the sierras where it had eaten many school-children. Another woman said that it had been captured in the company of a young boy who had run away naked into the woods. A third said that the hunters who had brought the wolf down out of the sierras had been followed by other wolves who howled at night from the darkness beyond their fire and some of the hunters had said that these wolves were no right wolves.

The road left the river and the river flats and led away to the north through a broad mountain valley. With dusk the company fell out in a high meadow and built a fire and set about cooking their supper. The boy tied his horse and sat in the grass, not quite one of them and not quite apart. He twisted the cap from his canteen and drank the last of his water and put the cap back and sat holding the empty container in his hands. After a while a boy came up to him and invited him to the fire.

They were elaborately polite. They called him caballero for all his sixteen years and he sat with his hat pushed back and his boots crossed before him and ate beans and napolitos and a machaca made from dried goatmeat that was rank and black and stringy and dusted with dry red pepper for traveling. Le gusta? they said. He said he liked it very much. They asked him where he came from and he said Nuevo Mexico and they glanced at one another and they said that he must be very sad to be so far from his home.

In the dusk the meadow looked a camp of gypsies or refugees. Their number had swelled with new arrivals along the road and there were new fires built and figures drifted back and forth across the darkened spaces between. Burros grazed on the meadow slope where it banked away against the dark lilac sky to the west and the little carretas stood tilted on their tongues in silhouette one behind the next like orecarts. Several men were in the company by now and were passing a bottle of mescal among themselves. In the dawn two of them were sitting yet before the cold dead ashes. The women turned out to cook breakfast, building back the fire and setting about slapping tortillas from the masa and laying them out on a comal cut from roofingtin. They worked around the seated drunks and around the packsaddles over which blankets had been hung to dry all with equal disregard.

It was midmorning before the caravan was under way. Those too drunk to travel were shown every consideration and room made for them among the chattels in the carts. As if some misfortune had befallen them that could as easily have visited any among them.

The road they traveled led through wilderness enough that they passed no habitation nor met upon it any other traveler at all. They made no stop at noon but soon thereafter passed through a gap in the mountains where two miles below them the river ran and the sparse houses of Colonia Morelos stood along the quadrature of its four streets like markers in a child's game drawn in the dust.

He left the company while they set up their camp on the floodplain south of the town and he turned his horse into the road downriver to see if he could find the wolf. The road was dried clay corrugated with cart tracks set so hard they would not break under the horse's hooves. The river was clear and cold where it came out of the high sierras to the south and it turned at the settlement to run south again under the western wall of the Pilares. He turned off the road and followed a path out along the river and stood the horse to drink from the cold riffles. An old man with a burro was gathering driftwood out on the gravel flats. The pale and twisted shapes of wood arranged atop the burro looked like some tapestry of bones. The boy put his horse forward upriver, the horse's hooves trudging in the round river gravels.

The town that he entered was an old Mormon settlement from the century before and he passed brick buildings with tin roofs, a brick store with a false wood front. In the alameda opposite the store bunting had been strung tree to tree and the members of a small brass band sat in the little kiosk as if perhaps awaiting the arrival of some dignitary. Along the streetfront and in the alameda were vendors selling cacahuates and ears of steamed corn dusted with red pepper and buñuelos and natillas and paper spills of fruit. He dismounted and tied the horse and took the rifle from the scabbard lest it be stolen and walked toward the alameda. Among the fairgoers in that little park of dried mud and starveling trees were visitors more alien than even he, families in rags that moved agape among the patched canvas pitchtents and Mennonites got up like medicineshow rubes in their straw hats and bib overalls and a row of children halted half dumbstruck before a painted canvas drop depicting garish human abnormalities and Tarahumara indians and Yaquis carrying bows and quivers of arrows and two Apache boys in deerskin boots with grave and coalblack eyes who'd come from their camp in the sierras where the last free remnants of their tribe lived like shadowfolk of the nation they had been and all of them with such gravity that the shabby circus of their beholding could as well have been the pageantry of some dread new dispensation visited upon them.

He found the wolf readily enough but he lacked the ten centavos required to see her. They'd rigged a makeshift tent of sheeting over the little tumbril of a cart and they'd put up a sign at the front that gave her history and the number of people she was known to have eaten. He stood and watched the few people filing in and out. They did not seem much animated by what they'd seen. When he asked them about the wolf they shrugged. They said a wolf was a wolf. They did not believe that she'd eaten anyone.

The man collecting the money at the fly of the pitchtent listened with his head bowed while the boy explained to him his situation. He raised his head and looked into the boy's eyes. Pásale, he said.

She was lying in the floor of the cart in a bed of straw. They'd taken the rope from her collar and fitted the collar with a chain and run the chain through the floorboards of the cart so that it was all that she could do to rise and stand. Beside her in the straw was a clay bowl that perhaps held water. A young boy stood with his elbows hung over the top board of the cart with a jockeystick held loosely across his shoulder. When he saw enter what he took for a paying customer he stood up and began to prod the wolf with the stick and to hiss at her.

She ignored the prodding. She was lying on her side breathing in and out quietly. He looked at the injured leg. He stood the rifle against the cart and called to her.

She rose instantly and turned and stood looking at him with her ears erect. The boy holding the jockeystick looked up at him across the top of the cart.

He talked to her a long time and as the boy tending the wolf could not understand what it was he said he said what was in his heart. He made her promises that he swore to keep in the making. That he would take her to the mountains where she would find others of her kind. She watched him with her yellow eyes and in them was no despair but only that same reckonless deep of loneliness that cored the world to its heart. He turned and looked at the boy. He was about to speak when the pitchman ducked inside under the canopy and hissed at them. Él viene, he said. Él viene.

Maldicíon, the boy said. He threw aside his stick and he and the pitchman set about taking down the sheets and untying the cords from the stakes they'd driven into the mud. As the sheets fell the carretero came at a trot across the alameda and fell in to help them, snatching up the sheets and hissing at them to hurry. Soon they were backing the little blindfold mule between the shafts of the cart and fitting the harness and buckling it about.

La tablilla, cried the carretero. The boy snatched up the sign and pushed it under the pile of ropes and sheeting and the carretero mounted up into the cart and called out to the pitchman and the pitchman snatched away the blindfold from the mule's eyes and mule and cart and wolf and driver went rattling and clattering out into the street. Fairgoers scattered away before them and the carretero looked back wildly up the road where the alguacil and his entourage were just entering the town from the south—alguacil and attendants and retainers and friends and mozos de estribo and mozos de cuadra all with their equipage winking in the sun and trotting among the legs of the horses upwards of two dozen hunting dogs.

The boy had already turned and started toward the street to get his horse. By the time he'd untied it and shoved the rifle into the scabbard and mounted up and swung the horse into the street the alguacil and his party were passing along the alameda four and six abreast, calling out to one another, many of them garbed in the gaudy attire of the norteño and of the charro all spangled and trimmed with silver braid, the seams of their trousers done with silver shells. They rode saddles worked in silver with flat pommels the size of plates and some were drunk riding and doffed their enormous hats in gestures of outlandish courtliness at women their horses had forced against buildings or into doorways. The hunting dogs trotting neat of foot beneath them seemed alone sober and purposive and they paid no mind at all to the town dogs that sallied out bristling behind them or indeed to anything at all. They were some of them black in color or black and tan but for the most part they were bluetick dogs brought into the country from the north years before and some were so like in pattern and color to the speckled horses they paced that they seemed tailored from the same piece of hide. The horses sidled and stepped and tossed their heads and the riders pulled them about but the dogs trotted steadily upon the road before them as if they had a lot on their minds.

He waited in the crossroads for them to pass. Some nodded to him and wished him a good day as to a fellow horseman but if the alguacil in passing recognized him sitting his horse in this new wayplace he gave no sign so. When they had passed horses dogs and all he put his horse into the road again and set out behind them and behind the carreta now vanished upriver in the distance.

THE HACIENDA through whose gates they passed was sited on a level plain between the road and the braided flats of the Bato-pito River and it was named for the mountains to the east through which they'd ridden. It lay hazy in the distance in a long thin bight of limewashed walls under the thin green spires of a cypress grove. Downriver were groves of fruit trees and pecans in ordered rows. He turned down the long drive as the hunting party was entering the gates of the portal ahead of him. In the fields were crossbred bulls with long ears and humped backs of a kind new to the country and workers raised up and stood with their short hoes in their hands and watched him pass. He raised his hand in greeting but they only bent to their work again.

When he rode through the standing gate of the portal there was no sign of the party. A mozo came to take his horse and he stepped down and handed over the reins. The mozo appraised him by his clothes and nodded toward the kitchen door and a few minutes later he was seated at a table along with the retainers of the newly arrived party some dozen in number and all of them eating great slabs of fried steak with beans and flour tortillas hot from the comal. At the end of the table sat the carretero.

He stepped over the bench with his plate and sat and the carretero nodded to him but when he asked about the wolf the

carretero said only that the wolf was for the feria and more he
would not say.

When he'd eaten he rose and carried his plate to the sideboard
and asked the cocinera where the patrón might be but she only
glanced at him and then made a sweeping gesture that took in
the thousands of hectares of land running north along the river
which comprised the hacienda. He thanked her and touched his
hat and walked out and crossed the compound. On the far side
stood stables and a bodega or granary and the long row of mud
houses where the workers were billeted.

He found the wolf chained in an empty stall. She was standing
backed into the corner and two boys were leaning over the stall
door hissing at her and trying to spit on her. He went down the
stable hall looking for his horse but there were no horses in the
stable. He walked back out into the compound. From upriver
where they'd gone to course the dogs the alguacil and his party
were returning toward the house. In the yard behind the house
the carretero had harnessed the little mule into his cart again
and had mounted up into the box. The flat pop of the reins
carried across the compound like a distant pistolshot and mule
and cart set forth. They passed out through the portal gate just
as the first of the riders and the first of the dogs swung into the
road before them.

Such a company makes no way for mules and carts and the
carretero pulled his rig off into the grass by the side of the road
to let them pass, standing in the box and taking off his hat with
a flourish and searching with his eyes among the approaching
riders for the alguacil. He slapped the reins again. The mule
trudged sullenly and the cart tilted and creaked and rattled over
the bad ground by the roadside. As the dogs and riders passed
the lead dog raised its nose and caught the scent from the cart
on the wind and let out a deep bay and turned and swung in
behind the cart where it trundled past just off the road. The
other dogs surged about, the hair bristling along their shoulders,
swinging their muzzles in the air. The carretero looked back in
alarm. As he did so the mule humped and kicked and snatched

the little cart about and set off across the fields at a gallop with the dogs in full cry behind.

The alguacil and his minions stood in their stirrups and shouted after them, laughing and whooping. Some of the younger horsemen of the company roweled their mounts forward and set out after the runaway mule and cart, calling out to the carretero and laughing. The carretero clutched the boards and leaned over the side with his hat to slap at the dogs leaping and scrabbling at the cart. Tall as the cart was they yet began to leap in, three or four of them, and to rummage through the straw howling and whining and finally raising a leg and urinating and lurching and falling against the side of the cart and spraying the carretero and spraying each other and fighting briefly and then standing with their forefeet along the top boards of the cart and barking down at the dogs that raced beside.

The riders overtook them laughing and circled the cart at a full gallop until one of them took down his reata and dropped a loop over the mule's head and brought it to a halt. They whooped and called out to one another and beat away the dogs with their doubled rope ends and led the cart back to the road. The dogs coursed out over the fields and the girls and young women working there squealed and put their hands atop their heads while the men stood with their hoes clubbed in their hands. In the road the alguacil called to the carretero and fished a silver coin from his pocket and pitched it to him with great accuracy. The carretero caught the coin and touched the brim of his hat with it and stood down into the road to inspect the cart and the rudely cottered wooden wheels and the harness and the fresh repair to the cartshaft. The alguacil looked past the riders to where the boy stood afoot in the road. He took another coin from his pocket and pitched it spinning.

Por el Americano, he called.

No one caught it. It fell in the dust and lay there. The alguacil sat his horse. He nodded to the boy.

Es for you, he said.

The riders watched him. He stooped and picked up the coin

and the alguacil nodded and smiled but there was no thanking or touching the hat. The boy walked up to him and held the coin up.

No puedo aceptarlo, he said.

The alguacil arched his brow and nodded his head vigorously. Sí, he said. Sí.

The boy stood at the alguacil's stirrup and gestured at him with the outheld coin. No, he said.

No? said the alguacil. Y cómo no?

The boy said that he wanted the wolf. He said that he could not sell her. He said that if there was a fine that he would work to pay the fine or if there was a fee for a permit or a toll to cross into the country he would work for that but that he could not part with the wolf because the wolf had been put in his care.

The alguacil heard him out and when he was done he accepted the coin and then pitched it to the watching carretero as a coin once given cannot be taken back and then he turned his horse in the road and called to his men and driving the dogs before them they all rode on toward the hacienda and vanished through the standing gates of the portal.

The boy looked at the carretero. The carretero had climbed again into his cart and he unwrapped the reins and looked down at the boy. He said that the alguacil had given the coin to him. He said that if the boy had wanted the coin he should have taken it when it was offered. The boy said he did not want the man's money then or now. He said that the carretero might work for such a man but he did not. But the carretero only nodded as if to say he did not expect the boy would understand but that someday with luck he might. Nadie sabe para quien trabaja, he said. Then he slapped the drivingreins against the mule's rump and set off down the road.

He walked back out to the stable where they'd chained the wolf. An old mozo from the house had been set to guard her and to see that she not be molested. He sat with his back to the stable door in the half dark smoking a cigarette. His hat lay in the straw beside him. When the boy asked if he could see the wolf he drew deeply on the cigarette as if contemplating the request. Then he said that no one could see the wolf without the permission of the hacendado and in any case there was no light to see her by.

The boy stood in the doorway. The mozo spoke no more and after a while he turned and went out again. He walked back across the compound to the house and stood looking in at the patio gates. Men were laughing and drinking and there was a veal calf roasting on a spit under the wall at the far side of the enclosure and under the smoky light of the cressetlamps burning in the long blue desert dusk were tables laden with savories and sweets and fruits to feed a hundred people and more. He turned and went back around the side of the house to find one of the mozos de cuadra and to see about his horse. Mariachi music struck up behind him in the courtyard and new arrivals were dismounting at the gates, coming out of the darkening shapes of the mountains to the east along the road accompanied by dogs at their horses' heels and hoving up in the light at the gateposts where torches burned in iron pipes driven into the ground.

The horses of the lesser guests such as himself were tied by halter ropes along a rail at the rear of the establos and he found Bird standing among them. He was still saddled and the bridle and bridlereins hung from the pommel and he was eating feed from a two-board tinsheathed trough nailed along the wall. He raised his head when Billy spoke to him and looked back chewing.

Es su caballo? said the mozo.

Sí. Claro.

Todo está bien?

Sí. Bien. Gracias.

The mozos were working their way along the line of horses pulling off saddles and brushing horses and pouring feed. He asked that they leave his horse saddled and they said that they would do as he wished. He looked at his horse again. You fell into it pretty good, didnt you? he said.

He walked around to the stable and entered the door at the

far end and stood. It was almost dark in the stable hall and the mozo in charge of the wolf seemed to be sleeping. He found an empty stall and walked in and kicked up the hay in one corner with his boots and lay down with his hat on his chest and closed his eyes. He could hear the cries of the mariachis and the howling of the chained hounds in an outbuilding somewhere and after a while he slept.

He slept and as he slept he dreamt and the dream was of his father and in the dream his father was afoot and lost in the desert. In the dying light of that day he could see his father's eyes. His father stood looking toward the west where the sun had gone and where the wind was rising out of the darkness. The small sands in that waste was all there was for the wind to move and it moved with a constant migratory seething upon itself. As if in its ultimate granulation the world sought some stay against its own eternal wheeling. His father's eyes searched the coming of the night in the deepening redness beyond the rim of the world and those eyes seemed to contemplate with a terrible equanimity the cold and the dark and the silence that moved upon him and then all was dark and all was swallowed up and in the silence he heard somewhere a solitary bell that tolled and ceased and then he woke.

Men with torches were passing singlefile down the stable past the open door of the stall where he'd been sleeping, their figures reeling outsized across the farther walls. He rose and put on his hat and went out. They were dragging the wolf from her stall by her chain and she cringed in the smoky light and drew back and tried to keep low to the ground to protect her underbelly. Someone with an old rakehandle fell in behind her to goad her on and in the distance somewhere beyond the domicilios the hounds had set up a fresh clamor.

He followed them out and across the darkened lot. They passed through an open wooden carriage gate where the doors were hung in stone piers and the howling of the hounds grew louder and the wolf shrank back and struggled against the chain.

Some of the men following behind were stumbling drunk and they kicked at her and called her cobarde. They passed along the stone bodega where the light from the eaves fell along the upper walls and carried the shadows of the interior rafters out into the dark of the yard. The illumination from within seemed to bow the walls and in the apron of light before the open doors the shadows of figures inside reeled and fell away and the company entered dragging the wolf over the packed clay. A way was made for them with much cheering and calling out. They handed off their torches to mozos who snuffed them in the dirt of the floor and when all had entered and were inside the mozos pushed shut the heavy wooden doors and dropped the bar.

He made his way along the edge of the crowd. They were a strange egality of witnesses there gathered and among the merchants from adjacent towns and the neighboring hacendados and the petty hidalgos de gotera come from as far as Agua Prieta and Casas Grandes in their tightly fitted suits there were tradesmen and hunters and gerentes and mayordomos from the haciendas and from the ejidos and there were caporals and vaqueros and a few favored peons. There were no women. Along the far side of the building were bleachers or stands scaffolded up on poles and in the center of the bodega was a round pit or estacada perhaps twenty feet in diameter defined by a low wooden palisade. The boards of the palisade were black with the dried blood of the ten thousand gamecocks that had died there and in the center of the pit was an iron pipe newly driven into the ground.

He shouldered his way through from the rear just as they were dragging the wolf over the boards and into the pit. Those along the bleachers stood to see. The man in the pit chained the wolf to the pipe and then dragged her to the end of the chain and stretched her out while they removed the homemade muzzle. Then they stepped back and slipped the noose of the rope they'd stretched her with. She stood up and looked about. She looked small and ragged and she stood with her back bowed like a cat. The wrapping was gone from her leg and she favored it as she moved sideways to the end of the chain and back, her white teeth shining in the light from the tin reflectors overhead.

The first casts of dogs had already been brought in by their handlers and they leaped and tugged at their leads and bayed and stood upright against their collars. Two of them were led forward and spectators in the crowd called out to the owners and whistled and named their wagers. The hounds were young and uncertain. The handlers boosted them over the parapet into the pit where they circled bristling and bayed at the wolf and looked at each other. The handlers hissed them on and they circled the wolf warily. The wolf crouched and bared her teeth. The crowd began to hoot and catcall and after a while a man at the far side of the pit blew a whistle and the handlers came forward and grabbed the ends of the trailing chains and hauled the dogs back and dragged them over the parapet and led them away, the dogs standing at their collars again and baying back at the wolf.

The wolf paced and circled limping on three legs and then crouched by the iron stake where it seemed she'd made her querencia. Her almond eyes ran the circle of faces beyond the pit and she glanced briefly up at the lights. She crouched on her elbows and then rose and circled and came back and crouched again. Then she stood. A fresh cast of dogs was being handed scrabbling over the parapet.

When the handlers slipped loose the dogs they sprang forward with their backs roached and bowled into the wolf and the three of them rolled into a ball of snarling and popping teeth and a rattle of chain. The wolf fought in absolute silence. They scrabbled over the ground and then there was a high yip and one of the dogs was circling and holding up one foreleg. The wolf had seized the other dog by the lower jaw and she threw it to the ground and straddled it and snatched her grip from the dog's jaw and buried her teeth in its throat and bit again to improve her grip where the muscled neck slid away in the loose folds of skin.

The boy had worked his way around to the bleachers. He stood by one of the stone piers and he took off his hat so that

those behind could see but then he realized no one else had
taken off theirs so he put it back on. Left alone the wolf might
well have killed the dog but the arbitro blew his whistle and one
of the handlers came forward with a sixfoot length of cane and
with it blew into the wolf's ear. She abandoned her hold and
leaped back and spun on her haunches. The handlers got hold
of their dogs by the chains and led them away. A man came
forward and stepped over the low wooden barricade and began
to circle about with a pail out of which he laved and flung water
like some bemused and halfwitted horticulturist, methodically
slaking the dust in the floor of the pit while the wolf lay panting.
The boy turned and made his way along the edge of the crowd
to the door at the rear through which the hounds had gone and
stepped outside into the cool dark. A handler with two fresh
dogs was already coming through the door.

Some boys smoking cigarettes at the back wall of the bodega
turned and looked at him in the light of the door's opening. The
howling of the dogs in the crib beyond was loud and continuous.

Cuántos perros tienen? he asked them.

The nearest boy looked at him. He said they had four dogs.
Y usted? he said.

He explained that he meant all the dogs how many but they
only shrugged.

Quién sabe? they said. Bastante.

He walked past them and out to the crib. It was a long
building with a tin roof and he took a lantern down from a pole
and lifted the wooden stake from out of the doorhasp and pushed
open the door and entered with the lantern aloft. Along the wall
the hounds leaped and bayed and lunged at their chains. There
were upwards of thirty of them in the shed, mostly redbone
and bluetick dogs bred in the country to the north but also
nondescript animals from new-world bloodlines and dogs that
were little more than pitbulls bred to fight. Chained at the end
of the shed separate from the others were two enormous
airedales and when the light from the lantern ignited their eyes
the boy saw a thing that not even the pit dogs possessed in such

absolute purity and he backed away mistrustful of the chains that held them. He backed out and shut the door and dropped the stake into the hasp and rehung the lantern on the pole. He nodded to the boys standing along the wall and went past and entered the bodega again.

The crowd seemed actually to have swelled in his brief absence. On the far side of the arena stood the members of the mariachi band in their white and illfitting suits. Through the crowd he could glimpse the wolf. She was squatting on her haunches with her mouth wide and she was alternately darting at one and then the other of the two dogs circling her. One of the dogs had been bitten through the ear and both handlers were freckled with blood where it had circled shaking its head. He pushed his way through the crowd and when he reached the wooden parapet he stepped over it and walked out into the pit.

He was taken at first for yet another handler but it was the handlers he approached. There were now at the farther side of the pit crouching and feinting in such postures of attack and defense as they would have the dogs adopt and calling out in highpitched chants to seek the dogs on and twisting and gesturing with their hands in an antic simulation of the contest before them. When the nearer of them saw him coming he raised up and looked toward the árbitro. The árbitro stood with the whistle to his mouth but he seemed not to know what to make of what he saw. The boy stepped past the handlers and entered the perimeter of the twelvefoot circle of torn ground defined by the chain to which the wolf was tethered. Someone called out a warning and the árbitro blew his whistle and then there was a hush fell over the bodega. The wolf stood panting. The boy stepped past her and seized the first dog by the loose skin of the saddle and hauled its hindquarters up off the ground and squatted and got hold of its chain and backed away with it and turned and handed the chain to the handler. The handler took the chain and pulled the lunging dog against his leg. Qué pasó? he said.

But the boy had already started after the second dog. By now some of the spectators had begun to call out and there was an ugly murmur running through the bodega. The handlers looked toward the árbitro. The árbitro blew the whistle again and gestured toward the intruder. He in turn hauled up the second dog by its chain and walked it on its hindlegs to the other handler and then turned and went back after the wolf.

She stood spraddlelegged with her sides heaving and her black mouth pleated back from the white and perfect teeth. He crouched and spoke to her. He had no way to know if she would bite him or not. A handful of men had climbed over the estacada and were advancing toward him but when they reached the perimeter of the torn ground they stopped as if they'd come to a wall. No one spoke to him. All seemed to be watching to see what he would do. He rose and stepped to the iron stake piked in the ground and wrapped a turn of chain about his forearm and squatted and seized the chain at the ring and tried to rise with it. No one moved, no one spoke. He doubled his grip and tried again. The beaded sweat on his forehead shone in the light. He tried yet a third time but he could not pull the stake and he rose and turned back and took hold of the actual wolf by the collar and unsnapped the swivelhook and drew the bloody and slobbering head to his side and stood.

That the wolf was loose save for his grip on her collar did not escape the notice of the men who had entered the ring. They looked at one another. Some began to back away. The wolf stood against the güero's thigh with her teeth bared and her flanks sucking in and out and she made no move.

Es mía, the boy said.

People in the stands began to call out but those in any proximity to the unchained wolf seemed hesitant as to what course to take. In the end it was neither the alguacil nor the hacendado who came forward but the hacendado's son. They gave way before him, a young man who bore on the braided jacket he wore the scent of the young women he'd so recently danced with. He stepped into the pit and advanced and stood with his boots spread and his thumbs hung loosely in the blue sash about his waist. If he was afraid of the wolf he gave no evidence so.

Qué quieres, joven? he said.

The boy repeated what he'd said to the riders he'd met with on the Cajón Bonita in the mountains to the north. He said that he was custodian to the wolf and charged with her care but the young hacendado smiled ruefully and shook his head and said that the wolf had been caught in a trap in the Pilares Teras which mountains are barbarous and wild and that the deputies of Don Beto had encountered him crossing the river at the Colonia de Oaxaca and that he had been intent on taking the wolf to his own country where he would sell the animal at some price.

He spoke in a high clear voice like one declaiming to the crowd and when he was done he stood with his hands folded one across the other before him as if there were no more to be said.

The boy stood holding the wolf. He could feel the movement of her breathing and the light tremor of her body against him. He looked at the young don and he looked at the ring of faces in the light. He said that he had come from Hidalgo County in the state of New Mexico and that he had brought the wolf with him from that place. He said that he had caught her in a steeltrap and that he and the wolf had been on the trail six days coming into this country and had not come out of the Pilares at all but were in the act of attempting to cross the river and enter those same mountains when they were turned back because of the swiftness of the water.

The young hacendado took his hands from before him and clasped them behind. He turned and took a few steps in contemplation and turned again and looked up.

Para qué trajo la loba aquí? De que sirvió?

He stood holding the wolf. All waited for him to answer but he had no answer. His eyes ran the assemblage, searching the eyes that watched him. The árbitro stood with his pocketwatch still outheld before him. The handlers stood with doubled grip upon the collars of the dogs. The man with the watercan waited. The young hacendado turned to look at the gallery.

He smiled and turned again to the boy. Then he spoke in english.

You think that this country is some country you can come here and do what you like.

I never thought that. I never thought about this country one way or the other.

Yes, said the hacendado.

We was just passin through, the boy said. We wasnt botherin nobody. Queríamos pasar, no más.

Pasar o traspasar?

The boy turned and spat into the dirt. He could feel the wolf lean against his leg. He said that the tracks of the wolf had led out of Mexico. He said the wolf knew nothing of boundaries. The young don nodded as if in agreement but what he said was that whatever the wolf knew or did not know was irrelevant and that if the wolf had crossed that boundary it was perhaps so much the worse for the wolf but the boundary stood without regard.

The spectators nodded and murmured among themselves. They looked to the boy to see how he would reply. The boy only said that if he were allowed to go he would return with the wolf to America and that he would pay whatever fine he had incurred but the hacendado shook his head. He said that it was too late for that and that anyway the alguacil had taken the wolf into custody and it was forfeit in lieu of the portazgo. When the boy said that he had not known that he would be required to pay in order to pass through the country the hacendado said that then he was in much the same situation as the wolf.

They waited. The boy looked aloft toward the roofbeams where the dust and the smoke had risen and where it moved slowly in slow coils across the lights. He looked among the faces for any there to whom he might plead his case but he saw nothing. He reached down and unbuckled the leather dogcollar from about the wolf's neck and pulled it away and stood. Those nearest tried to back into the crowd. The young gentryman drew a small revolver from his waistband.

Agárrala, he said.

He stood. Some several other of the spectators had also drawn their arms. He looked like a man standing on a scaffold seeking in the crowd some likeness to his own heart. Nothing to come of the looking even though all there might arrive at their own such standing soon or late. He looked at the young don. He knew that he would shoot the wolf. He reached down and pulled the collar back around the bloodied ruff of the wolf's neck and rebuckled it.

Ponga la cadena, said the hacendado.

He did so. Stooping and picking up the snap end of the chain and hooking it through the ring of the collar. Then he dropped the chain into the dirt and stepped away from the wolf. The little pistols disappeared as silently as they had come.

They made a path for him and watched him as he went. Outside the night had grown colder yet and the air smelled of woodsmoke from the cookfires over in the domicilios of the workers. Someone closed the door behind him. The square of the light in which he stood drew narrow slowly in the door's shadow to darkness. The tranca dropped woodenly into place within. He walked back up in the dark to the establo where the horses were being tended. A young mozo stood up and greeted him. He nodded and walked down and got his horse and slipped off the halter and hung it over the hitchrail and bridled the horse. He unrolled his blanket from behind the saddle and pulled it around his shoulders. Then he mounted up and rode out past the standing horses and nodded down to the mozo and touched his hat and rode toward the house.

The gate to the patio was closed. He stood down and opened it and then mounted up again. He bent forward in the saddle to clear the gateway arch and rode through with the stirrups dragging along the plaster and clicking off the iron jambs. The patio was paved with clay tiles and the sound of the horse's hooves upon them caused the servant girls to look up from their tasks. They stood holding tablecloths and plates and wicker baskets. Along the wall the oil lamps still burned atop their poles and the staccato shadows of hunting bats crossed the tiles and vanished and reappeared and crossed back. He crossed the courtyard horseback and nodded to the women and leaned from the saddle and took an empanada from a platter and sat eating it. The horse leaned its long nose down over the table but he pulled it away. The empanada was filled with seasoned meat and he ate it and leaned down and took another. The women went on with their work. He finished the empanada and then took a sweet pastry from a tray and ate that, putting the horse forward along the tables. The women moved away before him. He nodded to them again and wished them a good evening. He took another pastry and rode the circuit of the courtyard eating it while the horse shied at the passing bats and then he rode out through the gate again and down the drive. After a while one of the women crossed the patio and shut the gate behind him.

When he struck the road he turned south toward the town riding slowly. The howling of the dogs receded behind him. A half moon hung cocked in the east over the mountains like an eye narrowed in anger.

He'd reached the outer lights of the colonia before he halted the horse in the road. Then he reined it about and turned back.

When he pulled up before the door of the bodega he slid one foot out of the stirrup and slammed at the door with the heel of his boot. The door rattled against the crossbar within. He could hear the shouts of the men and he could hear the snarling of the dogs in the shed at the far side of the bodega. No one came. He rode around to the rear of the building and down along the narrow walled passageway between the bodega and the crib where the hounds were penned. Some men who had been squatting along the wall stood up. He nodded to them and stepped down and slid the rifle out of the scabbard and tied the reins together and dropped them over the post at the corner of the shed and walked past the men and pushed open the door and entered.

No one paid him any mind. He made his way through the crowd and when he reached the estacada the wolf was alone in the pit and she was a sorry thing to see. She'd returned to the stake and crouched by it but her head lay in the dirt and her tongue lolled in the dirt and her fur was matted with dirt and blood and the yellow eyes looked at nothing at all. She had been fighting for almost two hours and she had fought in casts of two the better part of all the dogs brought to the feria. At the far side of the estacada a pair of handlers were holding on to the airedales and there was a discussion going on with the árbitro and with the young hacendado. No one was anywhere near the airedales and they stood at their leashes and popped their wet teeth and jerked the handlers roughly about. The dust hanging in the lights glistened like silica. The aguador stood by with his pail of water.

He stepped over the parapet and walked toward the wolf and levered a shell into the chamber of the rifle and halted ten feet from her and raised the rifle to his shoulder and took aim at the bloodied head and fired.

The echo of the shot in the closed space of the barn rattled all else into silence. The airedales dropped to all fours and whined and circled behind the handlers. No one moved. The blue riflesmoke hung in the air. The wolf lay stretched out dead.

He lowered the rifle and ratcheted the spent casing out and caught it where it spun and put it in his pocket and levered the breech of the rifle shut again and stood with his thumb over the hammer. He looked at the crowd surrounding him. No one spoke. Some of them were looking toward the rear but it was not the young don who made his way to the estacada but the alguacil's deputy last seen hazing the carretero with his own coat down the street of the upriver colonia. He stepped over the barricade and walked out into the pit and demanded of the boy his rifle. The boy stood. The deputy unsnapped the flap on his holster and drew the 45 automatic already cocked.

Déme la carabina, he said.

The boy looked at the wolf. He looked at the crowd. His eyes were swimming but he did not let down the hammer of the rifle or move to relinquish it. The deputy raised the pistol and sighted it upon his upper chest. Spectators at the far side of the estacada squatted or dropped to their knees and some of them lay face down in the dirt with their hands over their heads. In the silence the only sound was the low whining of one of the dogs. Then someone spoke from the bleachers. Bastante, he said. No le moleste.

It was the alguacil. All turned to him. He was standing in the upper tiers of the rough board scaffolding with men at either side of him in their seven x beaver hats, some smoking puros as was the alguacil. He gestured with one hand. He said it was finished. He said for the boy to put up his rifle and that he would not be harmed. The deputy lowered the pistol, the watchers in the gallery rose from the ground and dusted themselves off. The boy laid the barrel of the rifle across his shoulder and lowered the hammer with his thumb. He turned and looked up at the alguacil. The alguacil made a small sweeping motion with the back of his hand. Whether to him or to the crowd at large he knew not but the spectators began to talk among themselves once more and someone opened the doors of the bodega onto the cool Mexican night.

The man to whom the hide had been promised had stepped across the boards and come forward. He walked around the dead wolf and stood facing her with his beltknife in his hand. The boy asked him what the hide was worth and he shrugged. He watched the boy carefully.

Cuánto quiere por él? the boy said.

El cuero?

La loba.

The claimant to the hide looked at the wolf and he looked at the boy. He said that the hide was worth fifty pesos.

Acepta la carabina? the boy said.

The claimant's eyebrows rose but he regained his composure. Es un huinche? he said.

Claro. Cuarenta y cuatro.

He unlimbered the rifle from his shoulder and pitched it across to the man. The claimant jacked open the lever and closed it again. He bent and picked up the ejected cartridge from the dirt and wiped it on his shirtsleeve and fed it back into the receiver. He raised the rifle and sighted at the lights overhead. It was worth a dozen mutilated wolfhides but he held it and weighed it in his hand and looked at the boy before nodding. Bueno, he said. He put the rifle over his shoulder and held out his hand. The boy looked down at the hand, then slowly took it and they sealed their barter by handclasp in the center of the pit while the populace filed past toward the open door. They studied him with their dark eyes in passing but if they were disappointed in their sport they gave no notice for they also were guests of hacendado and alguacil and they kept their own counsel as the custom of the country decreed. The claimant of the hide asked the boy if he had any more cartridges for the rifle but he only shook his head and knelt down and gathered up the limp shape of the shewolf in his arms which thin as she was yet was all he could carry and he crossed the pit and stepped over the barricade and went on toward the door at the rear with the head lolling and the slow blood dripping in his tracks.

When he rode out from the shadow of the building with the wolf across the bow of the saddle he had wrapped her in the remainder of the sheeting the rancher's wife had given him. The yard was filled with departing horsemen and with their shouts to each other. Dogs swarmed baying about the legs of his horse and the horse shied and stamped and kicked out at them and he rode past the open door of the bodega and on through the gate and out across the fields toward the river, leaning from the saddle and batting away the last of the dogs with his hat. To the south over the town rockets were rising in long sputtering arcs and breaking open in the darkness and falling in a slow hot confetti. The crack of their bursting reached him well behind the flare of light and in each flare of light hung the smudged ghosts of those gone before. He reached the river and turned downstream and rode through the shallow riffles and out along the broad gravel flats. A flight of ducks passed him going downriver in the dark. He could hear their wings. He could see them where they rose against the sky and flared away over the dark country to the west. He rode past the town and the small lights of the carnival and the shapes of the lights that lay slurred in the slow black coils of water along the river shore. A burntout catherinewheel stood smoking beyond the willow bracken. He studied the rise of the mountains, how they lay. The wind coming off the water smelled like wet metal. He could feel the blood of the wolf against his thigh where it had soaked through the sheeting and through his breeches and he put his hand to his leg and tasted the blood which tasted no different than his own. The fireworks died away. The moon's half hung over the black cape of the mountains.

At the junction of the rivers he rode across the broad gravel beach and sat the horse at the ford and he and the horse looked away to the north where the river was running clear and cold down out of the darkness of the country. He almost reached to draw the rifle from the scabbard to keep it out of the river but then he just put the horse forward into the shoals.

He could feel the horse's hooves muted on the cobbled rocks of the river floor and hear the water sucking at the horse's legs. The water came up under the animal's belly and he could feel the cold of it where it leaked into his boots. A last lone rocket rose over the town and revealed them midriver and revealed all the country about them, the shoreland trees strangely enshadowed, the pale rocks. A solitary dog from the town that had caught the scent of the wolf on the wind and followed him out stood frozen on the beach on three legs standing in that false light and then all faded again into the darkness out of which it had been summoned.

They crossed through the ford and rode dripping up out of the river and he looked back at the darkening town and then put the horse forward through the shore willows and standing cane and rode west toward the mountains. As he rode he sang old songs his father once had sung in the used to be and a soft corrido in spanish from his grandmother that told of the death of a brave soldadera who took up her fallen soldierman's gun and faced the enemy in some old waste of death. The night was clear and as he rode the moon dropped under the rim of the mountain and stars began to come up in the east where it was darkest. They rode up the dry course of a creekbed in a night suddenly colder, as if the moon had had warmth to it. Up through the low hills where he would ride all night singing softly as he rode.

By the time he reached the first talus slides under the tall escarpments of the Pilares the dawn was not far to come. He reined the horse in a grassy swale and stood down and dropped the reins. His trousers were stiff with blood. He cradled the wolf in his arms and lowered her to the ground and unfolded the sheet. She was stiff and cold and her fur was bristly with the blood dried upon it. He walked the horse back to the creek and left it standing to water and scouted the banks for wood with which to make a fire. Coyotes were yapping along the hills to the south and they were calling from the dark shapes of the rimlands above him where their cries seemed to have no origin other than the night itself.

He got the fire going and lifted the wolf from the sheet and took the sheet to the creek and crouched in the dark and washed the blood out of it and brought it back and he cut forked sticks from a mountain hackberry and drove them into the ground with a rock and hung the sheet on a trestlepole where it steamed in the firelight like a burning scrim standing in a wilderness where celebrants of some sacred passion had been carried off by rival sects or perhaps had simply fled in the night at the fear of their own doing. He pulled the blanket about his shoulders and sat shivering in the cold and waiting for the dawn that he could find the place where he would bury the wolf. After a while the horse came up from the creek trailing the wet reins through the leaves and stood at the edge of the fire.

He fell asleep with his hands palm up before him like some dozing penitent. When he woke it was still dark. The fire had died to a few low flames seething over the coals. He took off his hat and fanned the fire with it and coaxed it back and fed the wood he'd gathered. He looked for the horse but could not see it. The coyotes were still calling all along the stone ramparts of the Pilares and it was graying faintly in the east. He squatted over the wolf and touched her fur. He touched the cold and perfect teeth. The eye turned to the fire gave back no light and he closed it with his thumb and sat by her and put his hand upon her bloodied forehead and closed his own eyes that he could see her running in the mountains, running in the starlight where the grass was wet and the sun's coming as yet had not undone the rich matrix of creatures passed in the night before her. Deer and hare and dove and groundvole all richly empaneled on the air for her delight, all nations of the possible world ordained by God of which she was one among and not separate from. Where she ran the cries of the coyotes clapped shut as if a door had closed upon them and all was fear and marvel. He took up her stiff head out of the leaves and held it or he reached to hold what cannot be held, what already ran among the mountains at once terrible and of a great beauty, like flowers that feed on flesh. What blood and bone are made of but can themselves not make on any altar nor by any wound of war. What we may well believe has power to cut and shape and hollow out the dark form of the world surely if wind can, if rain can. But which cannot be held never be held and is no flower but is swift and a huntress and the wind itself is in terror of it and the world cannot lose it.

II

DOOMED ENTERPRISES divide lives forever into the then and the now. He'd carried the wolf up into the mountains in the bow of the saddle and buried her in a high pass under a cairn of scree. The little wolves in her belly felt the cold draw all about them and they cried out mutely in the dark and he buried them all and piled the rocks over them and led the horse away. He wandered on into the mountains. He whittled a bow from a holly limb, made arrows from cane. He thought to become again the child he never was.

They rode the high country for weeks and they grew thin and gaunted man and horse and the horse grazed on the sparse winter grass in the mountains and gnawed the lichens from the rock and the boy shot trout with his arrows where they stood above their shadows on the cold stone floors of the pools and he ate them and ate green nopal and then on a windy day traversing a high saddle in the mountains a hawk passed before the sun and its shadow ran so quick in the grass before them that it caused the horse to shy and the boy looked up where the bird turned high above them and he took the bow from his shoulder and nocked and loosed an arrow and watched it rise with the wind rattling the fletching slotted into the cane and watched it turning and arcing and the hawk wheeling and then flaring suddenly with the arrow locked in its pale breast.

The hawk turned and skated off down the wind and vanished beyond the cape of the mountain, a single feather fell. He rode out to look for it but he never found it. He found a single drop of blood that had dried on the rocks and darkened in the wind and nothing more. He dismounted and sat on the ground beside the horse where the wind blew and he made a cut in the heel of his hand with his knife and watched the slow blood dropping on the stone. Two days later he sat the horse on a promontory overlooking the Bavispe River and the river was running backwards. That or the sun was setting in the east behind him. He made his rough camp in a windbreak of juniper and waited out the night to see what the sun would do or what the river and in the morning when day broke over the distant mountains and across the broad plain before him he realized that he had crossed back through the mountains to where the river ran north again along the eastern side of the sierras.

He rode deeper into the mountains. He sat on a windfall tree in a high forest of madroño and ash and with his knife cut to length a piece of rope while the horse watched. He stood and strung the rope through the beltloops of his jeans where they hung from his hips and folded away the knife. It aint nothin to eat, he told the horse.

In that wild high country he'd lie in the cold and the dark and listen to the wind and watch the last few embers of his fire at their dying and the red crazings in the woodcoals where they broke along their unguessed gridlines. As if in the trying of the wood were elicited hidden geometries and their orders which could only stand fully revealed, such is the way of the world, in darkness and ashes. He heard no wolves. Ragged and half starving and his horse dismayed he rode a week later into the mining town of El Tigre.

A dozen houses sited senselessly along a slope overlooking a small mountain valley. There was no one about. He sat the horse in the middle of the mud street and the horse stared bleakly at the town, at the rude jacales of mud and sticks with their cowhide doors. He put the horse forward and a woman came out into the street and approached him and stood at his stirrup and looked up into the child's face under the hat and asked if he were sick. He said that he was not. That he was only hungry. She told him to get down and he did so and slid the

bow from his shoulder and hung it over the horn of the saddle
and followed her down to her house while the horse walked
behind.

He sat in a kitchen that was all but dark so sheltered was it
from the sun and he ate frijoles from a clay bowl with a huge
spoon of enameled tin. The sole light fell from a smokehole in
the ceiling and the woman knelt there at a low clay brasero and
turned tortillas on a cracked and ancient clay comal while the
thin smoke rose up the blackened wall and vanished overhead.
He could hear chickens clucking outside and in a room darker
yet beyond a curtain of pieced sacking some sleeper was sleeping. The house smelled of smoke and rancid grease and the
smoke bore the faintly antiseptic odor of piñon wood. She
turned the tortillas with her bare fingers and put them on a clay
plate and brought them to him. He thanked her and folded one
of the tortillas and dipped it into the beans and ate.

De dónde viene? she said.

De los Estados Unidos.

De Tejas?

Nuevo Mexico.

Qué lindo, she said.

Lo conoce?

No.

She watched him eat.

Es minero? she said.

Vaquero.

Ay, vaquero.

When he'd finished and wiped the bowl clean with the last
piece of tortilla she took the dishes and carried them across the
room and put them in a bucket. When she came back she sat
down on the slab-board bench across the table from him and
studied him. Adónde va? she said.

He didnt know. He looked vaguely around the room. Pinned
to the bare mud wall with a wooden peg was a calendar with a
color print of a 1927 Buick. A woman in a fur coat and a turban

stood beside it. He said that he did not know where he was going. They sat. He nodded toward the curtained doorway. Es su marido? he said.

She said that it was not. She said that it was her sister.

He nodded. He looked about the room again which his first look had in any case exhausted and then he reached over his shoulder and took his hat from the stile of the chair at his back and pushed the chair back on the clay floor and stood.

Muchísimas gracias, he said.

Clarita, called the woman.

She hadnt taken her eyes from him and it occurred to him that she might be a little bit crazy. She called again. She turned and looked toward the darkened room beyond the curtain, she held up one finger. Momentito, she said. She rose and went into the other room. In a few minutes she appeared again. She held aside the sacking against the doorjamb in a faintly theatrical gesture. The woman who had been asleep stepped through and stood before him in a wrapper of stained pink rayon. She looked at him and turned and looked back at her sister. She was perhaps the younger but they looked much alike. She looked again at the boy. He stood with his hat in his hands. The sister stood behind her in the doorway with the frayed and dusty sacking pulled against her in a way to suggest perhaps that the emergence of the sleeper was a rare and transitory thing. She herself no more than a herald of coming good. The sleeping sister pulled her wrap about herself and reached and touched the boy's face with one hand. Then she turned and passed back through the doorway to be seen no more. The boy thanked his hostess and put on his hat and pushed open the clattery hide door and walked outside into the sunlight where the horse stood waiting.

Riding out the road wherein were neither ruts nor hoofprints nor any sign of commerce at all he passed two men standing in a doorway who called out and made signs to him. He'd hung the bow again across his shoulder and he thought that riding so armed in his blackened rags atop the bony horse he must cut a sad or foolish figure but when he regarded his hecklers more

closely he reckoned he could scarce look worse than they and
he rode on.

He crossed the small valley and rode west into the mountains.
He'd no way to know how long he'd been in that country but
for all he'd seen of it good or ill which he pondered as he rode
he knew that he no longer feared whatever he might find there.
Days to come he would encounter wild indians deep in the
sierras living in the chozas and wickiups of their squalid
rancherías and indians wilder yet who lived in caves and all of
whom may well have thought him mad for the regard with
which they treated him. They fed him and the women washed
his clothes and mended them and sewed his boots with a homemade awl and ligaments from a hawk's foot. They spoke among
themselves in their own tongue or with him in their broken
spanish. They said that most of their young people had gone to
work in the mines or in the cities or on the haciendas of the
Mexicans but that they did not trust the Mexicans. They traded
with them in the small villages along the river and sometimes
they would stand in the outer ring of light and watch them at
their festivals but otherwise they kept to themselves. They said
that it was the way of the Mexicans to blame them for the crimes
they committed among themselves and that the Mexicans would
get drunk and kill each other and then send soldiers into the
mountains to seek them out. When he told them where he came
from he was surprised to find that they knew that country also
but of it they would not speak. No one tried to trade horses
with him. No one asked him why he had come. They cautioned
him only to lay clear of the Yaqui country to the west because
the Yaqui would kill him. Then the women packed for him a
dinner of some dried and leathern meat or machaca and parched
corn and sootstained tortillas and an old man came forward
and addressed him in a spanish he could scarcely understand,
speaking with great earnestness into the boy's eyes and holding
his saddle fore and aft so that the boy sat almost in his arms.
He was dressed in odd and garish fashion and his clothes were
embroidered with signs that had about them the geometric look

of instructions, perhaps a game. He wore jewelry of jade and silver and his hair was long and blacker than his age would seem to warrant. He told the boy that although he was huérfano still he must cease his wanderings and make for himself some place in the world because to wander in this way would become for him a passion and by this passion he would become estranged from men and so ultimately from himself. He said that the world could only be known as it existed in men's hearts. For while it seemed a place which contained men it was in reality a place contained within them and therefore to know it one must look there and come to know those hearts and to do this one must live with men and not simply pass among them. He said that while the huérfano might feel that he no longer belonged among men he must set this feeling aside for he contained within him a largeness of spirit which men could see and that men would wish to know him and that the world would need him even as he needed the world for they were one. Lastly he said that while this itself was a good thing like all good things it was also a danger. Then he removed his hands from the boy's saddle and stepped away and stood. The boy thanked him for his words but he said that he was in fact not an orphan and then he thanked the women standing there and turned the horse and rode out. They stood watching him go. As he passed the last of the brush wickiups he turned and looked back and as he did so the old man called out to him. Eres, he said. Eres huérfano. But the boy only raised one hand and touched his hat and rode on.

In two days he struck a wagonroad passing east and west across the sierras. The woods were green with ilex and madroño, the road seemed little used. In a day's travel he passed no soul. He crossed through a high pass where the way was so narrow that the rocks bore old scars of wagonhubs and below the pass were scattered stone cairns, the mojoneras de muerte of that country where travelers had been slain by indians years before. The country seemed depopulate and barren and he saw no game and saw no birds and there was nothing about but the wind and the silence.

At the eastern escarpment he dismounted and led the horse along a shelf of gray rock. The scrub juniper that grew along the rim leaned in a wind that had long since passed. Along the face of the stone bluffs were old pictographs of men and animals and suns and moons as well as other representations that seemed to have no referent in the world although they once may have. He sat in the sun and looked out over the country to the east, the broad barranca of the Bavispe and the ensuing Carretas Plain that was once a seafloor and the small pieced fields and the new corn greening in the old lands of the Chichimeca where the priests had passed and soldiers passed and the missions fallen into mud and the ranges of mountains beyond the plain range on range in pales of blue where the terrain lay clawed open north and south, canyon and range, sierra and barranca, all of it waiting like a dream for the world to come to be, world to pass. He saw a single vulture hanging motionless in some high vector that the wind had chosen for it. He saw the smoke of a locomotive passing slowly downcountry over the plain forty miles away.

He took a handful of piñon nuts from one tattered pocket and spread them on a rock and cracked them with a handstone. He'd taken to talking to the horse and he talked to it now as he cracked the nuts and when he had them free of their hulls he scooped them up and held them out. The horse looked at him and looked at the piñon nuts and shuffled forward two steps and placed its rubbery mouth in his palm.

He wiped the slobber from his hand on the leg of his trousers and sat cracking and eating the rest of the nuts himself while the horse watched. Then he stood and walked to the edge of the escarpment and threw the handstone. It sailed out turning and fell and fell and vanished in the silence. He stood listening. From far below the faint clatter of stone on stone. He walked back and stretched out on the warm rock shelving and cradled his head in the crook of his arm and stared into the dark of his hatcrown. His home had come to seem remote and dreamlike. There were times he could not call to mind his father's face.

He slept and in his sleep he dreamt of wild men who came to

him with clubs and their teeth were filed to points and they gathered round him and warned him of their work before they even set about it. He woke and lay listening. As if they might yet be there just beyond the darkness of his hat. Squatting among the rocks. Chiseling in stone with stones those semblances of the living world they'd have endure and the world dead at their hands. He lifted his hat and placed it on his chest and looked at the blue sky. He sat up and looked for the horse but the horse was only a few feet away standing waiting for him. He rose and rolled the stiffness out of his shoulders and put on his hat and took up the trailing reins and ran his hand down the horse's foreleg till it lifted its foot and he cradled the hoof between his knees and looked at it. The horse had long since shed its shoes and the hooves were long and broomed and he took out his pocketknife and pared back the hoof wall where the edges were splayed and then let down the horse's foot and walked around the animal inspecting and paring the other hooves in turn. The constant currying of the brush and greenwood in the mountains had carried off all trace of the stable and the horse gave off a warm and rooty smell. The horse had dark hooves with heavy hoof walls and the horse had in him enough grullo blood to make a mountain horse by both conformation and inclination and as the boy had grown up where talk of horses was more or less continual he knew that where the blood carries the shape of a hock or the breadth of a face it carries also an inner being of a certain design and no other and the wilder their life became in the mountains the more he felt the horse subtly at war with itself. He didnt think the horse would quit him but he was sure the horse had thought about it. He pared the last hind hoof and led the animal back out to the narrow track and mounted up and turned and started down into the gorge.

The road descended the granite face of the sierra like a hairspring. He was amazed that wagons could have negotiated those narrow switchbacks. There were caveouts along the edges of the road where he dismounted and led the horse and there were rocks in the road no man could move. The way descended down out of the pine forests through oak and juniper. A wild and jumbled terrain. Everywhere the green spring invasive in the barrancas. In the evening light a trembling celadon. He was at the descent some seven hours, the last of them in darkness.

He slept that night in a wash in the river sand with the cane and willow thick about him and in the morning he rode north along the river track until he came to a ford. Shored up on the red alluvial plain on the far side of the river were the ruins of a town slumping back into the mud out of which it had been raised. A single smoke stood in the blue air. He put the horse into the ford and halted to let the animal drink and he leaned down from the saddle and raised a palmful of water and passed it over his face and raised another to drink. The water was cold and clear. Upriver swifts or swallows were circling and flaring low over the water and the morning sun was warm on his face. He pressed the heels of his boots into the horse's flank and the horse raised its dripping mouth out of the river and waded slowly out into the ford. Midstream he halted again and slid the bow from his shoulder and let it go in the river. It turned and jostled in the riffles and floated out into the pool below. A crescent of pale wood, turning and drifting, lost in the sun on the water. Legacy of some drowned archer, musician, maker of fire. He rode on through the ford and up through the shore willows and carrizal and into the town.

Most of those buildings still standing were at the farther end of the town and toward these he rode. He passed the wreckage of an ancient coach half crushed in a zaguán where the doors were fallen in. He passed a mud horno in a yard from within which the eyes of some animal watched and he passed the ruins of a huge adobe church whose roofbeams lay in the rubble. The man who stood in the doorway at the rear of the church was paler of skin than even he and had sandy hair and pale blue eyes and the man called out to him first in spanish and then in english. He told him to get down and to come in.

He left the horse at the door of the church and followed the man into a small room where a fire burned in a homemade sheetiron stove. The room contained a small bed or cot and a long pine table with turned legs and several ladderback chairs such as were made by the Mennonites of that country. A number of cats of every color lay about the room. The man gestured at the cats vaguely as if they were to be excused in some way and then motioned for the boy to take a chair. The boy pulled the blanket from about his shoulders and stood holding it. The room was very warm and yet the man had bent and opened the stove door and was at chunking in more wood. On top of the stove stood an iron skillet and a kettle and a few blackened pans together with a clawfooted silver teapot deeply dented and dark with tarnish that sorted oddly with the other housewares. He rose and shut the stove door with his foot and reached and took down a pair of china cups and saucers and set them on the table. One of the cats got up and walked down the table and looked into each of the cups in turn and then sat. The man took the teapot from the stove and poured the cups and put the pot back and looked at the boy.

Eres puros huesos, he said.

Tengo miedo es verdad.

Please. Be comfortable. Would you like some eggs?

I guess I could eat some eggs.

How many will you eat?

I'll eat three.

There is no bread.

I'll eat four.

You must sit.

Yessir.

He took down a small enameled pail and went out through the low door. The boy pulled back a chair and sat. He folded the blanket roughly and laid it in the chair beside him and took up the nearer cup and sipped the coffee. It wasnt real coffee. He didnt know what it was. He looked around the room. The cats watched him. After a while the man returned with eggs rolling around in the floor of the pail. He picked up the frypan and held it by the handle and peered into it as into some black looking-glass and then set it down again and spooned grease into it from a clay jar. He watched the grease melt and then broke the eggs into the pan and stirred them about with the same spoon. Four eggs, he said.

Yessir.

The man turned and looked at him and then turned back to his cooking. It occurred to the boy that he hadnt been speaking to him. When the eggs were done he took down a plate and scooped them out onto it and placed a blackened silver fork on the edge of the plate and set it on the table in front of the boy. He poured more coffee and put the pot back on the stove and sat down across the table to watch him eat.

You are lost, he said.

The boy paused with a forkful of the eggs and studied the question. I dont think so, he said.

The last man to come here was sick. He was a sick man.

When was that?

The man gestured vaguely in the air with one hand.

What happened to him? the boy said.

He died.

The boy went on eating. I aint sick, he said.

He is buried in the churchyard.

The boy ate. I aint sick, he said, and I aint lost.

He is the first to be buried there in many a year, I can tell you.

How many a year?

I dont know.

What did he come here for?

He was a miner from the mountains. A barretero. He became sick and so he came here. But it was too late. No one could do anything for him.

How many other people live here?

No one. Only me.

Then you was the only one that tried?

Tried what?

To do anything for him.

Yes.

The boy looked up at the man. He ate. What day is it? he said.

It is Sunday.

I meant what day of the month.

I dont know.

Do you know what month it is?

No.

How do you know it's Sunday.

Because it comes every seven days.

The boy ate.

I am a Mormon. Or I was. I was a Mormon born.

He wasnt sure what a Mormon was. He looked at the room. He looked at the cats.

They came here many years ago. Eighteen and ninety-six. From Utah. They came because of the statehood. In Utah. I was a Mormon. Then I converted to the church. Then I became I dont know what. Then I became me.

What do you do here?

I am the custodian. The caretaker.

What do you take care of?

The church.

It's done fell down.

Yes. Of course. It fell down in the terremoto.

Were you here then?

I was not born.

When was it?

In eighteen eighty-seven.

The boy finished the eggs and put the fork on the plate. He looked at the man.

How long have you been here?

Since six years now.

It was like this when you got here.

Yes.

He raised and drained his cup and set it back in the saucer. I thank you for the breakfast, he said.

You are welcome.

He looked like he might be getting ready to rise and leave. The man reached into his shirtpocket and took out tobacco and a small cloth folder in which were papers cut from cornhusks. One of the cats on the bunk had risen and stretched, hindleg and fore, and it leapt silently to the table and walked to the boy's plate and sniffed at it and squatted on bowed elbows and began delicately to pick bits of egg from the tines of the fork. The man had pinched tobacco into a paper and sat rolling it back and forth. He pushed the makings across the table toward the boy.

Thanks, the boy said. I aint never took it up.

The man nodded and twisted the cigarette he'd made into the corner of his mouth and rose and went to the stove. He took a long splinter of wood from a can of them in the floor and opened the stove door and leaned and lit the splinter and with it lit the cigarette. Then he blew out the splinter and put it back in the can and shut the stove door and returned to the table with the pot and refilled the boy's cup. His own cup stood black and cold untouched. He set the pot back on the stove and walked around the table and sat as before. The cat rose and looked at itself in the white porcelain of the plate and stepped away and sat and yawned and set about cleaning itself.

What did you come here for? the boy said.

What did you?

Sir?

What did you come here for?

I didnt come here. I'm just passin through.

The man drew on the cigarette. Myself also, he said. I am the same.

You been passin through for six years?

The man gestured with a small toss of one hand. I came here as a heretic fleeing a prior life. I was running away.

You come here to hide out?

I came because of the devastation.

Sir?

The devastation. From the terremoto.

Yessir.

I was seeking evidence for the hand of God in the world. I had come to believe that hand a wrathful one and I thought that men had not inquired sufficiently into miracles of destruction. Into disasters of a certain magnitude. I thought there might be evidence that had been overlooked. I thought He would not trouble himself to wipe away every handprint. My desire to know was very strong. I thought it might even amuse Him to leave some clue.

What sort of clue?

I dont know. Something. Something unforeseen. Something out of place. Something untrue or out of round. A track in the dirt. A fallen bauble. Not some cause. I can tell you that. Not some cause. Causes only multiply themselves. They lead to chaos. What I wanted was to know his mind. I could not believe He would destroy his own church without reason.

You think maybe the people that lived here had done somethin bad?

The man smoked thoughtfully. I thought it possible, yes. Possible. As in the cities of the plain. I thought there might be evidence of something suitably unspeakable such that He might be goaded into raising his hand against it. Something in the rubble. In the dirt. Under the vigas. Something dark. Who could say?

What did you find?

Nothing. A doll. A dish. A bone.

He leaned and stubbed out the cigarette in a clay bowl on the table.

I am here because of a certain man. I came to retrace his steps. Perhaps to see if there were not some alternate course. What was here to be found was not a thing. Things separate from their stories have no meaning. They are only shapes. Of a certain size and color. A certain weight. When their meaning has become lost to us they no longer have even a name. The story on the other hand can never be lost from its place in the world for it is that place. And that is what was to be found here. The corrido. The tale. And like all corridos it ultimately told one story only, for there is only one to tell.

The cats shifted and stirred, the fire creaked in the stove. Outside in the abandoned village the profoundest silence.

What is the story? the boy said.

In the town of Caborca on the Altar River there was a man who lived there who was an old man. He was born in Caborca and in Caborca he died. Yet he lived once in this town. In Huisiachepic.

What does Caborca know of Huisiachepic, Huisiachepic of Caborca? They are different worlds, you must agree. Yet even so there is but one world and everything that is imaginable is necessary to it. For this world also which seems to us a thing of stone and flower and blood is not a thing at all but is a tale. And all in it is a tale and each tale the sum of all lesser tales and yet these also are the selfsame tale and contain as well all else within them. So everything is necessary. Every least thing. This is the hard lesson. Nothing can be dispensed with. Nothing despised. Because the seams are hid from us, you see. The joinery. The way in which the world is made. We have no way to know what could be taken away. What omitted. We have no way to tell what might stand and what might fall. And those seams that are hid from us are of course in the tale itself and the tale has no abode or place of being except in the telling only and there it lives and makes its home and therefore we can never be done with the telling. Of the telling there is no end. And whether in Caborca or in Huisiachepic or in whatever other place by whatever other name or by no name at all I say again all tales are one. Rightly heard all tales are one.

The boy looked into the dark disc of liquid in his cup that was not coffee. He looked at the man and he looked at the cats. They seemed to be sleeping to a cat and it occurred to him that the man's voice was to them no novelty and that he must talk to himself in the absence of any godsent ear from the outer world. Or talk to the cats.

What about the man that used to live here? he said.

Yes. This man's parents were killed by a cannonshot in the church at Caborca where they had gone with others to defend themselves against the outlaw American invaders. Perhaps you know something of the history of this country. When the stones and rubble were cleared away the boy lay in the arms of his dead mother. The boy's father lay nearby and he tried to speak. They raised him up. The blood ran from his mouth. They bent to hear what he would say but he said nothing. His chest was crushed and he breathed blood and he lifted one hand as if in farewell and then he died.

The boy was brought to this town. Of Caborca he remembered little. He remembered his father. Certain things. He remembered his father lifting him in his arms to see puppets performing in the alameda. Of his mother he remembered less. Perhaps nothing. The particulars of his life are strange particulars. This is a story of misfortune. Or so it would seem. The end is not yet told.

Here he grew to manhood. In this town. Here he married a wife and all in God's good time was himself blessed with a son.

In the first week of May in the year eighteen eighty-seven this man takes his son and sets out on a journey. He will go to Bavispe and there leave the boy in the care of an uncle who is also the boy's padrino. From Bavispe he will continue on to Batopite where he will arrange for the sale of sugar from certain estancias to the south. In Batopite he will stay the night. This is a journey I have thought of many times. This journey and this man. He is youthful. Perhaps not thirty years of age. He rides a mule. The boy rides in the bow of the saddle before him. It is in the springtime and the wildflowers are blooming in the meadows along the river. He has promised to return with a gift for his young wife. He sees her standing there. She waves goodbye to him as he sets out. He has no likeness of her other than that which he carries in his heart. Think of that. Perhaps she is crying. Standing there watching him out of sight. Standing in the very shadow of this church that is doomed to fall. Life is a memory, then it is nothing. All law is writ in a seed.

The man had arched his fingers above the table to place the scene. He passed one hand from left to right to show where things had been and how it must have been with the sun and with the rider or with the woman where she stood. As if he'd shape out in the present air the spaces where such things had been.

At Bavispe there was a fair. A traveling circus. And the man held his young son aloft under the paper lanterns as his father before him so that the child might see. A clown, a magician, a man who held up serpents in his naked hands. The next morning he departed alone for Batopite as told, leaving the child behind. And there in Bavispe the child died, crushed in the terremoto. The padrino held the boy in his arms and wept. The town of Batopite was spared. Even today you can see the great crack in the mountain wall across the river like an enormous laugh. And that was all the news they had of disaster in Batopite. Nothing else was known. Returning to Bavispe the following day this man met a traveler afoot who told him the news. He could not believe the man's words and he urged the mule on and when he arrived at Bavispe all was in ruin as the traveler had told and death was everywhere in great abundance.

He entered the town already in terror of what he should find. He heard gunshots. Dogs ran out that had been at the bodies in the rubble and scampered past him and men with guns ran out and stood in the street shouting. In the alameda the dead lay on mats of river reed and old women dressed in black walked to and fro among the rows with green fronds to keep the flies away. The padrino came to him and wept at the mule's stirrup and could not speak but only took the reins in his own hands and led him sobbing. Through the alameda where lay dead merchants and farmers and the wives of merchants and farmers. Dead schoolgirls. Lying on reeds in the alameda of Bavispe. A dead dog in a carnival costume. A dead clown. Youngest of them all his son crushed and lifeless. He dismounted and there he knelt and clasped the bloody ruin of the child to his breast. The year is eighteen eighty-seven.

What thoughts must have been his? Who cannot feel his anguish? He returns to Huisiachepic bearing across the mule's haunches the corpse of the child with which God had blessed his house. Waiting for him in Huisiachepic is the mother of the child and this is the gift he brings her.

Such a man is like a dreamer who wakes from a dream of grief to a greater sorrow yet. All that he loves is now become a torment to him. The pin has been pulled from the axis of the universe. Whatever one takes one's eye from threatens to flee away. Such a man is lost to us. He moves and speaks. But he is himself less than the merest shadow among all that he beholds. There is no picture of him possible. The smallest mark upon the page exaggerates his presence.

Who would seek the company of such a man? That which speaks in us one to another and is beyond our words or beyond the lifting or the turning of a hand to say that this is the way my heart is, or this. That thing was lost in him. So.

The boy watched him. His eyes were bright and he had placed one hand palm upward on the table as if within it lay the very thing lost. He closed his fist upon it.

We lose sight of him for some years. He abandons his wife in the ruins of this town. Many friends are dead. Of his wife nothing more is known. He is in Guatemala. He is in Trinidad. How could he return? Had he but saved some part of the burial of his life then perhaps there would have been no need to come with flowers and grief. And yet as it was there was no part of him left to do so. You see?

Men spared their lives in great disasters often feel in their deliverance the workings of fate. The hand of Providence. This man saw in himself again what he'd perhaps forgot. That long ago he'd been elected out of the common lot of men. For what he was asked now to reckon with was that he'd been called forth twice out of the ashes, out of the dust and rubble. For what?

You must not suppose such elections to be happy ones for they are not. In his sparing he found himself severed from both antecedents and posterity alike. He was but some brevity of a being. His claims to the common life of men became tenuous, insubstantial. He was a trunk without root or branch. Perhaps there was yet even then a moment when he would have gone to the church to pray. But the church lay in pieces on the ground. And in the darkened chancel within him had the ground also shifted, also cracked. There also was a ruin. A waste had opened in his soul and perhaps he saw with some new clarity how like the church he was himself but a thing of clay and perhaps he thought that the church would not be raised again as to do such work requires first that God be in men's hearts for it is there alone that it truly has its being and there failing no power can build it back again. He became a heretic. So.

After many a youthful wandering this man appeared at last in the capital and there he worked for some years. He was a bearer of messages. He carried a satchel of leather and canvas secured with a lock. He had no way to know what the messages said nor had he any curiosity concerning them. The stone facades of the buildings among which he went on his daily rounds were pitted with the marks of old gunfire. In places above the reach of people to collect them there yet remained smeared here and there the thin dark medallions of lead which had been rounds from machinegun emplacements in the streets. The rooms in which he stood waiting were rooms from which men in high office had been dragged to their execution. Need one say he was a man without politics? He was simply a messenger. He had no faith in the power of men to act wisely in their own behalf. It was his view rather that every act soon eluded the grasp of its propagator to be swept away in a clamorous tide of unforeseen consequence. He believed that in the world was another agenda, another order, and with this power lay whatever brief he may have held. In the meantime he waited to be called to he knew not what.

The man leaned back, he looked up at the boy and smiled.

Do not misunderstand me, he said. The events of the world can have no separate life from the world. And yet the world itself can have no temporal view of things. It can have no cause to favor certain enterprises over others. The passing of armies and the passing of sands in the desert are one. There is no favoring, you see. How could there be? At whose behest? This man did not cease to believe in God. Nor did he come to have some modern view of God. There was God and there was the world. He knew that the world would forget him but that God could not. And yet that was the very thing he wished for.

Easy to see that naught save sorrow could bring a man to such a view of things. And yet a sorrow for which there can be no help is no sorrow. It is some dark sister traveling in sorrow's clothing. Men do not turn from God so easily you see. Not so easily. Deep in each man is the knowledge that something knows of his existence. Something knows, and cannot be fled nor hid from. To imagine otherwise is to imagine the unspeakable. It was never that this man ceased to believe in God. No. It was rather that he came to believe terrible things of Him.

By now he is a pensioner in Mexico. He has no friends. By day he sits in the park. The very ground under his feet is composted with the blood of the ancients. He watches passersby. He has become convinced that those aims and purposes with which they imagine their movements to be invested are in reality but a means by which to describe them. He believes that their movements are the subject of larger movements in patterns unknown to them and these in turn to others. He finds no comfort in these speculations I can tell you. He sees the world slipping away. All about him an enormous emptiness without echo. It was at this time that he began to pray. From no very pure motive perhaps. But then what would such a motive look like? Can God be cajoled? Can He be pled with or asked to see the reason in one's argument? Can anything from his own hand do aught to please Him more than had it acted otherwise? Can He be surprised? In his heart this man had already begun to plot against God but he did not know it yet. He would not know it until he began to dream of Him.

Who can dream of God? This man did. In his dreams God was much occupied. Spoken to He did not answer. Called to did not hear. The man could see Him bent at his work. As if through a glass. Seated solely in the light of his own presence. Weaving the world. In his hands it flowed out of nothing and in his hands it vanished into nothing once again. Endlessly. Endlessly. So. Here was a God to study. A God who seemed a slave to his own selfordinated duties. A God with a fathomless capacity to bend all to an inscrutable purpose. Not chaos itself lay outside of that matrix. And somewhere in that tapestry that was the world in its making and in its unmaking was a thread that was he and he woke weeping.

On a certain day he rose and put his few possessions into an old valise he'd kept beneath his bed these years and descended the stairwell for the last time. He carried his bible beneath his arm. Like the peregrine minister of some paltry sect. In three days' time he was in the town of Caborca of sacred memory. Standing there by the river squinting up in the sunshine where the dome of the broken transept of the church of La Purísima Concepción de Nuestra Señora de Caborca floated in the pure desert air. So.

The man shook his head slowly. He'd taken up his makings from the table and begun to roll another cigarette. Very thoughtfully. As if its construction were a puzzle to him. He rose and went to the stove and lit the cigarette with the same blackened splinter of wood and inspected the fire and shut the stove door and returned to the table and sat as before.

Perhaps you know the town of Caborca. The church is very beautiful. By the flooding of the river through the years much has been destroyed. The sanctuary and two bell towers. The rear of the nave and most of the south transept. What remains of it stands on three legs, so to speak. The dome hangs in the sky like an apparition and so it has hung for many years. Most improbably. No mason could devise such a structure. For years the people of Caborca waited for it to fall. It was like a thing unfinished in their lives. Events of doubtful outcome were made subject to its standing. It was said of certain old and venerable men that when they died the dome would fall and they died and their children died and the dome floated on in the pure air until at last it came to bear such import in the minds of the people of that town that they scarce would speak of it at all.

This was what he came to. Perhaps he did not even consider the question as to how he had been brought to this place. Yet it was the very thing he sought. Beneath that perilous roof he threw down his pallet and made his fire and there he made ready to receive that which had eluded him. By whatever name. There in the ruins of that church out of whose dust and rubble he had been raised up seventy years before and sent forth to live his life. Such as it was. Such as it had become. Such as it would be.

He drew slowly on the cigarette. He studied the rising smoke. As if in its slow uncoiling lay the lineaments of the history he told. Dream or memory or builded stone. He tapped the ash into the bowl.

The people of the town came and they stood about. At a certain distance. They were interested to see what God would do with such a man. Perhaps he was a crazy person. Perhaps a saint. He paid them no mind. He paced and muttered into his bible and he thumbed the pages. Overhead in the vault were frescoes depicting the very events he pondered. On the west wall of the dome the clay nests of golondrinas mortared up among the fading vestments of the saints. From time to time in his circling he'd pause and hold his book aloft and thump at a page with his finger and address his God at large. This is what they saw. An old hermit. A man with no history. Some said a holy man come among them and some a lunatic and many were scandalized who'd not heard God addressed before in such a manner. Not seen God bearded in his very house.

It seemed that what he wished, this man, was to strike some colindancia with his Maker. Assess boundaries and metes. See that lines were drawn and respected. Who could think such a reckoning possible? The boundaries of the world are those of God's devising. With God there can be no reckoning. With what would one bargain?

They sent for the priest. The priest came and spoke with the man. The priest outside the church. The solitary parishioner within. Beneath the shadow of the perilous vault. The priest spoke to this misguided man of the nature of God and of the spirit and the will and of the meaning of grace in men's lives and the old man heard him out and nodded his head at certain salient points and when the priest was done this old man raised his book aloft and shouted at the priest. You know nothing. That is what he shouted. You know nothing.

The people looked at the priest. To see how he would respond. The priest studied the man and then went away again. The conviction with which the old man spoke had jarred his heart and he weighed the old man's words and was troubled because of course the old man's words were true ones. And if the old man knew that then what else must he know?

He returned the next day. And the day after. People came to attend. Scholars of the town. To hear what was said on either side. The old man at his pacing under the shadow of the vault. The priest outside. The old man thumbing his book with a terrible dexterity. Like a moneycounter. The priest countering from those high canonical principles to which he gave such latitude. Both of them heretics to the bone.

He leaned forward and stubbed out the cigarette. He held up a finger. As if to countenance caution. The sun had entered the room by the south window and certain of the cats had risen to stretch, to rearrange themselves.

With this difference, he said. With this difference. The priest wagered nothing. He'd nothing at hazard. He stood on no such ground as the crazed old man. Under no such shadow. Rather he chose to stand outside the critical edifice of his own church and by this choice he sacrificed his words of their power to witness.

The old man by whatever instinct stood on ground at once blessed and fraughtful. This was his choice, this his gesture. All agreed his testimony was a powerful one. The strength of his conviction was plain to them. In his words there was little measure and little of restraint. In his new life the libertine was out. Do you see? By his arrogance he had engaged the living thing. On that perilous ground he had made of himself the only witness there can ever be and if some saw in his eyes the rapture of madness what else would one look for in one who had enjoined the God of the universe on ground of that God's own choosing? For that is always the nature of such ground, perilous and transitory. And it is indeed so that you must make your case there or nowhere.

And the priest? A man of broad principles. Of liberal sentiments. Even a generous man. Something of a philosopher. Yet one might say that his way through the world was so broad it scarcely made a path at all. He carried within himself a great reverence for the world, this priest. He heard the voice of the Deity in the murmur of the wind in the trees. Even the stones were sacred. He was a reasonable man and he believed that there was love in his heart.

There was not. Nor does God whisper through the trees. His voice is not to be mistaken. When men hear it they fall to their knees and their souls are riven and they cry out to Him and there is no fear in them but only that wildness of heart that springs from such longing and they cry out to stay his presence for they know at once that while godless men may live well enough in their exile those to whom He has spoken can contemplate no life without Him but only darkness and despair. Trees and stones are no part of it. So. The priest in the very generosity of his spirit stood in mortal peril and knew it not. He believed in a boundless God without center or circumference. By this very formlessness he'd sought to make God manageable. This was his colindancia. In his grandness he had ceded all terrain. And in this colindancia God had no say at all.

To see God everywhere is to see Him nowhere. We go from day to day, one day much like the next, and then on a certain day all unannounced we come upon a man or we see this man who is perhaps already known to us and is a man like all men but who makes a certain gesture of himself that is like the piling of one's goods upon an altar and in this gesture we recognize that which is buried in our hearts and is never truly lost to us nor ever can be and it is this moment, you see. This same moment. It is this which we long for and are afraid to seek and which alone can save us.

So. The priest went away. He returned to the town. The old man to his testament. To his pacing and to his argufying. He'd become something like a barrister. He pored over the record not for the honor and glory of his Maker but rather to find against Him. To seek out in nice subtleties some darker nature. False favors. Small deceptions. Promises forsaken or a hand too quickly raised. To make cause against Him, you see. He understood what the priest could not. That what we seek is the worthy adversary. For we strike out to fall flailing through demons of wire and crepe and we long for something of substance to oppose us. Something to contain us or to stay our hand. Otherwise there were no boundaries to our own being and we too must extend our claims until we lose all definition. Until we must be swallowed up at last by the very void to which we wished to stand opposed.

The church at Caborca continued to stand as before. Even the priest could see that the ragged pensioner encamped in the rubble was all of parishioner it was ever like to have. He went away. He left the old man to his claim there under the shadow of that dome which some said could be seen to yaw visibly in the wind. He tried to smile at the old man's posture. What news of God that this church should stand or fall? What more than the wind's whim whether the faltering dome should prove sanctuary or sepulchre to a deranged old anchorite? Nothing would be changed. Nothing known. In the end all would be as before.

Acts have their being in the witness. Without him who can speak of it? In the end one could even say that the act is nothing, the witness all. It may be that the old man saw certain contradictions in his position. If men were the drones he imagined them to be then had he not rather been appointed to take up his brief by the very Being against whom it was directed? As has been the case with many a philosopher that which at first seemed an insurmountable objection to his theories came gradually to be seen as a necessary component to them and finally the centerpiece itself. He saw the world pass into nothing in the very multiplicity of its instancing. Only the witness stood firm. And the witness to that witness. For what is deeply true is true also in men's hearts and it can therefore never be mistold through all and any tellings. This then was his thought. If the world was a tale who but the witness could give it life? Where else could it have its being? This was the view of things that began to speak to him. And he began to see in God a terrible tragedy. That the existence of the Deity lay imperiled for want of this simple thing. That for God there could be no witness. Nothing against which He terminated. Nothing by way of which his being could be announced to Him. Nothing to stand apart from and to say I am this and that is other. Where that is I am not. He could create everything save that which would say him no.

Now we may speak of madness. Now it is safe to do so. Perhaps one could say that only a madman could pace and rend his clothes over the accountability of God. What then to make of this man with claim that God had preserved him not once but twice out of the ruins of the earth solely in order to raise up a witness against Himself?

The fire ticked in the stove. He leaned back in his chair. He pressed the tips of his fingers together five to five and flexed his hands thoughtfully against each other. As if testing the strength of some membranous proposition. A large gray cat came up the table and stood looking at him. It had one ear missing almost entirely and its teeth hung down outside. The man pushed back slightly from the table and the cat stepped down into his lap and curled up and subsided and turned its head and gravely regarded the boy across the table in the manner of a consultant. A cat of counsel. The man placed one hand upon it as if to secure it there. He looked at the boy. The task of the narrator is not an easy one, he said. He appears to be required to choose his tale from among the many that are possible. But of course that is not the case. The case is rather to make many of the one. Always the teller must be at pains to devise against his listener's claim—perhaps spoken, perhaps not—that he has heard the tale before. He sets forth the categories into which the listener will wish to fit the narrative as he hears it. But he understands that the narrative is itself in fact no category but is rather the category of all categories for there is nothing which falls outside its purview. All is telling. Do not doubt it.

The priest visited the old man no more, the story stood unfinished. The old man of course in no wise ceased to pace and rail. He at least had no plans for forgetting the injustices of his past life. The ten thousand insults. The catalog of woes. He had the mind of the injured party, you see. Nothing was lost to him. Of the priest what can be said? As with all priests his mind had become clouded by the illusion of its proximity to God. What priest will denounce his robes even to save himself? And yet the old man was not so far from his thoughts and one day they sent for him and they told him that the old man had fallen ill. That he lay on his pallet and spoke to no one. Not even God. The priest went to see him and it was as they said. He stood without the transept and addressed the old man. He asked if he were indeed ill. The old man lay staring at the fading frescoes. At the coming and going of the golondrinas. He cast his eyes upon the priest and his look was haggard and hollow and he looked away again. The priest seeing opportunity in the weakness of others in the normal human way took up where he'd left off those weeks before and began to declaim to the old man con-

cerning the goodness of God. The old man clapped his hands
to his ears but the priest only drew nearer. At last the old man
staggered up from his pallet and began to scrabble up stones
from the rubble and to pelt the priest with them and so drove
him away.

He returned in three days' time and spoke again to the old
man but the old man no longer heard him. The food, the pitcher
of milk—which the people of Caborca had become accustomed
to leave for him at the edge of the shadowline—these remained
untouched. God had outwitted him, of course. How could there
have been another possibility? In the end it seemed He'd turned
even the old man's heretical usurpations to his own service. The
sense of election which had at once sustained and tormented the
pensioner these years now stood fulfilled in a way he'd not
foreseen and before his troubled gaze stood the truth in its awful
purity. He saw that he was indeed elect and that the God of the
universe was yet more terrible than men reckoned. He could
not be eluded nor yet set aside nor circumscribed about and it
was true that He did indeed contain all else within Him even
to the reasoning of the heretic else He were no God at all.

The priest was greatly moved by what he saw and this surprised him. In the end he even overcame his fears and ventured
in beneath the dome of the ruinous church to the old man's side.
Perhaps this gave the old man heart. Perhaps even at this late
juncture he thought the priest might bring the structure toppling
down where he himself had failed. But the dome of course only
hung in the air and after a while the old man began to speak.
He took the priest's hand as of the hand of a comrade and he
spoke of his life and what it had been and what it had become.
He told the priest what he had learned. In the end he said that
no man can see his life until his life is done and where then to
make a mending? It is God's grace alone that we are bound by
this thread of life. He held the priest's hand in his own and he
bade the priest look at their joined hands and he said see the
likeness. This flesh is but a memento, yet it tells the true.
Ultimately every man's path is every other's. There are no

separate journeys for there are no separate men to make them. All men are one and there is no other tale to tell. But the priest only took his telling for confession and when the old man was done he began the words of absolution. At this the old man seized his arm midway in its crossing there in the still air by his deathbedside and stayed him with his eyes. He let go the priest's other hand and raised his own. Like a man going on a journey. Save yourself, he hissed. Save yourself. Then he died.

Outside in the weedgrown streets all was silence. The man passed his cupped hand over the cat's head, sleeking back its ears. The good, the damaged. The cat lay with its forepaws curled against its chest, its eyes half closed. This is my warrior cat, the man said. Pero es el más dulce de todo. Y el más simpático.

He looked up. He smiled. The storyteller's task is not so simple. You will have guessed by now of course who was the priest. Or perhaps not so much priest as advocate of priestly things. Priestly views. This priest for a while yet would strive to cling to his calling but in the end he was no longer able to bear the look in the eyes of those who came to him for counsel. What counsel had he to give, this man of words? He'd no answers to the questions the old messenger had brought from the capital. The more he considered them the more knotted they became. The more he attempted even to formulate them the more they eluded his every representation and finally he came to see that they were not the old pensioner's queries at all but his own.

The old man was buried in the churchyard at Caborca among those of his own blood. Such was the working out of God's arrangement with this man. Such was his colindancia and such perhaps is every man's. At his dying he had told the priest that he'd been wrong in his every reckoning of God and yet had come at last to an understanding of Him anyway. He saw that his demands upon God resided intact and unspoken also in even the simplest heart. His contention. His argument. They had their being in the humblest history. For the path of the world also is one and not many and there is no alter course in any least part of it for that course is fixed by God and contains all consequence in the way of its going and outside of that going there is neither path nor consequence nor anything at all. There never was. In the end what the priest came to believe was that the truth may often be carried about by those who themselves remain all unaware of it. They bear that which has weight and substance and yet for them has no name whereby it may be evoked or called forth. They go about ignorant of the true nature of their condition, such are the wiles of truth and such its stratagems. Then one day in that casual gesture, that subtle movement of divestiture, they wreak all unknown upon some ancillary soul a havoc such that that soul is forever changed, forever wrenched about in the road it was intended upon and set instead upon a road heretofore unknown to it. This new man will hardly know the hour of his turning nor the source of it. He will himself have done nothing that such great good befall him. Yet he will have the very thing, you see. Unsought for and undeserved. He will have in his possession that elusive freedom which men seek with such unending desperation.

What the priest saw at last was that the lesson of a life can never be its own. Only the witness has power to take its measure. It is lived for the other only. The priest therefore saw what the anchorite could not. That God needs no witness. Neither to Himself nor against. The truth is rather that if there were no God then there could be no witness for there could be no identity to the world but only each man's opinion of it. The priest saw that there is no man who is elect because there is no man who is not. To God every man is a heretic. The heretic's first act is to name his brother. So that he may step free of him. Every word we speak is a vanity. Every breath taken that does not bless is an affront. Bear closely with me now. There is another who will hear what you never spoke. Stones themselves are made of air. What they have power to crush never lived. In the end we shall all of us be only what we have made of God. For nothing is real save his grace.

* * *

When he had mounted up the man stood at his stirrup and squinted up at him in the midmorning sun. You ride to America? he said.

Yessir.

To return to your family.

Yes.

How long since you have seen them?

I dont know.

He looked out down the street. Lost in weeds between the rows of fallen buildings. The mudbrick rubble slumped by the episodic rains of the region into shapes suggesting the work of enormous insect colonies. There was no sound anywhere. He looked down at the man. I dont even know what month it is, he said.

Yes. Of course.

Spring's comin.

Go home.

Yessir. I aim to.

The man stepped back. The boy touched his hat.

I thank you for the breakfast.

Vaya con Dios, joven.

Gracias. Adiós.

He turned the horse and rode out down the street. At the end of the town he reined the horse toward the river and he looked back a last time but the man was gone.

He would cross and recross the river countless times in the days following where the road went ford by ford or along those alluvial fans stepped into the base of the hills where the river shoaled and bended and ran. He passed through the town of Tamichopa which was leveled and burned by the Apaches on the day before Palm Sunday in the year seventeen fifty-eight and in the early afternoon he entered the town of Bacerac which was the old town of Santa María founded in the year sixteen forty-two and where a child came out unbidden and took his horse by the headstall and led him through the street.

They passed through a portal where he was obliged to bend low over the horse's neck and they went on through a white-washed zaguán into a patio where a burro tethered to a pole turned a stone wheatmill. He dismounted and was given a cloth with which to wash and then he was taken into the house and given his supper.

He sat at a scrubbed wooden table with two other young men and they ate very well on baked squash and onion soup and tortillas and beans. The boys were even younger than he and they eyed him furtively and waited for him to speak as the oldest but he did not and so they ate in silence. They fed his horse and at nightfall he was put to bed on an iron cot with a shuck tick at the rear of the house. He'd spoken to no one other than to say thank you. He thought he'd been mistaken for someone else. He woke once at some unknown hour and started up to see a figure watching him from the doorway but it was only the clay olla hanging there in the half darkness to cool the water in the night and not some other kind of figure of some other kind of clay. The next sound he heard was the slapping of hands making the tortillas for breakfast at daylight.

One of the boys brought him coffee in a bowl on a tray. He walked out into the patio drinking it. He could hear women talking somewhere in another part of the house and he stood in the sun drinking the coffee and watching the hummingbirds that tilted and darted and stood among the flowers hanging down over the wall. After a while a woman came to the door and called him to his breakfast. He turned holding the cup and turning saw his father's horse pass in the street.

He walked out through the zaguán and stood in the street but it was empty. He walked up to the corner and looked east and west and he walked up to the square and looked out along the main road north but horse or rider there was none. He turned and started back to the house. He listened as he went for the sound of a horse anywhere behind the walls or the portals that he passed. He stood in front of the house for a long time and then he went in to get his breakfast.

He ate alone in the kitchen. There seemed no one about. He finished and rose and went out to see about his horse and then returned to the house to thank the women but he could not find them. He called but no one answered. He stood in the doorway to a room with high ceilings sheathed in cane and furnished with an old dark wood armoire from another country and two wooden beds painted blue. On the far wall in a niche a painted tin retablo of the Virgin with a slender daycandle burning before it. In the corner a child's cradle and in the cradle a small dog with clouded eyes that raised its head and listened for his presence. He went back to the kitchen and looked for something with which to write. In the end he dusted flour from the bowl on the sideboard over the wooden table and wrote his thanks in that and went out and got his horse and led it afoot down the zaguán and out through the portal. Behind in the patio the little mule turned the pugmill tirelessly. He mounted up and rode out down the little dusty street nodding to those he passed on his way. Riding like a young squire for all his rags. Carrying in his belly the gift of the meal he'd received which both sustained him and laid claim upon him. For the sharing of bread is not such a simple thing nor is its acknowledgement. Whatever thanks be given, however spoke or written down.

Midmorning he rode through the town of Bavispe. He did not stop. A meatvendor's cart stood in the plaza before the church and old women in black muslin wraps were at lifting the dull red strips that hung from the racks and looking underneath with a strange prurience. He rode on. By noon he was in Colonia de Oaxaca and he halted his horse in the road before the alguacil's house and then spat quietly in the dust and rode on. Noon of the day following he passed again through the town of Morelos and took the road north toward Ojito. All day black thunderclouds were making up to the north. He crossed the river a final time and rode up through the low broken hills where the storm overtook him in a hail of ice. He and the horse took shelter in a compound of old abandoned buildings by the roadside. The hail passed and a steady rain set in. Water ran everywhere down through the clay roof overhead and the horse was restless and stood uneasily. Some scent of old troubles or perhaps just the closeness of the walls. It grew dark and he pulled the saddle from the horse and made a bed in the corner out of the loose straw he kicked up. The horse walked out into the rain and he lay under his blanket where he could see out through the broken walls the shape of the horse standing by the side of the road and the shape of the horse in the mute erratic glare of the lightning where the storm moved off to the west. He slept. Late in the night he woke but what had woke him was only the rain's ceasing. He rose and walked out. The moon was in the east over the dark escarpment of the mountains. Sheetwater standing in the flats beyond the narrow road. There was no wind and yet the dead flat of the water shimmered in the bonecolored light as if something had passed over it and the galled moon in the water shivered and yawed and righted itself again and then all lay as before.

In the morning he rode the horse through the border crossing at Douglas Arizona. The guard nodded to him and he nodded back.

You look like maybe you stayed a little longer than what you intended, the guard said.

The boy sat the horse, his hands resting on the pommel of the saddle. He looked down at the guard. You wouldnt loan a man a half dollar to eat on would you? he said.

The guard stood a minute. Then he reached into his pocket.

I live over towards Cloverdale, the boy said. You tell me your name and I'll see that you get it back.

Here you go.

The boy cupped the spinning coin out of the air and nodded and dropped it into his shirtpocket. What's your name?

John Gilchrist.

You aint from around here.

No.

I'm Billy Parham.

Well I'm pleased to meet you.

I'll send you that half dollar soon as I catch somebody comin back this way. You neednt to worry about it.

I aint worried about it.

The boy sat holding the reins loosely. He looked out up the broad street lying before him and at the barren hills about. He looked at Gilchrist again.

How do you like this country? he said.

I like it fine.

The boy nodded. I do too, he said. He touched the brim of his hat. Thanks, he said. I appreciate it. Then he touched the wildlooking horse with his heels and rode off up the street into America.

HE WAS ALL DAY on the old road from Douglas to Cloverdale. By evening he was high in the Guadalupes and it was cold and cold in the pass with the early dark coming and the wind that shunted through the gap. He rode slouched loosely in the saddle with his elbows at his side. He read names and dates where they'd been written in the rock by men long dead who'd passed the same as he. Below him in the long enshadowed twilight lay the beautiful Animas Plain. Coming down the eastern side of the pass the horse suddenly knew where it was and it raised its nose and nickered and quickened its step.

It was past midnight when he reached the house. There were no lights. He went to the barn to put the horse up and there were no horses in the barn and there was no dog and before he'd even traversed half the length of the barn bay he knew that something was bad wrong. He pulled the saddle off the horse and hung it up and pulled down some hay and shut the stall door and walked down to the house and opened the kitchen door and walked in.

The house was empty. He walked through all the rooms.

Most of the furniture was gone. His own small iron bed stood alone in the room off the kitchen, bare save for the tick. In the closet a few wire hangers. He went into the pantry and found some canned peaches and he stood in the dark at the sink eating them out of the glass jar with a cookingspoon and looking out through the window at the pastureland to the south blue and silent under the rising moon and the fence running out into the darkness under the mountains and the shadow of the fence crossing the land in the moonlight like a suture. He turned on the tap at the sink but it gave only a dry gasp and then nothing. He finished the peaches and went to his parents' room and stood in the doorway looking at the empty bedstead, the few rags of clothes in the floor. He went to the front door and opened it and walked out onto the porch. He walked down to the creek and stood listening. After a while he went back to the house and went to his room and lay down on his bed and after a while he slept.

He was up in the morning at daylight sorting through the jars on the shelves in the pantry. He found some stewed tomatoes and ate them and he walked out to the barn and found a brush and led the horse out into the sun and stood brushing him for a long time. Then he led him back into the barn bay and saddled him and mounted up and rode out through the standing gate and took the road north toward the SK Bar.

When he rode into the yard old man Sanders was sitting on the porch much as he'd left him. He didnt know the boy. He didnt even know the horse. He called for him to get down anyway.

It's Billy Parham, the boy called. The old man didnt answer for a minute. Then he called into the house. Leona, he called. Leona.

The girl came to the door and shaded her eyes with one hand and looked at the rider. Then she came out and stood with her hand on her grandfather's shoulder. As if it was the rider had come with bad news for the old man.

* * *

WHEN HE GOT BACK to the house again it was past noon. He left the horse saddled and standing in the yard and walked in and took off his hat. He walked through all the rooms. He thought the old man was crazy but he couldnt account for the girl. He walked into his parents' room and stood. He stood for a long time. He saw how the ticking of the mattress bore the rusty imprint of the springcoils and he looked at that for a long time. Then he hung his hat on the doorknob and walked over to the bed. He stood beside it. He reached down and got hold of the mattress and dragged it off the bed and stood it up and let it fall over backwards in the floor. What came to light beneath was an enormous bloodstain dried near black and soaked so thick it cracked and splintered like some dark ceramic glaze. A faint sour dust rose. He stood there. His hands reached about in the air and finally he took hold of the bedpost and gripped it for support. After a while he looked up and after a while he walked over to the window. Where the noon light lay over the fields. Over the new green of the cottonwoods along the creek. Bright on the Animas Peaks. He looked at it all and he fell to his knees in the floor and sobbed into his hands.

When he rode through Animas the houses seemed deserted. He stopped at the store and filled his canteen from the spigot at the side of the building but he didnt go in. He slept that night on the plains north of the town. He'd nothing to eat and he made no fire. He woke all night and at each waking the signature of Cassiopeia had swung further about the polestar and at each wakening all was as it had been and would forever be. At noon the following day he rode into Lordsburg.

THE SHERIFF LOOKED UP from his desk. He pursed his thin lips.

My name's Billy Parham, the boy said.

I know who you are. Come on in. Set down.

He sat in a chair opposite the sheriff's desk and put his hat on his knee.

Where have you been, son?

Mexico.

Mexico.

Yessir.

What caused you to run off?

I didnt run off.

Were you havin trouble at home?

No sir. Pap never allowed it.

The sheriff leaned back in his chair. He tapped his lower lip with his forefinger and contemplated the ragged figure before him. Pale with road dust. Thin to emaciation. A rope holding up his trousers.

What were you doin in Mexico?

I dont know. I just went down there.

You just got a wild hair up your ass and there wouldnt nothin else do but for you to go off to Mexico. Is that what you're tellin me?

Yessir. I reckon.

The sheriff reached and pushed a stapled set of papers from the edge of the desk and squared them with this thumb. He looked at the boy.

What do you know about this business, son?

I dont know nothin about it. I come here to ask you.

The sheriff sat watching him. All right, he said. If that's your story you'll be held to it.

It aint a story.

All right. We took trackers down there. There was six horses left out of there. Mr Sanders says he thinks that's all the horses there was on the place. Is that right?

Yessir. There was seven countin mine.

Jay Tom and his boy said that there was two of em and that they left out with the horses about two hours before daylight.

They could tell that?

They could tell that.

They showed up down there on foot.

Yes.

What does Boyd say?

Boyd dont say nothin. He run off and hid. He laid out in the cold all night and walked up to Sanders' the next day and they couldnt get no sense out of him. Miller had to get in the truck and drive down there and find that mess. They'd been shot with a shotgun.

Billy looked past the sheriff out to the street. He tried to swallow but he couldnt. The sheriff watched him.

First thing they done was they caught the dog and cut its throat. Then they set and waited to see would anybody come out. They waited there long enough that one of em went to take a leak. They waited to see that everbody was asleep again after the dog quit barkin and all.

Were they Mexicans?

They was indians. Or Jay Tom says they was indians. I reckon he would know. The dog never died.

What?

I said the dog never died. Boyd's got it. It's mute as a stone.

The boy sat looking at the greasestained hat cocked on his knee.

What kind of guns did they get? the sheriff said.

There wasnt any to get. The only gun on the place was a forty-four forty carbine and I had that with me.

It wasnt much use to em, was it?

No sir.

We got nothin to go on. You know that.

Yessir.

Have you?

Have I what?

Do you know anything you aint told me.

Have you got jurisdiction in Mexico?

No.

Then what difference does it make?

That aint much of a answer.

No it aint. It's about like yours.

The sheriff watched him for a while.

If you think I dont care about this, he said, you're wrong as hell.

The boy sat. He put the back of his forearm to one eye and then the other and turned and looked out the window again. There was no traffic in the street. Out on the sidewalk two women were talking in spanish.

Could you give me a description of the horses?

Yessir.

Was any of em branded?

One of em was. That Niño horse. Pap bought him off of a Mexican.

The sheriff nodded. All right, he said. He leaned down and pulled out a drawer in his desk and took out a tin deedbox and put it on top of the desk and opened it.

I dont guess I'm supposed to give you this stuff, he said. But I dont always do what I'm told. You got any place to keep it?

I dont know. What's in there?

Papers. Marriage license. Birth certificates. There's some papers on horses in here but most of em goes back a few years. Your mama's weddin ring is in here.

What about Pap's watch?

There wasnt no watch. There's some household effects out at the Websters'. If you want I'll put these papers in the bank. They aint even appointed a conservator so I dont know what else to do with em.

There ought to be papers on Niño and on that Bailey horse.

The sheriff turned the box around and slid it across the desk. The boy began to thumb through the documents.

Who's Margarita Evelyn Parham? the sheriff said.

My sister.

Where is she at?

She's dead.

How come her to have a Mexican name?

She was named after my grandmother.

He pushed the deedbox back on the desk and refolded the two papers he'd removed from it along their three lines and slid them inside his shirt.

Is that everthing you want? the sheriff said.

Yessir.

He closed the lid on the box and put it back in the drawer of his desk and shut the drawer and leaned back in his chair and looked at the boy. You aint fixin to go back down there are you? he said.

I aint decided what all I'm goin to do. First thing I got to do is go get Boyd.

Go get Boyd?

Yessir.

Boyd aint goin nowhere.

If I am he is.

Boyd's a juvenile. They aint goin to turn him over to you. Hell. You're a juvenile yourself.

I aint askin.

Son, dont get crosswise of the law over this.

I dont intend to. I dont intend for it to get crosswise of me neither.

He took his hat off his knee and held it briefly in both hands and then stood. I thank you for the papers, he said.

The sheriff put his hands on the arms of his chair as if he might be going to rise but he didnt. What about the descriptions on them horses? he said. You want to write them out for me?

What would be the use in it?

You didnt learn no manners down there while you was gone, did you?

No sir. I guess not. I learned some things but they sure wasnt manners.

The sheriff nodded toward the window. Is that your horse out there?

Yessir.

I see that scabbard boot. Where's the rifle at?

I traded it.

What did you trade it for?

I dont think I could say.

You mean you wont say.

No sir. I mean I aint sure I could put a name to it.

When he walked out into the sun and untied the horse from the parking meter people passing in the street turned to look at him. Something in off the wild mesas, something out of the past. Ragged, dirty, hungry in eye and belly. Totally unspoken for. In that outlandish figure they beheld what they envied most and what they most reviled. If their hearts went out to him it was yet true that for very small cause they might also have killed him.

THE HOUSE where his brother was staying was out on the east side of town. A small stucco house with a fenced yard and a front porch. He tied Bird at the fence and pushed open the gate and started up the walk. The dog came around the corner of the house and bared its teeth at him and raised its hackles.

It's me, numbnuts, he said.

When it heard his voice it flattened its ears and began to squirm across the yard toward him. It hadnt barked and it didnt whine.

Hello the house, he called.

The dog twisted itself against him. Git away, he said.

He called the house again and then went up on the porch and knocked at the front door and stood. No one came. He walked around to the back. When he tried the kitchen door it was unlocked and he pushed it open and looked in. It's Billy Parham, he called.

He entered and shut the door. Hello, he called. He walked through the kitchen and stood in the hallway. He was about to call again when the kitchen door opened behind him. He turned and Boyd was standing there. He stood with a steel pail in one hand and his other hand on the doorknob. He was taller. He leaned against the jamb.

I reckon you thought I was dead, Billy said.

If I'd of thought you was dead I wouldnt be here.

He shut the door and set the pail on the kitchen table. He looked at Billy and he looked out the window. When Billy spoke to him again his brother wouldnt look at him but Billy could see that his eyes were wet.

Are you ready to go? he said.

Yeah, said Boyd. Just waitin on you.

They took a shotgun from a closet in the bedroom and they took nineteen dollars in coins and small bills from a white china box in a bureau drawer and stuffed it all into an oldfashioned leather changepurse. They took the blanket off the bed and they found Billy a belt and some clothes and they took all the shotshells out of a Carhart coat hanging on the wall at the back door, one double-ought buckshot and the rest number five and number seven shot, and they took a laundry bag and filled it with canned goods and bread and bacon and crackers and apples from the pantry and they walked out and tied the bag to the horn of the saddle and mounted up and rode out the little sandy street riding double with the dog trotting after them. A woman with clothespins in her mouth in a yard they passed nodded to them. They crossed the highway and they crossed the tracks of the Southern Pacific Railway and turned west. Come dark they were camped on the alkali flats fifteen miles west of Lordsburg before a fire made of fenceposts they'd dragged out of the ground with the horse. East and to the south there was water on the flats and two sandhill cranes stood tethered to their reflections out there in the last of the day's light like statues of such birds in some waste of a garden where calamity had swept all else away. All about them the dry cracked platelets of mud lay curing and the fencepost fire ran tattered in the wind and the balled papers from the groceries they opened loped away one by one downwind into the gathering dark.

They fed the horse on oatmeal they'd taken from the house

and Billy skewered bacon along a length of fencewire and hung it to cook. He looked at Boyd where he sat with the shotgun across his lap.

You and Pap ever get your differences patched up?

Yeah. About half way.

Which half?

Boyd didn't answer.

What is that you're eatin?

A raisin sandwich.

Billy shook his head. He poured water from the canteen into a fruitcan and set it in the coals.

What happened to your saddle? Boyd said.

Billy looked at the saddle with the mutilated offside fender but he didnt answer.

They'll be huntin us, Boyd said.

Let em hunt.

How are we goin to pay em back for what all we took?

Billy looked up at him. Maybe you better just get used to the idea of bein a outlaw, he said.

Even a outlaw dont rob them that's took him in and befriended him.

How much of this are we goin to have to listen to?

Boyd didnt answer. They ate and unrolled their beds and turned in to sleep. The wind blew all night. It burned up the fire and burned up the coals of the fire and the balled and twisted shape of redhot wire burned briefly like the incandescent armature of an enormous heart in the night's darkness and then faded to black and the wind blew the coals to ash and blew the ash away and scoured the clay where coals and ash had been till other than the blackened wire there was no trace of fire at all and all night things passed in the dark that had of themselves no articulation yet had a destination for that.

Are you awake? Billy said.

Yeah.

What did you tell em?

Nothin.

Why?
What would be the use in it?
The wind blew. The migrant sands seethed past.
Billy?
What?
They knew my name.
Knew your name?
They called for me. Called Boyd. Boyd.
It dont mean nothin. Go to sleep.
Like we was friends.
Go to sleep.
Billy?
What?
You dont have to try and make it better than what it is.
Billy didnt answer.
It is what it is.
I know it. Go to sleep.

In the morning they sat eating and they watched across the
flats where something was articulating in the sunrise far out on
the steelcolored clay of the playa. After a while they could see
that it was a rider. He was perhaps a mile out and he approached
in a series of thin and trembling images which in those places
where the footground was flooded would suddenly augment in
their length and then shrivel and draw up again so that the rider
appeared to advance and recede and advance again. The sun
rose into the red reefs of cloud along the eastern shore and the
rider came on, crossing a lake ten miles wide and three inches
deep. Billy got up and got the shotgun and came back and put
it under the blanket and sat again.

The horse was either the color of the terrain or was stained
so by it. The rider advanced over the shallow standing water
and the water displaced under the hooves of the horse brightened
in the light and vanished instantly like lead dishing in a vat. He
rode off of the lake and threaded a path along the sandy soda
shore through the sparse tussocks of grass until he sat the clay-
colored horse before them and looked down at them from under

the shade of his hat. He didnt speak. He looked at them and he looked back across the playa and leaned and spat and looked at them again. You aint who I thought you was, he said.

Who'd you think we was?

The rider ignored him. What are you all doin out here? he said.

Aint doin nothin.

He looked at Boyd. He looked at the horse. What have you got under that blanket? he said.

A shotgun.

Are you fixin to shoot me?

No sir.

Is that your brother?

He can answer for hisself.

Are you his brother?

Yeah.

What are you all doin out here?

Passin through.

Passin through?

Yeah.

Passin through to where?

We're goin to Douglas Arizona.

Yeah?

We got friends over there.

You aint got none over here?

We aint cut out for town life.

Is that your all's horse?

Yeah.

I know who you are, the man said.

They didnt answer. The man looked back out across the flats of the dry lake where the thin standing water lay like lead in the windless morning. He leaned and spat again and looked at Billy.

I'm goin to tell Mr Boruff what you told me. That it's just a pair of drifters. Or if you want I'll wait on you and you can ride back with me.

We aint ridin back. I appreciate it.

I'll tell you somethin else if you dont know it.

Tell it.

You got a long row to hoe.

Billy didnt answer.

How old are you?

Seventeen.

The man shook his head. Well, he said. You all take care.

Tell me somethin, Billy said.

All right.

How could you see us from way out yonder?

I seen your reflection. Certain times you can see things out on a playa that's too far to see. Some of the boys claimed you all was a mirage but Mr. Boruff knowed you wasnt. He studies this country. He knows what's in it and what aint in it. So do I.

You study it again in about a hour and see if you see us.

I aim to.

He nodded to them each separately where they sat on that barren inland strand and he looked at the mute dog.

He aint much shucks as a watchdog, is he?

He's had his throat cut.

I know it, the rider said. You all take care. Then he turned the horse and rode back out across the flats and across the lake. He rode into the sun and he rode in silhouette but even though the sun was well up and no longer in their eyes when they themselves were mounted and set out south along the edge of the pan they still could see nothing at all on the far shore of the lake where the rider had vanished.

Some time midmorning they crossed the boundary line into the state of Arizona. They rode through a low range of mountains and descended into the San Simon Valley where it ran down from the north and they nooned at the river in a grove of cottonwoods. They hobbled and watered the horse and sat naked in the shallow gravel pool. Pale, thin, dirty. Billy watched his brother until his brother raised up and looked at him.

It aint no use you askin me a bunch of stuff.

I wasnt going to ask you nothin.

You will.

They sat in the water. The dog sat in the grass watching them.

He's wearin daddy's boots, aint he? Billy said.

There you go.

You're lucky you aint dead too.

I dont know what's so lucky about it.

That's a ignorant thing to say.

You dont know.

What dont I know?

But Boyd didnt say what it was he didnt know.

They ate sardines and crackers in the shade of the cotton-woods and they slept and in the afternoon they rode on again.

I thought one time maybe you'd gone to California, Boyd said.

What would I do in California?

I dont know. They got cowboys in California.

California cowboys.

I wouldnt want to go to California.

I wouldnt either.

I might go to Texas.

What for?

I dont know. I aint never been.

You aint never been noplace. So what reason is that?

Only one I got.

They rode. In the long shadows jackrabbits bolted and loped and froze again. The mute dog paid them no mind.

Why caint the law go to Mexico? Boyd said.

Cause it's American law. It aint worth nothin in Mexico.

What about the Mexican law?

There aint no law in Mexico. It's just a pack of rogues.

Will number five shot kill a man?

It will if you get close enough. It'll make a hole you can run your arm through.

In the evening they crossed the highway just east of Bowie and struck the old road south through the Dos Cabezas range.

They made camp and Billy rustled wood out along a shallow stone arroyo and they ate and sat by the fire.

You reckon they will come after us? Boyd said.

I dont know. They might.

He leaned and jostled the coals with a stick and put the stick in the fire. Billy watched him.

They wont catch us.

I know it.

Why dont you say what's on your mind.

There aint nothin on my mind.

It wasnt nobody's fault.

Boyd sat staring into the fire. Coyotes were yapping out along the ridge to the north of the camp.

You'll just make yourself crazy, Billy said.

I done already have.

He looked up. His pale hair looked white. He looked fourteen going on some age that never was. He looked as if he'd been sitting there and God had made the trees and rocks around him. He looked like his own reincarnation and then his own again. Above all else he looked to be filled with a terrible sadness. As if he harbored news of some horrendous loss that no one else had heard of yet. Some vast tragedy not of fact or incident or event but of the way the world was.

The day following they crossed through the high gap at Apache Pass. Boyd sat behind him with his thin legs dangling on the horse's flanks and together they looked over the country to the south. The day was sunny and there was a wind blowing and there were ravens in the mountains riding the updrafts over the southfacing slopes.

This is one more place you aint been, Billy said.

They're everwhere, aint they?

You see that line yonder where the color changes?

Yeah.

That's Mexico.

It dont look like it's gettin no closer.

What does that mean?

It means let's ride if we're goin to.

Noon the following day they struck route 666 and followed the blacktop down out of the Sulphur Springs Valley. They rode through the town of Elfrida. They rode through the town of McNeal. In the evening they rode through the main street of Douglas and halted at the gateshack on the border. The guard stood in the doorway and nodded at them. He looked at the dog.

Where's Gilchrist at? said Billy.

He's off. He dont come on till in the mornin.

Can I leave some money for him?

Yeah. You can leave it.

Let me have a half dollar, Boyd.

Boyd dug the leather changepurse out of his pocket and unsnapped it. The money was all nickels and dimes and pennies and he counted the requisite coins out and cupped them and handed them across Billy's shoulder to him. Billy took the coins and poked them apart in his own hand and recounted them and then cupped them together again and leaned down and held out his fist.

I owe him a half dollar.

All right, said the guard.

Billy touched the brim of his hat with his forefinger and put the horse forward.

You takin that dog with you? the guard said.

If he wants to come.

The guard watched them go, the dog trotting after. They crossed the little bridge. The Mexican guard looked up at them and nodded them on and they rode into Agua Prieta.

I know how to count, Boyd said.

What?

I know how to count. There wasnt no need for you to count it a second time.

Billy turned and looked at him and turned back again.

All right, he said. I wont do it again.

They bought paletas of icecream from a streetvendor and sat on the curb at the horse's feet and watched the street coming to life in the evening. The dog lay uneasily in the dust in front of them while town dogs passed and circled with their backs roached taking his scent.

They bought meal and dried beans in a grocery and salt and coffee and dried fruit and dried peppers and they bought a small enameled frypan and a pot with a lid and a box of kitchen matches and a few utensils and they changed the remainder of their money into pesos.

Now you're rich, Billy said.

Nigger-rich, said Boyd.

It's moren what I had when I come down here.

That aint no big comfort.

They left the road at the south end of town and followed the river along its course of pale gray cobbles out into the desert and made camp in the dark. Billy fixed their supper and they ate and sat watching the fire.

You need to quit thinkin about it, Billy said.

I aint thinkin about it.

What are you thinkin about?

Nothin.

That's hard to do.

What if somethin was to happen to you?

Dont be thinkin all the time about what would happen.

What if it was?

You could go back.

To the Websters?

Yeah.

After we robbed em and all?

You didnt rob em. I thought you wasnt thinkin about nothin.

I aint. I just got a uneasy feelin.

Billy leaned and spat into the fire. You'll be all right.

I'm all right now.

They rode all the day following along the secular river in its bed of stones and in the early evening they entered the roadside hamlet of Ojito. Boyd had been sleeping with his face against his brother's back and he raised up all sweaty and rumpled and got his hat from where he'd crushed it in his lap between them and put it on.

Where are we at? he said.

I dont know.

I'm hungry.

I know it. I am too.

You reckon they got anything to eat here?

I dont know.

They halted the horse before a man in a crumbling mud doorway and asked if there was anything to eat in the town and the man reflected a moment and then offered to sell them a chicken. They rode on. Where the empty road ran out into the desert to the south a storm was making up and the country was bluelooking under the clouds and the thin wires of lightning that stood repeatedly over the raw blue mountains in the distance broke in utter silence like a storm in a belljar. It caught them just before dark. The rain came ripping across the desert driving flights of wild doves before it and they rode into a wall of water and were wet instantly. A hundred yards along they dismounted and stood in a grove of roadside trees and held the horse and watched the rain roar in the mud. By the time the storm had passed it was dead black of night about them and they stood shivering in the starless dark and listened to the water dripping in the silence.

What do you want to do now? Boyd said.

Mount up and ride, I reckon.

That's a awful wet horse to have to climb aboard.

He might say the same about you.

It was past midnight when they rode through the town of Morelos. Lamps dimmed out down the street as if they were bringing the darkness with them. He'd wrapped his coat around Boyd and Boyd was tottering asleep against his back and the horse went sucking through the mud with its head down and the dog tacked before them among the pools of standing water and they took the road south where he had followed the pilgrims to the fair in the spring of that same year so long ago.

They passed what was left of the night in a jacal just off the road and in the morning they built a fire and made breakfast and dried their clothes and then saddled the horse and set out again on the road south. In three more days of such riding and seven days into the country passing one by one through the squalid mud towns along the river they entered the town of Bacerac. In front of a whitewashed house under an elder tree were two horses standing head down. One was a big roan gelding with a fresh brand on its left hip and the other was their horse Keno wearing a tooled mexican saddle.

Look yonder, said Boyd.

I see him. Get down.

Boyd slid from the horse and Billy dismounted and passed him the reins and pulled the shotgun from the saddlescabbard. The dog had stopped in the road and stood looking back at them. Billy unbreeched the gun to see that it was loaded and breeched it shut again and looked at Boyd.

Take the horse over yonder and keep out of the way.

All right.

He watched while Boyd walked the horse across the road and then he turned and started for the house. The dog stood looking from one to the other until Boyd whistled for it.

He walked around Keno and patted his neck and the horse pushed its forehead against his shirt and breathed a long sweet breath against him. He stood the shotgun against the elder tree and lifted the stirrup and hung it over the horn and pulled the latigo and slid the strap free and pulled loose the backcinch and took hold of the saddle by horn and cantle and lifted it down and stood it in the dirt. Then he pulled off the saddleblanket and hung it over the horn of the saddle and picked up the shotgun and untied the horse and led it back across the street to where Boyd stood.

He jammed the shotgun back into the scabbard and looked again toward the house. Ride Bird, he said.

Boyd stood up into the saddle and looked down at him.

Take the horses up here and keep out of sight of the house.

I'll meet you at the south end of town. Just stay hid. I'll find you.

What do you aim to do?

I want to see who all's in there.

What if it's them?

It aint.

Who all do you think is in there?

I dont know. I think somebody has died. Go on now.

You better take the shotgun.

I dont need it. Go on.

He watched him ride up the narrow dirt street and then he turned and walked back to the house.

He knocked at the door and stood with his hat in his hands. No one came. He put his hat on and walked down and pushed at an old weathered carriage door in the wall but it was barred shut. He looked at the top of the wall. There were broken bottle ends set into the mud masonry there. He took out his knife and put it between the doors and began to walk the ancient wooden tranca a half inch at a time across the gates until the end of it slipped free of the cradle and he pushed the door open and stepped inside and pushed it shut again. There were no drag-marks in the dirt, nothing come and gone. There were chickens sitting in a tree in broad daylight. He crossed the patio to the rear of the house and stood in a doorway that gave onto a long hall. On a low bench were clay pots with plants in them which had been recently watered and the dirt was damp and the tiles under the bench were wet. He took off his hat again and walked down the hallway and stood in the door at the far end. In a darkened room a woman lay in a bed. About her were sister figures clothed in dark rebozos. On a table a candle burning.

The woman in the bed was lying with her eyes closed and she held a glass rosary in her hands. She was dead. One of the women kneeling turned her head and looked at him. Then she looked toward a part of the room he could not see. After a while a man came out pulling on his coat and he nodded politely to the boy standing at the door.

Quién es? he said.

He was tall and blond and he spoke spanish with a foreign accent. Billy stepped to one side and they stood in the hall.

Estaba su caballo enfrente de la casa?

The man stopped, his coat on one shoulder. He looked at Billy and he looked down the hallway. Estaba? he said.

HE FOUND BOYD laid up with the horses in a stand of carrizo cane at the river's edge south of the town.

Anybody could of tracked you here, he said.

Boyd didnt answer. Billy squatted on the ground and broke off a reed and broke it again in his hands.

He's a German doctor. He had a factura for the horse. Or said he did. He said he had papers from a broker in Casas Grandes named Soto.

Boyd had been standing holding the shotgun. He reholstered it in the scabbard and leaned and spat. Well, he said. Whatever papers he has it's moren what we got.

We got the horse.

Boyd stood looking past the horse at the river running. They're goin to shoot us, he said.

Come on, Billy said. Let's go.

You just walked in there?

Yeah.

What did you tell him?

Let's go. We aint down here for the fun of it.

What did you tell him.

Told him the truth. Told him his horse was stole by indians.

Where's he at now?

He took the mozo's horse and rode off downriver to hunt em.

Did he have a gun?

Yeah. He had a gun.

What are we goin to do?

Ride to Casas Grandes.

Where's it at?

I dont know.

They left Keno in the brake doublehobbled with the dog tied to him and rode back into the town. They sat on the ground in the dusty square while a thin old man squatted opposite and drew for them with a whittled stick a portrait of the country they said they wished to visit. He sketched in the dust streams and promontories and pueblos and mountain ranges. He commenced to draw trees and houses. Clouds. A bird. He penciled in the horsemen themselves doubled upon their mount. Billy leaned forward from time to time to question the measure of some part of their route whereupon the old man would turn and squint at the horse standing in the street and then give an answer in hours. All the while there sat watching on a bench a few feet away four men dressed in ancient and sunfaded suits. By the time the old man was done the map he'd drawn covered an area in the dirt the size of a blanket. He stood and dusted the seat of his trousers with a swipe of his flattened hand.

Give him a peso, Billy said.

Boyd dug out the pocketbook and unsnapped it and took out the coin and Billy gave it to the old man and the old man took it with grace and dignity and removed his hat and put it on again and they shook hands all around and the old man pocketed the coin and turned and walked out across the little blighted zócalo and disappeared up the street without looking back. When he was gone the men on the bench began to laugh. One of them rose to better see the map.

Es un fantasma, he said.

Fantasma?

Sí, sí. Claro.

Cómo?

Cómo? Porque el viejo está loco es como.

Loco?

Completamente.

Billy stood looking at the map. No es correcto? he said.

The man threw up his hands. He said that what they beheld was but a decoration. He said that anyway it was not so much a question of a correct map but of any map at all. He said that in that country were fires and earthquakes and floods and that one needed to know the country itself and not simply the landmarks therein. Besides, he said, when had that old man last journeyed to those mountains? Or journeyed anywhere at all? His map was after all not really so much a map as a picture of a voyage. And what voyage was that? And when?

Un dibujo de un viaje, he said. Un viaje pasado, un viaje antiguo.

He threw up one hand in dismissal. As if no more could be said. Billy looked at the other three men on the bench. They watched with a certain brightness of eye so that he wondered if he were being made a fool of. But the one seated at the right leaned forward and tapped the ash from his cigarette and addressed the man standing and said that as far as that went there were certainly other dangers to a journey than losing one's way. He said that plans were one thing and journeys another. He said it was a mistake to discount the good will inherent in the old man's desire to guide them for it too must be taken into account and would in itself lend strength and resolution to them in their journey.

The man who was standing weighed these words and then erased them in the air before him with a slow fanning motion of his forefinger. He said that the jóvenes could hardly be expected to apportion credence in the matter of the map. He said that in any case a bad map was worse than no map at all for it engendered in the traveler a false confidence and might easily cause him to set aside those instincts which would otherwise guide him if he would but place himself in their care. He said that to follow a false map was to invite disaster. He gestured at the sketching in the dirt. As if to invite them to behold its futility. The second man on the bench nodded his agreement in this and said that the map in question was a folly and that the dogs in the street would piss upon it. But man on the right only smiled and said that for that matter the dogs would piss upon their graves as well and how was this an argument?

The man standing said that what argued for one case argued for all and that in any event our graves make no claims outside of their own simple coordinates and no advice as to how to arrive there but only the assurance that arrive we shall. It may even be that those who lie in desecrated graves—by dogs of whatever manner—could have words of a more cautionary nature and better suited to the realities of the world. At this the man at the left who'd so far not spoke at all rose laughing and gestured for the two boys to follow and they went with him out of the square and into the street leaving the disputants to their rustic parkbench tertulia. Billy untied the horse and they stood while the man pointed out to them the track to the east and told them certain landmarks in the mountains and that the track terminated at a station called Las Ramadas and that they must trust in their luck or their friendship with God to make their way across the divide to Los Horcones. He shook hands with them and smiled and wished them luck and they asked how far it was to Casas Grandes and he held up one hand with his thumb folded across the palm. Cuatro días, he said. He looked toward the square where the other men were yet haranguing one another and he said that they must attend a funeral that very evening for the wife of a friend and that their mood was idiosincrático and to pay them no mind. He said that far from making men reflective or wise it was his experience that death often leads them to attribute great consequence to trivial things. He asked if they were brothers and they said that they were and he told them to care for one another in the world. He nodded again toward the mountains and he said that the serranos had good hearts but that elsewhere was another matter. Then he wished them luck again and called upon God to be with them and stepped back and raised his hand in farewell.

When they were out of sight of the old men they quit the road and went down to the river and followed the river path until they had picked up the other horse and the dog. Boyd mounted Keno and they rode on until they came to the ford where they crossed the river and took the road east into the mountains.

Such road as it was soon ceased to be road at all. Where it first left the river it was the width of a wagon or more and had in recent times been scraped or graded with a fresno and the brush cut back yet once clear of the town the heart seemed to have gone out of this enterprise and they found themselves on a common footpath following the course of a dry arroyo up into the hills. At just dark they came upon a small holding, a clutch of pole huts staked out upon a trinchera or terrace shored up with rock. They made their camp just above this place on the next level ground and hobbled the horses and made a fire. Below them through the scrub pine and juniper they could see a yellow houselamp. A little later as they were boiling their pail of beans a man came up the road carrying a lantern. He called to them from the road and Billy stepped to where the shotgun stood leaning against a tree and called back for him to approach. He came to the fire and stood. He looked at the dog.

Buenas noches, he said.

Buenas noches.

Son Americanos?

Sí.

He held the lantern up. He looked at the shapes of the horses in the dark beyond the fire.

Dónde está el caballero?

No hay otro caballero más que nosotros, Billy said.

The man's eyes wandered over their meager possessions. Billy knew that he'd been sent to invite them to the house but he did not do so. They spoke briefly of nothing at all and then he took his leave. He walked back out to the road and through the trees they saw him raise the lamp to his face and lift the glass in its bail and blow out the flame. Then he walked back down to the house in the dark.

The day following their way led them into the mountains shutting in the Bavispe River Valley under the western slope.

The trail grew more wretched yet with washouts where the riders were obliged to dismount and lead the horses clambering along the narrow floor of the arroyo and up along the switch-backs and there were places where the track diverged and where separate schools of thought wandered off through the pine and scrub oak. They camped that night in an old burn among the bones of trees and among the shapes of boulders that had broken open in the earthquake half a century before and slid down the mountain on the face of their cleavings and grinding stone on stone had struck the fire with which they'd burnt the woods alive. The trunks of the pollarded and broken trees stood at every angle pale and dead in the twilight and in the twilight small owls flew in utter silence hither and yon about the darkening glade.

They sat by the fire and cooked and ate the last of their bacon with beans and tortillas and they slept on the ground in their blankets and the wind in the dead gray pilings about them made no sound and the owls when they called in the night called with soft watery calls like the calls of doves.

They rode for two days through the high country. A fine rain fell. It was cold and they rode with their blankets about them and the dog trotted ahead like some mute and mindless bell-wether and the breath from the horses' nostrils plumed whitely in the thin air. Billy offered that they take turn about riding the saddled horse but Boyd said that he would ride the Keno horse by preference saddle or no. When Billy then offered to swap the saddle to the other horse Boyd only shook his head and booted the bareback horse forward.

They rode through the ruins of old sawmills and they rode through a mountain meadow dotted with the dark stumps of trees. Across a valley in the evening with the sun on it they could see the tailings of an old silvermine and camped in withy huts among the rusted shapes of antique machinery a family of gypsy miners working the abandoned shaft who now stood aligned all sizes of them before the evening cookfire watching the riders pass along the opposing slope and shading their eyes against the sun with their hands like some encampment of ragged and deranged militants at review. That same evening he shot a rabbit and they halted in the long mountain light and made a fire and cooked the rabbit and ate it and fed the guts to the dog and then the bones and when they were done they sat gazing into the coals.

You reckon the horses know where we're at? Boyd said.

What do you mean?

He looked up from the fire. I mean do you reckon they know where we're at.

What the hell kind of question is that?

Well. I reckon it's a question about horses and what they know about where they're at.

Hell, they dont know nothin. They're just in some mountains somewheres. You mean do they know they're in Mexico?

No. But if we was up in the Peloncillos or somewheres they'd know where they was at. They could find their way back if you turned em out.

Are you askin me if they could find their way back from here if you cut em loose?

I dont know.

Well what are you askin.

I'm askin if they know where they're at.

Billy stared at the coals. I dont know what the hell you're talkin about.

Well. Forget it.

You mean like they got a picture in their head of where the ranch is at?

I dont know.

Even if they did it wouldnt mean they could find it.

I didnt mean they could find it. Maybe they could and maybe they couldnt.

They couldnt backtrack the whole way. Hell.

I dont think they backtrack. I think they just know where things are.

Well you know moren me then.

I didnt say that.

No, I said it.

He looked at Boyd. Boyd sat with the blanket over his shoulders and his cheap boots crossed before him. Why dont you go to bed? he said.

Boyd leaned and spat into the coals. He sat watching the spittle boil. Why dont you, he said.

When they set forth in the morning it was still gray light. Mist moving through the trees. They rode out to see what the day would bring and within the hour they sat the horses on the eastern rim of the escarpment and watched while the sun ballooned like boiling glass up out of the plains of Chihuahua to make the world again from darkness.

By noon they were on the prairie again riding through better grass than any they had seen before, riding through bluestem and through sideoats grama. In the afternoon they saw far to the south a standing palisade of thin green cypress trees and the thin white walls of a hacienda. Shimmering in the heat like a white boat on the horizon. Distant and unknowable. Billy looked back at Boyd to see if he had seen it but Boyd was watching it as he rode. It shimmered and was lost in the heat and then it reappeared again just above the horizon and hung there suspended in the sky. When he looked again it had vanished altogether.

In the long twilight they walked the horses to cool them. There was a stand of trees in the middle distance and they mounted up again and rode toward them. The dog trotted ahead with lolling tongue and the darkening prairieland sank about them cool and blue and the shapes of the mountains they'd quit stood behind them black and without dimension against the evening sky.

They kept the trees skylighted before them and as they approached the glade they rode the groaning shapes of cattle up out of their beds. The cattle shook their necks and trotted off in the dark and the horses sniffed at the air and at the trampled grass. They rode into the trees and the horses slowed and stopped and then walked carefully out into the dark standing water.

They hobbled Bird and then staked Keno where he would keep the cows off of them while they slept. They'd nothing to eat and they made no fire but only rolled themselves in their blankets on the ground. Twice in the night in his grazing the horse passed the catchrope over them and he woke and lifted the rope over his brother where he slept and laid it in the grass again. He lay in the dark wrapped in the blanket and listened to the horses cropping the grass and smelling the good rich smell of the cattle and then he slept again.

In the morning they were sitting naked in the dark water of the ciénaga when a party of vaqueros rode up. They watered their mounts at the far end and nodded and wished them a good morning and sat astride the drinking horses rolling cigarettes and taking in the country.

Adónde van? they called.

A Casas Grandes, said Billy.

They nodded. Their horses raised their dripping muzzles and regarded the pale shapes crouched in the water with no great curiosity and lowered their heads and drank again. When they were done the vaqueros wished them a safe journey and turned the horses out of the ciénaga and rode them at a trot out through the trees and set off across the country south the way they'd come.

They washed their clothes out with soapweed and hung them in an acacia tree where they could not blow away for the thorns. Clothes much consumed by the country through which they'd ridden and which they had little way to repair. Their shirts all but transparent, his own coming apart down the center of the back. They spread their blankets and lay naked under the cottonwoods and slept with their hats over their eyes while the cows came up through the trees and stood looking at them.

When he woke Boyd was sitting up and looking out through the trees.

What is it?

Look yonder.

He raised up and looked across the ciénaga. Three indian children were crouched in the reeds watching them. When he stood up with the blanket about his shoulders they went trotting off.

Where the hell's the dog at?

I dont know. What's he supposed to do?

Beyond the trees woodsmoke was rising and he could hear voices. He pulled the blanket about him and walked out and got their clothes and came back.

They were Tarahumaras and they were afoot as their kind always were and they were headed back into the sierras. They drove no stock, they had no dogs. They spoke no spanish. The men wore white breechclouts and straw hats and little else but the women and girls had on brightly colored dresses with many petticoats. A few among them wore huaraches but for the most part they were barefoot and their feet shod or no were clublike and stubby and thick with callus. Their equipage was done up in bundles of handwoven cloth and all of it piled under a tree together with half a dozen morawood bows and goathide quivers with long reed arrows standing in them.

The women at the cookfire regarded them with little interest where they stood at the edge of the glade in their newly laundered rags. An old man and a young boy were playing homemade violins and the boy stopped playing but the old man played on. The Tarahumara had watered here a thousand years and a good deal of what could be seen in the world had passed this way. Armored Spaniards and hunters and trappers and grandees and their women and slaves and fugitives and armies and revolutions and the dead and the dying. And all that was seen was told and all that was told remembered. Two pale and wasted orphans from the north in outsized hats were easily accommodated. They sat on the ground a little apart from the others and ate from tin plates too hot to hold a kind of succotash in which they recognized the seeds of squash and mesquite beans and bits of wild celery. They ate with the plates balanced on the insides of their boots where they'd drawn them up before them heel to heel. While they were eating a woman came from the fire and dished up from a gourd a brickcolored mucilage made from God knew what. They sat looking at it. There was nothing to drink. No one spoke. The indians were dark almost to blackness and their reticence and their silence bespoke a view of a world provisional, contingent, deeply suspect. They had about them a wary absorption, as if they observed some hazardous truce. They seemed in a state of improvident and hopeless vigilance. Like men committed upon uncertain ice.

When they'd done eating they said their thanks and withdrew. Nothing was acknowledged. Nothing spoken. As they passed out through the trees Billy looked back but not even the children had been watching them leave.

The Tarahumara moved on in the evening. A great quiet settled over the glade. Billy took the shotgun and walked out through the grass with the dog and studied the country in the long red twilight. The lean and tallowcolored cattle watched from the cottonwoods and acacia and snorted and went trotting. There was nothing to shoot save the little ringdoves coming in to water and he would not waste a shell on them. He stood on a slight rise out on the prairie and watched the sun set beyond the mountains to the west and he walked back in the dark and in the morning they caught the horses and saddled Bird and set out once more.

They reached the Mormon settlement at Colonia Juárez in the late afternoon and rode the horses through the orchards and vineyards and picked apples from the trees and put them in their clothing. They crossed the Casas Grandes River on the narrow plank bridge and rode past the tidy whitewashed clapboard houses. Trees lined the little street and the houses were kept with garden and lawn and white picket fences.

What kind of a place is this? Boyd said.

I dont know.

They rode on to the end of the street and when they turned the first bend in the narrow dusty road they were on the desert again as if the little town were no more than a dream. In the evening on the road to Casas Grandes they rode past the walled ruins of the ancient mud city of the Chichimeca. Among those clay warrens and mazes there burned here and there in the dusk the fires of squatters and where the squatters rose and moved about they cast their shadows lurching across the crumbling walls like drunken stewards and the moon rose over the dead city and shone upon the terraced embattlements and shone upon the roofless crypts and the pitovens and upon the mud corrals and upon the darkened ballcourt where nighthawks were hunting and upon the dry acequias where bits of pottery and stone tools together with the bones of their makers lay enleavened in the cracked clay floors.

They rode into Casas Grandes across the high banked tracks of the Mexican Northeast Railroad and they rode past the depot and up the street and tied their horses in front of a cafe and entered. Screwed into their receptacles in the ceiling and casting a hard yellow light over the tables were the first electric lightbulbs they'd seen since leaving Agua Prieta on the American border. They sat at a table and Boyd took off his hat and put it on the floor. There was no one in the place. After a while a woman came from behind the curtained doorway at the rear and walked over and stood at their table and looked down at them. She had no pad to write on and there seemed to be no menu. Billy asked her if she had any steaks and she nodded and said that she did. They ordered and sat looking out the small window at the darkened street where the horses stood.

What do you think? Billy said.

About what?

About anything.

Boyd shook his head. His thin legs stretched out before him. On the far side of the street a family of Mennonites passed along before the dimly lighted shopfronts in their overalls with the women behind them in their sunfaded motherhubbards carrying marketbaskets.

You aint sullin up on me are you?

No.

What are you thinkin?

Nothin.

All right.

Boyd watched the street. After a while he turned and looked at Billy. I was thinkin it was too easy, he said.

What was?

Comin up on Keno thataway. Gettin him back.

Yeah. Maybe.

He knew that they wouldnt have the horse back until they crossed the border with it and that nothing was easy but he didnt say so.

You dont trust nothin, he said.

No.

Things change.

I know. Some things.

You worry about everthing. But that dont change nothin. Does it?

Boyd sat studying the street. Two riders passed in what looked to be band uniforms. They both looked at the horses tied in front of the cafe.

Does it, Billy said.

Boyd shook his head. I dont know, he said. I dont know how it would of turned out if I hadnt worried.

They slept that night in a field of dusty weeds just off the railroad right of way and in the morning they washed in an irrigation ditch and mounted up and rode back into town and ate at the same cafe. Billy asked the woman if she knew the whereabouts of the offices of a ganadero named Soto but she did not. They ate a huge breakfast of eggs and chorizo and tortillas made from wheat flour such as they had not seen before in that country and they paid with what proved to be very nearly the last of their money and walked out and mounted up and rode through the town. Soto's offices were in a brick building three blocks south of the cafe. Billy was watching the reflections of two riders passing in the glass of the building's window across the street where the gaunted horses slouched by segments through the wonky panes when he saw the illjoined dog appear also and realized that the rider at the head of this unprepossessing parade was he himself. Then he saw that the lettering on the glass above the rider's head said Ganaderos and above that it said Soto y Gillian.

Look yonder, he said.

I see it, said Boyd.

Why didnt you say somethin if you seen it?

I'm sayin it now.

They sat the horses in the street. The dog sat in the dirt and waited. Billy leaned and spat and looked back at Boyd.

You care for me to ask you somethin?

Ask it.

How long do you aim to stay sulled up like this?

Till I get unsulled.

Billy nodded. He sat looking at their reflections in the glass. He seemed at odds to account for their appearance there. I thought you might say that, he said. But Boyd had seen him studying the tableau of ragged pilgrims paired with their horses all askew in the puzzled grid of the ganadero's glass with the mute dog at their heels and he nodded toward the window. I'm lookin at the same thing you are, he said.

They returned twice more to the ganadero's office before they found him in. Billy left Boyd to tend the horses. You keep Keno out of sight, he said.

I aint ignorant, said Boyd.

He crossed the street and raised one hand at the door to break the glare on the glass and looked in. An oldfashioned office with dark varnished wainscotting, dark oak furniture. He opened the door and entered. The glass in the door rattled when he closed it and the man at the desk looked up. He was holding the receiver of an oldfashioned pedestal telephone to his ear. Bueno, he said. Bueno. He winked at Billy. He gestured with one hand for him to come forward. Billy took off his hat.

Sí, sí. Bueno, said the ganadero. Gracias. Es muy amable. He hung the receiver back in the cradle and pushed the telephone away from him. Bueno, he said. Pendejo. Completamente sin vergüenza. He looked up at the boy. Pásale, pásale.

Billy stood holding his hat. Busco al señor Soto, he said.

No está.

Cuándo regresa?

Todo el mundo quiere saber. Who are you?

Billy Parham.

And who is that?

I'm from Cloverdale New Mexico.

Is that a fact?

Yessir. It is.

And what was your business with señor Soto?

Billy turned his hat a quarter turn through his hands. He looked toward the window. The man looked with him.

I am Señor Gillian, he said. Perhaps I can help you.

He pronounced it Geeyan. He waited.

Well, Billy said. You all sold a horse to a German doctor named Haas.

The man nodded. He seemed anxious for the story to unfold.

And I was huntin the man you bought the horse off of. It might could of been a indian.

Gillian leaned back in his chair. He tapped his lower teeth.

It was a dark bay gelding about fifteen and a half hands high. What you might call a castaño oscuro.

I am familiar with the particulars of this horse. Needless to say.

Yessir. You might of sold him moren one horse.

Yes. I might have but I did not. What was your interest in this horse?

I aint really concerned about the horse. I was just huntin the man that sold him.

Who is the boy in the street?

Sir?

The boy in the street.

That's my brother.

Why is he outside?

He's all right outside.

Why dont you bring him in?

He's all right.

Why dont you bring him in?

Billy looked out the window. He put on his hat and went out.

I thought you was watchin the horses, he said.

Yonder they stand, said Boyd.

The horses were in the sidestreet tethered by their bridlereins to a spike in a telegraph pole.

That's a sorry way to leave a horse.

I aint left em. I'm right here.

He seen you settin out here. He wants you to come in.

What for?

I didnt ask him.

You dont think we might be better off to just keep ridin?

It'll be all right. Come on.

Boyd looked toward the ganadero's window but the sun was on the glass and he couldnt see in.

Come on, said Billy. We dont go back in he'll think somethin.

He thinks somethin now.

No he dont.

He looked at Boyd. He looked off up the street at the horses. Them horses look terrible, he said.

I know it.

He stood with his hands in the back of his overall pants and chopped his bootheel into the dirt of the street. He looked at Boyd. We come a pretty hard ride to see this man, he said.

Boyd leaned and spat between his boots. All right, he said.

Gillian looked up when they entered. Billy held the door for his brother and Boyd walked in. He didnt take off his hat. The ganadero leaned back and studied them once and then the other. As if he'd been called upon to judge their consanguinity.

This here's my brother Boyd, Billy said.

Gillian gestured for him to come forward.

He was worried about the way we look, Billy said.

He can tell me himself what are his worries.

Boyd stood with his thumbs in his belt. He still hadnt taken off his hat. I wasnt worried about how we look, he said.

The ganadero studied him anew. You are from Texas, he said.

Texas?

Yes.

Where'd you get a notion like that?

You came here from Texas, no?

I aint never been in Texas in my life.

How do you know Dr Haas?

I dont know him. I never laid eyes on the man.

What is your interest in his horse?

It aint his horse. The horse was stole off our ranch by indians.

And your father sent you to Mexico to recover this horse.

He didnt send us nowhere. He's dead. They killed him and my mother with a shotgun and stole the horses.

The ganadero frowned. He looked at Billy. You agree with this? he said.

I'm like you, said Billy. Just waitin to hear what's comin next.

The ganadero studied them for a long time. Finally he said that he had come to his present position by way of trading horses on the road in both their own country and his and that he had learned as all such traders must how to reconstruct the histories of those with whom he came in contact largely by eliminating their own alternatives. He said that he was seldom wrong and seldom surprised.

What you have told me is preposterous, he said.

Well, said Boyd. You have it your own way.

The ganadero swiveled slightly in his chair. He tapped his teeth. He looked at Billy. Your brother thinks I am a fool.

Yessir.

The ganadero arched his brows. You agree with him?

No sir. I dont agree with him.

How come you believe him and not me? said Boyd.

Who would not? the ganadero said.

I reckon you just enjoy to hear people lie.

The ganadero said that yes he did. He said that it was a prerequisite for being in this business at all. He looked at Billy.

Hay algo más, he said. Something else. What is it?

That's all I know to tell.

But not all there is to be told.

He looked at Boyd. Is it? he said.

I dont know what you'd be askin me for.

The ganadero smiled. He rose laboriously from his desk. He was a smaller man standing. He went to an oak filecabinet and opened a drawer and thumbed through some papers and came back with a folder and sat and placed the folder on the desk before him and opened it.

Do you read spanish? he said.

Yessir.

The ganadero was tracing the document with his forefinger.

The horse was purchased at auction on March the second. It was a lot purchase of twenty-three horses.

Who was the seller?

La Babícora.

He turned the open folder and pushed it across the desk. Billy didnt look at it. What's La Babícora? he said.

The ganadero's unkempt eyebrows lifted. What is the Babícora? he said.

Yessir.

It is a ranch. It is owned by one of your countrymen, a señor Hearst.

Do they sell a lot of horses?

Not so many as they buy.

Why did they sell the horse?

Quién sabe? The capón is not so popular in this country. There is a prejudice I think is how you would say.

Billy looked down at the sales sheet.

Please, said the ganadero. You may look.

He picked up the folder and scanned the list of horses detailed under lot number forty-one eighty-six.

Qué es un bayo lobo? he said.

The ganadero shrugged.

He turned the page. He scanned the descriptions. Ruano. Bayo. Bayo cebruno. Alazán. Alazán Quemado. Half the horses were colors he'd never heard of. Yeguas and caballos, capones and potros. He saw a horse he thought could have been Niño. Then he saw another that could also have been. He closed the folder and placed it back upon the ganadero's desk.

What do you think? said the ganadero.

What do I think about what?

You told me it was the seller of the horse that brought you here and not the horse itself.

Yessir.

Perhaps your friend works for señor Hearst. That could be.

Yessir. That could be.

It is not such an easy thing to find a man in Mexico.

No sir.

The monte is extensive.

Yessir.

A man can be lost.

Yessir. He can.

The ganadero sat. He tapped the arm of his chair with his forefinger. Like a retired telegrapher. Algo más, he said. What is it?

I dont know.

He leaned forward on his desk. He looked at Boyd and he looked down at Boyd's boots. Billy followed his gaze. He was looking for the marks of spur straps.

You are far from home, he said. Needless to say. He looked up at Billy.

Yessir, said Billy.

Let me advise you. I feel the obligation.

All right.

Return to your home.

We aint got one to return to, Boyd said.

Billy looked at him. He still hadnt taken off his hat.

Why dont you ask him why he wants us to go home, said Boyd.

I will tell you why he wants this, said the ganadero. Because he knows what perhaps you do not. That the past cannot be mended. You think everyone is a fool. But there are not so many reasons for you to be in Mexico. Think of that.

Let's go, said Boyd.

We are close to the truth here. I do not know what that truth is. I am no gypsy fortuneteller. But I see great trouble in store. Great trouble. You should listen to your brother. He is older.

So are you.

The ganadero leaned back in the chair again. He looked at Billy. Your brother is young enough to believe that the past still exists, he said. That the injustices within it await his remedy. Perhaps you believe this also?

I dont have a opinion. I'm just down here about some horses.

What remedy can there be? What remedy can there be for what is not? You see? And where is the remedy that has no unforeseen consequence? What act does not assume a future that is itself unknown?

I quit this country once before, Billy said. It wasnt the future that brought me back here.

The ganadero was holding his hands forward one above the other, a space between. As if he held something unseen shut within an unseen box. You do not know what things you set in motion, he said. No man can know. No prophet foresee. The consequences of an act are often quite different from what one would guess. You must be sure that the intention in your heart is large enough to contain all wrong turnings, all disappointments. Do you see? Not everything has such a value.

Boyd was standing at the door. Billy turned and looked at him. He looked at the ganadero. The ganadero dismissed the air before him with the back of his hand. Yes, yes, he said. Go.

In the street Billy looked back to see if the ganadero was watching from his window.

Dont be lookin back, said Boyd. You know he's watchin us.

They rode south out of the town and took the road toward San Diego. They rode in silence, the mute and footsore dog trotting and walking by turns before them down the center of the shadowless noon road.

Do you know what he was talkin about? said Billy.

Boyd turned slightly on the bareback horse he rode and looked back.

Yeah. I know what he was talkin about. Do you?

They rode out through the last of the small colonias south of the town. In the fields they passed there were men and women picking cotton among the gray and brittle plants. They watered the horses at a roadside acequia and loosed the latigos to let them blow. Across the pieced land they watched a man turning the earth with an ox yoked by its horns to a singlehanded plow. The plow was of a type that was old in Egypt and was little more than a treeroot. They mounted up and rode on. He looked back at Boyd. Thin atop the unfurnished horse. Thinner yet in shadow. The tall dark horse that trod the road with its great angular articulations arch and slanting in the dust more true of horse than horse he rode. Late in the day from the crest of a rise in the road they halted the horses and looked out over the broken plats of dark ground below them where the sluicegates had been opened into the newplowed fields and where the water standing in the furrows shone in the evening light like grids of burnished barmetal stretching away in the distance. As if the boundary gates to some ancient enterprise lay fallen there beyond the ditchside cottonwoods, the evening's singing birds.

By and by they overtook on the darkening road a young girl walking barefoot and carrying upon her head a cloth bundle that hung to either side like a great soft hat. So that as they clopped slowly past she was obliged to turn her whole body sideways to see them. They nodded and Billy wished her a good evening and she wished them one back and they rode on. A little farther and they came to a place where the overflow from the acequias had left water standing in the bar ditch and they dismounted and led the horses along the bank and sat in the grass and watched geese walk stiffly about on the darkening fields. The girl passed along the road. They thought at first that she was singing softly to herself but she was crying. When she saw the horses she stopped. The horses raised their heads and looked toward the road. She went on and they lowered their heads and drank again. When they led the horses back up into the road she was very small and almost motionless in the distance before them. They mounted up and set out and after a while they overtook her once again.

Billy crossed his horse to the far side of the road. So that she must turn her face to the west in the last of the light to answer him if he spoke to her as he rode past. But when she heard the horses on the road behind her she crossed also and when he spoke to her she did not turn at all and if she answered he did not hear it. They rode on. A hundred yards and he stopped and got down into the road.

What are you doin? said Boyd.

He looked back at the girl. She had stopped. There was nowhere for her to go. Billy turned and lifted the near stirrup and hung it over the horn and checked the latigo.

It's gettin dark, said Boyd.

It is dark.

Well let's go on.

We're goin.

The girl had begun to walk again. She approached slowly keeping to the farthest edge of the road. As she came abreast of them Billy asked her if she wanted to ride. She didnt answer. She shook her head under the bundle and then she hurried past. Billy watched her go. He stroked the horse and took up the reins and started down the road afoot leading the horse behind. Boyd sat Keno and watched him.

What's got into you? he said.

What?

Askin her to ride.

What's wrong with that?

Boyd put his horse forward and rode beside his brother. What are you doin? he said.

Walkin my horse.

What the hell's wrong with you?

Aint nothin wrong with me.

Well what are you doin?

I'm just walkin my horse. Like you're ridin yours.

The hell you are.

Are you scared of girls?

Scared of girls?

Yeah.

He looked up at Boyd. But Boyd just shook his head and rode on.

The girl's small figure receded into the darkness ahead. Doves were still coming into the fields to the west of the road. They could hear them cross overhead even after it was too dark to see. Boyd rode on, he waited in the road. After a while Billy caught him up. He was riding again and they went on side by side.

They passed out of the irrigated land and they passed in a grove of roadside trees a jacal of mud and sticks where the faint orange light of a slutlamp burned. They thought it must be the place where the girl lived and were surprised to come upon her in the road before them once again.

When they overtook her now it was black of night and Billy slowed the horse beside her and asked her if she had far to go and she hesitated for a moment and then said that she did not. He offered that he would carry her bundle behind him on the horse and she could walk beside but she refused politely. She called him señor. She looked at Boyd. It occurred to him that she could have hidden in the roadside chaparral but she had not done so. They wished her a good evening and rode on and a short while later they encountered two horsemen on the road riding back the way they'd come who spoke to them briefly out of the darkness and passed on. He halted his horse and sat watching after them and Boyd halted beside him.

Are you thinkin what I am? Billy said.

Boyd sat with his forearms crossed over the withers of his horse. You want to wait on her?

Yeah.

All right. You think they'll bother her?

Billy didnt answer. The horses shifted and stood. After a while he said: Let's just wait here a minute. She'll be along in a minute. Then we can go.

But she wasnt along in a minute and she wasnt along in ten minutes or in thirty.

Let's go back, Billy said.

Boyd leaned and spat slowly into the road and turned his horse.

They'd gone no more than a mile when they saw a fire somewhere ahead of them through the iron shapes of the brush. The road turned and the fire swung slowly off to the right. Then it swung back. A half mile further and they halted their horses. The fire was burning in a small grove of oaks off to the east. The light of it was caught under the dark canopy of the leaves and shadows moved and moved back and a horse nickered from the dark beyond.

What do you want to do? said Boyd.

I dont know. Let me think.

They sat their horses in the darkened road.

You thought yet?

I guess there aint nothin to do but just ride on in.

They'll know we backtracked em.

I know it. It caint be helped.

Boyd sat watching the fire through the trees.

What do you want to do? said Billy.

If we're goin to go on in there then let's just do it.

They got down and led the horses. The dog sat in the road and watched them. Then it got up and followed.

When they entered the clear ground under the trees the two men were standing on the far side of the fire watching them approach. Their horses were not in sight. The girl was sitting on the ground with her legs tucked under her and clutching the bundle in her lap. When she saw who it was she looked away and sat staring into the fire.

Buenas noches, called Billy.

Buenas noches, they said.

They stood holding the horses. They had not been invited forward. The dog when it struck the circle of light stopped in its tracks and then backed away slightly and stood waiting. The men were watching them. One of them was smoking a cigarette and he raised it to his lips and sucked thinly at it and blew a thin stream of smoke toward the fire. He made a circling motion with his arm, his finger pointed down. He told them to take their horses around and into the trees behind them. Nuestros caballos están allá, he said.

Está bien, said Billy. He stood.

The man said that it was not all right. He said that he did not want their horses soiling the ground on which they were to sleep.

Billy looked at him. He turned slightly and looked at his horse. He could see curved like a dark triptych in a glass paperweight the figures of the two men and the girl burning in the fugitive light of the fire at the black center of the animal's eye. He passed the reins behind him to Boyd. Take them out yonder, he said. Dont unsaddle Bird and dont loose the latigo and dont put them with their horses.

Boyd passed in front of him leading the horses and went on past the men and into the dark of the trees. Billy came forward and nodded to them and pushed his hat back slightly from his eyes. He stood before the fire and looked down into it. He looked at the girl.

Cómo está, he said.

She didnt answer. When he looked across the fire the man who was smoking had squatted on his heels and was watching him through the warp of heat with eyes the color of wet coal. On the ground at his side stood a bottle stoppered with a corncob.

De dónde viene? he said.

America.

Tejas.

Nuevo Mexico.

Nuevo Mexico, the man said. Adónde va?

Billy watched him. He had his right arm folded across his chest and held in place with the elbow of his left so that his left forearm stood vertically before him holding the cigarette in a pose strangely formal, strangely delicate. Billy looked at the girl again and he looked again at the man across the fire. He had no answer to his query.

Hemos perdido un caballo, he said. Lo buscamos.

The man didnt answer. He held the cigarette between his forefingers and dipped his wrist in a birdlike motion and smoked and then raised the cigarette aloft again. Boyd came out of the trees and circled the fire and stood but the man did not look at him. He pitched the butt of the cigarette into the fire before him and wrapped his arms around his knees and began to rock back and forth in a motion barely perceptible. He jutted his chin at Billy and asked if he had followed them in order to see their horses.

No, said Billy. Nuestro caballo es un caballo muy distinto. Lo conoceríamos en cualquier luz.

As soon as he'd said it he knew that he'd given up his only plausible answer to the man's next question. He looked at Boyd. Boyd knew it too. The man rocked, he studied them. Qué quieren pues? he said.

Nada, said Billy. No queremos nada.

Nada, said the man. He formed the word as if tasting it. He gave his chin a slight sideways turn as a man might in pondering likelihoods. Two horsemen who meet two others on a dark road and pass on and thereafter meet also a traveler afoot know that those riders have overtaken the foot-traveler and passed on. That was what was known. The man's teeth shone in the firelight. He picked something from between them and examined it and then ate it. Cuántos años tiene? he said.

Yo?

Quién más.

Diecisiete.

The man nodded. Cuántos años tiene la muchacha?

No lo sé.

Qué opina.

Billy looked at the girl. She sat staring into her lap. She looked to be maybe fourteen.

Es muy joven, he said.

Bastante.

Doce quizás.

The man shrugged. He reached and took up the bottle from the ground and pulled the stopper and drank and sat holding the bottle by the neck. He said that if they were old enough to bleed they were old enough to butcher. Then he held the bottle up over his shoulder. The man behind him stepped forward and took it from him and drank. Out in the road a horse was passing. The dog had stood to listen. The rider did not stop and the slow clop of the hooves on the dried mud of the roadway faded and the dog lay down again. The man standing drank a second time and then handed the bottle back. The other man took it and pushed the cob back into the neck of the bottle with the heel of his hand and then weighed the bottle.

Quiere tomar? he said.

No. Gracias.

He weighed the bottle in his hand again and then pitched it underhand across the fire. Billy caught it and looked at the man. He held the bottle to the light. The smoky yellow mescal rolled viscously inside the glass and the curled form of the dead gusano circled the floor of the bottle in a slow drift like a small wandering fetus.

No quiero tomar, he said.

Tome, the man said.

He looked at the bottle again. The greaseprints on the glass shone in the firelight. He looked at the man and then he twisted the cob out of the neck.

Get the horses, he said.

Boyd stepped behind him. The man watched him. Adónde vas? he said.

Go on, said Billy.

Adónde va el muchacho?

Está enfermo.

Boyd crossed and went on toward the trees. The dog stood up and looked after him. The man turned and looked at Billy again. Billy raised the bottle and began to drink. He drank and lowered the bottle. Water ran from his eyes and he wiped them with his forearm and looked at the man and raised the bottle and drank again.

When he lowered the bottle it was all but empty. He sucked in air and looked at the man but the man was looking at the girl. She'd stood and was looking toward the trees. They could feel the ground shudder. The man rose and turned. Behind him the second man had stepped away from the fire and went trotting holding up his arms in silent exhortation. He was trying to head the horses where they came out of the trees tossing their heads and trotting sideways to keep from treading on the trailing stakeropes.

Demonios, said the man. Billy dropped the bottle and pitched the cob stopper into the fire and reached and grabbed the girl by the hand.

Vámonos, he said.

She bent and scooped up her bundle. Boyd came out of the trees at a gallop. He was bent low over Keno's neck and he was holding the bridlereins of Billy's horse in one hand and the shotgun in the other and he carried the reins of his own horse in his teeth like a circus rider.

Vámonos, hissed Billy, but she was already clutching his arm.

Boyd rode the horses almost through the fire and pulled Keno up stamping and wild-eyed. He caught the reins in his teeth again and pitched the shotgun to Billy. Billy caught it and took the girl by the elbow and swung her toward the horse. The other two horses had vanished out on the darkened plain to the south of the camp and the man who'd pitched him the bottle of mescal was coming back out of the darkness carrying in his left hand a long thin knife. Other than the sound of the horses blowing and stamping all was silence. No one spoke. The dog circled nervously behind the horses. Vámonos, said Billy. When he looked the girl was already seated on the horse's crupper behind saddle and blanketroll. He grabbed the reins from Boyd and swung them over the horse's head and cocked the shotgun in one hand like a pistol. He didnt know whether it was loaded or not. The mescal sat in his stomach like some unholy incubus. He stepped into the stirrup and the girl flattened herself expertly along the horse's flank and he swung his leg over her and sawed the horse around. The man was already upon him and he pointed the shotgun at the man's chest. The man made a lunge for the bridle but the horse shied and Billy shucked his boot out of the stirrup and kicked at the man and the man ducked and passed the blade of the knife across the outside of Billy's leg cutting through his boot and trouser both. He hauled the horse around and dug his heels in and the man lunged at the girl and got a handful of her dress but the cloth ripped away and then they were pounding out across the low grass swale and out onto the roadway where Boyd sat his stamping horse in the starlight waiting for them. He pulled the horse up squatting and tossing its head and spoke to the girl over his shoulder. Está bien? he said.

Sí, sí, she whispered. She was leaning forward over her bundle with both arms around his waist.

Let's go, said Boyd.

They set out south down the road side by side at a hard gallop with the dog behind them losing ground by the yard. There was no moon but the stars in that country were so many that the riders cast shadows on the road anyway. Ten minutes later Boyd sat holding Billy's horse by the reins while Billy stood at the roadside and gripped his knees and vomited into the roadside grass. The dog came wheezing up out of the dark and the horses looked at Billy and stamped in the road. Billy looked up and

wiped his weeping eyes. He looked at the girl. She sat the horse
half naked, her bare legs hanging down the side of the horse's
haunches. He spat and wiped his mouth on the back of his sleeve
and looked at his boot. Then he sat in the road and pulled the
boot off and looked at his leg. He pulled the boot back on again
and got up and picked the shotgun up out of the road and walked
back to the horses. The leg of his jeans flapped about his ankle.

We need to get off this road, he said. It aint goin to take them
all that long to catch their horses.

Are you cut?

I'm all right. Let's go.

Let's listen a minute.

They listened.

You caint hear nothin for the damn dog pantin.

Listen a minute.

Billy took the reins and raised them over the horse's head and
put his boot in the stirrup and the girl ducked and he swung up
into the saddle. A crazy man, he said. I got a crazy man for a
brother.

Mande? said the girl.

Listen a minute, Boyd said.

What do you hear?

Nothin. How do you feel?

About like you'd expect.

She dont speak no english, does she?

Hell no. How would she speak english?

Boyd sat looking off up the road into the darkness. You know
they're goin to follow us.

Billy jammed the shotgun into the scabbard. Hell yes I know
it, he said.

Dont be cussin in front of her.

What?

I said dont be cussin in front of her.

You just now got done sayin she dont speak no english.

That dont make it not cussin.

You dont make no sense. And what made you think them

sumbucks back yonder didnt have pistols in their clothes somewheres?

I didnt think it. That's why I thowed you the shotgun.

Billy leaned and spat. Damn, he said.

What do you aim to do with her?

I dont know. Hell. How would I know?

They turned the horses off of the road and set out upon a
treeless plain. The flat black mountains in the distance made a
jagged hem along the lower reach of the heavens. The girl sat
small and erect with one hand holding on to Billy by his belt.
Trekking in the starlight between the dark boundaries of the
mountain ranges east and west they had the look of storybook
riders conveying again to her homeland some stolen backland
queen.

They made camp in the dry country on a rise where the night
sank about them in an infinite deep and they staked the horses
and left Bird saddled. The girl had yet to speak. She walked
out in the darkness and they saw her no more till morning.

When they woke there was a fire on the ground and she was
pouring water from the canteen and setting it to heat, moving
quietly about in the gray light. Billy lay in his blanket watching
her. She must have found more clothes among her possessions
for she was wearing a skirt again. She stirred the water in the
tin, though what she stirred he could not guess. He closed his
eyes. He heard his brother say something in spanish and when
he looked out from his blanket Boyd was squatting by the fire
crosslegged and drinking from his tinware cup.

He turned out and rolled his bedding and she brought him a
cup of hot chocolate and went back to the fire. She'd browned
tortillas in their small skillet and spooned them full of beans and
they sat by the fire and ate their breakfast while the day paled
about them.

Did you unsaddle Bird? Billy said.

No. She did.

He nodded. They ate.

How bad are you cut? Boyd said.

It's just a scratch. He cut through my boot pretty good.

This country's hell on clothes.

It's gettin that reputation with me. What possessed you to run their horses off thataway?

I dont know. I just took a notion to do it.

Did you hear what he said about her?

Yeah. I heard it.

By sunup they'd broke camp and were set out once more across the gravel and creosote plain south. They nooned at a well in the desert where oak and elder grew clumped in the flats and they turned the horses out and slept on the ground. Billy slept with the shotgun cradled in his arm and when he woke the girl was sitting watching him. He asked her if she could ride caballo en pelo and she said that she could. When they set out again she rode behind Boyd so as to spell the horses. He thought Boyd would have something to say about it but he didnt. When he looked back the girl was riding with both arms around his waist. When he looked back later her dark hair was spilled over his brother's shoulder and she was sleeping against his back.

In the evening they reached the hacienda of San Diego sited on a hill overlooking the tilled lands that ran on to the Casas Grandes River and to the Piedras Verdes. A windmill turned on the plain below them like a chinese toy and dogs barked in the distance. In the long steep light the raw umber mountains stood deeply shadowed in their folds and in the sky to the south a dozen buzzards turned in a slow crepe carousel.

III

I T WAS ALL BUT DARK when they rode past the main house and along the drive, past the porticoes with their slender carved iron posts, past the white plaster walls quoined with red sandstone blocks and the terracotta filigree along the upper parapets. The front of the house was faced with three stone arches and above them were carved the words Hacienda de San Diego in letters arched over the initials L.T. The tall palladian windows were shuttered and the shutters were weathered and broken and paint and plaster were flaking from the walls and the portico ceiling was no more than bare wood lath all water-stained and buckled. They went on across the yard toward what looked to be the domicilios where smoke was rising against the evening sky and rode through the standing wooden gates into the courtyard and sat the horses side by side.

In one corner of the enclosure stood the carcass of an antique Dodge touring car long stripped of wheels and axles, of glass and seats. At the far end of the compound a cookfire burned on the ground and by its light they could see two gaudy caravan wagons with wash hung between them and passing back and forth before the fire both men and women in robes and kimonos who appeared to belong to a circus.

Qué clase de lugar es éste? Billy said.

Es ejido, said the girl.

Qué clase de gente?

No lo sé.

He swung down and the girl slid from the back of Boyd's horse and came and took the reins.

What are them? said Boyd.

I dont know.

They entered the compound, Billy and the girl afoot, the girl leading the horse. Boyd rode behind them. The figures at the far end paid them no mind at all. Two boys were lighting lamps from a burning split of wood at the fire and passing the lit lamps by their bails on a forked pole to a boy on the azotea who moved against the deepening sky hanging the lamps from the parapet. The ground in the compound became more illuminated as he went and soon a rooster began to call. Other boys were stacking haybales against a wall and under the farther portal men were unrolling a painted canvas drop much cracked and weathered from its travels.

Two of the costumed figures seemed engaged in a controversy and one of them stepped back and flung his arms wide. As if to demonstrate the measure of something outsized. Then he burst into song in some alien tongue. All movement ceased until he had done. Then all began again.

Dónde están los domicilios? said Billy.

The girl nodded toward the dark beyond the walls. Afuera, she said.

Let's go.

I'd like to see it, Boyd said.

You dont even know what it is.

It's somethin.

Billy took the bridlereins from the girl. He looked back at the fire, at the figures there. We can come back, he said. They're just gettin set up.

They rode out to where the three long adobe buildings stood that housed the workers and they rode up the passageway between the first two paced the way by a gauntlet of bristling and snarling curdogs. The evening was warm and there were cookfires burning out of doors and in the soft light a muted clink of utensils and the delicate slapping of hands shaping out tortillas. People drifted from fire to fire and their voices carried on the darkness and more distantly yet the sound of a guitar on the sweetness of the summer night.

They were given rooms at the far end of the row and the girl unsaddled Billy's horse and led both animals off to water them. Billy fished a wooden match from his shirtpocket and struck it alight with his thumbnail. The two rooms had a single door and a single window and high ceilings of vigas with latillas of sticks. A low door connected them and in the corner of the second room was a fireplace and a small altar with a Virgin of painted wood. A jar that held dead weeds. A drinking glass in the bottom of which lay a medallion of blackened wax. Against the wall stood a contrivance of poles lashed together into a frame and webbed with strips of rawhide with the hair on. It had the look of some rude agrarian implement but was in fact a bed. He blew out the match and walked out and stood in the door. Boyd was sitting on the stoop watching the girl. She was at the watering trough at the far end of the compound holding the horses while they drank. She and the two horses and the dog were surrounded by a semicircle of sitting dogs of every stripe and color but she paid them no mind. She stood very patiently with the horses while they drank. While they raised their dripping mouths and looked about and while they drank again. She did not touch the horses nor talk to them. She just waited while they drank and they drank for a long time.

They ate with a family named Muñoz. They must have looked hard used by the road for the woman kept urging food upon them and the man made little lifting motions with his outheld hands that they take more. He asked Billy where it was that they had come from and received the news with a certain sadness or resignation. As of things that could not be helped. They ate squatting on the ground with spoons and clay plates. The girl offered nothing in the way of her own origins and no one asked. While they were eating a strong tenor voice came floating on the night over the roofs of the domicilios. It ran up the scales and down twice in succession. Silence fell over the camp. A dog began to howl. Only after it seemed there would be nothing more forthcoming did the ejiditarios commence to talk again. A little later a bell tolled from somewhere off in the compound and in the long afterclang they began to rise and call out to one another.

The woman had carried her comal and her pots to the house and she now stood in the lamplit doorway with a small child on one arm. She saw Billy still sitting on the ground and she motioned him up. Vámonos, she called. He looked up at her. He said that he had no money but she only stared at him as if she did not understand. Then she said that everyone was going and that those who had money would pay for those who did not. She said that everyone must go. There could be no thought of people being left behind. Who would permit such a thing?

He rose and stood. He looked for Boyd but he could not see him or the girl. Stragglers were hurrying through the smoke of the dying cookfires. The woman had shifted the child to her other hip and come forward and took him by the hand as if he were himself a child. Vámonos, she said. Está bien.

They followed the others up the hill, the crowd moving slowly for the old people and the old people urging them to pass and go on. None would. The empty house on the crest of the rise above them stood bleak and lightless but music was coming from the long walled compound where the shops and establos were once sited, the domiciles of the overseers. Light fell out through the tall bay doors and cressets of oil or pitch fashioned out of buckets burned at either side of the stone archway at the entrance and here the ejiditarios were queued and they shuffled forward with their centavos and their pesos clutched in their hands to offer them up to the doorman where he stood in his polished black suit. Two young men carrying a litter passed through the crowd. The litter was made from poles and sheeting and the old man lying on it was dressed in coat and tie and he clutched a wooden rosary and stared grimly at the arch of sky above him. Billy looked at the child the woman was carrying but the child was asleep. When they reached the gates the woman paid and the gatekeeper thanked her and rattled the coppers into a bucket on the ground beside him and they passed through into the courtyard.

The gaudy little wagons had been drawn up at the farther end of the enclosure. Lamps stood in a semicircle on the packed clay ground before them and lamps had been hung from a rope stretched overhead and in the uplight overhead the faces of young boys watched along the parapet like rows of theatrical masks displayed there. The mules that stood between the wagonshafts were fitted out in braid and tinsel and velvet trappings and the mules and caravans alike were the same that conveyed the little company over the back roads of the republic to stand at night in just these costumes while the lamps were lit and the crowds pushed forward in some backland plaza or alameda where a man passed up and back and swung before him like a censer a waterpail pierced with nailholes by which to lay the dust and the primadonna moved in lascivious silhouette behind a wagonsheet donning her costume or turning to regard herself in a mirror which none could see but all could imagine to be present.

He watched the play with interest but could make little of it. The company was perhaps describing some adventure of their own in their travels and they sang into each other's faces and wept and in the end the man in buffoon's motley slew the woman and slew another man perhaps his rival with a dagger and young boys ran forward with the curtain hems to draw them shut and the mules standing in their traces raised their heads up out of their sleep and began to shift and step.

There was no applause. The crowd sat quietly on the ground. Some of the women were crying. After a while the majordomo who had spoken to them prior to the performance stepped out through the curtain and thanked them for their attendance and stepped to one side and bowed as the boys carried the curtains open again. The actors stood before them hand in hand and bowed and curtseyed and there was a smattering of applause and then the curtain closed for good.

In the morning before it was quite light he walked out of the compound and down to the river. He walked out over the plank bridge on its stone piers and stood looking down at the clear cold waters of the Casas Grandes running out of the mountains to the south. He turned and looked downstream. A hundred feet away in water to her thighs stood the primadonna naked. Her hair was down and it was wet and clinging to her back and it reached to the water. He stood frozen. She turned and swung her hair before her and bent and lowered it into the river. Her breasts swung above the water. He took off his hat and stood with his heart laboring under his shirt. She raised up and gathered her hair and twisted out the water. Her skin so white. The dark hair under her belly almost an indelicacy.

She bent once more and trailed her hair in the water with a swaying motion sideways and then stood and swung it about her in a great hoop of spray and stood with her head back and her eyes closed. The sun rising over the gray ranges to the east lit the upper air. She held one hand up. She moved her body, she swept both hands before her. She bent and caught her falling hair in her arms and held it and she passed one hand over the surface of the water as if to bless it and he watched and as he watched he saw that the world which had always been before him everywhere had been veiled from his sight. She turned and he thought she might sing to the sun. She opened her eyes and saw him there on the bridge and she turned her back and walked slowly up out of the river and was lost to his view among the pale standing trunks of the cottonwoods and the sun rose and the river ran as before but nothing was the same nor did he think it ever would be.

He walked slowly back up to the compound. In the new sunrise the shadows of workers setting out for the fields with their shouldered hoes passed one by one along the eastern facing wall of the granary like figures in some agrarian drama. He got his breakfast from the Muñoz woman and walked out with his saddle over his shoulder and caught his horse and saddled him and mounted up and rode out to see the country.

It was midday before the caravans bearing the opera company sallied forth out through the gates and down the hill and across the bridge to set out south along the road to Mata Ortíz, to Las

Varas and Babícora. In the hard noon light the faded gilt of the
lettering and the weathered red paint and sunbleached tapestries
seemed some fallen grace from the pageantry of the prior night
and the caravans in their trundling and swaying slowly south
and in their diminishing in the heat and desolation seemed
charged with some new and more austere enterprise. As if the
light of God's day had sobered their hopes. As if the light
and the country thereby made visible were alien to their true
purpose. He watched from a rise in the rolling lands south of
the hacienda where the grass seethed in the wind underfoot.
The caravans moved slowly through the cottonwoods on the far
side of the river, the little mules plodded. He leaned and spat
and put the horse forward with his heels.

In the afternoon he walked through the empty rooms of the
old residencia. The rooms were stripped of their fixtures and
chandeliers and the parquet flooring was mostly gone. Turkeys
stepped and moved away through the rooms before him. The
house smelled of damp and old straw and waterstains had
wrought upon the swagged and crumbling plasterwork great
freeform sepia maps as of old antique kingdoms, ancient worlds.
In the corner of the parlor a dead animal, dry hide and bones.
A dog perhaps. He walked out into the courtyard. The raw
mud brickwork showing through the plaster of the enclosing
walls. In the center of the open space a stonework well. A bell
rang in the distance.

In the evening the men smoked and talked and drifted in
small groups from fire to fire. The Muñoz woman brought his
boot to him and he examined it in the firelight. The long slice
in the leather had been mended back with awl and cord. He
thanked her and pulled it on. The women knelt on the packed
dirt and leaned over the coals and turned with their bare hands
the tortillas off the hot sheetiron comals leaving along the unleav-
ened edges like tallymarks fingerprints of black from where
they'd fed the charcoal fire. An endless ritual endlessly repeated,
the propagation of the great secular host of the Mexicans. The
girl helped the woman prepare the meal and after the men had

been fed she came and sat beside Boyd and ate in silence. Boyd seemed to pay her little mind. He'd told Boyd that they'd be leaving in two days' time and in the way she raised her eyes to look at him across the fire he knew that Boyd had told her.

She worked all the day following in the fields and in the evening she came in and went to wash herself with bowl and rag behind the curtain and then went out to sit and watch small boys playing ball in the clay court between the buildings. When he rode in she stood and came over and took the bridlereins and she asked him if she could go with them.

He stepped down and took off his hat and clawed his fingers through his sweaty hair and put his hat back on again and looked at her. No, he said.

She stood holding the horse. She looked away. Her dark eyes swimming. He asked her why she wanted to go with them but she only shook her head. He asked her if she was afraid, if there was something here of which she was afraid. She didnt answer. He asked how old she was and she said fourteen. He nodded. He punched a crescent in the dirt underfoot with the heel of his boot. He looked at her.

Alguien le busca, he said.

She didnt answer.

No se puede quedar aquí?

She shook her head. She said she could not stay. She said she had no place to go.

He looked out across the compound in the tranquil evening light. He said that he had no place to go either so what help could he be to her but she only shook her head and said that she would go wherever they went she didnt care.

At dawn the day following while he saddled his horse the workers came out bringing gifts of food. They brought tortillas and chiles and carne seca and live chickens and whole hoops of cheese until they were burdened with provisions beyond their means to carry them. The Muñoz woman gave Billy something which when she stepped back he saw was a clutch of coins knotted into a rag. He tried to give it back but she turned away and walked back to her house without speaking. When they rode out of the compound the girl was riding behind Boyd on the bareback horse with her arms around his waist.

They rode all day south and nooned by the river and ate an enormous lunch out of the provisions they carried and slept under the trees. Late in the day a few miles south of Las Varas on the Madera road they came to a place where the horses balked and stood blowing in the road.

Look yonder, said Boyd.

The opera company was camped beyond the road in a field of wildflowers. The caravans were parked side by side and a canvas awning had been hung between them for a ramada and in the afforded shade the primadonna was taking her ease in a great canvas hammock with a pot of tea on the table at her side and a japanese fan. A victrola was playing from the open door of the caravan and in the field beyond their encampment a number of workers leaned on their implements with their hats in their hands and listened to the music.

She'd heard the horses on the road and she sat in her hammock and raised one hand to shade her eyes and look out although the sun was behind her and the awning shaded her anyway.

I guess they just camp out like gypsies, Billy said.

They are gypsies.

Who says?

Everbody.

The horse's ears quartered the compass for the source of the music.

They're broke down.

What makes you say that?

They'd of got farthern this.

Maybe they just decided to stop here.

What for? There aint nothin here.

Billy leaned and spat. You reckon she's here just by herself?

I dont know.

What do you reckon's got into the horses?

I dont know.

She's done went and put the spyglasses to us now.

The primadonna had fetched up from the table a small pair of lorgnette operaglasses and was peering toward the road with them.

Let's get down.

All right.

They walked the horses along the road and he sent the girl over to see if the woman needed anything. The music stopped. The woman called into the caravan and after a while the music began again.

There's a mule's died, Boyd said.

How do you know?

There just has.

Billy looked over the camp. There were no animals of any description about.

Likely the mules is hobbled up in them oaks yonder, he said.

No they aint.

When the girl came back she said that one of the mules had died.

Shit, said Billy.

What, said Boyd.

You all set that up.

Set what up?

About the mule. She's made a signal or somethin.

A dead mule signal.

Yeah.

Boyd leaned and spat and shook his head. The girl stood with one hand shading her eyes waiting. Billy looked at her. Her thin clothes. Her dusty legs. Her feet in huaraches made from strapleather and rawhide. He asked her how long the men had been gone and she said two days.

We better go over and see if she's all right.

What do you aim to do if she aint? Boyd said.

Hell if I know.

Well why dont we just keep ridin.

I thought you was the one liked to go around rescuin people.

Boyd didnt answer. He mounted up and Billy turned and looked up at him. He shucked one boot out of the stirrup and leaned down and gave the girl his hand and she put her foot in the stirrup and he swung her up and then put the horse forward. Well let's go, he said. If they aint nothin else will satisfy you.

He followed them out across the field. When the workers saw them coming they began once again to grub in the ground with their short hoes. He rode up alongside Boyd and they sat their horses side by side before the reclining primadonna and wished her a good afternoon. She nodded. She studied them across the top of the splayed fan. It was painted with some oriental scene and the bolsters were of ivory inlaid with silver wire.

Los hombres han salido por Madero? said Billy.

She nodded. She said that they would be returning at any moment. She lowered the fan slightly and looked out down the road south. As if they might be appearing even now.

Billy sat his horse. He didnt seem to be able to think what else to say. After a while he took his hat off.

You are Americans, the woman said.

Yes mam. I reckon the girl told you.

There is nothing to hide.

We dont have nothin to hide. I just come over to see if there was anything we could do for you.

She arched her painted brows in surprise.

I thought maybe you all was broke down out here.

She looked at Boyd. Boyd looked off toward the mountains to the south.

We're headed yonway, Billy said. If you wanted us to carry a message or anything.

She sat up slightly in the hammock and called out into the caravan. Basta, she called. Basta la música.

She sat listening, one hand balanced on the table. In a moment the music ceased and she subsided again into the hammock and spread the fan and looked across the top of it at the young jinete who sat his horse before her. Billy looked toward the caravan thinking someone might appear in the doorway but no one did.

What all did the mule die of? he said.

That mule, she said. That mule died because its blood all fell out in the road.

Mam?

She raised a hand languidly before her, her ringed and tapered fingers weaving. As if she described the ascending of the animal's soul.

That mule was having his troubles but no one could reason with that mule. Gasparito should not have been put to attend to the wants of that mule. He had no temperament for such a mule. Now you see what has come to pass.

No mam.

Drinking too. In these matters drinking is always present. And then the fear. The other mules are screaming. Tienen mucho miedo. Screaming. Sliding and falling in the blood and screaming. What does one say to these animals? How does one put their minds at rest?

She made a peremptory gesture to one side. As of some casting to the winds in the dry hot solitude, the birdcalls in the little glade, the evening's onset. Can such animals ever be restored to their former state? There can be no question. Especially in the case of dramatic mules such as these mules. These mules can have no peace now. No peace. You see?

What was it he done to the mule?

He tried to cut off the head with a machete. Of course. What did the girl say to you? She speaks no english?

No mam. She just said it died was all.

The primadonna looked at the girl suspiciously. Where did you find this girl?

She was just walkin along the road. I wouldnt of thought you could cut off a mule's head with a machete.

Of course not. Only a drunken fool would attempt such a feat. When the hacking availed not he began to saw. When Rogelio seized him he would have hacked at Rogelio. Rogelio was disgusted. Disgusted. They fell in the road. In the blood and the dust. Rolling about under the feet of the animals. The carriage threatening to overturn and all in it. Disgusting. What if someone should come along on this road? What if people appeared on this road at such a time to see this spectacle?

What happened to the mule?

The mule? The mule died. Of course.

They wouldnt nobody shoot it or nothin?

Yes. There is a story. I myself was the one. I came forward to shoot this mule, what do you think? Rogelio prohibited this act. Because it will frighten the other mules he says to me. Can you imagine this? At this point in history? Then he wishes to dismiss Gasparito. He says that Gasparito is a lunatic but Gasparito is only a borrachón. From Vera Cruz of course. And a gypsy. Can you imagine this?

I thought you was all gypsies.

She sat up in the hammock. Cómo? She said. Cómo? Quién lo dice?

Todo el mundo.

Es mentira. Mentira. Me entiendes? She leaned over and spat twice into the dirt.

At this moment the door did darken and a small dark man in shirtsleeves stood glaring out. The primadonna turned in her hammock and looked up at him. As if his appearance in the doorway had cast a shadow visible to see. He looked over the visitors and their mounts and took from his shirtpocket a package of El Toro cigarettes and put one in his mouth and fished about in his pocket for a match.

Buenas tardes, Billy said.

You think a gypsy can sing an opera? the woman said. A gypsy? All gypsies can do is play the guitar and paint horses. And dance their primitive dances.

She sat upright in the hammock and hiked her shoulders and spread her hands before her. Then she uttered a long piercing note that was not quite a cry of pain and not quite anything else. The horses shied and arched their necks and the riders had to haul them around and still they twisted and stepped and rolled their eyes. Out in the fields the workers stood stock still in their furrows.

Do you know what that was? she said.

No mam. It sure was loud.

That was the do agudo. You think some gypsy can sing that note? Some croaking gypsy?

I guess I never give it a lot of thought.

Show me this gypsy, said the primadonna. This gypsy I wish to see.

Who would paint a horse?

Gypsies of course. Who else? Horsepainters. Dentists of horses.

Billy took off his hat and wiped his forehead with the back of his shirtsleeve and put the hat back on. The man in the door had come partway down the painted wooden steps and sat smoking. He leaned and snapped his fingers at the dog. The dog backed away.

Where abouts did this happen about the mule? Billy said.

She raised up and pointed with the folded fan. On the road, she said. Not one hundred meters. We could go no farther. A trained mule. A mule with theatrical experience. Slaughtered in its traces by a drunken fool.

The man on the steps took a last deep draw on his cigarette and flipped the stub at the dog.

You got any message for your party if we see em? said Billy.

Tell Jaime that we are well and that he is to come at his own pace.

Who is Jaime?

Punchinello. He is Punchinello.

Mam?

The payaso. The clowen.

The clown.

Yes. The clown.

In the show.

Yes.

I wont know him without his warpaint.

Mande?

How will I know him.

You will know him.

Does he make people laugh?

He makes people do what he wishes them to do. Sometimes he makes the young girls cry but that is another history.

Why does he kill you?

The primadonna leaned back in her hammock. She studied him. She looked out at the workers in the field. After a while she turned to the man on the steps.

Díganos, Gaspar. Por qué me mata el punchinello?

He looked up at her. He looked at the riders. Te mata, he said, porque él sabe tu secreto.

Paff, said the primadonna. No es porque yo sé el de él?

No.

A pesar de lo que piensa la gente?

A pesar de cualquier.

Y qué es este secreto?

The man raised one foot before him and turned his boot to examine it. It was a boot of black leather with lacing up the side, a kind seldom seen in that country. El secreto, he said, es que en este mundo la máscara es la que es verdadera.

Le entendió? said the primadonna.

He said that he understood. He asked her if that was her opinion also but she only waved one hand languidly. So says the arriero, she said. Quién sabe?

He said it was your secret.

Paff. I have no secret. Anyway it no longer interests me. To be killed night after night. It drains one's strength. One's powers of speculation. It is better to concentrate on small things.

I reckon I would of thought he was just jealous.

Yes. Of course. But even to be jealous is a test of one's strength. Jealous in Durango and again in Monclova and in Monterrey. Jealous in heat and in rain and in cold. Such a jealousy must empty out the malice of a thousand hearts, no? How is one to do this? I think it is better to make a study of smaller things.

Then the larger will follow. In smaller things one can progress. There one's efforts are repaid. Perhaps just the attitude of the head. The movement of a hand. The arriero is only a spectator in these matters. He cannot see that for the wearer of the mask nothing is changed. The actor has no power to act but only as the world tells him. Mask or no mask is all one to him.

She picked up the operaglasses by their stem and scanned the countryside. The road. The long shadows upon the road. And where do you go, you three? she said.

We're down here huntin some horses that was stole.

In whose charge were these horses?

No one answered.

She looked at Boyd. She spread the fan. Painted across the folded bellows of the ricepaper was a dragon with great round eyes. She folded it shut. For how long will you seek these horses? she said.

Ever how long it takes.

Podría ser un viaje largo.

Quizás.

Long voyages often lose themselves.

Mam?

You will see. It is difficult even for brothers to travel together on such a voyage. The road has its own reasons and no two travelers will have the same understanding of those reasons. If indeed they come to an understanding of them at all. Listen to the corridos of the country. They will tell you. Then you will see in your own life what is the cost of things. Perhaps it is true that nothing is hidden. Yet many do not wish to see what lies before them in plain sight. You will see. The shape of the road is the road. There is not some other road that wears that shape but only the one. And every voyage begun upon it will be completed. Whether horses are found or not.

I reckon we better get on, Billy said.

Ándale pues, said the primadonna. May God go with you.

I see this Punchinello on the road I'll tell him you're waitin on him.

Paff, said the primadonna. Do not waste your breath.

Adiós.

Adiós.

He looked at the man on the steps. Hasta luego, he said.

The man nodded. Adiós, he said.

Billy reined the horse around. He looked back and touched the brim of his hat. The primadonna opened the fan in a graceful falling gesture. The arriero leaned forward with his hands on his kneecaps and tried a last time to spit upon the dog and then they all rode out across the field to the road. When he looked back at the primadonna she was watching them through the spyglasses. As if she might better assess them in that way where they set forth upon the shadowbanded road, the coming twilight. Inhabiting only that ocular ground in which the country appeared out of nothing and vanished again into nothing, tree and rock and the darkening mountains beyond, all of it contained and itself containing only what was needed and nothing more.

THEY MADE CAMP in an oakgrove beside the river and built a fire and sat while the girl prepared their dinner out of the bounty they'd carried off from the ejido. When they'd eaten she fed the dog the scraps and washed the plates and the pot and went to see about the horses. They rode out again late the next morning and at noon they turned the horses out of the dirt roadway and took a path along the lower edge of a field of peppers and on to the trees and to the river where it shimmered quietly in the heat. The horses quickened their pace. The path turned and ran along an irrigation ditch and then descended into the trees and out again and along a growth of river willows and through a stand of cane. A cool wind was coming off the water, the white tassels of the cane bending and hissing gently in the wind. Beyond the bracken the sound of water falling.

They came out of the canebrake at a trodden ford in the runoff from the irrigation channel. Above them was a pool where water ran from an old corrugated culvertpipe. The water spilled heavily into the pool and splashing there in the water were half a dozen boys stark naked. They saw the riders at the ford and they saw the girl but they paid them no mind.

Damn, said Boyd.

He clapped his heels into the horse's ribs and put it forward through the sandy shallows. He didnt look back at the girl. She was watching the boys with goodnatured interest. She looked behind at Billy and put her other arm around Boyd's waist and they rode on.

When they reached the river she slid from the horse and took the reins and led both animals out into the water and loosed the latigo on Bird and stood with the horses while they drank. Boyd sat on the bank of the river with one of his boots in his hand.

What's the matter? said Billy.

Nothin.

He limped down along the gravel bar carrying his boot and got a round rock and sat and ran his arm down into the boot and began to pound with the rock.

You got a nail?

Yeah.

Tell her to bring the shotgun.

You tell her.

The girl was standing in the river with the horses.

Tráigame la escopeta, Billy called.

She looked at him. She waded around to the offside of his horse and took the shotgun out of the scabbard and brought it to him. He pried off the forearm and unbreeched the gun and took out the shell and lifted away the barrel and squatted in front of Boyd.

Here, he said. Let me have it.

Boyd handed him the boot and he set it on the ground and reached down and felt inside for the nail and then dropped the breech end of the barrel down into the boot and pounded down the nail with the barrel lug and reached in and felt again and then handed the boot back to Boyd.

Them things smell awful, he said.

Boyd pulled on the boot and stood and walked up and back.

Billy put the shotgun back together and pushed the shell into the chamber with his thumb and breeched the gun and stood it upright on the gravels and sat holding it. The girl was back out in the river with the horses.

You reckon she seen em? Boyd said.

Seen what?

Them boys naked.

He squinted up at Boyd where he stood against the sun. Well, he said, I reckon she did. She aint been struck blind since yesterday has she?

Boyd looked out to where the girl stood in the river.

She didnt see nothin she aint seen before, Billy said.

What's that supposed to mean?

It dont mean nothin.

The hell it dont.

It dont mean nothin. People see people naked, that's all. Dont start gettin crazy on me again. Hell. I seen that opera woman in the river naked as a jaybird.

You never.

The hell I didnt. She was takin a bath. She was washin her hair.

When was all this?

She washed her hair and wrung it out like a shirt.

You mean buck naked?

I mean not stitch one.

How come you never said nothin about it?

You dont need to know everthing.

Boyd stood chewing his lip. You went up and talked to her, he said.

What?

You went up and talked to her. Just like you never seen nothin.

Well what did you want me to do? Tell her I seen her jaybird naked and then start talkin to her?

Boyd had squatted on the gravel spit and he took off his hat and sat holding it in both hands before him. He looked out at the passing river. You think maybe we ought to of stayed back yonder? he said.

At the ejido?

Yeah.

And wait for the horses to come to us I reckon.

He didnt answer. Billy rose and walked out along the gravel bar. The girl brought the horses up and he put the shotgun back in the scabbard and looked at Boyd.

Are you ready to ride? he called.

Yeah.

He pulled the cinches on his horse and took the reins from the girl. When he looked at Boyd Boyd was still sitting there.

What is it now? he said.

Boyd got up slowly. It aint nothin now, he said. It aint nothin from what it was before.

He looked at Billy. You know what I mean?

Yeah, said Billy. I know what you mean.

In three days' riding they reached the crossing where the old wagonroad came down out of La Norteña in the western sierras and crossed the high plains of the Babícora and on through the valley of the Santa María to Namiquipa. The days were hot and dry and the riders and their horses by each day's end were the color of the road. They'd ride the horses out across the fields to the river and Billy would throw down the saddle and bedrolls and while the girl made camp he'd take the horses downriver and strip off his boots and clothes and ride bareback into the river leading Boyd's horse by the reins and sit the horse naked save for his hat and watch the dust of the road leach away in a pale stain downstream in the clear cold water.

The animals drank. They lifted their heads and looked out downriver. After a while an old man came through the woods on the far side driving a pair of oxen with a jockeystick. The oxen were yoked with a homemade yoke of poplar wood so

whitened by the sun it seemed some ancient weathered bone
they bore upon their necks. They waded out into the river with
their slow rolling motion and looked upstream and down and
across at the horses before they bent to drink. The old man
stood at the water's edge and looked at the naked boy horseback.

Cómo le va? said Billy.

Bien, gracias a Dios, said the old man. Y a usted?

Bien.

They spoke of the weather. They spoke of the crops, of which
the old man knew a great deal and the boy nothing. The old
man asked the boy if he was a vaquero and he said he was and
the old man nodded. He said that the horses were good horses.
Everyone could see that. His eyes drifted upstream to where
the thin blue column of smoke from their camp stood in the
windless air.

Mi hermano, said Billy.

The old man nodded. He was dressed in the dirty white
manta of that country in which the workers tended the fields
like soiled inmates wandered from some ultimate Bedlam to
stand at last hacking in slow and mindless rage at the earth itself.
The oxen raised their dripping mouths out of the river first one
and then the other. The old man tilted his stick toward them as
if to bless.

Le gustan, he said.

Claro, said Billy.

He watched them drink. He asked the old man if the oxen
were willing workers and the old man weighed the question and
then said that he did not know. He said that the oxen had no
choice. He looked at the horses. Y los caballos? he said.

The boy said he thought that horses were willing enough. He
said that some horses enjoyed their work. They enjoyed working
cattle. He said that horses were different from oxen.

A kingfisher flew up the river and veered and chattered and
then swung back above the river again and continued upstream.
No one looked at it. The old man said that the ox was an animal
close to God as all the world knew and that perhaps the silence

and the rumination of the ox was something like the shadow of a greater silence, a deeper thought.

He looked up. He smiled. He said that in any case the ox knew enough to work so as to keep from being killed and eaten and that that was a useful thing to know.

He came forward and hazed the animals up out of the river. They clambered out along the gravel shore and blew and craned their necks. The old man turned, his stick on one shoulder.

Está lejos de su casa? he said.

The boy said that he had no home.

The old man's face grew troubled. He said that the boy must have a home but the boy said that he did not. The old man said that there was a place for everyone in the world and that he would pray for the boy. Then he drove the oxen out through the willows and the sycamore wood in the new dusk and was soon gone from sight.

When he got back to the fire it was almost dark. The dog stood up and the girl came forward to take the sleek and dripping animals. He walked around the fire and turned his saddle where it stood to dry.

She wants to go to Namiquipa to see her mother, Boyd said.

He stood looking down at his brother. I guess she can go wherever she's a mind to, he said.

She wants me to go with her.

Wants you to go with her?

Yeah.

What for?

I dont know. Because she's afraid.

Billy stared into the coals. Is that what you want to do? he said.

No.

Then what are we jawin about?

I told her she could take the horse.

Billy squatted slowly with his elbows on his knees. He shook his head. No, he said.

She aint got no other way to go.

What the hell do you think is goin to happen if somebody sees her ridin a stolen horse? Hell. Any horse.

It aint stole.

The hell it aint. And how do you aim to get it back?

She'll bring it back.

It and the sheriff. What did she run off for if she wants to go back?

I dont know.

I dont either. We come a long ways to get that horse.

I know it.

Billy spat into the fire. I sure would hate to be a woman in this country. What does she aim to do after she gets back?

Boyd didnt answer.

Does she know the kind of shape we're in?

Yeah.

Why wont she talk to me?

She's afraid you'll leave her.

That's why she wants to take the horse.

Yeah. I guess.

What if I wont let her take it?

I reckon she'd go anyways.

Then let her.

The girl came back. They stopped talking even though she could not have understood what they said. She arranged their cookware in the coals and went off to the river for water. Billy looked at Boyd.

You aint above runnin off with her. Are you?

I aint goin nowheres.

If push come to shove.

I dont know what that would be.

If you thought she'd be left on her own or they wouldnt be nobody to look after her or somebody would bother her. Like that. You aint above just goin with her. Are you?

Boyd leaned and pushed the blackened billet ends of two

sticks forward into the small coals with his fingers and wiped his fingers on the leg of his jeans. He didnt look at his brother. No, he said. I guess I aint.

In the morning they rode out to the crossroads and here they took leave of the girl.

How much money have we got? Boyd said.

Damn near none.

Why dont you give it to her?

I knew this was comin. What do you propose to eat on?

Give her half of it.

All right.

She sat the horse bareback and looked down at Boyd with her black eyes brimming and then she slid from the horse and put her arms around him. Billy watched them. He looked at the sky to the south all troubled with weather clouds. He leaned and spat dryly into the road. Let's go, he said.

Boyd boosted her onto the horse and she turned and looked down at him with her hand to her mouth and then reined the horse around and set off on the narrow dirt road east.

THEY RODE ON SOUTH along the dusty road, doubled once more upon Billy's horse. The dust blew off the crown of the road before them and the roadside acacias twisted and hissed in the wind. Late in the afternoon it darkened over and rain began to splatter in the dirt and to rattle in their hatbrims. They passed three men in the road riding. Illsorted horses and worse tack. When Billy looked back two of them were looking back at him.

Would you know them Mexicans we took the girl off of? he said.

I dont know. I dont think so. Would you?

I dont know. Probably not.

They rode on in the rain. After a while Boyd said: They'd know us.

Yeah, said Billy. They'd know us.

The road narrowed going up into the mountains. The country

was all barren pinewood and the spare and reedy grass in the parklands looked poor fare for the sustenance of a horse. They took turns walking on the switchbacks, leading the horse or walking beside it. They camped in the pinewoods at night and the nights were cold again and when they rode into the town of Las Varas they had not eaten in two days. They crossed the railroad tracks and rode past the big adobe warehouses with their mud buttresses and their signs that said puro maíz and compro maíz. There were stacks of raw yellow slabcut pine lumber along the sidings and the air was rank with piñon smoke. They rode past the low stuccoed railstation with its tin roof and descended into the town. The houses were adobe with pitched roofs of wood shake and there were stacks of firewood in the yards and fences made from pine slabs. A boldlooking dog with one leg off limped into the street before them and turned to stand them off.

Sic him, Trooper, said Boyd.

Shit, said Billy.

They ate in what passed for a cafe in that rawlooking country. Three tables in an empty room and no fire.

I believe it's warmer outside than what it is in here, Billy said.

Boyd looked out the window at the horse standing in the street. He looked toward the rear of the cafe.

You reckon this place is even open?

After a while a woman came through the door at the rear and stood before them.

Qué tiene de comer? Billy said.

Tenemos cabrito.

Qué más?

Enchiladas de pollo.

Qué más?

Cabrito.

I aint eatin no goat, Billy said.

I aint either.

Dos ordenes de las enchiladas, Billy said. Y café.

She nodded and went away.

Boyd sat with his hands between his knees to warm them. Outside gray smoke blew through the streets. No one was about.

You think it's worse to be cold or be hungry?

I think it's worse to be both.

When the woman brought the plates she set them down and then made a shooing motion toward the front of the cafe. The dog was standing at the window looking in. Boyd took off his hat and made a pass at the glass with it and the dog went away. He put his hat back on again and picked up his fork. The woman went to the rear and returned with two mugs of coffee in one hand and a basket of corn tortillas in the other. Boyd pulled something from his mouth and laid it on the plate and sat looking at it.

What's that? said Billy.

I dont know. It looks like a feather.

They poked the enchiladas apart trying to find something edible inside. Two men came in and looked at them and went on to sit at the table at the back.

Eat the beans, Billy said.

Yeah, said Boyd.

They spooned the beans into the tortillas and ate them and drank the coffee. The two men at the rear sat quietly waiting for their meal.

She's goin to ask us what was wrong with the enchiladas, Billy said.

I dont know if she will or not. You reckon people eat them things?

I dont know. We can take em and give em to the dog.

You propose to take the woman's food out and feed it to the dog right in front of her own cafe?

If the dog'll eat it.

Boyd pushed back his chair and rose. Let me go out and get the pot, he said. We can feed the dog down the road.

All right.

We'll just tell her we're takin it with us.

When he came back in with the pot they scraped the food off the plates and put the lid on and sat drinking their coffee. The woman came out with two platters of richlooking meat with gravy and rice and pico de gallo.

Damn, said Billy. Dont that look good.

He called for the bill and the woman came over and told them it was seven pesos. Billy paid and nodded toward the rear and asked the woman what those men were eating.

Cabrito, she said.

When they walked out into the street the dog got up and stood waiting.

Hell, said Billy. Just go on and give it to him.

In the evening on the road to Boquilla they encountered a bunch of vaqueros looseherding perhaps a thousand head of raw corriente steers upcountry toward the Naco pens at the border. They'd been trailing the herd three days from the Quemada deep at the southern end of La Babícora and they were dirty and outlandishlooking and the cattle wild and spooky. They passed bawling in a sea of dust and the ghostcolored horses trod among them sullen and red-eyed with their heads lowered. A few of the riders raised a hand in greeting. The young güeros had pulled to a piece of high ground and swung down and they stood with the horse and watched the slow pale chaos drift west with the sun leaving the ground behind them smoking gently and the last cries of the riders and the last moans of the cattle drifting away into the deep blue silence of the evening. They mounted up and rode on again. At dark they passed through a hamlet on that high plain where the houses were of logs with woodshingle roofs. Smoke and the smell of cooking drifted on the cold air. They rode through the bands of yellow light that fell over the road from the lamplit windows and on into the dark and the cold again. In the morning on that same road they encountered wet and sleek coming up from the high-country laguna south of the road the horses Bailey and Tom and Niño.

They'd clambered up into the road with half a dozen other horses all of them still dripping water and they trotted and tossed their heads in the cool of the morning. Two riders came into the road behind them and hazed them up out of their cropping at the roadside grass and drove them on.

Billy neckreined the horse to the side of the road and swung his leg over the pommel of the saddle and slid down and handed the reins up to Boyd. The bunched horses advanced curiously, their ears up. Their father's horse tossed its head and let out a long whicker.

Aint this somethin? said Billy. Aint this somethin?

He watched the riders. Young boys themselves. Perhaps his age. They were wet to the knees and the horses they rode were wet. They'd seen the riders and seen them rein to the side and they came on more cautiously. Billy pulled the shotgun from the scabbard and unbreeched it to see that it was loaded and breeched it shut again with a quick upward jerk. The advancing horses stopped in the road.

Shake out a loop, he said. Dont let that Niño by.

He stepped out into the road with the shotgun in the crook of his arm. Boyd boosted himself over the cantle and pulled the lasso tie and paid out the rope in his hands. The other horses had stopped but Niño came on along the edge of the road, his head up, testing the air.

Whoa Niño, Billy said. Whoa boy.

The two riders coming along behind stopped. They sat their horses uncertainly. Billy had crossed the road to head Niño and Niño tossed his head and came back into the road.

Qué pasa? called the vaqueros.

Drop a loop on that son of a bitch or take the shotgun one, Billy said.

Boyd brought the loop up. Niño had already sized up the space between the man afoot and the man horseback and he bolted forward. When he saw the rope come up he tried to check but he lost footing on the packed clay of the roadway and Boyd swung the loop once and dropped it over his head and dallied the rope to the saddlehorn. Bird turned and planted himself in the road and squatted on his haunches but the Niño horse stopped when the rope hit him and stood and whinnied and looked back at the riders and the horses behind.

Qué están haciendo? the riders called. They were sitting their horses where they'd first stopped. The other horses had turned and taken to grazing by the roadside again.

Pull a piece of that small rope and build me a hackamore, Billy said.

You aim to ride him?

Yes.

I can ride him.

I'll ride him. Make it longer. Longer.

Boyd looped and tied the hackamore and cut the rope with his claspknife and pitched the hackamore to Billy. Billy caught it and walked Niño down along the length of the catchrope talking softly to him. The two riders put their horses forward.

He slipped the hackamore over Niño's head and loosed the catchrope. He talked to the horse and patted it and then pulled the catchrope off over the horse's head and let it fall to the ground and led the horse over to where Boyd sat the other horse. The loop of rope went scurrying over the dirt. The riders stopped again. Qué pasa? they called.

Billy pitched the shotgun up to Boyd and then jumped and pulled himself up over the horse's back with both hands and swung a leg over and reached for the shotgun again. Niño stamped in the road and tossed his head.

Dab your twine on old Bailey yonder, Billy said.

Boyd looked out down the road at the two riders. He put the horse forward.

No moleste a esos caballos, the riders called.

Billy reined Niño to the side of the road. Boyd advanced upon the horses where they stood leisurely cropping the roadside grass and threw his loop. The throw anticipated the Bailey horse and as he raised his head to move away he raised it into the loop. Billy sat his father's horse watching. I could do that, he told the horse. In about nine tries.

Quiénes son ustedes? the riders called.

Billy rode forward. Somos proprietarios de estos caballos, he called.

The vaqueros sat their horses. Behind them a truck had appeared in the road coming from Boquilla. It was too far off to hear but they must have seen the gaze of the other two riders shift for they turned and looked behind them. No one moved. The truck came on slowly in a thin and augmenting gearwhine. The dust from the wheels drifted slowly out over the country. Billy turned his horse out of the road and sat with the shotgun upright on his thigh. The truck came on. It labored past. The driver looked at the horses and at the boy sitting with the shotgun. In the bed of the truck were eight or ten workers all huddled like conscriptees and as the truck passed they sat looking out back down the road through the dust and motorsmoke at the horses and riders with no expression at all.

Billy nudged Niño forward. But when he looked for the vaqueros there was only one of them in the road. The other one was already riding back south across the campo. He crossed to the standing horses and cut the Tom horse out of the bunch and hazed the rest of the horses up out of the road and turned and looked at Boyd. Let's go, he said.

They advanced upon the lone rider with the loose horse trotting before them and Boyd trailing the Bailey horse behind by the catchrope. The young vaquero watched them come. Then he turned his horse off the road and out onto the grass swales and there he sat watching them pass. Billy looked off across the campo for the other rider but he had dropped from sight behind a rise. He slowed his horse and called out to the vaquero.

Adónde se fué su compadre?

The young vaquero did not answer.

He put the horse forward again, the shotgun upright against his shoulder. He looked back at the horses grazing by the roadside and he looked again at the vaquero and then he fell in alongside Boyd and they rode on. A quarter mile on when he looked back the vaquero was in the road riding slowly behind them. A little way more he stopped and sat the horse quarterwise in the road with the shotgun on his knee. The vaquero stopped also. When they rode on again he rode as well.

Well we're in it now.

We were in it when we left home, Boyd said.

The other old boy's gone for help.

I know it.

Old Niño aint been rode much, has he.

Not much.

He looked at Boyd. Dirty and ragged with his hat forward against the sun and his face enshadowed. He looked some new breed of child horseman left in the wake of war or plague or famine in that country.

At noon with the low walls of the hacienda at Boquilla shimmering in the distance five riders appeared in the road before them. Four of them had rifles which they carried across the bow of their saddles or held loosely in one hand. They curbed their horses sharply and the animals stamped and sidled in the road and the riders called loudly back and forth although they were none at any distance from another.

The two brothers checked their horses. The Tom horse went trotting forward with its ears up. Billy turned and looked back. There were three more riders in the road behind them. He looked at Boyd. The dog walked over to the edge of the road and sat down. Boyd leaned and spat and looked south across the unfenced grasslands, the shape of the lake in the distance palely blown where it mirrored the cloudcover overhead. Five or six lean duncolored steers had raised their heads to stare at the horses in the road. He looked back at the riders behind and he looked at Billy.

You want to make a run for it?

No.

We got the fresher horses.

You dont know what kind of horses they got. Bird couldnt keep up with Niño anyways.

He studied the advancing horsemen. He handed the shotgun across to Boyd. Put this up, he said. Find the papers.

Boyd reached back and began to unwrap the thong from the rosette on the saddlebag pocket.

Dont set there with that thing, said Billy. Put it up.

He sheathed the shotgun in the scabbard. You got a lot more confidence in papers than what I got, he said.

Billy didnt answer. He was watching the riders advance along the road all five abreast now with their rifles upright save one. The Tom horse stood at the side of the road and neighed at the approaching horses. One of the riders scabbarded his rifle and took down his rope. The Tom horse watched him approach and then turned and started out of the road but the rider spurred forward and swung his loop and dropped it over the horse's neck. The horse stopped and stood just off the road and the rider let the coil of rope fall in the road and all came on.

Boyd handed Billy the brown envelope with Niño's papers and Billy sat holding them and holding the hackamore rope loosely in his other hand. The insides of his legs were wet from the horse and he could smell him and the horse stamped and nodded and whinnied at the approaching riders.

They halted a few feet out. The older man among them looked them over and nodded. Bueno, he said. Bueno. He was one-armed and his right shirtsleeve was pressed and pinned to his shoulder. He rode his horse with the reins tied and he wore a pistol at his belt and a plain flatcrowned hat of a type no longer much seen in that country and he wore tooled boots to his knees and carried a quirt. He looked at Boyd and he looked again at Billy and at the envelope he was holding.

Déme sus papeles, he said.

Dont give him them papers, Boyd said.

How else is he goin to see em?

Los papeles, said the man.

Billy nudged the horse forward and leaned and handed the

envelope over and then backed the horse and sat. The man put the envelope in his teeth and undid the tieclasp and then took out the papers and unfolded them and examined the seals and held them to the light. He looked through the papers and then refolded them and took the envelope from his armpit and put the papers back in the envelope and handed the envelope to the rider on his right.

Billy asked him if he could read the papers for they were in english but the man didnt answer. He leaned slightly to better see the horse that Boyd was riding. He said that the papers were of no value. He said that in consideration of their youth he would not bring charges against them. He said that if they wished to pursue the matter further they could see Señor Lopez at Babícora. Then he turned and spoke to the man on his right and this man put the envelope inside his shirt and he and another man rode forward with their rifles upright in their left hands. Boyd looked at Billy.

Turn the horse loose, Billy said.

Boyd sat holding the rope.

Do like I told you, Billy said.

Boyd leaned and slacked the noose of the catchrope under Bailey's jaw and pulled the rope off over the animal's head. The horse turned and crossed through the roadside ditch and set off at a trot. Billy stepped down from Niño and pulled the hackamore off and slapped the animal across the rump with it and it turned and set out after the other horse. By now the riders behind them had come up and they set off after the horses without being told. The jefe smiled. He touched his hat at them and picked up the reins and turned his horse sharply in the road. Vámanos, he said. Then he and the four mounted riflemen set off back down the road toward Boquilla from whence they'd come. Out on the plain the young vaqueros had headed the loose horses and were driving them back into the road west again as they had first intended and soon all were lost to sight in the noon heatshimmer and there was only the silence left. Billy stood in the road and leaned and spat.

Say what's on your mind, he said.

I aint got nothin to say.

Well.

You ready?

Yeah.

Boyd shucked his boot backward out of the stirrup and Billy put his foot in and swung up behind him.

Bunch of damned ignorance if you ask me, Boyd said.

I thought you didnt have nothin to say.

Boyd didnt answer. The mute dog had gone to hide in the roadside weeds and now it reappeared and stood waiting. Boyd sat the horse.

Now what are you waitin on? said Billy.

Waitin on you to tell me which way you want to go.

Well what the hell way do you think we're goin?

We're supposed to be in Santa Ana de Babícora in three days' time.

Well we might just be late.

What about the papers?

What the hell good are the papers without the horse? Anyway you just got done seein what papers are worth in this country.

One of them boys that left out of here with the horses had a rifle in a boot.

I seen it. I aint blind.

Boyd turned the horse and they set out back west along the road. The dog fell in and trotted at the horse's offside in the horse's shadow.

You want to quit? Billy said.

I never said nothin about quittin.

It aint like home down here.

I never said it was.

You dont want to use common sense. We come too far down here to go back dead.

Boyd pressed the horse's flanks with the heels of his boots and the horse stepped out more smartly. You think there is a place that far? he said.

They picked up the tracks of the two riders and the three horses where they'd returned to the road and an hour later they were back at the place above the lake where they'd first seen the horses. Boyd rode slowly along the side of the road studying the ground underfoot until he saw where horses shod and shoeless had left the road and set out north across the high rolling grasslands.

Where do you reckon they're headed? he said.

I dont know, said Billy. I dont know where they come from for that matter.

They rode north all afternoon. From a rise just at twilight they saw the riders looseherding the horses now some dozen in number before them five miles away on the blue and cooling prairie.

You reckon that's them? Boyd said.

Pret near got to be, said Billy.

They rode on. They rode into the dark and when it was too dark to see they halted the horse and sat listening. There was no sound save the wind in the grass. The evening star sat low in the west round and red like a shrunken sun. Billy slid to the ground and took the bridlereins from his brother and led the horse.

It's dark as the inside of a cow.

I know it. It's all overcast.

That's a damned favorable way to get snakebit.

I got boots on. The horse dont.

They crested out on a knoll and Boyd stood in the stirrups.

Can you see em? said Billy.

No.

What do you see?

I dont see nothin. There aint nothin to see. It's just dark on dark and then more of it.

Maybe they aint had time to build a fire yet.

Maybe they aim to drive all night.

They moved on along the crest of the rise.

Yonder they are, said Boyd.

I see em.

They crossed down the far side into a low swale and looked for some sheltered place out of the wind. Boyd got down and stood in the grassy bajada and Billy handed him the reins.

Find somethin to tie him to. Dont hobble him and dont try to stake him. He'll wind up in their remuda.

He pulled down the saddle and blankets and saddlebag.

You want to build a fire? said Boyd.

What would you build it with?

Boyd walked off into the night with the horse. After a while he came back.

There aint nothin to tie him to that I can find.

Let me have him.

He looped the catchrope and slid it over the horse's head and dallied the other end to the saddlehorn.

I'll sleep with the saddle for a pillow, he said. He'll wake me if he gets farthern forty foot.

I never seen it no darker, said Boyd.

I know it. I think it's fixin to rain.

In the morning when they walked out along the crest of the rise and looked off to the north there was no fire nor smoke of fire. The weather had moved on and the day was clear and still. There was nothing at all out there on the rolling grasslands.

This is some country, said Billy.

You reckon they've done skeedaddled?

We'll find em.

They rode out and began to cut for sign a mile to the north. They found the cold dead fire and Billy squatted and blew into the ashes and spat into the coals but there was no faintest hiss to them.

They never built a fire this mornin.

You reckon they seen us?

No.

No tellin how early they might of left out of here.

I know it.

What if they're laid up somewheres fixin to drygulch us?

Drygulch us?

Yeah.

Where'd you hear that at?

I dont know.

They aint laid up noplace. They just got a early start is all.

They mounted up and rode on. They could see the trace of the horses where they'd gone through the grass.

We need to be careful and not top one of these rises and just come up on em, Boyd said.

I thought about that.

We could lose their track.

We wont lose it.

What if the ground turns off hard and rocky? You thought about that?

What if the world ends, said Billy. You thought about that?

Yeah. I thought about it.

Midmorning they saw the riders entrained along a ridge two miles to the east driving the horses before them. An hour later they came into a road running east and west and they sat the horse in the road and studied the ground. In the dust were the tracks of a large remuda of horses and they looked out down the road to the east the way the remuda had gone. They turned east along the road and by noon they could see before them the sometime haze of dust drifting off the low places in the road where the horses had gone. An hour later and they came to a crossroads. Or they came to a place where a gullied rut ran down out of the mountains from the north and crossed and continued on over the rolling country to the south. Sitting in the road astride a good american saddlehorse was a small dark man of indeterminate age in a John B Stetson hat and a pair of expensive latigo boots with steeply undershot heels. He'd pushed the hat back on his head and he was quietly smoking a cigarette and watching them approach along the road.

Billy slowed the horse, he studied the terrain about for other horses, other riders. He halted the horse at a small distance and thumbed back his own hat. Buenos días, he said.

The man studied them briefly with his black eyes. His hands were folded loosely over the pommel of his saddle before him and the cigarette burned loosely between his fingers. He shifted slightly in the saddle and looked off down the rutted track behind him where the faint dust of the driven remuda yet hung lightly in the air like a haze of summer pollen.

What are your plans? he said.

Sir? said Billy.

What are your plans. Tell me your plans.

He raised the cigarette and drew slowly upon it and blew the smoke slowly before him. He seemed not to be in a hurry about anything.

Who are you? said Billy.

My name is Quijada. I work for Mr Simmons. I am superintendent of the Nahuerichic.

He sat his horse. He drew slowly on the cigarette again.

Tell him we're huntin our horses, Boyd said.

I'll be the judge of what to tell him, Billy said.

What horses? the man said.

Horses stole off our ranch in New Mexico.

He studied them. He jutted his chin at Boyd. Is that your brother?

Yes.

He nodded. He smoked. He dropped the cigarette in the road. The horse looked at it.

You understand this is a serious matter, he said.

It is to us.

He nodded again. Follow me, he said.

He reined the horse about and set off up the road. He did not look back to see if they would follow but they did follow. Nor did they presume to ride beside him.

By midafternoon they were full in the dust of the driven horses. They could hear them on the road ahead although they could not see them. Quijada reined his horse off the road and out through the pine trees and reentered the road ahead of the remuda. The caporal was riding point and when he saw Quijada he raised one hand and the vaqueros rode forward and headed the herd and the caporal came up and he and Quijada sat their horses and talked. The caporal looked back at the two boys doubled on the bony horse. He called to the vaqueros. The horses in the road were bunching and milling nervously and one of the riders had gone back down the line hazing horses out of the trees. When the horses had all come to rest and stood contained in the road Quijada turned to Billy.

Which are your horses? he said.

Billy turned in the saddle and looked over the remuda. Some thirty horses standing or shifting sullenly from foot to foot in the road, lifting and ducking their heads in the golden dust where it shimmered in the sun.

The big bay, he said. And that lightcolored bay with him. The one with the blaze. And that speckled horse at the back. The tigre.

Cut them out, said Quijada.

Yessir, Billy said. He turned to Boyd. Get down.

Let me do it, said Boyd.

Get down.

Let him do it, said Quijada.

Billy looked at Quijada. The caporal had turned his horse and the two men sat side by side. He swung his leg over the fork of the saddle and slid to the ground and stepped back. Boyd boosted himself into the saddle and took down the rope and began to build a loop, putting the horse forward with his knees and riding back along the edge of the remuda. The vaqueros sat smoking, watching him. He rode slowly and he did not look at the horses. He rode with the loop hanging down the near side of the horse and then he swung it low along the roadside balk of pines and brought up a hoolihan backhanded over the heads of the now stirring horses and dropped the loop over Niño's neck and raised his arm aloft to carry the slack rope off of the backs of the interim horses all in one gesture and dallied and began to cluck to the roped horse and talk him gently out of the bunch. The vaqueros watched, they smoked.

Niño came forward. The Bailey horse followed, the two of them shouldering their way haltingly and wide of eye out through the strange horses. Boyd brought them close in behind him and continued on along the edge of the road. He undallied and fashioned a jimsaw loop from the home end of the rope and when he reached the rear of the bunch he dropped the loop over the head of the Tom horse without even looking at it. Then he led the three horses back up along the edge of the road past the remuda and stopped with the horses pressed up against Bird and against each other, raising and ducking their heads.

Quijada turned and spoke to the caporal and the caporal nodded. Then he turned and looked at Billy.

Take your horses, he said.

Billy reached and took the bridlereins from his brother and stood in the road holding the horses. I need you to write me a paper, he said.

What kind of paper.

A quitclaim or a conducta or a factura. Some kind of a voucher with your name on it till I can get these horses off of this range.

Quijada nodded. He turned and unfastened the flap on his saddlebag and rummaged through his possibles and came up with a small black leather notebook. He opened it and took a pencil from the binding and sat writing.

What is your name? he said.

Billy Parham.

He wrote. When he was done he tore the page from the notebook and put the pencil back in the binding and closed the book and handed the paper down to Billy. Billy took it and folded it without reading it and took off his hat and put the folded paper inside the sweatband and put the hat back on again.

Thank you, he said. I appreciate it.

Quijada nodded again and spoke again to the caporal. The caporal called to the vaqueros. Boyd leaned down and took the reins and walked the horse out into the dusty roadside pines and turned and sat the horse and he and the horses watched while the vaqueros hazed the remuda into motion again. They passed.

The horses bunched and sorted and rolled their eyes and the vaquero riding drag looked at Boyd sitting his horse with the horses among the trees and he raised one hand and made a small tossing motion with his jaw. Adiós, caballero, he said. Then he fell in behind the remuda and they all passed on up the road into the mountains.

IN THE EVENING they watered the horses at an abrevadero masoned up out of hewn limestone. The vanes of the mill turned slowly above them and the long and skewed shadow of the vanes lay turning out on the high prairie in a slow dark carousel. They'd saddled Niño to ride and Billy dismounted and loosed the cinch to let him blow and Boyd slid down from the Bailey horse he'd been riding and they drank from the pipe and then squatted and watched the horses drink.

You like to watch horses drink, Billy said.

Yeah.

He nodded. I do too.

What would you say that paper's worth?

On this spread I'd say it's worth gold.

And not much off of it.

No. Not much off of it.

Boyd pulled a grass stem and put it in his teeth.

Why do you reckon he let us have the horses?

Cause he knowed they was ours.

How did he know it?

He just knew it.

He could of kept em anyways.

Yeah. He could of.

Boyd spat and put the grass stem back in his teeth. He watched the horses. That was more blind luck, he said. Us runnin up on the horses.

I know it.

How much more luck you reckon we got comin?

You mean like findin the other two horses?

Yeah. That. Or anything.

I dont know.

I dont either.

You think the girl will be there like she said?

Yeah. She'll be there.

Yeah, Billy said. I guess she will be.

Doves coming in across the drylands to the south veered and flared away from the tank when they saw them sitting there. The water from the pipe ran with a cold metallic sound. The western sun descending under the banked clouds had sucked away the golden light and left the land all blue and cool and silent.

You think they've got the other horses, dont you? Boyd said.

Who.

You know who. Them riders that come out of Boquilla.

I dont know.

But that's what you think.

Yeah. That's what I think.

He took the paper Quijada had given him from the sweatband of his hat and unfolded it and read it and refolded it and put it back in his hat and put his hat on. You dont like it, do you? he said.

Who would like it?

I dont know. Hell.

What do you think the old man would of done?

You know what he'd of done.

Boyd took the stem from his teeth and threaded it through the buttonhole on the pocket of his ragged shirt and looped and tied it.

Yeah. He aint here to say though, is he?

I dont know. Someways I think he'll always have a say.

NOON THE FOLLOWING DAY they rode into Boquilla y Anexas looseherding the horses before them. Boyd stayed with the

horses while Billy went into the tienda and bought forty feet of
half inch grass rope to make hackamores out of. The woman at
the counter was measuring cloth off of a bolt. She held the cloth
to her chin and measured down the length of her arm and she
cut the cloth with a straightedge and a knife and folded it and
pushed it across the counter to a young girl. The young girl
doled out coppers and ancient tlacos and pesos and crumpled
bills and the woman counted the sum and thanked her and the
girl left with the cloth folded under her arm. When she'd left
the woman went to the window and watched her. She said that
the cloth was for the girl's father. Billy said it would make a
pretty shirt but the woman said that it was not to make a shirt
but to line his coffinbox with. Billy looked out the window. The
woman said that the girl's family was not rich. That she had
learned these extravagances working for the wife of the hacendado and had spent the money she was saving for her boda.
The girl was crossing the dusty street with the cloth under her
arm. At the corner were three men and they looked away when
she approached and two of them looked after her when she
passed.

THEY SAT in the shade of a whitewashed mud wall and ate
tacos off of greasy brown papers that they'd bought from a
streetvendor. The dog watched. Billy balled the empty paper
and wiped his hands on his jeans and got his knife out and
measured a length of rope between his outstretched arms.

Are we goin to set here? said Boyd.

Yeah. Why? You got a appointment somewheres?

Why dont we go over yonder and set in the alameda?

All right.

How come do you reckon they never branded the horses?

I dont know. They probably been traded all over the country.

Maybe we ought to brand em.

What the hell you goin to brand em with?

I dont know.

Billy cut the rope and laid the knife by and looped the bosal. Boyd put the last corner of the taco in his mouth and sat chewing.

What do you reckon is in these tacos? he said.

Cats.

Cats?

Sure. You see how the dog was lookin at you?

They aint done it, said Boyd.

You see any cats in the street?

It's too hot for cats in the street.

You see any in the shade?

There could be some laid up in the shade somewheres.

How many cats have you seen anywheres?

You wouldnt eat a cat, Boyd said. Even to get to watch me eat one.

I might.

No you wouldnt.

I would if I was hungry enough.

You aint that hungry.

I was pretty hungry. Wasnt you?

Yeah. I aint now. We aint eat no cats have we?

No.

Would you know it if we had?

Yeah. You would too. I thought you wanted to go over in the alameda.

I'm waitin on you.

Lizards now, Billy said. You caint tell them from chicken hardly.

Shit, said Boyd.

They hazed the horses across the street and under the shade of the painted trees and Billy tied hackamores with trailing rope ends for the horses to walk on if they took a mind to quit them and Boyd lay in the parched and ratty grass with the dog for a pillow and his hat over his eyes and slept. The street was empty all through the afternoon. Billy put the hackamores on the horses and tied them and walked over and stretched out in the grass and after a while he was asleep too.

Toward evening a solitary rider on a horse somewhat above his station stopped in the street opposite the alameda and looked them over where they slept and looked their horses over. He leaned and spat. Then he turned and rode back the way he'd come.

When Billy woke he raised up and looked at Boyd. Boyd had turned on his side and had his arm around the dog. He reached and picked his brother's hat up out of the dust. The dog opened one eye and looked at him. Coming up the street were five riders.

Boyd, he said.

Boyd sat up and felt for his hat.

Yonder they come, said Billy. He rose and stepped into the street and cinched up the latigo on Bird and undid the reins and stepped up into the saddle. Boyd pulled on his hat and walked out to where the horses were standing. He untied Niño and walked him past one of the little ironslatted benches and stood onto the bench and forked one leg over the animal's bare back all in one motion without even stopping the horse and turned and rode past the trees and out to the street. The riders came on. Billy looked at Boyd. Boyd was sitting his horse leaning slightly forward with his hands palm down on the horse's withers. He leaned and spat and wiped his mouth with the back of his wrist.

They approached slowly. They didnt even look at the horses standing under the trees. Save for the one-armed rider they were all of them young men and they did not appear to be carrying guns.

Yonder's our buddy, said Billy.

The jefe.

I dont believe he's all that much of a jefe.

Why is that?

He wouldnt be here. He'd of sent somebody. You recognize any of them others?

No. Why?

I just wondered how big of a outfit it is that we're dealin with here.

The same man in the same tooled boots and the same flat hat turned his horse slightly sideways before them as if he might be going to ride past. Then he turned the horse back. Then he halted the horse in front of them and nodded. Bueno, he said.

Quiero mis papeles, Billy said.

The young men behind looked at each other. The manco studied the two boys. He asked them if they might perhaps be crazy. Billy didnt answer. He took the paper from his pocket and unfolded it. He said that he had a factura for the horses.

Factura de donde? said the manco.

De la Babícora.

The man turned his head and spat into the dust of the street without taking his eyes off Billy. La Babícora, he said.

Sí.

Firmado por quién?

Firmado por el señor Quijada.

He sat without expression. Quijada no es alguacil, he said.

Es gerente, said Billy.

The manco shrugged. He dropped the loop of the reins over the saddlehorn and held out his one hand. Permítame, he said.

Billy folded the paper and put it in his shirtpocket. He said that they had come for the other two horses. The man shrugged again. He said that he could not help them. He said that he could not help the young Americans.

We dont need your help, Billy said.

Cómo?

But Billy had already reined his horse to the right and put the horse forward into the middle of the street. Stay there, Boyd, he said. The jefe turned to the rider on his right. He told him to take the horses in charge. Te los encargo, he said.

No toque esos caballos, said Billy.

Cómo? said the jefe. Cómo?

Boyd rode out from under the trees.

Stay there, said Billy. Do like I said.

Two of the riders had advanced upon the tied horses. The third moved to head Boyd's horse but Boyd booted past him and put his horse out into the street.

Stay back, said Billy.

The rider reined his horse about. He looked at the jefe. Niño had begun to roll his eyes and to stamp in the street. The manco had taken the reins of his horse in his teeth and he had reached across and was in the act of unbuttoning the flap on the holster of his sidearm. Niño's rolling eye must have communicated some unwelcome intelligence to the other horses in the street for the jefe's horse also had begun to skitter and to jerk its head. Billy snatched off his hat and booted his horse forward and hazed his hat in front of the eyes of the jefe's horse and the jefe's horse stood bolt upright and squatted and took two steps backward. The jefe grabbed the great flat pommel of his saddle and when he did so the horse stepped again and made a quarter turn and fell backwards in the street. Billy sawed his horse about and the horse stepped in the jefe's hat and turned and sent it skittering. In turning Billy saw Niño stand and saw Boyd standing with his bootheels in the horse's flanks. The jefe's horse was on its knees scrabbling and it struggled and lunged up and set off down the street with the looped reins hanging and the stirrups flapping. The jefe lay in the road. His eyes moved from side to side taking in the rancorous movements of the horses all about him. He looked at his hat crushed in the road.

The pistol lay in the dirt. Of the riders in the jefe's party two were trying to snub down the horses under the trees where they lunged and jerked at their hackamore leads and one had dismounted and was coming to the assistance of the fallen man. The fourth rider turned and looked at the pistol. Boyd slid from his horse and swung the reins down over the horse's head all in one movement and kicked the pistol out into the middle of the street. Niño tried to rear again and snatched him half off the ground but he pulled the horse down and stepped in front of the mounted rider and cut him off where he had already turned and he ran two fingers up the nostrils of the man's horse which set it to backing and fighting its head. Then he trotted Niño out into the street behind him and bent and picked up the pistol and jammed it into his belt and grabbed a handful of mane and swung himself up and pulled the horse around.

Billy was standing in the street. One of the other vaqueros had also dismounted and now two of them were kneeling in the dust trying to get the jefe to sit up. But the jefe couldnt sit. They raised him up but he sloughed bonelessly to one side and fell over into their arms. They must have thought him only addled because they kept talking to him and patting his cheeks. Out in the street a collection of onlookers had begun to assemble. The other two riders stepped down and dropped their reins and came running.

There aint no use in that, Billy said.

One of the vaqueros turned and looked at him. Cómo? he said.

Es inútil, said Billy. Se quebró el espinazo.

Mande?

His back's broke.

THEY LEFT THE ROAD a mile north of the town and traveled west till they came to the river. Boyd had hazed the other horses off while the riders were kneeling in the street and they now had all the horses with them. It was almost dark. They sat on a gravel bar and watched the horses standing in the water against the cooling sky. The dog walked into the water and drank and raised its head and looked back at them.

You got any ideas now? Boyd said.

No. I aint.

They sat looking at the horses, nine in number.

They probably got some old boy can track a lizard across a rockslide.

Probably.

What are we goin to do with their horses?

I dont know.

Boyd spat.

Maybe if they get their own horses back they'll leave us be.

Bullshit.

They aint goin to wait till in the mornin.

I know it.

You know what they'll do to us?

I got a pretty good notion.

Boyd threw a stone into the water. The dog turned and looked at the place where it had gone.

We caint looseherd these horses across this country in the dark, he said.

I dont intend to.

Well why dont you tell us what you do intend.

Billy rose and stood looking at the drinking horses. I think we ought to cut out their horses and drive em out to that rise yonder and chouse em back towards Boquilla. They'll get there sooner or later.

All right.

Let me have the pistol.

What do you aim to do with it?

Put it in the man's mochila it belongs to.

You think he's dead?

If he aint he will be.

Then what difference does it make?

Billy looked at the horses in the river. He looked down at Boyd. Well, he said, if it dont make no difference then just let me have it.

Boyd pulled the pistol out of his belt and handed it up. Billy stuck it in his own belt and waded out into the river and mounted Bird and cut the five Boquilla horses out and hazed them up from the river.

Dont let our horses foller, he said.

They aint goin to foller.

Dont entertain no company while I'm gone.

Go on.

Dont build no fires nor nothin.

Go on. I aint a idjit.

He rode out and disappeared over the rise. The sun was down and the long cool evening of the high country had set in. The other three horses came up out of the river one by one and began to graze in the good grass along the bank. It was dark by the time Billy got back. He rode directly in off the plain to their camp.

Boyd stood. You must of give him his head, he said.

I did. Are you ready.

Just waitin on you.

Well let's go.

They sorted out the horses and drove them across the river and set out upcountry. The plains about them blue and devoid of life. The thin horned moon lay on its back in the west like a grail and the bright shape of Venus hung directly above it like a star falling into a boat. They kept to the open country clear of the river and they rode all night and toward the morning they made a dry camp in a quemada of burned trees clustered dead and black and ragged on a slight rise a mile west of the river. They dismounted and looked for some sign of water but there was none.

There's got to of been water here at one time, Billy said.

Maybe the fire dried it up.

A spring or a seep. Somethin.

There aint no grass. There aint nothin.

It's a old burn. Years old.

What do you want to do?

Let's just tough it out. It'll be daylight directly.

All right.

Get your soogan. I'll watch for a while.

I wish I had a soogan.

Outlaws travel light.

They staked the horses and Billy sat with the shotgun in the dark ruin of trees about. The moon long down. No wind.

What was he goin to do with Niño's papers and no horse? Boyd said.

I dont know. Find a horse to fit them. Go to sleep.

Papers aint worth a damn noways.

I know it.

I'm a hungry son of a bitch.

When did you take to cussin so much?

When I quit eatin.

Drink some water.

I did.

Go to sleep.

It was already growing light in the east. Billy stood and listened.

What do you hear? said Boyd.

Nothin.

This is a spooky kind of place.

I know it. Go to sleep.

He sat and cradled the shotgun in his lap. He could hear the horses cropping grass out on the prairie.

You asleep? he said.

No.

I got the papers back.

Niño's papers?

Yeah.

Bullshit.

No, I did.

Where'd you get em from.

They were in the mochila. When I went to put his pistol back they were in the mochila.

I'll be damned.

He sat holding the shotgun and listening to the horses and to the silence of the world beyond. After a while Boyd said: Did you put the pistol back?

No.

How come?

I just didnt.

Have you got it?

Yeah. Go to sleep.

When it was light he rose and walked out to see what sort of country it was that they were in. The dog rose and followed. He walked out to the top of the rise and squatted and leaned on the shotgun. A mile away on the plain a band of palecolored rangecattle were grazing toward the north. Otherwise nothing. When he got back to the trees he stood looking down at his sleeping brother.

Boyd, he said.

Yeah.

Are you ready to ride?

His brother sat up and looked out at the country. Yeah, he said.

We could head back north to the hacienda. The old lady would hide us out.

Till what?

I dont know.

We're supposed to meet her tomorrow.

I know it. It caint be helped.

How long would it take to ride to the hacienda?

I dont know. Let's go.

They set out north and rode till they came in view of the river. There were cattle grazing along the edge of the trees at the river breaks. They sat the horses and looked back across the rolling high prairie to the south.

Could you kill a cow with a shotgun? said Boyd.

Get close enough. Yeah.

What about with a pistol?

You'd have to get close enough to where you could hit it.

How close would you have to get?

We aint shootin no cow. Come on.

We got to eat somethin.

I know it. Come on.

When they reached the river they crossed through the shallows and looked for a road on the other side but there was no road. They followed the river north and in the early afternoon they rode into the pueblito of San José, a clutch of low and graylooking mud hovels. As they passed along the rutted track with their string of horses a few women peered warily from out of the low doorways.

What do you think's wrong here? said Boyd.

I dont know.

Maybe they think we're gypsies.

Maybe they think we're horsethieves.

A goat watched them from a low roof with its agate eyes.

Ay cabrón, said Billy.

This is a hell of a place, said Boyd.

They found a woman to feed them and they sat on a mat of woven rushes on the clay floor and ate cold atole out of home-made bowls of unfired clay. When they wiped the bottoms of the bowls their tortillas came up gritty and stained with mud. They tried to pay the woman but she would take no money. Billy offered again for the niños but she said there were no niños.

They camped that night in a grove of cottonwoods by the river and staked out the horses in the river grass and they stripped off and swam in the river in the dark. The water was cold and silky. The dog sat on the bank and watched them. In the morning Billy rose before daybreak and walked out and unstaked Niño and led him back to camp and saddled him and mounted up with the shotgun.

Where you goin? said Boyd.

See if I can rustle us up somethin to eat.

All right.

Just stay here. I wont be gone long.

Where would I go?

I dont know.

What am I supposed to do if somebody comes?

There wont nobody come.

What if they do?

Billy looked at him. He was crouched with his blanket around his shoulders and he was so thin and ragged. He looked at him and he looked out past the pale boles of the cottonwoods and over the rolling desert grassland emerging in the gray dawn light.

I guess what it is is you want me to leave you the pistol.

I think it might be a good idea.

Do you know how to shoot it?

Yes, damn it.

It's got two safeties.

I know it.

All right.

He took the pistol out of the bag and handed it down to him.

There's one in the chamber.

All right.

Dont shoot it. That and what's in the clip is all the shells we got for it.

I aint goin to shoot it.

All right.

How long will you be gone?

I wont be gone long.

All right.

He rode off downriver with the shotgun across the bow of the saddle. He'd taken the buckshot shell from the chamber and rummaged through the shells in the bag and come up with a couple of number five shot and loaded the gun with one of them and buttoned the other into the pocket of his shirt. He rode slowly and he watched the river through the trees as he rode. A mile down he saw ducks on the water. He dismounted and dropped the reins and took the shotgun and began to stalk them through the shore willows. He took off his hat and laid it on the ground. The horse whinnied behind him and he looked back and swore at it under his breath and then raised up and looked out down the river. The ducks were still there. Three dark scaup motionless on the pewter calm of the tailwater. The mist rising off the river like smoke. He made his way carefully through the willows, crouching as he went. The horse nickered again. The ducks flew.

He stood up and looked back. Damn you, he said. But the horse was not looking at him. It was looking across the river. He turned and there he saw five men riding.

He dropped to his hands and knees. They were coming upriver singlefile through the trees on the far side. They had not seen him. The ducks wheeled overhead in the new sunlight and swung away downriver. The riders looked up, they rode on. Niño stood in plain sight among the willows but they did not see him and he did not whinny again and they passed on and disappeared upriver among the trees.

He rose and grabbed up his hat and jammed it on his head and walked carefully back out to where the horse stood that he not spook it and he caught the reins and mounted up and swung the horse around and put it into a lope.

He cut away from the river and made a swing out over the prairie. The upper branches of the cottonwoods were already in sunlight. He fished about in the mochila behind him as he rode trying to find the buckshot shell. He did not see the riders anywhere across the river and when he saw his own horses grazing at their stakeropes among the trees he turned toward the camp.

Boyd knew what was happening without he said a word and set off to get the horses. Billy swung down and grabbed their blankets and rolled and tied them. Boyd came up the river afoot at a run hazing the horses before him.

Get the ropes off of em, Billy called. We're goin to have to make a run for it.

Boyd turned. He put up one hand as if to reach for the first of the horses as they came up out of the trees and then his shirt belled out behind him redly and he fell down on the ground.

Billy knew afterward that he had seen the actual riflebullet. That the suck and whiff at his ear had been the bullet passing and that he had seen it for one frozen moment before his eyes with the sun on the side of the small revolving core of metal, the lead wiped bright by the rifling of the bore, slowed from having passed through his brother's body but still moving faster than sound and passing his left ear with the suck of the air like a whisper from the void and the small jar of the shockwave and then the bullet caroming off of a treebranch and singing away over the desert behind him that by a hairsbreadth had not carried his life away with it and then the sound of the shot come lagging after.

It rang out across the river lean and flat and echoed back from the desert. He was already running among the frantic and careening horses and he knelt and turned his brother over where he lay in the bloodstained dirt. Oh God, he said. Oh God.

He lifted his head out of the dust. His ragged shirt wet with blood. Boyd, he said. Boyd.

It hurts, Billy.

I know it.

It hurts.

The rifle cracked again from across the river. All of the horses had run out of the trees save Niño who stood stamping at the dropped reins. He turned toward the sound and raised one hand. No tire, he called. No tire. Nos rendimos. Nos rendimos aquí.

The rifle cracked again. He laid Boyd down and ran for the horse and caught the trailing reins just as the animal turned to quit the place. He hauled the horse around and trotted with it to where his brother lay and he stood on the reins while he picked his brother up and then he turned and pushed him up into the saddle and threw the reins over the horse's head and grabbed the pommel and swung up behind him and seized him around the waist where he sat tottering and leaned and dug his heels into Niño's belly.

Three more shots rang out as they came out of the trees and into the open country but by now he had put the horse into a gallop. His brother lolled against him all loose and bloody and he thought that he had died. He could see the other horses running on the plain before them. One of them had dropped back and appeared to be injured. The dog was nowhere in sight.

The horse he overtook was Bailey and he had been shot just above the rear hock and when they passed him he stopped altogether. When Billy looked back he was just standing there. As if the heart had gone out of him.

He overtook the other two horses in the length of perhaps a mile and they fell in behind. When he looked back he could see all five horsemen on the plain coming hard after him in a thin line of dust, some of them whipping over and under, all carrying their rifles held out at their side, all of it clear and stark in the new morning sun. When he looked ahead he saw nothing but grass and the sporadic palmilla that dotted the plain stretching away to the blue sierras. There was nowhere to run and nowhere to stand. He whacked Niño with the heels of his boots. Bird and the Tom horse were already beginning to fall back and he turned and called to them. When he looked ahead again he saw in the distance a small dark form crossing the landscape left to right in a trail of dust and he knew that there was a road there.

He leaned forward clutching his brother to him and he talked to Niño and dug in with his heels under the horse's flanks and they went pounding over the empty plain with the stirrups flapping and kicking out. When he looked back Bird and the Tom horse were still with him and he knew that Niño was tiring under the double riders he carried. He thought that the horsemen behind had dropped back some and then he saw that one of them had stopped and he saw the white puff of smoke from the rifle and heard the thin dead crack of it lost in the open space but that was all. Ahead the carrier on the road had vanished in the distance and left only a pale hovering of dust to mark its passage.

The road was raw dirt and as there was neither selvedge nor bar ditch to mark it he was in it before he knew it. He reined up skidding and hauled the gasping horse around. Bird was coming hard behind him and he tried to head him but then when he looked to the south he saw laboring towards him out of the emptiness an ancient flatbed truck carrying farmworkers. He forgot Bird and turned and put the horse south along the road toward the truck waving his hat.

The truck had no brakes and when the driver saw him he began to grind slowly down through the gears. The workers crowded forward along the bed looking down at the wounded boy.

Tómelo, he called to them. Tómelo. The horse stamped and rolled its eyes and a man reached and took the reins and half-hitched them about one of the stakes in the truckbed and other hands reached for the boy and some clambered down into the road to help lift him up. Blood was a condition of their lives and none asked what had befallen him or why. They called him el güerito and passed him up into the truck and wiped the blood from their hands on the front of their shirts. A lookout was standing with one hand on top of the cab watching the riders out on the plain.

Pronto, he called, pronto.

Vámonos, Billy shouted to the driver. He leaned and pulled the reins loose and hammered the truckdoor with the side of his fist. The men in the truck reached down their hands to help aboard those in the road and the driver put the truck in gear and they lurched forward. One of the men held out a blood-stained hand and Billy clasped it. They'd made a place for Boyd on the rough boards of the truckbed with shirts and serapes. He couldnt tell if he was alive or dead. The man gripped his hand. No te preocupes, he shouted.

Gracias, hombre. Es mi hermano.

Vámonos, the man shouted. The truck labored forward up the road in a low whine of gears. Out on the prairie the riders were already dividing, two of them cutting away to the north to follow the truck. The workers waved and whistled at him where he sat the horse in the road and they gestured with their hands in great circles over their heads to motion to him to go on. He'd already boosted himself forward into the saddle and found the stirrups and the blood was soaking cold through his trousers. He booted Niño forward. Bird was a mile ahead on the prairie. When he looked back the riders were less than a hundred yards out and he leaned along Niño's neck and called upon him to give his life.

He rode Bird down on the prairie but when he overtook him he had in his eye much the same look as the Bailey horse and he knew that he had lost him. He looked back at the riders and he called one last time to his old horse to give him heart and then he rode on. He heard again that distant flat report that a rifle makes over open ground and when he looked back one of the riders had dismounted and was kneeling beside his horse firing. He leaned low in the saddle and rode on. When he looked back again the two riders had diminished on the plain and when he looked one final time they were smaller yet and Bird was nowhere in sight. He never did see the Tom horse again.

Midmorning alone in that country he led the drenched and bottomed horse afoot up a cobbled arroyo. He talked to the horse and kept to the rocks and where the horse put a foot in the sand of the arroyo floor he dropped the reins and went back and repaired the mark with a whisk of grass. His trouserlegs were stiff with dried blood and he knew that both he and the horse were going to have to find water very soon.

He left the horse standing with the latigo loosed and climbed up and lay in the arroyo breaks and studied the country to the east and to the south. He saw nothing. He climbed back down and picked up the reins of the standing horse and took hold of the pommel of the saddle and he looked at the dark shape of the blood in the leather and he stood for a moment with the reins doubled in his fist and his forearm across the wet salt withers of his father's horse. Why couldnt the sons of bitches have shot me? he said.

In the blue dusk of that day he saw a light far to the north that first he took for the polestar. He watched to see if it would lift off of the horizon but it did not and he turned slightly in his course and leading the exhausted horse afoot set out across the desert prairie toward it. The horse faltered behind him and he dropped back and took hold of the bridle cheekstrap and walked beside the horse and talked to it. The horse so crusted with white salt rime it shone like some prodigy embarked upon the darkening plain. When he'd said all he knew to say he told it stories. He told it stories in spanish that his grandmother had told him as a child and when he'd told all of those that he could remember he sang to it.

The last thin paring of the old moon hung over the distant mountains to the west. Venus had moved away. With dark a gauzy swarm of stars. He could not guess what they were for, so many. He trekked on for another hour and then halted and felt the horse to see that it was dry and swung up into the saddle and rode on. When he looked for the light it was gone and he fixed his position by the stars and after a while the light appeared again out of the dark cape of desert headland that had obscured it. He'd quit singing and he tried to think how to pray. Finally he just prayed to Boyd. Dont be dead, he prayed. You're all I got.

IT WAS NEAR MIDNIGHT when they struck the fence and he turned east and rode till he came to a gate. He dismounted and led the horse through and closed the gate again and remounted and rode up the pale clay track toward the light where dogs had already risen and come forward howling.

The woman who came to the door was not young. She lived in this remote station with her husband who she said had given his eyes for the revolution. She shouted back the dogs and they slank away and when she stood aside for him to pass this husband was standing in the small lowceilinged room as if he'd risen to greet some dignitary. Quién es? he said.

She said that it was an American who had lost his way and the man nodded. He turned away and the weathercreased face caught for a moment the light from the oil lamp. There were no eyes in his sockets and the lids were pinched shut so that he wore a constant look of painful selfabsorption. As if old errors preoccupied him.

They sat at a pine table painted green and the woman brought him milk in a cup. He'd about forgotten that people even drank milk. She struck a match to the circular wick of the burner in the kerosene stove and adjusted the flame and put on a kettle and when it had boiled she spooned eggs one by one down into the kettle and put the lid back again. The blind man sat stiff and erect. As if he himself were the guest in his own house. When the eggs had boiled the woman brought them steaming in a bowl and sat down to watch the boy eat. He picked one up and put it down quickly. She smiled.

Le gustan los blanquillos? said the blind man.

Sí. Claro.

They sat. The eggs steamed in the bowl. In the unshaded light of the coaloil lamp their faces hung like masks.

Dígame, said the blind man. Qué novedades tiene?

He told them that he was in the country seeking to recover horses stolen from his family. He said that he was traveling with his brother but that he had become separated from him. The blind man inclined his head to hear. He asked for news of the revolution but the boy had no news to give. Then the blind man said that although the countryside was tranquil this was not necessarily a good sign. The boy looked at the woman. The woman nodded her head solemnly in agreement. She seemed to set great store by her husband. He took an egg from the bowl and cracked it on the rim and began to peel it. While he was eating the woman began to tell of their life.

She said that the blind man had been born of humble origins. Orígenes humildes, she said. She said that he had lost his eyes in the year of our Lord nineteen thirteen in the city of Durango. He'd ridden east in late winter of that year and joined Maclovio Herrera and on the third of February they had fought at Nami-quipa and taken the town. In April he had fought at Durango with the rebels under Contreras and Pereyra. In the federal arsenal was an antique demiculverin of french manufacture which he was placed in charge of. They did not take the city. He could have saved himself, the woman said. But he would not leave his post. He was taken prisoner along with many others. The prisoners were given the opportunity to swear oaths of loyalty to the government and those who would not do so were stood against a wall and shot without ceremony. Among them were men of many nations. American and English and German. And men from lands no one had even heard of. Yet they went also to the wall and there they died in the terrible volleys of riflefire, the terrible smoke. They fell down soundlessly beside each other, their hearts' blood on the plasterwork behind them. He saw this.

Among the defenders of Durango there were of course few foreigners yet there was one such. A German Huertista named Wirtz who was a captain in the federal army. The captured rebels stood in the street chained together with fencewire like toys and this man walked their enfilade and bent to study each in turn and note in their eyes the workings of death as the assassinations continued behind him. The man spoke spanish well for all that he spoke it with a german accent and he told the artillero that only the most pathetic of fools would die for a cause that was both wrong and doomed and the captive spat in his face. The German then did something very strange. He smiled and licked the man's spittle from about his mouth. He was a very large man with enormous hands and he reached and seized the young captive's head in both these hands and bent as if to kiss him. But it was no kiss. He seized him by the face and it may well have looked to others that he bent to kiss him on each cheek perhaps in the military manner of the French but what he did instead with a great caving of his cheeks was to suck each in turn the man's eyes from his head and spit them out again and leave them dangling by their cords wet and strange and wobbling on his cheeks.

And so he stood. His pain was great but his agony at the disassembled world he now beheld which could never be put right again was greater. Nor could he bring himself to touch the

eyes. He cried out in his despair and waved his hands about
before him. He could not see the face of his enemy. The archi-
tect of his darkness, the thief of his light. He could see the
trampled dust of the street beneath him. A crazed jumble of
men's boots. He could see his own mouth. When the prisoners
were turned and marched away his friends steadied him by the
arm and led him along while the ground swang wildly underfoot. No one had ever seen such a thing. They spoke in awe.
The red holes in his skull glowed like lamps. As if there were a
deeper fire there that the demon had sucked forth.

They tried to put his eyes back into their sockets with a spoon
but none could manage it and the eyes dried on his cheeks like
grapes and the world grew dim and colorless and then it vanished forever.

Billy looked at the blind man. He sat erect and impassive.
The woman waited. Then she continued.

Some said of course that this man Wirtz had saved his life for
had he not been blinded he'd have surely gone to the wall. Some
others said that would have been the better course. None asked
the blind man for his views. He sat in the cold stone cárcel while
the light did fade about him till at last he sat in darkness. The
eyes dried and wrinkled and the cords they hung by dried and
the world vanished and he slept at last and dreamt of the country
through which he'd ridden in his campaigns in the mountains
and the brightly colored birds thereof and the wildflowers and
he dreamt of young girls barefoot by the roadside in the mountain towns whose own eyes were pools of promise deep and dark
as the world itself and over all the taut blue sky of Mexico where
the future of man stood at dress rehearsal daily and the figure
of death in his paper skull and suit of painted bones strode up
and back before the footlights in high declamation.

Hace veintiocho años, the woman said. Y mucho ha cambi-
ado. Y a pesar de eso todo es lo mismo.

The boy reached and took the last egg from the bowl and
cracked it and began to peel it. As he did so the blind man
spoke. He said that on the contrary nothing had changed and

all was different. The world was new each day for God so made it daily. Yet it contained within it all the evils as before, no more, no less.

The boy bit into the egg. He looked at the woman. She seemed to be waiting for the blind man to say more and when he did not she continued as before.

The rebels returned and took Durango on June the eighteenth and he was led from the cárcel and he stood in the street while the sounds of gunfire echoed from the outskirts where the routed federal soldiers were being hunted down and shot. He stood and he listened for any voice he might know.

Quién es usted, ciego? they said. He told his name but none knew him. Someone cut and gave to him a greenwood stave and with this as his sole possession he set out alone afoot on the road to Parral.

He told the time of day by turning his face to the sightless sun like a worshipper. By the sounds of the countryside. The coolness of the night, the damp. By the calls of birds and by the first warmth of the rumored light upon his skin. People brought him water and food from the houses he passed and provisioned him for the road ahead. Dogs that came bristling into the road to challenge him slank away again. He was surprised at the authority which his blindness conferred upon him. He seemed to want for nothing.

There had been rain in the country and wildflowers bloomed by the roadside. He made his way slowly, tracking the ruts with his greenwood stick. He'd no boots for they'd long been stolen and those first days he walked barefoot and his heart was filled with despair. More than filled. Despair was in him like a lodger. Like a parasite that had turned out his very being from its abode and taken up the shape of that space within him where it once had been. He could feel it lodged against his throat. He could not eat. He sipped water from a cup proffered anonymously out of the world's dark and handed the cup away into that dark again. His liberation from the cárcel meant little to him and there were days his freedom seemed to him no more than just

some further curse and in this condition he tapped his way
slowly north along the road to Parral.

In the cool dark of his first night alone in the country it had
rained and he stopped and listened and he could hear the rain
coming across the desert. Borne on the wind the smell of wet
creosote bush. He lifted his face and stood by the roadside and
his thoughts were that other than wind and rain nothing would
ever come again to touch him out of that estrangement that was
the world. Not in love, not in enmity. The bonds that fixed him
in the world had become rigid. Where he moved the world
moved also and he could never approach it and he could never
escape it. He sat in the roadside weeds in the rain and wept.

On the morning of his third day abroad he entered the town
of Juan Ceballos and there he stood in the road with his cane
aloft and turned, listening, squinting his terrible squint. But
the dogs had already crept away and a woman spoke to him at
his right side and asked that she might take his hand and he
gave it.

Y adónde va? she said.

He said he did not know. He said that he was going where
the road went. The wind. The will of God.

La voluntad de Dios, she said. As if choosing.

She took him to her house. He sat at a rough board table and
she gave him a pozole with fruit to eat but he could not eat it
for all that she urged him. She asked him to tell her from whence
he'd come but he was ashamed of his condition and he would
not say how his calamity had befallen him. She asked him had
he always been blind and he weighed this question and after a
while he said that yes he had.

When he left he wore on his feet a pair of old patched huaraches and he carried over his shoulder a thin serape. In the pocket
of his ragged breeches a few copper coins. Men talking in the
street fell silent at his approach and spoke again when he had
passed. As if it might be that he were some deputy of darkness
sent to spy among them. As if words carried away by a blind
man might thereby come to have a life unreckoned with and be

met with elsewhere in the world bearing a meaning never intended by those who'd uttered them. He turned in the road and
held his cane aloft. Ustedes no saben nada de mí, he shouted.
They fell silent and he turned and went on and after a while he
could hear them talking again.

That night he heard the sounds of battle far distant on the
plain and he stood in the dark and listened. He tested the wind
for the smell of cordite and listened for sounds of men and horses
but all he could hear was the faint rattle of riflefire and the
periodic heavy dull report of a howitzer firing cannister shot
and after a while nothing.

The next morning early his cane clattered before him on the
boards of a bridge. He stopped. He reached and tapped forward.
He stepped carefully onto the boards and stood and listened.
He could hear much muted beneath him the sound of water
running.

He made his way down along the small river bank and pushed
through the rushes till he came to the water. He reached out
and touched it with his cane. He slashed at the water and then
he stopped. He raised his head to listen.

Quién está? he called.

No one answered back.

He laid aside his serape and stripped out of his rags and took
up his cane again and thin and naked and filthy he waded into
the river.

He waded out wondering if the water might perhaps be deep
enough to bear him away. He imagined that in his estate of
eternal night he might somehow have already halved the distance to death. That the transition for him could not be so great
for the world was already at some certain distance and if it were
not death's terrain he encroached upon in his darkness then
whose?

The water came but to his knees. He stood in the river, he
steadied himself with his staff. Then he sat. The water was
cool, it moved slowly about him. He lowered his face to take
its odor, to taste it. He sat for a long time. In the distance he

heard a bell that tolled slowly three times and ceased. He got to his knees and then leaned forward and lay facedown in the water. He placed the staff yokewise across his neck and held it in his two hands. He held his breath. He gripped his staff and he held it for a long time. When he could hold it no longer he breathed out and then tried to breathe the water in but he could not and the next thing he was kneeling in the river gasping and coughing. He'd let go his cane and it had drifted away and he rose and floundered about coughing and sucking in air and flailing at the river surface with the flat of his hand. To the man standing on the bridge he must have seemed deranged. Must have seemed to be attempting to calm the river, or something in the river. Until he saw those barren eyecups.

A la izquierda, he called.

The blind man stopped. He crouched with his arms crossed before him.

A su izquierda, called the man.

The blind man patted the water to his left.

A tres metros, called the man. Pronto. Se va.

He lurched forward. He groped about. The man on the bridge called out coordinates and finally his hand closed upon his staff and he sat down in the river for modesty and clutched the cane to him.

Qué hace, ciego? the man called.

Nada. No me molesta.

Yo? Le molesto? Ciego, ciego.

He said that he had thought the blind man was drowning and was on the point of coming to his rescue when he saw him raise up sputtering.

The blind man sat with his back turned to the bridge and the road. He could smell tobacco smoke and after a while he asked the man if he could have a cigarette.

Por supuesto.

He rose and waded ashore. Dónde está mi ropa? he called.

The man directed him to his clothes. When he had dressed he made his way up to the road and he and the man sat on the bridge smoking. The sun felt good on his back. The man said that there was not enough water in the river to drown oneself and the blind man nodded. He said that in any case there was not enough privacy.

The blind man said that there was a church nearby, no? His friend told him that there was no church. That there was nothing at all anywhere in sight. The blind man said that he had heard a bell and the man said that he had had an uncle who was blind and he too often heard things which were not.

The blind man shrugged. He said he was only newly blinded. The man asked him why he thought the sound of bells must be from a church but the blind man only shrugged again and smoked. He asked what other sound a church would make.

The man asked him why he wished to die but the blind man said that it was not important. The man asked if it was because he could not see and he said that it was a reason among reasons. They smoked. Finally the blind man told him about his conjecture that the blind had already partly quit the world anyway. He said that he had become but a voice to speak in a darkness incommensurable with the motives of life. He said that the world and all in it had become to him but a rumor. A suspicion. He shrugged. He said that he did not wish to be blind. That he had outlived his estate.

The man heard him out, they sat in silence. The blind man heard the faint hiss of the other's cigarette in the water beneath him. Finally the man said that it was a sin to lose heart and anyway the world remained as it had always been. That much was undeniable. When the blind man did not answer he told the blind man to touch him but the blind man was loath to do so.

Con permiso, the man said. He took the blind man's hand and placed his fingers on his lips. There the blind man's fingers lay. In the gesture of one adjuring another to silence.

Toca, the man said. The blind man would not. He took the blind man's hand again and he moved it upon his face. Toca, he said. Si el mundo es ilusión la pérdida del mundo es ilusión también.

The blind man sat with his hand to the man's face. Then he began to move it. A face of no determinate age. Dark or fair. He touched the narrow nose. The coarse straight hair. He touched the balls of the man's eyes beneath the thin closed lids. No sound in the high desert morning save their breathing. He felt the eyeballs move under his fingers. Small quick movements like the movements in a tiny womb. He drew his hand away. He said that he could tell nothing. Es una cara, he said. Pues qué?

The other man sat in silence. As if contemplating how to answer. He asked the blind man could he weep. The blind man said that any man could weep but what the man wished to know was could the blind weep tears from the places where their eyes had been, how could they do this? He did not know. He took a last draw from the cigarette and let it fall into the river. He said again that the world in which he made his way was very different from what men suppose and in fact was scarcely world at all. He said that to close one's eyes told nothing. Any more than sleeping told of death. He said that it was not a matter of illusion or no illusion. He spoke of the broad dryland barrial and the river and the road and the mountains beyond and the blue sky over them as entertainments to keep the world at bay, the true and ageless world. He said that the light of the world was in men's eyes only for the world itself moved in eternal darkness and darkness was its true nature and true condition and that in this darkness it turned with perfect cohesion in all its parts but that there was naught there to see. He said that the world was sentient to its core and secret and black beyond men's imagining and that its nature did not reside in what could be seen or not seen. He said that he could stare down the sun and what use was that?

These words seemed to silence his friend. They sat side by side on the bridge. The sun shone upon them. Finally the man asked him how he had come by such views and he answered that they were things he'd long suspected and that the blind have much to contemplate.

They rose to go. The blind man asked his friend which way he was going. The man hesitated. He asked the blind man which way he. The blind man pointed with his stave.

Al norte, he said.

Al sur, said the other.

He nodded. He offered his hand into the darkness and they said their farewell.

Hay luz en el mundo, ciego, the man said. Como antes, así ahora. But the blind man only turned away and set out as before on the road to Parral.

Here the woman broke off her narrative and looked at the boy. The boy's eyelids were heavy. His head jerked.

Está despierto, el joven? said the blind man.

The boy sat upright.

Sí, the woman said. Está despierto.

Hay luz?

Sí. Hay luz.

The blind man sat erect and formal. His hands outspread palm down on the table before him. As if to steady the world, or himself in it. Continuá, he said.

Bueno, the woman said. Como en todos los cuentos hay tres viajeros con quienes nos encontramos en el camino. Ya nos hemos encontrado la mujer y el hombre. She looked at the boy. Puede acertar quién es el tercero?

Un niño?

Un niño. Exactamente.

Pero es verídica, esta historia?

The blind man broke in to say that indeed the tale was a true one. He said that they had no desire to entertain him nor yet even to instruct him. He said that it was their whole bent only to tell what was true and that otherwise they had no purpose at all.

Billy asked how it could be that on the long road to Parral he

should meet only three people but the blind man said that he
did meet other people on that road and that he received from
them many kindnesses but that the three strangers at issue were
those with whom he spoke of his blindness and that they must
therefore be the principals in a cuento whose hero was a blind
man, whose subject was sight. Verdad?

Es héroe, este ciego?

For a while the blind man forbore to answer. Finally he said
that it was best to wait and see. That it was best to judge for
oneself. Then he gestured with one hand to the woman and she
continued as before.

He'd made his way north along the road as told until in
nine days' time he reached the town of Rodeo on the Río Oro.
Everywhere he attracted gifts. Women came out to him. They
stopped him in the road. They pressed upon him their own
possessions and they offered to attend him some part of the way
along the road. Walking at his elbow they described to him the
village and the fields and the condition of the crops and they
named to him the names of the persons who lived in the houses
they passed and confided to him details of their domestic arrangements or spoke of the illnesses of the old. They told him
of the sorrows in their lives. The death of friends, the incon-
stancy of lovers. They spoke of the faithlessness of husbands in
a way that was a trouble to him and they clutched his arm and
hissed the names of whores. None swore him to secrecy, none
asked his name. The world unfolded to him in a way it had not
before in his life.

On the twenty-sixth of June of that year a company of Huer-
tistas had passed through the town of Rodeo on their way east
to Torreón. They arrived late in the night many of them drunk
and all of them afoot and they bivouacked in the alameda and
burned the benches for firewood and in the gray dawn rounded
up those they said were rebel sympathizers and stood them
against the mud wall of the granja and gave them cigarettes to
smoke and then shot them dead while their children watched
and their wives and mothers wailed and tore out their hair.

When the blind man arrived the following day he fell unwittingly into a funeral enfiled along the gray mud street and before he could properly judge the events occurring about him a young girl had taken his hand and he was led out to the dusty cemetery at the outskirts of the town. There amid the poor wooden crosses and the crockery jars and cheap glass dishes that stood for offertory the first of the three cratewood coffins imperfectly blacked with coaloil and chimneysoot was placed upon the ground while the attending trumpeter played a melancholy martial air and an elder of the village spoke in lieu of priest for there was none. The girl clutched his hand, she leaned to him.

Era mi hermano, she whispered.

Lo siento, said the blind man.

They lifted the dead man from the box and lowered him into the arms of two men who had scrambled down into the grave. There they laid him out on the raw dirt and composed his arms again upon his chest where they had fallen free and they laid a cloth across his face. Then these rude provisional sextons reached up and took the hands of their waiting friends and were helped up from the grave and the men shoveled each a spadeful of dirt down upon the dead man in his poor clothes, the gray caliche rattling dully and the women sobbing, and shouldered up the empty box and the lid to carry back to the village for the conveying of yet another body. The blind man could hear new people arriving in the little cemetery and soon he was led away a short distance through the shouldering crowd to stand again and hear yet another simple country oration.

Quién es? he hissed.

The girl clutched his hand. Otro hermano, she whispered.

As they stood for the third burial the blind man leaned and asked how many of her family were to be buried but she said that this was the last.

Otro hermano?

Mi padre.

The clods rattled, the women wailed anew. The blind man put on his hat.

Returning they passed in the road another cortege bound out for the cemetery and the blind man heard yet other weeping and other feet shuffling along under the dire weight of the dead they bore. No one spoke. When they had passed the girl led him forth into the road again and they went on as before.

He asked the girl if there were any left alive of her household but she said there were none save only she for her mother was dead years since.

It had rained in the night past and rained in the dead fire left by the assassins and the blind man could smell the wet ashes. They passed the clay granja where the wall that had been dark with blood was all washed clean again by women of the town as if no blood had ever been there. The girl told him of the executions and named each man who died and told who he was and how he stood and how he fell. The women were held back until the last man was shot and then the captain had stood aside and they rushed forward to try to hold the men in their arms as they died.

Y tú? said the blind man.

She'd gone first to her father but he was already dead. Then to each of her brothers in turn, the elder first. But they also were dead. She walked among the women where they squatted on the ground and held the dead bodies to themselves and rocked and wept. The soldiers went away. A dogfight broke out in the street. After a while some men came with carretas. She walked about carrying her father's hat. She didnt know what to do with it.

She was still holding the hat in her lap at midnight sitting in the church when the sepulturero stopped to speak to her. He told her that she should go home but she said that her father and her brothers were dead in her house on their mats and a candle burned in the floor and that she had nowhere to sleep. She said that all her house was taken up with the dead and so she had come to the church. The sepulturero listened. Then he sat beside her on the raw wood bench. The hour was late, the church empty. They sat side by side holding their hats, she the sombrero of woven straw, he the dusty black fedora. She was crying. He sighed and seemed himself weary and cast down. He said that while one would like to say that God will punish those who do such things and that people often speak in just this way it was his experience that God could not be spoken for and that men with wicked histories often enjoyed lives of comfort and that they died in peace and were buried with honor. He said that it was a mistake to expect too much of justice in this world. He said that the notion that evil is seldom rewarded was greatly overspoken for if there were no advantage to it then men would shun it and how could virtue then be attached to its repudiation? It was the nature of his profession that his experience with death should be greater than for most and he said that while it was true that time heals bereavement it does so only at the cost of the slow extinction of those loved ones from the heart's memory which is the sole place of their abode then or now. Faces fade, voices dim. Seize them back, whispered the sepulturero. Speak with them. Call their names. Do this and do not let sorrow die for it is the sweetening of every gift.

The girl respoke these words to the blind man where they stood before the granja wall. She said that the young girls had come and dipped their pañuelos in the blood of the slain where it pooled in the dirt or torn off strips from the hems of their pettiskirts. There was a great coming and going in this commerce as of some band of witless nurses wrenched from all memory of their right function. The blood soon soaked into the earth and with fall of dark before the rain began packs of dogs arrived and gouged up mouthfuls of the bloodsoaked mud and ate it down and snapped and quarreled and slank away again and in the day once more there was no sign remaining of death and blood and murder.

They stood in silence and then the blind man touched the girl, her face and cheek and lips. He did not ask to do so. She stood very still. He touched her eyes each in turn. She asked if he had been a soldier and he said that he had been and she asked if he had killed many men and he said none. She asked that he lean down so that she could close her eyes and touch his own face to see what could be known in that way and he did so. He did not say that it would not be the same for her. When she came to the eyes she hesitated.

Ándale, he said. Está bien.

She touched the wrinkled lids caved into the sockets. She touched them gently with the tips of her fingers and she asked if there were any pain there but he said there was only the pain of memory and that sometimes in the night he would dream that this darkness were itself a dream and he would wake and he would touch those eyes that were not there. He said such dreams were a torment to him and yet he would not wish them away. He said that as the memory of the world must fade so must it fade in his dreams until soon or late he feared that he would have darkness absolute and no shadow of the world that was. He said that he feared what that darkness held for he believed that the world hid more than it revealed.

In the street people were shuffling past. Persínese, the girl whispered. The blind man would not turn loose her hand but leaned his staff against his waist and blessed himself clumsily with his left hand. The cortege passed. The girl gripped his hand anew and they went on.

Among her father's clothes she found him coat and shirt and trousers. She put what few other clothes were in the house into a muslin sack and tied it shut and she took the kitchen knife and molcajete and some spoons together with what food there was and tied them up in an old Saltillo serape. The house was cool and smelled of the earth. Outside among the cloistered walls and warrens he could hear yardfowl, a goat, a child. She brought water in a bucket for him to wash himself and he did so with a rag and then put on the clothes. He stood in the one small room that was the house entire and waited for her to return. The door stood open to the road and people going past in the street on their way to the cemetery could see him standing there. When she came back she took his hand again and she said that he was guapo in his new clothes and she gave him an apple of those she had bought and they stood in the room eating the apples and then shouldered up the bundles and set out together.

The woman leaned back. The boy thought that she would continue but she did not. They sat in silence.

Era la muchacha, he said.

Sí.

He looked at the blind man. The blind man sat with his drawn face half enshadowed in the light of the oil lamp. He must have sensed the boy studying him. Es una carantoña, no? he said.

No, Billy said. Y además, no me dijo que los aspectos de las cosas son engañosas?

Because the blind man's face lacked all expression one could not tell when he would speak or if he would at all. After a while he raised one hand from the table in that odd gesture of blessing or despair. Para mí, sí, he said.

Billy looked at the woman. She sat as before, her hands folded upon the table. He asked the blind man had he heard of others who had suffered the same calamity as he at that man's hands but the blind man only said that he had heard, yes, but had not seen nor met. He said that the blind do not seek each other's company. He told how once in the alameda in Chihuahua he had heard a cane come tapping and he'd called out his own condition and asked if another such were there in that mutual darkness. The tapping ceased. No one spoke. Then the tapping commenced again and withdrew down the walkway and faded among the sounds of traffic in the street.

He leaned slightly forward. Entienda que ya existe este ogro. Este chupador de ojos. Él y otros como él. Ellos no han desaparecido del mundo. Y nunca lo haran.

Billy asked him if such men as had stole his eyes were only products of the war but the blind man said that since war itself was their very doing that could hardly be the case. He said that in his opinion no one could speak for the origins of such men nor where they might appear but only of their existence. He said that who steals one's eyes steals a world and himself remains thereby forever hidden. How to speak of his locality?

Y sus sueños, said the boy. Se han hecho más pálidos?

The blind man sat for some time. He could have been sleeping. He could have been waiting for word to be brought to him. Finally he said that in his first years of darkness his dreams had been vivid beyond all expectation and that he had come to thirst for them but that dreams and memories alike had faded one by one until they were no more. Of all that once had been no trace remained. The look of the world. The faces of loved ones. Finally even his own person was lost to him. Whatever he had been he was no more. He said that like every man who comes to the end of something there was nothing to be done but to begin again. No puedo recordar el mundo de luz, he said. Hace muchos años. Ese mundo es un mundo frágil. Ultimamente lo que vine a ver era más durable. Más verdadero.

He spoke of the first years of his blindness in which the world about him awaited his movements. He said that men with eyes may select what they wish to see but for the blind the world appears of its own will. He said that for the blind everything was abruptly at hand, that nothing ever announced its approach. Origins and destinations became but rumors. To move is to abut against the world. Sit quietly and it vanishes. En mis primeros años de la oscuridad pensé que la ceguera fué una forma de la muerte. Estuve equivocado. Al perder la vista es como un sueño de caída. Se piensa que no hay ningún fondo en este abismo. Se cae y cae. La luz retrocede. La memoria de la luz. La memoria del mundo. De su propia cara. De la carantoña.

He raised one hand slowly and held it before him. As if in measure of something. He said that if this falling were a falling to death then it was death itself that was different than men supposed. Where is the world in this falling? Is it also receding away with the light and the memory of the light? Or does it not fall also? He said that in his blindness he had indeed lost himself and all memory of himself yet he had found in the deepest dark of that loss that there also was a ground and there one must begin.

En este viaje el mundo visible es no más que un distraimiento. Para los ciegos y para todos los hombres. Ultimamente sabemos que no podemos ver el buen Dios. Vamos escuchando. Me entiendes, joven? Debemos escuchar.

When he spoke no more the boy asked him if the advice then which the sepulturero had given to the girl in the church had been false advice but the blind man said that the sepulturero had advised according to his lights and should not be faulted. Such men even took it upon themselves to advise the dead. Or to commend them to God once priest and friends and children all have gone to their houses. He said that the sepulturero might presume to speak of a darkness of which he had no knowledge, for had he such knowledge he could not then be a sepulturero. When the boy asked him if this knowledge were a special knowledge only to the blind the blind man said that it was not. He said that most men were in their lives like the carpenter whose work went so slowly for the dullness of his tools that he had not time to sharpen them.

Y las palabras del sepulturero acerca de la justicia? the boy said. Qué opina?

At this the woman reached and took up the bowl of eggshells and said that it was late and that her husband should not tire himself. The boy said that he understood but the blind man said for them not to preoccupy themselves. He said that he had given a certain amount of thought to the question which the boy asked. As had many men before him and as men would after he was gone. He said that even the sepulturero would understand that every tale was a tale of dark and light and would perhaps not have it otherwise. Yet there was still a further order to the narrative and it was a thing of which men do not speak. He said the wicked know that if the ill they do be of sufficient horror men will not speak against it. That men have just enough stomach for small evils and only these will they oppose. He said that true evil has power to sober the smalldoer against his own deeds and in the contemplation of that evil he may even find the path of righteousness which has been foreign to his feet and may have no power but to go upon it. Even this man may be appalled at what is revealed to him and seek some order to stand against it. Yet in all of this there are two things which perhaps he will not know. He will not know that while the order which the righteous seek is never righteousness itself but is only order, the disorder of evil is in fact the thing itself. Nor will he know that while the righteous are hampered at every turn by their ignorance of evil to the evil all is plain, light and dark alike. This man of which we speak will seek to impose order and lineage upon things which rightly have none. He will call upon the world itself to testify as to the truth of what are in fact but his desires. In his final incarnation he may seek to indemnify his words with blood for by now he will have discovered that words pale and lose their savor while pain is always new.

Quizás hay poca de justicia en este mundo, the blind man said. But not for the reasons which the sepulturero supposes. It is rather that the picture of the world is all the world men know and this picture of the world is perilous. That which was given him to help him make his way in the world has power also to blind him to the way where his true path lies. The key to heaven has power to open the gates of hell. The world which he imagines to be the ciborium of all godlike things will come to naught but dust before him. For the world to survive it must be replenished daily. This man will be required to begin again whether he wishes to or no. Somos dolientes en la oscuridad. Todos nosotros. Me entiendes? Los que pueden ver, los que no pueden.

The boy studied the mask in the lamplight. Lo que debemos entender, said the blind man, es que ultimamente todo es polvo. Todo lo que podemos tocar. Todo lo que podemos ver. En esto tenemos la evidencia más profunda de la justicia, de la misericordia. En esto vemos la bendición más grande de Dios.

The woman rose. She said that it was late. The blind man made no move to do so. He sat as before. The boy looked at him. Finally he asked him why this was such a blessing and the blind man did not answer and did not answer and then at last he said that because what can be touched falls into dust there can be no mistaking these things for the real. At best they are only tracings of where the real has been. Perhaps they are not even that. Perhaps they are no more than obstacles to be negotiated in the ultimate sightlessness of the world.

In the morning when he walked out to saddle his horse the woman was scattering grain from a bota to the birds in the yard. Wild blackbirds flew down from the trees and stalked and fed among the poultry but she fed all without discrimination. The boy watched her. He thought she was very beautiful. He saddled the horse and left it standing and said his goodbyes and then mounted up and rode out. When he looked back she raised her hand. The birds were all about her. Vaya con Dios, she called.

He turned the horse into the road. He'd not gone far when the dog came out of the chaparral and fell in beside the horse. He had been in a fight and he was cut and bloody and held one paw to his chest. Billy halted the horse and looked down at him. The dog limped forward a few steps and stood.

Where's Boyd? Billy said.

The dog pricked its ears and looked about.

You dumb-ass.

The dog looked toward the house.

He was in the truck. He aint here.

He put the horse forward and the dog fell in behind and they set out north along the road.

Before noon they struck the main road north to Casas Grandes and he sat in that empty desert crossroads and looked off upcountry and back to the south but there was nothing to be seen save sky and road and desert. The sun stood almost overhead. He slid the shotgun out of the dusty leather scabbard and unbreeched it and took out the shell and looked at the wad end to see what size shot it held. It was number five and he thought about putting in the buckshot load but in the end he put the number five shell back in the chamber and breeched the gun shut and put it back in the scabbard and set out north along the road to San Diego, the dog limping at the horse's heels. Where's Boyd? he said. Where's Boyd?

That night he slept in a field wrapped in the blanket the woman had given him. The breaks of a river lay across the plain perhaps a mile distant and that was the way the horse would have gone. He lay on the cooling earth and watched the stars. The dark shape of the horse off to his left where he'd staked it. The horse raising its head above the skyline to listen among the constellations and then bending to graze again. He studied those worlds sprawled in their pale ignitions upon the nameless night and he tried to speak to God about his brother and after a while he slept. He slept and woke from a troubling dream and could not sleep again.

He'd trudged in his dream through a deep snow along a ridge toward a darkened house and the wolves had followed him as far as the fence. They ran their lean mouths against each other's flanks and they flowed about his knees and furrowed the snow with their noses and tossed their heads and in the cold their pooled breath made a cauldron about him and the snow lay so blue in the moonlight and those eyes were palest topaz where they crouched and whined and tucked their tails and they fawned and shuddered as they drew close to the house and their teeth shone that were so white and their red tongues lolled. At the gate they would go no further. They looked back toward the dark shapes of the mountains. He knelt in the snow and reached out his arms to them and they touched his face with their wild muzzles and drew away again and their breath was warm and it smelled of the earth and the heart of the earth. When the last of them had come forward they stood in a crescent before him and their eyes were like footlights to the ordinate world and then they turned and wheeled away and loped off through the snow and vanished smoking into the winter night. In the house his parents slept and when he crawled into his bed Boyd turned to him and whispered that he'd had a dream and in the dream Billy had run away from home and when he woke from the dream and seen his empty bed he'd thought that it was true.

Go to sleep, Billy said.

You wont run off and leave me will you Billy?

No.

You promise?

Yes. I promise.

No matter what?

Yes. No matter what.

Billy?

Go to sleep.

Billy.

Hush. You'll wake them.

But in the dream Boyd only said softly that they would not wake.

The dawn was long in coming. He rose and walked out on the desert prairie and scanned the east for light. In the gray beginnings of the day the calls of doves from the acacias. A wind coming down from the north. He rolled the blanket and ate the last of the tortillas and the boiled eggs she'd given him and he saddled the horse and rode out as the sun came up out of the ground to the east.

Within the hour it was raining. He untied the blanket from behind him and pulled it over his shoulders. He could see the rain coming across the country in a gray wall and soon it was pounding the flat gray clay of the bajada through which he rode. The horse plodded on. The dog walked beside. They looked like what they were, outcasts in an alien land. Homeless, hunted, weary.

He rode all day the broad barrial between the breaks of the river and the long straight bight of the roadway to the west. The rain slacked but it did not stop. It rained all day. Twice he saw riders ahead on the plain and he halted the horse but the riders rode on. In the evening he crossed the railroad tracks and entered the pueblo of Mata Ortíz.

He halted before the door of a small blue tienda and got down and halfhitched the reins to a post and entered and stood in the partial darkness. A woman's voice spoke to him. He asked her if there was a doctor in this place.

Médico? she said. Médico?

She was sitting in a chair at the end of the counter with what looked like a flywhisk cradled in her arms.

En éste pueblo, he said.

She studied him. As if trying to ascertain the nature of his illness. Or his wounds. She said that there was no doctor nearer than Casas Grandes. Then she half rose out of the chair and began to hiss and make shooing gestures at him with the whisk.

Mam? he said.

She fell back laughing. She shook her head and put her hand to her mouth. No, she said. No. El perro. El perro. Dispénsame. He turned and saw the dog standing in the doorway behind him. The woman rose heavily still laughing and came forward tugging at a pair of old wirerimmed spectacles. She set them on the bridge of her nose and took him by the arm and turned him to the light.

Güero, she said. Busca el herido, no?

Es mi hermano.

They stood in silence. She had not turned loose of his arm. He tried to see into her eyes but the light played off the glass of her spectacles and one of the panes was half opaque with dirt as if perhaps she had no vision in that eye and saw no need to clean it.

El vivía? he said.

She said that he was living when he passed by her door and that people had followed the truck to the end of the town and that he was alive to the limits of Mata Ortíz and beyond that who could say?

He thanked her and turned to go.

Es su perro? she said.

He said that it was his brother's dog. She said that she'd

guessed as much for the dog wore a worried look. She looked out into the street where the horse stood.

Es su caballo, she said.

Sí.

She nodded. Bueno, she said. Monte, caballero. Monte y vaya con Dios.

He thanked her and walked out to the horse and untied it and mounted up. He turned and touched the brim of his hat to the old woman where she stood in the door.

Momento, she called.

He waited. In a moment a young girl came out and eased past the woman and came to the stirrup of his horse and looked up at him. She was very pretty and very shy. She held up one hand, her fist closed.

Qué tiene? he said.

Tómelo.

He held out his hand and she dropped into it a small silver heart. He turned it to the light and looked at it. He asked her what it was.

Un milagro, she said.

Milagro?

Sí. Para el güero. El güero herido.

He turned the heart in his hand and looked down at her.

No era herido en el corazón, he said. But she only looked away and did not answer and he thanked her and dropped the heart into his shirtpocket. Gracias, he said. Muchas gracias.

She stepped back from the horse. Que jovén tan valiente, she said and he agreed that indeed his brother was brave and he touched his hat again and raised his hand to the old woman where she stood in the doorway still clutching the whisk and he put the horse forward down the single mud street of Mata Ortíz north toward San Diego.

It was dark and starless from the overcast of rain when he crossed the bridge and rode up the hill toward the domicilios. The same dogs sallied forth howling and circled the horse and he rode past the dimly lighted doorways and past the remains of the evening fires where the haze of woodsmoke hung over the compound in the damp air. He saw no one run to carry news of his arrival yet when he arrived at the door of the Muñoz house the woman was standing there waiting for him. People were coming out of the houses. He sat the horse and looked down at her.

Él está? he said.

Sí. Él está.

Él vive?

Él vive.

He dismounted and handed the reins to the boy standing nearest in the company gathered about him and took off his hat and entered the low doorway. The woman followed him. Boyd lay on a pallet at the far side of the room. The dog was already curled on the pallet with him. About him on the floor stood gifts of food and gifts of flowers and holy images of wood or clay or cloth and little handmade wooden boxes that held milagros and ollas and baskets and glass bottles and figurines. In the wall niche above him a candle in a glass burned at the feet of the poor wooden Madonna but there was no light other.

Regalos de los obreros, the woman whispered.

Del ejido?

She said that some of the gifts were from the ejido but that mostly they were from the workers who had carried him here. She said the truck had returned and the men had filed in holding their hats and placed these gifts before him.

Billy squatted and looked down at Boyd. He pulled back the blanket and pushed up the shirt he wore. Boyd was wrapped in muslin windings like someone dressed for death and he'd bled through the cloth and the blood was dry and black. He put his hand on his brother's forehead and Boyd opened his eyes.

How you doin, pardner? he said.

I thought they got you, Boyd whispered. I thought you was dead.

I'm right here.

That good Niño horse.

Yeah. That good Niño horse.

He was pale and hot. You know what I am today? he said.

No, what are you?

Fifteen. If I dont make it another day.

Dont you worry about that.

He turned to the woman. Qué dice el médico?

The woman shook her head. There was no doctor. They'd sent for an old woman no more than a bruja and she had bound his wounds with a poultice of herbs and given him a tea to drink.

Y qué dice la bruja? Es grave?

The woman turned away. In the light from the niche he could see the tears on her dark face. She bit her lower lip. She did not answer. Damn you, he whispered.

It was three oclock in the morning when he rode into Casas Grandes. He crossed the high embankment of the railroad track and rode up Alameda Street until he saw a light in a cantina. He dismounted and went in. At a table near the bar a man lay asleep in his crossed arms and otherwise the room was empty.

Hombre, Billy said.

The man jerked upright. The boy before him had every air of those bearing grave news. He sat warily with his hands on the table at either side.

El médico, Billy said. Dónde vive el médico.

THE DOCTOR'S MOZO unlocked and unlatched the door cut into the wooden gate and stood there just inside the darkened zaguán. He did not speak but only waited to hear the supplicant's tale. When Billy was done he nodded. Bueno, he said. Pásale.

He stepped aside and Billy entered and the mozo resecured the door. Espere aquí, he said. Then he went padding away over the cobbles and disappeared in the dark.

He waited a long time. From the rear of the zaguán came the smell of green plants and earth and humus. A rustle of wind. Of things disturbed that had been sleeping. Outside the gate

Niño whinnied softly. Finally a light came on in the patio and the mozo reappeared. Behind him the doctor.

He was not dressed but came forward in his robe, one hand in his robe pocket. A small and unkempt man.

Dónde está su hermano? he said.

En el ejido de San Diego.

Y cuándo ocurrió ese accidente?

Hace dos días.

The doctor studied the boy's face in the pale and yellow light.

He is very hot?

I dont know. Yes. Some.

The doctor nodded. Bueno, he said. He told the mozo to start the car and then turned back to Billy. I will need some minutes, he said. Five minutes.

He held up one hand and spread his fingers.

Yessir.

You have nothing to pay of course.

I got a good horse outside. I'll give you the horse.

I dont want your horse.

I got papers on him. Tengo los papeles.

The doctor had already turned to go. Bring in the horse, he said. You can put the horse here.

Have you got room to where we can take the saddle with us?

The saddle?

I'd like to keep the saddle. My daddy give it to me. I got no way to carry it back.

You can carry it back on the horse.

You wont take the horse?

No. It is all right.

He stood outside in the street holding Niño while the mozo slid back the bars and opened the tall wooden gates. He started through leading the horse but the mozo cautioned him back and told him to wait and then turned and disappeared. After a while he heard the car start up and the mozo came driving up through the zaguán in an old Dodge opera coupe. He drove out into the street and got out and left the motor running and took the bridlereins and led the horse in through the gates and on toward the rear.

In a few minutes the doctor appeared. He was dressed in a dark suit and the mozo followed behind carrying his medical bag.

Listo? the doctor said.

Listo.

The doctor walked around the car and climbed in. The mozo handed in the bag and shut the door. Billy climbed in the other side and the doctor turned on the lights and the motor died.

He sat waiting. The mozo opened the door and reached under the seat and got the crank and walked around in front of the car and the doctor turned the lights off. The mozo bent and fitted the crank into the slot and raised up and gave it a turn and the motor started again. The doctor ran the engine up loudly and turned the lights back on and rolled down the window and took the crank from the mozo. Then he pulled the shiftlever in the floor down into first and they pulled away.

The street was narrow and ill lit and the yellow beams of the headlamps ran out to a wall at the end of it. A family of people were just entering the street, the man walking ahead, behind him a woman and two halfgrown girls carrying baskets and shabbily tied bundles. They froze in the headlights like deer and their postures mimicked the shadows volunteered outsized upon the wall behind them, the man standing upright and erect and the woman and the older girl throwing up one arm as if to protect themselves. The doctor levered the big wooden steering wheel to the left and the headlights swung away and the figures vanished once more into the indenominate dark of the Mexican night.

Tell me of this accident, the doctor said.

My brother got shot in the chest with a rifle.

And when did this happen?

Two days ago.

Does he speak?

Sir?

Does he speak? Is he awake?

Yessir. He's awake. He never did talk much.

Yes, said the doctor. Of course. He lit a cigarette and smoked quietly on the road south. He said that the car had a radio and that Billy could play it if he wished but Billy thought that the doctor would play it himself if he wanted to hear it. After a while the doctor did so. They listened to american hillbilly music coming out of Acuña on the Texas border and the doctor drove and smoked in silence and the hot eyes of cattle feeding in the bar ditches at the side of the road floated up in the carlights and everywhere the desert stretched away in the dark beyond.

They turned up the ejido road through the river loam and the pale shapes of the cottonwood trunks passing in the lights and lumbered over the wooden bridge and up the hill and into the compound. The ejido dogs crossed back and forth in the lights howling. Billy pointed their way and they drove up past the darkened doors of the sleeping communals and halted before the dim yellow light where his brother lay within among his offerings like some feastday icon. The doctor shut off the engine and the lights and reached for the bag but Billy had already taken it to carry. He nodded and stepped out of the car and adjusted his hat and entered the house with Billy behind him.

The Muñoz woman had already come from the other room and she stood in the frail light of the votive candle in the only dress Billy had ever seen her in and wished the doctor a good evening. The doctor handed her his hat and then unbuttoned his coat and slipped it from his shoulders and held it up and turned it and reached his glasses in their case from the inside pocket. Then he handed the coat to the woman and removed his cufflinks left and right and put them in his trouser pocket and turned up his starched white shirtsleeves two turns each and sat on the low pallet and took the glasses from their case and put them on and looked at Boyd. He placed one hand on Boyd's forehead. Cómo estás? he said. Cómo te sientes?

Nunca mejor, wheezed Boyd.

The doctor smiled. He turned to the woman. Hiérvame algo de agua, he said. Then he took from his pocket a small nickel-plated flashlight and leaned over Boyd. Boyd closed his eyes but the doctor pulled down the lower lid of each eye in turn and examined them. He waved the light slowly back and forth across the pupils and looked in. Boyd tried to turn his head away but the doctor had placed his hand alongside his cheek. Véame, he said.

He pulled back the blanket. Something small scurried away over the muslin. Boyd was wearing one of the white cotton jumpers the workers in the field wore and it had neither collar nor buttons. The doctor pushed it up and pulled Boyd's right elbow down from the sleeve and pulled it over his head and then very carefully pulled the garment down off of Boyd's left arm and handed it to Billy without even looking at him. Boyd lay wrapped in cotton sheeting and his wound had bled through the winding and the blood had dried and blackened. The doctor slid the flat of his hand up under the wrappings and placed his hand on Boyd's chest. Respire, he said. Respire profundo. Boyd breathed but his breathing was shallow and labored. The doctor slid his hand to the left side of his chest near to the dark stains in the sheeting and told him to breathe again. He bent and unsnapped the clasps on his bag and took out his stethoscope and hung it around his neck and he took out a pair of spade-ended scissors and cut through the filthy windings and lifted back the severed ends all stiff with blood. He placed his fingers on Boyd's naked chest and tapped his left middle finger with his right and listened. He moved his hand and thumped again. He moved his hand down to Boyd's caved and sallow abdomen and probed gently with his fingers. He watched the boy's face.

Tienes muchos amigos, he said. No?

Cómo? wheezed Boyd.

Tantos regalos.

He lifted the earpieces of the stethoscope into place and put the cone on Boyd's chest and listened. He moved it from the right to the left. Respire profundo, he said. Por la boca. Otra vez. Bueno. He placed the cone over Boyd's heart and listened. He listened with his eyes closed.

Billy, Boyd wheezed.

Shh, said the doctor. He put his fingers to his lips. No habla.

He dropped the earpieces of the stethoscope down about his neck and he lifted by its chain a gold casewatch from his waistcoat pocket and snapped it open with his thumb. He sat with two fingers pressed to the side of Boyd's neck beneath his jaw and he tilted the white porcelained face of the watch toward the votive lamp and sat watching quietly while the needlethin sweepsecond hand sectored the dial with its small black roman numbers.

Cuándo puedo yo hablar? Boyd whispered.

The doctor smiled. Ahora si quieres, he said.

Billy?

Yeah.

You dont have to stay.

I'm all right.

You dont have to stay if you dont want. It's all right.

I aint goin nowheres.

The doctor slid the watch back into his waistcoat. Saca la lengua, he said.

He examined Boyd's tongue and he put his finger inside Boyd's mouth and felt the inner face of his cheek. Then he bent and picked up the bag and set it on the pallet beside him and opened the bag and tilted it slightly toward the light. The bag was of heavy pebbled leather dyed black and it was scuffed and worn at the corners and the leather there and along the edges had gone brown again. The brass catches were worn from eighty years of use for his father had carried it before him. He took out a bloodpressure cuff and wrapped it around Boyd's thin upper arm and pumped the contrivance with the bulb. He placed the cone of the stethoscope in the crook of Boyd's arm and listened. He watched the needle drop and watched it bounce. In

the panes of his antique eyeglasses the thin and upright flame of
the votive lamp stood centered. Very small, very steadfast.
Like the light of holy inquiry burning in his aging eyes. He
unwound the cloth and turned to Billy.

Hay una mesa chica en la casa? O una silla?

Hay una silla.

Bueno. Tráigala. Y tráigame una contenedor de agua. Una
bota o cualquiera cosa que tenga.

Sí señor.

Y traiga un vaso de agua potable.

Yessir.

Él debe tomar agua. Me entiendes?

Yessir.

Y deja abierta la puerta. Necesitamos aire.

Yessir. I will.

He came back carrying the chair upside down over his arm
by the rung and he had a clay olla of water in one hand and
a cup of wellwater in the other. The doctor had risen and he
had donned a white apron and he was holding a towel and a
bar of darklooking soap. Bueno, he said. He folded the soap
in the towel and stuck it beneath his arm and took the chair
from Billy carefully and righted it and set it in the floor and
turned it slightly in the place he wished for it to go. He took
the olla from Billy and set it on the chair and he bent and sorted
through his bag and came up with a bent glass straw and stood
it in the cup Billy was holding. He said for him to give his
brother the water to drink. He said for him to see that he drank
slowly.

Yessir, Billy said.

Bueno, said the doctor. He took the towel from under his
arm and rolled his sleeves up each another turn. He looked
down at Billy.

No te preocupes, he said.

Yessir, said Billy. I'll try.

The doctor nodded and turned and left to go wash his hands.
Billy sat on the pallet and leaned forward and held the cup and

the straw for Boyd to drink. I can pull these covers up, he said. Are you cold? You aint cold are you?

I aint cold.

Here you go.

Boyd drank.

Dont drink too fast, Billy said. He tilted the cup. You looked like one of these dirtfarmers in that rig.

Boyd drank deeply through the straw and then turned away coughing.

Dont drink so fast.

He lay getting his breath. He drank again. Billy took the cup away and waited and then offered it again. The glass pipe rattled and sucked. He tilted the cup. When Boyd had drunk all the water he lay getting his breath and he looked up at Billy. There's worse things to look like, he said.

Billy set the cup on the chair. I didnt take much care of you did I? he said.

Boyd didnt answer.

The doctor says you're goin to be all right.

Boyd lay breathing shallowly, his head back. He stared at the dark vigas of the ceiling overhead.

He says you're goin to be good as new.

I didnt hear him say it, Boyd said.

When the doctor came back Billy picked up the cup and rose and stood holding it. The doctor was drying his hands. Él tenía sed, verdad?

Yessir, Billy said.

The woman came through the door carrying a pail of steaming water. Billy went to her and took the bucket by the bail and the doctor gestured for him to place it on the hearth. He folded the towel and laid it by his bag and laid the soap on top of it and sat. Bueno, he said. Bueno. He turned to Billy. Ayúdame, he said.

Together they turned Boyd on his side. Boyd gasped and clutched about in the air with one hand. He seized Billy's shoulder.

Easy pardner, Billy said. I know it hurts.

No you dont, wheezed Boyd.

Está bien, said the doctor. Está bien así.

He gently pulled away the stained and blackened sheeting from Boyd's chest and lifted it free and handed it up to the woman. He left the black and weedy poultices in place, the one on his chest and the larger one behind his shoulder. He leaned over the boy and pressed the poultices gently each in turn to see if anything should run from beneath them and he tested the air tentatively with his nose for any hint of rot. Bueno, he said. Bueno. He touched gently the area under Boyd's arm between the poultices where the skin was blue and swollenlooking.

La entrada es en el pecho, no?

Sí, said Billy.

He nodded and took up the towel and soap and dipped the towel in the olla of water and soaped it and set about cleaning Boyd's back and chest, washing carefully around the poultices and under his arm. He rinsed the towel in the olla and squeezed it out and bent and wiped away the soap. The towel where he turned it was dark with grime. No estás demasiado frío? he said. Estás cómodo? Bueno. Bueno.

When he was done he laid the towel by and set the olla in the floor and leaned and took from his bag a folded towel which he laid on the chair and opened carefully with just his fingertips. Inside was a second towel cured in the autoclave and done up in a bundle fastened with tape. He gently pried loose and lifted away the tape and holding the edges delicately between thumb and finger he spread the towel open upon the chair seat. Inside were gauze squares and squares of muslin and cottonballs. Small folded towels. Rolls of cloth bandage. He lifted his hands away without touching anything and he took two small enameled pans nested together from his bag and one he laid near the bag and the other he leaned and dipped partly full of hot water from the bucket and then conveyed it carefully in both hands to the chair and set it at the edge of the chair away from the bandages. He selected from their fitted compartments in his case his tools of nickel steel. Sharpnosed scissors and forceps and hemostats some dozen in number. Boyd watched. Billy watched. He dropped the instruments into the pan and he took from the bag a small red bulb syringe and placed that in the pan and he took out a small tin of bismuth and he took out two small sticks of silver nitrate and unwrapped them from out of their foil coverings and laid them on the towel beside the pan. Then he took out a bottle of iodine and loosed the cap and passed the bottle up to the woman and he held his hands over the pan and instructed her to pour the iodine over his hands. She stepped forward and took the cap from the bottle.

Ándale, he said.

She poured.

Más, he said. Un poquito más.

Because the outer door was open the flame in the glass fluttered and twisted and the little light that it afforded waxed and waned and threatened to expire entirely. The three of them bent over the poor pallet where the boy lay looked like ritual assassins. Bastante, the doctor said. Bueno. He held up his dripping hands. They were dyed a rusty brown. The iodine moved in the pan like marbling blood. He nodded to the woman. Ponga el resto en el agua, he said.

She poured the remainder of the iodine into the pan and the doctor tested the water with one finger and then quickly fished a hemostat from the pan and with the hemostat he took up a packet of the muslin squares and dipped them and held them up to drain. He turned to the woman again. Bueno, he said. Quita la cataplasma.

She put one hand to her mouth. She looked at Boyd and she looked at the doctor.

Ándale pues, he said. Está bien.

She blessed herself and bent and reached and took hold of the rag that bound the poultice and lifted it and slid her thumb beneath the poultice and pulled it away. It was of matted weeds and dark with blood and it came away unwillingly. Like something that had been feeding there. She stepped back and folded it from sight in the dirty sheeting. Boyd lay in the flickering light of the votive candle with a small round hole a few inches above and to the left of his left nipple. The wound was dry and crusted and palelooking. The doctor bent and swabbed it carefully with the cotton. The iodine stained Boyd's skin. Blood welled slowly in the hole and a thin line of it ran across Boyd's chest. The doctor laid a clean gauze square over the wound. They watched it slowly darken with blood. The doctor looked up at the woman.

La otra? she said.

Sí. Por favor.

She leaned and freed the poultice from Boyd's back with her thumb and lifted it away. Larger, blacker, uglier. Beneath it was a ragged hole that yawned redly. About it the flesh was crusted with scale and blackened blood. The doctor placed a sheaf of the gauze squares over the wound and placed a square of muslin over them and pressed upon it with the tips of his fingers and held it there. Slowly the cloth darkened. The doctor placed more patches. A thin trickle of blood ran down Boyd's back. The doctor swabbed it up and pressed again with the tips of his fingers against the wound.

When the bleeding had stopped he took a cloth and dipped in the iodine solution in the pan and while he held the packing against the wound in the boy's back he set to cleaning closely about both wounds. He dropped the soiled swabs in the dry tray beside him and when he was done he pushed his glasses up on the bridge of his nose with the back of his wrist and looked at Billy.

Take his hand, he said.

Mande?

Take his hand.

No sé si me va permitir.

Él te permite.

He sat on the edge of the pallet and took hold of Boyd's hand and Boyd clasped it in his grip.

Do your damndest, Boyd whispered.

Qué dice?

Nada, said Billy. Ándale.

The doctor took a sterile cloth and wrapped it around the little flashlight and turned the flashlight on and picked it up and put it in his mouth. Then he dropped the cloth into the pan with the swabs and leaned and took a hemostat from the pan and bent over Boyd and gently lifted away the pads from the exit wound and trained his light upon it. The blood was already beginning to well anew and he placed the hemostat in the wound and snapped it shut.

Boyd bowed and threw his head back but he did not cry out. The doctor took another hemostat from the pan and he dabbed up the blood with a cloth patch and studied the wound with the light and then clamped again. The tendons in Boyd's neck shone taut in the lamplight. The doctor gripped the flashlight in his teeth. Unos pocos minutos más, he said. Unos pocos minutos.

He placed two more hemostats and then he took the red bulb syringe from the pan and filled it with the solution and he instructed the woman to take the towel and hold it against the boy's back. Then he slowly flooded the wound. He cleaned the wound with a swab and flooded it again washing out clots of blood and bits of matter. He reached into the pan with his hand and brought up a hemostat and clamped it in place.

Pobrecito, said the woman.

Unos pocos minutos más, said the doctor.

He flooded the wound out once again with the syringe and he took up one of the sticks of silver nitrate and with a muslin swab held in a hemostat in one hand he cleaned away clots and debris while with the other he cauterized with the silver nitrate. The silver nitrate left pale gray tracks in the tissue. He clamped one more hemostat and again flooded the wound. The woman doubled the towel against Boyd's back and held it. With the forceps the doctor picked out something small from the wound and held it to the light. It was about the size of a grain of wheat and he held it and turned it in the small cone of light.

Qué es eso? Billy said.

The doctor leaned with the flashlight in his teeth so that the boy could see better. Plomo, he said. But it was a small chip flaked off from Boyd's sixth rib and he was referring to the faint metal coloring along the conchoidal edge of the bone. He laid it on the towel together with the forceps and with his forefinger he felt along Boyd's ribs from front to back. He watched Boyd's face while he did so. Te duele? he said. Allá? Allá? Boyd lay with his face turned away. He sounded as if he could hardly breathe.

The doctor took a pair of small sharpnosed scissors from the pan and glanced at Billy and then began to snip away the dead tissue along the edges of the wound. Billy reached and took Boyd's hand in both of his.

Le interesa el perro, the doctor said.

Billy looked toward the door. The dog sat watching them. Git, he said.

Está bien, the doctor said. No lo molesta. Es de su hermano, no?

Sí.

The doctor nodded.

When he was done he instructed the woman to hold the towel beneath the wound in the boy's chest and then he flooded and cleaned it also. He flooded it again and he probed it with a swab. Finally he sat back and took the flashlight from his mouth and laid it on the towel and looked at Billy.

Es un muchacho muy valiente, he said.

Es grave? said Billy.

Es grave, the doctor said. Pero no es muy grave.

Qué sería muy grave?

The doctor adjusted his spectacles, pushing them back again with his wrist. It had grown cold in the room. You could see very faintly the doctor's breath plume and lapse in the lapsing light. A light bead of sweat lay across his forehead. He made the sign of the cross in the air before him. Eso, he said. Eso es muy grave.

He reached and took up the flashlight again, holding it in one of the muslin squares. He put it in his teeth and took up the bulb and refilled it and laid it by and then slowly unclamped the first of the hemostats that lay in a circle of hardware about the wound in Boyd's back. He drew it away very slowly. Then he unclamped the next.

He took up the bulb and gently washed the wound and swabbed it and took up the silver nitrate stick and gently touched it in the wound. He worked from the top of the wound downward. When he had removed the last hemostat and dropped it into the pan he sat for a moment with both hands over Boyd's back as if exhorting him to heal. Then he took up the tin of bismuth and unscrewed the lid and held it over the wounds and shook the white powder over them.

He laid gauze squares on the wounds and over the wound in the boy's back he placed a small clean towel from among his sterile dressings and he taped them down and then he and Billy eased Boyd up and the doctor quickly wrapped him about with a roll of cloth bandaging, passing the roll under his arms, until he reached the end of it. He fastened the end with two small steel clamps and they pulled Boyd's jumper back over him and eased him down again. His head lolled and he sucked a long rasping breath.

Fué muy afortunado, the doctor said.

Cómo?

Que no se le han punzando los pulmones. Que no se le ha quebrado la gran arteria cual era muy cerca de la dirección de la bala. Pero sobre todo que no hay ni gran infección. Muy afortunado.

He wrapped his instruments in the towel and placed them in his bag and he emptied the basins into the bucket and swabbed them out and put them away and closed the bag. He rinsed and dried his hands and stood and took his cufflinks from his pocket and rolled down his sleeves and fastened them. He told the woman that he would return the following day and change the dressings and that he would leave the supplies with her and show her how he wished it to be done. He said that the boy must drink plenty of water. That they must keep him warm. Then he handed Billy his bag and turned and the woman helped him on with his coat and he took his hat and thanked her for her help and ducked out through the low door.

Billy followed him out with the bag and intercepted the doctor coming around to the front of the car with the crank. He handed him the bag and took the crank from him. Permítame, he said.

He bent in the dark and found the slot in the radiator grill with his fingers and fitted the crank and pushed it into the socket. Then he stood and swung the crank. The motor started and the doctor nodded. Bueno, he said. He stepped back along the fender and idled down the throttle and turned and took the crankhandle from Billy and bent and stowed it under the seat.

Gracias, he said.

A usted.

The doctor nodded. He looked toward the doorway where the woman stood and he looked again at Billy. He took a cigarette from his pocket and put it in his mouth.

Se queda con su hermano, he said.

Sí. Acepte el caballo, por favor.

The doctor said that he would not. He said that he would send his mozo with the horse in the morning. He looked at the sky to the east where the first gray light was shaping out the roofline of the hacienda from the accommodate darkness. Ya es de mañana, he said. Viene la madrugada.

Yes, said Billy.

Stay with your brother. I will send the horse.

Then he climbed into the car and pulled shut the door and switched on the lights. There was nothing to see yet the ejiditarios had come to their doorways all down the wall of dwellings, men and women pale in the lights, pale in their clothes of unbleached cotton, children clutching at their knees and all of them watching while the car trundled slowly past and swung around in the compound and went out and down the road with the dogs running alongside howling and leaning to nip at the softly rumpling tires where they turned on the clay.

* * *

WHEN BOYD AWOKE late in the morning Billy was sitting there and when he woke midday and when he woke again in the evening he was there. He sat nodding and tottering on into the twilight and he was surprised to hear his name called.

Billy?

He opened his eyes. He leaned forward.

I dont have no water.

Let me get it. Where's the glass?

Right here. Billy?

What?

You got to go to Namiquipa.

I aint goin nowheres.

She'll think we just ditched her.

I caint leave you.

I'll be all right.

I caint go off down there and leave you.

Yeah you can.

You need somebody to look after you.

Listen, Boyd said. I've done got over all that. Go on like I asked you. You was worried about the horse anyways.

The mozo arrived at noon the day following riding a burro and leading Niño on a rope halter. The workers were in the fields and he rode across the bridge and up past the row of their habitations calling out as he went for señor Páramo. Billy went out and the mozo halted the burro and nodded to him. Su caballo, he said.

He looked at the horse. The horse had been fed and curried and watered and rested and looked another horse altogether and he told the mozo so. The mozo nodded easily and undallied the end of the halter rope from the horn of his saddle and slid from the burro.

Por qué no montaba el caballo? Billy said.

The mozo shrugged. He said that it was not his horse to ride.

Quiere montarlo?

He shrugged again. He stood with the halter rope.

Billy stepped to the horse and unlooped the bridlereins from the saddlehorn where they'd been hung and bridled the horse and let the reins fall and slid the halter off Niño's neck.

Ándale, he said.

The mozo coiled the rope and hung it over the horn of the burro's saddle and walked around the horse and patted him and took up the reins and stepped into the stirrup and swung up. He turned the horse and rode out down the paseo between the row houses and put the horse into a trot and rode up the hill past the hacienda and turned there for he would not take the horse out of sight. He backed the horse and turned it and rode a few figure eights and then galloped the horse down the hill and stopped it in a sliding squat before the door and stepped down all in one motion.

Le gusta? said Billy.

Claro que sí, said the mozo. He leaned and put the flat of his hand on the horse's neck and then nodded and turned and climbed aboard the burro and rode out down the paseo without looking back.

IT WAS ALMOST DARK when he left. The Muñoz woman tried to have him wait until morning but he would not. The doctor had arrived in the late afternoon and he had left the dressings for the woman and a package of epsom salts and the woman had fixed Boyd a tea made from manzanilla and árnica and the root of the golondrina bush. She'd put up provisions for Billy in an old canvas moral and he slung it over the horn of the saddle and mounted up and turned the horse and looked down at her.

Dónde está la pistola? he said.

She said that it was under the pillow beneath his brother's head. He nodded. He looked out down the road toward the bridge and the river and he looked at her again. He asked her if any men had been to the ejido.

Sí, she said. Dos veces.

He nodded again. Es peligroso para ustedes.

She shrugged. She said that life was dangerous. She said that for a man of the people there was no choice.

He smiled. Mi hermano es un hombre del pueblo?

Sí, she said. Claro.

He rode south along the road through the riverside cotton-woods, riding through the town of Mata Ortíz and riding the moon up out of the west to its cool meridian before he turned off and put up for the remainder of the night in a grove of trees he'd skylighted from the road. He rolled himself in his serape and hung his hat over the tops of his standing boots and did not wake till daylight.

He rode all day the day following. Few cars passed and he saw no riders. In the evening the truck that had carried his brother to San Diego came lumbering down the road from the north in a slow uncoiling of road dust and ground to a stop. The workers on the bed of the truck waved and called out to him and he rode up and pushed his hat back on his head and held up his hand to them. They gathered along the edge of the truckbed and held out their hands and he leaned from the horse and shook hands with them every man. They said that it was dangerous for him to be on the road. They did not ask about Boyd and when he began to tell them they waved away his words for they had been to see him that very day. They said that he had eaten and that he'd drunk a small glass of pulque for the vigor in it and that all signs were of the most affirmative nature. They said that only the hand of the Virgin could have sustained him through such a terrible wound. Herida tan grave, they said. Tan horrible. Herida tan fea.

They spoke of his brother lying with the pistol under his pillow and spoke in a high whisper. Tan joven, they said. Tan valiente. Y peligroso por todo eso. Como el tigre herido en su cueva.

Billy looked at them. He looked out across the cooling country to the west, the long bands of shadow. Doves were calling from the acacias. The workers believed that his brother had killed the manco in a gunfight in the streets of Boquilla y Anexas. That the manco had fired upon him without provocation and what folly for the manco who had not reckoned upon the great heart of the güerito. They pressed him for details. How the güerito had risen from his blood in the dust to draw his pistol and shoot the manco dead from his horse. They addressed Billy with great reverence and they asked him how it was that he and his brother had set out upon their path of justice.

He scanned their faces. What he saw in those eyes was very moving to him. The driver and the two other men in the cab of the truck had got down and were standing along the bed of the truck at the rear. All waited to see what he would say. In the end he told them that the accounts of the conflict were greatly exaggerated and that his brother was only fifteen years and that he himself was to blame for he should have cared better for his brother. He should not have carried him off to a strange country to be shot down in the street like a dog. They only shook their heads and repeated among themselves Boyd's age. Quince años, they said. Qué guapo. Qué joven tan esforzado. In the end he thanked them for their care of his brother and touched the brim of his hat at which they all crowded again with their hands outstretched and he shook their hands again and the hands of the driver and the other two men standing in the road and then reined the horse around and rode past the truck and out along the road south. He heard the truckdoors slam behind him and heard the driver put the truck in gear and they rumbled slowly past him in the augmenting dust. The workers on the bed of the truck waved and some took off their hats and then one of them stood and steadied himself by one hand on the shoulder of his companion and raised one fist in the air and shouted to him. Hay justicia en el mundo, he called. Then they all rode on.

He woke that night with the ground trembling beneath him and he sat up and looked for the horse. The horse stood with its head raised against the desert nightsky looking toward the west. A train was going downcountry, the pale yellow cone of

the headlight boring slowly and sedately down the desert and
the distant clatter of the wheeltrucks outlandish and mechanical
in that dark waste of silence. Finally the small square windowlight of the caboose trailing after. It passed and left only the
faint pale track of boilersmoke hanging over the desert and
then came the long lonesome whistle echoing across the country
where it called for the crossing at Las Varas.

He rode into Boquilla at noon with the shotgun across the
pommel of the saddle. There was no one about. He took the
road south to Santa Ana de Babícora. Towards dark he began
to come upon riders riding north toward Boquilla, young men
and boys with their black hair slicked down on their skulls and
their boots polished and the cheap cotton shirts they wore that
had been pressed with hot bricks. It was Saturday night and
they were going to a dance. They nodded gravely, mounted on
burros or on the little distaff mules from the mines. He nodded
back, his eyes watching every movement, the shotgun upright
against him with the buttstock cradled against his inner thigh.
The good horse he rode flaring its nostrils at them. When he
rode through La Pinta on the high juniper plain above the Santa
María River Valley the moon was up and when he rode into
Santa Ana de Babícora it was midnight and the town was dark
and empty. He watered the horse in the alameda and took the
road west to Namiquipa. An hour's ride he came to a small
stream that was part of the headwaters of the Santa María and
turned the horse off down out of the road and hobbled him in
the river grass and rolled himself into his serape and slept in
dreamless exhaustion.

When he woke the sun was hours high. He walked down to
the creek carrying his boots and stood in the water and bent and
washed his face. When he raised up and looked for the horse the
horse was standing looking toward the road. In a few minutes a
rider came along. Coming down the road on the horse his mother
used to ride was the girl wearing a new dress of blue cotton and
a small straw hat with a green ribbon that hung down her back.
Billy watched her pass and when she was out of sight he sat in

the grass and studied his boots standing there and the slow passing of the small river and the tops of the grass that bent and recovered constantly in the morning breeze. Then he reached for the boots and pulled them on and stood and walked up and bridled and saddled the horse and mounted up and rode out into the road and set out behind her.

When she heard the horse on the road she put her hand on top of her hat and turned and looked back. Then she stopped. He slowed the horse and rode up to her. She fixed him with her dark eyes.

Está muerto? she said. Está muerto?

No.

No me mienta.

Le juro por Dios.

Gracias a Dios. Gracias a Dios. She slid from the horse and dropped the reins and knelt in her new clothes in the dry rutted clay of the road and blessed herself and closed her eyes and folded her hands to pray.

An hour later when they rode back through Santa Ana de Babícora she'd still hardly spoken. It was almost noon and they rode up the one mud street past the lowslung rows of slumped mud buildings and the half dozen painted trees that composed the alameda and on across the upland desert plain again. He saw nothing that looked like a tienda in the town and he'd nothing with which to buy anything if there had been one. She rode a sedate dozen paces behind him and he looked back at her once or twice but she did not smile nor acknowledge him in any way and after a while he didn't look anymore. He knew she'd not left her house without provisions but she didnt mention it and neither did he. A little ways north of the town she spoke behind him and he stopped and turned the horse in the road.

Tienes hambre? she said.

He thumbed his hat back and looked at her. I could eat the runnin gears of a bull moose, he said.

Mánde?

They ate in a grove of acacia by the roadside. She spread her serape and laid out tortillas in a cloth and tamales in their corded wraps of cornhusk and a small jar of frijoles from which she unscrewed the lid and in which she stood a wooden spoon. She opened a cloth containing four empanadas. Two ears of cold corn dusted with red chile powder. The quarter part of a small wheel of goatcheese.

She sat with her legs tucked under her, her head turned for the brim of the hat to shade her face. They ate. When he asked her didnt she want to know about Boyd she said she already knew. He watched her. She seemed fragilely wrapped in her clothing. On her left wrist there was a blue discoloration. Other than that her skin was so perfect it appeared oddly false. As if it had been painted on.

Tienes miedo de los hombres, he said.

Cuáles hombres?

Todos los hombres.

She turned and looked at him. She looked down. He thought that she was reflecting upon the question but she only brushed an escarabajo from the serape and reached and took up one of the empanadas and bit delicately into it.

Y quizás tienes razón, he said.

Quizás.

She looked off to where the horses stood in the roadside grass, their tails whisking. He thought she would say no more but she began to talk about her family. She said that her grandmother had been widowed by the revolution and married again and was widowed again within the year and married a third time and was a third time widowed and wed no more although there were opportunities enough for her to do so as she was a great beauty and not yet twenty years of age when the last husband fell as detailed by his own uncle at Torreón with one hand over his breast in a gesture of fidelity sworn, clutching the rifleball to him like a gift, the sword and pistol he carried falling away behind him useless in the palmettos, in the sand, the riderless horse stepping about in the melee of shot and shell and the cries of men, trotting off with the stirrups flapping, coming back, wandering in silhouette with others of its kind among the bodies of the dead on that senseless plain while the dark drew down around them all about and small birds driven from their arbors in the thorns returned and flitted about and chittered and the moon rose blind and white in the east and the little jackal wolves came trotting that would eat the dead from out of their clothes.

She said that her grandmother was skeptical of many things in this world and of none more than men. She said that in every trade save war men of talent and vigor prosper. In war they die. Her grandmother spoke to her often of men and she spoke with great earnestness and she said that rash men were a great temptation to women and this was simply a misfortune like others and there was little that could be done to remedy it. She said that to be a woman was to live a life of difficulty and heartbreak and those who said otherwise simply had no wish to face the facts. And she said that since this was so nor could it be altered one was better to follow one's heart in joy and in misery than simply to seek comfort for there was none. To seek it was only to welcome in the misery and to know little else. She said that these were things all women knew yet seldom spoke of. Lastly she said that if women were drawn to rash men it was only that in their secret hearts they knew that a man who would not kill for them was of no use at all.

She had finished eating. She sat with her hands folded in her lap and the things she'd said sorted oddly with her composure. The road was empty, the country silent. He asked her if she thought that Boyd would kill a man. She turned and studied him. As if he were someone for whom words must be weighed so as to accommodate their understanding. Finally she said that the word was abroad in the country. That all the world knew that the güerito had killed the gerente from Las Varitas. The man who had betrayed Socorro Rivera and sold out his own people to the Guardia Blanca of La Babícora.

Billy listened to all this and when she was done he said that the manco had fallen from his horse and broken his back and that he himself had seen it happen.

He waited. After a while she looked up.

Quieres algo más? she said.

No. Gracias.

She began to pack up the remains of their picnic. He watched her but he made no move to help. He rose and she folded the serape and rolled the remainder of the provisions in it and retied it with the cords.

No sabes nada de mi hermano, he said.

Quizás, she said.

She stood with the rolled serape over her shoulder.

Por qué no me contesta? he said.

She looked up at him. She said that she had answered him. She said that in every family there is one who is different and the others believe that they know that person but they do not know that person. She said that she herself was such a one and knew whereof she spoke. Then she turned and walked out to where the horses were grazing in the dusty roadside weeds and tied the serape on behind the cantle and tightened the cinch and stood up into the saddle.

He mounted up and rode the horse past her into the road. Then he stopped and looked back. He said that there were things about his brother that only his family could know and that as his family was dead there was no one who knew save he. Every small thing. Any time that he was sick as a child or the day he was bitten by a scorpion and thought he was going to die or any of his life in another part of the country that even Boyd remembered little of or none at all including his grandmother and his twin sister dead and buried in that long ago in a place he'd likely never see again.

Sabías que él tenía una gemela? he said. Que murió cuando tenía cinco años?

She said that she did not know that Boyd had once had a twin sister or that she died but that it was not important for now he had another. Then she put the horse forward and went past him and into the road.

An hour later they overtook three young girls afoot. Two of

them carried a basket between them with a cloth over it. They were on their way to the pueblo of Soto Maynez and they had yet a ways to go. They looked back when they heard the riders on the road behind them and they huddled together laughing and when the riders passed they pushed one another to the verge of the road and looked up with their quick dark eyes and laughed behind their hands. Billy touched his hat and rode on but the girl stopped and walked the horse beside them and when he looked back she was talking to them. They were little younger than she but she was calling them to task in that same low flat voice. Finally they stopped and stood back against the roadside chaparral but here she halted the horse entirely and continued until she was done. Then she turned and put the horse forward and did not look back.

They rode all day. It was dark when they entered La Boquilla and he rode through the town as he had come with the shotgun upright before him. When they passed the spot where the manco had fallen she made the sign of the cross and kissed her fingers. Then they rode on. The sparse trunks of the painted alameda trees stood pale as bone in the light from the windows. Some windows of glass but mostly oiled butcherpaper tacked up in frames and behind them neither movement nor shadow but only those sallow squares like parchments or old barren maps long weathered of any trace of their terrains or routes upon them. On the outskirts of the settlement there was a fire burning just off the roadside and they slowed and rode past cautiously but the fire appeared to be only a trashfire and there was no one about and they rode on into the dark country to the west.

That night they camped in a swale at the edge of the lake and shared the last of the provisions she'd brought. When he asked her would she not have been afraid to ride through this country by herself at night she said that there was no remedy for it and that one must put oneself in the care of God.

He asked if God always looked after her and she studied the heart of the fire for a long time where the coals breathed bright and dull and bright again in the wind from the lake. At last she said that God looked after everything and that one could no more evade his care than evade his judgment. She said that even the wicked could not escape his love. He watched her. He said that he himself had no such idea of God and that he'd pretty much given up praying to Him and she nodded without taking her eyes from the fire and said that she knew that.

She took her blanket and went off down by the lake. He watched her go and then shucked off his boots and rolled his serape about him and fell into a troubled sleep. He woke sometime in the night or in the early morning and turned and looked at the fire to see how long he'd slept but the fire was all but cold on the ground. He looked to the east to see if there were any trace of dawn graying over the country but there was only the darkness and the stars. He prodded the ashes with a stick. The few red coals that turned up in the fire's black heart seemed secret and improbable. Like the eyes of things disturbed that had best been left alone. He rose and walked down to the lake with the serape about his shoulders and he looked at the stars in the lake. The wind had died and the water lay black and still. It lay like a hole in that high desert world down into which the stars were drowning. Something had woke him and he thought perhaps he'd heard riders on the road and that they'd seen his fire but there was no fire to see and then he thought perhaps the girl had risen and come to the fire and stood over him where he slept and he remembered tasting rain on his face but there was no rain nor had there been and then he remembered his dream. In the dream he was in another country that was not this country and the girl who knelt by him was not this girl. They knelt in the rain in a darkened city and he held his dying brother in his arms but he could not see his face and he could not say his name. Somewhere among the black and dripping streets a dog howled. That was all. He looked out at the lake where there was no wind but only the dark stillness and the stars and yet he felt a cold wind pass. He crouched in the sedge by the lake and he knew he feared the world to come for in it were already written certainties no man would wish for. He saw pass as in a slow tapestry unrolled images of things seen and unseen. He saw the shewolf dead in the mountains and the hawk's blood on the stone and he saw a glass hearse with black drapes pass in a street carried on poles by mozos. He saw the castaway bow floating on the cold waters of the Bavispe like a dead serpent and the solitary sexton in the ruins of the town where the terremoto had passed and the hermit in the broken transept of the church at Caborca. He saw rainwater dripping from a lightbulb screwed into the sheetiron wall of a warehouse. He saw a goat with golden horns tethered in a field of mud.

Lastly he saw his brother standing in a place where he could not reach him, windowed away in some world where he could never go. When he saw him there he knew that he had seen him so in dreams before and he knew that his brother would smile at him and he waited for him to do so, a smile which he had evoked and to which he could find no meaning to ascribe and he wondered if what at last he'd come to was that he could no longer tell that which had passed from all that was but a seeming. He must have knelt there a long time because the sky in the east did grow gray with dawn and the stars sank at last to ash in the paling lake and birds began to call from the far shore and the world to appear again once more.

They rode out early with nothing to eat save the last few tortillas dried and hardening at the edges. She rode behind him and they did not speak and in this manner they rode at noon across the wooden river bridge and into Las Varas.

There were few people about. They bought beans and tortillas at a small tienda and they bought four tamales from an old woman who sold them in the street out of a steel oildrum sashed up in a wooden frame with castiron wheels from off an orecart. The girl paid the woman and they sat in a stack of piñon firewood behind a store and ate in silence. The tamales smelled and tasted of charcoal. While they were eating a man approached them and smiled and nodded. Billy looked at the girl, she looked at him. He looked at the horse and at the stock of the shotgun jutting from the boot under the saddle.

No me recuerdas, the man said.

Billy looked at him again. He looked at his boots. It was the arriero last seen on the steps of the opera caravan in the roadside grove south of San Diego.

Le conozco, Billy said. Cómo le va?

Bien. He looked at the girl. Dónde está su hermano?

Ya está en San Diego.

The arriero nodded sagely. As if he understood some situation.

Dónde está la caravana? said Billy.

He said he did not know. He said that they had waited by the side of the road but that no one had ever returned.

Cómo no?

The arriero shrugged. He made a chopping motion with the heel of his hand out through the air. Se fué, he said.

Con el dinero.

Claro.

He said that they'd been left without resources or any means to travel. At the time of his own departure the dueña had sold all the mules save one and bickering had broken out. When Billy asked what she would do he shrugged again. He looked away down the street. He looked at Billy. He asked him if he could spare him a few pesos so that he could get something to eat.

Billy said that he had no money but the girl had already risen and walked out to the horse and when she returned she gave the arriero some coins and he thanked her a number of times and bowed and touched his hat and put the coins in his pocket and wished them a good voyage and turned and went off down the street and disappeared into the sole cantina in that upland pueblo.

Pobrecito, the girl said.

Billy spat into the dry grass. He said that the arriero was probably lying and besides he was only a drunk and she should not have given him money. Then he got up and walked out to where the horses were standing and buckled the latigo and took up the reins and mounted up and rode out up through the town toward the railroad tracks and the road north without even looking back to see if she would follow.

In the three days' riding that took them to San Diego she spoke hardly at all. The last night she had wanted to keep riding on in the dark to reach the ejido but he would not. They camped on the river some miles south of Mata Ortíz and he built a fire of driftwood on a gravel bar in the river and she cooked the last of the dried beans and tortillas which was all the rations they'd had to eat since they left Las Varas. They ate seated across from each other while the fire burned down to a frail basket of coals and the moon rose in the east and overhead very high and very faint they could hear the calls of birds moving south and they could see them trail in slender cipherings across the deeply smoldering western rim and into the dusk and the darkness beyond.

Las grullas llegan, she said.

He watched them. The cranes were moving south and he watched their thin echelons trail along those unseen corridors writ in their blood a hundred thousand years. He watched them until they were gone and the last thin fluted cry like a child's horn floated away on the night's onset and then she rose and took her serape and walked off down the gravel bar and vanished among the cottonwoods.

They rode across the plankwood bridge and up to the old hacienda at noon the day following. People stood all along in the doorways of the domicilios who should have been in the fields and he realized that it was some feastday of the calendar. He rode past her and pulled the horse up in front of the Muñoz door and dismounted and dropped the reins and pulled off his hat and ducked and entered the low doorway.

Boyd was sitting on the pallet with his back against the wall. The flame of the votive candle heeled about in the glass above his head and swathed as he was in his wraps of sheeting he looked like someone sat suddenly upright at his own vigil. The mute dog had been lying down and it stood and moved against him. Dónde estabas? Boyd said. He wasnt talking to his brother.

He was talking to the girl who came smiling through the doorway behind him.

THE NEXT DAY he rode out down the river and he was gone all day. High thin skeins of wildfowl were moving downcountry and leaves were falling in the river, willow and cottonwood, coiling and turning in the current. Their shadows where they skated over the river stones looked like writing. It was dark when he returned, riding the horse up through the smoke of the cookfires from pool to pool of light like a mounted sentry posted to patrol the watchfires of a camp. In the days to follow he worked with the herders, driving sheep down from the hills and through the high vaulted gate of the compound where the animals milled and climbed against each other and the esquiladores stood at the ready with their shears. They drove the sheep half a dozen at a time into the highceilinged and ruinous storeroom and the esquiladores stood them between their knees and clipped them by hand and young boys gathered the wool up from off the raincupped boards of the floor and stamped it into the long cotton bags with their feet.

It was cool in the evening and he would sit by the fire and drink coffee with the ejiditarios while the dogs of the compound moved from fire to fire scavenging for scraps. By now Boyd was riding out in the evening, sitting the horse stiffly and riding at a walk with the girl riding Niño close beside him. He'd lost his hat in the fray on the river and he wore an old straw hat they'd found for him and a shirt made from striped ticking. After they'd come back Billy would walk out to where the horses were hobbled below the domicilios and ride Niño bareback down to the river and wade the horse out into the darkening shallows where he'd seen the naked dueña at her bath and the horse would drink and raise its dripping muzzle and they would listen together to the river passing and to the sound of ducks somewhere on the water and sometimes the high thin cranking of the flights of cranes still passing south a mile above the river. He rode down the far bank in the twilight and he could see in the river loam among the cottonwoods the tracks of the horses where Boyd had passed and he followed the tracks to see where they had gone and he tried to guess the thoughts of the rider who had made them. When he walked back up to the compound it was late and he entered the low door and sat on the pallet where his brother lay sleeping.

Boyd, he said.

His brother woke and turned and lay in the pale candlelight and looked up at him. It was warm in the room from the day's heat seeping back out of the mud walls and Boyd was naked to the waist. He'd taken the wrapping from about his chest and he was paler than his brother could ever remember and so thin with the rack of his ribs stark against the pale skin and when he turned in the reddish light Billy could see the hole in his chest for just a moment and he turned his eyes away like a man unwittingly made privy to some secret thing to which he was in no way entitled, for which he was in no way prepared. Boyd pulled the muslin cover up and lay back and looked at him. His long pale uncut hair all about him and his face so thin. What is it? he said.

Talk to me.

Go to bed.

I need for you to talk to me.

It's okay. Everthing's okay.

No it aint.

You just worry about stuff. I'm all right.

I know you are, said Billy. But I aint.

THREE DAYS LATER when he woke in the morning and walked out they were gone. He walked out to the end of the row and looked down toward the river. His father's horse standing in the field raised its head and looked at him and looked out down the road toward the river and the river bridge and the road beyond.

He got his things from the house and saddled the horse and

rode out. He said goodbye to no one. He sat the horse in the road beyond the river cottonwoods and he looked off downcountry at the mountains and he looked to the west where thunderheads were standing sheared off from the thin dark horizon and he looked at the deep cyanic sky taut and vaulted over the whole of Mexico where the antique world clung to the stones and to the spores of living things and dwelt in the blood of men. He turned the horse and set out along the road south, shadowless in the gray day, riding with the shotgun unscabbarded across the bow of the saddle. For the enmity of the world was newly plain to him that day and cold and inameliorate as it must be to all who have no longer cause except themselves to stand against it.

He looked for them for weeks but he found only shadow and rumor. He found the little heartshaped milagro in the watchpocket of his jeans and he hooked it out with his forefinger and held it in the palm of his hand and he studied it long and long. He rode as far south as Cuauhtémoc. He rode north again to Namiquipa but could find no one who owned to know the girl and he rode as far west as La Norteña and the watershed and he grew thin and gaunted in his travels and pale with the dust of the road but he never saw them again. He sat the horse at dawn in the crossroads at Buenaventura and watched waterfowl trailing over the river and the lonely lagunas, the dark liquid movement of their wings against the red sunrise. He passed back north through the small mud hamlets of the mesa, through Alamo and Galeana, settlements through which he'd passed before and where his return was remarked upon by the poblanos so that his own journeying began to take upon itself the shape of a tale. It was cold at night on the high plains in these early days of December and he had little to keep him warm. When he rode once more into Casas Grandes he'd not eaten in two days and it was past midnight and a cold rain falling.

He rapped long at the zaguán gates. Toward the rear of the house a dog barked. Finally a light came on.

When the mozo opened the gate and looked out to see him

standing there in the rain holding the horse he did not seem surprised. He asked after his brother and Billy said that his brother had recovered from his wounds but that he had disappeared and he apologized for the hour but wished to know if he might see the doctor. The mozo said that the hour was of no consequence for the doctor was dead.

He didnt ask the mozo when had the doctor died or of what cause. He stood with his hat and held it in both hands before him. Lo siento, he said.

The mozo nodded. They stood there in silence and then the boy put on his hat and turned and put one foot into the stirrup and stood up into the saddle and sat the dark wet horse and looked down at the mozo. He said that the doctor had been a good man and he looked off down the street toward the lights of the town and he looked again at the mozo.

Nadie sabe lo que le espera en este mundo, said the mozo.

De veras, the boy said.

He nodded and touched his hat and turned and rode back down the darkened street.

IV

HE CROSSED THE BORDER at Columbus New Mexico. The guard in the gateshack studied him briefly and waved him through. As if he saw his like too often these days to be in doubt about him. Billy halted the horse anyway. I'm an American, he said, if I dont look like it.

You look like you might of left some bacon down there, the guard said.

I aint come back rich, that's for sure.

I guess you come back to sign up.

I reckon. If I can find a outfit that'll have me.

You neednt to worry about that. You aint got flat feet have you?

Flat feet?

Yeah. You got flat feet they wont take you.

What the hell are you talkin about?

Talkin about the army.

Army?

Yeah. The army. How long you been gone anyways?

I dont have no idea. I dont even know what month this is.

You dont know what's happened?

No. What's happened?

Hell fire, boy. This country's at war.

He took the long straight clay road north to Deming. The day was cold and he wore the blanket over his shoulders. The knees were out of his trousers and his boots were falling apart. The pockets which had hung by threads from his shirt he'd long ago torn off and thrown away and the back of the shirt where it had separated was sewn with agave and the collar of his jacket had separated and the shredded facing stood about his neck like some tawdry sort of lace and gave him the improbable look of a ruined dandy. The few cars that passed gave him all the berth that narrow road afforded and the people looked back at him through the rolling dust as if he were a thing wholly alien in that landscape. Something from an older time of which they'd only heard. Something of which they'd read. He rode all day and he crossed in the evening through the low foothills of the Florida Mountains and he rode on across the upland plain into the dusk and into the dark. In that dark he passed a file of five horsemen riding south back the way he'd come and he spoke to them in spanish and wished them a good evening and they spoke back to him each one in their soft voices as they passed. As if the closeness of the dark and the straitness of the way had made of them confederates. Or as if only there would confederates be found.

He rode into Deming at midnight and rode the main street from one end to the other. The horse's shoeless hooves clapping dully on the blacktop in the silence. It was bitter cold. Nothing was open. He spent the night in the bus station at the corner of Spruce and Gold, sleeping on the tile floor wrapped in the filthy serape with his warbag for a pillow and the stained and filthy hat over his face. The sweatblackened saddle stood against the wall along with the shotgun in its scabbard. He slept with his boots on and he got up twice in the night and went out to see about his horse where he'd left it tethered to a lampstandard by the catchrope.

In the morning when the cafe opened he went up to the counter and asked the woman where you went to join the army. She said that the recruiting office was at the armory on South Silver Street but she didnt think they'd be open this early.

Thank you mam, he said.

You want some coffee?

No mam. I aint got no money.

Set down, she said.

Yes mam.

He sat on one of the stools and she brought him a cup of coffee in a white china mug. He thanked her and sat drinking it. After a while she came from the grill and set a plate of eggs and bacon in front of him and a plate of toast.

Dont tell nobody where you got it, she said.

The recruiting office was closed when he got there and he was waiting on the steps with two boys from Deming and a third from an outlying ranch when the sergeant arrived and unlocked the door.

They stood in front of his desk. He studied them.

Which one of you all aint eighteen, he said.

No one answered.

They's usually about one in four and I see four recruits in front of me.

I aint but seventeen, Billy said.

The sergeant nodded. Well, he said. You'll have to get your mama to sign for you.

I dont have no mama. She's dead.

What about your daddy?

He's dead too.

Well you'll have to get your next of kin. Uncle or whatever. He'll need to get a notarized statement.

I dont have no next of kin. I just got a brother and he's youngern me.

Where do you work at?

I dont work nowheres.

The sergeant leaned back in his chair. Where are you from? he said.

From over towards Cloverdale.

You got to have some kin.

Not that I know of I dont.

The sergeant tapped his pencil on the desk. He looked out the window. He looked at the other boys.

You all want to join the army? he said.

They looked at one another. Yessir, they said.

You dont sound real sure.

Yessir, they said.

He shook his head and swiveled his chair and rolled a printed form into his typewriter.

I want to join the cavalry, the boy from the ranch said. My daddy was in the cavalry in the last war.

Well son you just tell em when you get to Fort Bliss that that's what you want to do.

Yessir. Do I need to take my saddle with me?

You dont need to take a thing in the world. They're goin to look after you like your own mother.

Yessir.

He took their names and dates of birth and next of kin and their addresses one by one and he signed four mealvouchers and gave them to them and he gave them directions to the doctor's office where they were to get their physical examinations and he gave them the forms for that.

You all should be done and back here right after dinner, he said.

What about me? Billy said.

Just wait here. The rest of you all take off now. I'll see you back here this afternoon.

When they'd left the sergeant handed Billy his forms and his voucher.

You look there at the bottom of that second sheet, he said. That's a parental consent form. If you want to join this man's army you better bring it back with your mama's signature on it. If she has to come down from heaven to do it I dont have a problem in the world with that. You understand what I'm tellin you?

Yessir. I guess you want me to sign my dead mama's name on that piece of paper.

I didnt say that. Did you hear me say that?

No sir.

Go on then. I'll see you back here after dinner.

Yessir.

He turned and went out. There were people standing in the door behind him and they stood aside to let him pass.

Parham, the sergeant said.

He turned. Yessir, he said.

You come back here this afternoon now, you hear?

Yessir.

You aint got noplace else to go.

He walked across the street and untied his horse and mounted up and rode back up Silver Street and up West Spruce, holding the papers in his hand. All the streets east and west were trees, north and south minerals. He tied his horse in front of the Manhattan Cafe cattycorner from the bus station. Next to it was the Victoria Land and Cattle Company and two men in the narrowbrimmed hats and walkingheel boots that landowners wore were standing on the sidewalk talking. They looked at him when he passed and he nodded but they didnt nod back.

He slid into the booth and laid the papers on the table and looked at the menu. When the waitress came he started to order the plate lunch but she said that lunch didnt start till eleven oclock. She said he could get breakfast.

I've done eat one breakfast today.

Well we dont have no city ordinance about how many breakfasts you can eat.

How big of a breakfast can I get?

How big of a one can you eat?

I've got a mealticket from the recruitin office.

I know it. I see it layin yonder.

Can I get four eggs?

You just tell me how you want em.

She brought the breakfast on an oblong crockery platter with the four eggs over medium and a slice of fried ham and grits with butter and she brought a plate of biscuits and a small bowl of gravy.

You want anything else you let me know, she said.

All right.

You want a sweetroll?

Yes mam.

You need some more coffee?

Yes mam.

He looked up at her. She was about forty years old and she had black hair and bad teeth. She grinned at him. I like to see a man eat, she said.

Well, he said. You're lookin at one I believe ought to meet your requirements.

When he was done eating he sat drinking coffee and studying the form his mother was supposed to sign. He sat studying it and thinking about it and after a while he asked the waitress if she could bring him a fountainpen.

She brought it and handed it to him. Dont carry it off, she said. It aint mine.

I wont.

She left to go back to the counter and he bent over the form and wrote on the line Louisa May Parham. His mother's name was Carolyn.

When he walked out the other three boys were coming up the sidewalk toward the cafe. They were talking together like they'd all been friends forever. When they saw him they stopped talking and he spoke to them and asked them how they were doing and they said they were doing all right and entered the cafe.

The doctor's name was Moir and his office was out on West Pine. By the time he got there there were half a dozen people waiting, mostly young men and boys sitting holding their recruiting forms. He gave his name to the nurse at the desk and sat in a chair and waited along with the others.

When the nurse finally called his name he was asleep and he jerked awake and looked around and he didnt know where he was.

Parham, she said again.

He stood up. That's me, he said.

The nurse handed him a form and he stood in the hallway

while she held a card over his eye and told him to read the chart on the wall. He read it to the bottom letter and she tested the other eye.

You got good eyes, she said.

Yes mam, he said. I always did.

Well I guess so, she said. You dont normally start out with bad ones and they get better.

When he went into the doctor's office the doctor had him sit in a chair and he looked in his eyes with a flashlight and he put a cold instrument in his ear and looked in there. He told him to unbutton his shirt.

You came here horseback, he said.

Yessir.

Where did you come from.

Mexico.

I see. Have you got any history of disease in your family?

No sir. They're all dead.

I see, the doctor said.

He put the cool cone of the stethoscope against the boy's chest and listened. He thumped his chest with the tips of his fingers. He put the stethoscope to his chest again and listened with his eyes closed. He sat up and took the tubes from his ears and leaned back in his chair. You've got a heartmurmur, he said.

What does that mean?

It means you wont be joining the army.

He worked for a stable out on the highway for ten days and slept in a stall until he had money for clothes and for the busfare to El Paso and he left the horse with the owner of the lot and set out east in a new duckingcloth workcoat and a new blue shirt with pearl buttons.

It was a cold and blustery day in El Paso. He found the recruiting office and the clerk filled out the same forms over again and he stood in line with a number of men and they undressed and put their clothes in a basket and were given a brass chit with a number on it and then they stood in line naked holding their papers.

When he reached the examining station he handed the doctor his medical form and the doctor looked in his mouth and into his ears. Then he put the stethoscope to his chest. He told him to turn around and he put the stethoscope to his back and listened. Then he listened to his chest again. Then he picked up a stamp from the desk and stamped Billy's form and signed it and picked up the form and handed it to him.

I cant pass you, he said.

What's wrong with me.

You've got an irregularity in your heartbeat.

There aint nothin wrong with my heart.

Yes there is.

Will I die?

Sometime. It's probably not all that serious. But it will keep you out of the army.

You could pass me if you wanted to.

I could. But I wont. They'd find it somewhere down the line anyway. Sooner or later.

It was not yet noon when he walked out and down San Antonio Street. He went down South El Paso Street to the Splendid Cafe and ate the plate lunch and walked back to the bus station and he was in Deming again before dark.

In the morning when he walked up the barn bay Mr Chandler was sorting through tack in the saddleroom. He looked up.

Well, he said. Did you get in the army?

No sir, I didnt. They turned me down.

Well I'm sorry to hear it.

Yessir. I am too.

What do you aim to do?

I'm goin to try em in Albuquerque.

Son they got a awful lot of recruitin offices set up all over the country. A man could make a career out of it.

I know it. I'm goin to try it one more time.

He worked on to the end of the week and drew his pay and took the bus out on Sunday morning. He was all day on the road. Night set in just north of Socorro and the sky was filled with flights of waterfowl circling and dropping in to the river marshlands east of the highway. He watched with his face to the cold and darkening glass of the window. He listened for their cries but he could not hear them above the drone of the bus.

He slept at the YMCA and he was at the recruiting office when they opened in the morning and he was on the bus south again before noon. He'd asked the doctor if there was any medicine he could take but the doctor said that there was not. He asked if there was something you could take that would make it run all right just for a while.

Where are you from, the doctor said.

Cloverdale New Mexico.

How many different recruiting offices have you tried to enlist at?

This makes the third one.

Son, even if we did have a deaf doctor we wouldnt put him to listening to recruits with a stethoscope. I think you need to just go on home.

I dont have one to go to.

I thought you said you were from somethingdale. Where was it?

Cloverdale.

Cloverdale.

I was but I aint no more. I dont have anyplace to go. I think I need to be in the army. If I'm goin to die anyways why not use me? I aint afraid.

I wish I could, the doctor said. But I cant. It's not up to me. I have to follow regulations like everybody else. We turn away good men every day.

Yessir.

Who told you you were going to die?

I dont know. They never told me I wasnt goin to.

Well, the doctor said. They couldnt very well tell you that even if you had a heart like a horse. Could they?

No sir. I reckon not.

Go on now.

Sir?

Go on now.

When the bus pulled into the lot behind the bus station at Deming it was three oclock in the morning. He walked out to Chandler's and went to the saddleroom and got his saddle and went to the stall and led Niño out into the bay and threw the saddleblanket over him. It was very cold. The barn was oak batboards and he could see the horse's breath pass across the slats lit from the single yellow bulb outside. The groom Ruiz came and stood in the door with his blanket around his shoulders. He watched while Billy saddled the horse. He asked him if he had succeeded in joining the army.

No, Billy said.

Lo siento.

Yo también.

Adónde va?

No sé.

Regresa a Mexico?

No.

Ruiz nodded. Buen viaje, he said.

Gracias.

He led the horse out down the barn bay and through the door and mounted up and rode out.

He rode through the town and took the old road south to Hermanas and Hachita. The horse was newly shod and in good plight from the grain it had been fed on and he rode the sun up and he rode all day and rode it down again and rode on into the night. He slept on the high plain wrapped in his blanket and rose shivering before dawn and rode on again. He quit the road just west of Hachita and rode through the foothills of the Little Hatchet Mountains and struck the railroad coming out of the Phelps Dodge smelter to the south and crossed the tracks and reached the shallow salt lake at sunset.

There was water standing in the flats as far as he could see and the sunset on the water had turned it to a lake of blood. He tried to put the horse forward but the horse could not see across the lake and balked and would not go. He turned and rode south along the flats. Gillespie Mountain lay covered in snow and beyond that the Animas Peaks standing in the last of that day's sun with the snow lying red in the rincons. And far to the south the pale and ancient cordilleras of Mexico impounding the visible world. He came to the remnants of an old fence and dismounted and twisted out the staples from some of the spindly posts and made a fire and sat with his boots crossed before him staring into it. The horse stood in the dark at the edge of the fire and gazed bleakly at the barren salt ground. It's your own doin, the boy said. I got no sympathy for you.

They crossed the flat shallow lake in the morning and before noon they struck the old Playas road and followed it west into the mountains. There was snow in the pass and not a track in it. They rode down into the beautiful Animas Valley and took the road south from Animas and reached the Sanders ranch about two hours past nightfall.

He called from the gate and the girl came out on the porch.

It's Billy Parham, he called.

Who?

Billy Parham.

Come up Billy Parham, she called.

When he entered the parlor Mr Sanders stood. He was older, smaller, more frail. Get in this house, he said.

I'm awful dirty to come in.

You come on in. We thought you'd died.

No sir. Not yet I aint.

The old man shook his hand and held it. He was looking past him toward the door. Where's that Boyd at? he said.

They ate in the diningroom. The girl served them and then sat down. They ate roast beef and potatoes and beans and the girl passed him a bread dish covered with a linen cloth and he took a piece of cornbread and buttered it. This is awful good, he said.

She's a good cook, the old man said. I hope she dont decide

to get married and quit me. If I had to cook for myself the cats'd leave.

Oh Grandaddy, the girl said.

They wanted to put Miller four-F too, the old man said. On account of his leg. They took him up at Albuquerque. They run em through up there I reckon in wholesale lots.

They didnt me. Are they goin to put him in the cavalry?

I dont think so. I dont think they're even goin to have one.

He looked out across the table, chewing slowly. In the yellow light of the pressed glass chandelier the old photographs and portraits above the sideboard seemed like artifacts salvaged from some ancient removal. Even the old man seemed distant from them. From the sepia-tinted buildings, the old shake roofs. The people on horseback. Men sitting among cardboard cactus in a photographer's studio in suits and ties with the legs of their breeches stogged into their boottops and rifles standing upright before them. The antique dresses of the women. The wary or haunted cast to their eyes. Like people photographed at gunpoint.

That's John Slaughter in that picture at the end yonder.

Which one?

That last one on the top right under Miller's certificate. That was took in front of his house.

Who's the indian girl?

That's Apache May. They brought her back from a indian camp they raided, bunch of Apaches been stealin cattle. Eighteen ninety-five or six, somewhere in there. He may have killed some of em. He come back with her, she was just a little thing. She was wearin a dress made from an election poster and he took her and raised her as his own. He was just crazy about her. She died in a fire not long after that picture was took.

Did you know him?

I did. I worked for him at one time.

Did you ever kill a indian?

No. I come near it a time or two. Some that worked for me.

Who is that on the mule?

That's James Autry. He didnt care what he rode.

Who's that with the lion on the packhorse?

The old man shook his head. I know his name, he said. But I cant say it.

He drained his coffee and rose and got his cigarettes and an ashtray from the sideboard. The ashtray was from the Chicago World's Fair and it was cast from potmetal and it said 1833–1933. It said A Century of Progress. Let's go in here, he said.

They went in the parlor. There was a paneled oak pumporgan against the wall where they passed through from the diningroom. A lace throw on top of it. A framed handtinted portrait of the old man's wife as a young woman.

That thing dont play, the old man said. Aint nobody to play it noway.

My grandmama used to play one, Billy said. In the church.

Women used to play music. Anymore you just turn on a victrola.

He bent and opened the stove door with the poker and poked the fire up and put another split log in and shut the door.

They sat and the old man told him stories about rawhiding cattle in Mexico as a young man and about Villa's raid on Columbus New Mexico in nineteen sixteen and about sheriff's posses tracking badmen down into the bootheel as they fled toward the border and about the drought and die-up of eighty-six and trailing north the corriente cattle that they'd bought for next to nothing up out of that stricken ground across the high parched plains. Cattle so poor the old man said that at evening crossing before the sun where it burned upon the western desert shore you could all but see through them.

What do you aim to do? he said.

I dont know. Try and hire on somewheres I reckon.

We're about shut down here altogether.

Yessir. I wasnt askin.

This war, the old man said. There's no way to calculate what's to come.

No sir. I dont reckon there is.

The old man tried to get him to stay the night but he would not. They stood on the porch. It was cold and the prairie all about lay in a deep silence. The horse nickered at them from the gate.

You'd do just as well to start fresh in the mornin, the old man said.

I know it. I just need to get on.

Well.

I like ridin of a night anyways.

Yes, the old man said. I always did. You take care, son.

Yessir. I will. Thank you.

HE CAMPED THAT NIGHT on the broad Animas Plain and the wind blew in the grass and he slept on the ground wrapped in the serape and in the wool blanket the old man had given him. He built a small fire but he had little wood and the fire died in the night and he woke and watched the winter stars slip their hold and race to their deaths in the darkness. He could hear the horse step in its hobbles and hear the grass rip softly in the horse's mouth and hear it breathing or the toss of its tail and he saw far to the south beyond the Hatchet Mountains the flare of lightning over Mexico and he knew that he would not be buried in this valley but in some distant place among strangers and he looked out to where the grass was running in the wind under the cold starlight as if it were the earth itself hurtling headlong and he said softly before he slept again that the one thing he knew of all things claimed to be known was that there was no certainty to any of it. Not just the coming of war. Anything at all.

He went to work for the Hashknives except that it wasnt the Hashknives any more. They sent him out to a linecamp on the Little Colorado. In three months he saw three other human beings. When he got paid in March he went to the post office in Winslow and sent a money order to Mr Sanders for the twenty dollars he owed him and he went to a bar on First Street and sat on a stool and pushed back his hat with his thumb and ordered a beer.

What kind of beer you want? the barman said.

Just any kind. It dont matter.

You aint old enough to drink beer.

Then why did you ask me what kind I wanted?

It dont matter cause I aint servin you.

What kind is he drinkin?

The man down the bar that he'd nodded to studied him. This is a draft, son, he said. Just tell em you want a draft.

Yessir. Thank you.

Dont mention it.

He walked up the street and went in the next bar and sat on a stool. The barman wandered down and stood before him.

Give me a draft.

He went back down the bar and pulled the beer into a round glass mug and came back and set it on the bar. Billy put a dollar on the bar and the barman went to the cash register and rang it up and came back and clapped down seventy-five cents.

Where you from? he said.

Down around Cloverdale. I been workin for the Hashknives.

There aint no Hashknives. Babbitts sold it.

Yeah. I know it.

Sold it to a sheepherder.

Yeah.

What do you think of that?

I dont know.

Well I do.

Billy looked down the bar. It was empty save for a soldier who looked drunk. The soldier was watching him.

They never sold him the brand though, did they? the barman said.

No.

No. So there aint no Hashknives.

You want to flip for the jukebox? the soldier said.

Billy looked at him. No, he said. I wouldnt care to.

Set there then.

I aim to.

Is there somethin wrong with that beer? the barman said.

No. I dont reckon. Do you get a lot of complaints?

I just noticed you aint drinkin it is all.

Billy looked at the beer. He looked down the length of the bar. The soldier had turned slightly and was sitting with one hand on his knee. As if he might be deciding whether or not to get up.

I just thought there might be somethin wrong with it, the barman said.

Well I dont reckon there is, Billy said. But if there is I'll let you know.

You got a cigarette? the soldier said.

I dont smoke.

You dont smoke.

No.

The barman fished a pack of Lucky Strikes from his shirtpocket and palmed them onto the bar and slid them down to the soldier. There you go, soldier, he said.

Thanks, the soldier said. He shook a cigarette upright in the pack and pulled it free with his mouth and took a lighter from his pocket and lit the cigarette and put the lighter on the bar and slid the pack of cigarettes back to the barman. What's that in your pocket? he said.

Who are you talkin to? said Billy.

The soldier blew smoke down the bar. Talkin to you, he said.

Well, said Billy. I reckon its my business what I got in my pocket.

The soldier didnt answer. He sat smoking. The barman reached and got the cigarettes from the bar and took one and lit it and put the pack back in his shirtpocket. He stood leaning against the backbar with his arms crossed and the smoldering cigarette in his fingers. No one spoke. They seemed to be waiting for someone to arrive.

Do you know how old I am? the barman said.

Billy looked at him. No, he said. How would I know how old you are?

I'll be thirty-eight years old in June. June fourteenth.

Billy didnt answer.

That's how come I aint in uniform.

Billy looked at the soldier. The soldier sat smoking.

I tried to enlist, the barman said. Tried to lie about my age but they wasnt havin none of it.

He dont care, the soldier said. Uniform dont mean nothin to him.

The barman pulled on his cigarette and blew smoke toward the bar. I'll bet it'd mean somethin if it had that risin sun on the collar and they was comin down Second Street about ten abreast. I bet it'd mean somethin then.

Billy picked up the beermug and drank it dry and set it back on the bar and stood up and pulled his hat forward and looked a last time at the soldier and turned and went out into the street.

He worked another nine months for Aja and when he left he had a packhorse that he'd traded for and a regular bedroll and soogan and an old singleshot 32 caliber Stevens rifle. He rode south across the high plains west of Socorro and he rode through Magdalena and across the plains of Saint Augustine. When he rode into Silver City it was snowing and he checked into the Palace Hotel and sat in the room and watched the snow falling in the street. There was no one about. He went out after a while and walked down Bullard Street to the feed store but it was closed. He found a grocery store and bought six boxes of breakfast cereal and came back and fed them to the horses and put the horses in the yard behind the hotel and got his supper in the hotel diningroom and went up and went to bed. When he came down in the morning he was the only one at breakfast and when he went out to try and buy some clothes all the shops were closed. It was gray and cold in the streets and a mean wind blew out of the north and there was no one about. He tried the door of the drugstore because there was a light on inside but it was closed too. When he got back to the hotel he asked the clerk if today was Sunday and the clerk said it was Friday.

He looked out at the street. There aint no stores open, he said.

It's Christmas day, the clerk said. Aint no stores open on Christmas day.

He drifted into the north Texas panhandle and he worked out most of the following year for the Matadors and he worked for the T Diamond. He drifted south and he worked small spreads some no more than a week. By the spring of the third year of the war there was hardly a ranch house in all of that country that did not have a gold star in the window. He worked until March on a small ranch out of Magdalena New Mexico and then one day he got his pay and saddled his horse and tied his bedroll onto the packhorse and rode south again. He crossed the last blacktop highway just east of Steins and two days later rode up to the SK Bar gate. It was a cool spring day and the old man was sitting on the porch in his rocker with his hat on and a bible in his lap. He'd bent forward to see if he could tell who it was. As if the extra foot of proximity might bring the rider into focus. He looked older and more frail, much reduced from his former self in the two years since he'd seen him. Billy called his name and the old man said for him to get down and he did. When he got to the foot of the steps he stopped with one hand on the paintflaked baluster and looked up at the old man. The old man sat with the bible closed over one finger to mark its place. Is that you, Parham? he said.

Yessir. Billy.

He walked up the steps and took off his hat and shook hands with the old man. The old man's eyes had faded to a paler blue. He held Billy's hand a long time. Bless your heart, he said. I've thought about you a thousand times. Set down here where we can visit.

He pulled up one of the old canebottomed chairs and sat and

put his hat over his knee and looked out over the pasturelands toward the mountains and he looked at the old man.

I reckon you knew about Miller, the old man said.

No sir. I've not had much news.

He was killed on Kwajalein Atoll.

I'm awful sorry to hear that.

We've had it pretty rough here. Pretty rough.

They sat. There was a breeze coming up the country. A pot of asparagus fern hanging from the porch eaves at the corner swung gently and its shadow oscillated over the boards of the porch slow and random and uncentered.

Are you doin all right? Billy said.

Oh I'm all right. I had a operation for cataracts back in the fall but I'm makin it. Leona went off and got married on me. Now her husband's shipped out and she's livin in Roswell I dont know what for. Got a job. I tried to reason with her but you know how that goes.

Yessir.

By rights I got no business bein here atall.

I hope you live forever.

Dont wish that on me.

He'd leaned back and closed the bible shut. That rain is comin this way, he said.

Yessir. I believe it is.

Can you smell it?

Yessir.

I always loved that smell.

They sat. After a while Billy said: Can you smell it?

No.

They sat.

What do you hear from that Boyd? the old man said.

I aint heard nothin. He never come back from Mexico. Or if he did I never heard it.

The old man didnt speak for a long time. He watched the darkening country to the south.

I seen it rain on a blacktop road in Arizona one time, he said. It rained on one side of the white line for a good half mile and the other side bone dry. Right down the centerline.

I can believe that, Billy said. I've seen it rain thataway.

It was a peculiar thing to see.

I seen it thunder in a snowstorm one time, Billy said. Thunder and lightnin. You couldnt see the lightnin. Just everthing would light up all around you, white as cotton.

I had a Mexican one time to tell me that, the old man said. I didnt know whether to believe him or not.

It was in Mexico was where I seen it.

Maybe they dont have it in this country.

Billy smiled. He crossed his boots on the boards of the porch in front of him and watched the country.

I like them boots, the old man said.

I bought em in Albuquerque.

They look to be good'ns.

I hope they are. I give enough for em.

Everthing's higher than a cat's back with the war and all. What all you can even find to buy.

Doves were coming in and crossing the pasture toward the stockpond west of the house.

You aint got married on us have you? the old man said.

No sir.

People hate to see a man single. I dont know what there is about it. They used to pester me about gettin married again and I was near sixty when my wife died. My sister in law primarily. I'd done already had the best woman ever was. Aint nobody goin to be that lucky twice runnin.

No sir. Most likely not.

I remember old Uncle Bud Langford used to tell people, said: It would take one hell of a wife to beat no wife at all. Course then he was never married, neither. So I dont know how he would know.

I guess I've got to say that I dont understand the first thing about em.

What's that.

Women.

Well, said the old man. At least you aint took to lyin.

There wouldnt be no use in it.

Why dont you put your horses up fore your plunder gets wet out yonder.

I reckon I'd best be gettin on.

You aint goin to ride off in the rain. We're fixin to eat supper here in just a few minutes. I got a Mexican woman cooks for me.

Well. I probably need to move while the spirit's on me.

Just stay and take supper. Hell, you just got here.

When he came back from the barn the wind was blowing harder but it still had not begun to rain.

I remember that horse, the old man said. That was your daddy's horse.

Yessir.

He bought it off a Mexican. He claimed the horse when he bought it didnt know a word of english.

The old man pushed himself up from his rocker and clutched the bible under his arm. Even gettin up out of a chair gets to be work. You wouldnt believe that, would you?

Do you think horses understand what people say?

I aint sure most people do. Let's go in. She's done hollered twice.

He was up in the morning before daybreak and he went through the dark house to the kitchen where there was a light. The woman was sitting at the kitchen table listening to an old wooden radio shaped like a bishop's hat. She was listening to a station out of Ciudad Juárez and when he stood in the door she turned it off and looked at him.

Está bien, he said. No tiene que apagarlo.

She shrugged and rose. She said that it was over anyway. She asked him if he would like his breakfast and he said that he would.

While she was fixing it he walked out to the barn and brushed the horses and cleaned their hooves and then saddled Niño and left the latigo loose and he strapped the old visalia packframe onto his bedhorse and tied on his soogan and went back to the house. She got his breakfast out of the oven and set it on the table. She'd cooked eggs and ham and flour tortillas and beans and she set it in front of him and poured his coffee.

Quiere crema? she said.

No gracias. Hay salsa?

She set the salsa at his elbow in a small lavastone molcajete.

Gracias.

He thought that she would leave but she didnt. She stood watching him eat.

Es pariente del señor Sanders? she said.

No. Él era amigo de mi padre.

He looked up at her. Siéntate, he said. Puede sentarse.

She made a little motion with her hand. He didnt know what it meant. She stood as before.

Su salud no es buena, he said.

She said that it was not. She said that he had had trouble with his eyes and that he was very sad over his nephew who was killed in the war. Conoció a su sobrino? she said.

Sí. Y usted?

She said that she had not known the nephew. She said that when she came to work here the nephew was already dead. She said that she had seen his picture and that he was very handsome.

He ate the last of the eggs and wiped the plate with the tortilla and ate the tortilla and drank the last of the coffee and wiped his mouth and looked up and thanked her.

Tiene que hacer un viaje largo? she said.

He rose and put the napkin on the table and took his hat up from the other chair and put it on. He said that he did indeed have a long journey. He said he did not know what the end of his journey would look like or whether he would know it when he got there and he asked her in spanish to pray for him but she said she had already decided to do so before he even asked.

* * *

HE SIGNED the horses through the Mexican customs at Berendo and folded the stamped entry papers into his saddlebag and gave the aduanero a silver dollar. The aduanero saluted him gravely and addressed him as caballero and he rode south into old Mexico, State of Chihuahua. He'd last passed through this port of entry seven years ago when he was thirteen and his father rode the horse he now rode and they had taken delivery of eight hundred head of cattle from two Americans rawhiding the back acres of an abandoned ranch in the mountains to the west of Ascensión. At that time there had been a cafe here but now there was none. He rode down the little mud street and bought three tacos from a woman sitting beside a charcoal brazier in the dust of the roadside and ate them as he went.

Two days' riding brought him at evening to the town of Janos, or to the lights thereof sited on the darkening plain below him. He sat the horse in the old rutted wagonroad and looked off toward the western sierras black against the bloodred drop of the sky. Beyond lay the Bavispe River country and the high Pilares with the snow still clinging in the northern rincons and the nights still cold up there on the alto plano where he had ridden another horse in another time long ago.

He approached from the east in the dark, riding past one of the crumbling mud towers of the ancient walled town and riding slowly through a settlement composed wholly of mud and in ruins a hundred years. He rode past the tall mud church and past the old green spanish bells hung from their trestlepole in the yard and past the open doors of the houses where men sat smoking quietly. Behind them in the yellow light of the oil lamps the women moved at their tasks. Over the town hung a haze of charcoal smoke and from somewhere in those dusky warrens music was playing.

He followed the sound down the narrow mud corridors and hove up at last before a door nailed up out of raw pine boards crusted with dried rosin and hung on bullhide hinges. The room he entered was but one more in the row of cribs inhabited or abandoned that lined either side of the little street. When he entered the music ceased and the musicians turned and looked at him. There were several tables in the room and all had ornately turned legs that were stained with mud as if they'd stood outside in the rain. At one of the tables sat four men with glasses and a bottle. Along the back wall was an ornate Brunswick bar brought here from God knew where and on the shelves of the carved and dusty backbar there were half a dozen bottles, some with labels, some without.

Está abierto? he said.

One of the men pushed back his chair on the clay floor and stood. He was very tall and when he stood his head vanished into the darkness above the single shaded bulb that hung over the table. Sí, caballero, he said. Cómo no?

He went to the bar and took down an apron from a nail and tied it about his waist and stood before the dimly lit carved mahogany with his hands crossed before him. He looked like a butcher standing in a church. Billy nodded at the other three men at the table and wished them a good evening but none spoke back. The musicians rose with their instruments and filed out into the street.

He pushed his hat back slightly on his head and crossed the room and put his hands on the bar and studied the bottles on the back wall.

Déme un Waterfills y Frazier, he said.

The barman held up one finger. As if agreeing with the wisdom of this choice. He reached and took down a tumbler from among a varied collection and righted it on the bar and reached down the whiskey and poured the glass half full.

Agua? he said.

No gracias. Tome algo para usted.

The barman thanked him and reached down another tumbler and poured it and set the bottle on the bar. On the dust of the bottle his hand had left an imprint visible in the sallow glare from the lamp. Billy held up his glass and looked at the barman across the rim of it. Salud, he said.

Salud, said the barman. They drank. Billy set his glass down and gestured at it with a circling motion of his finger that included the barman's glass also. He turned and looked at the three men sitting on the table. Y sus amigos también, he said.

Bueno, said the barman. Cómo no.

He crossed the room in his apron with the bottle and poured their glasses and they toasted his health and he raised his own glass and they drank. The barman returned to the bar where he stood uncertainly, glass and bottle in hand. Billy set his glass on the bar. Finally a voice from the table spoke to ask that he join them. He picked up the glass and turned and thanked them. He did not know who had spoken.

When he pulled back the chair which the barman had earlier vacated and sat in it and looked up he could see that the oldest of the three men was very drunk. He wore a sweatstained guayabera and he slouched in his chair with his chin resting in the open collar of it. The black eyes in their redrimmed cups were sullen and depthless. Like lead slag poured into borings to seal away something virulent or predacious. In the slow shuttering of the lids an overlong interval. It was the younger man on his right who spoke. He said that it was a long distance between drinks of whiskey for a traveler in this country.

Billy nodded. He looked at the bottle standing on their table. It was slightly yellow, slightly misshapen. There was no stopper to it nor label and it held a thin lees of fluid, a thin sediment. A thinly curved agave worm. Tomamos mescal, the man said. He leaned back in his chair and called to the barman. Venga, he called. Siéntate con nosotros.

The barman set the whiskey bottle on the bar but Billy said for him to bring it. He untied his apron and took it off and hung it back on the nail and came over with the bottle. Billy waved at the glasses on the table. Otra vez, he said.

Otra vez, said the barman. He poured the glasses round.

When he had filled all save the glass of the man who was drunk he hesitated for the prior pouring yet stood before him. The younger man touched his elbow. Alfonso, he said. Tome.

Alfonso drank not. He stared leadenly at the pale newcomer. He seemed not so much reduced by drink as restored to some atavistic state once lost to him. The younger man looked across the table at the American. Es un hombre muy serio, he said.

The barman stood the bottle before them and dragged a chair across from a nearby table and sat. All raised their glasses. They would have drunk except that Alfonso chose that moment to speak. Quién es, joven? he said.

They paused. They looked at Billy. Billy lifted his glass and drank and sat the empty glass down and looked across the table at those eyes again.

Un hombre, he said. No más.

Americano.

Claro. Americano.

Es vaquero?

Sí. Vaquero.

The drunk man did not move. His eyes did not move. He could have been speaking to himself.

Tome, Alfonso, said the younger man. He raised his own glass and looked around the table. The others raised their glasses. All drank.

Y usted? said Billy.

The drunk man did not answer. His wet red underlip hung loosely away from the perfect white teeth. He seemed not to have heard.

Es soldado? he said.

Soldado no.

The younger man said that the drunk man had been a soldier in the revolution and that he had fought at Torreón and at Zacatecas and that he had been wounded many times. Billy looked at the drunk man. The opaque black of his eyes. The younger man said that he had received three bullets in the chest at Zacatecas and lain in the dirt of the streets in darkness and cold while the dogs drank his blood. He said that the holes were there in the patriot's chest for all to see.

Otra vez, said Billy. The barman leaned forward with the bottle and poured.

When all the glasses were filled the younger man raised his glass and offered a toast to the revolution. They drank. They set their glasses down and wiped their mouths with the backs of their hands and looked at the drunk man. Por qué viene aquí? the drunk man said.

They looked at Billy.

Aquí? said Billy.

But the drunk man did not respond to questions, he only asked them. The younger man leaned slightly forward. A este país, he whispered.

A este país, said Billy. They waited. He leaned forward and reached across the table and took the drunk man's glass of mescal and slung its contents out across the room and set the glass back on the table. No one moved. He gestured to the barman. Otra vez, he said.

The barman reached slowly for the bottle and slowly poured the glasses once again. He set the bottle down and wiped his hand on the knee of his trousers. Billy picked up his glass and held it before him. He said that he was in their country to find his brother. He said that his brother was a little crazy and he should not have abandoned him but he did.

They sat holding their glasses. They looked at the drunk man. Tome, Alfonso, said the younger man. He gestured with his glass. The barman raised his own glass and drank and set the empty glass on the table again and leaned back. Like a player who has moved his piece and sits back to await the results. He looked across the table at the youngest man who sat slightly apart with his hat down over his forehead and his full glass in both hands before him like an offering. Who'd so far said no word at all. The whole room had begun to hum very slightly.

The ends of all ceremony are but to avert bloodshed. But the drunk man by his condition inhabited a twilight state of responsibility and to this the man at his side made silent appeal. He smiled and shrugged and raised his glass to the norteamericano and drank. When he set his glass down again the drunk man stirred. He leaned slowly forward and reached for his glass and the younger man smiled and raised his glass again as if to welcome him back from his morbidities. But the drunk man clutched the glass and then slowly held it out to the side of the table and poured the whiskey on the floor and set the glass back upon the table once more. Then he reached unsteadily for the bottle of mescal and turned it up and poured the oily yellow fuel into his glass and set the bottle back on the table with the sediment and the worm coiling slowly clockwise in the glass floor of it. Then he leaned back as before.

The younger man looked at Billy. Outside in the darkened town a dog barked.

No le gusta el whiskey? Billy said.

The drunk man did not answer. The glass of mescal sat as it had sat when Billy first entered the bar.

Es el sello, said the younger man.

El sello?

Sí.

He said that he objected to the seal which was the seal of an oppressive government. He said that he would not drink from such a bottle. That it was a matter of honor.

Billy looked at the drunk man.

Es mentira, the drunk man said.

Mentira? said Billy.

Sí. Mentira.

Billy looked at the younger man. He asked him what it was that was a lie but the younger man told him not to preoccupy himself. Nada es mentira, he said.

No es cuestión de ningún sello, the drunk man said.

He spoke slowly but not without facility. He had turned and addressed his statement to the younger man beside him. Then he turned back and continued to stare at Billy. Billy made a circle with his finger. Otra vez, he said. The barman reached and took up the bottle.

You want to drink that stinkin catpiss in favor of good american whiskey, Billy said, you be my guest.

Mande? said the drunk man.

The barman sat uncertainly. Then he leaned and poured the empty glasses and picked up the cork and pushed it back into the bottle. Billy raised his glass. Salud, he said. He drank. All drank. Save for the drunk man. Out in the street the old spanish bells rang once, rang twice. The drunk leaned forward. He reached past the glass of mescal standing before him and seized the bottle of mescal again. He picked it up and poured Billy's glass full with a slight circular movement of his hand. As if the small tumbler must be filled in some prescribed fashion. Then he tipped the bottle up and set it on the table and leaned back.

The barman and the two younger man sat holding their glasses. Billy sat looking at the mescal. He leaned back in the chair. He looked toward the door. He could see Niño standing inn the street. The musicians who had fled were already playing again somewhere in another street, another taverna. Or perhaps it was other musicians. He reached and took up the mescal and held it to the light. A smokelike sediment curled in the glass. Small bits of debris. No one moved. He tilted the glass and drank.

Salud, called the younger man. They drank. The barman drank. They clapped their empty tumblers on the table and they smiled around. Then Billy leaned to one side and spat the mescal in the floor.

In the ensuing silence the pueblo itself seemed to have been sucked up by the desert round. There was no sound anywhere. The drunk man sat stilled in the act of reaching for his glass. The younger man lowered his eyes. In the shadow of the lamp his eyes even looked closed and may have been. The drunk man balled his reaching hand and lowered it to the table. Billy circled one finger in the air slowly. Otra vez, he said.

The barman looked at Billy. He looked at the leaden-eyed patriot sitting with his fist upright beside his glass. Era demasiado fuerte para él, he said. Demasiado fuerte.

Billy didnt take his eyes from the drunk man. Más mentiras, he said. He said that it was not at all the case that the mescal was too strong for him as the barman claimed.

They sat looking at the mescal bottle. At the black half moon of the bottle's shadow beside the bottle. When the drunk man did not move or speak Billy reached across the table for the whiskey bottle and poured the glasses round once more and set the bottle back on the table. Then he pushed back his chair and stood.

The drunk man placed both hands on the edge of the table.

The man who had so far not spoken at all said in english that if he reached for his billfold the man would shoot him.

I dont doubt that for a minute, Billy said. He spoke to the bartender without taking his eyes from the man across the table. Cuánto debo? he said.

Cinco dolares? said the barman.

He reached into his shirtpocket with two fingers and took out his money and dealt it open with his thumb and slid loose a five-dollar bill and laid it on the table. He looked at the man who'd spoken to him in english. Will he shoot me in the back? he said.

The man looked up at him from under his hatbrim and smiled. No, he said. I dont think so.

Billy touched the brim of his hat and nodded to the men at the table. Caballeros, he said. And turned to start for the door leaving his filled glass on the table.

If he calls to you do not turn around, the young man said.

He did not stop and he did not turn and he'd very nearly reached the door when the man did call. Joven, he said.

He stopped. The horses out in the street raised their heads and looked at him. He looked at the distance to the door which was no more than his own length. Walk, he said. Just walk. But he didnt walk. He turned around.

The drunk man had not moved. He sat in his chair and the

young man who spoke english had risen and stood beside him with one hand on his shoulder. They looked to be posed for some album of outlawry.

Me llama embustero? said the drunk man.

No, he said.

Embustero? He clawed at his shirt and ripped it open. It was fastened with snaps and it opened easily and with no sound. As if perhaps the snaps were worn and loose from just such demonstrations in the past. He sat holding his shirt wide open as if to invite again the trinity of rifleballs whose imprint lay upon his smooth and hairless chest just over his heart in so perfect an isoscelian stigmata. No one at the table moved. None looked at the patriot nor at his scars for they had seen it all before. They watched the güero where he stood framed in the door. They did not move and there was no sound and he listened for something in the town that would tell him that it was not also listening for he had a sense that some part of his arrival in this place was not only known but ordained and he listened for the musicians who had fled upon his even entering these premises and who themselves perhaps were listening to the silence from somewhere in those cratered mud precincts and he listened for any sound at all other than the dull thud of his heart dragging the blood through the small dark corridors of his corporeal life in its slow hydraulic tolling. He looked at the man who'd warned him not to turn but that was all the warning that man had. What he saw was that the only manifest artifact of the history of this negligible republic where he now seemed about to die that had the least authority or meaning or claim to substance was seated here before him in the sallow light of this cantina and all else from men's lips or from men's pens would require that it be beat out hot all over again upon the anvil of its own enactment before it could even qualify as a lie. Then it all passed. He took off his hat and stood. Then for better or for worse he put it on again and turned and walked out the door and untied the horses and mounted up and rode out down the narrow street leading the packhorse and he did not look back.

* * *

HE'D NOT GOT CLEAR of the town before a drop of rain the size of a middle taw landed in the brim of his hat. Then another. He looked up into a cloudless sky. The visible planets burning in the east. There was no wind nor smell of rain in the air yet the drops fell the more. The horse wanted to stop in the road and the rider looked back at the dark town. The few small window squares of dim and reddish light. The smack of the rain falling on the hard clay of the road sounded like horses somewhere in the darkness crossing a bridge. He was beginning to feel drunk. He halted the horse and then turned and rode back.

He rode the horse through the first door he came to, dropping the packhorse's rope and leaning low along his horse's neck to clear the doorbeam. Inside he sat the animal in the selfsame rain and he looked up to see the selfsame stars above him. He reined the horse about and rode out again and entered another doorway and at once the muted clatter of the raindrops on the crown of his hat ceased. He got down and stomped about in the dark to see what was underfoot. He went out and brought in the pack-horse and untied the diamondhitch and pulled his soogan off onto the ground and unbuckled and pulled down the packframe and hobbled the animal and drove it back out into the rain. Then he pulled loose the latigo on his saddlehorse and pulled off the saddle and saddlebags and stood the saddle against the wall and knelt down and felt out the ropes on the soogan and untied and unrolled it and sat and pulled off his boots. He was feeling drunker. He took off his hat and lay down. The horse walked past his head and stood looking out the door. Dont you step on me damn you, he said.

When he woke in the morning the rain had stopped and it was full daylight. He felt awful. He'd risen sometime in the night and staggered out to vomit and he remembered casting about with his weeping eyes for some sign of the horses and then staggering in again. He might not have remembered it except that when he sat up and looked around for his boots they were on his feet. He picked up his hat and put it on and looked toward the door. Several children who had been crouched there watching him stood up and backed away.

Dónde están los caballos? he said.

They said that the horses were eating.

He stood too fast and leaned against the doorjamb holding his eyes. He was afire with thirst. He raised his head again and stepped out through the door and looked at the children. They were pointing down the road.

He walked out past the last of the row of low mud dwellings with the children following behind and walked the horses down in a grassy field on the south side of the town where a small stream crossed the road. He stood holding Niño's reins. The children watched.

Quieres montar? he said.

They looked at one another. The youngest was a boy of about five and he held both arms straight up in the air and stood waiting. Billy picked him up and set him astride the horse and then the little girl and lastly the oldest boy. He told the oldest boy to hold on to the younger ones and the boy nodded and he picked up the reins again and the packhorse's trailing rope and led both horses back up toward the road.

A woman was coming along from the town. When the children saw her they whispered among themselves. She was carrying a blue pail with a cloth over it. She stood by the side of the road holding the pail by the bailwire in both hands before her. Then she started down through the field towards them.

Billy touched his hat and wished her a good morning. She stopped and stood holding the pail. She said that she had been looking for him. She said that she knew he'd not gone far because his bed and his saddle were where he'd left them. She said that the children had told her that there was a horseman asleep in the caídas at the edge of town who was sick and she had brought him some menudo hot from the fire and if he would eat it he would then have strength for his journey.

She bent and set the pail on the ground and lifted away the cloth and handed the cloth to him. He stood holding it and looking down at the pail. Inside sat a bowl of speckled tinware covered with a saucer and beside the bowl were wedged some folded tortillas. He looked at her.

Ándale, she said. She gestured toward the pail.

Y usted?

Ya comí.

He looked at the children aligned upon the horse's back. He handed up the reins and the catchrope to the boy.

Toma un paseo, he said.

The boy reached forward and took the reins and he handed the end of the catchrope to the girl and then handed the half rein over the girl's head and booted the horse forward. Billy looked at the woman. Es muy amable, he said. She said for him to eat before it grew cold.

He squatted on the ground and tried to lift out the bowl but it was too hot. Con permiso, she said. She reached down and took the bowl from the pail and lifted off the saucer and set the bowl in the saucer and handed it to him. Then she reached down and took out a spoon and handed him that.

Gracias, he said.

She knelt in the grass opposite to watch him eat. The ribbons of tripe swam in the clear and oily broth like slow planarians. He said that he was not really sick but only somewhat crudo from his night in the tavern. She said that she understood and that it was of no consequence and that sickness had no way to know who'd caused it thanks be to God for all of us.

He took a tortilla from the pail and tore it and refolded it and dipped it in the broth. He spooned up a piece of tripe and it sloughed from the spoon and he cut it in two against the side of the bowl with the edge of the spoon. The menudo was hot and rich with spice. He ate. She watched.

The children rode up on the horse behind him and sat waiting. He looked up at them and made a circling motion with his finger and they set off again. He looked at the woman.

Son suyos?

She shook her head. She said that they were not.

He nodded. He watched them go. The bowl had cooled somewhat and he took it by the rim and tipped it up and drank from it and took a bite of the tortilla. Muy sabroso, he said.

She said that she had had a son but that he was dead twenty years.

He looked at her. He thought that she did not look old enough to have had a child twenty years ago but then she seemed no particular age at all. He said that she must have been very young and she said that she had indeed been very young but that the grief of the young is greatly undervalued. She put one hand to her chest. She said that the child lived in her soul.

He looked out across the field. The children sat astride the horse at the edge of the river and the boy seemed to be waiting for the horse to drink. The horse stood waiting for whatever next thing might be required of it. He drained the last of the menudo and folded the last quadrant of the tortilla and wiped the bowl with it and ate it and set bowl and spoon and saucer back in the bucket and looked at the woman.

Cuánto le debo, señora, he said.

Señorita, she said. Nada.

He took the folded bills from his shirtpocket. Para los niños.

Niños no tengo.

Para los nietos.

She laughed and shook her head. Nietos tampoco, she said.

He sat holding the money.

Es para el camino, she said.

Bueno. Gracias.

Déme su mano.

Cómo?

Su mano.

He gave her his hand and she took it and turned it palm up and held it in hers and studied it.

Cuántos años tiene? she said.

He said that he was twenty.

Tan joven. She traced his palm with the tip of her finger. She pursed her lips. Hay ladrones aquí, she said.

En mi palma?

She leaned back and closed her eyes and laughed. She laughed with an easy enthusiasm. Me lleva Judas, she said. No. She shook her head. She had on only a thin flowered shift and her breasts swung inside the cloth. Her teeth were white and perfect. Her legs bare and brown.

Dónde pues? he said.

She caught her lower lip with her teeth and studied him with her dark eyes. Aquí, she said. En este pueblo.

Hay ladrones en todos lados, he said.

She shook her head. She said that in Mexico there were villages where robbers lived and villages where they did not. She said that it was a reasonable arrangement.

He asked her if she was a robber and she laughed again. Ay, she said. Dios mio, qué hombre. She looked at him. Quizás, she said.

He asked her what sorts of things she would steal if she were a robber but she only smiled and turned his hand in hers and studied it.

Qué ve? he said.

El mundo.

El mundo?

El mundo según usted.

Es gitana?

Quizás sí. Quizás no.

She placed her other hand over his. She looked out across the field where the children were riding.

Qué vio? he said.

Nada. No vi nada.

Es mentira.

Sí.

He asked her why she would not tell what she had seen but she only smiled and shook her head. He asked if there were no good news at all and she became more serious and nodded yes and she turned his palm up again. She said that he would live a long life. She traced the line where it circled under the base of his thumb.

Con mucha tristeza, he said.

Bastante, she said. She said that there was no life without sadness.

Pero usted ha visto algo malo, he said. Qué es?

She said that whatever she had seen could not be helped be it good or bad and that he would come to know it all in God's good time. She studied him with her head slightly cocked. As if there were some question he must ask if only he were quick enough to ask it but he did not know what it was and the moment was fast passing.

Qué novedades tiene de mi hermano, he said.

Cuál hermano?

He smiled. He said that he had but one brother.

She uncovered his hand and held it. She did not look at it. Es mentira, she said. Tiene dos.

He shook his head.

Mentira tras mentira, she said. She bent to study his palm.

Qué ve? he said.

Veo dos hermanos. Uno ha muerto.

He said that he had a sister who had died but she shook her head. Hermano, she said. Uno que vive, uno que ha muerto.

Cuál es cual?

No sabes?

No.

Ni yo tampoco.

She let go his hand and rose and took up the bucket. She looked again across the field at the children and the horse. She said that he had perhaps been fortunate in the night for the rain may have kept those indoors who might otherwise have been abroad but she said that the rain which befriends can also betray one. She said also that while the rain fell by the will of God evil chose its own hour and that those whom it sought out were perhaps not entirely lacking of some certain darkness in themselves. She said that the heart betrayed itself and the wicked often had eyes to see that which was hidden from the good.

Y sus ojos?

She tossed her head, her black hair flowed about her shoulders. She said that she had seen nothing. She said that it was only a game. Then she turned and walked across the field and up toward the road.

He rode south all day and in the evening he passed through the town of Casas Grandes and set out south along the road that he'd first ridden with his brother three years before, out past the darkening ruins in the dusk, past the ancient ballcourts where the nighthawks were hunting yet. The day following he reached the hacienda at San Diego and sat the horse in the old cottonwoods by the river. Then he rode the horse across the board bridge and up to the domicilios.

The Muñoz house stood empty. He walked through the rooms. There were no furnishings of any kind. In the niche where the Virgin had stood nothing but a gray scale of old candlewax pooled on the dusty plaster.

He stood in the door, then he walked out and mounted up and rode up to the compound and through the gates.

In the courtyard an old man who sat weaving baskets told him that they were gone. He asked the old man if he knew where they had gone but the old man seemed not to have a clear understanding of the idea of destination. He gestured widely at the world. The rider sat the horse and looked about the courtyard. The old touring car. The ruining buildings. A hen turkey roosting in a sashless window. The old man had bent again to his basket and he wished him a good day and turned the horse and leading the packhorse rode out through the tall arched gate and past the tenants' quarters and down the hill to the river and across the bridge again.

Two days later he rode through Las Varas and turned east toward La Boquilla on the road where he and his brother had first seen their father's horse come up from the lake into the road wet and dripping. There'd been no rain in the high country and the road was dusty underfoot. A dry wind blowing down from the north. On the distant plain beyond the lake the dust blowing out of Babícora as if it were afire. In the evening the big red Waco plane came in from the west and circled and dropped among the trees.

He camped on the plain and made a small fire that seethed in the wind like a forgefire and swallowed up his meager hoard of sticks and limbs. He watched it burn and watched it burn. The rags of flame that fled downcountry broke and vanished like a shout in the darkness. The next day he rode through Babícora and Santa Ana de Babícora and took the road north to Namiquipa.

The town was little more than a mining camp sited on a bluff above the river and he staked his horses below the town to the east in a grove of river willows and bathed in the river and washed his clothes. In the morning when he rode up into the town he encountered a wedding party coming along the road. A common wood carreta hung with bunting. A tarp of manta tied over a rickety bowframe of willow poles to keep the bride from the sun. The cart was drawn by a single small mule, gray and shambling, the bride sat alone in the cart holding a parasol open beneath the teetering canopy. In the road beside her walked a company of men in suits of black or suits of gray that had perhaps once been black and as they passed the bride turned and looked at him sitting the horse by the roadside like some pale witness of ill omen and she blessed herself and turned away again and they went on. He would see the cart again in the village. The wedding was not till after noon and they had ridden in so early solely to take advantage of the dustless condition of the road at that hour.

He followed them down into the town and he rode his horse through the small dusty streets. No one was about. He leaned from his horse and rapped at a random door and sat listening. No one came. He shucked his boot backwards out of the stirrup and kicked at the door by way of knocking louder but the door was imperfectly latched and it swung slowly open into the low darkness.

Hola, he called.

No one answered. He looked out down the narrow street. He looked in through the top of the door. Against the far wall of the hovel a candle burned in a dish and lying on a trestle with wildflowers from the mountains about him lay an old man dressed in his burial suit.

He got down and dropped the reins and stepped through the low door and doffed his hat. The old man had his hands composed upon his chest and he had no shoes on and his bare feet had been tied together at the toes with twine so that they would not lie asplay. Billy called softly into the darkness of the house but that room was all the house there was. Four empty chairs stood against one wall. A fine dust lay over everything. High in the rear wall was one small window and he crossed the room and looked out into the patio behind the house. An old horse-drawn hearse stood with the wagonshafts tilted back against the box. In an open shed at the far side of the enclosure stood a raw wood coffin on sawhorses made from pine poles. The lid of the coffin leaned against the wall of the shed. The coffin and the lid had been blacked on the outside but the inside of the box was raw new wood and no cloth or any lining to it.

He turned and looked at the old man on his coolingboard. The old man had a moustache and his moustache and his hair were silver gray. The hands crossed at his chest were broad and sturdy. His nails had not been cleaned. His skin was dark and dusty, his bare feet square and knotty. The suit he wore seemed small for him and was of a cut no longer seen even in that country and the old man had most likely had it all his life.

He picked up a small yellow flower in shape like a daisy and which he'd seen grow by the roadside and he looked at the flower and at the old man. In the room the smell of wax, a faint hint of rot. A frail afterscent of burnt copal. Qué novedades ahora viejo? he said. He put the flower in the buttonhole of his shirtpocket and went out and pulled the door shut behind him.

NONE IN THAT TOWN knew what had become of the girl. Her mother had moved away. Her sister had gone to Mexico years since, who knew what happened to such girls? In the afternoon the wedding party came up the street with the bride and groom sitting on the box of the covered carreta. They passed slowly, accompanied by drum and cornet, the cart creaking, the bride in her veil of white, the groom in black. Their smiles like grimaces, terror in their eyes. In appearance they were like certain folk figures of that country who dance together with their own pale bones painted on their costumes. The cart in its slow creaking like that which fords the dreams of the paisano in his weary sleep, passing slowly from left to right through the irrestorable night for which alone he labors, dying away toward the dawn in a faint rattle, a tenuous dread.

In the evening they carried the old man up from the dead-house and interred him in the cemetery among the tilted weath-ered boards that passed for tombstones in that austere upland country. No one questioned the right of the güero to be among the mourners and he nodded silently to them and entered the low house where a table had been laid with much of the best that the country had to offer. While he was standing against the wall eating tamales a woman came up to him and said to him that the girl would not be so easy to find as she was a notorious bandida and that many people were looking for her. She said it was rumored that at La Babícora they had put a price on her head. She said that some believed that the girl made gifts of silver and jewels to the poor and others believed that she was a witch or demon. It was also possible that the girl was dead although it was certainly not true that she had been killed at Ignacio Zaragosa.

He studied her. She was just a young woman of the campo.

Dressed in a poor black shift of cotton imperfectly mordant, imperfectly dyed. The blacking of it had left dark rings at her wrists.

Y por qué me dice esto pues? he said.

She stood with her upper lip in her lower teeth. Finally she said that it was because she knew who he was.

Y quién soy? he said.

She said that he was the brother of the güerito.

He lowered his foot from the wall behind him and looked at her and he looked beyond her at the dark mourners who filed past and foraged from the board like those same figures of death at the feast and he looked at her again. He asked her if she knew where he could find his brother.

She didnt answer. The movement of figures in the room slowed, the low mutterings of the condolent died to a whisper. The mourners wished one another that they profit from their meal and then all of it ground away in the history of its own repetition and he could hear those antecedent ceremonies dropping somewhere like wooden blocks into their slots. Like tumblers in a lock or like the wooden gearteeth in old machinery slipping one by one into the mortices cut in the cogwheel rolling up to meet them. No sabe? she said.

No.

She put her hand forefinger first against her mouth. Almost in such a gesture as to admonish one to silence. She held her hand out as if she might touch him. She said that his brother's bones lay in the cemetery at San Buenaventura.

It was dark when he went out and untied the horse and mounted up. He rode out past the sallow waxen windowlights and took the road south the way he'd come. Beyond the first rise the town vanished behind him and the stars swarmed everywhere in the blackness overhead and there was no sound at all in the night save the steady clop of the hooves in the road, the faint creak of leather, the breath of the horses.

He rode that country for weeks making inquiry of anyone willing to be inquired of. In a bodega in the mountain town of

Temosachic he first heard lines from that corrido in which the young güero comes down from the north. Pelo tan rubio. Pistola en mano. Qué buscas joven? Que te levantas tan temprano. He asked the corridero who was this joven of which he sang but he only said that it was a youth who sought justice as the song told and that he had been dead many years. The corridero held the fretted neck of his instrument with one hand and raised his glass from the table and toasted silently his inquisitor and toasted aloud the memory of all just men in the world for as it was sung in the corrido theirs was a bloodfilled road and the deeds of their lives were writ in that blood which was the world's heart's blood and he said that serious men sang their song and their song only.

Late April in the town of Madera he stabled his horse and went afoot through a fair in the field beyond the railtracks. It was cold in that mountain town and the air was filled with the smoke of piñon wood and the smell of pitch from the sawmill. In the field the lights were strung overhead and barkers called out their nostrums or called out the wonders hid within the shabby stenciled pitchtents staked with guyropes in the trampled grass. He bought a cup of cider from a vendor and watched the faces of the townsfolk, the faces dark and serious, the black eyes that seemed on the point of ignition beneath the feria lights. The girls that passed holding hands. The naive boldness of their glances. He stood before a painted caravan where a man in a red and gilded pulpit chanted to a gathering of men. A wheel with the figures from the lotería was fastened to the wall of the caravan and a girl in a red sheath and a black and silver bolero jacket stood on a wood platform ready to turn the wheel. The man in the pulpit turned to the girl and held out his cane and the girl smiled and pulled down on the side of the wheel and set it clacking. All faces turned to watch. The nails in the rim of the wheel went ratcheting over the leather pawl and the wheel slowed and came to a stop and the woman turned to the crowd and smiled. The pitchman held up his cane again and named the fading figure on the wheel whose turn had come.

La sirena, he cried.

No one moved.

Alguien?

He surveyed the crowd. They stood within a makeshift cuadra of rope. He held the cane out over them as if to ordain them into some sort of collective. The cane was black enamel and the silver head of it was in the form of a bust that may have been a likeness of the pitchman himself.

Otra vez, he cried.

His eyes swept over them. They swept over Billy where he stood alone at the edge of the crowd and they swept back. The wheel clacked and spun on its slightly eccentric track, the figures wheeled into a blur. The leather stop chattered.

A small toothless man sidled up to him and tugged at his shirt. He fanned before him the deck of cards. On the backs a pattern of arcane symbols woven into a damascene. Tome, he said. Pronto, pronto.

Cuánto?

Está libre. Tome.

He took a peso coin from his pocket and tried to hand it to the man but the man shook his head. He looked toward the wheel. The wheel slapped slowly.

Nada, nada, he said. Tenga prisa.

The wheel slapped, slapped. He took a card.

Espere, cried the pitchman. Espere . . .

The wheel turned a last soft click and stopped.

La calavera, cried the pitchman.

He turned over his card. Printed on it was the calavera.

Alguien? cried the pitchman. In the crowd they looked from one to the other.

The small man at his side seized his elbow. Lo tiene, he hissed. Lo tiene.

Qué gano?

The man shook his head impatiently. He tried to hold up his hand that held the card. He said that he would get to see.

Ver qué?

Adentro, hissed the man. Adentro. He reached and snatched

the card from his grip and held it aloft. Aquí, he called. Aquí
tenemos la calavera.

The pitchman swept his cane in a slow acceleration over the
heads of the crowd and then suddenly pointed the silver cap
toward Billy and the shill.

Tenemos ganador, he cried. Adelante, adelante.

Venga, wheezed the shill. He tugged at Billy's elbow. But
Billy had already seen bleeding through the garish paintwork
old lettering from a prior life and he recognized the caravan of
the traveling opera company that he'd seen standing with its
gilded wheelspokes in the smoky courtyard of the hacienda at
San Diego when he and Boyd had first ridden through the gates
there in that long ago and the caravan he'd seen stranded by the
roadside while the beautiful diva sat beneath her awning and
waited for men and horses to return who would not return ever.
He pushed the shill's hand from his sleeve. No quiero ver, he
said.

Sí, sí, slurred the shill. Es un espectáculo. Nunca ha visto
nada como esto.

He seized the shill's thin wrist and held it. Oiga, hombre, he
said. No quiero verlo, me entiende?

The shill shrank in his grip, he cast a despairing look back
over his shoulder toward the pitchman who stood waiting with
his cane resting across the rostrum before him. All had turned
to see the winner at the outermost reach of the lights. The
woman by the wheel stood coquettishly, her forefinger twisted
into the dimple in her cheek. The pitchman raised his cane and
made with it a sweeping motion. Adelante, he cried. Qué pasó?

He pushed the shill from him and released his wrist but the
shill far from being cast down only crept to his side and plucking
with small motions of his fingers at his clothes began to whisper
at his ear of the attractions of the spectacle within the caravan.
The pitchman called out to him again. He said that everyone
was waiting. But Billy had already turned to go and the pitchman called after him a last time and made some comment to the
crowd which set them laughing and trying to see over their

shoulders. The shill stood forlornly with the barata in his hands but the pitchman said that there would be no third assay with the wheel but rather the woman who turned the wheel would make a selection herself as to who should enter free. She smiled and scanned the faces with her painted eyes and pointed out a young boy at the forefront of the crowd but the pitchman said that he was too young and that it would not be permitted and the woman made a pout and said that all the same he was muy guapo and then she selected a brownskinned peon who stood stiffly before her in what may have been rented clothes and came down the steps and took him by the hand and the pitchman held up a roll of tickets in his fist and the men pressed forward to purchase them.

He walked out beyond the strung lights and crossed the field to where he'd left his horse and he paid the establero and led Niño clear of the other animals and mounted up. He looked back at the haze of the carnival lights burning in the crisp and smoky air and then rode out across the railtracks and took the road south out of Madera toward Temosachic.

A week later he rode again through Babícora in the early morning dark. Cool and quiet. No dogs. The hoofclop of the horses. The blue moonshadow of the horses and the rider passing slant along the street in a constant headlong falling. The road north had been freshly graded with a fresno and he rode along the selvedge through the soft dirt of the endspill. Dark junipers out on the plain islanded in the dawn. Dark cattle. A white sun rising.

He watered the horses at a grassy ciénaga where ancient cottonwoods stood in an elfin round and rolled himself into his soogan and slept. When he woke a man was sitting a horse watching him. He sat up. The man smiled. Te conozco, he said.

Billy reached and got his hat and put it on. Yeah, he said. And I know you.

Mande?

Dónde está su compañero?

The man lifted one hand from the pommel in a vague gesture.
Se murió, he said. Dónde está la muchacha?

Lo mismo.

The man smiled. He said that God's ways were strange ones.

Tiene razón.

Y su hermano?

No sé. Muerto también, tal vez.

Tantos, said the man.

Billy looked toward where the horses were grazing. He'd
been sleeping with his head on the mochila where his pistol was
buckled away. The man's eyes followed his where they looked.
He said for every man that death selects another is reprieved
and he smiled in a conspiratorial manner. As one met with
another of his kind. He leaned forward with his hands squared
on the pommel of his saddle and spat.

Qué piensa? he said.

Billy wasnt sure what it was that he was being asked. He said
men die.

The man sat his horse and weighed this soberly. As if there
might be some deeper substrate to this reflection with which he
must reckon. He said that men believe death's elections to be a
thing inscrutable yet every act invites the act which follows and
to the extent that men put one foot before the other they are
accomplices in their own deaths as in all such facts of destiny.
He said that moreover it could not be otherwise that men's ends
are dictated at their birth and that they will seek their deaths in
the face of every obstacle. He said that both views were one
view and that while men may meet with death in strange and
obscure places which they might well have avoided it was more
correct to say that no matter how hidden or crooked the path to
their destruction yet they would seek it out. He smiled. He
spoke as one who seemed to understand that death was the
condition of existence and life but an emanation thereof.

Qué piensa usted? he said. Billy said that he had no opinion
beyond the one he'd given. He said that whether a man's life
was writ in a book someplace or whether it took its form day

by day was one and the same for it had but one reality and that was the living of it. He said that while it was true that men shape their own lives it was also true that they could have no shape other for what then would that shape be?

Bien dicho, the man said. He looked across the country. He said that he could read men's thoughts. Billy didnt point out to him that he'd already asked him twice for his. He asked the man could he tell what he was thinking now but the man only said that their thoughts were one and the same. Then he said he harbored no grudge toward any man over a woman for they were only property afoot to be confiscated and that it was no more than a game and not to be taken seriously by real men. He said that he had no very high opinion of men who killed over whores. In any case, he said, the bitch was dead, the world rolled on.

He smiled again. He had something in his mouth and he rolled it to one side and sucked at his teeth and rolled it back. He touched his hat.

Bueno, he said. El camino espera.

He touched his hat again and roweled the horse and sawed it around until its eyes rolled and it squatted and stamped and then went trotting out through the trees and into the road where it soon disappeared from sight. Billy unbuckled the mochila and took out the pistol and thumbed open the gate and turned the cylinder and checked the chambers and then lowered the hammer with his thumb and sat for a long time listening and waiting.

On the fifteenth of May by the first newspaper he'd seen in seven weeks he rode again into Casas Grandes and stabled his horse and took a room at the Camino Recto Hotel. He rose in the morning and walked down the tiled hallway to the bath. When he came back he stood in the window where the morning light fell slant upon the raw cords in the worn carpet underfoot and listened to a girl singing in the garden below. She was sitting on a cloth of white canvas and piled on the canvas were nueces or pecans some bushels in quantity. She sat with a flat stone in the crook of her knees and she was breaking the pecans with a stone mano and as she worked she sang. Leaning forward with her dark hair veiled about her hands she worked and sang. She sang:

> Pueblo de Bachiniva
> Abril era el mes
> Jinetes armados
> Llegaron los seis

She crushed the hulls between the stones, she separated out the meats and dropped them in a jar at her side.

> Si tenía miedo
> No se le veía en su cara
> Cuantos vayan llegando
> El güerito les espera

Splitting out with her fineboned fingers the meat from the hulls, the delicate fissured hemispheres in which is writ we must believe each feature of the tree which bore them, each feature of the tree they'd come to bear. Then she sang the same two verses over. He buttoned his shirt and got his hat and went down the stairs and out into the courtyard. When she saw him coming across the cobbles she stopped singing. He touched his hat and wished her a good day. She looked up and smiled. She was a girl of perhaps sixteen. She was very beautiful. He asked her if she knew any more verses of the corrido which she sang but she did not. She said that it was an old corrido. She said that it was very sad and that at the end the güerito and his novia die in each other's arms for they have no more ammunition. She said that at the end the patrón's men ride away and the people come from the town and carry the güerito and his novia to a secret place and bury them there and the little birds flew away but that she did not remember all the words and anyway she was embarrassed that he had been listening to her sing. He smiled. He told her that she had a pretty voice and she turned away and clucked her tongue.

He stood looking out across the courtyard toward the moun
tains to the west. The girl watched him.

Déme su mano, she said.

Mande?

Déme su mano. She held out her own hand in a fist before
her. He squatted on his bootheels and held out his hand and
she gave him a handful of the shelled pecans and then closed his
hand with hers and looked about as if it were some secret gift
and someone might see. Ándale pues, she said. He thanked her
and stood and walked back across the courtyard and up to his
room but when he looked from the window again she was gone.

Days to come he rode up through the high country of the
Babícora. He'd build his fire in some sheltered swale and at
night sometimes he'd walk out over the grasslands and lie on
the ground in the world's silence and study the burning firmament above him. Walking back to the fire those nights he often
thought about Boyd, thought of him sitting by night at just such
a fire in just such country. The fire in the bajada no more than
a glow, hid in the ground like some secret glimpse of the earth's
burning core broke through into the darkness. He seemed to
himself a person with no prior life. As if he had died in some
way years ago and was ever after some other being who had no
history, who had no ponderable life to come.

He saw in his riding occasional parties of vaqueros crossing
the high grasslands, sometimes mounted on mules for their
good footing in the mountains, sometimes driving beeves before
them. It was cold in the mountains at night but they seemed
thinly dressed and had only their serapes in which to sleep.
They were called mascareñas for the whitefaced cattle bred
on the Babícora and they were called agringados because they
worked for the white man. They crossed in silent defile over
the talus slopes and rode up through the passes toward the high
grassy vegas, sitting their horses with their easy formality, the
low sun catching the tin cups tied to their saddlehorns. He saw
their fires burning on the mountain at night but never did he go
to them.

On a certain evening just before dark he entered into a road and turned and followed it west. The red sun that burned in the broad gap of the mountains before him sloughed out of its form and was slowly sucked away to light all the sky in a deep red afterflash. When darkness had come there stood in the distance on the plain the single yellow light from a dwelling and he rode on until he came to a small weatherboard cabin and sat the horse before it and called out.

A man came to the door and stepped out onto the gallery. Quién es? he said.

Un viajero.

Cuántos son ustedes?

Yo sólo.

Bueno, the man said. Desmonte. Pásale.

He stepped down and tied the bridlereins about the porch post and mounted the steps and removed his hat. The man held the door for him and he entered and the man followed and shut the door and nodded toward the fire.

They sat and drank coffee. The man's name was Quijada and he was a Yaqui indian from western Sonora and he was the same gerente of the Nahuerichic division of the Babícora who'd told Boyd to cut their horses out of the remuda and take them. He'd seen the lone güero riding in the mountains and told the alguacil not to molest him. He told his guest that he knew who he was and why he'd come. Then he leaned back in his chair. He raised the cup to his lips and drank and watched the fire.

You're the man give us back our horses, Billy said.

He nodded. He leaned forward and he looked at Billy and then he sat looking into the fire. The thick handleless porcelain cup from which he drank looked like a chemist's mortar and he sat with his elbows on his knees and held it before him in both hands and Billy thought that he would say something more but he did not. Billy drank from his cup and sat holding it. The fire ticked. Outside in the world all was silence. Is my brother dead? he said.

Yes.

He was killed in Ignacio Zaragosa?

No. In San Lorenzo.

The girl too?

No. When they took her away she was covered in blood and she was falling down and so it was natural that people thought that she had been shot but it was not so.

What became of her?

I dont know. Perhaps she went back to her family. She was very young.

I asked about her in Namiquipa. They didnt know what had become of her.

They would not tell you in Namiquipa.

Where is my brother buried?

He is buried at Buenaventura.

Is there a stone?

There is a board. He was very popular with the people. He was a popular figure.

He didnt kill the manco in La Boquilla.

I know.

I was there.

Yes. He killed two men in Galeana. No one knows why. They did not even work for the latifundio. But the brother of one was a friend to Pedro Lopéz.

The alguacil.

The alguacil. Yes.

He'd seen him once in the mountains, he and his henchmen, the three of them descending a ridgeline in the twilight. The alguacil carried a short sword in a beltscabbard and he answered to no one. Quijada leaned back and sat with his boots crossed before him. The cup in his lap. Both watched the fire. As if some work were there annealing. Quijada raised his cup as if to drink. Then he lowered it again.

There is the latifundio of Babícora, he said. With all the wealth and power of Mr Hearst to call upon. And there are the campesinos in their rags. Which do you believe will prevail?

I dont know.

His days are numbered.

Mr Hearst?

Yes.

Why do you work for the Babícora?

Because they pay me.

Who was Socorro Rivera?

Quijada tapped the rim of his cup softly with the gold band on his finger. Socorro Rivera tried to organize the workers against the latifundio. He was killed at the paraje of Las Varitas by the Guardias Blancas five years ago along with two other men. Crecencio Macías and Manuel Jiménez.

Billy nodded.

The soul of Mexico is very old, said Quijada. Whoever claims to know it is either a liar or a fool. Or both. Now that the yankees have again betrayed them the Mexicans are eager to reclaim their indian blood. But we do not want them. Most particularly the Yaqui. The Yaqui have long memories.

I believe you. Did you ever see my brother again after we left with the horses?

No.

How do you know about him?

He was a hunted man. Where would you go? Inevitably he was taken in by Casares. You go to the enemy of your enemies.

He was only fifteen. Sixteen, I guess.

All the better.

They didnt take very good care of him, did they?

He didnt want to be taken care of. He wanted to shoot people. What makes one a good enemy also makes one a good friend.

Yet you work for Mr Hearst?

Yes.

He turned and looked at Billy. I am not a Mexican, he said. I dont have these loyalties. These obligations. I have others.

Would you have shot him yourself?

Your brother?

Yes.

If it had come to that. Yes.

Maybe I ought not to be drinkin your coffee.

Maybe not.

They sat for a long time. Finally Quijada leaned forward and studied his cup. He should have gone home, he said.

Yes.

Why didnt he?

I dont know. Maybe the girl.

The girl would not have gone with him?

I suppose she would have. He didnt rightly have a home to go to.

Maybe you are the one who should have cared for him better.

He wasnt easy to care for. You said it yourself.

Yes.

What does the corrido say?

Quijada shook his head. The corrido tells all and it tells nothing. I heard the tale of the güerito years ago. Before your brother was even born.

You dont think it tells about him?

Yes, it tells about him. It tells what it wishes to tell. It tells what makes the story run. The corrido is the poor man's history. It does not owe its allegiance to the truths of history but to the truths of men. It tells the tale of that solitary man who is all men. It believes that where two men meet one of two things can occur and nothing else. In the one case a lie is born and in the other death.

That sounds like death is the truth.

Yes. It sounds like death is the truth. He looked at Billy. Even if the güerito in the song is your brother he is no longer your brother. He cannot be reclaimed.

I aim to take him back with me.

It will not be permitted.

Who would I go to?

There is no one to go to.

Who would I go to if there was someone?

You could apply to God. Otherwise there is no one.

Billy shook his head. He sat regarding his own dark visage

where it yawed in the white ring of the cup. After a while he looked up. He looked into the fire. Do you believe in God? he said.

Quijada shrugged. On godly days, he said.

No one can tell you what your life is goin to be, can they?

No.

It's never like what you expected.

Quijada nodded. If people knew the story of their lives how many would then elect to live them? People speak about what is in store. But there is nothing in store. The day is made of what has come before. The world itself must be surprised at the shape of that which appears. Perhaps even God.

We come down here to get our horses. Me and my brother. I dont think he even cared about the horses, but I was too dumb to see it. I didnt know nothin about him. I thought I did. I think he knew a lot more about me. I'd like to take him back and bury him in his own country.

Quijada drained his cup and sat holding it in his lap.

I take it you dont think that's such a good idea.

I think you may have some problems.

But that aint all you think.

No.

You think he belongs where he's at.

I think the dead have no nationality.

No. But their kin do.

Quijada didnt answer. After a long time he stirred. He leaned forward. He turned the white porcelain bowl up and held it in the palm of his hand and regarded it. The world has no name, he said. The names of the cerros and the sierras and the deserts exist only on maps. We name them that we do not lose our way. Yet it was because the way was lost to us already that we have made those names. The world cannot be lost. We are the ones. And it is because these names and these coordinates are our own naming that they cannot save us. That they cannot find for us the way again. Your brother is in that place which the world has chosen for him. He is where he is supposed to be. And yet the place he has found is also of his own choosing. That is a piece of luck not to be despised.

GRAY SKY, gray land. All day he slouched north on the wet and slouching horse through the sandy muck of the upcountry roads. The rain went harrying over the road before him in the gusts of wind and rattled over his slicker and the hooftracks oozed shut behind him. In the evening he heard again the cranes overhead, passing high above the overcast, balancing beneath them the bight of the earth's curve, earth's weather. Their metal eyes grooved to the pathways which God has chosen for them to follow. Their hearts in flood.

He rode into the town of San Buenaventura in the evening and he rode through pools of standing water past the alameda with its whitepainted treetrunks and the old white church and out along the old road to Gallego. The rain had stopped and rain dripped from the alameda trees and dripped from the high canales in the mudwalled houses he passed. The road led up through the low hills to the east of the town and set in a bench of land there a mile or so above the town lay the cemetery.

He turned off and slogged out along the muddy lane and halted his horse before the wooden gates. The cemetery was a large and wild enclosure set in a field filled with loose stones and brambles and surrounded by a low mud wall already then in ruins. He halted and looked out over this desolation. He turned and looked back at the packhorse and he looked at the gray scud of clouds and at the evening light failing in the west. A wind was blowing down from the gap in the mountains and he stepped down and dropped the reins and passed through the gate and started out across the rough cobbled field. A raven flew up out of the bracken and parried away on the wind croaking thinly. The red sandstone dolmens that stood upright among the low tablets and crosses on that wild heath looked like the distant ruins of some classic enclave ringed about by the blue mountains, the closer hills.

Most of the graves were no more than cairns of rock without marker of any kind. Some held a simple wooden cross composed of two slats nailed together or twisted together with wire. The cobbled rocks everywhere underfoot were the scattered remains of these cairns and ignoring the red stone steles this place looked the burial of some aftermath of battle. Other than the wind in the wild rough grass there was no sound at all. He walked out along a narrow and uncertain footpath winding among the graves, among the slabs and sepulchre tablets blacked over with lichen. In the middle distance a red stone pillar in the shape of a pollarded treetrunk.

His brother was buried against the southmost wall under a board cross in which had been burned with a hot nail the words Fall el 24 de febrero 1943 sus hermanos en armas dedican este recuerdo D E P. A ring of rusted wire that once had been a wreath leaned against the board. There was no name.

He squatted and took off his hat. Off to the south a pile of trash was smoldering in the damp and a black smoke rose into the dark overcast. The desolation of that place was a thing exquisite.

It was dark when he rode back into Buenaventura. He dismounted before the church door and walked in and took off his hat. At the altar a few small candles burned and in that half fugitive light knelt a solitary figure bent at prayer. He walked up the aisle. There were loose tiles in the floor that rocked and clicked under his boots. He bent and touched the kneeling figure on the arm. Señora, he said.

She raised her head, a dark seamed face faintly visible in the darker folds of her rebozo.

Dónde está el sepulturero?

Muerto.

Quién está encargado del cementerio?

Dios.

Dónde está el sacerdote.

Se fué.

He looked about at the dim interior of the church. The woman

seemed to be waiting for further questions but he could think
of none to put.

Qué quiere, joven? she said.

Nada. Está bien. He looked down at her. Por quién está
orando? he said.

She said that she only prayed. She said that she left it to God
as to how the prayers should be apportioned. She prayed for
all. She would pray for him.

Gracias.

No puedo hacerlo de otro modo.

He nodded. He knew her well enough, this old woman of
Mexico, her sons long dead in that blood and violence which
her prayers and her prostrations seemed powerless to appease.
Her frail form was a constant in that land, her silent anguishings.
Beyond the church walls the night harbored a millennial dread
panoplied in feathers and the scales of royal fish and if it yet fed
upon the children still who could say what worse wastes of war
and torment and despair the old woman's constancy might not
have stayed, what direr histories yet against which could be
counted at last nothing more than her small figure bent and
mumbling, her crone's hands clutching her beads of fruitseed.
Unmoving, austere, implacable. Before just such a God.

When he rode out the next morning early the rain had stopped
but the day had not cleared and the landscape lay gray under a
gray sky. To the south the raw peaks of the Sierra del Nido
loomed out of the clouds and closed away again. He dismounted
at the wooden gate and hobbled the packhorse and untied the
spade and mounted up again and rode out down the footpath
among the cobbled rocks with the spade over his shoulder.

When he reached the gravesite he stood down and chucked
the spade in the ground and took his gloves from the saddlebag
and looked at the gray skies and finally he unsaddled the horse
and hobbled it and left it to graze among the stones. Then he
turned and squatted and rocked the fragile wooden cross loose
in its clutch of rocks and lifted it away. The spade was a primi-

tive thing helved in a long paloverde pole and the tang bore the marks where it had been beaten out over a pritchel and the seam rudely welded shut at the forge. He hefted it in his hand and looked again at the sky and bent and began to shovel away the cairn of loose rock over his brother's grave.

He was a long time at his work. He'd taken off his hat and after a while he took off his shirt and laid it across the wall. By what he reckoned to be noon he'd dug down some three feet and he stood the shovel in the dirt and walked back to where he'd left the saddle and the bags and he got out his lunch of beans wrapped in tortillas and sat in the grass eating and drinking water from the canvascovered zinc bottle. There had been no one along the road all morning except for a solitary bus, grinding slowly up the grade and on through the gap toward Gallego to the east.

In the afternoon three dogs appeared and sat down among the stones to watch him. He bent to pick up a rock but they ducked and vanished among the bracken. Later a car came out the cemetery road and stopped at the gate and two women came out along the path and went on to the far west corner of the burial ground. After a while they came back. The man who had driven them sat on the wall and smoked and watched Billy but he did not speak. Billy dug on.

Midafternoon the blade struck the box. He'd thought maybe there would be none. He dug on. By the time he had the top of the box dug clear there was little left of the day. He dug down along the side and felt along the wood for handles but he couldnt find any. He dug on until he had one end of the box clear and by then it was growing dark. He stood the spade in the loose dirt and went to get Niño.

He saddled the horse and led him back to the grave and took down the catchrope and doubled and dallied it and then worked the free end around the box, forcing it along the wood with the blade of the shovel. Then he pitched the shovel to one side and climbed out and untracted the horse and led him slowly forward.

The rope grew taut. He looked back. Then he eased the horse forward again. There was a muffled explosion of wood in the hole and the rope went slack. The horse stopped.

He walked back. The box had collapsed and he could see Boyd's bones in their burial clothes through the broken boards. He sat down in the dirt. The sun had set and it was growing dark. The horse stood at the end of the rope waiting. He felt suddenly cold and he got up and walked over to the wall and got his shirt and pulled it on and came back and stood.

You could just shovel the dirt back in, he said. It wouldnt take a hour.

He walked over to the saddlebags and got out his matches and came back and lit one and held it out over the grave. The box was badly caved. A musty cellar odor rose from the dark ground. He shook out the match and walked over to the horse and unhitched the rope and came back coiling it in his hand and he stood with the coiled rope in the blue and windless dusk and looked off to the north where under the overcast the earliest stars were burning. Well, he said. You could do that.

He worked the end of the rope loose from the coffinbox and laid the rope by on the mound of loose dirt. Then he took up the spade and with the blade of it he split away a long sliver of wood from one of the broken boards and knocked the dirt loose from it against the box and struck a match and got it lit and stood it slantwise in the ground. Finally he climbed down into the grave and by that pale and fluttering light he began to pry apart the boards with the spade and cast them out until the remains of his brother lay wholly to sight, composed on a pallet of rotting rags, lost in his clothes as always.

He rode the horse back out through the gate and got down and skylighted the packhorse off to the south and remounted and rode out and brought the animal back and led it through the gates and back to the grave. He dismounted and untied the bedroll and unrolled it on the ground and pulled loose the tarp and spread it out. It was a windless night and his cryptboard taper was still burning at the side of the grave. He climbed down into the excavation and gathered his brother up in his arms and lifted him out. He weighed nothing. He composed the bones upon the soogan and folded them away and tied the bundle shut at the ends with lengths of pigginstring while the horse stood watching. Over on the gravel highway he could hear the whine of a truck on the grade and the lights came up and swept slowly across the desert and over the bleak headlands and then the truck passed on in its pale wake of dust and ground on toward the east.

By the time he'd filled the grave back in it was close to midnight. He trod down the dirt with his boots and then shoveled the loose rocks back over the top and lastly he took the cross from where he'd leaned it against the wall and stood it in the rocks and piled rocks about it to support it. The wooden torch had long since burned out and he took the charred end of it up and threw it across the wall. Then he threw the spade after it.

He lifted Boyd and laid him across the wooden packframe and he rolled up the blankets from his bedroll and laid them across the horse's haunches and tied everything down. Then he walked over and picked up his hat and put it on and picked up the waterbottle and hung it by its strap over the saddlehorn and mounted up and turned the horse. He sat there for a minute taking a last look around. Then he got down again. He walked over to the grave and pulled the wooden cross loose from the cobbles and carried it back to the packhorse and tied it down on the leftside forks of the packtree and then mounted up again and leading the packhorse rode out through the cemetery and through the gate and down the road. When he reached the highway he crossed it and struck out crosscountry toward the watershed of the Santa María, keeping the polestar to his right, looking back from time to time to see how rode the canvas that held his brother's remains. The little desert foxes barking. The old gods of that country tracing his progress over the darkened ground. Perhaps logging his name into their ancient daybook of vanities.

In two nights' riding he passed the lights of Casas Grandes off to the west, the small city receding away behind him on the plain. He crossed the old road coming down from Guzmán and Sabinal and struck the Casas Grandes River and took the trail north along the river bank. In the early morning hours and before it was quite light he passed through the pueblo of Corralitos, half abandoned, half in ruins. The houses of the town loopholed against the vanished Apaches. The naked slagheaps dark and volcanic against the skyline. He crossed the railroad tracks and an hour north of the town in the gray dawn four horsemen sallied forth from a grove of trees and halted their mounts in the track before him.

He reined the horse. The riders sat silently. The dark animals they rode raised their noses as if to search him out on the air. Beyond the trees the bright flat shape of the river lay like a knife. He studied the men. He'd not seen them move yet they seemed closer. They sat divided before him on the track two and two.

Qué tiena allá? they said.

Los huesos de mi hermano.

They sat in silence. One of the riders detached himself and rode forward. He crossed the track in his riding forward and then crossed it back. Riding erect, archly. As if at some sinister dressage. He halted the horse almost within armreach and he leaned forward with his forearms crossed on the pommel of his saddle.

Huesos? he said.

Sí.

The new light in the east was behind him and his face was a shadow under the shape of his hat. The other riders were darker figures yet. The rider sat upright in the saddle and looked back towards them. Then he turned to Billy again.

Ábralo, he said.

No.

No?

They sat. There was a flash of white beneath his hat as if he'd smiled. What he'd done was to seize his horse's reins in his teeth. The next flash was a knife that had come from somewhere in his clothing and caught the light in turning for just a moment like a fish deep in a river. Billy dropped down from the offside of his horse. The bandolero caught up the packhorse's leadrope but the packhorse balked and squatted on its haunches and the man booted his horse forward and made a pass at the hitchropes with his knife while the packhorse sawed about on the end of the lead. Some among his companions laughed and the man swore and he hauled the packhorse forward and dallied the leadrope to his saddlehorn again and reached and cut the ropes and pulled the soogan of bones to the ground.

Billy was trying to undo the tie on the flap of the saddlebag to get to his pistol but Niño turned and stamped and backed away sawing his head. The bandolero undallied and cast off the leadrope and stepped down. The packhorse turned and went trotting. The man bent above the shrouded form on the ground and unseamed with a single long pass of the knife ropes and soogan all from end to end and kicked aside the coverings to reveal in the graying light Boyd's poor form in the loosely fitting coat with his hands crossed at his chest, the withered hands with the bones imprinted in the leather skin, lying there with his caven face turned up and clutching himself like some fragile being fraught with cold in that indifferent dawn.

You son of a bitch, said Billy. You son of a bitch.

Es un engaño? said the man. Es un engaño?

He kicked at the poor desiccated thing. He turned with the knife.

Dónde está el dinero?

Las alforjas, called out one of the riders. Billy had swung under Niño's neck and he reached again for the flap of the saddlebag on the horse's offside. The bandolero cut open the bedroll under his feet and kicked it apart and trod in it with his boots and turned and then reached and seized Niño's bridle-reins. But the horse must have begun to see the loosening of some demoniac among them for he reared and backed and in his backing trod among the bones and he reared again and pawed and the bandolero was snatched off balance and one forehoof caught his belt and ripped it from him and tore open the front of his trousers. He scrambled from under the horse and swore wildly and made a grab again for the swinging reins and the men behind him laughed and before anyone would have thought of such a thing occurring he plunged his knife into the horse's chest.

The horse stopped and stood quivering. The point of the blade had bedded itself in the animal's breastbone and the bandolero stepped back and threw out his hands.

Goddamn you to hell, Billy said. He held the trembling horse by the throatlatch and took hold of the handle of the knife and pulled the blade from the horse's chest and flung it away. Blood welled, blood ran down the front of the horse. He snatched off his hat and pushed it against the wound and looked wildly back at the mounted men. They sat their horses as before. One of them leaned and spat and jerked his chin at the others. Vámonos, he said.

The bandolero was demanding that Billy go fetch the knife. Billy didnt answer. He held his hat against the horse's chest and tried once more to reach back and unfasten the saddlebag pocket but he could not reach it. The bandolero reached and got hold of the tiestraps and pulled down the saddlebags onto the ground and dragged them from under the horse.

Vámonos, called the rider.

But the bandolero had already found the pistol and he held it up to show to them. He dumped the bags out and kicked Billy's possibles over the ground, his spare clothes, his razor. He picked up a shirt and held it up and then draped it across his shoulder and he cocked the pistol and spun the cylinder and let the hammer down again. He stepped across the wreckage of the bones unshrouded from out of the soogan and cocked the pistol and put it to Billy's head and demanded his money. Billy could feel his hat going warm and sticky with blood where he held it to the horse's chest. The blood was seeping through the felt and running on his arm. You go to hell, he said.

Vámonos, called the rider. He turned his horse

The man with the pistol looked at them. Tengo que encontrar mi cuchillo, he called.

He uncocked the pistol and went to shove it in his belt but he had no belt. He turned and looked upriver where the day was coming beyond the brambly river breaks. The breath of the standing horses plumed and vanished. The leader told him to get his horse. He said that he did not need his knife and that he had killed a good horse for no reason.

Then they were gone. Billy stood holding the crushed and bloodsogged hat and he heard the horses crossing the river upstream and then he just heard the river and the first birds that were waking in that country and his own breath and the labored breathing of the horse. He put his arm around the horse's neck and held it and he could feel it trembling and feel it lean against him and he was afraid that it would die and he could feel in the horse's breast a despair much like his own.

He wrung the blood from the hat and wiped his hand on his trousers and unbuckled and pulled down the saddle and left it lying where it fell in the track along with the other wreckage there and he led the horse slowly out through the trees and across a gravel bar and into the river. The water was cold running into his boots and he talked to the horse and bent and lifted a hatful of water and poured it over the animal's chest. The horse steamed in the cold and its breathing had begun to suck and rattle and it sounded all wrong. He put the palm of his hand over the hole but the blood ran between his fingers. He stripped off his shirt and folded it and pushed it against the animal's chest but the shirt soon filled with blood and still the blood ran.

He'd let the reins trail in the river and he patted the horse and spoke to it and left it standing there while he waded to the river bank and clawed up a handful of wet clay from under the roots of the willows. He came back and plastered the clay over the wound and troweled it down with the flat of his hand. He rinsed out the shirt and wrung the water from it and folded it over the plaster of mud and waited in the gray light with the steam rising off the river. He didnt know if the blood would ever stop running but it did and in the first pale reach of sunlight across the eastern plain the gray landscape seemed to hush and the birds to hush and in the new sun the peaks of the distant mountains to the west beyond the wild Bavispe country rose out of the dawn like a dream of the world. The horse turned and laid its long bony face upon his shoulder.

He led the animal ashore and up into the track and turned it to face the light. He looked in its mouth for blood but there was none that he could see. Old Niño, he said. Old Niño. He left the saddle and the saddlebags where they'd fallen. The trampled bedrolls. The body of his brother awry in its wrappings with one yellow forearm outflung. He walked the horse slowly at his elbow and held the mudstained shirt against its chest. His boots sloshed with river water and he was very cold. They walked up the track and into a grove of wild mahogany where he'd be partly hid from sight of any parties passing along the river and then he went back and got the saddle and the saddlebags and the bedroll. Lastly he went to fetch the remains of his brother.

The bones seemed held together only by the dry outer covering of hide and by their integuments but they were of a piece and nothing scattered. He knelt in the road and refolded the weightless arms and wrapped the soogan about and sorted the ropes and tied the ends to make the severed pieces do. By the time he had all this done the sun was well up and he gathered the bones in his arms and carried them up into the trees and laid them on the ground. Lastly he walked back out to the river and washed and wrung out his hat and filled it with river water and carried it back to the horse to see if it would drink. The horse would not. It was lying in the leaves and the shirt was lying in the leaves and the clay compress had begun to break away and blood was running from the wound again and pooling darkly in the little jagged cups of the dry mahogany leaves and the horse would not raise its head.

He walked out and looked for the packhorse but he couldnt see it. He went to the river and squatted and rinsed out the shirt and put it on and he got a fresh handful of clay from under the willows and carried it back and caked the new mud over the old and sat shivering in the leaves watching the horse. After a while he went back out and down the track to hunt for the other horse.

He couldnt find it. When he came back up the river he picked up the waterbottle where it lay by the side of the trail and he picked up his cup and his razor and walked back up to the trees. The horse was shivering in the leaves and he pulled one of the blankets from the bedroll and spread it over the horse and sat with his hand on the horse's shoulder and after a while he fell asleep.

He woke with a start from some half desperate dream. He bent over the horse where it lay quietly breathing among the leaves and he looked at the sun to see how far the day had got to. His shirt was almost dry on him and he unbuttoned the pocket and took out his money and spread it out to dry. Then he got the box of wood matches out of the saddlebags and spread them also. He walked out down the track to the spot where the ambuscade had occurred and cast about in the trackside chaparral until he found the knife. It was an oldfashioned dirk ground down out of a cheap military knife with an edge honed into both sides of the blade. He wiped it on his trousers and went back and put the knife with his other plunder. Then he walked out to where he'd left Boyd. A column of red ants had found the bones and he squatted in the leaves and studied them and then rose and trod them into the dirt and picked up the soogan and carried it out and lodged it in the fork of one of the trees and walked back and sat beside the horse.

No one passed the day long. In the afternoon he went once more to look for the other horse. He thought maybe it had gone upriver or that the highwaymen had taken it but in any case he never saw it again. By dark the matches had dried and he built a fire and put some beans to boil and sat by the fire and listened to the river passing in the dark. The cottoncolored moon that had stood in the daysky to the east rose overhead and he lay in his blankets and watched to see if any birds might cross before it on their way upriver north but if they did he did not see them and after a while he slept.

In the night as he slept Boyd came to him and squatted by the deep embers of the fire as he'd done times by the hundreds and smiled his soft smile that was not quite cynical and he took off his hat and held it before him and looked down into it. In the dream he knew that Boyd was dead and that the subject of his being so must be approached with a certain caution for that which was circumspect in life must be doubly so in death and he'd no way to know what word or gesture might subtract him back again into that nothingness out of which he'd come. When finally he did ask him what it was like to be dead Boyd only smiled and looked away and would not answer. They spoke of other things and he tried not to wake from the dream but the ghost dimmed and faded and he woke and lay looking up at the stars through the bramblework of the treelimbs and he tried to think of what that place could be where Boyd was but Boyd was dead and wasted in his bones wrapped in the soogan upriver in the trees and he turned his face to the ground and wept.

He was asleep in the morning when he heard the shouts of arrieros and the crack of whips and a wild singing in the woods downriver. He pulled on his boots and walked out to where the horse lay in the leaves. Its side rose and fell beneath the blanket that he had feared would be stiff and cold and it turned up one eye to him as he knelt over it. An eye in which lay cupped the sky and arching trees and his own nearing face. He placed one hand over the animal's chest where the mud had caked and dried and broken. The hair was stiff and bristly with dried blood. He stroked the muscled shoulder and spoke to the horse and the horse exhaled slowly through its nose.

He fetched water again in his hat but the horse could not drink without rising. He sat and wet its mouth with his hand and listened to the arrieros on the track drawing nearer and after a while he rose and walked out and stood waiting for them.

They appeared out of the trees driving a team of six yoked oxen and they wore costumes such as he'd never seen before. Indians or gypsies perhaps by the bright colors of the shirts and the sashes that they wore. They drove the oxen with jerkline and jockeystick and the oxen labored and swayed in the traces and their breath steamed in the morning cold. Behind them on a handmade float built from green lumber and carried on old truckaxles was an airplane. It was of some ancient vintage and it was disassembled and the wings tied down with ropes alongside the fuselage. The rudder in the vertical stabilizer swung back and forth in small erratic movements with the jostling of the float as if to make corrections in their course and the oxen swayed heavily in their harness and the mismatched rubber tires rumpled softly over the stones and through the weeds on either side of the narrow track.

The drovers when they saw him raised their hands in greeting and cried out. Almost as if they'd been expecting to come upon him soon or late. They wore necklaces and silver bracelets and some wore hooplets of gold in their ears and they called out to him and pointed along the narrow road upstream in the river's bend to a grassy flat where they would stop and rendezvous. The airplane was little more than a skeleton with sunbleached shreds of linen the color of stewed rhubarb clinging to the steambent ashwood ribs and stays and inside you could see the wires and cables that ran aft to the rudder and elevators and the cracked and curled and sunblacked leather of the seats and in their tarnished nickel bezels the glass of instrument dials glaucous and clouded from the pumicing of the desert sands. The wingstruts were tied in bundles alongside and the blades of the propellor were bent back along the cowling and the landingstruts were bent beneath the fuselage.

They passed on and halted in the flat and they left the youngest among them to tend the animals and then they came back down the track rolling cigarettes and passing among them an esclarajo made from a 50 caliber shellcasing in which burned a bit of tow. They were gypsies from Durango and the first thing that they asked him was what was the matter with the horse.

He told them that the horse was wounded and that he thought its condition was serious. One of them asked him when this had occurred and he said that it was the day before. He sent one of the younger men back to the float and in a few minutes he returned with an old canvas musette bag. Then they all walked up through the trees to look at the horse.

They gypsy knelt in the leaves and looked first into the animal's eyes. Then he pinched away the cracked mud from its chest and looked at the wound. He looked up at Billy.

Herida de cuchillo, said Billy.

The gypsy's expression did not change and he did not take his eyes from Billy. Billy looked at the other men. They were squatting on their haunches about the horse. He thought that if the horse died they might eat it. He said that the horse had been attacked by a lunatic one of four among a band of robbers. The man nodded. He passed his hand across the underside of his chin. He did not look at the horse again. He asked Billy if he wanted to sell the horse and Billy knew for the first time that the horse would live.

They squatted there, all watching him. He looked at the drover. He said that the horse had belonged to his father and that he could not part with him and the man nodded and opened the bag.

Porfirio, he said. Tráigame agua.

He looked down through the trees toward Billy's camp where a thin wisp of smoke stood in the morning air motionless as rope. He called after the man to put the water to boil and then looked at Billy again. Con su permiso, he said.

Por supuesto.

Ladrones.

Sí. Ladrones.

The drover looked down at the horse. He gestured with his chin out toward the tree where Boyd's bones were lodged in their trussings.

Qué tiene allá? he said.

Los huesos de mi hermano.

Huesos, said the gypsy. He turned and looked toward the river where his man had gone with the bucket. The other three men crouched waiting. Rafael, he said. Leña. He turned to Billy and smiled. He looked about at the little grove of trees and he put the flat of his hand to his cheek in a curious gesture such as a man might make who remembers he has forgotten something. He wore on one forefinger an ornate ring of gold and jewels and he wore a golden rope about his throat. He smiled again and gestured toward the fire that they proceed there.

They collected wood and built back the fire and they fetched rocks to make a trivet and there they set the bucket to boil. Soaking in the pail were several handfuls of small green leaves and the waterbearer had covered the bucket with what looked to be an old brass cymbal and all sat about the fire and watched the bucket and after a while it began to steam among the flames.

The one called Rafael lifted the cover with a stick and laid the cover by and stirred the green froth within and then put the cover back again. A pale green tea ran down the sides of the bucket and hissed in the fire. The chief of the drovers sat rolling a cigarette. He passed the cloth pouch on to the man beside him and he leaned and took a burning branch from the fire and with his head cocked to one side lit the cigarette and then put the branch back in the fire. Billy asked him if he himself was not afraid of robbers in that country but the man only said that the robbers were loath to molest the gitanos for they also were men of the road.

Y adónde van con el aeroplano? said Billy.

The gypsy gestured with his chin. Al norte, he said.

They smoked. The bucket steamed. The gypsy smiled.

Con respecto al aeroplano, he said, hay tres historias. Cuál quiere oír?

Billy smiled. He said that he wished to hear the true history.

The gypsy pursed his lips. He seemed to be considering the plausibility of this. Finally he said that it was necessary to state that there were two such airplanes, both of them flown by young Americans, both lost in the mountains in the calamitous summer of nineteen fifteen.

He drew deeply upon the cigarette and blew the smoke toward the fire. Certain facts were known, he said. There was common ground and there one could begin. This airplane had sat in the high desert mountains of Sonora and the wind and the blowing sand had flayed it of its fabric and passing indians had pried away and carried off the brass inspection plate from the instrument panel for amulet and there it had languished on in that wild upcountry lost and unclaimed and indeed unclaimable for nearly thirty years. Thus far all was a single history. Whether there be two planes or one. Whichever plane was spoken of it was the same.

He drew carefully at the stub of the cigarette between his thumb and forefinger, one dark eye asquint against the smoke rising past his nose in the motionless air. Finally Billy asked him whether it made any difference which plane it was since there was no difference to be spoken of. The gypsy nodded. He seemed to approve of the question although he did not answer it. He said that the father of the dead pilot had contracted for the removal of the airplane to a place on the border just east of Palomas. He had sent his agent to the town of Madera—pueblo que conoce—and this agent was himself such a man as might ask just such a question.

He smiled. He smoked the last of the cigarette to an ash and let the ash fall into the fire and blew the smoke slowly after. He licked his thumb and wiped it on the knee of his trousers. He said that for men of the road the reality of things was always of consequence. He said that the strategist did not confuse his devices with the reality of the world for then what would become of him? El mentiroso debe primero saber la verdad, he said. De acuerdo?

He nodded toward the fire. The watercarrier rose and jostled the coals with a stick and fed more wood under the pail and returned to his place again. The gypsy waited till he was done. Then he continued. He spoke of the identity of the little canvas biplane as having no meaning except in its history and he said that since this tattered artifact was known to have a sister in the same condition the question of identity had indeed been raised. He said that men assume the truth of a thing to reside in that thing without regard to the opinions of those beholding it while that which is fraudulent is held to be so no matter how closely it might duplicate the required appearance. If the airplane which their client has paid to be freighted out of the wilderness and brought to the border were in fact not the machine in which the son has died then its close resemblance to that machine is hardly a thing in its favor but is rather one more twist in the warp of the world for the deceiving of men. Where then is the truth of this? The reverence attached to the artifacts of history is a thing men feel. One could even say that what endows any thing with significance is solely the history in which it has participated. Yet wherein does that history lie?

The gypsy looked away upriver to where the airplane sat beyond the trees. He seemed to ponder its shape there. As if were contained in that primitive construction some yet uncoded clue to the campaigns of the revolution, the strategies of Angeles, the tactics of Villa. Y por qué lo quiere el cliente? he said. Que después de todo no es nada más que el ataúd de su hijo?

No one answered. After a while the gypsy continued. He said that he'd thought at one time that the client wished simply to have the aircraft as a memento. He whose son's bones were themselves long scattered on the sierra. Now his thought was different. He said that as long as the airplane remained in the mountains then its history was of a piece. Suspended in time. Its presence on the mountain was its whole story frozen in a single image for all to contemplate. The client thought and he thought rightly that could he remove that wreckage from where it lay year after year in rain and snow and sun then and then only could he bleed it of its power to commandeer his dreams. The gypsy gestured with one hand in a slow suave gesture. La historia del hijo termina en las montañas, he said. Y por allá queda la realidad de él.

He shook his head. He said that simple tasks often prove most difficult. He said that in any case this gift from the mountains had no real power to quiet an old man's heart because once more its journey would be stayed and nothing would be changed. And the identity of the airplane would be brought into question which in the mountains was no question at all. It was forcing a decision. It was a difficult matter. And as is so often the case God had finally taken a hand and decided things himself. For ultimately both airplanes were carried down from the mountain and one was in the Río Papigochic and the other was before them. Como lo ve.

They waited. Rafael rose again and prodded the fire and he lifted the lid from the pail and stirred the steaming soup within and re-covered it. The gypsy in the meantime had rolled another cigarette and lit it. He considered how to continue.

Town of Madera. A stained and whimsical map printed on poor paper already severing at the folds. A canvas bankbag full of silver pesos. Two men met almost by chance neither of whom would ever trust the other. The gypsy thinned his lips in what would not quite pass for a smile. He said that where expectations are few disappointments are rare. They had gone into the mountains in the fall two years ago and they had built a sled from the limbs of trees and by this conveyance had brought the wreckage to the rim of the great gorge of the Papigochic River. There with rope and windlass they would lower the thing to the river and there build a raft by which to ferry it carcass and wings and struts all down to the bridge on the Mesa Tres Ríos road and from there overland to the border west of Palomas. Snow drove them from the high country before they ever reached the river.

The other men about that pale dayfire seemed to attend his words closely. As if they themselves were only recent conscriptees to this enterprise. The gypsy spoke slowly. He described to them the nature of the country where the airplane had gone down. The wildness of it and the high grassy vegas and the deep barrancas where the days were polar in their brevity, barrancas in the floor of which great rivers looked no more than bits of string. They quit the country and returned again in the spring. They had no money left. A seeress tried to warn them back. One of their own. He had weighed the woman's words, but he knew what she did not. That if a dream can tell the future it can also thwart that future. For God will not permit that we shall know what is to come. He is bound to no one that the world unfold just so upon its course and those who by some sorcery or by some dream might come to pierce the veil that lies so darkly over all that is before them may serve by just that vision to cause that God should wrench the world from its heading and set it upon another course altogether and then where stands the sorcerer? Where the dreamer and his dream? He paused that all might contemplate this. That he might contemplate it himself. Then he continued. He spoke of the cold in the mountains at that season. He populated the terrain for them with certain birds and animals. Parrots. Tigers. Men of another time living in the caves of that country so remote that the world had overlooked to kill them. The Tarahumara standing half naked along the sheer rock wall of the void while the fuselage and the wingstructure of the broken plane dangled in the blue and grew small and turned slowly in the deepening gulf of the barranca silent and chimeless and far below them the shapes of vultures in slow spirals like bits of ash in an updraft.

He spoke of the rapids in the river and the great rocks that stood in the gorge and the rain in the mountains in the night and the way the river went howling through the narrows like a train and at night the rain which had fallen for miles into that ultimate sundering of the earth's rind hissed in their driftwood fires and the solid rock about them through which the water roared would shudder like a woman and if they spoke to one another no words formed in the air for the awful noise in that nether world.

They passed nine days in the gorge while the rain fell and the river rose until at last they were socketed high in a rocky crevice like refugent woodmice seven of them without food or fire and the whole gorge trembling as if the world itself were like to cleave beneath them and swallow up all and they posted watches in the night until he himself asked what it was they watched for? What do if it came?

The brass cymbal over the bucket rose slightly along one edge and a green froth belched forth and ran down the side of the bucket and the cymbal fell again soundlessly. The gitano reached and tipped the end of ash from his cigarette thoughtfully into the coals.

Nueve días. Nueve noches. Sin comida. Sin fuego. Sin nada. The river rose and they tied the raft with the windlass ropes and then with vines and the river rose and ate away the raft by pole and by plank and nothing to be done for it and the rain fell. First the wings were swept away. They hung he and his men from the rocks in the howling darkness like beleaguered apes and screamed mutely to one another in the maelstrom and his primo Macio descended to secure the fuselage although what use it could be without the wings none knew and Macio himself was nearly swept away and lost. On the morning of the tenth day the rain ceased. They made their way along the rocks in the wet gray dawn but all sign of their enterprise had vanished in the flood as if it had never been at all. The river continued to rise and on the morning of the day following while they sat staring at the hypnotic flume below them a drowned man shot out of the cataract upriver like a pale enormous fish and circled once facedown in the froth of the eddywater beneath them as if he were looking for something on the river's floor and then he was sucked away downriver to continue his journey. He'd come already a long way in his travels by the look of him for his clothes were gone and much of his skin and all but the faintest nap of hair upon his skull all scrubbed away by his passage over the river rocks. In his circling in the froth he moved all loosely and disjointed as if there were no bones to him. Some incubus or mannequin. But when he passed beneath them they could see revealed in him that of which men were made that had better been kept from them. They could see bones and ligaments and they could see the tables of his smallribs and through the leached and abraded skin the darker shapes of organs within. He circled and gathered speed and then exited in the roaring flume as if he had pressing work downriver.

The gypsy blew softly through his teeth. He studied the fire.

Y entonces qué? said Billy.

He shook his head. As if the recollection of these things were a trial to him. Ultimately they had climbed out of the gorge and made their way out of the mountains as far as Sahuaripa and there they had waited until at last a truck came droning down the all but impassable road from Divisaderos and they rode in the bed of this truck for four days, sitting with shovels across their knees, shapeless with mud, climbing down times un-counted to dig and pitch in the muck like convicts while the driver shouted at them from the cab and then groaning on again. To Bacanora. To Tonichi. North again out of Nuri to San Nicolás and Yécora and on through the mountains to Temo-sachic and Madera where the man with whom they had first contracted would demand the return of the monies advanced them.

The gypsy pitched the stub of his cigarette into the fire and crossed his boots before him and drew them to him in his hands and sat leaning forward studying the flames. Billy asked him if the airplane had ever been found and he said that it had not for indeed there was nothing to find. Billy then asked him why they had returned to Madera at all and the man weighed this question. Finally he said that he did not believe that it was by chance that he had first met this man and been hired to go into the mountains nor was it chance that sent the rains and flooded the Papigochic. They sat. The tender of the pail rose a third time and stirred it and set it by to cool. Billy looked at the solemn faces about the fire. The bones beneath the olive skin. World wanderers. They squatted lightly there in that ring in the wood, at once vigilant and unconstrained. They stood in no proprietary relationship to anything, scarcely even to the space they occupied. Out of their anterior lives they had arrived at the same understanding as their fathers before them. That movement itself is a form of property. He looked at them and he said that the airplane they now freighted north along the road was then some other airplane.

The black eyes all shifted to the leader of their small clan. He sat for a long time. It was very quiet. Out on the road one of the oxen began to piss loudly. Finally he shaped his mouth and said that he believed that fate had intervened in the matter for its own good reasons. He said that fate might enter into the affairs of men in order to contravene them or set them at naught but to say that fate could deny the true and uphold the false would seem to be a contradictory view of things. To speak of a will in the world that ran counter to one's own was one thing. To speak of such a will that ran counter to the truth was quite another, for then all was rendered senseless. Billy then asked him if it was his notion that the false plane had been swept away by God in order to single out the true and the gypsy said that it was not. When Billy said that he had understood him to say that it was God who had ultimately made the decision concerning the two planes the gypsy said that he believed that to be so but he did not believe that by this act God had spoken to anyone. He said that he was not a superstitious man. The gypsies heard this out and then turned to Billy to see how he would respond. Billy said that it seemed to him that the freighters did not hold the identity of the airplane to be of any great consequence but the gitano only turned and studied him with those dark and troubled eyes. He said that it was indeed of consequence and that it was in fact the whole burden of their inquiry. From a certain perspective one might even hazard to say that the great trouble with the world was that that which survived was held in hard evidence as to past events. A false authority clung to what persisted, as if those artifacts of the past which had endured had done so by some act of their own will. Yet the witness could not survive the witnessing. In the world that came to be that which prevailed could never speak for that which perished but could only parade its own arrogance. It pretended symbol and summation of the vanished world but was neither. He said that in any case the past was little more than a dream and its force in the world greatly exaggerated. For the world was made new each day and it was only men's clinging to its vanished husks that could make of that world one husk more.

La cáscara no es la cosa, he said. It looked the same. But it was not.

Y la tercera historia? said Billy.

La tercera historia, said the gypsy, es ésta. Él existe en la historia de las historias. Es que ultimadamente la verdad no puede quedar en ningún otro lugar sino en el habla. He held his hands before him and looked at his palms. As if they may have been at some work not of his own doing. The past, he said, is always this argument between counterclaimants. Memories dim with age. There is no repository for our images. The loved ones who visit us in dreams are strangers. To even see aright is effort. We seek some witness but the world will not provide one. This is the third history. It is the history that each man makes alone out of what is left to him. Bits of wreckage. Some bones. The words of the dead. How make a world of this? How live in that world once made?

He looked toward the pail. The steam had ceased rising and he nodded and stood. Rafael rose and took up the musette bag and slung it over one shoulder and picked up the pail and all followed the gypsy up through the river woods to where the horse lay and there one of the men knelt and raised up the horse's head from the ground while Rafael took from the bag a leather funnel and a length of rubber hose and they gripped the horse's mouth and opened up its jaws while he greased the hose and ran it down the horse's gullet and twisted the funnel over the end and then they poured with no ceremony the contents of the pail into the horse.

When they had done the gypsy washed again the dried blood

from the horse's chest and examined the wound and then
dredged up a double handful of the cooked leaves from the floor
of the bucket and packed them against the wound in a poultice
which he bound up with burlap sacking and tied with cord over
the horse's neck and behind its forelegs. When he was done he
rose and stepped back and stood looking down at the animal
with long contemplation. The horse looked very strange indeed.
It half raised its head and blinked at them and then wheezed
and stretched its neck in the leaves and lay there. Bueno, said
the gypsy. He looked at Billy and smiled.

They stood in the road and the gitano pulled the brim of his hat
down level and slid the scrimshawed length of birdbone which he
used for a drawtie up under his chin and looked at the oxen and at
the float and the airplane. He looked out through the trees to where
the rolled soogan that held Boyd's body was wedged in the low
branches of the tascate tree. He looked at Billy.

Estoy regresándole a mi país, Billy said.

The gypsy smiled again and looked north along the road.
Otros huesos, he said. Otros hermanos. He said that as a child
he had traveled a good deal in the land of the gavacho. He said
he'd followed his father through the streets of western cities and
they collected odds of junk from the houses there and sold them.
He said that sometimes in trunks and boxes they would come
upon old photographs and tintypes. These likenesses had value
only to the living who had known them and with the passage of
years of such there were none. But his father was a gypsy and
had a gypsy mind and he would hang these cracked and fading
likenesses by clothespins from the crosswires above the cart.
There they remained. No one ever asked about them. No one
wished to buy them. After a while the boy took them for a
cautionary tale and he would search those sepia faces for some
secret thing they might divulge to him from the days of their
mortality. The faces became very familiar to him. By their
antique clothing they were long dead and he pondered them
where they sat posed on porchsteps, seated in chairs in a yard.
All past and all future and all stillborn dreams cauterized in that

brief encapture of light within the camera's closet. He searched those faces. Looks of vague discontent. Looks of rue. Perhaps some burgeoning bitterness at things in fact not yet come to be which yet were now forever past.

His father said that the gorgios were an inscrutable lot and so he found them to be. In and out of all depicting. The photographs that hung from the wire became for him a form of query to the world. He sensed in them a certain power and he guessed that the gorgios considered them bad luck for they would scarcely look at them but the truth was darker yet as truth is wont to be.

What he came to see was that as the kinfolk in their fading stills could have no value save in another's heart so it was with that heart also in another's in a terrible and endless attrition and of any other value there was none. Every representation was an idol. Every likeness a heresy. In their images they had thought to find some small immortality but oblivion cannot be appeased. This was what his father meant to tell him and this was why they were men of the road. This was the why of the yellowing daguerreotypes swinging by their clothespegs from the cross-wire of his father's cart.

He said that journeys involving the company of the dead were notorious for their difficulty but that in truth every journey was so accompanied. He said that in his opinion it was imprudent to suppose that the dead have no power to act in the world, for their power is great and their influence often most weighty with just those who suspect it least. He said that what men do not understand is that what the dead have quit is itself no world but is also only the picture of the world in men's hearts. He said that the world cannot be quit for it is eternal in whatever form as are all things within it. In those faces that shall now be forever nameless among their outworn chattels there is writ a message that can never be spoken because time would always slay the messenger before he could ever arrive.

He smiled. Pensamos, he said, que somos las víctimas del tiempo. En realidad la vía del mundo no es fijada en ningún lugar. Cómo sería posible? Nosotros mismos somos nuestra propia jornada. Y por eso somos el tiempo también. Somos lo mismo. Fugitivo. Inescrutable. Desapíadado.

He turned and spoke in romany to the others and one of them took a bullwhip from the keepers nailed to the sideboards of the float and uncoiled it and sent it looping through the air where the crack of it echoed like a gunshot in the woods and the caravan lurched into motion. The gypsy turned and smiled. He said that perhaps they would meet again upon some other road for the world was not so wide as men imagined. When Billy asked him how much he owed him for his services he dismissed the debt with a wave of his hand. Para el camino, he said. Then he turned and set off up the road after the others. Billy stood holding the thin sheaf of bloodstained banknotes he'd taken from his pocket. He called out to the gypsy and the gypsy turned.

Gracias, he called.

The gypsy raised one hand. Por nada.

Yo no soy un hombre del camino.

But the gypsy only smiled and waved one hand. He said that the way of the road was the rule for all upon it. He said that on the road there were no special cases. Then he turned and strode on after the others.

IN THE EVENING the horse rose and stood on trembling legs. He did not halter it but only walked alongside the animal out to the river where it stepped very carefully into the water and drank endlessly. In the evening while he was fixing his supper from the tortillas and goatcheese the gypsies had left him a rider came along the road. Solitary. Whistling. He stopped among the trees. Then he came on more slowly.

Billy stood and walked out to the road and the rider halted and sat his horse. He pushed his hat back slightly, the better to see, the better to be seen. He looked at Billy and at the fire and at the horse lying in the woods beyond.

Buenas tardes, said Billy.

The rider nodded. He was riding a good horse and he wore good boots and a good Stetson hat and he was smoking a small black puro. He took the puro out of his mouth and spat and put it back.

You speak american? he said.

Yessir. I do.

I thought you looked about halfway sensible. What the hell are you doin out here? What's wrong with that horse?

Well sir, I guess I'm mindin my own business. I reckon I could even say the same about the horse.

The man paid no attention. He aint dead is he?

No. He aint. He got cut by roadagents.

Cut by roadagents?

Yessir.

You mean they nutted him?

No. I mean they stabbed him in the chest with a pigsticker.

Whatever in the hell for?

You tell me.

I dont know.

Well I dont either.

The rider sat smoking contemplatively. He looked out across the landscape to the west of the river. I dont understand this country, he said. Not the first thing about it. You aint got any coffee anywheres about your person I dont reckon?

I got some perkin. You want to light I got some supper fixin. It aint much but you're welcome.

Well I'd take it as a kindness.

He stepped down wearily and passed the bridlereins behind his back and adjusted his hat again and came forward leading the horse. Not the first damn thing, he said. Did you see my airplane come through here?

They squatted by the fire as the woods darkened and they waited for the coffee to boil. I never would of thought about them gypsies stickin the way they done, the man said. I had my doubts about em. One thing about me, when I'm wrong I'll admit it.

Well. That's a good trait to have.

Yes it is.

They ate the beans rolled up in the tortillas together with the melted cheese. The cheese was rank and goaty. Billy lifted the lid from the coffeepot with a stick and looked in and put the lid back. He looked at the man. The man was seated tailorwise on the ground holding the soles of his boots together with one hand.

You look like you might of been down here a while, the man said.

I dont know. What does that look like?

Like you need to get back.

Well. You probably right about that. This is my third trip. It's the only time I was ever down here that I got what I come after. But it sure as hell wasnt what I wanted.

The man nodded. He didnt seem to need to know what that was. I'll tell you what, he said. It will be one cold day in hell when you catch me down here again. A frosty son of a bitch. I'll tell you that flat out.

Billy poured the coffee. They drank. The coffee was vilely hot in the tin cups but the man seemed not to notice. He drank and sat looking out through the dark woods toward the river and the silver panels of the river plaited over the gravel bars in the moonlight. Downriver the nacre bowl of the moon sat swaged into the reefs of cloud like a candled skull. He flipped the dregs of coffee into the darkness. I better get on, he said.

You welcome to stay.

I enjoy to ride of a night.

Well.

I believe a man can even cover more ground.

There's robbers all in this country, Billy said.

Robbers, the man said. He contemplated the fire. After a while he took one of the thin black cigars from his pocket and studied that. Then he bit the tip from it and spat it into the fire.

You smoke cigars?

I aint never took it up.

It aint against your religion?

Not that I know of.

The man leaned and pulled a burning billet from the fire and lit the cigar with it. It took some lighting to get it to burn. When he had it going he put the piece of wood back in the fire and blew a smoke ring and then blew a smaller one through the center of it.

What time did they leave out of here? he said.

I dont know. Noon maybe.

They wont make ten mile.

It might of been later.

Ever time I lay over somewheres they have a breakdown. They aint failed a time. My own fault. I keep gettin sidetracked by them señoritas. I liked them mamselles over yonder awful well too. I like it when they dont speak no english. Did you get over there?

No.

He reached into the fire and took out the stick he'd used to light his cigar and whipped away the flame and then turned and drew in the dark behind him with the red and smoldering end of it like a child. After a while he put it back in the fire again.

How bad's your horse? he said.

I dont know. He's been down two days.

You ought to of got that gypsy to see about him. They're supposed to know everthing there is about a horse.

Is that right?

I dont know. I know they're good at makin a sick one look well long enough to sell it.

I aint lookin to sell it.

I'll tell you what you better do.

What's that?

Keep this here fire built up.

Why is that.

Mountain lions is why. Horsemeat's their favorite kind.

Billy nodded. I always heard that, he said.

You know why you always heard it?

Why I always heard it?

Yeah.

No. Why?

Cause it's right is why.

You think most of what a man hears is right?

That's been my experience.

It aint been mine.

The man sat smoking and contemplating the fire. After a while he said: It aint been mine neither. I just said that. I wasnt over yonder like I said neither. I'm a four-F. Always was, always will be.

Did those gypsies bring that airplane out of the sierras and down the Papigochic River?

Is that what they said?

Yeah.

That airplane come out of a barn on the Taliafero Ranch out of Flores Magón. It couldnt even fly where you're talkin about. The ceiling on that plane aint but six thousand feet.

Was the man that flew it killed in it?

Not that I know of.

Was that why you come down here? To find that plane and take it back?

I come down here cause I'd knocked up a girl in McAllen Texas and her daddy wanted to shoot me.

Billy stared into the fire.

You talk about runnin into the arms of that which you have fled from, the man said. You ever been shot?

No.

I have twice. The last time was in downtown Cuauhtémoc broad daylight on a Saturday afternoon. Everbody run. There was two Mennonite women picked me up out of the street and loaded me into a wagon or I'd still be layin there.

Where'd they shoot you at?

Right here, he said. He turned and pushed the hair back above his right temple. See there? You can see it.

He leaned and spat into the fire and looked at the cigar and put it back in his mouth. He smoked. I aint crazy, he said.

I never said you was.

No. You might of thought it though.

You might of thought it about me.

Might.

Did that happen or did you just say it?

No. It happened.

My brother was shot and killed down here. I'd come down to take him home. He was shot and killed south of here. Town called San Lorenzo.

You can get killed down here about as quick as anything else you might decide to do.

My daddy was shot and killed in New Mexico. That's his horse layin over yonder.

It's a cruel world, the man said.

He come out of Texas in nineteen and nineteen. He was about the age I am now. He was not born there. He was born in Missouri.

I had a uncle was born in Missouri. His daddy fell off a wagon drunk in the mud one night goin through there and that's how it come about that he was born in Missouri.

My mama was from off a ranch up in De Baca County. Her mother was a fullblooded Mexican didnt speak no english. She lived with us up until she died. I had a younger sister died when I was seven but I remember her just as plain. I went to Fort Sumner to try and find her grave but I couldnt find it. Her name was Margaret. I always liked that name for a girl. If I ever had a girl that's what I'd name her.

I better get on.

Well.

Mind what I said about your fire.

Well.

You sound like you've had your share of troubles in this world.

I just got to jabberin. I been more fortunate than most. There aint but one life worth livin and I was born to it. That's worth all the rest. My bud was better at it than me. He was a born natural. He was smarter than me too. Not just about horses. About everthing. Daddy knew it too. He knew it and he knew I knew it and that's all there was to say about it.

I better get on.

You take care.

I will do it.

He rose, he adjusted his hat. The moon was high and the sky had cleared. The river where it lay behind the trees looked like poured metal.

This world will never be the same, the rider said. Did you know that?

I know it. It aint now.

FOUR DAYS LATER he set out north along the river with the remains of his brother trestled up in a travois he'd made from sapling poles dragging behind the horse. They were three days reaching the border. He rode past the first of the white obelisks marking the international boundary line west of Dog Springs and he crossed the ancient dry reservoir there. The old earthworks were broken out in places and he rode across the cracked clay floor of the reservoir with the travois poles rasping behind him. There were prints in the clay of cattle and antelope and of coyotes that had crossed after some recent rain and he came upon a place that was runed over all about with the random trident of cranetracks where the birds had glided in and stalked about upon that barren mud. He slept that night in his own country and he had a dream wherein he saw God's pilgrims laboring upon a darkened verge in the last of the twilight of that day and they seemed to be returning from some deep enterprise that was not of war nor were they yet in flight but rather seemed coming from some labor to which perhaps these and all other things stood subjugate. A dark arroyo separated him from the place where they were going and he looked to see if he could tell by the nature of their implements what it was that they had been about but they carried none and they toiled on in silence against a sky that was darkening all around and then they were gone. When he woke in the round darkness about he thought that something had indeed passed in the desert night and he was awake a long time but he had no sense that it would ever return again.

The day following he rode through Hermanas and out along the dusty road west and that evening he sat the horse in the crossroads in front of the store in Hatchita and he looked away toward the southwest where the late sun was on the Animas Peaks and he knew that he would not be going there again. He crossed the Animas Valley slowly dragging the travois and he was all day in the doing of it. When he entered the town of Animas the morning of the following day it was Ash Wednesday by the calendar and the first folk he saw were Mexicans with sootmarks on their foreheads, five children and a woman walking singlefile along the dusty edge of the road out from the town. He wished them a good day but they only blessed themselves on seeing the body in the travois and passed on. He bought a spade at the hardware store and set out south from the town till he came to the little cemetery and he hobbled the horse and left it to graze outside the gates while he worked at digging the grave.

He was down to his waist in the dry dirt and caliche when the sheriff pulled up and got out and walked down through the gate.

I suspicioned it was you, he said.

Billy paused and leaned on the spade and squinted up at him. He'd taken off his rag of a shirt and he reached and picked it up off the ground and wiped the sweat from his forehead with it and stood waiting.

That's your brother layin yonder I take it, the sheriff said.

Yessir.

The sheriff shook his head. He looked off out over the country. As if there was something about it that you just couldnt quite lay your hand on. He looked down at Billy.

There aint much to say, is there?

No sir. Not much.

Well. You caint just travel around the country buryin people. Let me go see the judge and see if I can get him to issue a death certificate. I aint even sure whose property that is you're diggin in.

Yessir.

You come see me in Lordsburg tomorrow.

All right.

The sheriff pulled his hat down and shook his head again and turned and walked back out through the gate toward his car.

Days to come he rode north to Silver City and west to Duncan Arizona and north again through the mountains to Glenwood, to Reserve. He worked for the Carrizozos and for the GS's and he left for no reason he could name and in July of that year he drifted south again to Silver City and took the old road east past the Santa Rita mines and on through San Lorenzo and the Black Range. A wind was coming off the mountains to the north and the prairie before him had darkened under the moving clouds. The horse shuffled along with its head down and the rider rode very erect with his hat pulled low across his eyes. The country was all catclaw and creosote on a gravel plain and there were no fences and little grass. A few miles on and he struck the blacktop road and sat the horse. A truck whined past and drew away into the distance. Eighty miles away the raw rock ranges of the Organ Mountains shining under the clouds in the paneled light of the late sun. As he watched they faded into shadow. The wind coming off the desert had spits of rain in it. He crossed through the bar ditch and rode up onto the blacktop and slowed the horse and looked back. The panicgrass volunteered along the selvedge of the road heeled and twisted in the wind. He turned back along the highway toward some buildings he'd seen. The castoff tirecasings from the overland trucks lay coiled and corrugated by the highwayside like the sloughed and sunblacked hides of old dryland saurians shed along the tarmac roadway there. The wind blew down from the north and then the rain blew down and went gusting in sheets across the road before him.

They were three building of adobe set just off the road that had at one time been a waystation in that country and the roofs were all but gone and most of the vigas carried off. There was an old rusty orange gaspump out front with the glass broken out of the top of it. He led the horse into the largest of the buildings and unsaddled it and stood the saddle in the floor. In one corner was a pile of hay and he kicked at it to loosen it up or perhaps just to see what it might contain. It was dry and dusty and held a depression where something had been sleeping. He went out and walked around behind the building and came back with an old hubcap and poured water in it from the canvas waterbag and held it for the horse to drink. Out through the wrecked wood sash of the windowframe he could see the road shining blackly in the rain.

He got his blankets and spread them in the hay and he was sitting eating sardines out of a tin and watching the rain when a yellow dog rounded the side of the building and entered through the open door and stopped. It looked first at the horse. Then it swung its head and looked at him. It was an old dog gone gray about the muzzle and it was horribly crippled in its hindquarters and its head was askew someway on its body and it moved grotesquely. An arthritic and illjoined thing that crabbed sideways and sniffed at the floor to pick up the man's scent and then raised its head and nudged the air with its nose and tried to sort him from the shadows with its milky half blind eyes.

Billy set the sardines carefully beside him. He could smell the thing in the damp. It stood there inside the door with the rain falling in the weeds and gravel behind it and it was wet and wretched and so scarred and broken that it might have been patched up out of parts of dogs by demented vivisectionists. It stood and then it shook itself in its grotesque fashion and hobbled moaning to the far corner of the room where it looked back and then turned three times and lay down.

He wiped the blade of the knife on his breeches leg and laid the knife across the tin and looked about. He pried a loose clod of mud from the wall and threw it. The dog made a strange moaning sound but it did not move.

Git, he shouted.

The dog moaned, it lay as before.

He swore softly and rose to his feet and cast about for a weapon. The horse looked at him and it looked at the dog. He crossed the room and went out in the rain and walked around the side of the building. When he came back he had in his fist a threefoot length of waterpipe and with it he advanced upon the dog. Go on, he shouted. Git.

The dog rose moaning and slouched away down the wall and limped out into the yard. When he turned to go back to his blankets it slank past him into the building again. He turned and ran at it with the pipe and it scrabbled away.

He followed it. Outside it had stopped at the edge of the road and it stood in the rain looking back. It had perhaps once been a hunting dog, perhaps left for dead in the mountains or by some highwayside. Repository of ten thousand indignities and the harbinger of God knew what. He bent and clawed up a handful of small rocks from the gravel apron and slung them. The dog raised its misshapen head and howled weirdly. He advanced upon it and it set off up the road. He ran after it and threw more rocks and shouted at it and he slung the length of pipe. It went clanging and skittering up the road behind the dog and the dog howled again and began to run, hobbling brokenly on its twisted legs with the strange head agoggle on its neck. As it went it raised its mouth sideways and howled again with a terrible sound. Something not of this earth. As if some awful composite of grief had broke through from the preterite world. It tottered away up the road in the rain on its stricken legs and as it went it howled again and again in its heart's despair until it was gone from all sight and all sound in the night's onset.

HE WOKE in the white light of the desert noon and sat up in the ranksmelling blankets. The shadow of the bare wood windowsash stenciled onto the opposite wall began to pale and fade as he watched. As if a cloud were passing over the sun. He kicked out of the blankets and pulled on his boots and his hat and rose and walked out. The road was a pale gray in the light and the light was drawing away along the edges of the world. Small birds had wakened in the roadside desert bracken and begun to chitter and to flit about and out on the blacktop bands of tarantulas that had been crossing the road in the dark like landcrabs stood frozen at their articulations, arch as marionettes, testing with their measured octave tread the sudden jointed shadows of themselves beneath them.

He looked out down the road and he looked toward the fading light. Darkening shapes of cloud all along the northern rim. It had ceased raining in the night and a broken rainbow or watergall stood out on the desert in a dim neon bow and he looked again at the road which lay as before yet more dark and darkening still where it ran on to the east and where there was no sun and there was no dawn and when he looked again toward the north the light was drawing away faster and that noon in which he'd woke was now become an alien dusk and now an alien dark and the birds that flew had lighted and all had hushed once again in the bracken by the road.

He walked out. A cold wind was coming down off the mountains. It was shearing off the western slopes of the continent where the summer snow lay above the timberline and it was crossing through the high fir forests and among the poles of the aspens and it was sweeping over the desert plain below. It had ceased raining in the night and he walked out on the road and called for the dog. He called and called. Standing in that inexplicable darkness. Where there was no sound anywhere save only the wind. After a while he sat in the road. He took off his hat and placed it on the tarmac before him and he bowed his head and held his face in his hands and wept. He sat there for a long time and after a while the east did gray and after a while the right and godmade sun did rise, once again, for all and without distinction.

CITIES
OF THE
PLAIN

I

THEY STOOD in the doorway and stomped the rain from their boots and swung their hats and wiped the water from their faces. Out in the street the rain slashed through the standing water driving the gaudy red and green colors of the neon signs to wander and seethe and rain danced on the steel tops of the cars parked along the curb.

Damned if I aint half drowned, Billy said. He swung his dripping hat. Where's the all-american cowboy at?

He's done inside.

Let's go. He'll have all them good fat ones picked out for hisself.

The whores in their shabby deshabille looked up from the shabby sofas where they sat. The place was all but empty. They stomped their boots again and crossed to the bar and stood and thumbed back their hats and propped their boots on the rail above the tiled drainway while the barman poured their whiskies. In the bloodred barlight and the drifting smoke they raised their glasses briefly and nodded as if to salute some fourth companion now lost to them and they tilted back the shots and set the empty glasses on the bar again and wiped their mouths with the backs of their hands. Troy jutted his chin at the barman and made a circling gesture with one finger at the empty glasses. The barman nodded.

John Grady you look like a goddamned wharf rat.

I feel like one.

The barman poured their whiskies.

I never seen it rain no harder. You want a beer back? Give us three beers.

You got one of them little darlins picked out?

The boy shook his head.

Which one you like, Troy?

I'm like you. I come down here for a fat woman and that's what I'm havin. I'm goin to tell you right now cousin, when the mood comes on you for a fat woman they just wont nothin else satisfy.

I know the feelin well. You better pick you one out, John Grady.

The boy turned and looked across the room at the whores.

How about that old big'n in the green pajamas?

Dont be puttin him on my gal, said Troy. You'll be the cause of a fight breakin out here in a minute.

Go on. She's lookin over here.

They're all lookin over here.

Go on. I can tell she likes you.

She'd bounce John Grady off the ceilin.

Not the all-american cowboy she wouldnt. The cowboy'd stick like a cocklebur. What about the one with the blue windercurtain wrapped around her?

Dont pay no attention to him, John Grady. She looks like her face caught fire and they beat it out with a rake. I'm goin to say that blond on the end is more your style.

Billy shook his head and reached for his whiskey. They aint no reasonin with the man. He just aint got no taste in women and that's a mathematical fact.

You stick with your old dad, said Troy. He'll get you onto somethin with some substance to it. Parham yonder actually claimed that a man ought not to date anything he couldnt lift. Said what if the house caught fire.

Or the barn.

Or the barn.

You remember the time we brought Clyde Stapp down here?

I do and he was a man of judgment. Picked him out a gal with some genuine heft to her.

JC and them slipped the old woman a couple of dollars to let em go back there and peek. They was goin to take his picture but they got to laughin and blew the deal.

We told Clyde he looked like a monkey fuckin a football. I thought we was goin to have him to whip. What about that one in the red yonder?

Dont listen to him, John Grady.

Value per pound on a dollar basis. He dont even want to consider a thing like that.

You all go on, said John Grady.

Pick you one out.

That's all right.

You see there Troy? All you done is got the boy confused.

JC told everbody that Clyde fell in love with the old gal and wanted to take her back with him but all they had was the pickup and they'd of had to send for the flatbed. By then Clyde had done sobered up and fell out of love and JC said he wasnt takin him to no more whorehouses. Said he hadnt acted in a manly and responsible fashion.

You all go on, said John Grady.

From the rear of the premises he could hear the rain rattling on a metal roof. He ordered another shot of whiskey and stood turning the glass slowly on the polished wood and watching the room behind him in the yellowing glass of the old Brunswick backbar. One of the whores crossed the room and took him by the arm and asked him to buy her a drink but he said he was only waiting for his friends. After a while Troy came back and sat on the barstool and ordered another whiskey. He sat with his hands folded on the bar before him like a man at church. He took a cigarette from his shirtpocket.

I dont know, John Grady.

What dont you know?

I dont know.

The barman poured his whiskey.

Pour him anothern.

The barman poured.

Another whore had come up to take John Grady's arm. The powder on her face had cracked like sizing.

Tell her you got the clap, said Troy.

John Grady was speaking to her in spanish. She tugged at his arm.

Billy told that to one down here one time. She said that was all right she had it too.

He lit the cigarette with a Third Infantry Zippo lighter and laid the lighter on top of his cigarettes and blew smoke down along the polished wood and looked at John Grady. The whore had gone back to the sofa and John Grady was studying something in the backbar glass. Troy turned and followed his gaze. A young girl of no more than seventeen and perhaps younger was sitting on the arm of the sofa with her hands cupped in her lap and her eyes cast down. She fussed with the hem of her gaudy dress like a schoolgirl. She looked up and looked toward them. Her long black hair fell across her shoulder and she swept it slowly away with the back of her hand.

She's a goodlookin thing, aint she? Troy said.

John Grady nodded.

Go on and get her.

That's all right.

Hell, go on.

Here he comes.

Billy stepped up to the bar and adjusted his hat.

You want me to go get her? said Troy.

I can get her if I want her.

Otra vez, said Billy. He turned and looked across the room.

Go on, said Troy. Hell, we'll wait on you.

That little girl the one you're lookin at? I bet she aint fifteen.

I bet she aint either, said Troy.

Get that one I had. She's five gaited or I never rode.

The barman poured their whiskies.

She'll be back over there directly.

That's all right.

Billy looked at Troy. He turned and picked up his glass and contemplated the reddish liquor welling at the brim and raised and drank it and took his money from his shirtpocket and jerked his chin at the watching barkeep.

You all ready? he said.

Yeah.

Let's go get somethin to eat. I think it's fixin to quit rainin. I dont hear it no more.

They walked up Ignacio Mejía to Juárez Avenue. The gutters ran with a grayish water and the lights of the bars and cafes and curioshops bled slowly in the wet black street. Shopowners called to them and streetvendors with jewelry and serapes sallied forth to attend them at either side. They crossed Juárez Avenue and went up Mejía to the Napoleón and sat at a table by the front window. A liveried waiter came and swept the stained white tablecloth with a handbroom.

Caballeros, he said.

They ate steaks and drank coffee and listened to Troy's war stories and smoked and watched the ancient yellow taxicabs ford the water in the streets. They walked up Juárez Avenue to the bridge.

The trolleys had quit running and the streets were all but empty of trade and traffic. The tracks shining in the wet lamplight ran on toward the gateshack and beyond to where they lay embedded in the bridge like great surgical clamps binding those disparate and fragile worlds and the cloudcover had moved off down from the Franklins and south toward the dark shapes of the mountains of Mexico standing against the starlit sky. They crossed the bridge and pushed through the turnstile each in turn, their hats cocked slightly, slightly drunk, and walked up south El Paso Street.

IT WAS STILL DARK when John Grady woke him. He was up and dressed and had already been to the kitchen and back and had spoken to the horses and he stood in the doorway of Billy's bunkroom with the canvas curtain pushed back against the jamb and a cup of coffee in one hand. Hey cowboy, he said.

Billy groaned.

Let's go. You can sleep in the winter.

Damn.

Let's go. You been layin there damn near four hours.

Billy sat up and swung his feet onto the floor and sat with his head in his hands.

I dont see how you can lay there like that.

Damn if you aint a cheerful son of a bitch in the mornin. Where's my by god coffee at?

I aint carryin you no coffee. Get your ass up from there. Grub's on the table.

Billy reached up and took his hat from a wallpeg over the bed and put the hat on and squared it. Okay, he said. I'm up.

John Grady walked back out up the barn bay toward the house. The horses nickered at him from their stalls as he passed. I know what time it is, he told them. At the end of the barn a length of hayrope hung from the loft overhead and he drained the last of his coffee and slung the dregs from the cup and leaped up and batted the rope and set it swinging and went out.

They were all at the table eating when Billy pushed open the door and came in. Socorro came and took the plate of biscuits and carried them to the oven and dumped them into a pan and put the pan in the warmer and took hot biscuits from the warmer and put them on the plate and carried the plate back to the table. On the table was a bowl of scrambled eggs and one of grits and there was a plate of sausage and a boat of gravy and bowls of preserves and pico de gallo and butter and honey. Billy washed his face at the sink and Socorro handed him the towel and he dried his face and laid the towel on the counter and came to the table and stepped over the back of the empty chair and sat and reached for the eggs. Oren glanced at him over the top of his paper and continued reading.

Billy spooned the eggs and set the bowl down and reached for the sausage. Mornin Oren, he said. Mornin JC.

JC looked up from his plate. I guess you been fightin that bear all night too.

Fightin that bear, said Billy. He reached and took a biscuit and refolded the cloth back over the plate and reached for the butter.

Let's see them eyes again, said JC.

Aint nothin wrong with these eyes. Pass the salsa yonder.

He spooned the hot sauce over his eggs. Fight fire with fire. Aint that right John Grady?

An old man had come into the kitchen with his braces hanging. He wore an oldfashioned shirt of the kind the collar buttoned to and it was open at the neck and no collar to it. He had just shaved and there was shaving cream on his neck and on the lobe of one ear. John Grady pushed back his chair.

Here Mr Johnson, he said. Set here. I'm all done.

He rose with his plate to take it to the sink but the old man waved him down and went on toward the stove. Set down, he said, set down. I'm just gettin me some coffee.

Socorro unhooked one of the white porcelain mugs from the underside of the cabinet shelf and poured it and turned the handle facing out and handed it to the old man and he took it and nodded and went back across the kitchen. He stopped at the table and spooned two huge scoops of sugar out of the bowl into his cup and left the room taking the sugarspoon with him. John Grady put his cup and plate on the sideboard and got his lunchbucket off the counter and went out.

What's wrong with him? said JC.

Aint nothin wrong with him, said Billy.

I meant John Grady.

I know who you meant.

Oren folded the paper and laid it on the table. Dont you all even start, he said. Troy, you ready?

I'm ready.

They pushed back from the table and rose and went out. Billy sat picking his teeth. He looked at JC. What are you doin this mornin?

I'm goin into town with the old man.

He nodded. Out in the yard the truck started. Well, he said. It's light enough to see, I reckon.

He rose and crossed the kitchen and got his lunchpail from the counter and went out. JC reached across the table and got the paper.

John Grady was sitting behind the wheel of the idling truck. Billy got in and set the lunchpail on the floor and shut the door and looked at him.

Well, he said. You ready to put in a day's work for a day's wages?

John Grady put the truck in gear and they pulled away down the drive.

Daybreak to backbreak for a godgiven dollar, said Billy. I love this life. You love this life, son? I love this life. You do love this life dont you? Cause by god I love it. Just love it.

He reached into his shirtpocket and shook out a cigarette from the pack there and lit it with his lighter and sat smoking while they rolled down the drive through the long morning shadows of fence and post and oaktree. The sun was blinding white on the dusty windshield glass. Cattle standing along the fence called after the truck and Billy studied them. Cows, he said.

They nooned on a grassy rise on the red clay ranges ten miles south of the ranch house. Billy lay with his rolled jacket under his head and his hat over his eyes. He squinted out at the gray headlands of the Guadalupes eighty miles to the west. I hate comin out here, he said. Goddamn ground wont even hold a fencepost.

John Grady sat crosslegged chewing a weedstem. Twenty miles to the south a live belt of green ran down the Rio Grande valley. In the foreground fenced gray fields. Gray dust follow-

ing a tractor and cultivator down the gray furrows of a fall cot-
tonfield.

Mr Johnson says the army sent people out here with orders
to survey seven states in the southwest and find the sorriest
land they could find and report back. And Mac's ranch was settin right in the middle of it.

Billy looked at John Grady and looked back at the mountains.

You think that's true? said John Grady.

Hell, who knows.

JC says the old man is gettin crazier and crazier.

Well he's still got more sense crazy than JC's got sane so
what does that make JC?

I dont know.

There aint nothin wrong with him. He's just old is all.

JC says he aint been right since his daughter died.

Well. There aint no reason why he should be. He thought
the world of her.

Yeah.

Maybe we ought to ask Delbert. Get Delbert's view of
things.

Delbert aint as dumb as he looks.

I hope to God he aint. Anyway the old man always had a few
things peculiar about him and he's still got em. This place aint
the same. It never will be. Maybe we've all got a little crazy. I
guess if everbody went crazy together nobody would notice,
what do you think?

John Grady leaned and spat between his teeth and put the
stem back in his mouth. You liked her, didnt you?

Awful well. She was as nice to me as anybody I ever knew.

A coyote came out of the brush and trotted along the crest of
a rise a quarter mile to the east. I want you to look at that son
of a bitch, said Billy.

Let me get the rifle.

He'll be gone before you get done standin up.

The coyote trotted out along the ridge and stopped and looked back and then dropped off down the ridge into the brush again.

What do you reckon he's doin out here in the middle of the day?

He probably wonders the same about you.

You think he seen us?

Well I didnt see him walkin head first into them nopal bushes yonder so I dont expect he was completely blind.

John Grady watched for the coyote to reappear but the coyote didnt.

Funny thing, said Billy, is I was fixin to quit about the time she took sick. I was ready to move on. After she died I had a lot less reason to stay on but I stayed anyways.

I guess maybe you figured Mac needed you.

Horseshit.

How old was she?

I dont know. Late thirties. Forty maybe. You'd never of knowed it though.

You think he's gettin over it?

Mac?

Yeah.

No. You dont get over a woman like that. He aint gettin over nothin. He never will.

He sat and put his hat on and adjusted it. You ready, cousin?

Yeah.

He rose stiffly and reached down and got his lunchpail and he swiped at the seat of his trousers with one hand and then bent and got his jacket. He looked at John Grady.

There was a old waddy told me one time he never knowed a woman raised on indoor plumbin to ever turn out worth a damn. She come up the hard way. Old man Johnson was never nothin but a cowboy and you know what that pays. Mac met her at a church supper in Las Cruces when she was seventeen years old and that was all she wrote. He aint goin to be gettin over it. Not now, not soon, not never.

It was dark when they got back. Billy rolled up the window of the truck and sat looking toward the house. I'm a wore-out sumbuck, he said.

You want to just leave the gear in the truck?

Let's bring in the come-along. It might rain. Might. And that box of staples. They'll rust up.

I'll get em.

He got the stuff from the bed of the truck. The lights came on in the barn bay. Billy was standing there shaking his hand up and down.

Ever time I reach for that son of a bitch I get shocked.

It's the nails in them boots.

Then why dont it shock my feet?

I dont know.

He hung the come-along on a nail and set the box of staples on a framing crossbrace just inside the door. The horses whinnied from their stalls.

He went on down the barn bay and at the last stall pounded the flat of his hand against the stall door. There was an instant explosion against the boards on the other side. Dust drifted in the light. He looked back at Billy and grinned. Egg it on, said Billy. He'll put a foot through that son of a bitch.

JOAQUÍN STEPPED BACK with both hands atop the board he was leaning on and lowered his head as if he'd seen something in the corral too awful to watch. But he was only stepping back to spit and he did so in his slow and contemplative way and then stepped forward and looked through the boards again. Caballo, he said. The shadow of the trotting horse passed across the boards and across his face and passed on. He shook his head.

They walked on down to where some two by twelves were nailed and braced along the top of the corral and climbed up and sat with their bootheels wedged in the board below and smoked and watched John Grady work the colt.

What does he want with that owlheaded son of a bitch anyway?

Billy shook his head. Maybe it's like Mac says. Ever man winds up with the horse that suits him.

What is that thing he's got on its head?

It's called a cavesson halter.

What's wrong with a plain hackamore?

You'd have to ask the cowboy.

Troy leaned and spat. He looked at Joaquín. Qué piensas? he said.

Joaquín shrugged. He watched the horse circle the corral at the end of the longeline.

That horse has been broke with a bit, Troy said.

Yeah.

I guess he aims to break it and start over.

Well, Billy said, I got a suspicion that whatever it is he aims to do he'll most likely get it done.

They watched the horse circle.

He aint trainin it for the circus is he?

No. We had the circus yesterday evenin when he forked up on it.

How many times did he get thowed?

Four.

How many times did he get back up on it?

You know how many times.

Is he supposed to be some sort of specialist in spoiled horses?

Let's go, Billy said. He's liable to walk that son of a bitch all afternoon.

They went on toward the house.

Ask Joaquín yonder, Billy said.

Ask me what?

If the cowboy knows horses.

The cowboy says he dont know nothin.

I know it.

He claims he just likes it and works hard at it.

What do you think? said Billy.

Joaquín shook his head.

Joaquín thinks his methods is unorthodox.

So does Mac.

Joaquín didnt answer till they reached the gate. Then he stopped and looked back at the corral. Finally he said that it didnt make much difference if you liked horses or not if they didnt like you. He said the best trainers he ever knew, horses couldnt stay away from them. He said horses would follow Billy Sánchez to the outhouse and stand there and wait for him.

WHEN HE GOT BACK from town John Grady was not in the barn and when he walked up to the house to get his supper he was not there either. Troy was sitting at the table picking his teeth. He sat down with his plate and reached for the salt and pepper. Where's everbody at? he said.

Oren just left. JC's gone out with his girl. John Grady I reckon is laid up in the bed.

No he aint.

Well maybe he's gone off somewheres to think things over.

What happened?

That horse fell backwards on him. Like to broke his foot.

Is he all right?

I reckon. They carried him in to the doctor, him cussin and carryin on. Doctor wrapped it up and give him a pair of crutches and told him to stay off of it.

He's on crutches?

Yep. Supposed to be.

All this happened this afternoon?

Yep. It was lively as you could ever wish for here for a while. Joaquín come and got Oren and he went down there and told him to come on and he wouldnt do it. Oren said he thought he was goin to have to whip him. Hobblin around after the damned horse wantin to get up on it again. Finally got him to take his boot off. Oren said another two minutes and they'd of had to cut it off of him.

Billy nodded his head and bit thoughtfully into a biscuit.

He was ready to fight Oren?

Yep.

Billy chewed. He shook his head.

How bad is his foot?

He's sprained his ankle.

What did Mac say?

Nothin. He's the one carried him in to the doctor's.

I guess he cant do no wrong where Mac's concerned.

You got that right.

Billy shook his head again. He reached for the salsa. I miss ever show that comes to town, he said. I guess this might whittle down his reputation as a pure D peeler some though, mightnt it?

I dont know if it will or not. Joaquín says he stood in one stirrup and rode the son of a bitch down like a tree.

What for?

I dont know. I reckon he just dont like to quit a horse.

HE'D BEEN ASLEEP maybe an hour when the commotion in the dark of the barn bay woke him. He lay listening a minute and then he rose and reached for the cord and pulled on the overhead light and put on his hat and stepped to the door and pushed back the curtain and looked out. The horse hove past a foot from his face and went hammering down the bay and turned and stood breathing and stamping in the dark.

Damn, he said. Bud?

John Grady went limping past.

What the hell are you doin?

He hobbled on out of the lightfall. Billy stepped into the bay.

You are a goddamned idjit, aint you? What in the hell is wrong with you?

The horse began to run again. He heard it coming and knew it was coming but he'd no more than just got back inside the doorframe before it exploded into the space of light from the single bulb in his cubicle, running with its mouth open and its eyes like eggs in its head.

Goddamn it, he said. He got his pants off of the iron footrail of his cot and pulled them on and squared his hat and stepped out again.

The horse had started down the bay again. He flattened himself against the stall door next to his bunkroom. The horse went by as if the barn were afire and slammed up against the door at the end of the bay and turned and stood shrieking.

Goddamn it will you leave that squirrelheaded son of a bitch alone? What the hell's got into you?

John Grady came limping past into the dusty light again trailing a loop of rope and limped on out the other side.

You cant even see to rope the son of a bitch, Billy called.

The horse came pounding down the far side of the bay. It was saddled and the stirrups were kicking out. One of them must have caught on a board toward the far end where it turned in the thin slats of light from the yardlamp because there was a crack of breaking wood and a clattering in the dark and then the horse stood on its forefeet and jackslammed the boards at the end of the barn. A minute later the lights came on at the house. The dust in the barn drifted like smoke.

There you go, called Billy. The whole damn house is up.

The dark shape of the horse shifted in the barred light. It leaned its long neck and screamed. The door opened at the end of the barn.

John Grady limped past again with the rope.

Someone threw the lightswitch. Oren was standing there flapping his hand about. Goddamn it, he said. Why dont somebody fix that thing.

The crazed horse stood blinking at him ten feet away. He looked at the horse and he looked at John Grady standing in the middle of the barn bay with the catchrope.

What in hell's thunder is goin on out here? he said.

Go on, said Billy. Tell him somethin. I sure as hell dont have no answer for him.

The horse turned and trotted partway down the bay and stopped and stood.

Put the damn horse up, said Oren.

Let me have the rope, said Billy.

John Grady looked back at him. You think I cant even catch him?

Go on then. Catch him. I hope the son of a bitch runs over you.

One of you all catch him, said Oren, and lets quit this damn nonsense.

The door opened behind Oren and Mr Johnson stood there in his hat and boots and nightshirt. Shut the door, Mr Johnson, said Oren. Come in if you want.

John Grady dropped the loop over the horse's neck and walked the horse down along the rope and reached up through the loop and took hold of the trailing bridlereins and threw the rope off.

Dont get on that horse, said Oren.

It's my horse.

Well you can tell that to Mac then. He'll be out here in a minute.

Go on bud, said Billy. Put the damn horse up like the man asked you.

John Grady looked at him and he looked at Oren and then he turned and led the horse back down the barn bay and put it up in the stall.

Bunch of damned ignorance, said Oren. Come on, Mr Johnson. Damn.

The old man turned and went out and Oren followed and pulled the door shut behind him. When John Grady came limping out of the stall he was carrying the saddle by the horn, the stirrups dragging in the dirt. He crossed the bay toward the tackroom. Billy leaned against the jamb watching him. When he came out of the tackroom he passed Billy without looking at him.

You're really somethin, said Billy. You know that?

John Grady turned at the door of his bunkroom and he looked at Billy and he looked down the hall of the lit barn and spat quietly in the dirt and looked at Billy again. It wasnt any of your business, he said. Was it.

Billy shook his head. I will be damned, he said.

IN THE MOUNTAINS they saw deer in the headlights and in the headlights the deer were pale as ghosts and as soundless. They turned their red eyes toward this unreckoned sun and sidled and grouped and leapt the bar ditch by ones and twos. A small doe lost her footing on the macadam and scrabbled wildly and sank onto her hindquarters and rose again and vanished with the others into the chaparral beyond the roadside. Troy held the whiskey up to the dashlights to check the level in the bottle and unscrewed the cap and drank and screwed the cap back on and passed the bottle to Billy. Be no lack of deer to hunt down here it looks like.

Billy unscrewed the cap from the bottle and drank and sat watching the white line down the dark road. I dont doubt but what it's good country.

You dont want to leave Mac.

I dont know. Not without some cause to.

Loyal to the outfit.

It aint just that. You need to find you a hole at some point. Hell, I'm twenty-eight years old.

You dont look it.

Yeah?

You look forty-eight. Pass the whiskey.

Billy peered out at the high desert. The bellied lightwires raced against the night.

They wont care for us drinkin?

She dont particularly like it. But there aint much she can do about it. Anyway it aint like we was goin to show up down there kneewalkin drunk.

Will your brother take a drink?

Troy nodded solemnly. Quicker than a minnow can swim a dipper.

Billy drank and handed over the bottle.

What was the kid goin to do? said Troy.

I dont know.

Did you and him have a fallin out?

No. He's all right. He just said he had somethin he needed to do.

He can flat ride a horse. I'll say that.

Yes he can.

He's a salty little booger.

He's all right. He's just got his own notions about things.

That horse he thinks so much of is just a damned outlaw if you want my opinion.

Billy nodded. Yep.

So what's he want with it?

I guess that's what he wants with it.

You still think he's going to have it follerin him around like a dog?

Yeah. I think it.

I'll believe it when I see it.

You want to lay some money?

Troy shook a cigarette from the pack on the dash and put it in his mouth and pushed in the lighter. I dont want to take your money.

Hell, dont be backwards about takin my money.

I think I'll pass. He aint goin to like them crutches.

Not even a little bit.

How long is he supposed to be on em?

I dont know. A couple of weeks. Doctor told him a sprain could be worse than a break.

I'll bet he aint on em a week.

I'll bet he aint either.

A jackrabbit froze in the road. Its red eye shone.

Go on dumb-ass, Billy said.

The rabbit made a soft thud under the truck. Troy took the

lighter from the dashboard and lit his cigarette with it and put the lighter back in the receptacle.

When I got out of the army I went up to Amarillo with Gene Edmonds for the rodeo and stock show. He'd fixed us up with dates and all. We was supposed to be at their house to pick em up at ten oclock in the mornin and it was after midnight fore we left out of El Paso. Gene had a brand new Olds Eighty-eight and he pitched me the keys and told me to drive. Quick as we hit highway eighty he looked over at me, told me to shower down on it. That thing would strictly motivate. I pushed it up to about eighty, eighty-five. Still had about a yard of pedal left. He looked over again. I said: How fast do you want to go? He said just whatever you feel comfortable with. Hell. I didnt do nothin but roll her on up to about a hundred and ten and here we went. Old long flat road. Had about six hundred miles of it in front of us.

Well there was all these jackrabbits in the road. They'd set there and freeze in the lights. Blap. Blap. I looked over at Gene and I said: What do you want to do about these rabbits? He looked at me and he said: Rabbits? I mean if you were lookin for somebody to give a shit I can tell you right now it sure as hell wasnt Gene. He didnt care if syrup went to thirty cents a sop.

We pulled into a filling station at Dimmitt Texas just about daybreak. Pulled up to the pumps and shut her down and set there and there was a car on the other side of the pumps and the old boy that worked there was fillin the tank and cleanin the windshield. Woman settin there in the car. The old boy drivin had gone in to take a leak or whatever. Anyway we pulled in facin this other car and I'm kindly layin there with my head back waitin on the old boy and I wasnt even thinkin about this woman but I could see her. Just settin there, sort of lookin around. Well directly she sat straight up and commenced to holler like she was bein murdered. I mean just a hollerin. I raised up, I didnt know what had happened. She was lookin over at us and I thought Gene had done somethin. Exposed hisself or somethin. You never knew what he was goin to do. I looked at Gene but he didnt know what the hell was goin on any more than I did. Well here come the old boy out of the men's room and I mean he was a big son of a bitch too. I got out and walked around the car. I thought I was goin crazy. The Oldsmobile had this big ovalshaped grille in the front of it was like a big scoop and when I got around to the front of the car it was just packed completely full of jackrabbit heads. I mean there was a hundred of em jammed in there and the front of the car the bumper and all just covered with blood and rabbit guts and them rabbits I reckon they'd sort of turned their heads away just at impact cause they was all lookin out, eyes all crazy lookin. Teeth sideways. Grinnin. I cant tell you what it looked like. I come damn near hollerin myself. I'd noticed the car was overheatin but I just put that down to the speed we was makin. This old boy wanted to fight us over it. I said: Damn, Sam. Rabbits. You know? Hell. Gene got out and started mouthin at him and I told him to get his ass back in the car and shut up. Old boy went over and told the woman to hush up and quit slobberin and all but I like to never got him pacified. I started to just go on and hit the big son of a bitch and be done with it.

Billy sat watching the night spool past. The roadside chaparral, the flat black scrim of the mountains cut into the starblown desert sky above them. Troy smoked. He reached for the whiskey and unscrewed the cap and sat holding the bottle.

I got discharged in San Diego. Took the first bus out. Me and another old boy got drunk on the bus and like to got throwed off. I got off in Tucson and went in a store and bought a new pair of Judson boots and a suit. I dont know what the hell I bought the suit for. I thought you was supposed to have one. I got on another bus and come on to El Paso and went up that evenin to Alamogordo and got my horses. I wandered all over this country. Worked in Colorado. Worked up in the panhandle. Got throwed in jail in this little old chickenshit town I wont even name it to you. State of Texas though. State of Texas. I hadnt done nothin. Just in the wrong place at the wrong time. I like to never got out of there. I'd got in a fight with a Mexican and like to killed him. I was in jail up there for nine months to the day. I wouldnt of wrote home for nothin. Time I got out and went to see about my horses they'd been sold for the feedbill. I didnt care about the one but I did the other cause I'd had him a long time. Nobody seemed to know nothin about it. I knew if I grabbed the old boy I'd be right back in the damn jail again. Asked all around. Finally somebody told me they'd sold my horse out of the state. They thought the buyer was from Alabama or some damn place. I'd had that horse since I was thirteen years old.

I lost a horse in Mexico I was awful partial to, Billy said. I'd had him since I was nine.

It's easy to do.

What, lose a horse?

Troy had tipped the bottle up and he drank and lowered it and screwed the cap back on and wiped his mouth with the back of his hand and laid the bottle on the seat. No, he said. Get partial to one.

Half an hour later they pulled off the highway and rumbled over the pipes of a cattleguard and drove up the mile-long dirt road to the ranch house. The porchlight was on and three heeler dogs came out and ran beside the truck barking. Elton came out and stood on the porch with his hands in his back pockets and his hat on.

They ate at a long table in the kitchen, passing bowls of hominy and okra and a great platter of fried steaks and biscuits.

This is awful good, mam, Billy said.

Elton's wife looked at him. You wouldnt mind not callin me mam would you?

No mam.

It makes me feel like a old woman.

Yes mam.

He cant help hisself, Troy said.

That's all right, the woman said.

You never let me off that easy.

Bein let off easy was never somethin you needed more of, the woman said.

I'll try not to say it, Billy said.

There was a seven year old girl at the table and she watched them with wide eyes. They ate. After a while she said: What's wrong with it?

What's wrong with what?

Sayin mam.

Elton looked up. There aint nothin wrong with it, honey. Your mama's just one of them modern kinds of women.

What's a modern kind of woman?

Eat your supper, the woman said. If your daddy had his way we wouldnt even have the wheel yet.

They sat in old canebottomed chairs on the porch and Elton set the three glass tumblers on the board floor between his feet and unscrewed the cap from the bottle and poured three measures and put the cap back and stood the bottle on the floor and passed the glasses round and leaned back in his rocker. Salud, he said.

He'd turned off the porchlight and they sat in the soft square of light from the window. He raised his glass to the light and looked through it like a chemist. You wont guess who's back at Bell's, he said.

Dont even say her name.

Well you did guess.

Who else would it be?

Elton leaned back in the chair and rocked. The dogs stood in the yard at the foot of the steps looking up at him.

What, said Troy. Did her old man finally run her off?

I dont know. She's supposed to be visitin. It's turned out to be kindly a long visit.

Yeah.

For whatever consolation there might be in that.

It aint no consolation.

Elton nodded. You're right, he said. It aint.

Billy sipped the whiskey and looked out at the shapes of the mountains. Stars were falling everywhere.

Rachel run smack into her in Alpine, said Elton. Little darlin just smiled and hidied like butter wouldnt melt in her mouth.

Troy sat leaning forward with his elbows on his knees, the glass in both hands before him. Elton rocked.

You remember we used to go down to Bloy's to try and pick up girls? That's where he met her at. Camp meetin. That'll make you ponder the ways of God. He asked her out and she told him she wouldnt go out with a man that drank. He looked her straight in the eye and told him he didnt drink. She like to fell over backwards. I guess it come as somethin of a shock to her to meet a even bigger liar than what she was. But he told the naked truth. Of course she called his hand on it. Said she knew for a fact he drank. Said everbody in Jeff Davis County knew he drank and drank plenty and was wild as a buck. He never batted a eye. Said he used to but he quit. She asked him when did he quit and he said I just now did. And she went out with him. And as far as I know he never took another drink. Till she quit him of course. By then he had a lot of catchin up to do. Tell me about the evils of liquor. Liquor aint nothin. But he was changed from that day.

Is she still as good lookin?

I dont know. I aint seen her. Rachel said she was. Satan hath power to assume a pleasing form. Them big blue eyes. Knew more ways to turn a man's head than the devil's grandmother. I dont know where they learn it at. Hell, she wasnt but seventeen.

They're born with it, Troy said. They dont have to learn it.

I hear you.

What they dont seem to learn is not to just run over the top of some poor son of a bitch for the pure enjoyment of it.

Billy sipped his whiskey.

Let me have your glass, Elton said.

He set it on the floor between his feet and poured the

whiskey and recapped the bottle and reached and passed the glass across.

Thanks, said Billy.

Were you in the war? Elton said.

No. I was four-F.

Elton nodded.

I tried to enlist three different times but they wouldnt take me.

I know you did. I tried to get overseas but I spent the whole war at Camp Pendleton. Johnny fought all over the Pacific theatre. He had whole companies shot out from under him. Never got a scratch. I think it bothered him.

Troy handed across his glass and Elton set it on the floor and poured it and passed it back. Then he poured his own. He sat back. What are you lookin at? he asked the dog. The dog looked away.

The thing that bothers me and then I'll shut up about it is that we had a hell of a row that mornin and I never had the chance to make it up. I told him to his face that he was a damn fool—which he was—and that the worst thing he could do to the old boy was to let him have her. Which it was. I knew all about her by then. We like to come to blows over it. I never told you that. It was bad. I never saw him alive again. I should of just kept out of it. Anybody in the state he was in you cant talk to em noway. No use to try even.

Troy watched him. You told me, he said.

Yeah. I guess I did. I dont dream about him anymore. I used to all the time. I'd have these conversations with him.

I thought you was goin to get off the subject.

All right. It still seems like about the only subject there is, though. Dont it?

He rose heavily from the chair with bottle and glass in hand. Let's walk out to the barn. I'll show you the foal that Jones mare throwed you never did think much of. Just bring your all's glasses. I got the bottle.

* * *

THEY RODE ALL MORNING through the open juniper country, keeping to the gravelly ridges. A storm was making up over the Sierra Viejas to the west and over the broad plain that ran south from the Guadalupes down around the Cuesta del Burro range and on to Presidio and the border. They crossed the upper reaches of the creek at noon and sat among the yellow leaves and watched leaves turn and drift in a pool while they ate the lunch that Rachel had packed for them.

Look at this, said Troy.

What is it?

A tablecloth.

Damn.

He poured coffee from a thermos into their cups. The turkey sandwiches they ate were wrapped in cloth.

What's in the other thermos?

Soup.

Soup?

Soup.

Damn.

They ate.

How long has he been manager down here?

About two years.

Billy nodded. Did he not offer to hire you on before now?

He did. I told him I didnt mind workin with him but I wasnt all that sure about workin for him.

What made you change your mind?

I aint changed it. I'm just thinkin about it.

They ate. Troy nodded downcountry. They say there's been a white man ambushed ever mile of this draw.

Billy studied the country. Looks like they'd of learned to stay out of it.

When they'd done eating Troy poured the rest of the coffee into their cups and screwed the cap back on the thermos and laid it by with the soup and the sandwich cloths and the still folded tablecloth to pack back in the saddlebags. They sat sipping the coffee. The horses standing downstream side by side looked up from their drinking in the creek. They had wet leaves stuck to their noses.

Elton's got his own notions about what happened, Troy said. Johnny if he hadnt of found that girl would of found somethin else. You couldnt head him. Elton says he changed. He never changed. He was four years older than me. Not a lot of years. But he walked ground I'll never see. Glad not to see. People always said he was bullheaded, but it wasnt just that. He fought Daddy one time he wasnt but fifteen. Fistfought him. Made the old man fight him. Told him to his face that he respected him and all but that he wasnt goin to take what he'd said. Somethin the old man had chewed him out over. I cried like a baby. He didnt cry. Kept gettin up. Nose all busted and all. The old man kept tellin him to stay down. Hell, the old man was cryin. I hope I never see nothin like it again. I can think about it now and it makes me sick. And there was nothin any mortal man could of done to of stopped it.

What happened?

The old man finally walked off. He was beat and he knew it. Johnny standin there. Couldnt hardly stand up. Callin to him to come back. The old man wouldnt even turn around. He just went on to the house.

Troy looked into the bottom of his cup. He slung the dregs out across the leaves.

It wasnt just her. There's a kind of man that when he cant have what he wants he wont take the next best thing but the worst he can find. Elton thinks he was that kind and maybe he was. But I think he loved that girl. I think he knew what she was and he didnt care. I think it was his own self he was blind to. I think he was just lost. This world was never made for him. He'd outlived it before he could walk. Get married. Hell. He couldnt even stand to wear lace-up shoes.

You liked him though.

Troy looked off down through the trees. Well, he said. I dont guess like really says it. I cant talk about it. I wanted to be like him. But I wasnt. I tried.

He was your dad's favorite I reckon.

Oh yeah. It wasnt a problem with anybody. It was just known. Accepted. Hell. It wasnt even a contest. You ready?

I'm ready.

He rose. He placed the flat of his hand in the small of his back and stretched. He looked at Billy. I loved him, he said. So did Elton. You couldnt not. That was all there was to it.

He folded the cloths under his arm together with the thermos bottles. They hadnt even looked to see what the soup was. He turned and looked back at Billy. So how do you like this country?

I like it.

I do too. Always have.

So you comin down here?

No.

It was dusk when they rode into Fort Davis. Nighthawks were circling over the old parade grounds when they passed and the sky over the mountains behind them was blood red. Elton was waiting with the truck and horsetrailer in front of the Limpia Hotel. They unsaddled the horses in the graveled parking lot and put the saddles in the bed of the truck and wiped the horses down and loaded them in the trailer and went into the hotel and through the lobby to the coffeeshop.

How did you like that little horse? said Elton.

I liked him fine, said Billy. We got along good.

They sat and studied the menus. What are you all havin? said Elton.

They left around ten oclock. Elton stood in the yard with his hands in his back pockets. He was still standing there, just the silhouette of him against the porchlight, when they rounded the curve at the end of the drive and went on toward the highway.

Billy drove. He looked over at Troy. You goin to stay awake aint you?

Yeah. I'm awake.

You've done decided?

Yeah, I think so.

We're goin to have to go somewheres.

Yeah. I know it.

You aint asked me what I thought.

Well. You aint comin down here unless I do and I aint. So what would be the use in me askin?

Billy didnt answer.

After a while Troy said: Hell, I knew I wasnt comin back down here.

Yeah.

You go back home and everthing you wished was different is still the same and everthing you wished was the same is different.

I know what you mean.

I think especially if you're the youngest. You wasnt the youngest in your family was you?

No. I was the oldest.

You dont want to be the youngest. I can tell you right now. There aint no percentage in it.

They drove on through the mountains. About a mile past the intersection with highway 166 there was a truckload of Mexicans pulled off onto the grass. They stood almost into the road waving their hats. Billy slowed.

The hell with that, said Troy.

Billy drove past. He looked in the rearview mirror but he could see nothing but the dark of the road and the deep of the desert night. He pulled the truck slowly to a halt.

Damn it, Parham, Troy said.

I know. I just cant do it.

You're fixin to get us in a jackpot here we wont get home till daylight.

I know it.

He put the truck into reverse and began to grind slowly back down the highway, using the white line running from under the front of the truck to steer by. When the other truck hove into view alongside them he could see that the right front tire was down.

They gathered around the cab. Punchada, they said. Tenemos una llanta punchada.

Puedo verlo, said Billy. He pulled off the road and climbed out. Troy lit a cigarette and shook his head.

They needed a jack. Did they have a spare? Sí. Por supuesto.

He got the jack out of the bed and they carried it back to the truck and commenced to jack the front end up. They had two spares and neither of them would hold air. They spelled each other at the antique tirepump. Finally they raised up and looked at Billy.

He got the tiretools out of the truckbed and came around and got the patchkit and a flashlight from under the seat. They carried one of the spares out into the road and laid it down and stood on it to break the bead and then the man who'd taken the tools from Billy stepped forward and began to pry the tire up off the rim while the others watched. The innertube that he snaked out of the tire's inner cavity was made of red rubber and there was a whole plague of patches upon it. He laid it out on the macadam and Billy trained the light over it. Hay parches sobre los parches, he said.

Es verdad, the man said.

La otra?

Está peor.

One of the younger men manned the tirepump and the tube bloated slowly up in the road and sat hissing. He knelt and put his ear to the various leaks. Billy flipped open the tin lid of the patchcan and thumbed the number of repairs it contained. Troy had climbed out of the truck and he walked back and stood smoking quietly and looking at the tire and the tube and the Mexicans.

The Mexicans wheeled the blown tire around the side of the truck and Billy put the light on it. There was a great ragged hole in the sidewall. It looked like it had been chewed by bulldogs. Troy spat quietly in the road. The Mexicans threw the tire up onto the bed of the truck.

Billy took the stub of chalk from the patchkit and circled the leaks in the tube and they unscrewed the valvestem from the valve and sat on the tube and then walked it down till it was dead flat. Then they sat in the road with the white line running past their elbows and the gaudy desert night overhead, the myriad constellations moving upon the blackness subtly as sealife, and they worked with the dull red shape of rubber in their laps, squatting like tailors or menders of nets. They scuffed the rubber with the little tin grater stamped into the lid of the kit and they laid on the patches and fired them with a match one by one till all were fused and all were done. When they had the tube pumped up again they sat in the road in the quiet desert dark and listened.

Oye algo? said Billy.

Nada.

They sat listening.

He unscrewed the valvestem again and when they had the tube deflated the man slid it down inside the tire and worked it around the rim and fitted the valve and the boy came forward with the pump and began to pump up the tire. He was a long time pumping. When the bead popped on the rim he stopped and they unscrewed the hose from the valve and the man took the valvestem from his mouth and screwed it into the hissing valve and then they stepped back and looked at Billy. He spat and turned and walked back to the truck to get the tiregauge.

Troy was asleep in the front seat. Billy got the gauge out of the glovebox and walked back and they gauged the tire and then rolled it over to the truck and slid it onto the hub and tightened down the lugnuts with a wrench made from a socket welded onto a length of heavy iron pipe. Then they let down the jack and pulled it from under the truck and handed it to Billy.

He took the jack and tiretools and put the patchkit and the

gauge in his shirtpocket and the flashlight in the back pocket of his jeans. Then they shook hands all the way around.

Adónde van? said Billy.

The man shrugged. He said that they were going to Sanderson Texas. He turned and looked off across the dark headlands to the east. The younger men stood about them.

Hay trabajo allá?

He shrugged again. Espero que sí, he said. He looked at Billy. Es vaquero?

Sí. Vaquero.

The man nodded. It was a vaquero's country and other men's troubles were alien to it and that was about all that could be said. They shook hands again and the Mexicans clambered aboard the truck and the truck cranked and coughed and started and lumbered slowly out onto the roadway. The men and boys in the bed of the truck stood and raised their hands. He could see them above the dark hump of the cab, against the deep burnt cobalt of the sky. The single taillight had a short in the wiring and it winked on and off like a signal until the truck had rounded the curve and vanished.

He put the jack and tools in the pickup and opened the door and nudged Troy awake.

Let's go, cowboy.

Troy sat and stared out at the empty road. He looked back behind them.

Where'd they go?

They're done gone.

What time is it do you reckon?

I dont know.

Are you done bein a Samaritan?

I'm done.

He leaned and opened the glovebox door and put the patchkit and the tiregauge and the flashlight in and shut the door and started the engine.

Where were they headed? Troy said.

Sanderson.

Sanderson?

Yeah.

Where were they comin from?

I dont know. They didnt say.

I bet they aint even goin to Sanderson, Troy said.

Where do you think they're goin?

Hell, who knows.

Why would anybody lie about goin to Sanderson Texas?

I dont know.

They drove on. Rounding a curve with a steep bank to the right of the road there was a sudden white flare and a solid whump of a sound. The truck veered, the tires squealing. When they got stopped they were halfway off the road into the bar ditch.

What in the hell, said Troy. What in the hell.

A large owl lay cruciform across the driver's windshield of the truck. The laminate of the glass was belled in softly to hold him and his wings were spread wide and he lay in the concentric rings and rays of the wrecked glass like an enormous moth in a web.

Billy shut off the engine. They sat looking at it. One of its feet shuddered and drew up into a claw and slowly relaxed again and it moved its head slightly as if to better see them and then it died.

Troy opened the door and got out. Billy sat looking at the owl. Then he turned off the headlights and got out too.

The owl was all soft and downy. Its head slumped and rolled. It was soft and warm to the touch and it felt loose inside its feathers. He lifted it free and carried it over to the fence and hung it from the wires and came back. He sat in the truck and turned the lights on to judge if he could drive with the windshield in that condition or whether he might have to kick it out completely. There was a clear place in the lower right corner and he thought he could see if he hunkered down and looked through the windshield there. Troy had walked up the road and was standing taking a leak.

He started the truck and pulled back onto the road. Troy had walked further up and was sitting in the roadside grass. He drove up and rolled down the window and looked at him.

What's wrong with you? he said.

Nothin, Troy said.

Are you ready to go?

Yeah.

He rose and walked around in front of the truck and got in. Billy looked over at him.

Are you all right?

Yeah. I'm all right.

It was just a owl.

I know. It aint that.

Well what is it?

Troy didnt answer.

He pulled the shiftlever in the floor down into first and let the clutch out. They moved down the highway. He could see pretty well. He could lean over and see through the glass on the other side of the division bar. Are you all right? he said. What is it?

Troy sat looking out the window at the passing darkness. Just everthing, he said. Just ever goddamned thing. Hell. Dont pay no attention to me. I ought not to drink whiskey in the first place.

They drove on to Van Horn and stopped for gas and coffee and by then the country that Troy'd grown up in and that he thought he might go back to and where his dead brother was buried was all behind them and it was two oclock in the morning.

Mac will have a few things to say when he sees the truck.

Billy nodded. I might be able to run into town and get it fixed in the mornin.

What do you reckon it'll cost?

I dont know.

You want to just split it?

That would suit me.

All right.

You sure you're okay?

Yeah. I'm all right. I just get to thinkin about things is all.

Yeah.

It dont help none though, does it?

Nope.

They sat drinking their coffee. Troy shook out a cigarette and lit it and put his cigarettes and his Zippo lighter on the table. How come you had to stop back there?

I just did.

You said you had to.

Yeah.

What is it? Some sort of religious thing?

No. It aint nothin like that. It's just that the worst day of my life was one time when I was seventeen years old and me and my bud—my brother—we was on the run and he was hurt and there was a truckload of Mexicans just about like them back yonder appeared out of nowhere and pulled our bacon out of the fire. I wasnt even sure their old truck could outrun a horse, but it did. They didnt have no reason to stop for us. But they did. I dont guess it would of even occurred to em not to. That's all.

Troy sat looking out the window. Well, he said. That's a pretty good reason.

Well. It was all the one I needed anyways. You ready?

Yeah. He drained his cup. I'm ready.

HE PAID HIS TWO PENNIES at the gate and pushed through the turnstile and went on across the bridge. On the banks of the river under the bridge small boys held up tin buckets nailed to the ends of poles and called out for money. He crossed the bridge into a sea of waiting vendors hustling cheap jewelry, leather goods, blankets. They followed him along for a distance and were spelled by others in a relay of huckstering down Juárez Avenue and up Ignacio Mejía to Santos Degollado where they fell away and watched him go.

He stood at the end of the bar and ordered a whiskey and propped his foot on the rail and looked across the room at the whores.

Dónde están sus compañeros? said the barman.

He raised the glass of whiskey and turned it in his hand. En el campo, he said. He drank.

He stood there for two hours. The whores came across the room one by one to solicit him and one by one returned. He didnt ask about her. When he left he'd had five whiskies and he paid for them with a dollar and put another dollar on top of it for the barman. He crossed Juárez Avenue and went limping up Mejía to the Napoleón and took a seat in front of the cafe and ordered a steak. He sat and drank coffee while he waited and he watched the life in the streets. A man came to the door and tried to sell him cigarettes. A man tried to sell him a Madonna made of painted celluloid. A man with a strange device with dials and levers asked him if he wished to electrocute himself. After a while the steak arrived.

He went again the following night. There were half a dozen soldiers from Fort Bliss there, young recruits, their heads all but shaved. They eyed him drunkenly, they looked at his boots. He stood at the bar and drank three whiskies slowly. She did not appear.

He walked up Juárez Avenue through the hucksters and pimps. He saw a boy selling stuffed armadillos. He saw a tourist drunk laboring up the sidewalk carrying a full suit of armor. He saw a beautiful young woman vomit in the street. Dogs turned at the sound and ran toward her.

He walked up Tlaxcala and up Mariscal and entered another such place and sat at the bar. The whores came to tug at his arm. He said that he was waiting for someone. After a while he left and walked back to the bridge.

HE'D PROMISED MAC he wouldnt ride the horse again until his ankle was better. Sunday after breakfast he worked the animal in the corral and in the afternoon he saddled Bird and rode up into the Jarillas. Atop a raw rock bluff he sat the horse and studied the country. The flooded saltflats shining in the evening sun seventy miles to the east. The peak of El Capitan beyond. All the high mountains of New Mexico paling away to the north beyond the red plains, the ancient creosote. In the steeply canted light the laddered shadows of the fences looked like railtracks running up the country and doves were crossing below him toward a watertank on the McNew spread. He could see no cattle anywhere in that cowtrodden scrubland. The doves called everywhere and there was no wind.

When he got back to the house it was dark and by the time he'd unsaddled the horse and put it up and gone to the kitchen Socorro had already cleared away and was washing the dishes. He got a cup of coffee and sat down and she brought him his supper and while he was eating Mac came and stood in the hallway door and lit a cigar.

You about ready? he said.

Yessir.

Take your time. Take your time.

He walked back up the hallway. Socorro brought the pot from the stove and spooned the last of the caldillo onto his plate. She brought him more coffee and poured a cup for Mac and left it steaming on the far side of the table. When he was done eating he rose and carried his plate and cup to the sink and he poured more coffee and then went to the old cherrywood press hauled overland in a wagon from Kentucky eighty years ago and opened the door and took out the chess set from among the old cattleman's journals and the halfbound ledgers and leather daybooks and the old green Remington boxes of shotgun shells and rifle cartridges. On the upper shelf a dovetailed wooden box that held brass scaleweights. A leather folder of drawing instruments. A glass horsecarriage that once held candy for a Christmas in the long ago. He shut the door and carried the board and the wooden box to the table and unfolded the board and slid back the lid of the box and spilled out the pieces, carved walnut, carved holly, and set them up. Then he sat drinking his coffee.

Mac came out and pulled back the chair opposite and sat and dragged the heavy glass ashtray forward from among the bottles of ketchup and hotsauce and laid his cigar in the ashtray and took a sip of the coffee. He nodded toward John Grady's left hand. John Grady opened his hand, he set the pawns on the board.

I'm white again, said Mac.

Yessir.

He moved his pawn forward.

JC came in and got a cup of coffee from the stove and came to the table and stood.

Set down, said Mac. You're makin the room untidy.

That's all right. I aint stayin.

Better set down, said John Grady. He needs all his powers of concentration.

You got that right, said Mac.

JC sat down. Mac studied the board. JC glanced at the pile of white chesspieces at John Grady's elbow.

Son, you better cut the old man some slack. You might could be replaced with somebody that cowboys better and plays chess worse.

Mac reached and moved his remaining bishop. John Grady moved his knight. Mac took up his cigar and sat puffing quietly.

He moved his queen. John Grady moved his other knight and sat back. Check, he said.

Mac sat studying the board. Damn, he said. After a while he looked up. He turned to JC. You want to play him?

No sir. He's done made a believer out of me.

I know the feelin. He's beat me like a rented mule.

He looked at the wallclock and picked up his cigar again and put it in his teeth. I'll play you one more, he said.

Yessir, said John Grady.

Socorro took off her apron and hung it up and stood at the door.

Goodnight, she said.

Night Socorro.

JC rose from his chair. You all want some more coffee?

They played. When John Grady took the black queen JC pushed back his chair and got up.

I've tried to tell you, son. There's a cold winter comin.

He crossed the kitchen and set his cup in the sink and went to the door.

Night, he said.

Mac sat quietly studying the board. The cigar lay dead in the ashtray.

Night, said John Grady.

He pushed open the door and went out. The screendoor flapped shut. The clock ticked. Mac leaned back. He picked up the cigar stub and then he put it back in the ashtray. I believe I'll concede, he said.

You could still win.

Mac looked at him. Bullshit, he said.

John Grady shrugged. Mac looked at the clock. He looked at John Grady. Then he leaned and carefully turned the board around. John Grady moved Mac's remaining black knight.

Mac pursed his lips. He studied the board. He moved.

Five moves later John Grady mated the white king. Mac shook his head. Let's go to bed, he said.

Yessir.

He began to put away the pieces. Mac pushed back his chair and picked up the cups.

What time did Troy and Billy say they'd be back?

I dont reckon they said.

How come you not to go with em?

I just thought I'd stick around here.

Mac carried the cups to the sink. Did they ask you to go?

Yessir. I dont need to go everwhere they go.

He slid the cover shut on the box and folded the board and rose.

Is Troy fixin to go down there and go to work for his brother?

I dont know sir.

He crossed the room and put the chess set back in the press and closed the door and got his hat.

You dont know or you aint sayin?

I dont know. If I wasnt sayin I'd of said so.

I know you would.

Sir.

Yes.

I feel kind of bad about Delbert.

What do you feel bad about?

Well. I guess I feel like I took his job.

Well you didnt. He'd of been gone anyways.

Yessir.

You let me run the place. All right?

Yessir. Goodnight sir.

Switch on the barnlight yonder.

I can see all right.

You could see better with the light on.

Yessir. Well. It bothers the horses.

Bothers the horses?

Yessir.

He put on his hat and pushed open the door. Mac watched him cross the yard. Then he switched off the kitchen light and turned and crossed the room and went up the hallway. Bothers the horses, he said. Damn.

WHEN HE GOT UP in the morning and went down to Billy's room to wake him Billy wasnt there. The bed looked slept in

and he limped out past the horse stalls and looked across the
yard toward the kitchen. Then he went around to the side of
the barn where the truck was parked. Billy was sitting in the
seat leaning over the steering wheel taking the screws out of
the metal sashframe that held the windshield and dropping the
screws into the ashtray.

Mornin cowboy, he said.

Mornin. What happened to the windshield?

Owl.

Owl?

Owl.

He took the last screws out and pried up and lifted away the
frame and began to pry the edges of the caved-in glass out of
the rubber molding with the blade of the screwdriver.

Walk around and push in on this thing from the outside.
Wait a minute. There's some gloves here.

John Grady pulled on the gloves and hobbled around and
pushed on the edges of the glass while Billy pried with the
screwdriver. They got the glass worked out of the molding
along the bottom and one side and then Billy borrowed the
gloves and pulled the whole thing out in one piece and lifted it
over the steering wheel and laid it in the floor of the truck on
the passenger side.

What did you do, drive with your head out the window?

No. I just sort of sat in the middle and looked out the good
side.

He pushed at the windshield wiper lying inside across the
dashboard.

I thought maybe you'd not got in yet.

We got in around five. What'd you do?

Nothin much.

You aint been rodeoin in the barn while I was gone have you?

Nope.

How's your foot?

It's all right.

Billy pushed the wiper up on its spring and pried the wiper

arm off the capstan with the screwdriver and laid it on the seat.

You goin to get a new glass for it?

I'll get Joaquín to bring one when he goes in. I dont want the old man to see it if I can help it.

Hell, anybody could run into a owl.

I know. But anybody didnt.

John Grady was leaning through the open window of the standing truck door. He turned and spat and leaned some more. Well, he said. I dont know what that means.

Billy laid the screwdriver in the seat. I dont either, he said. I dont know why I said it. Let's go in and see if she's got breakfast ready. I could eat the runnin gears of a bull moose.

When they sat down Oren looked up from his paper and studied John Grady over the tops of his glasses. How's your foot? he said.

It's all right.

I'll bet.

It's all right enough to ride a horse. That's what you wanted to know isnt it?

Can you get that in a stirrup?

I dont have to.

Oren went back to his paper. They ate. After a while he put the paper down and took off his glasses and laid them on the table.

There's a man sendin a two year old filly out here that he aims to give to his wife. I kept my own counsel on that. He dont know nothin about the horse other than its blood. Or any other horse I reckon probably you could say.

Is she broke?

The wife or the horse?

I'll lay eight to five they aint either one, said JC. Sight unseen.

I dont know, said Oren. Green broke or some kind of broke. He wants to leave her here two weeks. I said we'd give her all the trainin she was capable of absorbin in that length of time and he seemed satisfied with that.

All right.

Billy, are you all workin with us this week?

I reckon.

What time did the man say they'd be here? said John Grady.

He said after breakfast. JC. You all ready?

I was born that way.

Well the day advanceth, said Oren. He put his glasses in his shirtpocket and pushed back his chair.

THEY PULLED INTO the yard in a pickup truck towing a new single trailer at about eight-thirty. John Grady walked out to meet them. The trailer was painted black and had the name of a ranch somewhere up in New Mexico that he'd never heard of painted on the side in gold. The two men unlatching and taking down the gate on the trailer nodded at him and the taller of the two looked briefly around the yard and then they backed the horse down the ramp.

Where's Oren at? the tall man said.

John Grady watched the filly. She had a nervous look to her which was all right for a young mare offloaded onto strange terrain. He limped around to see her from the other side. Her eye followed him.

Walk her around.

What?

Walk her around.

Is Oren here?

No sir. He's not. I'm the trainer. Just walk her around a minute and let me watch her.

The man stood for a minute. Then he handed the halter rope to the other man. Walk her around some there, Louis. He looked at John Grady. John Grady was watching the filly.

What time you expect him back?

Not till this evenin.

They watched the little filly walk up and back.

Are you the trainer sure enough?

Yessir.

What is it you're lookin for?

John Grady studied the filly and he looked at the man. That horse is lame, he said.

Lame.

Yessir.

Shit, the man said.

The man walking the horse looked back over his shoulder.

Did you hear that, Louis? the man called to him.

Yeah. I heard it. You want to just go on and shoot her?

What makes you think that horse is lame? the man said.

Well sir. It's not really a matter of what I think. She's lame in the left foreleg. Let me look at her.

Bring her over here, Louis.

You reckon she can make it that far?

I dont know.

He brought the horse over and John Grady walked up to her and leaned against her with his shoulder and lifted her foreleg between his knees and examined the hoof. He ran his thumb around the frog and he examined the hoof wall. He leaned against the animal to feel her breathing and he talked to her and pulled his kerchief from his back pocket and wet it with spittle and began to clean the wall of the hoof.

Who put this on here? he said.

Put what?

This dressing. He held up the handkerchief to show them the stain from the hoof.

I dont know, the man said.

John Grady took out his pocketknife and opened it and ran the point of it down the side wall of the hoof. The man had come closer to watch him. He held up the knifeblade. See that? he said.

Yeah?

She's got a sandcrack in that hoof and somebody has filled it in with wax and then put that hoofdressing over it.

He rose and let the filly's foot down and stroked her shoulder and the three of them stood looking at the filly. The tall man put his hands in his back pockets. He turned and spat. Well, he said.

The man holding the horse toed the ground and looked away.

The old man will shit when he hears this.

Where did you all buy her at?

The man took one hand out of his back pocket and adjusted his hat. He looked at John Grady and he looked at the filly again.

Can I leave her with you? he said.

No sir.

Well let me leave her here till Oren gets back and me and him can talk about it.

I cant do that.

Why not?

I cant do it.

You're tellin me to load her and get her off the place.

John Grady didnt answer. He didnt take his eyes off the man either.

You can do better than that, the man said.

I dont believe I can.

He looked at the man holding the horse. He looked toward the house and he looked at John Grady again. Then he reached to his hip and took out his wallet and opened it and took out a tendollar bill and folded the bill and put the wallet back and tendered the bill toward the boy. Here, he said. Put that in your pocket and dont tell nobody where you got it.

I dont believe I can do that.

Go on.

No sir.

The man's face darkened. He stood holding out the bill. Then he stuck it in the pocket of his shirt.

It wouldnt be no skin off your ass.

John Grady didnt answer. The man turned and spat again.

I didnt have nothin to do with doctorin it thataway if that's what you're thinkin.

I never said you did.

You wouldnt help a man out though, would you?

Not that way I wouldnt.

The man stood looking at John Grady. He spat once more. He looked at the other man and he looked out across the spread.

Let's go, Carl, the other man said. Hell.

They walked the horse back across the lot toward the truck and trailer. John Grady stood watching them. They loaded the horse and raised the gate and shut the doors and latched them. The tall man walked around the side of the truck. Hey kid, he called.

Yessir.

You go to hell.

John Grady didnt answer.

You hear me?

Yessir. I hear you.

Then they got in the truck and turned and drove out across the lot and down the drive.

HE DROPPED THE REINS of his horse in the yard at the kitchen door and went in. Socorro was not in the kitchen and he called her and waited and then went back out. As he was mounting the horse she came to the door. She put her hands to her eyes against the sun. Bueno, she said.

A qué hora regresa el Señor Mac?

No sé.

He nodded. She watched him. She asked him what time he would be back and he said by dark.

Espérate, she said.

Está bien.

No. Espérate.

She went in. He sat the horse. The horse stamped at the bare ground and shook its head. All right, he said. We're goin.

When she came back out she had his lunch done up in a cloth and she handed it up to him at the stirrup. He thanked her and reached behind him and put it in the gamepocket of his duckingjacket and nodded and put the horse forward. She watched him ride to the gate and lean and undo the latch and push the gate open horseback and ride through and turn the horse and close the gate horseback and then set off down the road at a jog with the morning sun on his shoulders, his hat pushed back. Sitting very straight in the saddle. The wrapped and bootless foot at one side, the empty stirrup. The herefords and their calves following along the fence and calling after him.

He rode among the half wild cattle in the Bransford pasture all day and a cold wind blew down from the mountains of New Mexico. The cattle trotted off before him or ran with their tails up over the gravel plains among the creosote and he studied them for culls as they went. He was horsetraining as much as he was sorting cattle and the little blue horse he rode had the cuttinghorse's contempt for cows and would closeherd them along the crossfence and bite them. John Grady gave him his head and he cut out a big yearling calf and John Grady roped the calf and dallied but the calf didnt go down. The little horse stood spraddlelegged backed into the rope with the calf standing and twisting at the end of it.

What do you want to do now? he asked the horse.

The horse turned and backed. The calf went bucking.

I guess you think I'm goin to get down and flank that big son of a bitch and me on one leg.

He waited until the calf had bucked itself into a clear space among the creosote and then he put the horse forward at a gallop. He paid the slack rope over the horse's head and overtook the calf on its off side. The calf went trotting. The rope ran from its neck along the ground on the near side and trailed in a curve behind its legs and ran forward up the off side following the horse. John Grady checked his dally and then stood in one stirrup and cleared his other leg of the trailing rope. When the rope snapped taut it jerked the calf's head backward and snatched its hind legs from under it. The calf turned endwise in the air and slammed to the ground in a cloud of dust and lay there.

John Grady was already off the horse and hobbling back along the rope to where the calf lay and he knelt on its head before it could recover and grabbed its hind leg and yanked the pigginstring from his belt and tied it and waited till it quit struggling. Then he leaned and pulled the leg up to take a closer look at the swelling on the inside of its leg that had made it run oddly and caused him to cut it out and rope it in the first place.

The calf had a stob of wood embedded under the skin. He tried to get hold of it with his fingers but it was broken off almost flush. He felt along the length of it and pushed on the end of it with his thumb and tried to feed it forward. He got a bit more of it exposed and finally leaned forward and got hold of it with his teeth and pulled it out. A watery serum ran. He held the stick under his nose and sniffed it and then pitched it away and went back to the horse to get his bottle of Peerless and his swabs. When he turned the calf loose it was running worse than before but he thought it would be all right.

He ate his lunch at noon in an outcropping of lava rock with a view across the floodplain to the north and to the west. There were ancient pictographs among the rocks, engravings of animals and moons and men and lost hieroglyphics whose meaning no man would ever know. The rocks were warm in the sun and he sat sheltered from the wind and watched the silent empty land. Nothing moved. After a while he folded away the wrappings from his lunch and rose and went down and caught the horse.

He was still currying the sweated animal by the light from the barn stall when Billy walked down picking his teeth and stood watching him.

Where'd you go?

Cedar Springs.

You up there all day?

Yep.

The man called that owned that filly.

I figured he would.

He wasnt pissed off or nothin.

He had no reason to be.

He asked Mac if he could get you to look at some horses for him.

Well.

He moved along the horse brushing. Billy watched him. She says she's fixin to throw it out if you dont come.

I'll be there in a minute.

All right.

What did you think about that country down there?

I thought it was some pretty nice country.

Yeah?

I aint goin nowheres. Troy aint either.

John Grady ran the brush down the horse's loins. The horse shuddered. We'll all be goin somewhere when the army takes this spread over.

Yeah, I know it.

Troy aint leavin?

Billy looked at the end of his toothpick and put it back in his mouth. The shadow of a bat come to hunt in the barnlight passed across the horse, across John Grady.

I think he just wanted to see his brother.

John Grady nodded. He leaned with both forearms across the horse and stripped the loose hairs from the brush and watched them drop.

When he entered the kitchen Oren was still at the table. He looked up from his paper and then went back to reading. John Grady went to the sink and washed and Socorro opened the warmer door over the oven and got down a plate.

He sat eating his supper and reading the news on the back side of Oren's paper across the table.

What's a plebiscite? said Oren.

You got me.

After a while Oren said: Dont be readin the back of the paper.

What?

I said dont be readin the back of the paper.

All right.

He folded the paper and slid it across the table and raised his coffee and sipped it.

How did you know I was readin the back of the paper?

I could feel it.

What's wrong with it?

Nothin. It just makes me nervous is all. It's a bad habit people got. If you want to read a man's paper you ought to ask him.

All right.

The man that owned that filly you wouldnt have on the property called out here tryin to hire you.

I already got a job.

I think he just wanted you to ride out to Fabens with him to look at a horse.

John Grady nodded. That aint what he wants.

Oren watched him. That's what Mac said.

Or it aint all he wants.

Oren lit a cigarette and laid the pack back on the table. John Grady ate.

What did Mac say?

Said he'd tell you.

Well. I been told.

Hell, call the man. You could do a little horsetradin on the weekend. Make yourself some money.

I guess I dont know how to work for but one man at a time.

Oren smoked. He watched the boy.

I went up to Cedar Springs. Worked them scrubs up there.

I wasnt askin.

I know it. I took that little blue horse of Watson's.

How did he do?

I thought he done awful good. Not braggin or nothin. He was a good horse fore I ever put a saddle on him.

You could of bought that horse.

I know it.

What didnt you like about him?

There wasnt nothin I didnt like about him.

You wont buy him now.

Nope.

He finished eating and wiped his plate with the last piece o tortilla and ate that and pushed the plate back and drank his coffee and set the cup down and looked at Oren.

He's just a good all around horse. He aint a finished horse but I think he'll make a cow horse.

I'm pleased to hear it. Of course your preference is for one that'll bow up like a bandsaw and run head first into the barn wall.

John Grady smiled. Horse of my dreams, he said. It aint exactly like that.

How is it then?

I dont know. I think it's just somethin you like. Or dont like. You can add up all of a horse's good points on a sheet of paper and it still wont tell you whether you'll like the horse or not.

What about if you add up all his bad ones?

I dont know. I'd say you'd probably done made up your mind at that point.

You think there's horses so spoiled you cant do nothin with em?

Yes I do. But probably not as many as you might think.

Maybe not. You think a horse can understand what a man says?

You mean like the words?

I dont know. Like can he understand what he says.

John Grady looked out the window. Water was beaded on the glass. Two bats were hunting in the barnlight. No, he said. I think he can understand what you mean.

He watched the bats. He looked at Oren.

I guess my feelin about a horse is that he mostly worries about what he dont know. He likes to be able to see you. Barring that, he likes to be able to hear you. Maybe he thinks that if you're talkin you wont be doin somethin else he dont know about.

You think horses think?

Sure. Dont you?

Yes I do. Some people claim they dont.

Well. Some people could be wrong.

You think you can tell what a horse is thinkin?

I think I can tell what he's fixin to do.

Generally.

John Grady smiled. Yeah, he said. Generally.

Mac always claimed a horse knows the difference between right and wrong.

Mac's right.

Oren smoked. Well, he said. That's always been a bit much for me to swallow.

I think if they didnt you couldnt even train one.

You dont think it's just gettin em to do what you want?

I think you can train a rooster to do what you want. But you wont have him. There's a way to train a horse where when you get done you've got the horse. On his own ground. A good horse will figure things out on his own. You can see what's in his heart. He wont do one thing while you're watchin him and another when you aint. He's all of a piece. When you've got a horse to that place you cant hardly get him to do somethin he knows is wrong. He'll fight you over it. And if you mistreat him it just about kills him. A good horse has justice in his heart. I've seen it.

You got a lot higher opinion of horses than I got, Oren said.

I really dont have all that much in the way of opinions where horses are concerned. When I was a kid I thought I knew all there was to know about a horse. Where horses are concerned I've just got dumber and dumber.

Oren smiled.

If a man really understood horses, John Grady said. If a man really understood horses he could just about train one by lookin at it. There wouldnt be nothin to it. My way is a long way from workin one over with a tracechain. But it's a long way from what's possible too.

He stretched his legs out. He crossed the sprained foot over his boot.

You're right about one thing, he said. They're mostly ruint before they ever bring em out here. They're ruined at the first saddle. Before that, even. The best horses are the ones been around kids. Or maybe even just a wild horse in off the range that's never even seen a man. He's got nothin to unlearn.

You might have a hard time gettin anyone to agree with you on that last one.

I know it.

You ever break a wild horse?

Yeah. You hardly ever train one though.

Why not?

People dont want em trained. They just want em broke. You got to train the owner.

Oren leaned and stubbed out his cigarette. I hear you, he said.

John Grady sat studying the smoke rising into the lampshade over the table. That probably aint true what I said about the one that aint never seen a man. They need to see people. They need to just see em around. Maybe what they need is to just think people are trees until the trainer comes along.

IT WAS STILL LIGHT OUT, a gray light with the rain falling in the streets again and the vendors huddled in the doorways looking out at the rain without expression. He stomped the water from his boots and entered and crossed to the bar and took off his hat and laid it on the barstool. There were no other customers. Two whores lounging on a sofa watched him without much interest. The barman poured his whiskey.

He described the girl to the barman but the barman only shrugged and shook his head.

Eres muy joven.

He shrugged again. He wiped the bar and leaned back and took a cigarette from his shirtpocket and lit it. John Grady motioned for another whiskey and doled his coins onto the counter. He took his hat and his glass over to the sofa and queried the whores but they only tugged at his clothing and asked him to buy them a drink. He looked into their faces. Who they might be behind the caked sizing and the rouge, the black greasepaint lining their dark indian eyes. They seemed alien and sad. Like madwomen dressed for an outing. He looked at the neon deer hanging on the wall behind them and the garish tapestries of plush, of foil and braid. He could hear the rain on the roof to the rear and the steady small drip of water falling from the ceiling into puddles in the bloodred carpeting. He drained his whiskey and set the glass on the low table and put on his hat. He nodded to them and touched the brim of his hat to go.

Joven, said the oldest.

Sí.

She looked furtively about but there was no one there to hear.

Ya no está, she said.

He asked where she had gone but they did not know. He asked if she would return but they did not think so.

He touched his hat again. Gracias, he said.

Ándale, said the whores.

At the corner a sturdy cabdriver in a blue suit of polished serge hailed him. He held an antique umbrella, rare to see in that country. One of the panels between the ribs had been replaced by a sheet of blue cellophane and under it the driver's face was blue. He asked John Grady if he wanted to go see the girls and he said that he did.

They drove through the flooded and potholed streets. The driver was slightly drunk and commented freely on pedestrians that crossed before them or that stood in the doorways. He commented on aspects of their character deducible from their appearance. He commented on crossing dogs. He talked about what the dogs thought and where they might be going and why.

They sat at a whorehouse bar on the outskirts of the city and the driver pointed out the virtues of the various whores that were in the room. He said that men out for an evening were often likely to accept the first proposal but that the prudent man would be more selective. That he would not be misled by appearances. He said that it was best to move freely where whores were concerned. He said that in a healthy society choice should always be the prerogative of the buyer. He turned to regard the boy with dreamy eyes.

De acuerdo? he said.

Claro que sí, said John Grady.

They drank up and moved on. Outside it was dark and in the streets the colored lights lay slurred and faintly peened in the fine rain. They sat at the bar of an establishment called the Red Cock. The driver saluted with his glass aloft and drank. They studied the whores.

I can take you some other places, the driver said. Maybe she is go home.

Maybe.

Maybe she is get married. Sometimes these girls is get married.

I seen her down here two weeks ago.

The driver reflected. He sat smoking. John Grady finished his drink and rose. Vamos a regresar a La Venada, he said.

In the Calle de Santos Degollado he sat at the bar and waited. After a while the driver returned and leaned and whispered to him and then looked about with studied caution.

You must talk to Manolo. Manolo only can give us this information.

Where is he?

I take you to him. I take you. It is arrange. You have to pay.

John Grady reached for his wallet. The driver stayed his arm.

He looked toward the barman. Afuera, he said. No podemos hacerlo aquí.

Outside he again reached for his billfold but the driver said for him to wait. He looked about theatrically. Es peligroso, he hissed.

They got into the cab.

Where is he? said John Grady.

We go to him now. I take you.

He started the engine and they pulled away down the street and turned right. They drove half way up the block and turned again and pulled into an alley and parked. The driver cut the engine and switched off the lights. They sat in the darkness. They could hear a radio in the distance. They could hear rainwater from the canales dripping in the puddles in the alley. After a while a man appeared and opened the rear door of the cab and got in.

The domelight was out in the cab and John Grady could not see the man's face. He was smoking a cigarette and he cupped his hand over it when he smoked in the manner of country people. John Grady could smell the cologne he wore.

Bueno, the man said.

You pay him now, said the cabdriver. He will tell you where the girl is.

How much do I pay him?

You pay me fifty dollars, the man said.

Fifty dollars?

No one answered.

I dont have fifty dollars.

The man sat for a moment. Then he opened the door again and got out.

Wait a minute, said John Grady.

The man stood in the alley, one hand on the door. John Grady could see him. He was wearing a black suit and a black tie. His face was small and wedgeshaped.

Do you know this girl? said John Grady.

Of course I know this girl. You waste my time.

What does she look like?

She is sixteen years old. She is the epiléptica. There is only one. She is gone two weeks now. You waste my time. You have no money and you waste my time.

I'll get the money. I'll bring it tomorrow night.

The man looked at the driver.

I'll come to the Venada. I'll bring it to the Venada.

The man turned his head slightly and spat and turned back. You cant come to the Venada. On this business. What is the matter with you? How much do you have?

John Grady took out his billfold. Thirty somethin, he said. He thumbed through the bills. Thirty-six dollars.

The man held out his hand. Give it to me.

John Grady handed him the money. He wadded it into his shirtpocket without even looking at it. The White Lake, he said. Then he shut the door and was gone. They couldnt even hear his footsteps going back up the alley. The driver turned in his seat.

You want to go to the White Lake?

I dont have any more money.

The driver drummed his fingers on the back of the seat. You dont have no monies?

No.

The driver shook his head. No monies, he said. Okay. You want to go back to the Avenida?

I cant pay you.

Is okay.

He started the engine and backed down the alley toward the street. You pay me next time. Okay?

Okay.

Okay.

WHEN HE PASSED Billy's room the light was on and he stopped and pushed open the canvas and looked in. Billy was ying in bed. He lowered the book he was reading and looked over the top of it and then laid it down.

What are you readin?

Destry. Where you been?

You ever been to a place called the White Lake?

Yes I have. One time.

Is it real expensive?

It's real expensive. Why?

I was just wonderin about it. See you in the mornin.

He let the canvas fall and turned and went on down the bay to his room.

You better stay out of the White Lake, son, Billy called.

John Grady pushed open the curtain and felt for the lightchain.

It aint no place for a cowboy.

He found the chain and pulled the light on.

You hear me?

HE LIMPED DOWN the hallway after breakfast with his hat in his hand. Mr Mac? he called.

McGovern came to the door of his office. He had some papers in his hand and some more wedged under his elbow. Come on in, son, he said.

John Grady stood in the door. Mac was at his desk. Come on in, he said. What do you need that I aint got?

He looked up from his papers. John Grady was still standing in the doorway.

I wonder if I could draw some on next month's pay.

Mac reached for his billfold. How much did you need.

Well. I'd like to get a hundred if I could.

Mac looked at him. You can have it if you want, he said. What did you aim to do next month?

I'll make out.

He opened the billfold and counted out five twenties. Well,

he said. I guess you're big enough to handle your own affairs. I aint none of my business, is it?

I just needed it for somethin.

All right.

He shuffled the bills together and leaned and laid them on the desk. John Grady came in and picked them up and folded them and stuck them in his shirtpocket.

Thank you, he said.

That's all right. How's your foot?

It's doin good.

You're still favorin it I see.

It's all right.

You still intend to trade for that horse?

Yessir. I do.

How did you know Wolfenbarger's filly had a bad hoof?

I could see it.

She didnt walk lame.

No sir. It was her ear.

Her ear?

Yessir. Ever time that foot hit the ground one ear would move a little. I just kept watchin her.

Sort of like a poker tell.

Yessir. Sort of.

You didnt want to go off horsetradin with the old man though.

No sir. Is he a friend of yours?

I know him. Why?

Nothin.

What were you goin to say?

That's all right.

You can say it. Go ahead.

Well. I guess I was goin to say that I didnt think I could keep him out of trouble on no part time basis.

Like it would be a full time job?

I didnt say that.

Mac shook his head. Get your butt out of here, he said.

Yessir.

You didnt tell him that did you?

No sir. I aint talked to him.

Well. That's a shame.

Yessir.

He put on his hat and turned but stopped again at the door.

Thank you sir.

Go on. It's your money.

When he came in that evening Socorro had already left the kitchen and there was no one at the table except the old man. He was smoking a homerolled cigarette and listening to the news on the radio. John Grady got his plate and his coffee and set them on the table and pulled back the chair and sat.

Evenin Mr Johnson, he said.

Evenin son.

What's the news?

The old man shook his head. He leaned across the table to the windowsill where the radio sat and turned it off. It aint news no more, he said. Wars and rumors of wars. I dont know why I listen to it. It's a ugly habit and I wish I could get broke of it but I think I just get worse.

John Grady spooned pico de gallo over his rice and his flautas and rolled up a tortilla and commenced to eat. The old man watched him. He nodded at the boy's boots.

You look like you been in some pretty mirey country today.

Yessir. I was. Some.

That old greasy clay is hard to clean off of anything. Oliver Lee always said he come out here because the country was so sorry nobody else would have it and he'd be left alone. Of course he was wrong. At least about bein left alone.

Yessir. I guess he was.

How's your foot doin.

It's all right.

The old man smiled. He drew on his cigarette and tapped the ash into the ashtray on the table.

Dont be fooled by the good rains we've had. This country is fixin to dry up and blow away.

How do you know?

It just is.

You want some more coffee?

No thanks.

The boy got up and went to the stove and filled his cup and came back.

Country's overdue, the old man said. Folks have got short memories. They might be glad to let the army have it fore they're done.

The boy ate. How much do you think the army will take?

The old man drew on his cigarette and stubbed it out thoughtfully. I think they'll take the whole Tularosa basin. That's my guess.

Can they just take it?

Yeah. They can take it. Folks will piss and moan about it. But they dont have a choice. They ought to be glad to get shut of it.

What do you think Mr Prather will do?

John Prather will do whatever he says he'll do.

Mr Mac said he told em the only way he'd leave was in a box.

Then that's how he'll leave. You can take that to the bank.

John Grady wiped his plate and sat back with his cup of coffee. I ought not to ask you this, he said.

Ask it.

You dont have to answer.

I know it.

Who do you think killed Colonel Fountain?

The old man shook his head. He sat for a long time.

I ought not to of asked you.

No. It's all right. You know his daughter's name was Maggie too. She was the one told Fountain to take the boy with him. Said they wouldnt bother a eight year old boy. But she was wrong, wasnt she?

Yessir.

A lot of people think Oliver Lee killed him. I knew Oliver

pretty well. We was the same age. He had four sons himself. I just dont believe it.

You dont think he could of done it?

I'll say it stronger than that. I'll say he didnt.

Or cause it to be done?

Well. That's another matter. I'll say he never shed no tears over it. Over the colonel, leastways.

You didnt want some more coffee?

No thank you son. I'd be up all night.

Do you think they're still buried out there somewheres?

No. I dont.

What do you think happened?

I always thought the bodies were taken to Mexico. They had a choice to bury em out there somewhere south of the pass where they might be discovered or to go another thirty miles to where they could drop em off the edge of the world and I think that's what they done.

John Grady nodded. He sipped his coffee. Were you ever in a shooting scrape?

I was. One time. I was old enough to know better too.

Where was it?

Down on the river east of Clint. It was in nineteen and seventeen just before my brother died and we were on the wrong side of the river waitin for dark to cross some stolen horses we'd recovered and we got word they was layin for us. We waited and waited and after a while the moon come up—just a piece of a moon, not even a quarter. It come up behind us and we could see it reflected in the windshield of their car over in the trees along the river breaks. Wendell Williams looked at me and he said: We got two moons in the sky. I dont believe I ever seen that before. And I said: Yes, and one of em is backwards. And we opened fire on em with our rifles.

Did they shoot back?

Sure they did. We laid there and shot up about a box of shells apiece and then they left out.

Was anybody hit?

Not that I ever heard of. We hit the car a time or two. Knocked the windshield out.

Did you get the horses across?

We did.

How many head was it?

It was a few. About seventy head.

That's a lot of horses.

It was a lot of horses. We was paid good money, too. But it wasnt worth gettin shot over.

No sir. I guess not.

It does funny things to a man's head.

What's that, sir?

Bein shot at. Havin dirt thowed on you. Leaves cut. It changes a man's perspective. Maybe some might have a appetite for it. I never did.

You didnt fight in the revolution?

No.

You were down there though.

Yes. Tryin to get the hell out. I'd been down there too long. I was just as glad when it did start. You'd wake up in some little town on a Sunday mornin and they'd be out in the street shootin at one another. You couldnt make any sense out of it. We like to never got out of there. I saw terrible things in that country. I dreamt about em for years.

He leaned and put his elbows on the table and took his makings from his shirtpocket and rolled another smoke and lit it. He sat looking at the table. He talked for a long time. He named the towns and villages. The mud pueblos. The executions against the mud walls sprayed with new blood over the dried black of the old and the fine powdered clay sifting down from the bulletholes in the wall after the men had fallen and the slow drift of riflesmoke and the corpses stacked in the streets or piled into the woodenwheeled carretas trundling over the cobbles or over the dirt roads to the nameless graves. There were thousands who went to war in the only suit they owned. Suits in which they'd been married and in which they would be

buried. Standing in the streets in their coats and ties and hats
behind the upturned carts and bales and firing their rifles like
irate accountants. And the small artillery pieces on wheels that
scooted backwards in the street at every round and had to be
retrieved and the endless riding of horses to their deaths bearing flags or banners or the tentlike tapestries painted with portraits of the Virgin carried on poles into battle as if the mother
of God herself were authoress of all that calamity and mayhem
and madness.

The tallcase clock in the hallway chimed ten.

I reckon I'd better get on to bed, the old man said.

Yessir.

He rose. I dont much like to, he said. But there aint no help
for it.

Goodnight sir.

Goodnight.

THE CABDRIVER would see him through the wroughtiron
gate in the high brick wall and up the walk to the doorway. As
if the surrounding dark that formed the outskirts of the city
were a danger. Or the desert plains beyond. He pulled a velvet
bellpull in an alcove in the archway and stood back humming.
He looked at John Grady.

You like for me to wait I can wait.

No. It's all right.

The door opened. A hostess in evening attire smiled at them
and stood back and held the door. John Grady entered and took
off his hat and the woman spoke with the driver and then shut
the door and turned. She held out her hand and John Grady
reached for his hip pocket. She smiled.

Your hat, she said.

He handed her his hat and she gestured toward the room and
he turned and went in, brushing down his hair with the flat of
his hand.

There was a bar to the right up the two stairs and he stepped up and passed along behind the stools where men were drinking and talking. The bar was mahogany and softly lit and the barmen wore little burgundy jackets and bowties. Out in the salon the whores lounged on sofas of red damask and gold brocade. They wore negligees and floorlength formal gowns and sheath dresses of white satin or purple velvet that were split up the thigh and they wore shoes of glass or gold and sat in studied poses with their red mouths pouting in the gloom. A cutglass chandelier hung overhead and on a dais to the right a string trio was playing.

He walked to the far end of the bar. When he put his hand on the rail the barman was already there placing a napkin.

Good evening sir, he said.

Evenin. I'll have a Old Grandad and water back.

Yessir.

The barman moved away. John Grady put his boot on the polished brass footrail and he watched the whores in the glass of the backbar. The men at the bar were mostly welldressed Mexicans with a few Americans dressed in flowered shirts of an intemperately thin cloth. A tall woman in a diaphanous gown passed through the salon like the ghost of a whore. A cockroach that had been moving along the counter behind the bottles ascended to the glass where it encountered itself and froze.

He ordered another drink. The barman poured. When he looked into the glass again she was sitting by herself on a dark velvet couch with her gown arranged about her and her hands composed in her lap. He reached for his hat, not taking his eyes from her. He called for the barman.

La cuenta por favor.

He looked down. He remembered that he'd left his hat with the hostess at the door. He took out his wallet and pushed a fivedollar bill across the mahogany and folded the rest of the bills and put them in his shirtpocket. The barman brought the change and he pushed a dollar back toward him and turned and looked across the room to where she sat. She looked small and lost. She sat with her eyes closed and he realized that she was listening to the music. He poured the shot of whiskey into the glass of water and set the shotglass on the bar and took his drink and set out across the room.

His faint shadow under the lights of the great glass tiara above them may have brought her from her reveries. She looked up at him and smiled thinly with her painted child's mouth. He almost reached for his hatbrim.

Hello, he said. Do you care if I set down?

She recomposed herself and smoothed her skirt to make room on the couch beside her. A waiter moved out from the shadows along the walls and laid down two napkins on the low glass table before them and stood.

Bring me a Old Grandad and water back. And whatever she's drinkin.

He nodded and moved away. John Grady looked at the girl. She leaned forward and smoothed her skirt again.

Lo siento, she said. Pero no hablo inglés.

Está bien. Podemos hablar español.

Oh, she said. Qué bueno.

Qué es su nombre?

Magdalena. Y usted?

He didnt answer. Magdalena, he said.

She looked down. As if the sound of her name were troubling to her.

Es su nombre de pila? he said.

Sí. Por supuesto.

No es su nombre . . . su nombre profesional.

She put her hand to her mouth. Oh, she said. No. Es mi nombre propio.

He watched her. He told her that he had seen her at La Venada but she only nodded and did not seem surprised. The waiter arrived with the drinks and he paid for them and tipped the man a dollar. She did not pick up her drink then or later. She spoke so softly he had to lean to catch her words. She said that the other women were watching but that it was nothing. It was only that she was new to this place. He nodded. No importa, he said.

She asked why he had not spoken to her at La Venada. He said that it was because he was with friends. She asked him if he had a sweetheart at La Venada but he said that he did not.

No me recuerda? he said.

She shook her head. She looked up. They sat in silence.

Cuántos años tiene? he said.

Bastantes.

He said it was all right if she did not wish to say but she didnt answer. She smiled wistfully. She touched his sleeve. Fue mentira, she said. Lo que decía.

Cómo?

She said that it was a lie that she did not remember him. She said that he was standing at the bar and she thought that he would come to talk to her but that he had not and when she looked again he was gone.

Verdad?

Sí.

He said that she had not really lied. He said she'd only shook her head, but she shook her head again and said that these were the worst lies of all. She asked him why he had come to the White Lake alone and he looked at the drinks untouched on the table before them and he thought about that and about lies and he turned and looked at her.

Porque la andaba buscando, he said. Ya tengo tiempo buscándola.

She didnt answer.

Y cómo es que me recuerda?

She half turned away, she almost whispered. También yo, she said.

Mande?

She turned and looked at him. También yo.

In the room she turned and closed the door behind them. He

couldnt even remember how they got there. He remembered her hand in his, small and cold, so strange to feel. The prism-broken light from the chandelier that ran in a river over her naked shoulders when they passed beneath. Half stumbling after her like a child.

She went to the bedside and lit two candles and then turned off the lamp. He stood in the room with his hands at his sides. She reached to the back of her neck and undid the clasp of her gown and reached behind and pulled down the zipper. He began to unbutton his shirt. The room was small and the bed all but filled it. It was a fourpost bed with a canopy and curtains of winecolored organza and the candles shone through onto the pillows with a winey light.

There was a light knock at the door.

Tenemos que pagar, she said.

He took the folded bills from his pocket. Para la noche, he said.

Es muy caro.

Cuánto? He was counting out the bills. He had eighty-two dollars. He held it out to her. She looked at the money and she looked at him. The knock came again.

Dame cincuenta, she said.

Es bastante?

Sí, sí. She took the money and opened the door and held it out and whispered to the man on the other side. He was tall and thin and he smoked a cigarette in a silver holder and he wore a black silk shirt. He looked at the client for just a moment through the partly opened door and he counted the money and nodded and turned away and she shut the door. Her bare back was pale in the candlelight where the dress was open. Her black hair glistened. She turned and withdrew her arms from the sleeves of the dress and caught the front of it before her. She stepped from the pooled cloth and laid the dress across a chair and stepped behind the gauzy curtains and turned back the covers and then she pulled the straps of her chemise from her shoulders and let it fall and stepped naked into the bed and pulled the satin quilt to her chin and turned on her side and put her arm beneath her head and lay watching him.

He took off his shirt and stood looking for some place to put it.

Sobre la silla, she whispered.

He draped the shirt over the chair and sat and pulled off his boots and put his socks in the tops of them and stood them to one side and stood and unbuckled his belt. He crossed the room naked and she reached and turned back the covers for him and he slid beneath the tinted sheets and lay back on the pillow and looked up at the softly draped canopy. He turned and looked at her. She'd not taken her eyes from him. He raised his arm and she slid against him the whole length of her soft and naked and cool. He gathered her black hair in his hand and spread it across his chest like a blessing.

Es casado? she said.

No.

He asked her why she wished to know. She was silent a moment. Then she said that it would be a worse sin if he were married. He thought about that. He asked her if that was really why she wished to know but she said he wished to know too much. Then she leaned and kissed him. In the dawn he held her while she slept and he had no need to ask her anything at all.

She woke while he was dressing. He pulled on his boots and crossed to the bedside and sat and put his hand against her cheek and smoothed her hair. She turned sleepily and looked up at him. The candles in their holders had burned out and the bits of wick lay blackened in the scalloped shapes of wax.

Tienes que irte?

Sí.

Vas a regresar?

Sí.

She studied his eyes to see if he spoke the truth. He leaned and kissed her.

Vete con Dios, she whispered.

Y tú.

She put her arms around him and held him against her breast and then she let him go and he rose and walked to the door. He turned and stood looking back at her.

Say my name, he said.

She reached and parted the canopy curtain. Mande? she said.

Di mi nombre.

She lay there holding the curtain. Tu nombre es Juan, she said.

Yes, he said. Then he pulled the door closed and went down the hall.

The salon was empty. It smelled of stale smoke and sweet ferment and the fading lilac rose and spice of the vanished whores. There was no one at the bar. In the gray light there were stains on the carpet, worn places on the arms of the furniture, cigarette burns. In the foyer he unlatched the painted half door and entered the little cloakroom and retrieved his hat. Then he opened the front door and walked out into the morning cold.

A landscape of low shacks of tin and cratewood here on the outskirts of the city. Barren dirt and gravel lots and beyond them the plains of sage and creosote. Roosters were calling and the air smelled of burning charcoal. He took his bearings by the gray light to the east and set out toward the city. In the cold dawn the lights were still burning out there under the dark cape of the mountains with that precious insularity common to cities of the desert. A man was coming down the road driving a donkey piled high with firewood. In the distance the churchbells had begun. The man smiled at him a sly smile. As if they knew a secret between them, these two. Something of age and youth and their claims and the justice of those claims. And of the claims upon them. The world past, the world to come. Their common transiencies. Above all a knowing deep in the bone that beauty and loss are one.

THE OLD ONE-EYED CRIADA was the first to reach her, trotting stoically down the hallway in her broken slippers and pushing open the door to find her bowed in the bed and raging as if some incubus were upon her. The old woman carried her keys tied by a thong to a short length of broomstick and she wrapped the stick with a quick turn of the bedclothes and forced it between the girl's teeth. The girl arched herself stiffly and the criada climbed up onto the bed and pinned her down and held her. A second woman had come to the doorway bearing a glass of water but she waved her away with a toss of her head.

Es como una mujer diabólica, the woman said.

Vete, called the criada. No es diabólica. Vete.

But the housewhores were gathering in the doorway and they began to push through into the room all of them in face-cream and hairpapers and dressed in their varied nightwear and they gathered clamoring about the bed and one pushed forward with a statue of the Virgin and raised it above the bed and another took one of the girl's hands and commenced to tie it to the bedpost with the sash from her robe. The girl's mouth was bloody and some of the whores came forward and dipped their handkerchiefs in the blood as if to wipe it away but they hid the handkerchiefs on their persons to take away with them and the girl's mouth continued to bleed. They pulled her other arm free and tied it as well and some of them were chanting and some were blessing themselves and the girl bowed and thrashed and then went rigid and her eyes white. They'd brought little figures from their rooms and votive shrines of gilt and painted plaster and some were at lighting candles when the owner of the establishment appeared in the doorway in his shirtsleeves.

Eduardo! Eduardo! they cried. He strode into the room backhanding them away. He swept icons and candles to the floor and seized the old criada by one arm and flung her back.

Basta! he cried. Basta!

The whores huddled whimpering, clutching their robes about their rolling breasts. They retreated to the door. The criada alone stood her ground.

Por qué estás esperando? he hissed.

Her solitary eye blinked. She would not move.

He'd brought from somewhere in his clothes an italian switchblade knife with black onyx handles and silver bolsters and he leaned and cut the sashes from the girl's wrists and seized the covers and pulled them up over her nakedness and folded the knife away as silently as it had appeared.

No la moleste, hissed the criada. No la moleste.

Cállate.

Golpéame si tienes que golpear a alguien.

He turned and seized the old woman by the hair and forced her to the door and shoved her into the hallway with the whores and shut the door behind her. He'd have latched it but those doors latched only from without. The old woman nevertheless did not enter again but stood outside calling that she needed her keys. He stood looking at the girl. The piece of broomstick had fallen from her mouth and lay on the blood-stained sheets. He picked it up and went to the door and opened it. The old woman shrank back and raised one arm but he only threw the keys rattling and clattering down the corridor and then slammed the door shut again.

She lay breathing quietly. There was a cloth lying on the bed and he picked it up and held it for a moment almost as if he might bend to wipe the blood from her mouth but then he flung it away also and turned and looked once more at the wreckage of the room and swore softly to himself and went out and shut the door behind him.

WARD BROUGHT THE STALLION out of the stall and started down the bay with it. The stallion stopped in the middle of the bay and stood trembling and took small steps as if the ground had got unsteady under its feet. Ward stood close to the stallion and talked to it and the stallion jerked its head up and down in a sort of frenzied agreement. They'd been through it all before but the stallion was no less crazy for that and Ward no less patient. He led the horse prancing past the stalls where the other horses circled and rolled their eyes.

John Grady was holding the mare by a twitch and when the stallion entered the paddock she tried to stand upright. She turned at the end of the rope and shot out one hindfoot and then she tried to stand again.

That is a pretty decent lookin mare, Ward said.

Yessir.

What happened to her eye?

Man that owned her knocked it out with a stick.

Ward led the walleyed stallion around the perimeter of the paddock. Knocked it out with a stick, he said.

Yessir.

He couldnt put it back though, could he?

No sir.

Easy, said Ward. Easy now. That's a sweet mare.

Yessir, said John Grady. She is.

He walked the stallion forward by fits and starts. The little mare rolled her good eye till it was white as the blind one. JC and another man had entered the paddock and closed the gate behind them. Ward turned and looked past them toward the paddock walls.

I aint tellin you all again, he called. You go on to the house like I told you.

Two teen-age girls came out and started across the yard toward the house.

Where's Oren at? said Ward.

John Grady turned with the skittering mare. He was leaning all over her and trying to keep her from stepping on his feet.

He had to go to Alamogordo.

Hold her now, Ward said. Hold her.

The stallion stood, his great phallus swinging.

Hold her, said Ward.

I got her.

He knows where it's at.

The mare bucked and kicked one leg. On the third try the stallion mounted her, clambering, stamping his hindlegs, the great thighs quivering and the veins standing. John Grady stood holding all of this before him on a twisted tether like a child holding by a string some struggling and gasping chimera invoked by sorcery out of the void into the astonished day-world. He held the twitchrope in one hand and laid his face against the sweating neck. He could hear the slow bellows of her lungs and feel the blood pumping. He could hear the slow dull beating of the heart within her like an engine deep in a ship.

He and JC loaded the mare in the trailer. She look knocked up to you? JC said.

I dont know.

He bowed her back, didnt he?

They raised the tailgate on the trailer and latched it at either side. John Grady turned and leaned against the trailer and wiped his face with his kerchief and pulled his hat back down.

Mac's done got the colt sold.

I hope he aint spent the money.

Yeah?

She's been bred twice before and it didnt take.

Ward's stud?

No.

I got my money on Ward's studhorse.

So does Mac.

Are we done?

We're done. You want to swing by the cantina?

Are you buyin?

Hell, said JC. I thought I'd get you to back me on the shuffleboard. Give us a chance to improve our financial position.

Last time I done that the position we wound up in wasnt financial.

They climbed into the truck.

Are you broke sure enough? said JC.

I aint got a weepin dime.

They started slowly down the drive. The horsetrailer clanked behind. Troy was counting change in his hand.

I got enough for a couple of beers apiece, he said.

That's all right.

I'm ready to blow in the whole dollar and thirty-five cents.

We better get on back.

HE WATCHED BILLY RIDE down along the fenceline from where it crested against the red dunes. He rode past and then sat the horse and looked out across the windscoured terrain and he turned and looked at John Grady. He leaned and spat.

Hard country, he said.

Hard country.

This used to be grama grass to a horse's stirrups.

I've heard that. Did you see any more of that bunch?

No. They're scattered all to hell and gone. Wild as deer. A man needs three horses to put in a day up here.

Why dont we ride up Bell Springs Draw.

Were you up there last week?

No.

All right.

They crossed the red creosote plain and picked their way up along the dry arroyo over the red rock scree.

John Grady Cole was a rugged old soul, Billy sang.

The trail crossed through the rock and led out along a wash. The dirt was like red talc.

With a buckskin belly and a rubber asshole.

An hour later they sat their horses at the spring. The cattle had been and gone. There were wet tracks at the south end of the ciénega and wet tracks in the trail leading out south down the side of the ridge.

There's at least two new calves with this bunch, Billy said.

John Grady didnt answer. The horses raised their dripping mouths from the water one and then the other and blew and leaned and drank again. The dead leaves clinging to the pale and twisted cottonwoods rattled in the wind. Set in a flat above the springs was a small adobe house in ruins these many years. Billy took his cigarettes from his shirtpocket and shook one out and hunched his shoulders forward and lit it.

I used to think I'd like to have a little spread up in the hills somewhere like this. Run a few head on it. Kill your own meat. Stuff like that.

You might one day.

I doubt it.

You never know.

I wintered one time in a linecamp up in New Mexico. You get a pretty good ration of yourself after a while. I wouldnt do it again if I could help it. I like to froze in that damn shack. The wind would blow your hat off inside.

He smoked. The horses raised their heads and looked out. John Grady pulled the latigo on his catchrope and retied it. You think you'd of liked to of lived back in the old days? he said.

No. I did when I was a kid. I used to think rawhidin a bunch of bony cattle in some outland country would be just as close to heaven as a man was likely to get. I wouldnt give you much for it now.

You think they were a tougher breed back then?

Tougher or dumber?

The dry leaves rattled. Evening was coming on and Billy buttoned his jacket against the cold.

I could live here, John Grady said.

Young and ignorant as you are you probably could.

I think I'd like it.

I'll tell you what I like.

What's that?

When you throw a switch and the lights come on.

Yeah.

If I think about what I wanted as a kid and what I want now they aint the same thing. I guess what I wanted wasnt what I wanted. You ready?

Yeah. I'm ready. What do you want now?

Billy spoke to the horse and reined it around. He sat and looked back at the little adobe house and at the blue and cooling country below them. Hell, he said. I dont know what I want. Never did.

They rode back in the dusk. The dark shapes of cattle moved off sullenly before them.

This is the tag end of that bunch, Billy said.

Yep.

They rode on.

When you're a kid you have these notions about how things are goin to be, Billy said. You get a little older and you pull back some on that. I think you wind up just tryin to minimize the pain. Anyway this country aint the same. Nor anything in it. The war changed everthing. I dont think people even know it yet.

The sky to the west darkened. A cold wind blew. They could see the aura of the lights from the city come up forty miles away.

You need to wear more clothes than that, Billy said.

I'm all right. How did the war change it?

It just did. It aint the same no more. It never will be.

EDUARDO STOOD at the rear door smoking one of his thin cigars and looking out at the rain. There was a sheetiron warehouse behind the building and there was nothing much there to see except the rain and black pools of water standing in the alley where the rain fell and the soft light from the yellow bulb screwed into the fixture over the back door. The air was cool. The smoke drifted in the light. A young girl who limped on a withered leg passed carrying a great armload of soiled linen down the hall. After a while he closed the door and walked back up the hallway to his office.

When Tiburcio knocked he did not even turn around. Adelante, he said. Tiburcio entered. He stood at the desk and counted out money. The desk was of polished glass and fruitwood and there was a white leather sofa against one wall and a low coffeetable of glass and chrome and there was a small bar against the other wall with four white leather stools. The carpeting on the floor was a rich cream color. The alcahuete counted out the money and stood waiting. Eduardo turned and looked at him. The alcahuete smiled thinly under his thin moustache. His black greased hair shone in the soft light. His black shirt bore a glossy sheen from the pressings of an iron too hot.

Eduardo put the cigar between his teeth and came to the desk. He stood looking down. He fanned with one slender jeweled hand the bills on the glass and he took the cigar from his teeth and looked up.

El mismo muchacho?

El mismo.

He pursed his lips, he nodded. Bueno, he said. Ándale.

When Tiburcio had gone he unlocked his desk drawer and took from it a long leather wallet with a chain hanging from it and put the bills in the wallet and put the wallet back in the drawer and locked it again. He opened his ledgerbook and made an entry in it and closed it. Then he went to the door and stood smoking quietly and looking out up the hallway. His hands clasped behind him at the small of his back in a stance he had perhaps admired or read of but a stance native to some other country, not his.

THE MONTH OF NOVEMBER passed and he saw her but once more. The alcahuete came to the door and tapped and went away and she said that he must leave. He held her hands in his, both of them sitting tailorwise and fully dressed in the center of the canopy bed. Leaning and talking to her very quickly and with great earnestness but she would only say it was too dangerous and then the alcahuete rapped at the door again and did not go away.

Prométeme, he said. Prométeme.

The alcahuete rapped with the heel of his fist. She clutched his hand, her eyes wide.

Debes salir, she whispered.

Prométeme.

Sí. Sí. Lo prometo.

When he passed through the salon it was all but empty. The blind pianist who sat in for the string trio at these late hours was at the bench but he was not playing. His young daughter stood beside him. On the piano lay the book which she had been reading to him as he played. John Grady crossed the room and took his last dollar but one and dropped it into the barglass atop the piano. The maestro smiled and bowed slightly. Gracias, he said.

Cómo estás, said John Grady.

The old man smiled again. My young friend, he said. How are you? You are well?

Yes, thank you. And you?

He shrugged. His thin shoulders rose in the dull black stuff of his suit and fell again. I am well, he said. I am well.

Are you done for the night?

No. We go for our supper.

It is very late.

Oh yes. It is late.

The blind man spoke an old-world english, a language from another place and time. He steadied himself and rose and turned woodenly.

Will you join us?

No thank you sir. I need to get on.

And how is your suit advancing?

He wasnt sure what that meant. He turned the words over in his mind. The girl, he said.

The old man bowed his head in affirmation.

I dont know, John Grady said. All right, I think. I hope so.

It is an uncertain business, the old man said. You must persevere. To persevere is everything.

Yessir.

The girl had taken her father's hat from the piano and stood holding it. She took his hand but he made no motion to leave. He faced the room, empty save for two whores and a drunk at the bar. We are friends, he said.

Yessir, John Grady said. He wasnt sure of whom the old man spoke.

May I speak in confidence?

Yes.

I believe she is favorable. He placed one delicate and yellowed finger to his lips.

Thank you sir. I appreciate that.

Of course. He held out one hand palm up and the girl placed the brim of his hat in his grip and he took it in both hands and turned and placed it on his head and looked up.

Do you think she's a good person? John Grady said.

Oh my, said the blind man. Oh my.

I think she is.

Oh my, said the blind man.

John Grady smiled. I'll let you get on to your supper. He nodded to the girl and turned to go.

Her condition, the blind man said. You know her condition?

He turned back. Sir? he said.

Little is known. There is a great deal of superstition. Here they are divided in two camps. Some take a benign view and others do not. You see. But this is my belief. My belief is that she is at best a visitor. At best. She does not belong here. Among us.

Yessir. I know she dont belong here.

No, said the blind man. I do not mean in this house. I mean here. Among us.

He walked back through the streets. Carrying the blind man's words concerning his prospects as if they were a contract with the world to come. Cold as it was the Juárenses stood in the open doorways and smoked or called to one another. Along the sandy unpaved streets nightvendors trundled their carts or drove their small burros before them. They called out leeen-ya. They called out quero-seeen-a. Plying the darkened streets and calling out like old suitors in search themselves of maids long lost to them.

II

H E WAITED but she didnt come. He stood at the window with the hangings of old lace gathered back in his hand and watched the life in the streets. Anyone who would have looked up to see him there behind the untrue panes of dusty glass could have told his story. The afternoon grew quiet. Across the street a merchant closed and locked the iron shutters of his hardware shop. A taxi stopped in front of the hotel and he leaned with his face against the cold pane but he could not see if anyone got out. He turned and went to the door and opened it and walked out to the head of the stairwell where he could look down into the lobby. No one came. When he went back and stood at the window again the taxi was gone. He sat on the bed. The shadows grew long. After a while it was dark in the room and the green neon of the hotel sign came on outside the window and after a while he rose and took his hat from the top of the bureau and went out. He turned at the door and looked back into the room and then pulled the door shut behind him. If he'd stood longer he'd have passed the criada La Tuerta in the shabby stairwell instead of the lobby as he did, he any lodger, she any old woman with one clouded eye struggling in from the street. He stepped out into the cool evening and she labored up the stairs and knocked at the door and waited and knocked again. A door down the hallway opened and a man looked out. He told her that he had no towels.

HE WAS LYING on his bunk staring up at the roughsawed boards of the ceiling of the bunkroom when Billy came and stood in the doorway. He was slightly drunk. His hat was pushed back on his head. What say, cowboy, he said.

Hey Billy.

How you doin?

I'm doin all right. Where'd you all go?

We went to a dance at Mesilla.

Who all went?

Everybody but you.

He sat in the doorway and jacked one boot against the jamb and took off his hat and put it on his knee and leaned his head back. John Grady watched him.

Did you dance?

Danced my ass off.

I didnt know you were a big dancer.

I aint.

I guess you give it your best.

It's a thing that's got to be seen. Oren tells me that squirrel-headed horse you think so much of is eatin out of your hand.

That might be a bit of an exaggeration.

What do you tell em?

Who?

Horses.

I dont know. The truth.

I guess it's a trade secret.

No.

How can you lie to a horse?

He turned and looked at John Grady. I dont know, the boy said. Do you mean how do you go about it or how can you bring yourself to do it?

Go about it.

I dont know. I think it's just what's in your heart.

You think a horse knows what's in your heart?

Yeah. Dont you?

Billy didnt answer. After a while he said: Yeah. I do.

I aint a very good liar.

You just aint had enough practice at it.

Down the barn bay in the stalls they could hear the wheeze and stir of the animals.

Have you got a girl you're seein?

John Grady crossed his boots one over the other. Yeah, he said. Tryin to.

JC said you did.

How did JC know?

He just said you manifested all the symptoms.

Manifested?

Yeah.

What are they?

He didnt say. You intend to bring her around some time where we can get a look at her?

Yeah. I'll bring her around.

Well.

He took his hat from his knee and put it on his head and rose.

Billy?

Yeah.

I'll tell you about it. It's kind of a mess. Right now I'm just a bit wore out.

I dont doubt it for a minute, cowboy. I'll see you in the mornin.

HE WENT the following week with no more money in his pocket than would buy a drink at the bar. He watched her in the mirror. She sat upright alone on the dark velvet couch with her hands composed in her lap like a debutante. He drank the whiskey slowly. When he looked in the mirror again he thought she had been watching him. He finished the whiskey and paid for it and turned to go. He had not meant to look directly at her but he did. He could not even imagine her life.

He got his hat and gave the woman the last of his change and she smiled and thanked him and he put his hat on and turned. He had his hand on the ornate onyx handle of the door when one of the waiters stepped in front of him.

Un momento, he said.

He stopped. He looked at the hatcheck girl and he looked at the waiter.

The waiter stood between him and the door. The girl, he said. She say you no forget her.

He looked toward the salon but he could not see her from the door.

Dígame? he said.

She say you no . . .

En español, por favor. Dígame en español lo que dice ella.

The man would not. He repeated the words again in english and then he turned and was gone.

He sat the next night in the Moderno and waited for the maestro and his daughter. He waited for a long time and he thought perhaps they had already been or perhaps they were not coming. When the little girl pushed open the door she saw him and looked up at her father but she said nothing. They took a table near the door and the waiter came and poured a glass of wine.

He rose and crossed the room and stood at their table. Maestro, he said.

The blind man turned his face up and smiled at the space alongside John Grady. As if some unseen double stood there.

Buenas noches, he said.

Cómo está?

Ah, said the blind man. My young friend.

Yes.

Please. You must join us. Sit down.

Thank you.

He sat. He looked at the girl. The blind man hissed at the waiter and the waiter came over.

Qué toma? said the maestro.

Nothing. Thank you.

Please. I insist.

I cant stay.

Traiga un vino para mi amigo.

The waiter nodded and moved away. John Grady thumbed back his hat and leaned forward with his elbows on the table. What is this place? he said.

The Moderno? It is a place where the musicians come. It is a very old place. It has always been here. You must come on Saturday. Many old people come. You will see them. They come to dance. Very old people dancing. Here. In this place. The Moderno.

Are they going to play again?

Yes, yes. Of course. It is early. They are my friends.

Do they play every night?

Yes. Every night. They will play soon now. You will see.

Good as the maestro's word the violinists began to tune their instruments in the inner room. The cellist leaned listening with his head inclined and drew his bow across the strings. A couple who had been sitting at a table against the far wall rose and stood in the archway holding hands and then sallied forth onto the concrete floor as the musicians struck up an antique waltz. The maestro leaned forward to hear. Are they dancing? he said. Are any dancing now?

The little girl looked at John Grady. Yes, John Grady said. They're dancing.

The old man leaned back, he nodded. Good, he said. That is good.

THEY SAT AGAINST a rock bluff high in the Franklins with a fire before them that heeled in the wind and their figures cast up upon the rocks behind them enshadowed the petroglyphs carved there by other hunters a thousand years before. They could hear the dogs running far below them. Their cries trailed off down the side of the mountain and sounded again more faintly and then faded away where they coursed out along some rocky draw in the dark. To the south the distant lights of the city lay strewn across the desert floor like a tiara laid out upon a jeweler's blackcloth. Archer had stood and turned toward the running dogs the better to listen and after a while he squatted again and spat into the fire.

She aint goin to tree, he said.

I dont believe she will either, said Travis.

How do you know it's the same lion? said JC.

Travis had taken his tobacco from his pocket and he smoothed and cupped a paper with his fingers. She's done us thisaway before, he said. She'll run plumb out of the country.

They sat listening. The cries grew faint and after a while there were no more. Billy had gone off up the side of the mountain to look for wood and he came back dragging a dead cedar stump. He picked it up and dropped it on top of the fire. A shower of sparks rose and drifted down the night. The stump sat all black and twisted over the small flames. Like some amorphous thing come in out of the night to warm itself among them.

Couldnt you find a bigger chunk of wood, Parham?

It'll take here in a minute.

Parham's put the fire plumb out, said JC.

The darkest hour is just before the storm, said Billy. It'll take here in a minute.

I hear em, Travis said.

I do too.

She's crossed at the head of that big draw where the road cuts back.

We wont get that Lucy dog back tonight.

What dog is that?

Bitch out of that Aldridge line. Them dogs was bred by the Lee Brothers. They just forgot to build in the quit.

Best dog we ever had was her grandaddy, said Archer. You remember that Roscoe dog, Travis?

Of course I do. People thought he was part bluetick but he was a full leopard cur with a glass eye and he did love to fight. We lost him down in Nyarit. Jaguar caught him and bit him damn near in two.

You all dont hunt down there no more.

No.

We aint been back since before the war. It got to be a long ways to go them last few trips. Lee Brothers had about quit goin. They brought a lot of jaguars out of that country, too.

JC leaned and spat into the fire. The flames were snaking up along the sides of the stump.

You all didnt care bein way off down there in old Mexico thataway?

We always got along with them people.

You dont need to go far to get in trouble, said Archer. You want trouble you can find all you can say grace over right across that river yonder.

That's an amen on that.

You cross that river you in another country. You talk to some of these old waddies along this border. Ask em about the revolution.

Do you remember the revolution, Travis?

Archer here can tell you moren what I can.

You was in swaddlin clothes wasnt you, Travis?

Just about it. I do remember bein woke up one time and goin to the window and we looked out and you could see the guns goin off over there like it was the fourth of July.

We lived on Wyoming Street, said Archer. After Daddy died. Mama's Uncle Pless worked in a machine shop on Alameda and they brought in the firingpins out of two artillery pieces and asked him could he turn new ones and he turned em and wouldnt take a dime for it. They was all on the side of the rebels. He brought the old pins home and give em to us boys. There was one shop turned some cannon barrels out of railroad axles and they dragged em back across the river behind a team of mules. The trunnions was made out of Ford truck axle housings and they set em in wood sashes and used the wheels off of fieldwagons to mount em in. That was in November of nineteen and thirteen. Villa come into Juárez at two oclock in the mornin on a train he'd highjacked. It was just a flat-out war. Lots of folks in El Paso had their windowlights shot out. Some people killed, for that matter. They'd go down and stand along the river there and watch it like it was a ballgame.

Villa come back in nineteen and nineteen. Travis can tell ye. We'd slip over there and hunt for souvenirs. Empty shellcases and what not. There was dead horses and mules in the street. Storewindows shot out. We seen bodies laid out in the alameda with blankets over em or wagonsheets. That sobered us up, I can tell you. They made us take showers with the Mexicans fore they'd let us back in. Disinfected our clothes and all. There was typhus down there and people had died of it.

They sat smoking quietly and looking out at the distant lights in the valley floor below them. Two of the dogs came in out of the night and passed behind the hunters. Their shadows trotted across the stone bluff and they crossed to a place in the dry dust under the rocks where they curled up and were soon asleep.

None of it done anybody any good, Travis said. Or if it did I never heard of it.

I been all over that country down there. I was a cattlebuyer for Spurlocks. Supposed to be one. I was just a kid. I rode all over northern Mexico. Hell, there wasnt no cattle. Not to speak of. Mostly I just visited. I liked it. I liked the country and I liked the people in it. I rode all over Chihuahua and a good part of Coahuila and some of Sonora. I'd be gone weeks at a time and not have hardly so much as a peso in my pocket but it didnt make no difference. Those people would take you in and put you up and feed you and feed your horse and cry when you left. You could of stayed forever. They didnt have nothin. Never had and never would. But you could stop at some little estancia in the absolute dead center of nowhere and they'd take you in like you was kin. You could see that the revolution hadnt done them no good. A lot of em had lost boys out of the family. Fathers or sons or both. Nearly all of em, I expect. They didnt have no reason to be hospitable to anybody. Least of all a gringo kid. That plateful of beans they set in front of you was hard come by. But I was never turned away. Not a time.

Three more dogs passed by the fire and sought out beds under the bluff. The stars swung west. The hunters talked of other things and after a while another dog came in. He was favoring a forefoot and Archer got up and walked up under the bluff to see about him. They heard the dog whine and when he came back he said they'd been in a fight.

Two more dogs came in and then all were in save one.

I'll wait a while if you all want to head back, Archer said.

We'll wait with ye.

I dont mind.

We'll wait a while. Wake up young Cole yonder.

Let him sleep, said Billy. He's been fightin that bear.

The fire burned down and it grew colder and they sat close to the flames and hand fed them with sticks and with old brittle limbs they broke from the windtwisted wrecks of trees along the rimrock. They told stories of the old west that once was. The older men talked and the younger men listened and light began to show in the gap of the mountain above them and then faintly along the desert floor below.

The dog they were waiting for came in limping badly and circled the fire. Travis called to her. She halted with her red eyes and looked at them. He rose and called her again and she came up and he took hold of her collar and turned her to the light. There were four bloody furrows along her flank. There was a flap of skin ripped loose at her shoulder exposing the muscle underneath and blood was dripping slowly from one ripped ear onto the sandy dirt where she stood.

We need to get that sewed up, Travis said.

Archer pulled a leash from among those he'd strung through his belt and he clipped it onto the D-ring of her collar. She carried the only news they would have of the hunt, bearing witness to things they could only imagine or suppose out there in the night. She winced when Archer touched her ear and when he let go of her she stepped back and stood with her forefeet braced and shook her head. Blood sprayed the hunters and hissed in the fire. They rose to go.

Let's go, cowboy, Billy said.

John Grady sat up and reached about on the ground for his hat.

Hell of a lionhunter you turned out to be.

Is the peeler awake? said JC.

The peeler's awake.

A man that's been huntin that bear I dont believe these old mountain lions hold much interest.

I think you got that right.

Chips all down and where was he? And us at the mercy of the old folks here. Could of used some help, son. We been outlied till it's pitiful. I mean sent to the showers. Wasnt even a contest, was it Billy?

Not even a contest.

John Grady squared his hat and walked out along the edge of the bluff. The desert plain lay cold and blue below them in the graying light and the shape of the river running down from the north through the break of gray winter trees lay in a pale serpentine of mist. To the south the cold gray grid of the distant city and the shape of the older city across the river like stampings in the desert soil. Beyond them the mountains of Mexico. The injured hound had come from the fire where the men were sorting and chaining the dogs and it walked out and stood beside John Grady and studied with him the plain below. John Grady sat and let his boots dangle over the edge of the rock and the dog lay down and rested its bloody head alongside his leg and after a while he put his arm around it.

BILLY SAT LEANING with his elbows on the table and his arms crossed. He watched John Grady. John Grady pursed his lips. He moved the remaining white knight. Billy looked at Mac. Mac studied the move and he looked at John Grady. He sat back in his chair and studied the board. No one spoke.

Mac picked up the black queen and held it a moment and

then set it back. Then he picked up the queen again and moved. Billy leaned back in his chair. Mac reached and took the cold cigar from the ashtray and put it in his mouth.

Six moves later the white king was mated. Mac sat back and lit the cigar. Billy blew a long breath across the table.

John Grady sat looking at the board. Good game, he said.

It's a long road, said Mac, that has no turning.

They walked out across the yard toward the barn.

Tell me somethin, Billy said.

All right.

And I know you'll tell me the truth.

I already know what the question is.

What's the answer.

The answer is no.

You didnt slack up on him just the littlest bit?

No. I dont believe in it.

The horses stirred and snuffled in their stalls as they passed down the bay. John Grady looked at Billy.

You dont reckon he thinks that do you?

I hope not. He damn sure wouldnt like it a bit.

He damn sure wouldnt.

HE WALKED into the pawnshop with the gun in the holster and the holster and belt slung over his shoulder. The pawnbroker was an old man with white hair and he was reading the paper spread out on the glass top of a display case at the rear of the shop. There were guns in racks along one wall and guitars hanging from overhead and knives and pistols and jewelry and tools in the cases. John Grady laid the gunbelt on the counter and the old man looked at it and looked at John Grady. He drew the pistol from the holster and cocked it and let the hammer down on the halfcock notch and spun the cylinder and opened the gate and looked at the chambers and closed the gate and cocked the hammer and let it back down with his thumb.

He turned it over and looked at the serial numbers on the frame and triggerguard and on the bottom of the backstrap and then slid it back into the holster and looked up.

How much do you want? he said.

I need about forty dollars.

The old man sucked his teeth and shook his head gravely.

I been offered fifty for it. I just need to pawn it.

I could let you have maybe twenty-five.

John Grady looked at the gun. Let me have thirty, he said.

The pawnbroker shook his head doubtfully.

I dont want to sell it, John Grady said. I just need to borrow on it.

The belt and holster too, yes?

Yes. It all goes together.

All right.

He brought out his pad of forms and slowly copied out the serial number and he wrote down John Grady's name and address and turned the paper on the glass for the boy to read and sign. Then he separated the sheets and handed a copy to John Grady and took the gun to his cage at the rear of the shop. When he returned he had the money and he laid it on the counter.

I'll be back for it, John Grady said.

The old man nodded.

It belonged to my grandfather.

The old man opened his hands and closed them again. A gesture of accommodation. Not quite a blessing. He nodded toward the glass case where half a dozen old Colt revolvers lay displayed, some nickelplated, some with grips of staghorn. One with old worn grips of guttapercha, one with the front sight filed away.

All of them belonged to somebody's grandfather, he said.

As he was going up Juárez Avenue a shineboy spoke to him. Hey cowboy, he said.

Hey.

Better let me shine those boots for you.

All right.

He sat on a little folding campstool and put his boot on the shineboy's homemade wooden box. The shineboy turned up the leg of his trousers and began to take out his rags and brushes and tins of polish and lay them to hand.

You goin to see your girl?

Yeah.

I hope you werent goin up there with these boots.

I guess it's a good thing you hollered at me. She might of run me off.

The boy dusted off the boot with his rag and lathered it. When are you gettin married? he said.

What makes you think I'm gettin married?

I dont know. You kind of got the look. Are you?

I dont know. Maybe.

Are you a cowboy sure enough?

Yep.

You work on a ranch?

Yeah. Small ranch. Estancia, you might say.

You like it?

Yeah. I like it.

He wiped off the boot and opened his can and began to slap polish onto the leather with the stained fingers of his left hand.

It's hard work, aint it?

Yeah. Sometimes.

What if you could be somethin else?

I wouldnt be nothin else.

What if you could be anything in the world?

John Grady smiled. He shook his head.

Were you in the war?

No. I was too young.

My brother was too young but he lied about his age.

Was he American?

No.

How old was he?

Sixteen.

I guess he was big for his age.

He was a big bullshitter for his age.

John Grady smiled.

The boy put the lid back on the tin and took out his brush.

They asked him if he was a pachuco. He said all the pachu-cos he knew of lived in El Paso. He told em he didnt know any Mexican pachucos.

He brushed the boot. John Grady watched him.

Was he a pachuco?

Sure. Of course he was.

He brushed the boot and then chucked the brush back into the box and took out his cloth and popped it and bent and began to rifle the cloth back and forth over the toe of the boot.

He joined the marines. He got two purple hearts.

What about you?

What about me what.

What did you join.

He glanced up at John Grady. He whipped the cloth around the counter of the boot. I sure didnt join no marines, he said.

What about the pachucos.

Nah.

You're not a pachuco?

Nah.

Are you a bullshitter?

Sure.

A big one?

Pretty big. Let me have the other foot.

What about the black around the edges?

I do that last. Dont worry about everything.

John Grady put his other foot on the box and turned up his trouserleg.

Appearance is important with women, the boy said. Dont think they dont look at your boots.

You got a girl?

Shit no.

You sound like you've had some bad experiences.

Who aint? You fool with em and that's the kind you'll have.

There'll be some sweet young thing nail you down one of these days.

I hope not.

How old are you?

Fourteen.

You lie about your age?

Yeah. Sure.

I guess if you admit it then it aint a lie.

The boy ceased rubbing in the polish for a moment and sat looking at the boot. Then he began again.

If there's somethin I want to be a different way from what it is then that's how I say it is. What's wrong with that?

I dont know.

Who else is goin to?

Nobody, I guess.

Nobody is right.

Is your brother married?

Which brother? I got three.

The one that was in the marines.

Yeah. He's married. They're all married.

If they're all married why did you ask which one?

The shineboy shook his head. Man, he said.

I guess you're the youngest.

No. I got a brother ten years old is married with three kids. Of course I'm the youngest. What do you think?

Well maybe marriage runs in the family.

Marriage dont run in families. Anyway I'm an outlaw. Oveja negra. You speak spanish?

Yeah. I speak spanish.

Oveja negra. That's me.

Black sheep.

I know what it is.

I am too.

The boy looked up at him. He reached and got his brush from the box. Yeah? he said.

Yeah.

You dont look like no outlaw to me.

What does one look like?

Not like you.

He brushed the boot and put away the brush and got his cloth out and popped it. John Grady watched him. What about you? What if you could be anything you wanted?

I'd be a cowboy.

Really?

The boy looked up at him with disgust. Shit no, he said. What's wrong with you? I'd be a rico and lay around on my ass all day. What do you think?

What if you had to do something?

I dont know. Maybe be a airplane pilot.

Yeah?

Sure. I'd fly everywhere.

What would you do when you got there?

Fly somewhere else.

He finished polishing the boot and got out his bottle of blacking and began to paint the heel and the edges of the sole with the swab.

Other boot, he said.

John Grady put his other foot up and the boy painted the edges. Then he put the swab back in the bottle and screwed the cap shut and pitched the bottle into the box. You're done, he said.

John Grady turned his cuffs back down and stood and reached into his pocket and took out a coin and handed it to the boy.

Thanks.

He looked down at his boots. What do you think.

She might let you in the door. Where's your flowers at?

Flowers?

Sure. You're goin to need all the help you can get.

You're probably right.

I shouldnt even be tellin you this stuff.

Why not?

You'd be better off just to be put out of your misery.

John Grady smiled. Where are you from? he said.

Right here.

No you're not.

I grew up in California.

What are you doin over here?

I like it over here.

Yeah?

Yeah.

You like shinin shoes?

I like it all right.

You like the street.

Yeah. I dont like goin to school.

John Grady adjusted his hat and looked off up the street. He looked down at the boy. Well, he said. I never much liked it myself.

Outlaws, the boy said.

Outlaws. I think maybe you're a bigger outlaw than me.

I think you're right.

I'm just kind of gettin the hang of it.

You need any pointers come see me. I'll be happy to show you the ropes.

John Grady smiled. Okay, he said. I'll see you around.

Adiós, vaquero.

Adiós, bolero.

The boy smiled and waved him on.

THE CRIADA STOOD behind her in the full-length mirror, her mouth bristling with hairpins. She looked at the girl in the mirror, so pale and so slender in her shift with her hair piled atop her head. She looked at Josefina. Josefina stood to the side with one arm crossed and her other elbow propped upon it, her fist to her chin. No, she said. No.

She shook her head and waved her hand as if to dismiss some

outrage and the criada began to withdraw the pins and combs from the girl's hair until the long black fall descended again over her shoulders and her back. She took her brush and began again to brush the girl's hair, following with the flat of her hand beneath, holding up the silky blackness with each stroke and letting it fall again. Josefina came forward and took a silver haircomb from the table and swept back the girl's hair along the side and held it there. She studied the girl and she studied the girl in the mirror. The criada had stepped back and stood holding the brush in both hands. She and Josefina studied the girl in the mirror, the three of them in the yellow light of the table-lamp standing there within the gilded plaster scrollwork of the mirror's frame like figures in an antique flemish painting.

Cómo es, pues, said Josefina.

She was speaking to the girl but the girl did not answer.

Es más joven. Más . . .

Inocente, said the girl.

The woman shrugged. Inocente pues, she said.

She studied the girl's face in the glass. No le gusta?

Está bien, the girl whispered. Me gusta.

Bueno, said the woman. She let go her hair and placed the comb in the criada's hand. Bueno.

When she was gone the old woman put the comb back on the table and came forward with her brush again. Bueno, she said. She shook her head and clucked her tongue.

No te preocupes, the girl said.

The old woman brushed her hair more fiercely. Bellísima, she hissed. Bellísima.

She assisted her with care. With solicitude. One by one the hooks and stays. Passing her hands across the lilac velvet, cupping her breasts each in turn and adjusting the border of the decolletage, pinning gown to undergarment. She brushed away bits of lint. She held the girl by her waist and turned her like a toy and she knelt at her feet and fastened the straps of her shoes. She rose and stood back.

Puedes caminar? she said.

No, said the girl.

No? Es mentira. Es una broma. No?

No, said the girl.

The criada made a shooing motion. The girl stepped archly about the room on the tall gold spikes of the slippers.

Te mortifican? said the criada.

Claro.

She stood again before the mirror. The old woman stood behind her. When she blinked only the one eye closed. So that she appeared to be winking in some suggestive complicity. She brushed the gathered hair with her hand, she plucked the shoulders of the sleeves erect.

Como una princesa, she whispered.

Como una puta, said the girl.

The criada seized her by the arm. She hissed at her, her eye glaring in the lamplight. She told her that she would marry a great rich man and live in a fine house and have beautiful children. She told her that she had known many such cases.

Quién? said the girl.

Muchas, hissed the criada. Muchas. Girls, she told her, with no such beauty as hers. Girls with no such dignity or grace. The girl did not answer. She looked across the old woman's shoulder into the eyes in the glass as if it were some sister there who weathered stoically this beleaguerment of her hopes. Standing in the gaudy boudoir that was itself a tawdry emulation of other rooms, other worlds. Regarding her own false arrogance in the pierglass as if it were proof against the old woman's entreaties, the old woman's promises. Standing like some maid in a fable spurning the offerings of the hag which do conceal within them unspoken covenants of corruption. Claims that can never be quit, estates forever entailed. She spoke to that girl standing in the glass and she said that one could not know where it was that one had taken the path one was upon but only that one was upon it.

Mande? said the criada. Cuál senda?

Cualquier senda. Esta senda. La senda que escoja.

But the old woman said that some have no choice. She said that for the poor any choice was a gift with two faces.

She was kneeling in the floor repinning the hem of the dress. She'd taken the pins from her mouth and now she laid them on the carpet and took them up one by one. The girl watched her image in the glass. The old woman's gray head bowed at her feet. After a while she said that there was always a choice, even if that choice were death.

Cielos, said the old woman. She blessed herself quickly and went on pinning.

When she entered the salon he was standing at the bar. The musicians were assembling their pieces on the dais and tuning them and the few notes or chords sounded in the quiet of the room as if some ceremony were at hand. Within the shadows of the niche beyond the dais Tiburcio stood smoking, his fingers laced about the thin niellate ebony holder of his cigarette. He looked at the girl and he looked toward the bar. He watched the boy turn and pay and take up his glass and come down the broad stairs where the velvetcovered rope railings led into the salon. He blew smoke slowly from his thin nostrils and then he opened the door behind him. The brief light framed him in silhouette and his long thin shadow fell briefly across the floor of the salon and then the door closed again as if he had not been there at all.

Está peligroso, she whispered.

Cómo?

Peligroso. She looked around the salon.

Tenía que verte, he said.

He took her hands in his but she only looked in anguish toward the door where Tiburcio had been standing. She took hold of his wrists and begged him to leave. A waiter glided forth from the shadows.

Estás loco, she whispered. Loco.

Tienes razón.

She took his hand and rose. She turned and whispered to the

waiter. John Grady rose and put money in the waiter's hand and turned toward her.

Debemos irnos, she said. Estamos perdidos.

He said that he would not. He said that he would not do that again and that she must meet him but she said that it was too dangerous. That now it was too dangerous. The music had begun. A long low chord from the cello.

Me matará, she whispered.

Quién?

She only shook her head.

Quién, he said. Quién te matará?

Eduardo.

Eduardo.

She nodded. Sí, she said. Eduardo.

HE DREAMT THAT NIGHT of things he'd heard and that were so although she'd never spoke of them. In a room so cold his breath smoked and where the corrugated steel walls were hung with bunting and a scaffolding covered with cheap red carpet rose in tiers for the folding slatwood chairs of the spectators. A raw wooden stage trimmed like a fairground float and BX cable running to a boom overhead made from galvanized iron pipe that held floodlights covered each in cellophanes of red and green and blue. Curtains of calendered velour in loops as red as blood.

The tourists sat in chairs with operaglasses hanging from their necks while waiters took their orders for drinks. When the lights dimmed the master of ceremonies strode onto the boards and doffed his hat and bowed and smiled and held up his whitegloved hands. In the wings the alcahuete stood smoking and behind him milled a great confusion of obscene carnival folk, painted whores with their breasts exposed, a fat woman in black leather with a whip, a pair of youths in ecclesiastical robes. A priest, a procuress, a goat with gilded horns and hooves who wore a ruff of purple crepe. Pale young debauchees with rouged cheeks and blackened eyes who carried candles. A trio of women holding hands, gaunt and thin as the inmates of a spitalhouse and attired the three alike in the same cheap finery, their faces daubed in fard and pale as death. At the center of all a young girl in a white gauze dress who lay upon a pallet-board like a sacrificial virgin. Arranged about her are artificial flowers that appear in their varied pale and pastel colors to be faded from the sun. As if perhaps replevined from some desert grave. Music has begun. Some ancient rondel, faintly martial. There is a periodic click in the piece from a scratch in the black bakelite plate turning under a stylus somewhere behind the curtains. The houselights dim till just the stage is lit. Chairs shuffle. A few coughs. The music fades until only the whisper of the stylus remains, the periodic click like a misset metronome, a clock, a portent. A measure of something periodic and otherwise silent and vastly patient which only darkness could accommodate.

When he woke it was not from this dream but from another and the pathway from dream to dream was lost to him. He was alone in some bleak landscape where the wind blew without abatement and where the presence of those who had gone before still lingered on in the darkness about. Their voices carried back to him, or perhaps the echo of those voices. He lay listening. It was the old man wandering the yard in his nightclothes and John Grady swung his legs over the side of the bunk and reached and got his trousers and pulled them on and stood and buckled his belt and reached and got his boots. When he went out Billy was standing in the doorway in his shorts.

I'll get him, said John Grady.

That's pitiful, Billy said.

He caught him going past the corner of the barn and on to God knows where. He had on his hat and his boots and dressed in these and his long white unionsuit he looked like the ghost of some ancient waddy wandering there.

John Grady took him by the arm and they started for the house. Come on, Mr Johnson, he said. You dont need to be out here.

The light had come on in the kitchen and Socorro was standing in the door in her robe. The old man stopped again in the yard and turned and looked again toward the darkness. John Grady stood holding his elbow. Then they went on to the house.

Socorro swung the screendoor wide. She looked at John Grady. The old man steadied himself with one hand against the doorjamb and entered the kitchen. He asked Socorro if she had any coffee. As if that was what he'd been in search of.

Yes, she said. I fix some coffee.

He's all right, said John Grady.

Quieres un cafecito?

No gracias.

Pásale, she said. Pásale. Puedes encontrar sus pantalones?

Sí. Sí.

He helped the old man to a chair at the table and went on down the hallway. Mac's light was on and he was standing in the door.

Is he all right?

Yessir. He's all right.

He went on to the end of the hall and entered the room on the left and got the old man's britches off the bedpost where he'd hung them. The pockets were weighted with change, with a pocketknife, a billfold. With a ring of keys to doors long since forgotten. He came back down the hallway holding them by the belt. Mac was still standing in the doorway. He was smoking a cigarette.

He aint got any clothes on?

Just his longjohns.

He'll take off out of here one of these nights naked as a jaybird. Socorro'll quit us for sure.

She wont quit.

I know it.

What time is it, sir?

It's after five. Damn near time to get up anyways.

Yessir.

Would you mind settin with him a bit?

No sir.

Make him feel better about it. Like he was gettin up anyways.

Yessir. I will.

You didnt know you'd hired on at a loonyfarm, did you?

He aint loony. He's just old.

I know it. Go on. Fore he catches cold. Them old dropseats he wears are probably drafty to set around in.

Yessir.

He sat with the old man and drank coffee until Oren came in. Oren looked at them but he didnt say anything. Socorro fixed breakfast and brought the eggs and biscuits and chorizo sausage and they ate. When John Grady took his plate to the sideboard and went out it was just breaking day. The old man was still sitting at the table in his hat. He'd been born in east Texas in eighteen sixty-seven and come out to this country as a young man. In his time the country had gone from the oil lamp and the horse and buggy to jet planes and the atomic bomb but that wasnt what confused him. It was the fact that his daughter was dead that he couldnt get the hang of.

THEY SAT IN THE FRONT ROW of the bleachers near the auctioneer's table and Oren leaned forward from time to time to spit carefully over the top boards into the dust of the arena. Mac had a small notebook in his shirtpocket and he took it out and consulted his notes and put it back again and then he took it out and sat holding it in his hand.

Did we look at this little horse? he said.

Yessir, said John Grady.

He studied his notebook again.

He said it was Davis but it aint.

No sir.

Bean, said Oren. It's a Bean horse.

I know what horse it is, said Mac.

The auctioneer blew into the microphone. The speakers were hung from the lightstandards at the far end of the arena and his voice quavered and echoed high in the auction barn.

Ladies and gentlemen a correction on that. This horse is entered by Mr Ryle Bean.

The bidding was started at five hundred. Someone at the far side of the arena touched the brim of his hat and the spotter raised one hand and turned and the auctioneer said now six now six I have six who'll give me seven seven seven. Seven now.

Oren leaned and spat thoughtfully into the dust. Over yonder's your buddy, he said.

I see him, said John Grady.

Who's that? said Mac.

Wolfenbarger.

Does he see us?

Yeah, said Oren. He sees us.

Did you know who that was, John Grady?

Yessir. He come out one afternoon.

I thought you wouldnt talk to him.

I didnt.

Just pretend like he aint even here.

Yessir.

When was he out?

Last week. I dont know. Wednesday maybe.

Just dont pay no attention to him.

Yessir. I aint.

I got more to do than worry about him.

Yessir.

Eighty, seven-eighty, called the auctioneer. Will you do it. The man wont take less.

The rider rode the horse around the arena. He crossed diagonally and stopped and backed.

That's a good usin horse and a good ropin horse, the auctioneer said. The horse is worth a thousand dollars. All right now. I've got eight got eight got eight. Eight and a half now. Eight-fifty eight-fifty eight-fifty.

The horse sold for eight and a quarter and they brought in an Arabian mare that sold for seventeen. Mac watched them lead her back out again.

I wouldnt have that crazy bitch on the place, he said.

They auctioned off a flashy palomino gelding that brought thirteen hundred dollars. Mac looked up from his notes. Where the hell do people get that kind of money? he said.

Oren shook his head.

Did Wolfenbarger bid on him?

You said not to look over there.

I know it. Did he?

Yep.

He didnt buy him though, did he.

No.

I thought you wasnt goin to look over there.

I didnt have to. He was wavin his hand like the place had caught fire.

Mac shook his head and sat looking at his notes.

They're fixin to run that rough string in here in a minute, Oren said.

What kind of money you think we're talkin about?

I would expect a man could buy them horses for a hundred dollars a head.

What would you do with the other three, run em back through?

Run em back through. Or you might do better to sell em off out at the place.

Mac nodded. Might, he said. He glanced across the stands. I hate that sumbuck goin to school on me.

I know it.

He lit a cigarette. They watched the stableboy bring in the next horse.

I'd say he's come to buy, said Oren.

I'd say he has too.

He'll bid on ever one of them horses of Red's. See if he dont.

I know it. We ought to shill him just a little bit.

Oren didnt answer.

A fool and his money, said Mac. John Grady what's wrong with that horse?

Not a thing that I know of.

I thought you said it was some kind of a mongrel outcross. A Martian horse or somethin.

Horse might be a little coldblooded.

Oren spat over the boards and grinned.

Coldblooded? said Mac.

Yessir.

The horse was bid in at three hundred dollars.

How old was that thing. You remember?

It was eleven.

Yeah, said Oren. About six years ago it was.

The bidding went to four and a half. Mac tugged at his ear. I'm just a horsetradin fool, he said. The spotter pointed to the auctioneer.

I got five got five got five got five now, called the auctioneer.

I thought you didnt like to do that, said Oren.

Do what? said Mac.

The bidding went to six and then six and a half.

He's not opened that mouth or shook his head or done nothin, the auctioneer said. Horse worth a little more money than that, folks.

The horse was sold at seven hundred. Wolfenbarger never bid. Oren glanced at Mac.

Cute sumbuck, aint he? Mac said.

You care if I say somethin.

Say it.

Why dont we do what we said and just trade like he wasnt here.

Damn if you aint awful hard on a man. Callin on him to follow his own advice.

It's hell, aint it.

You're probably right. Be the best strategy anyway for a ned like him.

The stableboy brought out the roan four year old from McKinney and they bid the horse in at six hundred.

Where's that string at? said Mac.

I dont know.

Well, we're fixin to get down to the nutcuttin.

He put one finger to his ear. The spotter raised his hand. The auctioneer's voice clapped back from the high speakers. I got six got six got six. Do we hear seven. Who'll give me seven. Seven now. Seven seven seven.

Yonder he goes with that hand.

I see him.

The horse went to seven and seven and a half and eight. The horse went to eight and a half.

Bidders all over the barn, aint they? said Oren.

All over the barn.

Well there aint nothin you can do about it. What's this horse worth?

I dont know. Whatever it sells for. John Grady?

I liked the horse.

I wish they'd of run that string through first.

I know you got a figure in mind.

I did have.

It's the same horse out here that it was in the paddock.

Spoke like a gentleman.

The bidding was stalled at eight and a half. The auctioneer took a drink of water. This is a nice horse, boys, he said. You're way off on this one.

The rider rode the horse down and turned it and came back. He rode it with no bridle but only a rope looped around its neck and he turned and sat the horse. I'll tell you what now, he called. I dont own a hair on him but this is a gaited horse.

It'll cost you a thousand dollars to breed to his mama, said the auctioneer. What do you say boys?

The spotter raised his hand.

I got nine got nine got nine. Now half half half. Nine and a half. Now half. Niner and now half.

Can I say somethin, said John Grady.

I wish you would.

You aint buyin him to sell, are you?

No, I aint.

Well then I think you ought to get the horse you want.

You think a lot of him.

Yessir.

Oren shook his head and leaned and spat. Mac sat looking in his book.

He's goin to cost me no matter what I do, one way of lookin at it.

The horse?

No, not the damn horse.

The bidding went to nine and a half and then a thousand.

John Grady looked at Mac and then looked out at the arena.

I know that old boy up yonder in the checked shirt, said Mac.

I do too, said Oren.

I'd like to see em buy back their own horse.

I would too.

Mac bought the horse for eleven hundred dollars. Put me in the damn poorhouse, he said.

That's a good horse, said John Grady.

I know how good a horse it is. Dont go tryin to make me feel better.

Dont pay no attention to him, son, said Oren. He wants you to brag on his horse only he's just a little backwards about it is all.

What do you think old highpockets cost me on that trade?

Probably didnt cost you nothin on that one, Oren said. He might be fixin to cost you on the next one though.

The groom was wetting down the dust in the barn with a waterhose. They brought in the four-horse string and Mac bought them too.

Like a thief in the dark, called the auctioneer. Number one c
four. Sold at five and a quarter.

That could of been more painful than what it was I reckon,
Mac said.

Skippin through the raindrops.

Yep.

He watched the groom lead the next horse out.

You remember this horse, John Grady.

Yessir. I remember all of em.

Mac thumbed his notes. You get in the habit of writin everthing down and after a while you cant remember nothin.

The reason you started writin stuff down in the first place
was cause you couldnt remember nothin, Oren said.

I know this little horse, said Mac. I'd sure like to sell him to
Wolfenbarger.

I thought you was goin to leave him be.

He could start a circus.

This is a smoothmouthed horse about eight year old, called
the auctioneer. A good usin horse and a good ropin horse and
he's worth quite a bit more than what you got him started at.

He needs to buy that horse. It'll do about anything except
travel in a straight line. Ought to suit him right down to the
ground.

The rider rode the horse hard up and back before the stands,
closereining the horse and doubling back.

Five five five, called the auctioneer. This is a good horse,
boys. Guaranteed to be sound. Work close like that. Like a cat
in a stovepipe, folks. Now half now half now half.

Mac tugged at his ear. Five and a half now six now six now
six, called the auctioneer.

Oren looked disgusted.

Hell, said Mac. We can have a little fun with the old boy
cant we?

The bidding went to seven. The owner stood up in the
stands. I'll tell you what, he said. If you can make him go
through the bridle I'll give him to you.

The bidding went to seven and a half, it went to eight.

John Grady did you hear about the preacher that sold the old boy the blind horse?

No sir.

He was always justifyin everthing with scripture. They come around wantin to know how he could do the old boy thataway and he told em, said: Well, he was a stranger and I took him in.

I think you told me that.

Mac nodded. He thumbed his notes.

He didnt know how to bid on that string. I think it just confused him.

Yessir.

He's ready to buy a horse.

He might be.

You a poker player, son?

I've sat in a time or two, yessir.

You think this horse will sell for under a thousand?

No sir. I kindly doubt it.

If it does bust a thousand what will it go to?

I dont know.

I dont know either.

Mac bid the horse to eight and a half and then to nine and a half. There it stopped. Oren leaned and spat.

What Oren dont understand is that the more money that nedhead is got in his pockets the more that Welburn horse is goin to cost me.

Oren understands that, said Oren. He just thinks you ought to go on and buy the horse for what the bid is and not risk not havin the money to do it with. Anyway, that sumbuck's got more money than Carter has liver pills.

The spotter raised his hand.

I got ten got ten got ten, called the auctioneer. Now eleven now eleven.

The horse went to eleven and Wolfenbarger bid it to twelve and Mac bid it to thirteen.

I aint responsible, said Oren.

The man's a horsebuyer.

You remember what the horse was bid in at?

Yeah. I remember.

Just go on then.

Old Oren, Mac said.

Wolfenbarger bought the horse for seventeen hundred dollars.

Fine piece of horseflesh, said Mac. Ought to suit him just about right.

He reached in his pocket and took out a dollar.

Why dont you run get us some Cokes, John Grady.

Yessir.

Oren watched him climb down through the stands.

You think he'd tout you off of a horse as well as he would on?

Yes. I do.

I think he would too.

I wish I had about six more just like him.

You know there's things about a horse he can only say in spanish?

I dont care if he only knows em in greek. Why?

I just thought it was curious. You think he's from San Angelo?

I think he's from wherever he says he's from.

I guess he is.

He learned it out of a book.

Out of a book?

Joaquín says he knows the name of ever bone a horse has got.

Oren nodded. Well, he said. He might at that. I know some things that he didnt learn out of no book.

I do too, said Mac.

The next horse they brought out the auctioneer read from the horse's papers at some length.

I believe this here is a biblical horse, Mac said.

Aint that the truth.

The horse was bid in at a thousand dollars and went to eighteen five and was a no sale. Oren leaned and spat. Man thinks a lot of his horse, he said.

The man does, said Mac.

They trotted in the Welburn horse and Mac bought him for fourteen hundred dollars.

Boys, he said. Let's go home.

You dont want to stick around and spend some more of Wolfenbarger's money?

Wolfenbarger who?

SOCORRO FOLDED and hung her towel, she untied and hung her apron. She turned at the door.

Buenas noches, she said.

Buenas noches, said Mac.

She shut the door. He could hear her winding her old tin clock. A little later he heard the faint ratcheting sound of his father-in-law winding the tallcase clock in the hallway. The glass doorcase closed softly. Then it was quiet. It was quiet in the house and it was quiet in the country about. He sat smoking. The cooling stove ticked. Far away in the hills behind the house a coyote called. When they had used to spend winters at the old house on the southeasternmost section of the ranch the last thing he would hear before he fell asleep at night was the bawl of the train eastbound out of El Paso. Sierra Blanca, Van Horn, Marfa, Alpine, Marathon. Rolling across the blue prairie through the night and on toward Langtry and Del Rio. The white bore of the headlamp lighting up the desert scrub and the eyes of trackside cattle floating in the dark like coals. The herders in the hills standing with their serapes about their shoulders watching the train pass below and the little desert foxes stepping into the darkened roadbed to sniff after it where the warm steel rails lay humming in the night.

That part of the ranch was long gone and the rest would soon follow. He drank the last of his coffee cold in the cup and lit his last cigarette before bed and then he rose from his chair and turned off the light and came back and sat smoking in the dark. A storm front had moved down from the north in the afternoon and it had turned off cold. No rain. Maybe in the eastern sections. Up in the Sacramentos. People imagined that if you got through a drought you could expect a few good years to try and get caught up but it was just like the seven on a pair of dice. The drought didnt know when the last one was and nobody knew when the next one was coming. He was about out of the cattle business anyway. He drew slowly on the cigarette. It flared and faded. His wife would be dead three years in February. Socorro's Candlemas Day. Candelaria. Something to do with the Virgin. As what didnt. In Mexico there is no God. Just her. He stubbed out the cigarette and rose and stood looking out at the softly lit barnlot. Oh Margaret, he said.

JC PULLED UP in front of Maud's and got out and slammed the truck door and he and John Grady went in.

Yonder come two good'ns, said Troy.

They stood at the bar. What'll you boys have, said Travis.

Give us two Blue Ribbons.

He got the bottles out of the cooler and opened them and set them on the bar.

I got it, said John Grady.

I got it, said JC.

He put forty cents on the bar and took the bottle by the neck and swigged down a long drink and wiped his mouth with the back of his hand and leaned against the bar.

You put in a hard day in the saddle? said Troy.

I'm mostly a nightrider, said JC.

Billy stood bent over the shuffleboard sliding the puck up and back. He looked at Troy and he looked at JC and then he slid the puck down the hardwood alleyway. The pins at the end swung up and the strike light lit up on the scoreboard and the small bells counted up the score. Troy grinned and put the cigar he was smoking in the corner of his mouth and stepped forward and took the puck and bent over the board.

You want to play?

JC'll play.

You want to play, JC?

Yeah, I'll play. What are we playin for?

Troy scored a strike on the bowling machine and stepped back and popped his fingers.

Me and JC'll play you and Askins.

Askins stood by the machine with one hand in his back pocket and the other holding a beer. Me and Jessie'll play you and Troy, he said.

Billy lit a cigarette. He looked at Askins. He looked at JC.

You and Troy play them, he said.

Go on and play.

You and Troy play. Go on.

What are we playin for? said JC.

I dont care.

Make it light on yourself.

What are we playin for, Troy?

Whatever they want to play for.

We'll play for a dollar.

High rollers. Get your quarters up. Jessie, you in?

I'm in, said Jessie.

Billy sat on the stool at the bar next to John Grady. They watched while the players put their quarters in the machine. The numbers rolled back and the bells chinged. Troy poured powdered wax from a can onto the alley and slid the puck back and forth and bent to shoot. Bowlin school is now open, he said.

Show us somethin.

You'd be surprised what all you can learn from a experienced player.

He slid the puck down the boards. The bells rang. He stepped back and popped his fingers. Things, he said, that will stand you in good stead all your life.

I need to talk to you, said John Grady.

Billy blew smoke across the room. All right, he said.

Let's go back in the back.

All right.

They took their beers and walked to the rear of the place where there were tables and chairs and a bandstand and a polished concrete dancefloor. They kicked back two chairs and sat at one of the tables and set their bottles down. The place was dim and musty.

I'll bet I know what this is about, said Billy.

Yeah. I know.

He sat peeling the label from his beerbottle with his thumbnail while he listened. He didnt even look up at John Grady. John Grady told him about the girl and about the White Lake and about Eduardo and he told him what the blind maestro had said. When he'd finished Billy still hadnt looked up but he'd stopped peeling the beerlabel. He didnt say anything. After a while he took his cigarettes from his pocket and lit one and laid the pack and his lighter on the table.

You are shittin me aint you? he said.

No. I guess I aint.

What the hell's wrong with you? Have you been drinkin paint thinner or somethin?

John Grady pushed his hat back. He looked out across the floor. No, he said.

Let me see if I got this straight. You want me to go to a whorehouse in Juárez Mexico and buy this whore cash money and bring her back across the river to the ranch. Is that about the size of it?

John Grady nodded.

Shit, said Billy. Smile or somethin, will you? Goddamn. Tell me you aint gone completely crazy.

I aint gone completely crazy.

The hell you aint.

I'm in love with her, Billy.

Billy slumped back in his chair. His arms hung uselessly by his side. Aw goddamn, he said. Goddamn.

I cant help what it sounds like.

My own damn fault. I never should of took you down there. Never in this world. It's my fault. Hell, I dont even know what I'm complainin about.

He leaned and took his lighted cigarette from the tin ashtray where he'd put it and took a pull on it and blew the smoke across the table. He shook his head. Tell me this, he said.

All right.

What in the goddamn hell would you do with her if you did get her away from down there? Which you aint.

Marry her.

Billy paused with the cigarette half way to his mouth. He put it down again.

Well that's it, he said. That's it. I'm havin your ass committed.

I mean it, Billy.

Billy leaned back in the chair. After a while he threw up one hand. I cant believe my goddamn ears. I think I'm the one that's gone crazy. I'm a son of a bitch if I dont. Have you lost your rabbit-assed mind? I'm an absolute son of a bitch, bud. I never in my goddamn life heard the equal of this.

I know. I cant help it.

The hell you cant.

Will you help me?

No and hell no. Do you know what they're goin to do with you? They're goin to hook your head up to one of them machines and throw a big switch and fry your brains to where you wont be a menace to yourself no more.

I mean it, Billy.

You think I dont mean it? I'm goin to help em hook up the wires.

I cant go down there. He knows who I am.

Look at me, son. You're not makin no sense. What the hell

kind of people do you think it is you're talkin about? Do you really think you can go down there and dicker with some greaser pimp that buys and sells people outright like you was goin down to the courthouse lawn to trade knives?

I cant help it.

Will you quit sayin that, goddamn it? What the hell do you mean you cant help it?

Just let it go. It's all right.

It's all right? Shit.

He slumped in the chair.

You want another beer?

No, I dont. I want a goddamn quart of whiskey.

I dont blame you for not wantin no part of it.

Well I'm glad as all hell to hear that.

He shook a cigarette out of the pack.

You got one lit, John Grady said.

Billy paid him no mind. You got no money, he said. So I dont know how in the hell you propose to go shoppin for whores.

I'll get it.

Get it where?

I'll get it.

How much were you plannin to offer him?

Two thousand dollars.

Two thousand dollars.

Yeah.

Well. If there was any doubt at all there sure aint now. You've gone completely crazy and that's all there is to be said about it. Aint it?

I dont know.

Well I do. Where in the hell, where in the goddamn hell, do you think you're goin to get two thousand dollars at?

I dont know. I'll get it.

You dont make that in a year.

I know it.

You're in a dangerous frame of mind, son. Did you know that?

Maybe.

I've seen it before. You know you been actin peculiar since you had that wreck? Have you thought about that? Look at me. I'm serious.

I aint crazy, Billy.

Well one of us is. Shit. I blame myself. That's all. Blame myself.

It dont have nothin to do with you.

The hell it dont.

It's all right. Just let it go.

Billy leaned back in his chair. He stared at the two cigarettes burning in the ashtray. After a while he pushed his hat back and passed his hand across his eyes and across his mouth and pulled the hat down again and looked across the room. Out at the bar the shuffleboard bells rang. He looked at John Grady.

How did you ever get in such a mess?

I dont know.

How did you let it get this far?

I dont know. I feel some way like I didnt have nothin to do with it. Like it's just the way it is. Like it always was this way.

Billy shook his head sadly. More craziness, he said. It aint too late, you know.

Yes it is.

It's never too late. You just need to make up your mind.

It's done made up.

Well unmake it. Start again.

Two months ago I'd of agreed with you. Now I know better. There's some things you dont decide. Decidin had nothin to do with it.

They sat for a long time. He looked at John Grady and he looked out across the room. The dusty dancefloor, the empty bandstand. The shapes of a covered drumset. He pushed back his chair and stood and set the chair back carefully at its place at the table and then he turned and walked out across the room and through the bar and out the door.

* * *

LATE THAT NIGHT lying in his bunk in the dark he heard the kitchen door close and heard the screendoor close after it. He lay there. Then he sat and swung his feet to the floor and got his boots and his jeans and pulled them on and put on his hat and walked out. The moon was almost full and it was cold and late and no smoke rose from the kitchen chimney. Mr Johnson was sitting on the back stoop in his duckingcoat smoking a cigarette. He looked up at John Grady and nodded. John Grady sat on the stoop beside him. What are you doin out here without your hat? he said.

I dont know.

You all right?

Yeah. I'm all right. Sometimes you miss bein outside at night. You want a cigarette?

No thanks.

Could you not sleep either?

No sir. I guess not.

How's them new horses?

I think he done all right.

Them was some boogerish colts I seen penned up in the corral.

I think he's goin to sell off some of them.

Horsetradin, the old man said. He shook his head. He smoked.

Did you used to break horses, Mr Johnson?

Some. Mostly just what was required. I was never a twister in any sense of the word. I got hurt once pretty bad. You can get spooked and not know it. Just little things. You dont hardly even know it.

But you like to ride.

I do. Margaret could outride me two to one though. As good a woman with a horse as I ever saw. Way bettern me. Hard thing for a man to admit but it's the truth.

You worked for the Matadors didnt you?

Yep. I did.

How was that?

Hard work. That's how it was.

I guess that aint changed.

Oh it probably has. Some. I was never in love with the cattle business. It's just the only one I ever knew.

He smoked.

Can I ask you somethin? said John Grady.

Ask it.

How old were you when you got married?

I was never married. Never found anybody that'd have me.

He looked at John Grady.

Margaret was my brother's girl. Him and his wife both was carried off in the influenza epidemic in nineteen and eighteen.

I didnt know that.

She never really knowed her parents. She was just a baby. Well, five. Where's your coat at?

I'm all right.

I was in Fort Collins Colorado at the time. They sent for me. I shipped my horses and come back on the train with em. Dont catch cold out here now.

No sir. I wont. I aint cold.

I had ever motivation in the world but I never could find one I thought would suit Margaret.

One what?

Wife. One wife. We finally just give it up. Probably a mistake. I dont know. Socorro pretty much raised her. She spoke better spanish than Socorro did. It's just awful hard. It liked to of killed Socorro. She still aint right. I dont expect she ever will be.

Yessir.

We tried ever way in the world to spoil her rotten but it didnt take. I dont know why she turned out the way she did. It's just a miracle I guess you could say. I dont take no credit for it, I'll tell you that.

Yessir.

Look yonder. The old man nodded toward the moon.

What?

You cant see em now. Wait a minute. No. They're gone.

What was it?

Birds flyin across the moon. Geese maybe. I dont know.

I didnt see em. Which way were they headed?

Upcountry. Probably headed for that marsh country on the river up around Belen.

Yessir.

I used to love to ride of a night.

I did too.

You'll see things on the desert at night that you cant understand. Your horse will see things. He'll see things that will spook him of course but then he'll see things that dont spook him but still you know he seen somethin.

What sort of things?

I dont know.

You mean like ghosts or somethin?

No. I dont know what. You just knows he sees em. They're out there.

Not just some class of varmint?

No.

Not somethin that will booger him?

No. It's more like somethin he knows about.

But you dont.

But you dont. Yes.

The old man smoked. He watched the moon. No further birds flew. After a while he said: I aint talkin about spooks. It's more like just the way things are. If you only knew it.

Yessir.

We was up on the Platte River out of Ogallala one night and I was bedded down in my soogan out away from the camp. It was a moonlit night just about like tonight. Cold. Spring of the year. I woke up and I guess I'd heard em in my sleep and it was just this big whisperin sound all over and it was geese just by the thousands headed up the river. They passed for the better part of a hour. They blacked out the moon. I thought the herd would get up off the grounds but they didnt. I got up and walked out and stood watchin em and some of the other young waddies in the outfit they had got up too and we was all standin out there in our longjohns watchin. It was just this whisperin sound. They was up high and it wasnt loud or nothin and I wouldnt of thought about somethin like that a wakin us wore out as we was. I had a nighthorse in my string named Boozer and old Boozer he come to me. I reckon he thought the herd'd get up too but they didnt. And they was a snuffy bunch, too.

Did you ever have a stampede?

Yes. We was drivin to Abilene in eighteen and eighty-five. I wasnt much more than a button. And we had got into it with a rep from one of the outfits and he followed us to where we crossed the Red River at Doane's store into Indian Territory. He knew we'd have a harder time gettin our stock back there and we did but we caught the old boy and it was him for you could still smell the coaloil on him. He come by in the night and set a cat on fire and thowed it onto the herd. I mean slung it. Walter Devereaux was comin in off the middle watch and he heard it and looked back. Said it looked like a comet goin out through there and just a squallin. Lord didnt they come up from there. It took us three days to shape that herd back and whenever we left out of there we was still missin forty some odd head lost or crippled or stole and two horses.

What happened to the boy?

The boy?

That threw the cat.

Oh. Best I remember he didnt make out too well.

I guess not.

People will do anything.

Yessir. They will.

You live long enough you'll see it.

Yessir. I have.

Mr Johnson didnt answer. He flipped the butt of his cigarette out across the yard in a slow red arc.

Aint nothin to burn out there. I remember when you could have grassfires in this country.

I didnt mean I'd seen everthing, John Grady said.

I know you didnt.

I just meant I'd seen things I'd as soon not of.

I know it. There's hard lessons in this world.

What's the hardest?

I dont know. Maybe it's just that when things are gone they're gone. They aint comin back.

Yessir.

They sat. After a while the old man said: The day after my fiftieth birthday in March of nineteen and seventeen I rode into the old headquarters at the Wilde well and there was six dead wolves hangin on the fence. I rode along the fence and ran my hand along em. I looked at their eyes. A government trapper had brought em in the night before. They'd been killed with poison baits. Strychnine. Whatever. Up in the Sacramentos. A week later he brought in four more. I aint heard a wolf in this country since. I suppose that's a good thing. They can be hell on stock. But I guess I was always what you might call superstitious. I know I damn sure wasnt religious. And it had always seemed to me that somethin can live and die but that the kind of thing that they were was always there. I didnt know you could poison that. I aint heard a wolf howl in thirty odd years. I dont know where you'd go to hear one. There may not be any such a place.

When he walked back through the barn Billy was standing in the doorway.

Has he gone back to bed?

Yeah.

What was he doin up?

He said he couldnt sleep. What were you?

Same thing. You?

Same thing.

Somethin in the air I reckon.

I dont know.

What was he talkin about?

Just stuff.

What did he say?

I guess he said cattle could tell the difference between a flight of geese and a cat on fire.

Maybe you dont need to be hangin around him so much.

You might be right.

You all seem to have a lot in common.

He aint crazy, Billy.

Maybe. But I dont know as you'd be the first one I'd come to for an opinion about it.

I'm goin to bed.

Night.

Night.

HE TOLD THE WOMAN in spanish that he intended to keep his hat and he carried it with him up the two steps to the bar and then he put it on again. There were some Mexican businessmen standing at the bar and he nodded to them as he passed. They nodded back curtly. The barman placed a napkin down. Señor? he said.

Old Grandad and water back.

The barman moved away. Billy took out his cigarettes and lighter and laid them on the bar. He looked in the backbar mirror. Several whores were draped about on the couches in the lounge. They looked like refugees from a costume ball. The barman returned with the shot of whiskey and set it and the glass of water on the bar and Billy picked up the whiskey and rocked it once in a slow circular motion and then raised it and drank. He reached for his cigarettes, he nodded to the barman.

Otra vez, he said.

The barman came with the bottle. He poured.

Dónde está Eduardo, said Billy.

Quién?

Eduardo.

The barman poured reflectively. He shook his head.

El patrón, said Billy.

El patrón no está.

Cuándo regresa?

No sé. He stood holding the bottle. Hay un problema? he said.

Billy shook a cigarette from the pack and put it in his mouth and reached for the lighter. No, he said. No hay un problema. I need to see him on a business deal.

What is your business?

He lit the cigarette and laid the lighter on top of the pack and blew smoke across the bar and looked up.

I dont feel like we're makin much progress here, he said.

The barman shrugged.

Billy took his money from his shirtpocket and laid a ten-dollar bill on the bar.

That aint for the drinks.

The barman looked down the bar to where the businessmen were standing. He looked at Billy.

Do you know what this job is worth? he said.

What?

I said do you know what this job is worth?

You mean you make pretty good on tips.

No. I mean do you know what it costs to buy a job like this?

I never heard of nobody buyin a job.

You do lots of business in Mexico?

No.

The barman stood with the bottle. Billy took out his money again and put down two fives on top of the ten. The barman palmed the money off the bar and put it in his pocket. Un momento, he said. Espérate.

Billy took up the whiskey and swirled it and drank. He set the glass down and passed the back of his wrist across his mouth. When he looked in the backbar glass the alcahuete was standing at his left elbow like Lucifer.

Sí señor, he said.

Billy turned and looked at him.

Are you Eduardo?

No. How may I help you?

I wanted to see Eduardo.

What do you want to see him about?

I wanted to talk to him.

Yes. Talk to me.

Billy turned to look at the barman but the barman had moved away to serve the other patrons.

It's just somethin personal, Billy said. Hell, I aint goin to hurt him.

The alcahuete's eyebrows moved slightly upward. That is good to know, he said. You find something you dont like?

I got a deal he might be interested in.

Who is the dealer.

What?

Who is the dealer.

Me. I'm the dealer.

Tiburcio studied him for a long time. I know who you are, he said.

You know who I am?

Yes.

Who am I?

You are the trujamán.

What's that?

You dont speak spanish?

I speak spanish.

You come with the mordida.

Billy took out his money and laid it on the bar. I got eighteen dollars. That's all I got. And I aint paid for the drinks yet.

Pay for the drinks.

What?

Pay for the drinks.

Billy left a five on the bar and put the thirteen dollars in his shirtpocket along with his cigarettes and lighter and stood.

Follow me.

He followed him out through the lounge past the whores in their whore's finery. Through the kaleidoscope of pieced light from the overhead chandelier and past the empty bandstand to a door at the rear.

The door was covered in winecolored baize and there was no doorknob to it. The alcahuete opened it anyway and they entered a corridor with blue walls and a single blue bulb screwed into the ceiling above the door. The alcahuete held the door and he stepped through and the alcahuete closed it behind them and turned and went down the corridor. The musky spice of his cologne hung in the air. At the farthest end of the corridor he stopped and tapped twice with his knuckles upon a door embossed with silver foil. He turned, waiting, his hands crossed before him at the wrist.

A buzzer buzzed and the alcahuete opened the door. Wait here, he said.

Billy waited. An old woman with one eye came down the corridor and tapped at one of the doors. When she saw him there she blessed herself with the sign of the cross. The door opened and she disappeared inside and the door closed and the corridor stood empty once again in the soft blue light.

When the silver door opened the alcahuete motioned him inside with a cupping motion of his thin ringed fingers. He stepped in and stood. Then he took off his hat.

Eduardo was sitting at his desk smoking one of his slender black cigars. He was sitting sideways with his feet crossed before him propped in the open lower drawer of his desk and he appeared to be examining his polished lizardskin boots. How may I help you? he said.

Billy looked back at Tiburcio. He looked again at Eduardo. Eduardo lifted his feet from the drawer and swiveled slowly in his chair. He was dressed in a black suit with a pale green shirt open at the neck. He rested his arm on the polished glass top of the desk, he held the cigar. He looked like he had nothing much on his mind.

I got a business proposition for you, Billy said.

Eduardo held up the little cigar and studied it. He looked at Billy again.

Somethin you might be interested in, Billy said.

Eduardo smiled thinly. He looked past Billy at the alcahuete and he looked at Billy again. My fortunes are to change for the better, he said. How very good.

He took a long slow pull on the cigar. He made a strange and graceful gesture with the hand that held it, turning it in an arc and holding it palm up. As if it cupped something unseen. Or were accustomed to holding something now absent.

Do you care if we talk alone? Billy said.

He nodded and the alcahuete withdrew and closed the door. When he was gone Eduardo leaned back in his chair and turned again and recrossed his boots in the drawer. He looked up and waited.

What I wanted, said Billy, was to buy one of these girls.

Buy, said Eduardo.

Yessir.

How do you mean, buy.

I give you the money and take her out of here.

You believe these girls are here against their will.

I dont know what they are.

But that's what you think.

I dont think anything.

Of course you do. Otherwise what would there be to buy?

I dont know.

Eduardo pursed his lips. He studied the end of the cigar. He doesnt know, he said.

You're tellin me that these girls are free to just walk out of here.

That is a good question.

Well what would be a good answer.

I would say that they are free in their persons.

In their what?

In their persons. They are free in their persons. Whether they are free here? He placed his forefinger alongside his temple. Well, who can say?

If one of em wanted to leave she could leave.

They are whores. Where would they go?

Suppose one of em wanted to get married.

Eduardo shrugged. He looked up at Billy.

Tell me this, he said.

All right.

Are you principal or agent?

Am I what?

Is it you who wishes to buy this girl?

Yes.

Do you come often to the White Lake?

I was here one time.

Where did you meet this girl?

At La Venada.

And now you wish to marry her.

Billy didnt answer.

The pimp pulled slowly on the cigar and blew the smoke slowly toward his boots. I think you are the agent, he said.

I aint no agent. I work for Mac McGovern at the Cross Fours out of Orogrande New Mexico and you can ask anybody.

I think you are not here on your own behalf.

I'm here to make you a offer.

Eduardo smoked.

Cash money, Billy said.

This girl has an illness. Does your friend know that?

I didnt say I had a friend.

She has not told him that, has she?

How do you know what girl it is.

Her name is Magdalena.

Billy studied him. You knew that because of what I said about La Venada.

This girl will not leave here. Perhaps your friend thinks that she will but she will not. Perhaps even she thinks it. She is very young. Let me ask you this.

Ask it.

What is wrong with your friend that he falls in love with whores?

I dont know.

Does he think she is not really a whore?

I couldnt tell you.

You cannot talk to him?

No.

Because she is whore to the bone. I know her.

I expect you do.

Your friend is very rich?

No.

What can he offer this girl? Why would she leave?

I dont know. I reckon he thinks she's in love with him.

Heavens, said Eduardo. Do you believe such a thing?

I dont know.

Do you believe such a thing?

No.

What are you going to do?

I dont know. What do you want me to tell him?

There is nothing to tell him. He drinks a great deal, your friend?

No. Not especially.

I am trying to help you.

Billy tapped his hat against the side of his leg. He looked at Eduardo and he looked around the room that was his office. In the corner against the far wall there was a small bar. A sofa upholstered in white leather. A glasstopped coffeetable.

You dont believe me, said Eduardo.

I dont believe you dont have some money invested in this girl.

Did I say that?

I thought you did.

She owes me a certain amount. Money that was advanced to her for her costumes. Her jewelry.

How much money.

Would I ask you such a question?

I dont know. I guess I wouldnt be in a position to be asked.

You think I am a whiteslaver.

I didnt say that.

That is what you think.

What do you want me to tell him.

What difference does it make?

I guess it might make a difference to him.

Your friend is in the grip of an irrational passion. Nothing you say to him will matter. He has in his head a certain story. Of how things will be. In this story he will be happy. What is wrong with this story?

You tell me.

What is wrong with this story is that it is not a true story. Men have in their minds a picture of how the world will be. How they will be in that world. The world may be many different ways for them but there is one world that will never be and that is the world they dream of. Do you believe that?

Billy put his hat on. I thank you for your time, he said.

You are welcome.

He turned to go.

You didnt answer my question, said Eduardo.

He turned back. He looked at the pimp. His cigar in his gracefully cupped fingers, his expensive boots. The windowless room. The furniture in it that looked as if it had been brought in and set in place solely for the purpose of this scene. I dont know, he said. I guess probably I do. I just dont like to say it.

Why is that?

It seems like a betrayal of some kind.

Can the truth be a betrayal?

Maybe. Anyway, some men get what they want.

No man. Or perhaps only briefly so as to lose it. Or perhaps only to prove to the dreamer that the world of his longing made real is no longer that world at all.

Yeah.

Do you believe that?

I'll tell you what.

Tell me.

Let me sleep on it.

The pimp nodded. Ándale pues, he said. The door opened by no visible means or signal. Tiburcio stood waiting. Billy turned again and looked back. You didnt answer mine, he said.

No?

No.

Ask it again.

Let me ask you this instead.

All right.

He's in trouble, aint he?

Eduardo smiled. He blew cigar smoke across the glass top of his desk. That is not a question, he said.

IT WAS LATE when he got back but the light was still on in the kitchen. He sat in the truck for a minute, then he shut off the engine. He left the key in the ignition and got out and walked across the yard to the house. Socorro had gone to bed but there was cornbread in the warmer over the oven and a plate of beans and potatoes with two pieces of fried chicken. He carried the plates to the table and went back and got silver out of the dishdrainer and got down a cup and poured his coffee and set the pot back over the eye of the stove where there was still a dull red glow of coals and he took his coffee to the table and sat and ate. He ate slowly and methodically. When he'd finished he carried the dishes to the sink and opened the refrigerator and bent to scout the interior for anything in the way of dessert. He found a bowl of pudding and took it to the sideboard and got down a small dish and filled it and put the pudding back in the refrigerator and got more coffee and sat eating the pudding and reading Oren's newspaper. The clock ticked in the hallway. The cooling stove creaked. When John Grady came in he went on to the stove and got a cup of coffee and came to the table and sat down and pushed back his hat.

You up for the day? said Billy.

I hope not.

What time is it?

I dont know.

Billy sipped his coffee. He reached in his pocket for his cigarettes.

Did you just get in? John Grady said.

Yep.

I reckon the answer was no.

You reckon right, little hoss.

Well.

It's about what you expected aint it?

Yeah. Did you offer him the money?

Oh we had a pretty good visit, take it all around.

What did he say.

Billy lit his cigarette and laid the lighter on top of the pack. He said she didnt want to leave there.

Well that's a lie.

Well that may be. But he says she aint leavin.

Well she is.

Billy blew smoke slowly across the table. John Grady watched him.

You just think I'm crazy, dont you?

You know what I think.

Well.

Why dont you take a good look at yourself. Look at what it's brung you to. Talkin about sellin your horse. It's just the old story all over again. Losin your head over a piece of tail. Cept in your case there aint nothin about it makes any sense. Nothin.

In your eyes.

In mine or any man's.

He leaned forward and began to count off on the fingers of the hand that held the cigarette: She aint American. She aint a citizen. She dont speak english. She works in a whorehouse. No, hear me out. And last but not least—he sat holding his thumb—there's a son of a bitch owns her outright that I guarangoddamntee you will kill you graveyard dead if you mess with him. Son, aint there no girls on this side of the damn river?

Not like her.

Well I'll bet that's the truth if you ever told it.

He stubbed out the cigarette. Well. I've gone as far as I can go with you. I'm goin to bed.

All right.

He pushed back his chair and rose and stood. Do I think you're crazy? he said. No. I dont. You've rewrote the book for crazy. If all you are is crazy then all them poor bastards in the loonybin that they're feedin under the door need to be set loose in the street.

He put the cigarettes and lighter in his shirtpocket and carried the cup and bowl to the sink. At the door he stopped again and looked back. I'll see you in the mornin, he said.

Billy?

Yeah.

Thanks. I appreciate it.

I'd say you're welcome but I'd be a liar.

I know it. Thanks anyway.

You aim to sell that stallion?

I dont know. Yeah.

Maybe Wolfenbarger will buy him.

I thought about that.

I expect you did. I'll see you in the mornin.

John Grady watched him walk across the yard toward the barn. He leaned and wiped the beaded water from the window glass with his sleeve. Billy's shadow shortened across the yard until he passed under the yellow light over the barn door and then he stepped through into the dark of the barn and was lost to view. John Grady let the curtains fall back across the glass and turned and sat staring into the empty cup before him. There were grounds in the bottom of the cup and he swirled the cup and looked at them. Then he swirled them the other way as if he'd put them back the way they'd been.

HE STOOD IN THE GROVE of willows with his back to the river and watched the road and the vehicles that moved along the road. There was little traffic. The dust of the few cars hung in the dry air long after the cars were gone. He walked on down to the river and squatted and watched the passing water murky with clay. He threw in a rock. Then another. He turned and looked back toward the road.

The cab when it came stopped at the turnoff and then backed and turned and came rocking and bumping down the rutted mud road and pulled up in the clearing. She got out on the far side and paid the driver and spoke briefly with him and the driver nodded and she stepped away. The driver put the cab in gear and put his arm across the seat and backed the cab and turned. He looked toward the river. Then he pulled away out to the road and went back toward town.

He took her hand. Tenía miedo que no vendrías, he said.

She didnt answer. She leaned against him. Her black hair falling about her shoulders. The smell of soap. The flesh and bone living under the cloth of her dress.

Me amas? he said.

Sí. Te amo.

He sat on a cottonwood log and watched her while she waded in the gravel shallows. She turned and smiled at him. Her dress gathered about her brown thighs. He tried to smile back but his throat caught and he looked away.

She sat on the log beside him and he took her feet in his hands each in turn and dried them with his kerchief and fastened with his own fingers the small buckles of her shoes. She leaned and put her head on his shoulder and he kissed her and he touched her hair and her breasts and her face as a blind man might.

Y mi respuesta? he said.

She took his hand and kissed it and held it against her heart and she said that she was his and that she would do whatever he asked her if it take her life.

She was from the State of Chiapas and she had been sold at the age of thirteen to settle a gambling debt. She had no family. In Puebla she'd run away and gone to a convent for protection. The procurer himself appeared on the convent steps the following morning and in the pure light of day paid money into the hand of the mother superior and took the girl away again.

This man stripped her naked and beat her with a whip made from the innertube of a truck tire. Then he held her in his arms and told her that he loved her. She ran away again and went to the police. Three officers took her to a room in the basement where there was a dirty mattress on the floor. When they were through with her they sold her to the other policemen. Then they sold her to the prisoners for what few pesos they could muster or traded her for cigarettes. Finally they sent for the procurer and sold her back to him.

He beat her with his fists and slammed her against the wall and knocked her down and kicked her. He said that if she ran away again he would kill her. She closed her eyes and offered him her throat. In his rage he seized her up by the arm but the arm broke in his hand. A muted snap, like a dry stick. She gasped and cried out with the pain.

Mira, he shouted. Mira, puta, que has hecho.

The arm was set by a curandera and now would not straighten. She showed him. Mires, she said. The house was called La Esperanza del Mundo. Where a painted child in a stained kimono with her arm in a sling wept in silence or went wordlessly with men to a room at the rear for a price of less than two dollars.

He had bent forward weeping with his arms around her. He

put his hand over her mouth. She took it away. Hay más, she said.

No.

She would tell him more but again he placed his fingers against her mouth. He said that there was only one thing he wished to know.

Lo que quieras, she said.

Te casas conmigo.

Sí, querido, she said. La respuesta es sí. I marry you.

WHEN HE ENTERED the kitchen Oren and Troy and JC were sitting there and he nodded to them and went on to the stove and got his breakfast and his coffee and came to the table. Troy scooted his chair slightly to make room. You aint about give out under this heavy courtin schedule are you son?

Shit, said JC. Dont even think about tryin to keep up with the cowboy.

I talked to Crawford about your horse, said Oren.

What did he say.

He said he thought he had a buyer if you could come to his figures.

Same figures?

Same figures.

I dont believe I can do it.

He might do a little better. But not much.

John Grady nodded. He ate.

You might do better to run him through the auction.

The auction aint for three more weeks.

Two and a half.

Tell him I'll take three and a quarter.

JC got up and carried his dishes to the sink. Oren lit a cigarette.

When will you see him? said John Grady.

I'll talk to him today if you want.

All right.

He ate. Troy got up and took his dishes to the sink and he and JC went out. John Grady wiped his plate with the last bite of biscuit and ate it and pushed back his chair.

These four-minute breakfasts are goin to get you in trouble with the union, Oren said.

I got to see the old man a minute.

He carried his plate and cup to the sink and wiped his hands on the sides of his trousers and crossed the room and went down the hall.

He knocked on the jamb of the office doorway and looked in but the room was empty. He went on down the hall to Mac's bedroom and tapped at the open door. Mac came out of the bathroom with a towel around his neck and his hat on.

Mornin son, he said.

Mornin sir. I wondered if I could talk to you for a minute.

Come on in.

He hung the towel over a chairback and went to the oldfashioned chifforobe and took out a shirt and shook it unfolded and stood undoing the buttons. John Grady stood in the doorway.

Come on in, Mac said. Put your damn hat back on.

Yessir. He took a couple of steps into the room and put his hat on and stood there. On the wall opposite were framed photographs of horses. On the dresser in an ornate silver frame a photograph of Margaret Johnson McGovern.

Mac pulled on his shirt and stood buttoning it. Set down, son, he said.

That's all right.

Go on. You look like you got a lot on your mind.

There was a heavy oak chair covered with dark leather at the far side of the bed and he crossed the floor and sat in it. Some of Mac's clothes were thrown across one arm of the chair. He put his elbow on the other arm. Mac swept up and tucked in his shirt front and back and buttoned his trousers and buckled his belt and got his keys and his change and his billfold from the dresser. He came over to the bed carrying his socks and sat and unrolled them and began to pull them on. Well, he said. You wont never have no better of a chance.

John Grady started to take off his hat again but then he put his hands back in his lap. Then he leaned forward with his elbows on his knees.

Just pretend it's a cold stockpond on a hot day and jump on in, said Mac.

Yessir. Well. I want to get married.

Mac stopped midsock. Then he pulled the sock on and reached down for his boot. Married, he said.

Yessir.

All right.

I want to get married and I thought for one thing if you didnt care I'd just go on and sell that horse.

Mac pulled on the boot and picked up the other boot and sat with it in his hand. Son, he said. I can understand a man wantin to get married. I lacked about a month bein twenty when I did. We kind of finished raisin one another. But I might of been fixed a little better than you. You think you can afford it?

I dont know. I thought maybe if I sold the horse.

How long have you been thinkin about this?

Well. A while.

This aint a have-to kind of thing is it?

No sir. It aint nothin like that.

Well why dont you hold off for a while. See if it wont keep.

I cant really do that.

Well, I dont know what that means.

There's some problems.

Well I got time to listen if you want to tell me about it.

Yessir. Well. For one thing she's Mexican.

Mac nodded. I've known that to work, he said. He pulled on the boot.

So I got the problem of gettin her over here.

Mac put his foot down on the floor and put his hands on his knees. He looked up at the boy. Over here? he said.

Yessir.

You mean across the river?

Yessir.

You mean she's a Mexican Mexican?

Yessir.

Damn, son.

He looked off across the room. The sun was just up over the barn. He looked at the white lace curtains on the window. He looked at the boy sitting stiffly there in his father's chair. Well, he said. That's somethin of a problem, I reckon. Aint the worst one I ever heard of. How old is she?

Sixteen.

Mac sat with his lower lip between his teeth. It keeps gettin worse, dont it? Does she speak english?

No sir.

Not word one.

No sir.

Mac shook his head. Outside they could hear the cattle calling along the fence by the road. He looked at John Grady. Son, he said, have you give this some thought?

Yessir. I sure have.

I take it you've pretty much made up your mind.

Yessir.

You wouldnt be here if you hadnt, would you?

No sir.

Where do you plan on livin at?

Well sir, I wanted to talk to you about that. I thought if you didnt care I'd see if I could fix up the old place at Bell Springs.

Damn. It dont even have a roof anymore does it?

Not much of a one. I looked it over. It could be fixed up.

It would take some fixin.

I could fix it up.

You probably could. Probably could. You aint said nothin about money. I cant raise you. You know that.

I aint asked for a raise.

I'd have to raise Billy and JC both. Hell. I might have to raise Oren.

Yessir.

Mac sat leaning forward with his fingers laced together. Son, he said, I think you ought to wait. But if you got it in your head to go on, then go ahead. I'll do whatever I can for you.

Thank you sir.

He put his hands on his knees and rose. John Grady rose. Mac shook his head, half smiling. He looked at the boy.

Is she pretty?

Yessir. She sure is.

I'll bet she is, too. You bring her in here. I want to see her.

Yessir.

You say she dont speak no english?

No sir.

Damn. He shook his head again. Well, he said. Go on. Get your butt out of here.

Yessir.

He crossed the room to the door and stopped and turned.

Thank you sir.

Go on.

HE AND BILLY rode to Cedar Springs. They rode to the top of the draw and rode back down again throwing all the cattle out downcountry before them and roping everything that looked suspicious, heading and heeling them and stretching the screaming animals on the ground and dismounting and dropping the reins while the horses backed and held the catchropes taut. There were new calves on the ground and some of them had worms in their navels and they doused them with Peerless and swabbed them out and doused them again and turned them loose. In the evening they rode up to Bell Springs and John Grady dismounted and left Billy with the horses while they drank and crossed through the swales of sacaton grass to the old adobe and pushed open the door and went in.

He stood very quietly. Sunlight fell the length of the room from the small sash set in the western wall. The floor was of packed clay beaten and oiled and it was strewn with debris, old clothes and foodtins and curious small cones of mud that had formed from water percolating down through the mud roof and dripping through the latillas to stand about like the work of old-world termites. In the corner stood an iron bedstead with random empty beercans screwed into the bare springs. On the back wall a 1928 Clay Robinson and Co. calendar showing a cowboy on nightherd under a rising moon. He passed on through the long core of light where he set the motes to dancing and went through the doorless framework into the other room. There was a small two-eyed woodburning stove against the far wall with the rusted pipes fallen into a pile behind it and there were a couple of old Arbuckle coffeeboxes nailed to the wall and a third one lying in the floor. A few jars of home-canned beans and tomatoes and salsa. Broken glass in the floor. Old newspapers from before the war. An old rotted Fish brand slicker hanging from a peg in the wall by the kitchen door and some pieces of old tackleather. When he turned around Billy was standing in the doorway watching him.

This the honeymoon suite? he said.

You're lookin at it.

He leaned in the doorframe and took his cigarettes from his shirtpocket and shucked one out and lit it.

The only thing you aint got here is a dead mule in the floor.

John Grady had crossed to the back door and stood looking out.

You think you're goin to be able to get the truck up here?

I think we might could comin up the other side.

What's this we shit? You got a rat in your pocket?

John Grady smiled. From the kitchen door you could see the late sun high on the bare ridgerock of the Jarillas. He shut the door and looked back at Billy and walked over to the stove and lifted one of the castiron eyeplates and looked in and lowered it again.

I may be wrong about this, said Billy, but it's my feelin that once they get used to lights and runnin water it's kindly hard to wean em back off again.

Got to start somewhere.

Is she goin to cook on that?

John Grady smiled. He went past Billy into the other room. Billy straightened up in the doorway to let him by and then stood looking after him. I hope she's a country girl, he said.

What do you say we ride back down on the back side and see what the old road looks like.

Whatever you want to do. We'll be late gettin in.

John Grady stood in the doorway looking out. Yeah, he said. All right. I can ride up on Sunday.

Billy watched him. He unlimbered himself out of the door-frame and crossed the room. Let's do it, he said. We're goin to be ridin back in the dark either way.

Billy?

Yeah.

It dont make any difference, you know. What anybody thinks.

Yeah. I know it too well.

That's a pretty picture, aint it.

He looked at the horses across the creek where they stood footed to their darkening shapes in the ford with their heads raised looking toward the house and the cottonwoods and the mountains and the red sweep of the evening sky beyond.

You think I'll outgrow whatever it is I got.

No. I dont. I used to but I dont no more.

I'm too far gone, is that it?

It aint just that. It's you. Most people get smacked around enough after a while they start to pay attention. More and more you remind me of Boyd. Only way I could ever get him to do anything was to tell him not to.

There used to be a pipe from the spring to the house.

You could run it again I would reckon.

Yeah.

I'd say the water's still good. There aint nothin above here.

Billy walked out in the yard and took a long drag on his cigarette and stood looking at the horses. John Grady pulled the door shut. Billy looked at him.

You never did tell me what Mac said.

He didnt say much. If he thought I was crazy he was too much of a gentleman to mention it.

What do you think he'd say if he knew she worked at the White Lake?

I dont know.

The hell you dont.

He wont know it unless you tell him.

I've thought about it.

Yeah?

He'd shit green apples.

Billy flipped the butt of the cigarette out across the yard. It was already dark enough that it made an arc in the fading light. Arcs within the arc. We better get on, he said.

HE DIDNT SELL the horse to Wolfenbarger. On Saturday two friends of McGovern's came out and they leaned on the fender of their truck and smoked and talked while he saddled the horse and led it out. They straightened up when they saw the horse. He nodded to them and took the animal out to the corral.

Mac came from the kitchen and nodded to the men.

Mornin.

He crossed the yard. Crawford introduced him to the other man and the three of them walked out to the corral.

That looks like the horse old man Chávez used to ride, the man said.

As far as I know there's no connection.

That was a funny story about that horse.

Yes it was.

You think a horse can grieve for a man?

No. Do you?

No. Still it was a funny kind of story.

It was.

The man walked around the horse while John Grady held it. He put his hand behind the horse's front leg and he looked into its eye. He backed up against the horse and picked up one hindleg and put it down again but he didnt look at the hoof and he didnt look into the horse's mouth.

You say this is a three year old?

Yessir.

Ride him around some.

They stood watching while John Grady rode the horse up and back and turned the horse and backed him and then cantered him around the corral.

How come the boy wants to sell him?

Mac didnt answer. They watched the horse. After a while he said: He just needs the money. The horse is sound.

What do you think, Junior?

You aint goin to pay no attention to me. Get me on Mac's wrong side.

It aint my horse, said Mac.

What do you think?

Crawford spat. Pretty good lookin horse I think.

What will he take for him?

What he's askin.

They stood.

I might go two and a half.

Mac shook his head.

It's his horse to sell aint it? the man said.

Mac nodded. Yes, he said. It is. But if he was to let that horse go for two hundred and fifty dollars I'd pay him off. I wouldnt want anybody that ignorant on the place. Liable to do themselves a injury.

The man toed the dirt. He looked at Crawford and he studied the horse again and he looked at Mac.

Will he take three?

Will you give three?

Yessir.

John Grady, called Mac.

Yessir?

Bring that man's horse over here and get your saddle off of him.

Yessir, said John Grady.

WHEN HE CAME IN that night Oren and Troy were still at the table drinking coffee and he got his plate from the warmer and filled his cup and joined them.

They tell me you're damn near afoot, said Oren.

Just about it.

I guess you decided that varmint was just too crazy to make a horse out of.

I just needed the money.

Mac said the man never even rode him.

He didnt.

I suppose the critter's reputation had done preceded him.

Could be.

You may not of heard the last from him.

Could be.

They watched him eat.

The cowboy thinks horses are sane and people are crazy, Troy said.

He might have a point.

You all have been around different horses from what I have.

More likely we been around different people.

I dont know, said Troy. I been acquainted with some lulus.

How did you all get along?

John Grady looked up. He smiled. Oren was shucking a cigarette out of the pack. All horses are crazy, he said. To a degree. Only thing to be said in their favor is that they dont try to hide it from you.

He reached down and popped a wooden match on the underside of his chair and lit his cigarette and shook the match out and laid it in the ashtray.

Why do you think they're crazy? said John Grady.

Why do I think it or why are they?

Why are they.

They're just made that way. A horse has got two brains. He dont see the same thing out of both eyes at once. He's got a eye for each side.

So does a fish, said Troy.

Well. That's true.

So does a fish have two brains?

I dont know. I dont know that a fish has got any brains at all to speak of.

Maybe a fish just aint smart enough to be crazy.

I think you got a point. A horse aint really all that dumb.

They're too dumb to shade up and a dumb-assed cow will do that.

So will a fish. Or a rattlesnake for that matter.

You think a snake is dumber than a fish?

Hell, Troy. I dont know. Who in the hell would know such a thing? They're both dumbern hell in my opinion.

Well I didnt mean to get you stirred up.

I aint stirred up.

Well go on with the story.

It aint a story. It was just a observation about horses.

Well what was it.

I dont know. I forgot.

No you aint.

You were talkin about a horse havin two brains, said John Grady.

Oren pulled on the cigarette. He looked at John Grady. He leaned and tapped the ash into the ashtray.

All I was sayin is that a horse is a different proposition from what a lot of people think. A lot of what people take for ignorance on the part of the horse is just confusion between the

righthand horse and the lefthand horse. Like if you was to saddle a horse and all and then walk around to his off side and start
to mount up. You know what's goin to happen.

Sure. All hell's goin to bust loose.

That's right. That particular horse aint even seen you yet.

Oren jerked up his elbows and drew back in alarm from his
own off side. Shit, he said. Who's that?

Troy grinned. John Grady drank from his cup and set it back
on the table. Why couldnt it be that he's just not used to bein
mounted from that side? he said.

It is. But the point is he cant ask the other half of the horse
if he's ever seen this man before or get his advice about what
to do.

Well it seems to me that if the two sides of the horse aint
even speakin to one another you'd have some real problems.
The whole horse wouldnt even start off together in the same
direction. What about that?

Oren smoked. He looked at Troy. I aint a authority on
horses' brains. I'm just tellin you what one cowboy's experience
has been. There's two sides to a horse and it's been my experience that what you got to do is work the one side and let the
other side go.

I've known some people the same way. Several, in fact.

Yes. I have too. But I think it's somethin they've worked at. A
horse comes by it natural.

You dont think you could train both sides of the horse the
same?

You're wearin me out.

Hell, that's a fair question.

I suppose you could. Maybe. It'd be hard to do. There would
just about have to be two of you.

Well suppose you had a twin brother.

I suppose in principle maybe you could work with a horse
thataway. I dont know. But what would you have when you got
done?

You'd have a two-sided balanced horse.

No you wouldnt. You'd just have a horse that thought there was two of you. Suppose one day he sees you both on the same side. What then?

I reckon he'd think you was quadruplets.

Oren stubbed out the cigarette. No, he said. He'd think the same thing as everbody else.

What's that?

That you're as crazy as a shithouse rat.

He pushed back his chair and rose. I'll see you all in the mornin.

The kitchen door closed. Troy shook his head. Old Oren is losin his sense of humor.

John Grady smiled. He thumbed his plate back from the edge of the table and leaned back in his chair. Through the window he could see Oren adjust his hat as he set out down the drive toward the small house he shared with his cat. As if the dead world past might take pains to notice. He'd not always been a cowboy. He'd been a miner in northern Mexico and he'd fought in wars and revolutions and he'd been an oilfield roustabout in the Permian Basin and a mariner under three different flags. He'd even been married once.

John Grady drained the last dark dregs from the bottom of the cup and set the cup on the table. Oren's all right, he said.

III

WHEN HE CROSSED at the top of the draw he smelled what the horse had been smelling. A reek of carrion wafted up on some vector of the cooling evening air. He sat the horse and turned in the saddle and tested the air with his nose but the smell had passed and vanished. He turned the horse and sat facing back down the draw and then he put the horse forward again down the narrow cattletrail. The horse watched the cattle moving out before them through the scrub and pricked his ears about.

I'll let you know what it is you need to do, John Grady told him.

A hundred yards down the far side of the draw he smelled it again and he halted the horse. The horse stood waiting.

You wouldnt scout out a dead cow for me, would you? he said.

The horse stood. He put him forward again and they rode down another quarter mile or so and the horse settled into his gait such as it was and paid no more mind to the distant cattle. A little further on and he halted the horse and tested the air. He sat the horse. Then he turned and started back up the way they'd come.

He cut for sign and finally picked up the scent ripe and strong and in the dusk he dismounted and stood looking down at the flyblown carcass of a new calf that had been dragged into the center of a ring of creosote bush in broad open country. There'd been no rain in two weeks and the dragmarks were visible across the gravel and he walked out a ways on the backtrack looking for sand or dirt where there might be a foot track but he didnt find one. He came back and picked up the reins and mounted up and looked out at the surrounding countryside to mark the spot and then rode out and back down the draw.

HE AND BILLY STOOD over the dead calf and Billy walked back out following the dragmarks and stood looking over the country.

How far out did you go? he said.

Not far.

It's been a stout somethin to drag that big calf.

You think it's been a lion?

No. A lion'd of covered it up. Or tried to.

They mounted up and rode out on the backtrack. They lost the track on the hard ground and picked it up again. Billy followed the track over the gravels by raising or lowering his head and catching a certain angle of the light. He said that the disturbed ground had a different look and after a while John Grady could see it too. The day was cool. The horses were fresh with the morning and the weather and seemed unworried.

Range riders, said Billy.

Range riders.

Detectives.

Pinkertons.

The calf had been cut out and run down and killed in open country. Billy dismounted and walked over the ground. There was blood on the rocks, black from the sun.

You dont think it's just been coyotes? said John Grady.

I dont think so.

What do you think it's been?

I know what it's been.

What?

Dogs.

Dogs?

Yep.

I aint never seen any dogs out here.

I aint either. But they're here.

In the days that followed they found two more dead calves. They rode the Cedar Springs pasture and they crossed the floodplain below it and they rode the surrounding traprock bluffs and the mesa that ran east toward the old mine. They found tracks of the dogs but they did not see them. Before the week was out they'd found another freshkilled calf not dead a day.

There were some old Oneida number three doublespring traps on a shelf in the saddleroom and Billy boiled and waxed them and they carried them out the next day and buried three of them around the carcass. They rode out before daybreak to check the sets and when they got to the kill the traps were all dug out and lying on the ground. One of them was not even sprung. The carcass itself was little more than skin and bones.

I didnt know dogs were that smart, said John Grady.

I didnt either. They probably didnt know we were that dumb.

You ever trap dogs before?

No.

What do you want to do?

Billy picked up the unsprung trap and reached under the jaw and sprang it with his thumb. It chopped shut with a dead metal sound in the quiet morning air. He cut the wires and wired the rings together and hung the traps over the horn of his saddle and mounted up. He looked at John Grady.

We just aint found where they're usin is all. They might walk in a blind set.

You think Travis's dogs would run em?

Billy sat looking out at the long morning light on the rocks of the mesa. I dont know, he said. That's a pretty good question.

They took a packhorse and carried a kitchen box and their soogans out to the mesa and made camp. They sat drinking coffee from tin cups and watching the coals flare and lapse in the wind's fanning of them. Far out on the plain below the lights of the cities lay shimmering in their grids with the dark serpentine of the river dividing them.

I thought you had other business to attend to, Billy said.

I do.

You think it can wait.

I hope it can wait. I aint sure this can.

Well I'm glad you aint forgot all of your raising.

I aint forgot anything.

You're tired of me gettin on your ass though.

You're entitled.

They sipped their coffee. The wind blew. They pulled their blankets about their shoulders.

I aint jealous you know.

I never said you were.

I know. You might of thought it. Truth is, I wouldnt pull your boots on at gunpoint.

I know.

Billy lit a cigarette with a brand from the fire and laid the brand back. He smoked. It looks a lot better from up here than it does down there, dont it?

Yes. It does.

There's a lot of things look better at a distance.

Yeah?

I think so.

I guess there are. The life you've lived, for one.

Yeah. Maybe what of it you aint lived yet, too.

They stayed out Saturday and they rode the country under the rim Sunday morning and midday they found a freshkilled calf lying in a gravel wash out on the floodplain. The mother was standing looking at it and they hazed her away and she walked off bawling and stood and looked back.

Them old-time brocklefaces wouldnt of give up a calf that-away, Billy said. I'll bet they aint a mark on her.

I'll bet there aint either, said John Grady.

You aint good for nothin but to eat and shit, are you? Billy told the cow. The cow stared dully.

You know they're holed up in them rocks somewhere under the rim.

Yeah. I know it. But you'd have a hell of a time tryin to ride it and I sure aint goin to walk it.

John Grady looked down at the dead calf. He leaned and spat. What do you want to do?

Why dont we just pack up and ride back and call Travis and see what he says.

All right. If he'd come out this evenin we could lay for em.

Well he wont be comin out this evenin, I can tell you that.

Why is that?

Shit, said Billy. That old man wont hunt on a Sunday.

John Grady smiled. What if our ox was in the ditch?

He wouldnt give a damn if the whole outfit was in the ditch and you and me and Mac with it.

Maybe he'd just let us borrow the dogs.

He wouldnt do that. Anyways the dogs wont hunt on Sunday either. They're Christian dogs.

Christian dogs.

Yep. Raised that way.

As they rode out along the upper end of the floodplain they heard another cow bawl and they halted and sat their horses and scanned the country below them.

Do you see her? said Billy.

Yeah. Yonder she is.

Is it that same one?

No.

Billy leaned and spat. Well, he said. You know what that means. You want to ride down there?

I dont see what would be the use in it.

THEY SET OUT across the broad creosote flats of the valley in the darkness before dawn on Tuesday. Archer had a set of six dogboxes that fitted atop the bed of the Reo truck they drove and the truck groaned along in low gear and the headlights swung up and down in pale yellow fulcrums picking up the riders that went before them in the dark and the shapes of the creosote bushes and the red eyes of the horses where they turned their heads or crossed ahead of the truck. The dogs jostling in their boxes rode in silence and the riders smoked or talked quietly among themselves. Their hats low, the corduroy collars of their duckingjackets turned up. Riding slowly up the broad flat valley ahead of the truck.

The truck pulled up in a gravel fan at the head of the valley and the riders dismounted and dropped the reins on their horses and helped Travis and Archer unload the dogs and snap them onto the big harnessleather gangleads. The dogs backed and danced and whined and some raised their mouths and howled and the howls echoed off of the rimrock and back again and Travis halfhitched the first cast of dogs to the front bumper of the truck where their collective breath clouded whitely in the headlamps and the horses standing along the edge of the dark stamped and snorted and leaned to test the yellow lightbeams with their noses. They handed down the dogs by their collars from the boxes on the other side of the truck and leashed them up as well and the stars in the east began to dim out one by one.

They walked the dogs baying out along the gravel and Billy and John Grady rode below them and cut back and forth until they located the dead calf in the wash. It had been eaten to the bones and the bones had been dragged about over the ground. The ribcage lay with its curved tines upturned on the gravel plain like some great carnivorous plant brooding in the barren dawn.

They called out to the doghandlers and Travis called back to the others and they came down the wash with the big bluetick and treeing walker hounds lunging at their leads and slobbering and sucking at the air with their noses. When they fetched up at the remains of the calf they drew back and shied and sniffed the ground and looked at Travis.

Keep the horses back, called Travis. Let's give em a chance.

He set about unleashing the dogs and urging them on. They padded about snuffing at the ground and the dogs that Archer was bringing down began to howl and moan and Archer turned them loose and they came barreling down the draw.

Travis walked over to where Billy sat his horse. He stood with the leads braided up together and slung across his shoulder and listened.

What do you think? said Billy.

I dont know.

I'll bet them calfkillin sons of bitches aint been gone from here long.

I bet they aint either.

What do you think?

I dont know. If Smoke wont run em they aint goin to be run.

Is that your best dog?

No. But he's the dog for the job.

Why is that?

Cause he's run dogs before.

What did he think about it?

He never said.

The dogs were casting about in the dark, returning and setting out again.

It looks to me like they've left out of here in ever direction. How many are they up here do you reckon?

I dont know. Three or four.

I'll bet they's moren that.

You may be right.

Yonder he goes now.

One of the dogs had sorted out the track and set off baying. The others came tearing out of the creosote and within seconds all eight hounds were in full cry.

That sounds pretty hot on that dry ground, said Travis. Where's my horse at?

JC did have him but I think he's gone on.

You know where they're headed dont you?

Up towards them rocks under the mesa yonder I'd say.

Archer came leading Travis's horse by the bridlereins. Travis stepped up into the saddle and looked toward the east. It's about to get light enough to see.

There's goin to be one godawful dogfight up in them rocks.

I hear you. Let's go boys.

John Grady and JC were sitting their horses at the upper end of the wash when Archer and Travis and Billy rode up.

Where's Troy and Joaquín?

Done gone on.

Let's go.

You hear that?

What?

Listen.

From the rimrock of the far western edge of the floodplain beyond the cries of the trailing hounds they could hear short chopping barks, a balesome howling.

Them ignorant sons of bitches is answerin back, said Billy.

I guess they want to be in on the race, Archer said. Dumb sumbucks dont know they are the race.

By the time they reached the foot of the stone palisades the hounds had already driven the dogs out of the rocks and they could hear them in a running fight and then a long howling chase up through the broken scree and boulders. It was by now gray light and they trotted the horses singlefile along the base of the cliffs, following a trail that wound among the fallen traprock. Travis put his horse alongside John Grady. He reached and put his hand on the horse's neck and John Grady slowed.

Listen, said Travis.

They halted and sat the horses and listened. Billy rode up.

Build your loops, boys, Travis said.

Think you all can see to rope?

We're fixin to find out.

They pulled the ties on their catchropes. Let's dont get in a hurry, said Travis. They're fixin to break out up here. Let em get out in the clear. Be careful now. Let's not rope our own dogs.

They ran their loops and nudged their horses forward.

Keep em small, said Travis. Keep em small. They'll go through one like a dose of salts through a cat.

The hounds' cries were suddenly just above them where the trail turned and angled up behind some large fallen boulders. They saw three shapes leaping from rock to rock. Then two more. John Grady was riding Watson's blue dun horse and he put his heels to the horse's ribs and the horse squatted and bolted. Billy was right behind him.

The trailing hounds came out of the rocks above them in full cry and John Grady reined off to the right. Both he and Billy were sitting up high in the saddle in an effort to see the running dogs. When they came out onto the upper trail John Grady looked back. Billy was whipping over and under with the small toy loop of his catchrope. A hundred feet behind him among the rocks several of Travis's appaloosa-colored dogs were coming hard. He leaned low over the horse's neck to talk it on and then raised up again to see. Three yellowlooking dogs were loping dead ahead in tandem before him up a long gravel wash. He leaned and spoke again to the horse but the horse had already seen them. He glanced back to check for Billy and when he looked ahead again the hindmost dog had broken away from the other two. He put the horse down the slope and went pounding out over the flat after it.

The loop being so small had no weight to it and he doubled it and swung it over his head and then caught it and doubled it again. When the horse saw the rope loft past its left ear it laid back its ears and came hauling down upon the running cur with its mouth open like some terrible vengeance.

The dog had no experience as quarry. It did not check or swerve but ran on and John Grady cranked the loop and leaned over the pommel of the saddle. He looked for the dog to cut back but the dog seemed to think it could outrun the horse. The coiled rope sailed out and the loop swiveled out of its turnings. The dun horse tossed up its head and set its forefeet in the gravel and squatted and John Grady dallied the home end of the rope about the polished leather of the pommel and the rope popped taut and the dog snapped into the air mutely. It cartwheeled soundlessly and landed on the gravel with a soft dead whump.

By now three more dogs had started across the plain with Travis and Joaquín after them. They passed a hundred feet out riding hard and John Grady punched the dun forward and set out after them with the yellow dog bouncing behind over the rocks and through the creosote at the end of the thirty-five foot maguey rope. Other hounds and riders had come out of the rocks to the west and were lined out upon the floodplain and he rode on dragging the dog a ways and then hauled the horse up short and jumped down and ran back to get his rope off of the dog. The dog was limp and bloody and it lay in the gravels grinning with its eyes half started from their sockets. He stood on it with his boot and pulled off the loop and trotted back to the waiting horse coiling the rope as he went.

By this time it was good daylight and there were already four riders out on the plain before him riding in a long sweep and he mounted up and slung the coiled rope over his shoulder and set out after them at a handgallop.

When he passed Joaquín the Mexican shouted something after him but he couldnt hear what it was. He quirted the horse on with the loop end of the rope, following Travis and JC and Travis's hounds. He almost ran over one of the outlaw dogs. It had crawled up and hidden in a clump of greasewood and he would have ridden past it had it not lost its nerve at the last moment and bolted. He reined the horse around so hard he nearly lost a stirrup. Billy came up on his right and passed him and the dog cut back and tried to cross in front of his horse and as it did so Billy rode it down and leaned and roped it and the horse squatted and slid to a stop in a boil of dust and the dog went sailing and bounced and skidded and then scrambled up and stood looking about. Billy turned his horse and pulled the dog down but it got up again and began to run at the end of the rope. When John Grady went past the dog was standing and twisting and pawing at the rope but Billy put his heels to the horse and the dog was snatched away. Out on the floodplain Joaquín was sawing his horse about and whooping and the dogs were scattered and baying and fighting. Travis rode up swinging his loop and John Grady reined to one side but the dog he was after cut in front of the horse and suddenly appeared in front of him. He put the horse after it and the dog tried to cut back but he swung his loop and dallied and reined the horse to the right. The dog spun in the air and landed and rose running and turned and was snatched up again. John Grady spurred the dun forward and the dog went bouncing and slamming mutely in a wide arc and then went dragging through the brush and gravel behind him.

He came back trailing the empty rope, paying it up and recoiling it as he rode. Travis and Joaquín and Billy were sitting the horses and letting them blow. The second cast of hounds were now tracking the dogs along the lower end of the floodplain, running them down among the boulders and scree and fighting and going on again. Joaquín was grinning.

I hogged your all's dog, I reckon, John Grady said.

Plenty of dogs, Joaquín said.

Watch JC, Billy said. Watch him now. He looks like he's fightin bees.

How many of these damn dogs are there?

I dont know. Archer started up a whole other bunch yonder where that big wash comes out.

Have they caught any?

I dont think so. Troy's afoot up in them rocks.

Two hounds appeared out of the chaparral and circled and sniffed the ground and stood uncertainly.

Hyeah, called Travis. Hunt em up.

Well pardner if your horse aint bottomed out completely why dont we ride on down there where the fun's at?

Billy booted his horse forward. You aint waitin on me, he said.

You all go on, said Travis. I'll catch you up.

Dogropers, called Billy. I knew it'd come to this.

Joaquín grinned and pressed his horse into a lope and raised one fist over his head. Adelante, muchachos, he called.

Perreros.

Tonteros.

Travis watched them go. He shook his head and leaned and spat and turned his horse to ride up toward where he'd last seen Archer.

Where they came up off the desert parkland there were great boulders fallen from the mesa above and they rode up the slope among them until John Grady halted his horse and held up his hand. They stopped to listen. John Grady stood in the saddle and scanned the slope above them. Billy rode up.

I think they're headed up towards the top of the mesa.

I do too.

Can they get up there?

I dont know. Probably. They seem to think so.

Can you see them?

No. There was one big yellow son of a bitch and another kindly spotted one. There may be three or four of em.

I guess they've thrown the dogs, aint they?

It looks like it.

You think we can get up there?

I think I might know a way.

Billy squinted up at the stone ramparts. He leaned and spat. I'd hate to get a horse half way up that draw and not be able to go either way.

So would I.

Plus I dont know how much good we're goin to do runnin these varmints without dogs. Do you?

We just need to get up there before they get gone. It's pretty open country up on top.

Well, lead on then.

All right.

Let's not get in too big a hurry.

All right.

Let's just cover the ground in front of us. Let's not get in a jackpot up here.

All right.

He followed John Grady back down the way they'd come and they rode for the better part of a mile and then turned up along the wash. The way grew steep, the path more narrow. They dismounted and led the horses. They crossed gray bands of midden soil from ancient campsites washed down out of the arroyo that carried bits of bone and pottery and they passed under pictographs upon the rimland boulders that bore images of hunter and shaman and meetingfires and desert sheep all picked into the rock a thousand years and more. They passed beneath a band of dancers holding hands like paper figures scissored out by children and stenciled on the stone. Under the caprock was a running shelf and they turned and looked back down over the floodplain and the desert. Troy was riding out toward Travis and JC and Archer and they were crossing toward the truck with most of the dogs in tow. They couldnt see Joaquín anywhere. In the distance they could see the highway through a gap in the low hills fifteen miles away. The horses stood blowing.

Where to now, cowboy? said Billy.

John Grady nodded toward the country above them and set out again leading the horse.

The shelf narrowed upward to a break in the strata of the rock and they led the horses into a defile so narrow that Billy's horse balked and would not follow. It backed and jerked at the bridlereins and skittered dangerously on the shales. Billy looked up the narrow passageway. The sheer rock walls rose up into the blue sky.

Bud are you real sure about this?

John Grady had dropped the reins on the blue horse and he peeled out of his jacket and made his way back to Billy.

Take my horse, he said.

What?

Take my horse. Or Watson's. He's been through here before.

He took the reins from Billy and calmed the horse and tied the jacket by the sleeves over the horse's eyes, leaning against the animal with his whole body. Billy worked his way up to where the dun horse stood and took up the reins and led it on up through the rocks, the horse scrabbling in the shale, the loose spurs clinking off the stone. At the top of the defile the horses lunged and clambered up and out onto the mesa and stood trembling and blowing. John Grady pulled the jacket off the horse's head and the horse blew and looked about. A mile away on the mesa three of the dogs were loping and looking back.

You want to ride that good horse? said John Grady.

Let me ride this good horse.

Well yonder they go.

They set off across the open tableland with their ropes popping and loud cries, leaning low in the saddle, riding neck and neck. In a mile they'd halved the dogs' lead. The dogs kept to the mesa and the mesa widened before them. If they'd kept to the rim they might have found a place to go down again where the horses could not follow but they seemed to think they could outrun anything that cared to follow and run they did, two of them side by side and the third behind, their long dogshadows beside them in the sun racing brokenly over the sparse taupe grass of the tableland.

Billy overhauled them on the dun horse before they could separate and leaned and roped the hindmost dog. He didnt even dally the rope but just caught two turns about his wrist and gave a yank and snatched the dog from the ground and rode on dragging it behind the horse with the rope in one hand.

He overtook the dogs again and rode past so as to head them. The running dogs looked up, their eyes lost, their tongues lolling. Their dead companion came sliding up beside them at the end of the trailing rope. Billy looked back and reined the horse to the right and dragged the dead dog in front of them and headed them in a long running arc. John Grady was coming hard across the mesa and Billy brought the dun horse to a halt in a series of hops and jumped down and freed his noose from the dog and rewound it on the run and mounted up again.

He reached the dogs first and snapped his loop around the big yellow dog in the lead. The speckled dog cut back almost under the horse's legs and headed toward the rim. The yellow dog rolled and bounced and got up again and continued running with the noose about its neck. John Grady came riding up behind Billy and swung his rope and heeled the yellow dog and quirted the horse on with the doubled rope end and then dallied. The slack of Billy's catchrope hissed along the ground and stopped and the big yellow dog rose suddenly from the ground in headlong flight taut between the two ropes and the ropes resonated a single brief dull note and then the dog exploded.

The sun was not an hour up and in the flat traverse of the light on the mesa the blood that burst in the air before them was as bright and unexpected as an apparition. Something evoked out of nothing and wholly unaccountable. The dog's head went cartwheeling, the ropes recoiled in the air, the dog's body slammed to the ground with a dull thud.

Goddamn, said Billy.

There was a long whoop from down the mesa. Joaquín was riding toward them with three of the blueticks. He'd seen them heel and head the dog and he waved his hat laughing. The hounds loped beside the horse. They still hadnt seen the spotted dog making for the rim of the mesa.

Ayeee muchachos, called Joaquín. He whooped and laughed

and leaned and hazed his hat at the heeling dogs.

Damn, said Billy. I didnt know you was goin to do that.

I didnt either.

Son of a bitch. He hauled his rope toward him, coiling it as it came. John Grady rode out to where the dog's headless body lay in the bloodstained grass and dismounted and freed his rope from the animal's hindquarters and mounted up again. The hounds came up circling the carcass and sniffing at the blood with their hackles up. One of them circled John Grady's horse and then backed and stood baying him but he paid it no mind. He coiled his rope and turned and dug his heels into the horse's flanks and set out across the mesa after the lone remaining dog. Joaquín by now had also seen the dog and he came riding after it, quirting his horse with the doubled rope and shouting to the dogs. Billy sat watching them go. He coiled the rope and tied it and wiped the blood from his hands on the leg of his jeans and then sat watching the race head out along the edge of the mesa. The spotted dog seemed to see no way down from the table-land and it looked to be tiring as it loped along the rim. When it heard the hounds it turned upcountry again and crossed behind Joaquín and Joaquín brought his horse around and in a flat race overtook it and roped it in less than a mile of ground. Billy rode out to the rimrock and dismounted and lit a cigarette and sat looking out over the country to the south.

They came riding back across the mesa with the hounds at the horses' heels. Joaquín trailed the dead dog through the grass at the end of his rope. The dog was bloody and half raw and its eyes were glazed and its lolling tongue was stuck with chaff and grass. They rode up to the rimrock and Joaquín dismounted and retrieved his rope from the dead dog.

Got some pups here somewhere, he said.

Billy walked up and stood looking at the dog. It was a bitch with swollen teats. He walked over and got his horse and mounted up and looked back at John Grady.

Let's take that long way back. Crawlin through them rocks gives me the fidgets.

John Grady had taken off his hat and set it in the fork of the saddle before him. His face was streaked with blood and there was blood on his shirt. He passed the back of his sleeve across his forehead and picked up his hat and put it on again. That's all right by me, he said. Joaquín?

Sure, said Joaquín. He eyed the sun. We'll be back for dinner.

You think we got em all?

Hard to say.

I'd say we broke a few of em of their habits.

I'd say we did too.

How many of Archer's dogs come up here with you?

Three.

Well we aint got but two.

They turned in their saddles and scanned the mesa.

Where do you reckon he's got to?

I dont know, said Joaquín.

He could of gone down the far side yonder.

Joaquín leaned and spat and turned his horse. Let's go, he said. He could be anywheres. There's always one that dont want to go home.

IT WAS STILL DARK in the morning when John Grady woke him. He groaned and turned and put the pillow over his head.

Wake up, cowboy.

What the hell time is it?

Five-thirty.

What's wrong with you?

You want to see if we can find them dogs?

Dogs? What dogs? What the hell are you talkin about?

Them pups.

Shit, said Billy.

John Grady sat in the doorway and propped one boot against the frame. Billy? he said.

What, damn it.

We could ride up there and take a look around.

He rolled over and looked at John Grady sitting sideways in the door in the dark. You're makin me completely crazy, he said.

Cut for sign. I guarantee you we could find em.

You couldnt find em.

We could get a couple of dogs from Travis.

Travis wont loan his dogs. We done been through all that.

I know about where that den's at.

Why wont you let me sleep?

We could be back by dinnertime. I guarantee you.

I'm beggin you to leave me alone, son. Beggin you. I dont want to have to shoot you. I'd never hear the end of it from Mac.

Where the dogs struck that first time just below that big slide of gravel? I'll bet we rode within fifty feet of that den. You know they're in those big rocks.

THEY RODE OUT carrying across the pommels of their saddles a longhanded spade, a mattock, a fourfoot iron prybar. Socorro had come to her door in wrapper and hairpapers while they were finding something to eat and shooed them to the table while she cooked eggs and sausage and made coffee. She packed their lunch while they ate.

Billy looked out the window to where the horses stood saddled at the kitchen door. Let's eat and get gone, he said. And do not tell her where we're goin.

All right.

I dont want to have to listen to it.

They crossed into the Valenciana pasture before the sun was up and rode past the old well. The cattle moved off before them in the gray half-light. Billy rode with the spade over his shoulder. I'll tell you one thing, he said.

What's that.

There's places up in them rocks where if they are denned you damn sure wont dig em out.

Yeah. I know it.

When they reached the trail along the western edge of the floodplain the sun was up behind the mesa and the light that overshot the plain crossed to the rocks above them so that they rode out the remnant night in a deep blue sink with the new day falling slowly down about them. They rode to the upper end and came back slowly, Billy in the lead studying the ground at either side of the horse, leaning with his forearm across the horse's withers.

Are you a tracker? said John Grady.

I'm a trackin fool. I can track lowflyin birds.

What do you see?

Not a damn thing.

The sun came down the rocks and over the broken ground toward them. They sat the horses.

They been runnin these cowtracks, Billy said. Or did run. I dont think they were all denned together. I think there was two separate bunches.

That could be.

Any close place like that right yonder?

Yeah?

There's doghair on ever rock. Let's just circle up here and keep our eyes open.

They came back up the valley close under the wall among the boulders and scree. They circled among the rocks and studied the ground. It was weeks since the last rain and what dogtracks had been printed in the clay trails below them had long since been trodden out by the cattle and in the dry ground the dogs made no track at all.

Let's go back up here, said Billy.

They rode along the upper slope close under the rock bluffs. They crossed the gravel slide and rode under the old shamans and the ledgerless arcana inscribed upon those outsize tablets.

I know where they're at, Billy said.

He turned the horse on the narrow trail and rode back down through the rocks. John Grady followed. Billy halted and dropped the reins and stood down. He passed afoot through a narrow place in the rocks and then he came back out again and pointed down the hill.

They've come in here from three sides, he said. Down yonder the cows have come right up to the rocks but they cant get in. See that tall grass?

I see it.

Reason it's tall is the cows couldnt get in there to eat it.

John Grady dismounted and followed him into the rocks. They walked up and back and they studied the ground. The horses stood looking in.

Let's just set a while, said Billy.

They sat. Within the rocks it was cool. The ground was cold. Billy smoked.

I hear em, John Grady said.

I do too.

They rose and stood listening. The mewling stopped. Then it began again.

The den was in a corner of the rocks and it angled back under a boulder. They lay on their bellies in the grass and listened.

I can smell em, Billy said.

I can too.

They listened.

How are we goin to get em out?

Billy looked at him. You aint, he said.

Maybe they'll come out.

What for?

We could get some milk and set it out for them.

I dont think they'll come out. Listen at how young they are. I'll bet their eyes aint open. What do you want with em anyway? he said.

I dont know. I hate leavin em down there.

We might could twist em out. Get a ocotillo long enough.

John Grady lay peering into the darkness under the rock. Let me have your cigarette, he said.

Billy handed it across.

There's another entrance, John Grady said. There's air blowin out of this one. See the smoke?

Billy reached and took the cigarette. Yeah, he said. But the den is still under that rock and the rock's the size of Mac's kitchen.

A kid could crawl down in there.

Where you goin to get a kid at? And suppose he got stuck down in there?

You could tie a rope to his legs.

They'd tie one to your neck if anything happened to him. Let me have your knife.

John Grady handed him his pocketknife and he rose and went off and after a while he came back with an ocotillo branch. It was a good ten feet long and he sat and trimmed the thorns off the lower couple of feet for a handhold and then they lay and took turns for the next half hour with the ocotillo down in the hole turning it in an effort to twist up the fur of the pups in the thorns.

We dont even know if this is long enough, Billy said.

I think what it is is that the hole's too big down there. You'd have to run the end of it underneath them some way to do any good and that would just be luck.

I aint heard one of em squeal for a while.

They might of moved back in a corner or somethin.

Billy sat up and pulled the ocotillo out of the hole and examined the end of it.

Is there any hair on it?

Yeah. Some. But there probably aint no shortage of hair down there.

What do you think that rock weighs?

Shit, said Billy.

All we'd have to do is tip it over.

I'll bet that damn rock weighs five tons. How in the hell are you goin to tip it over?

I dont believe it would be all that hard.

And where you goin to tip it to?

We could tip it this way.

Then it'd be layin over the hole.

So what? The pups are at the back.

What makes you so bullheaded? You cant get the horses in here and if you could they'd pull the damn rock over on top of theirselves.

They wouldnt have to be in here. They could be outside.

The ropes wont reach.

They will if we tie em end to end.

They still wont. It'd take near one just to go around the rock.

I think I can make it reach.

You got a ropestretcher in your saddlebags? Anyway, no two horses could tip that rock over.

They could with some leverage.

Bullheaded, Billy said. Worst case I believe I ever saw.

There's some fairsized saplin trees at the upper end of the wash. If we could cut one of em with the mattock we could use it for a prypole. Then we could tie the rope to the end of it and that would save havin to tie it around the rock. We'd be killin two birds with one stone.

Two horses and two cowboys is more like it.

We should of brought a axe.

You let me know when you're ready to go back. I'm goin to see if I can catch me a little nap.

All right.

John Grady rode up to the wash with the mattock across the saddle in front of him. Billy stretched out and crossed his boots one over the top of the other and pulled his hat over his face. It was totally silent in the basin. No wind, no bird. No call of cattle. He was almost asleep when he heard the first dull chock of the mattock blade. He smiled into the darkness of his hatcrown and slept.

When John Grady came back he was dragging behind the horse a cottonwood sapling he'd topped out and limbed. It was about eighteen feet long and close to six inches in diameter at the base and the weight of it hanging by the loop of rope from the saddlehorn was pulling his saddle over. He rode half standing in the offside stirrup with his left leg hanging over the sapling trunk and the horse was walking on eggshells. When he reached the rocks he stepped down and unlooped the rope and let the pole down on the ground and walked in and kicked Billy's bootsole.

Wake up and piss, he said. The world's on fire.

Let the son of a bitch burn.

Come on and give me a hand.

Billy shoved the hat back from his face and looked up. All right, he said.

They tied John Grady's catchrope to the end of the pole and stood it up behind the rock and made a cairn of rocks to bridge between the butt of it and the next ledge of rock up the slope. Then John Grady joined the home ends of the two reatas with a running splice and looped a broad Y in the end of Billy's rope that would afford loops for both pommels. They stood the horses side by side and dropped the loops over the horns and looked up at the rope bellying down from the end of the pole and they looked at each other and then they untracted the horses and walked them forward by the cheekstraps. The rope stretched taut. The pole bowed. They talked the horses forward and the horses leaned into their work. Billy looked up at the rope. If that sumbuck breaks, he said, we're goin to be huntin a hole.

The pole sawed suddenly sideways and stopped again and stood quivering.

Shit, said Billy.

I hear you. If that thing comes out of there you'll be huntin more than a hole.

We'll be huntin a undertaker.

What do you want to do?

It's your show, cowboy.

John Grady walked around and checked the pole and came back. Let's head the horses a little bit more to the left, he said.

All right.

They eased the horses forward. The rope stretched and began to unwind slowly on its axis. They looked at the rope and they looked at the horses. They looked at each other. Then the rock moved. It began to rear haltingly up out of its resting place these thousand years and it tilted and tottered and fell forward into the little grotto with a thud they could feel through their bootsoles. The pole clattered among the rocks, the horses recovered and stood.

Kiss my ass, said Billy.

They set to digging in the bare sunless earth that the rock had vacated and in twenty minutes they'd uncovered the den. The pups were back in the farthest corner huddled in a pile. John Grady lay on his stomach and reached down and back and brought one out and held it to the light. It just filled the palm of his hand and it was fat and it swung its small muzzle about and whined and blinked its pale blue eyes.

Hold him.

How many are they?

I dont know.

He ran his arm down the hole again and reached back and brought out another. Billy sat and piled the dogs together in the crook of his knee as they came. There were four of them. I'll bet these little shits are hungry, he said. Is that all of em?

John Grady lay with his cheek in the dirt. I think that's them, he said.

The dogs were trying to hide under Billy's knee. He held one up by its small nape. It hung like a sock, glaring bleakly at the world with its watery eyes.

Listen a minute, said John Grady.

They sat listening.

There's anothern.

He ran his arm down the hole and lay on the ground feeling

about in the dark beneath them. He closed his eyes. I got him, he said.

The dog he brought up was dead.

Yonder's your runt, Billy said.

The little dog was curled and stiff, its paws before its face. He put it down and pushed his shoulder deeper into the hole.

Can you find him?

No.

Billy stood. Let me try, he said. My arm's longern yours.

All right.

Billy lay in the dirt and ran his arm down into the hole. Come here you little turd, he said.

Have you got him?

Yeah. Damn if I dont think he's offerin to bite me.

The dog came up mewling and twisting in his hand.

This aint no runt, he said.

Let me see him.

He's fat as a butterball.

John Grady took the little dog and held it in his cupped hand.

Wonder what was he doin off back there by himself?

Maybe he was with the one that died.

John Grady held the dog up and looked into its small wrinkled face. I think I got me a dog, he said.

HE WORKED all through the month of December at the cabin. He carried tools horseback up the Bell Springs trail and he left a mattock and a spade beside the road and worked on the roadway by hand in the evenings when it was cool, filling the washes and cutting brush and ditching and filling in the gullies and squatting and eyeing the terrain for the way the water would run. In three weeks' time he had the worst of the trash hauled or burned and he had painted the stove and patched the roof and driven the truck for the first time up the old road all the way to the cabin with the new lengths of blue sheetmetal stovepipe in the truckbed and the cans of paint and whitewash and new pine shelving for the kitchen.

At the wreckingyard out on Alameda he went up and down the aisles of old stacked windowsash with a steel tape measuring by height and width and checking figures against those he'd jotted on the notepad in his shirtpocket. He dragged the windows he wanted out into the aisle and got the truck and backed it to the door and he and the yardman loaded the windows in the truck. The man sold him some panes of glass to replace the broken ones and showed him how to score and break them with a glasscutter and then gave him the glasscutter.

He bought an old Mennonite kitchen table made of pine and the man helped him carry it out and set it in the bed of the truck and the man told him to take the drawer out and stand it in the bed.

You go around a curve it'll come out of there.

Yessir.

Liable to go plumb overboard.

Yessir.

And take that glass and put it up there in the cab with you if you dont want it broke.

All right.

I'll see you.

Yessir.

He worked long into the nights and he'd come in and unsaddle the horse and brush it in the partial darkness of the barn bay and walk across to the kitchen and get his supper out of the warmer and sit and eat alone at the table by the shaded light of the lamp and listen to the faultless chronicling of the ancient clockworks in the hallway and the ancient silence of the desert in the darkness about. There were times he'd fall asleep in the chair and wake at some strange hour and stagger up and cross the yard to the barn and get the pup and take it and put it in its box on the floor beside his bunk and lie face down with his arm over the side of the bunk and his hand in the box so that it would not cry and then fall asleep in his clothes.

Christmas came and went. In the afternoon of the first Sunday in January Billy rode up and crossed the little creek and alloed the house and stood down. John Grady came to the door.

What are you doin? Billy said.

Paintin windowsash.

Billy nodded. He looked about. You aint goin to ask me in?

John Grady passed his sleeve along the side of his nose. He had a paintbrush in one hand and his hands were blue. I didnt know I had to, he said. Come on in.

Billy came in and stood. He took a cigarette from his pocket and lit it and looked around. He walked into the other room and he came back. The adobe brick walls had been whitewashed and the inside of the little house was bright and monastically austere. The clay floors were swept and slaked and he'd beaten them down with a homemade maul contrived from a fencepost with a section of board nailed to the bottom.

The old place dont look half bad. You aim to get you a santo to put in the corner yonder?

I might.

Billy nodded.

I'll take all the help I can get, John Grady said.

I hear you, said Billy. He looked at the bright blue of the sash of the windows. Did they not have any blue paint? he said.

They said this was about as close as they could get.

You fixin to paint the door the same color?

Yep.

You got another brush?

Yeah. I got one.

Billy took off his hat and hung it on one of the pegs by the door. Well, he said. Where's it at?

John Grady poured paint from his paintcan into an empty one and Billy squatted on one knee and stirred the brush into the paint. He passed the flat of the brush carefully across the rim of the can and painted a bright blue band down the center stile. He looked across his shoulder.

How come you to have a extra brush?

Just in case some fool showed up wantin to paint, I reckon.

They quit before dark. A cool wind was coming down from the gap in the Jarillas. They stood by the truck and Billy smoked and they watched the running fire deepening to darkness over the mountains to the west.

It's goin to be cold up here in the wintertime, pardner, Billy said.

I know it.

Cold and lonely.

It wont be lonely.

I'm talkin about her.

Mac says she can come down and work with Socorro whenever she wants.

Well that's good. I dont expect there'll be a lot of empty chairs at the table on them days.

John Grady smiled. I expect you're right.

When have you seen her?

Not for a while.

How long a while?

I dont know. Three weeks.

Billy shook his head.

She's still there, John Grady said.

You got a lot of confidence in her.

Yes I do.

What do you think is goin to happen when her and Socorro get their heads together?

She dont tell everthing she knows.

Her or Socorro?

Either one.

I hope you're right.

They aint goin to run her off, Billy. There's more to her than just she's good lookin.

Billy flipped the cigarette out across the yard. We better get on back.

You can take the truck if you want.

That's all right.

Go on. I'll ride that old crowbait of yours.

Billy nodded. Ride him blind through the brush tryin to beat me back. Get him snakebit and I dont know what all.

Go on. I'll ride behind the truck.

Horse like that it takes a special hand to ride him in the dark.

I'll bet it does.

A rider that can instill confidence in a animal.

John Grady smiled and shook his head.

A rider that's accustomed to the ways and the needs of the nighthorse. Ride the bedgrounds slow. Ride left to right. Sing to them snuffies. Dont pop no matches.

I hear you.

Did your grandaddy used to talk about goin up the trail?

Some. Yeah.

You think you'll ever go back to that country?

I doubt it.

You will. One of these days. Or I say you will. If you live.

You want to take the truck back?

Naw. Go on. I'll be along.

All right.

Dont eat my dessert.

All right. I appreciate you comin up.

I didnt have nothin else to do.

Well.

If I had I'd of done it.

I'll see you at the house.

See you at the house.

JOSEFINA WAS STANDING in the door watching. In the room the criada turned, one hand lofting the weight of the girl's dark hair for her to see.

Bueno, said Josefina. Muy bonita.

The criada smiled thinly, her mouth bristling with hairpins. Josefina looked back down the hall and then leaned in the door.

Él viene, she whispered. Then she turned and padded away down the corridor. The criada turned the girl quickly and studied her and touched her hair and stood back. She passed her thumb across her lips gathering the pins. Eres la china poblana perfecta, she said. Perfecta.

Es bella la china poblana? the girl said.

The criada arched her brows in surprise. The wrinkled lid fluttered over the pale blind eye. Sí, she said. Sí. Por supuesto. Todo el mundo lo sabe.

Eduardo stood in the doorway. The criada saw the girl's eyes and turned. He jerked his chin at her and she went to the dresser and laid down the hairbrush and put the pins in a china tray and went past him and out the door.

He came in and shut the door behind him. The girl stood quietly in the center of the room.

Voltéate, he said. He made a stirring motion with his forefinger.

She turned.

Ven aquí.

She came slowly forward and stood. He took her jaw in the palm of his hand and raised her face and looked into her painted eyes. When she lowered it again he put his hand into the gathered hair at her neck and pulled her head back. She turned her eyes up toward the ceiling. Her pale throat exposed. The visible bloodpulse in the thick arteries at either side of her neck and the small tic at the corner of her mouth. He told her to look at him and she did but she seemed to have power to cause those dark and hooded eyes of hers to go opaque. So that the visible depth in them was lost or shrouded. So that they hid the world within. He recaught his grip in her hair and the smooth skin tautened over her cheekbones and her eyes widened. He commanded again that she look at him but she was already looking at him and she did not answer.

A quién le rezas? he hissed.

A Dios.

Quién responde?

Nadie.

Nadie, he said.

That night she felt the cold pneuma come upon her as she lay naked in the bed. She turned and called to the cliente standing in the room.

I'm bein as quick as I can, he said.

By the time he'd slid into the bed beside her she'd cried out and gone rigid and her eyes white. In the muted light he could not see her but he placed his hand on her body and felt her bowed and trembling under his palm and taut as a snaredrum. He felt the tremor of her like the hum of a current running in her bones.

What is it? he said. What is it?

He came out into the hallway half dressed and pulling on his clothes. Tiburcio appeared from nowhere. He pushed the man aside and knelt in the girl's bed and unbuckled his belt and whipped it from about his waist and caught it and folded it and seized the girl's jaw and forced the leather between her teeth. The cliente watched from the doorway. I didnt do nothin, he said. I never even touched her.

Tiburcio rose and strode toward the door.

She just went that way, the cliente said.

Speak to no one, Tiburcio said. You understand me?

You got it, old buddy. Just you let me get my shoes.

The alcahuete shut the door after him. The girl was breathing harshly through the belt. He sat and pulled back the covers. He studied her without expression. He bent over her slightly in his black silk. The soft false whisper of it. A morbid voyeur, a mortician. An incubus of uncertain proclivity or perhaps just a dark dandy happened in from off the neon streets who aped imperfectly with his pale and tapered hands those ministrations of the healing arts that he had seen or heard of or as he imagined them to be. What are you? he said. You are nothing.

* * *

WHEN HE STEPPED OUT onto the porch and let the screen-door to behind him Mr Johnson was sitting on the edge of the porch with his elbows propped on his knees watching the sunset where it deepened and flared over the Franklins to the west. Distant flocks of geese were moving downriver along the jornada. They looked no more than bits of string against the raucous red of the sky and they were far too distant to be heard.

Where are you off to? said the old man.

John Grady walked to the edge of the porch and stood picking his teeth and looking out across the country along with him. What makes you think I'm off to somewhere?

Hair all slicked back like a muskrat. Boots.

He sat on the boards beside the old man. Goin to town, he said.

The old man nodded. Well, he said. I reckon it's still there.

Yessir.

You couldnt prove it by me.

When was the last time you were in El Paso?

I dont know. Been a year, I'd say. Maybe longer.

You dont get tired bein out here all the time?

I do. At times.

You dont ever want to make a run in to sort of see what's goin on?

I dont believe it would help. I dont believe there's anything goin on.

Did you used to go over to Juárez?

Yes I did. Back when I was a drinkin man. The last time I was in Juárez Mexico was in nineteen and twenty-nine. I seen a man shot in a bar. He was standin at the bar drinkin a beer and this man come in and walked up behind him and pulled a government forty-five out of his belt and shot him in the back of the head with it. Stuck the gun back in his breeches and turned and walked out again. He wasnt even in a hurry about it.

Shot him dead?

Yes. He was dead standin there. Thing I remember is how quick he fell down. Just dead weight. The movies dont ever get that part right neither.

Where were you?

I was standin almost next to him. I seen it in the bar mirror. I'm partially deaf to this day in this one ear on account of it. His head just damn near come off. Blood everwhere. Brains. I had on a brand new Stradivarius gabardine shirt and a pretty good Stetson hat and I burned everthing I had on save the boots. I bet I took nine baths handrunnin.

He looked out across the country to the west where the sky was darkening. Tales of the old west, he said.

Yessir.

Lot of people shot and killed.

Why were they?

Mr Johnson passed the tips of his fingers across his jaw. Well, he said. I think these people mostly come from Tennessee and Kentucky. Edgefield district in South Carolina. Southern Missouri. They were mountain people. They come from mountain people in the old country. They always would shoot you. It wasnt just here. They kept comin west and about the time they got here was about the time Sam Colt invented the sixshooter and it was the first time these people could afford a gun you could carry around in your belt. That's all there ever was to it. It had nothin to do with the country at all. The west. They'd of been the same it dont matter where they might of wound up. I've thought about it and that's the only conclusion I could ever come to.

How bad of a drinkin man did you used to be, Mr Johnson? If you dont care for me to ask.

Pretty bad. Maybe not as bad as some might like to remember it. But it was more than a passin acquaintance.

Yessir.

You can ask whatever you want.

Yessir.

You get my age you kindly get weaned off standin on ceremony. I think it embarrasses Mac at times. But dont worry about askin me stuff.

Yessir. Was that when you quit drinkin?

No. I was more dedicated than that. I quit and took it up again. Quit and took it up. Finally got around to quittin all together. Maybe I just got too old for it. There wasnt any virtue in it.

The drinkin or the quittin?

Either one. There aint no virtue in quittin what you aint able any longer to do in the first place. That's pretty, aint it.

He nodded toward the sunset. Deep laminar red. The cool of the coming dark was in it and it was all around them.

Yessir, said John Grady. It is.

The old man took his cigarettes from his shirtpocket. John Grady smiled. I see you aint quit smokin, he said.

I intend to be buried with a pack in my pocket.

You think you'll need em on the other side?

Not really. A man can hope though.

He watched the sky. Where do bats go in the wintertime? They got to eat.

I think maybe they migrate.

I hope so.

Do you think I ought to get married?

Hell, son. How would I know?

You never did.

That dont mean I didnt try.

What happened?

She wouldnt have me.

Why not?

I was too broke for her. Or maybe for her daddy. I dont know.

What happened to her?

It was a peculiar thing. She went on and married another old boy and she died in childbirth. It was not uncommon in them days. She was a awful pretty girl. Woman. I dont think she'd turned twenty. I think about her yet.

The last of the colors died in the west. The sky was dark and blue. Then just dark. The kitchen windowlights lay across the porch boards beside them where they sat.

I miss knowin whatever become of certain people. Where they're livin at and how they're gettin on or where they died at if they did die. I think about old Bill Reed. Sometimes I'll say to myself, I'll say: I wonder whatever happened to old Bill Reed? I dont reckon I'll ever know. Me and him was good friends, too.

What else?

What else what?

What else do you miss?

The old man shook his head. You dont want to get me started.

A lot?

Not all of it. I dont miss pullin a tooth with a pair of shoein tongs and nothin but cold wellwater to numb it. But I miss the old range life. I went up the trail four times. Best times of my life. The best. Bein out. Seein new country. There's nothin like it in the world. There never will be. Settin around the fire of the evenin with the herd bedded down good and no wind. Get you some coffee. Listen to the old waddies tell their stories. Good stories, too. Roll you a smoke. Sleep. There's no sleep like it. None.

He flipped the cigarette out into the dark. Socorro opened the door and looked out. Mr Johnson, she said, you ought to come in. It is too cold for you.

I'll be in directly.

I better go on I guess, John Grady said.

Dont keep one waitin, the old man said. They wont tolerate it.

Yessir.

Go on then.

He rose. Socorro had gone back in. He looked down at the old man. Still you dont think it's all that good a idea, do you?

What dont I think?

About gettin married.

I never said that.

Do you think it?

I think you ought to follow your heart, the old man said
That's all I ever thought about anything.

Going up Juárez Avenue among the crowds of tourists he
saw the shineboy at his corner and waved a hand to him.

I guess you're on your way to see your girl, the boy said.

No. I'm goin to see a friend of mine.

Is she still your novia?

Yes she is.

When you gettin married?

Pretty soon.

Did you ask her?

Yes.

She said yes?

She did.

The boy grinned. Otro más de los perdidos, he said.

Otro más.

Ándale pues, the boy said. I cant help you now.

He entered the Moderno and took off his hat and hung it
among the hats and instruments along the long wallrack by the
door and he took a table next to the one reserved for the maestro. The barman nodded to him across the room and raised one
hand. Buenas tardes, he called.

Buenas tardes, said John Grady. He folded his hands before
him on the tabletop. Two of the ancient musicians in their dull
black stage suits were sitting at a table in the corner and they
nodded to him politely who was a friend to the maestro and he
nodded back and the waiter came across the concrete floor in
his white apron and greeted him. He ordered a tequila and the
waiter bowed. As if the decision were a grave one well taken.
From outside in the street came the cries of children, the calls
of vendors. A square shaft of light fell slant from the barred
streetwindow above him and terminated out on the floor in a

pale trapezoid. In the center of it like a thing displayed in a bent and veering cage sat a large lemoncolored housecat washing itself. It shook its head and yawned. It turned and looked at him. The waiter brought the tequila.

He wet the top of his fist with his tongue and poured on salt from a tableshaker and he sipped the tequila and took a wedge of sliced lemon from the dish and crushed it between his teeth and laid it back in the dish and licked the salt from his fist. Then he took another sip of the tequila. The musicians watched him, sitting quietly.

He drank the tequila and ordered another. The cat was gone. The cage of light moved across the floor. After a while it started up the wall. The waiter had turned on the lights in the other room and a third musician had come in and joined the first two. Then the maestro entered with his daughter.

The waiter came over and helped him with his coat and held the chair. They spoke briefly and the waiter nodded and smiled at the girl and carried away the maestro's coat and hung it up. The girl turned slightly in her chair and looked at John Grady.

Cómo estás? she said.

Bien. Y tú?

Bien, gracias.

The blind man had tilted archly in his chair listening. Good evening, he said. Will you join us please?

Thank you. Yes. I would like to.

Then you must.

He pushed back his chair and rose. The maestro smiled at his approach and held out his hand into the darkness.

How are you?

Fine, thank you.

The blind man spoke to the girl in spanish. He shook his head. María is shy, he said. Por qué no hablas inglés con nuestro amigo? You see. She will not. It is of no use. Where is the waiter? What will you have please?

The waiter brought the drinks and the maestro ordered for

his guest. He put his hand on the girl's arm for her to wait till all were served. When the waiter had gone he turned. Now, he said. What has happened?

I asked her to marry me.

She has refused? Tell me.

No. She accepted.

But so solemn. You gave us a scare.

The girl rolled up her eyes and looked away. John Grady had no idea what it meant.

I came to ask you a favor.

Of course, said the maestro. By all means.

She has no family. No sponsor. I would like for you to be her padrino.

Ah, said the maestro. He put his folded hands to his chin and then placed them on the table again. They waited.

I am honored of course. But this is a serious matter. You understand.

Yes. I understand.

You will be living in America.

Yes.

America, the maestro said. Yes.

They sat. The blind man in his silence was twice silent. Even the three musicians in the corner were watching him. They could not hear what he was saying but they seemed to be waiting also for him to continue.

The office of the padrino is not a mere ceremony, he said. It is not some gesture of kinship or some way to bind friends.

Yes. I understand.

It is a serious matter and it is no insult that a man should refuse to accept it if his reasons are honorable.

Yessir.

One needs to be logical in these matters.

The maestro raised one hand before him and spread his fingers and he held it there. Like an evocation perhaps, or a gesture of fending away. Had he not been blind he would simply have been studying his nails. My health is poor, he said. But even were that not so this girl will be making a new life and she should have counsel in her new country. Dont you think this would be best?

I dont know. I feel like she needs all the help she can get.

Yes. Of course.

Is it because of your sight?

The blind man lowered his hand. No, he said. It is not a matter of sight.

He waited for the blind man to continue but he did not.

Is there something you cant say in front of the girl?

The girl? said the maestro. He smiled his blind smile, he shook his head. Oh my, he said. No no. We have no secrets. An old blind father with secrets? No, that would never do.

We dont have padrinos in America, John Grady said.

The waiter came and set John Grady's drink in front of him and the maestro thanked the waiter and slid his fingers across the wood of the table until they touched his own glass.

I drink to the boda, he said.

Gracias.

They drank. The girl bent down the straw in her bottle of refresco and leaned and sipped.

If a person could be found, said the maestro, of intelligence and heart, then perhaps the office could be explained to him. What do you think?

I think you are that person.

The blind man sipped his wine and set the glass back in the very ring upon the table it had vacated and folded his hands in thought.

Let me say this to you, he said.

Yessir.

In a matter such as this, once one is asked he is already responsible. Even should he refuse.

I'm just thinking about her.

I too.

She doesnt have anyone else. She has no friends.

But the padrino does not need to be a friend.

He has to be something.

He has to be a man of character who is willing to undertake certain duties. That is all. He could be a friend or not. He could be a rival from another house. He could be one to reunite families distanced by intrigue or bad blood or politics. You understand. He could be one with little connection to the family even. He could even be an enemy.

An enemy?

Yes. I know of such a case. In this very city.

Why would a man want an enemy for a padrino?

For the best of reasons. Or the worst. This man of whom we speak was a dying man when his lastborn came into the world. A son. His only son. So what did he do? He called upon that man who once had been a friend to him but now was his sworn enemy and he asked that man to be padrino to his son. The man refused of course. What? Are you mad? He must have been surprised. It had been years since last they spoke and their enemistad was a deep and bitter thing. Perhaps they had become enemies for the same reason they had once been friends. Which often happens in the world. But this man persisted. And he had the—how do you say—el naipe? En su manga.

The ace.

Yes. The ace up his sleeve. He told his enemy that he was dying. There was the naipe. Upon the table. The man could not refuse. All choosing was taken from his hands.

The blind man raised one hand into the smoky air in a thin upward slicing motion. Now comes the talk, he said. No end to it. Some say that the dying man wished to mend their friendship. Others that he had done this man some great injustice and wished to make amends before leaving this world forever. Others said other things. There is more than meets the eye. I say this: This man who was dying was not a man given to sentimentality. He also had lost friends to death. He was not a man given to illusions. He knew that those things we most desire to hold in our hearts are often taken from us while that which we would put away seems often by that very wish to become endowed with unsuspected powers of endurance. He knew how frail is the memory of loved ones. How we close our eyes and speak to them. How we long to hear their voices once again, and how those voices and those memories grow faint and faint until what was flesh and blood is no more than echo and shadow. In the end perhaps not even that.

He knew that our enemies by contrast seem always with us. The greater our hatred the more persistent the memory of them so that a truly terrible enemy becomes deathless. So that the man who has done you great injury or injustice makes himself a guest in your house forever. Perhaps only forgiveness can dislodge him.

Such then was this man's thinking. If we may believe the best of him. To bind the padrino to his cause with the strongest bonds he knew. And there was more. For in this appointment he also posted the world as his sentinel. The duties of a friend would come under no great scrutiny. But an enemy? You can see how nicely he has caught him in the net he has contrived. For this enemy was in fact a man of conscience. A worthy enemy. And this enemy-padrino now must carry the dying man in his heart forever. Must suffer the eyes of the world eternally on him. Such a man can scarce be said to author any longer his own path.

The father dies as die he must. The enemy become padrino now becomes the father of the child. The world is watching. It stands in for the dead man. Who by his audacity has pressed it into his service. For the world does have a conscience, however men dispute it. And while that conscience may be thought of as the sum of consciences of men there is another view, which is that it may stand alone and each man's share be but some small imperfect part of it. The man who died favored this view. As I do myself. Men may believe the world to be—what is the word? Voluble.

Fickle.

Fickle? I dont know. Voluble then. But the world is not voluble. The world is always the same. The man appointed the world as his witness that he might secure his enemy to his service. That this enemy would be faithful to his duties. That is what he did. Or that was my belief. At times I believe it yet.

How did it turn out?

Quite strangely.

The blind man reached for his glass. He drank and held the glass before him as if studying it and then he set it on the table before him once again.

Quite strangely. For the circumstance of his appointment came to elevate this man's padrinazgo to the central role of his life. It brought out what was best in him. More than best. Virtues long neglected began almost at once to blossom forth. He abandoned every vice. He even began to attend Mass. His new office seemed to have called forth from the deepest parts of his character honor and loyalty and courage and devotion. What he gained can scarcely be put into words. Who would have foreseen such a thing?

What happened? said John Grady.

The blind man smiled his pained blind smile. You smell the rat, he said.

Yes.

Quite so. It was no happy ending. Perhaps there is a moral to the tale. Perhaps not. I leave it to you.

What happened?

This man whose life was changed forever by the dying request of his enemy was ultimately ruined. The child became his life. More than his life. To say that he doted upon the child says nothing. And yet all turned out badly. Again, I believe that the intentions of the dying man were for the best. But there is another view. It would not be the first time that a father sacrificed a son.

The godchild grew up wild and restless. He became a criminal. A petty thief. A gambler. And other things. Finally, in the winter of nineteen and seven, in the town of Ojinaga, he killed

a man. He was nineteen years of age. Close to your own, perhaps.

The same.

Yes. Perhaps this was his destiny. Perhaps no padrino could
have saved him from himself. No father. The padrino squan-
dered all he owned in bribes and fees. To no avail. Such a road
once undertaken has no end and he died alone and poor. He
was never bitter. He scarcely seemed even to consider whether
he had been betrayed. He once had been a strong and even a
ruthless man, but love makes men foolish. I speak as a victim
myself. We are taken out of our own care and it then remains
to be seen only if fate will show to us some share of mercy. Or
little. Or none.

Men speak of blind destiny, a thing without scheme or purpose. But what sort of destiny is that? Each act in this world
from which there can be no turning back has before it another,
and it another yet. In a vast and endless net. Men imagine that
the choices before them are theirs to make. But we are free to
act only upon what is given. Choice is lost in the maze of generations and each act in that maze is itself an enslavement for it
voids every alternative and binds one ever more tightly into the
constraints that make a life. If the dead man could have forgiven his enemy for whatever wrong was done to him all would
have been otherwise. Did the son set out to avenge his father?
Did the dead man sacrifice his son? Our plans are predicated
upon a future unknown to us. The world takes its form hourly
by a weighing of things at hand, and while we may seek to puzzle out that form we have no way to do so. We have only God's
law, and the wisdom to follow it if we will.

The maestro leaned forward and composed his hands before
him. The wineglass stood empty and he took it up. Those who
cannot see, he said, must rely upon what has gone before. If I
do not wish to appear so foolish as to drink from an empty glass
I must remember whether I have drained it or not. This man
who became padrino. I speak of him as if he died old but he did

not. He was younger than I am now. I speak as if his conscience or the world's eyes or both led him to such rigor in his duties. But those considerations quickly fell to nothing. It was for love of the child that he came to grief, if grief it was. What do you make of that?

I dont know.

Nor I. I only know that every act which has no heart will be found out in the end. Every gesture.

They sat in silence. The room was quiet about them. John Grady watched the water beading upon his glass where it sat untouched before him. The blind man set his own glass back upon the table and pushed it from him.

How well do you love this girl?

I would die for her.

The alcahuete is in love with her.

Tiburcio?

No. The grand alcahuete.

Eduardo.

Yes.

They sat quietly. In the outer hall the musicians had arrived and were assembling their instruments. John Grady sat staring at the floor. After a while he looked up.

Can the old woman be trusted?

La Tuerta?

Yes.

Oh my, said the blind man softly.

The old woman tells her that she will be married.

The old woman is Tiburcio's mother.

John Grady leaned back in his chair. He sat very quietly. He looked at the blind man's daughter. She watched him. Quiet. Kind. Inscrutable.

You did not know.

No. Does she know? Yes, of course she knows.

Yes.

Does she know that Eduardo is in love with her?

Yes.

The musicians struck up a light baroque partita. Aging dancers moved onto the floor. The blind man sat, his hands before him on the table.

She believes that Eduardo will kill her, John Grady said.

The blind man nodded.

Do you believe he will kill her?

Yes, said the maestro. I believe he will kill her.

Is that why you wont be her godfather?

Yes. That is why.

It would make you responsible.

Yes.

The dancers moved with their stiff formality over the swept and polished concrete floor. They danced with an antique grace, like figures from a film.

What do you think I should do?

I cannot advise you.

You will not.

No. I will not.

I'd give her up if I thought I could not protect her.

Perhaps.

You dont think I could.

I think the difficulties might be greater than you imagine.

What should I do.

The blind man sat. After a while he said: You must understand. I have no certainty. And it is a grave matter.

He passed his hand across the top of the table. As if he were making smooth something unseen before him. You wish for me to tell you some secret of the grand alcahuete. Betray to you some weakness. But the girl herself is the weakness.

What do you think I should do?

Pray to God.

Yes.

Will you?

No.

Why not?

I dont know.

You dont believe in Him?

It's not that.

It is that the girl is a mujerzuela.

I dont know. Maybe.

The blind man sat. They are dancing, he said.

Yes.

That is not the reason.

What's not?

That she is a whore.

No.

Would you give her up? Truly?

I dont know.

Then you would not know what to pray for.

No. I wouldnt know what to ask.

The blind man nodded. He leaned forward. He placed one elbow on the table and rested his forehead against his thumb like a confessor. He seemed to be listening to the music. You knew her before she came to the White Lake, he said.

I saw her. Yes.

At La Venada.

Yes.

As did he.

Yes. I suppose.

That is where it began.

Yes.

He is a cuchillero. A filero, as they say here. A man of a certain rigor. A serious man.

I am serious myself.

Of course. If you were not there would be no problem.

John Grady studied that passive face. Closed to the world even as the world was closed to him.

What are you telling me?

I have nothing to tell.

He is in love with her.

Yes.

But he would kill her.

Yes.

I see.

Perhaps. Let me tell you only this. Your love has no friends. You think that it does but it does not. None. Perhaps not even God.

And you?

I do not count myself. If I could see what lies ahead I would tell you. But I cannot.

You think I'm a fool.

No. I do not.

You would not say so if you did.

No, but I would not lie. I dont think it. I never did. A man is always right to pursue the thing he loves.

No matter even if it kills him?

I think so. Yes. No matter even that.

HE WHEELED the last barrowload of trash from the kitchen yard out to the trashfire and tipped it and stood back and watched the deep orange fire gasping in the dark chuffs of smoke that rose against the twilight sky. He passed his forearm across his brow and bent and took up the handles of the wheelbarrow again and trundled it out to where the pickup was parked and loaded it and raised and latched the tailgate and went back into the house. Héctor was backing across the floor sweeping with the broom. They carried the kitchen table in from the other room and then brought in the chairs. Héctor brought the lamp from the sideboard and set it on the table and lifted away the glass chimney and lit the wick. He blew out the match and set back the chimney and adjusted the flame with the brass knob. Where is the santo? he said.

It's still in the truck. I'll get it.

He went out and brought in the rest of the things from the cab of the truck. He set the crude wooden figure of the saint on the dresser and unwrapped the sheets and set about making the bed. Héctor stood in the doorway.

You want me to help you?

No. Thanks.

He leaned against the doorjamb smoking. John Grady smoothed the sheets and unfolded the pillowcases and stuffed the feather pillows into them and then unfolded the pieced quilt that Socorro had given him. Héctor stuck the cigarette in his mouth and came around to the other side of the bed and they spread the quilt and stood back.

I think we're done, John Grady said.

They went back into the kitchen and John Grady leaned and cupped his hand at the top of the lamp chimney and blew out the flame and they went out and shut the door behind them. They walked out in the yard and John Grady turned and looked back toward the cabin. The night was overcast. Dark, cloudy, cold. They walked down to the truck.

Will they wait supper on you?

Yeah, said Héctor. Sure.

You can eat at the house if you want.

That's all right.

They climbed in and pulled the truck doors shut. John Grady started the engine.

Can she ride a horse? said Héctor.

Yeah. She can ride.

They pulled out down the rutted road, the tools sliding and clanking behind them in the truckbed. En qué piensas? said John Grady.

Nada.

They jostled on, the truck in second gear, the headlights rocking. When they rounded the first turn in the road the lights of the city appeared out on the plain below them thirty miles away.

It gets cold up here, Héctor said.

Yep.

You spent the night up here yet?

I was up here a couple of nights till past midnight.

He looked at Héctor. Héctor took his makings from his shirtpocket and sat rolling a cigarette.

Tienes tus dudas.

He shrugged. He popped a match with the nail of his thumb and lit the cigarette and blew the match out. Hombre de precaución, he said.

Yo?

Yo.

Two owls crouching in the dust of the road turned their pale and heartshaped faces in the trucklights and blinked and rose on their white wings as silent as two souls ascending and vanished in the darkness overhead.

Buhos, said John Grady.

Lechuzas.

Tecolotes.

Héctor smiled. He took a drag on the cigarette. His dark face glowed in the dark glass. Quizás, he said.

Pueda ser.

Pueda ser. Sí.

WHEN HE WALKED into the kitchen Oren was still at the table. He hung up his hat and went to the sink and washed and got his coffee. Socorro came out of her room and shooed him away from the stove and he took his coffee to the table and sat. Oren looked up from his paper.

What's the news, Oren?

You want the good or the bad?

I dont know. Just pick out somethin in the middle.

They dont have nothin like that in here. It wouldnt be news.

I guess not.

McGregor girl's been picked to be the Sun Carnival Queen. You ever see her?

No.

Sweet girl. How's your place comin?

Okay.

Socorro set his plate before him together with a plate of biscuits covered with a cloth.

She aint no city gal is she?

No.

That's good.

Yeah. It is.

Parham tells me she's pretty as a speckled pup.

He thinks I'm crazy.

Well. You might be a little crazy. He might be a little jealous.

He watched the boy eat. He sipped his coffee.

When I got married my buddies all told me I was crazy. Said I'd regret it.

Did you?

No. It didnt work out. But I didnt regret it. It wasnt her fault.

What happened?

I dont know. A lot of things. Mostly I couldnt get along with her folks. The mother was just a goddamned awful woman. I thought I'd seen awful but I hadnt. If the old man would of lived we might of had a chance. But he had a bad heart. I seen the whole thing comin. When I inquired after his health it was more than just idle curiosity. He finally up and died and here she come. Bag and baggage. That was pretty much the end of it.

He took his cigarettes from the table and lit one. He blew smoke thoughtfully out across the room. He watched the boy.

We was together three years almost to the day. She used to bathe me, if you can believe that. I liked her real well. She'd of been a orphan we'd be married yet.

I'm sorry to hear it.

A man gets married he dont know what's liable to happen. He may think he does, but he dont.

Probably right.

If you sincerely want to hear all about what is wrong with you and what you ought to do to rectify it all you need to do is

et them inlaws on the place. You'll get a complete rundown on
the subject and I guarantee it.

She aint got no family.

That's good, said Oren. That's your smartest move yet.

After Oren had gone he sat over his coffee a long time.
Through the window far to the south he could see the thin
white adderstongues of lightning licking silently along the rim
of the sky in the darkness over Mexico. The only sound was the
clock ticking in the hallway.

When he entered the barn Billy's light was still on. He went
down to the stall where he kept the pup and gathered it up all
twisting and whimpering in the crook of his arm and brought it
back to his bunkroom. He stood at the door and looked back.

Goodnight, he called.

He pushed aside the curtain and felt overhead in the dark for
the lightswitch chain.

Goodnight, called Billy.

He smiled. He let go the chain and sat on his bunk in the
darkness rubbing the pup's belly. He could smell the horses.
The wind was gusting up and a piece of loose roofingtin at the
far end of the barn rattled and the wind passed on. It was cold
in the room and he thought to light the little kerosene heater
but after a while he just pulled off his boots and trousers and
put the pup in his box and crawled under the blankets. The
wind outside and the cold in the room were like those winter
nights on the north Texas plains when he was a child in his
grandfather's house. When the storms blew down from the
north and the prairie land about the house stood white in the
sudden lightning and the house shook in the thunderclaps. On
just such nights and just such mornings in the year he'd gotten
his first colt he'd wrap himself in his blanket and go out and
cross to the barn, leaning into the wind, the first drops of rain
slapping at him hard as pebbles, moving down the long barn
bay like some shrouded refugee among the sudden slats of light
that stood staccato out of the parted board walls, moving

through those serried and electric prosceniums where they flared white and fugitive across the barn row on row until he reached the stall where the little horse stood waiting and unlatched the door and sat in the straw with his arms around its neck till it stopped trembling. He would be there all night and he would be there in the morning when Arturo came to the barn to feed. Arturo would walk with him back to the house before anyone else was awake, brushing the straw from his blanket as he walked beside him, not saying a word. As if he were a young lord. As if he were never to be disinherited by war and war's machinery. All his early dreams were the same. Something was afraid and he had come to comfort it. He dreamed it yet. And this: standing in the room in the black suit tying the new black tie he wore to his grandfather's funeral on the cold and windy day of it. And standing in his cubicle in Mac McGovern's horsebarn on another such day in the cold dawn before work in another such suit, the two halves of the box it came in lying on the bunk with the crepe tissue spilling out and the cut string lying beside it on the bunk together with the knife he'd cut it with that had belonged to his father and Billy standing in the doorway watching him. He buttoned the coat and stood. His hands crossed at the wrist in front of him. His face pale in the glass of the little mirror he'd propped on one of the two by fours that braced the rough stud wall of the room. Pale in the light of the winter that was on the country. Billy leaned and spat in the chaff and turned and went out down the barn bay and crossed to the house for breakfast.

THE LAST TIME he was to see her was in the same corner room on the second floor of the Dos Mundos. He watched from the window and saw her pay the driver and he went to the door so that he could watch her come up the stairs. He held her hands while she sat half breathless on the edge of the bed.

Estás bien? he said.

Sí, she said. Creo que sí.

He asked was she sure she had not changed her mind.

No, she said. Y tú?

Nunca.

Me quieres?

Para siempre. Y tú?

Hasta el fin de mi vida.

Pues eso es todo.

She said that she had tried to pray for them but that she could not.

Porqué no?

No sé. Creí que Dios no me oiría.

El oirá. Reza el domingo. Dile que es importante.

They made love and lay with her curled against him and not moving but breathing very quietly against his side. He did not know if she was awake but he told her the things about his life that he had not told her. He told her about working for the hacendado at Cuatro Ciénegas and about the man's daughter and the last time he saw her and about being in the prison in Saltillo and about the scar on his face that he had promised to tell her about and never had. He told her about seeing his mother on stage at the Majestic Theatre in San Antonio Texas and about the times that he and his father used to ride in the hills north of San Angelo and about his grandfather and the ranch and the Comanche trail that ran through the western sections and how he would ride that trail in the moonlight in the fall of the year when he was a boy and the ghosts of the Comanches would pass all about him on their way to the other world again and again for a thing once set in motion has no ending in this world until the last witness has passed.

The shadows were long in the room before they left. He told her that the driver Gutiérrez would pick her up at the cafe in la Calle de Noche Triste and take her to the other side. He would have with him the documents necessary for her to cross.

Todo está arreglado, he said.

She held his hands more tightly. Her dark eyes studied him. He told her that there was nothing to fear. He said that Ramón was their friend and that the papers were arranged and that no harm would come to her.

Él te recogerá a las siete por la mañana. Tienes que estar allí en punto.

Estaré allí.

Quédate adentro hasta que él llegue.

Sí, sí.

No le digas nada a nadie.

No. Nadie.

No puedes traer nada contigo.

Nada?

Nada.

Tengo miedo, she said.

He held her. Dont be afraid, he said.

They sat very quietly. Down in the street the vendors had begun to call. She pressed her face against his shoulder.

Hablan los sacerdotes español? she said.

Sí. Ellos hablan español.

Quiero saber, she said, si crees hay perdón de pecados.

He opened his mouth to speak but she put her hand to his lips. Lo que crees en tu corazón, she said.

He stared past her dark and shining hair toward the deepening dusk in the streets of the city. He thought about what he believed and what he did not believe. After a while he said that he believed in God even if he was doubtful of men's claims to know God's mind. But that a God unable to forgive was no God at all.

Cualquier pecado?

Cualquier. Sí.

Sin excepción de nada? She pushed her hand against his lips a second time. He kissed her fingers and took her hand away.

Con la excepción de desesperación, he said. Para eso no hay remedio.

Lastly she asked if he would love her all his life and she'd have touched her fingers to his mouth but he held her hand. No tengo que pensarlo, he said. Sí. Para todo mi vida.

She took his face in her hands and kissed him. Te amo, she said. Y seré tu esposa.

She rose and turned and held his hands. Debo irme, she said. He stood and put his arms around her and kissed her there in the darkening room. He would have walked her down the hallway to the head of the stairs but she stopped him at the door and kissed him and said goodbye. He listened to her steps in the stairwell. He went to the window to watch for her but she must have gone along the street beneath him because he could not see her. He sat on the bed in the empty room and listened to the sounds of all that alien commerce in the world outside. He sat a long time and he thought about his life and how little of it he could ever have foreseen and he wondered for all his will and all his intent how much of it was his own doing. The room was dark and the neon hotel sign had come on outside and after a while he rose and took his hat from the chair by the bed and put it on and went out and down the stairs.

AT THE INTERSECTION the cab stopped. A small man with a black crape armband stepped into the street and raised his hand and the cabdriver took off his hat and set it on the dashboard. The girl leaned forward to see. She could hear trumpets muted in the street, the clop of hooves.

The musicians who appeared were old men in suits of dusty black. Behind them came the pallbearers carrying upon their shoulders a flowerstrewn pallet. Wreathed among those flowers the pale face of a young man newly dead. His hands lay at his sides and he jostled woodenly on his coolingboard there astride the shoulders of his bearers and the wild notes from the dented gypsy horns carried back from the glass of the storefronts they passed and back from the old mud or stuccoed facades and a clutch of women in black rebozos passed weeping and children and men in black or with black armbands and among them led by the girl the blind maestro shuffling with his small steps and look of pained wonder. Behind them came two mismatched horses drawing to a weathered wooden cart and in the bed of it unswept of its straw and chaff a wooden coffinbox of handplaned boards pinned with wooden trunnels and no nails to it like some sephardic box of old and the wood blacked by scorching it and the blacking sealed with beeswax and lampoil so that save for the faint wood grain of it it looked a thing of burnished iron. Behind the cart came a man bearing the coffinlid and he carried it upon his back like death's penitent and his clothes and he were blackened with it wax or no. The cabdriver crossed himself silently. The girl crossed herself and kissed the tips of her fingers. The cart rattled past and the spoked wheels diced slowly the farther streetside and the solemn watchers there, a cardfan of sorted faces under the shopfronts and the long skeins of light in the street broken in the turning spokes and the shadows of the horses tramping upright and oblique before the oblong shadows of the wheels shaping over the stones and turning and turning.

She put up her hands and pressed her face into the musty back of the cabseat. She sat back, one hand over her eyes and her face averted into her shoulder. Then she sat bolt upright with her arms beside her and cried out and the driver wrenched himself around in the seat. Señorita? he said. Señorita?

THE CEILING of the room was of concrete and bore the impression of the boards used to form it, the concrete knots and nailheads and the fossil arc of the circlesaw's blade from some mountain sawmill. There was a single sooty bulb that burned there with a grudging orange light and a millermoth that patrolled it in random clockwise orbits.

She lay strapped to a steel table. The steel was cold against her back through the short white shift she wore. She looked at the light. She turned her head and looked at the room. After a while a nurse came in through the gray metal door and she turned her stained and dirty face toward her. Por favor, she whispered. Por favor.

The nurse loosed the straps and smoothed her hair back from her face and said she would return with something for her to drink, but when the door closed she sat upright on the table and climbed down. She looked for some place where they might have put her clothes but save for a second steel table against the far wall the room was empty. The door when she opened it led to a long green corridor dimly lit and stretching away to a closed door at the end. She went down the corridor and tried the door. It opened onto a flight of concrete steps, a rail of metal pipe. She descended three flights and exited into the darkened street.

She did not know where she was. At the corner she asked a man for directions to el centro and he stared at her breasts and continued to do so even as he spoke. She set out along the broken sidewalk. She watched the paving for glass or stones. The carlights that passed fetched her slight figure up onto the walls in enormous dark transparency with the shift burned away and the bones all but showing and then passing cast her reeling backwards to vanish once more into the dark. A man pulled up in a car and drove beside her and talked to her in low obscenities. He pulled ahead and waited. She turned into a dirt alley between two buildings and crouched shivering behind some battered steel oildrums. She waited a long time. It was very cold. When she went out again the car was gone and she went on. She passed a lot where a dog lunged at her silently along a fence and then stood in the fencecorner shrouded in its own breath silently watching her go. She passed a darkened house and a yard where an old man also in nightclothes stood urinating against a mud wall and these two nodded silently to each other across the darkened space like figures met in a dream. The sidewalk gave out and she walked on in the cold sand along the roadside and stopped from time to time to stand tottering while she picked the little goathead burrs from the soles of her bleeding feet. She kept the haze of light from the city before her and she walked a long time. When she crossed the Boulevard 16 de Septiembre she kept her arms folded tightly at her bosom and her eyes lowered in the glare of the headlights, crossing half naked in a hooting of carhorns like some tattered phantom routed out of the ordinal dark and hounded briefly through the visible world to vanish again into the history of men's dreams.

She went on through the barrios north of the city, along the old mud walls and the tin sides of warehouses where the sand streets were lit only by the stars. Someone was singing on the road a song from her own childhood and she soon passed a woman walking toward the city. They spoke good evening each to each and passed on but the woman stopped and turned and called after her.

Adónde va? she called.

A mi casa.

The woman stood quietly. The girl asked do I know you but the woman said that she did not. She asked the girl if this were her barrio and the girl said that it was and the woman then asked her how it could be that she did not know her. When she did not answer the woman came slowly back down the road toward her.

Qué pasó? she said.

Nada.

Nada, the woman said. She walked in a half circle around her where she stood shivering with her arms crossed over her breasts. As if to find some favored inclination in the blue light of the desert stars by which she would stand revealed for who she truly was.

Eres del White Lake, she said.

The girl nodded.

Y regresas?

Sí.

Por qué?

No sé.

No sabes.

No.

Quieres ir conmigo?

No puedo.

Porqué no?

She didnt know. The woman asked her again. She said that she could come with her and live in her house where she lived with her children.

The girl whispered that she did not know her.

Te gusta tu vida por allá? the woman said.

No.

Ven conmigo.

She stood shivering. She shook her head no. The sun was coming soon. In the dark above them a star fell and in the cold wind before the dawn papers loped and clutched and rattled briefly in the spines of the roadside growth and loped on again. The woman looked toward the desert sky to the east. She looked at the girl. She asked the girl if she was cold and she said that she was. She asked her again: Quieres ir conmigo?

She said that she could not. She said that in three days' time the boy she loved would come to marry her. She thanked her for her kindness.

The woman raised the girl's face in her hand and looked at her. The girl waited for her to speak but she only looked into her face as if to remember her. Perhaps to read at second hand the shapes of the roads that had led her to this place. What was lost or what was ruined. Whom bereft. Or what remained.

Cómo se llama? the girl said, but the woman did not answer. She touched the girl's face and took away her hand and turned and went on along the dark of the road out of the darkened barrio and did not look back.

Eduardo's car was gone. She crept shivering along the alley under the warehouse wall and tried the door but it was locked. She tapped and waited and tapped again. She waited a long time. After a while she went back out to the street. Her breath pluming in the light along the corrugated wall. She looked back down the alley again and then went around to the front of the building and through the gate and up the walkway.

The portress with her painted face seemed unsurprised to

see her standing there clutching herself in the stenciled shift. She stepped back and held the door and the girl entered and thanked her and went on through the salon. Two men standing at the bar turned to watch her. Pale and dirty waif drifted by mischance in from the outer cold to cross the room with eyes cast down and arms crossed at her breasts. Leaving bloody footprints in the carpet as if a penitent had passed.

HE SEEMED to have dressed with care for the occasion although it may have been that he had business elsewhere in the city. He slid back the goldlinked cuff of his shirt to consult his watch. His suit was of light gray silk shantung and he wore a silk tie of the same color. His shirt was a pale lemon yellow and he wore a yellow silk handkerchief in the breastpocket of the suit and the lowcut black boots with the zippers up the inner sides were freshly polished for he left his shoes outside his door several pair at a time as if the whorehouse hallway were a pullman car.

She sat in the saffroncolored robe he'd given her. Upon the antique bed where her feet did not quite reach the floor. She sat with her head bowed so that her hair cascaded over her thighs and she sat with her hands placed on the bed at either side of her as if she might be afraid of falling.

He spoke in reasoned tones the words of a reasonable man. The more reasonably he spoke the colder the wind in the hollow of her heart. At each juncture in her case he paused to give her space in which to speak but she did not speak and her silence only led inexorably to the next succeeding charge until that structure which was composed of nothing but the spoken word and which should have passed on in its very utterance and left no trace or residue or shadow in the living world, that bodiless structure stood in the room a ponderable being and within its phantom corpus was contained her life.

When he was done he stood watching her. He asked her what she had to say. She shook her head.

Nada? he said.

No, she said. Nada.

Qué crees que eres?

Nada.

Nada. Sí. Pero piensas que has traido una dispensa especial a esta casa? Que Dios te ha escogido?

Nunca creí tal cosa.

He turned and stood looking out the small barred window. Along the limits of the city where the roads died in the desert in sand washes and garbage dumps, out to the white perimeters at midday where smoke from the trashfires burned along the horizon like the signature of vandal hordes come in off the inscrutable wastes beyond. He spoke without turning. He said that she had been spoiled in this house. Because of her youth. He said that her illness was illness only and that she was a fool to believe in the superstitions of the women of the house. He said that she was twice a fool to trust them for they would eat her flesh if they thought it would protect them from disease or secure for them the affections of the lover of whom they dreamt or cleanse their souls in the sight of the bloody and bar-barous god to whom they prayed. He said that her illness was illness only and that it would so prove itself when at last it killed her as it soon would do.

He turned to study her. The slope of her shoulders and their movement with the rise and fall of her breath. The bloodbeat in the artery of her neck. When she looked up and saw his face she knew that he had seen into her heart. What was so and what was false. He smiled his hardlipped smile. Your lover does not know, he said. You have not told him.

Mande?

Tu amado no lo sabe.

No, she whispered. Él no lo sabe.

HE SET OUT the pieces loosely on the board and swiveled it about. I'll go you one more, he said.

Mac shook his head. He held the cigar and blew smoke slowly over the table and then picked up his cup and drained the last of his coffee.

I'm done, he said.

Yessir. You played a good game.

I didnt believe you'd sacrifice a bishop.

That was one of Schönberger's gambits.

You read a lot of chess books?

No sir. Not a lot. I read his.

You told me you played poker.

Some. Yessir.

Why do I think that means somethin else.

I never played that much poker. My daddy was a poker player. He always said that the problem with poker was you played with two kinds of money. What you won was gravy but what you lost was hard come by.

Was he a good poker player?

Yessir. He was one of the best, I reckon. He cautioned me away from it though. He said it was not any kind of a life.

Why did he do it if he thought that?

It was the only other thing he was good at.

What was the first thing?

He was a cowboy.

I take it he was pretty good at that.

Yessir. I've heard of some that was supposed to be better and I'm sure there were some better. I just never did see any of em.

He was on the death march, wasnt he?

Yessir.

There was a lot of boys from this part of the country was on it. Quite a few of em Mexicans.

Yessir. There was.

Mac pulled at his cigar and blew the smoke toward the window. Has Billy come around or are you and him still on the outs?

He's all right.

Is he still goin to stand up for you?

Yessir.

Mac nodded. She aint got nobody to stand on her side?

No sir. Socorro is bringin her family.

That's good. I aint been in my suit in three years. I'd better make a dry run in it, I reckon.

John Grady put the last of the pieces in the box and fitted and slid shut the wooden lid.

Might need Socorro to let out the britches for me.

They sat. Mac smoked. You aint Catholic are you? he said.

No sir.

I wont need to make no disclaimers or nothin?

No sir.

So Tuesday's the day.

Yessir. February seventeenth. It's the last day before Lent. Or I guess next to last. After that you cant get married till Easter.

Is that cuttin it kindly close?

It'll be all right.

Mac nodded. He put the cigar in his teeth and pushed back the chair. Wait here a minute, he said.

John Grady listened to him going down the hall to his room. When he came back he sat down and placed a gold ring on the table.

That's been in my dresser drawer for three years. It aint doin nobody any good there and it never will. We talked about everthing and we talked about that ring. She didnt want it put in the ground. I want you to take it.

Sir I dont think I can do that.

Yes you can. I've already thought of everthing you could possibly say on the subject so rather than go over it item by item let's just save the aggravation and you put it in your pocket and come Tuesday you put it on that girl's finger. You might need to get it resized. The woman that wore it was a beautiful woman. You can ask anybody, it wasnt just my opinion. But what you saw wouldnt hold a candle to what was on the inside. We would like to of had children but we didnt. It damn sure wasnt from not tryin. She was a woman with a awful lot of common sense. I thought she just wanted me to keep that ring for a remembrance but she said I'd know what to do with it when the time come and of course she was right. She was right about everthing. And there's no pride in it when I tell you that she set more store by that ring and what it meant than anything else she ever owned. And that includes some pretty damn fine horses. So take it and put it in your pocket and dont be arguin with me about everthing.

Yessir.

And now I'm goin to bed.

Yessir.

Goodnight.

Goodnight.

FROM THE PASS in the upper range of the Jarillas they could see the green of the benchland below the springs and they could see the thin standing spire of smoke from the fire in the stove rising vertically in the still blue morning air. They sat their horses. Billy nodded at the scene.

When I was a kid growin up in the bootheel me and my brother used to stop where we topped out on this bench south of the ranch goin up into the mountains and we'd look back down at the house. It would be snowin sometimes or snow on the ground in the winter and there was always a fire in the stove and you could see the smoke from the chimney and it was a long ways away and it looked different from up there. Always looked different. It was different. We'd be gone up in the mountains sometimes all day throwin them spooky cattle out of the draws and bringin em down to the feedstation where we'd put out cake. I dont think there was ever a time we didnt stop and look back thataway before we rode up into that country. From where we'd stop we were not a hour away and the coffee was still hot on the stove down there but it was worlds away. Worlds away.

In the distance they could see the thin straight line of the highway and a toysized truck running silently upon it. Beyond that the green line of the river breaks and range on range the distant mountains of Mexico. Billy watched him.

You think you'll ever go back there?

Where?

Mexico.

I dont know. I'd like to. You?

I dont think so. I think I'm done.

I came out of there on the run. Ridin at night. Afraid to make a fire.

Been shot.

Been shot. Those people would take you in. Hide you out. Lie for you. No one ever asked me what it was I'd done.

Billy sat with his hands crossed palm down on the pommel of his saddle. He leaned and spat. I went down there three separate trips. I never once come back with what I started after.

John Grady nodded. What would you do if you couldnt be a cowboy?

I dont know. I reckon I'd think of somethin. You?

I dont know what it would be I'd think of.

Well we may all have to think of somethin.

Yeah.

You think you could live in Mexico?

Yeah. Probably.

Billy nodded. You know what a vaquero makes in the way of wages.

Yep.

You might luck up on a job as foreman or somethin. But sooner or later they're goin to run all the white people out of that country. Even the Babícora wont survive.

I know it.

You'd go to veterinary school if you had the money I reckon. Wouldnt you?

Yep. I would.

You ever write to your mother?

What's my mother got to do with anything?

Nothin. I just wonder if you even know what a outlaw you are.

Why?

Why do I wonder it?

Why am I a outlaw.

I dont know. You just got a outlaw heart. I've seen it before.

Because I said I could live in Mexico?

It aint just that.

Dont you think if there's anything left of this life it's down there?

Maybe.

You like it too.

Yeah? I dont even know what this life is. I damn sure dont know what Mexico is. I think it's in your head. Mexico. I rode a lot of ground down there. The first ranchera you hear sung you understand the whole country. By the time you've heard a hundred you dont know nothin. You never will. I concluded my business down there a long time ago.

He hooked his leg over the pommel of the saddle and sat rolling a cigarette. They'd dropped the reins and the horses leaned and picked bleakly at the sparse tufts of grass trembling in the wind coming through the gap. He bent with his back to the wind and popped a match with his thumbnail and lit the cigarette and turned back.

I aint the only one. It's another world. Everbody I ever knew that ever went back was goin after somethin. Or thought they was.

Yeah.

There's a difference between quittin and knowin when you're beat.

John Grady nodded.

I guess you dont believe that. Do you?

John Grady studied the distant mountains. No, he said. I guess I dont.

They sat for a long time. The wind blew. Billy had long since finished his cigarette and stubbed it out on the sole of his boot.

He unfolded his leg back over the horn of the saddle and slid his boot into the stirrup and leaned down and took up the reins. The horses stepped and stood.

My daddy once told me that some of the most miserable people he ever knew were the ones that finally got what they'd always wanted.

Well, said John Grady. I'm willin to risk it. I've damn sure tried it the other way.

Yeah.

You cant tell anybody anything, bud. Hell, it's really just a way of tellin yourself. And you cant even do that. You just try and use your best judgment and that's about it.

Yeah. Well. The world dont know nothin about your judgment.

I know it. It's worse than that, even. It dont care.

QUINQUAGESIMA SUNDAY in the predawn dark she lit a candle and set the candledish on the floor beside the bureau where the light would not show beneath the doorway to the outer hall. She washed herself at the sink with soap and cloth and she leaned and let her black hair fall before her and passed the wet cloth the length of it a half a hundred times and brushed it as many more. She poured a frugal few drops of scent into her palm and pressed her palms together and scented her hair and the nape of her neck. Then she gathered her hair and twisted it into a rope and coiled and pinned it up.

She dressed with care in one of the three street dresses she owned and stood regarding herself in the dimly lit mirror. The dress was navy blue with white bands at the collar and sleeves and she turned in the mirror and reached over her shoulder and fastened the topmost buttons and turned again. She sat in the chair and pulled on the black pump shoes and stood and went to the bureau and got her purse and put into it the few toilet articles it would hold. No coja nada, she whispered. She folded in her clean underwear and her brush and combs and forced the catch shut. No coja nada. She took her sweater from the back of the chair and pulled it over her shoulders and turned to look at the room she would never see again. The crude carved santo stood as before. Holding his staff so crookedly glued. She took a towel from the rack by the washstand and she wrapped the santo in the towel and then she sat in the chair with the santo in her lap and the purse hanging from her shoulder and waited.

She waited a long time. She had no watch. She listened for the bells to toll in the distant town but sometimes when the wind was coming in off the desert you could not hear them. By and by she heard a rooster call. Finally she heard the slippered steps of the criada along the corridor and she rose as the door opened and the old woman looked in on her and turned and looked back down the hallway and then entered with her hand fanned before her and one finger to her lips and pressed the door shut silently behind her.

Lista? she hissed.

Sí. Lista.

Bueno. Vámonos.

The old woman gave a hitch of her shoulder and a sort of half jaunty cock of her head. Some powdered stepdam from a storybook. Some ragged conspiratress gesturing upon the boards. The girl clutched her purse and stood and put the santo under her arm and the old woman opened the door and peered out and then urged her forward with her hand and they stepped out into the hallway.

Her shoes clicked on the tiles. The old woman looked down and the girl bent slightly and raised her feet each in turn and slipped off the shoes and tucked them under her arm along with the santo.

The old woman shut the door behind them and they moved down the hallway, the crone holding her hand like a child's and tugging at her apron to sort forth her keys where they hung by their thong from the piece of broomhandle.

At the outer door she stood and put her shoes on again while

/ 221

the old woman muffled the heavy latch with her rebozo and turned it with her key. Then the door opened onto the cold and the dark.

They stood facing one another. Rápido, rápido, whispered the old woman and the girl pressed the money that she had promised into her hands and then threw her arms around her neck and kissed her dry and leather cheek and turned and stepped through the door. On the step she turned to take the old woman's blessing but the criada was too distraught to respond and before she could step away from out of the doorway light the old woman had reached and seized her arm.

No te vayas, she hissed. No te vayas.

The girl tore her arm away from the old woman's grip. The sleeve of her dress ripped loose along the shoulder seam. No, she whispered, backing away. No.

The old woman held out one hand. She called hoarsely after her. No te vayas, she called. Me equivoqué.

The girl clutched her santo and her purse and went down the alleyway. Before she reached the end she turned and looked back a last time. La Tuerta was still standing in the door watching her. Holding the clutch of pesos to her breast. Then her eye blinked slowly in the light and the door closed and the key turned and the bolt ran forever on that world.

She went down the alleyway to the road and turned toward the town. Dogs were barking and the air was smoky from the charcoal fires in the low mud hovels of the colonias. She walked along the sandy desert road. The stars in flood above her. The lower edges of the firmament sawed out into the black shapes of the mountains and the lights of the cities burning on the plain like stars pooled in a lake. She sang to herself softly as she went a song from long ago. The dawn was two hours away. The town one.

There were no cars on the road. From a rise she could see to the east across the desert five miles distant the random lights of trucks moving slowly upon the highway that came up from

Chihuahua. The air was still. She could see her breath in the dark. She watched the lights of a car that crossed from left to right somewhere before her and she watched the lights move on. Somewhere out there in the world was Eduardo.

When she reached the crossroads she studied the distance in either direction for any sign of approaching carlights before she crossed. She kept to the narrow streets down through the barrios in the outlying precincts of the city. Already there were windows lit with oil-lamps behind the walls of ocotillo or woven brush. She began to come upon occasional workmen with their lunches in lardcans they carried by the bail, whistling softly as they set forth in the early morning cold. Her feet were bleeding again in her shoes and she could feel the wet blood and the coldness of it.

The cafe held the only light along the Calle de Noche Triste. In the darkened window of the adjacent shoestore a cat sat silently among the footwear watching the empty street. It turned its head to regard her as she passed. She pushed open the steamed glass door of the cafe and entered.

Two men at a table by the window looked up when she came in and followed her with their eyes as she went by. She went to the rear and sat at one of the little wooden tables and put her purse and her parcel in the chair beside her and took up the menu from the chrome wire stand and sat looking at it. The waiter came over. She ordered a cafecito and he nodded and went back to the counter. It was warm in the cafe and after a while she took off the sweater and laid it in the chair. The men were still watching her. The waiter brought the coffee and set it before her with spoon and napkin. She was surprised to hear him ask where she was from.

Mande? she said.

De dónde viene?

She told him she was from Chiapas and he stood for a moment studying her as if to see how such people might be different from those he knew. He said that he'd been told to ask by one of the men. When she turned and looked at them they

smiled but there was no joy in it. She looked at the waiter.
Estoy esperando a un amigo, she said.

Por supuesto, said the waiter.

She sat over the coffee a long time. The street outside grew
gray in the February dawn. The two men at the front of the
cafe had long since finished their coffee and left and others had
come to take their place. The shops remained closed. A few
trucks passed in the street and people were coming in out of the
cold and a waitress was now going from table to table.

Shortly after seven a blue taxi pulled up at the door and
the driver got out and came in and canvassed the tables with
his eyes. He came to the rear of the cafe and looked down
at her.

Lista? he said.

Dónde está Ramón?

He stood picking at his teeth reflectively. He said that
Ramón could not come.

She looked toward the front of the cafe. The cab stood in the
street with the engine running in the cold.

Está bien, said the driver. Vámonos. Debemos darnos prisa.

She asked him if he knew John Grady and he nodded and
waved the toothpick. Sí, sí, he said. He said that he knew everyone. She looked again at the cab smoking in the street.

He had stepped back to allow her to rise. He looked down at
the chair where she'd put her purse. The santo wrapped in the
whorehouse towel. She placed her hand over these things.
Which he might wish to carry for her. She asked him who it
was who had paid him.

He put the toothpick back in his mouth and stood looking at
her. Finally he said that he had not been paid. He said that he
was cousin to Ramón and that Ramón had been paid forty dollars. He put his hand on the back of the empty chair and stood
looking down at her. Her shoulders were rising and falling with
her breath. Like someone about to attempt a feat of strength.
She said that she did not know.

He leaned down. Mire, he said. Su novio. Él tiene una cicatriz aquí. He passed his forefinger across his cheek to trace the path of the knife that had made the scar her lover carried from the fight three years ago in the comedor of the cárcel at Cuellar in the city of Saltillo. Verdad? he said.

Sí, she whispered. Es verdad. Y tiene mi tarjeta verde?

Sí. He took the greencard from his pocket and placed it on the table. On the card was printed her name.

Está satisfecha? he said.

Sí, she whispered. Estoy satisfecha. And rose and gathered up her things and left money on the table to pay for the coffee and followed him out into the street.

In the cold dawn all that halfsordid world was coming to light again and as she rode in silence in the rear of the cab through the waking streets she clutched the illcarved wooden relic and said a silent goodbye to everything she knew and to each thing she would not see again. She said goodbye to an old woman in a black rebozo come to a door to see what sort of day it was and she said goodbye to three girls her age stepping with care around the water standing in the street from the recent rains who were on their way to Mass and she said goodbye to dogs and to old men at streetcorners and to vendors pushing their carts through the street to commence their day and to shopkeepers opening their doors and to the women who knelt with pail and rag to wash the walkway tiles. She said goodbye to the small birds strung shoulder to shoulder along the lightwires overhead who had slept and were waking and whose name she would never know.

They passed through the outskirts of the city and she could see the river to the left through the river trees and the tall buildings of the city beyond that were in another country and the barren mountains where the sun would soon fall upon the rocks. They passed the old abandoned municipal buildings. Rusted watertanks in a yard strewn with trashpapers the wind had left. The sudden thin iron palings of a fence that ratcheted silently past the window from right to left and which in their

passing and in the period of their passing began to evoke the
dormant sorcerer within before she could tear her gaze away.
She put her hands to her eyes, breathing deeply. In the darkness inside the cups of her palms she saw herself on a cold white
table in a cold white room. The glass of the doors and the windows to that room were meshed with heavy wire and clamoring
there were whores and whores' handmaids many in number
and all crying out to her. She sat upright on the table and threw
back her head as if she would cry out or as if she would sing.
Like some young diva remanded to a madhouse. No sound
came. The cold pneuma passed. She should have called it back.
When she opened her eyes the cab had turned off the road and
was jostling over a bare dirt track and the driver was watching
her in the mirror. She looked out but she could not see the
bridge. She could see the river through the trees and the mist
coming off the river and the raw rock mountains beyond but
she could not see the city. She saw a figure moving among the
trees by the river. She asked the driver if they were to cross here
to the other side and he said yes. He said that she would be
going to the other side now. Then the cab pulled into the clearing and came to a stop and when she looked what she saw coming toward her across the clearing in the earliest light of
morning was the smiling Tiburcio.

HE'D LEFT THE RANCH around five and driven to the darkened front of the bar where he could see the dimly lit face of
the clock within. He backed the truck around on the gravel
apron so that he could watch the road and he tried not to turn
around to look at the clock every few minutes but he did.

Few cars passed. Shortly after six oclock a set of headlights
slowed and he sat upright over the steering wheel and cleared
the glass with the forearm of his jacket but the lights went past
and the car was not a taxi but a sheriff's prowlcar. He thought
they might come back and ask him what he was doing there but

they didnt. It was very cold sitting in the truck and after a while he got out and walked around and flailed at himself with his arms and stamped his boots. Then he got back in the truck. The bar clock said six-thirty. When he looked to the east he could see the gray shape of the landscape.

The lights of the gas station a half mile down the highway went out. A truck went down the highway. He wondered if he could drive down there and get a cup of coffee before the cab arrived. By eight-thirty he'd decided that if that was what it would take to make the cab arrive then that's what he would do and he started the engine. Then he shut it off again.

A half hour later he saw Travis's truck go by on the highway. In a few minutes it came back and slowed and pulled into the parking lot. John Grady rolled down the truck window. Travis pulled up and sat looking at him. He leaned and spat.

What'd they do, give you your time?

Not yet.

I thought maybe the truck was stole. You ain't broke down are you?

No. I was just waitin on somebody.

How long you been here?

I been here a while.

Has that thing got a heater in it?

Not much of a one.

Travis shook his head. He looked toward the highway. John Grady leaned and cleared the glass again with his sleeve. I better get on, he said.

Are you in some kind of trouble?

Yeah. Maybe.

Over a girl, I reckon.

Yeah.

They aint worth it, son.

I've heard that.

Well. Dont do nothin dumb.

It's probably too late.

It aint too late if you aint done it.

I'm all right.

He reached and turned the key and pushed the starter button. He turned and looked at Travis. I'll see you, he said.

He pulled out of the parking lot and headed back up the highway. Travis sat watching the truck until it was out of sight.

IV

WHEN HE got to the cafe in the Calle de Noche Triste the place was full and the girl was hurrying back and forth with orders of eggs and baskets of tortillas. She didnt know anything. She'd only come to work an hour ago. He followed her into the kitchen. The cook looked up from the stove and looked at the girl. Quién es? he said. The girl shrugged. She looked at John Grady. She balanced plates up her arm and pushed back out through the door. The cook didnt know anything. He said the waiter's name was Felipe but he wasnt here. He wouldnt be back until late afternoon. John Grady watched him for a few minutes while he turned the tortillas on the grill with his fingers. Then he pushed open the door and went back out through the restaurant.

He followed the trail of the cabdriver through the various sidestreet bars where he plied his trade. Bars where patrons from the prior night clutched their drinks and squinted in the light from the opening door like suspects under interrogation. He narrowly avoided two fights for refusing to accept a drink. He went to the Venada and knocked at the door but no one came. He stood outside the Moderno peering into the interior but all was closed and dark.

He went to the poolhall in Mariscal Street that was frequented by the musicians and where their instruments hung along the wall, guitars and mandolins and horns of brass or german silver. A mexican harp. He asked after the maestro but none had seen him. By noon he had nowhere else to go but to the White Lake. He sat in a cafe over a cup of black coffee. He sat for a long time. There was another place to go but he didnt want to go there either.

A dwarf of a man in a white coat led him down a corridor. The building smelled of damp concrete. Outside he could hear street traffic, a jackhammer.

The man pushed through a door at the end of the corridor and held the door and nodded him through and then reached and threw the lightswitch. The boy took off his hat. They stood in a room where the recent dead four in number lay on their coolingboards. The boards were trestled up on legs made from plumbing pipe and the dead lay upon them with their hands at their sides and their eyes closed and their necks in dark stained wooden chocks. None were covered over but all lay in their clothes as death had found them. They had the look of rumpled travelers resting in an anteroom. He walked along slowly past the tables. The overhead ceiling lights were covered with small wire baskets. The walls were painted green. In the floor a brass drain. Bits of gray mopstring twisted about the castered wheels under the tables.

The girl to whom he'd sworn his love forever lay on the last table. She lay as the rushcutters had found her that morning in the shallows under the shore willows with the mist rising off the river. Her hair damp and matted. So black. Hung with strands of dead brown weed. Her face so pale. The severed throat gaping bloodlessly. Her good blue dress was twisted about on her body and her stockings were torn. She'd lost her shoes.

There was no blood for it had all washed away. He reached and touched her cheek. Oh God, he said.

La conoce? said the orderly.

Oh God.

La conoce?

He leaned on the table, crushing his hat. He put his hand across his eyes, gripping his skull. Had he the strength he'd have crushed out all it held. What lay before him now and all else it might hold forever.

Señor, said the orderly, but the boy turned and pushed past him and stumbled out. The man called after him. He stood in the door and called down the hallway. He said that if he knew this girl he must make an identification. He said that there were papers to be filled out.

THE CATTLE in the long Cedar Springs Draw up through which he rode studied him as they stood chewing and then lowered their heads again. The rider knew they could tell his intentions by the attitude of the horse he rode. He passed on and rode up into the hills and crested out on the mesa and rode slowly along the rim. He sat the horse facing into the wind and watched the train going up the valley fifteen miles away. To the south the thin green line of the river lay like a child's crayon mark across that mauve and bistre waste. Beyond that the mountains of Mexico in paling blues and grays washing out in the distance. The grass along the mesa underfoot twisted in the wind. A dark head of weather was making up to the north. The little horse dipped its head and he pulled it about and rode on. The horse seemed uncertain and looked off to the west. As if to remember the way. The boy booted him forward. You dont need to worry about it, he said.

He crossed the highway and crossed through the westernmost section of the McGregor ranch. He rode through country he'd not seen before. In the early afternoon he came upon a rider sitting his horse with his hands crossed loosely over the pommel of his saddle. The horse was a goodlooking black gelding with a savvy look to its eye. It was ochred to the knees from the dust of that country and the rig was an old rimfire outfit with visalia stirrups and a flat saddlehorn the size of a coffeesaucer. The rider was chewing tobacco and he nodded as John Grady rode up. Can I help you? he said.

John Grady leaned and spat. Meanin I aint supposed to be on your land, he said. He looked at the rider. A man a few years older than he. The rider studied him back with his pale blue eyes.

I work for Mac McGovern, John Grady said. I reckon you know him.

Yes, the rider said. I know him. You all got stock drifted up this way?

No. Not that I know of. I just kindly drifted up this way myself.

The rider pushed the brim of his hat back slightly with his thumb. They were met upon a clay floodplain bereft of grass or any growing thing and the only sound the wind made was in their clothes. The dark clouds stood banked in a high wall to the north and a thin and soundless wire of lightning appeared there and quivered and vanished again. The rider leaned and spat and waited.

I was supposed to get married in two days' time, the boy said.

The rider nodded but the boy said no more.

I take it you changed your mind.

The boy didnt answer. The rider looked off to the north and looked back again.

We might get some rain out of that.

We might. It's rained over in town the last two nights.

Have you had your dinner?

No. I guess I aint.

Why dont you come on to the house.

I better get on back.

I reckon she changed hers.

The boy looked away. He didnt answer.

There'll be anothern along directly. You'll see.

No there wont.

Why dont you come on to the house and take dinner with us.

I appreciate it. I need to get back.

You remind me some of myself. Get somethin on your mind and just ride.

John Grady sat loosely holding the reins. He looked a long

time out at the running country before he spoke. When he did speak the rider had to lean to catch his words. I wish I could ride, he said. I wish I could.

The rider wiped the corners of his mouth with the heel of his thumb. Maybe you'd better ought not to go back just yet, he said. Maybe you ought to just wait a little while.

I'd ride and I'd never look back. I'd ride to where I couldnt find a single day I ever knew. Even if I was to turn back and ride over ever foot of that ground. Then I'd ride some more.

I've been thataway, said the rider.

I better get on.

You sure you wont change your mind? We feed pretty good.

No. I thank you.

Well.

I hope you get that rain up here.

I appreciate it.

He turned the horse and set out south down the broad flood-plain. The rider turned his own horse and started back upcountry but he stopped before he'd gone far. He sat the horse and watched the boy riding out down the broad valley and he watched him for a long time. When he could see him no more he raised himself slightly in the stirrups. As if he might call after him. The boy never looked back. When he was gone the rider stayed a while yet. He'd dropped the reins and he sat with one leg crossed over the fork of the saddle and he pushed back his hat and leaned and spat and studied the country. As if it ought to have something to tell him for that figure having passed through it.

It was late evening and almost dark when he rode the horse through the ford and dismounted under the cottonwoods in the glade at the far side. He let drop the reins and crossed to the cabin and pushed open the door. Inside it was dark and he stood in the doorway and looked back out at the evening. The darkening land. The sky to the west blood red where the sun had gone and the small dark birds blowing down before the storm. The wind in the flue moaned with a long dry sound. He went into the bedroom and stood. He got a match and lit the lamp and turned down the wick and put back the glass chimney and sat on the bed with his hands between his knees. The carved wooden santo leered from the shadows. His own shadow from the lamp rose up the wall behind him. A hulking shape which looked no description of him at all. After a while he took off his hat and let it drop to the floor and lowered his face into his hands.

When he rode out again it was dark and windy and starless and cold and the sacaton grass along the creek thrashed in the wind and the small bare trees he passed hummed like wires. The horse quivered and stepped and raised the flues of its nose to the wind. As if to sort what there might be in the coming storm that was not storm alone. They crossed the creek and set out down the old road. He thought he heard a fox bark and he looked for it along the rimrock skylined above the road to the left. Evenings in Mexico he used to see them come out and walk the traprock dikes above the plains for the vantage of the view there. To spy out what smaller life might venture forth in the dusk. Or they would simply sit upon those godlaid walls in silhouette like icons out of Egypt, silent and still against the deepening sky, sufficient to all that might be asked of them.

He'd left the lamp burning in the cabin and the softly lit window looked warm and inviting. Or it would have to other eyes. For himself he was done with all that and after he'd crossed the creek and taken the road he had to take he did not look back again.

When he rode into the yard it was raining lightly and he could see them all at supper through the rainbleared glass of the kitchen window. He rode on toward the barn and then halted the horse and looked back. He thought it was like seeing these people in some other time before he'd ever come to the ranch. Or they were like people in some other house of whose lives and histories he knew nothing. Mostly they all just seemed to be waiting for things to be a way they'd never be again.

He rode into the barn and dismounted and left the horse standing there and went to his room. The horses looked out over the stall doors and watched him as he passed. He did not turn on the light. He got his flashlight from the shelf and knelt and opened the footlocker and rummaged out his slicker and a dry shirt and he got the huntingknife that had belonged to his father from the bottom of the locker and the brown envelope that held his money and laid them on the bed. Then he stripped out of his shirt and put on the dry shirt and pulled on the slicker and put the huntingknife in the slicker pocket. He took some bills from the envelope and put the envelope back in the locker and closed the lid. Then he switched off the flashlight and set it back on the shelf and went out again.

When he reached the end of the road he dismounted and tied the reins together over the saddlehorn and led the horse a ways back up the road sliding in the mud and then let go the cheekstrap and stepped away and slapped the horse on the rump and stood watching as it trotted off up the road in the heavy muck to disappear in the rain and the dark.

The first lights that picked him up standing by the side of the highway slowed and stopped. He opened the car door and looked in.

My boots are awful muddy, he said.

Get in here, the man said. You cant hurt this thing.

He climbed in and pulled the door shut. The driver put the car in gear and leaned forward and squinted out at the road. I cant see at night worth a damn, he said. What are you doin out in the rain like this?

You mean aside from gettin wet?

Aside from gettin wet.

I just needed to get to town.

The driver looked at him. He was an old rancher, lean and rawboned. He wore the crown of his hat round the way some old men used to do. Damn, son, he said. You a desperate case.

It aint nothin like that. I just got some business to attend to.

Well I reckon it must be somethin that wont keep or you wouldnt be out here, would you?

No sir. I wouldnt.

Well I wouldnt either. It's a half hour past my bedtime right now.

Yessir.

Errand of mercy.

Sir?

Errand of mercy. I got a animal down.

He was bent over the wheel and the car was astraddle of the white center line. He looked at the boy. I'll get over if anything comes, he said. I know how to drive. I just cant see.

Yessir.

Who you work for?

Mac McGovern.

Old Mac. He's one of the good'ns. Aint he?

Yessir. He is.

You'd wear out a Ford pickup truck findin a better.

Yessir. I believe I would.

Got a mare down. Young mare. Tryin to foal.

You leave anybody with her?

My wife's at the house. At the barn, I should say.

They drove. The rain slashed over the road in the lights and the wipers rocked back and forth over the glass.

We'll be married sixty years April twenty-second.

That's a long time.

Yes it is. It dont seem like it, but it is. She come out here with her family from Oklahoma in a covered wagon. Got married we was both seventeen. We went to Dallas to the exposition on our honeymoon. They didnt want to rent us a room. Didnt neither one of us look old enough to be married. There aint been a day passed in sixty years I aint thanked God for that woman. I never done nothin to deserve her, I can tell you that. I dont know what you could do.

BILLY PAID HIS TOLL at the booth and walked across the bridge. The boys along the river beneath the bridge held up their buckets on poles and called out for money. He walked down Juárez Avenue among the tourists, past the bars and curioshops, the shills calling to him from the doorways. He went into the Florida and ordered a whiskey and drank it and paid and went out again.

He walked up Tlaxcala to the Moderno but it was closed. He tapped and waited under the green and yellow tiled arch. He walked around the side of the building and looked in through a broken corner in one of the barred windows. He could see the small light over the bar at the rear of the building. He stood in the rain looking out down the street where it lay in a narrow corridor of shops and bars and lowbuilt houses. The air smelled of dieselsmoke and woodfires.

He went back to Juárez Avenue and got a cab. The driver looked at him in the mirror.

Conoce el White Lake?

Sí. Claro.

Bueno. Vámonos.

The driver nodded and they pulled away. Billy sat back in the cab and watched the bleak streets of the bordertown pass in the rainy afternoon light. They left the paved road and went out through the mud roads of the outlying barrios. Vendors' burros piled high with cordwood turned away their heads as the taxi passed splashing through the potholes. Everything was covered with mud.

When they pulled up in front of the White Lake Billy got out and lit a cigarette and took his billfold from the hip pocket of his jeans.

I can wait for you, the driver said.

That's all right.

I can come in and wait.

I might be a while. What do I owe you?

Three dollars. You dont want me to wait for you?

No.

The driver shrugged and took the money and rolled the window back up and pulled away. Billy put the cigarette in his mouth and looked at the building there at the edge of the barrio between the mud and cratewood hovels and the pleated sheetiron walls of the warehouse.

He walked on to the rear of the place and turned up the alley past the warehouse and knocked at the first of two doors and waited. He flipped the butt of the cigarette into the mud. He'd reached to knock at the door again when it opened and the old criada looked out. As soon as she saw him she tried to shut the door but he shoved it back open and she turned and went scuttling down the hallway with one hand atop her head crying out. He shut the door behind him and looked down the hall. Whores' heads in curlingpapers ducked out and ducked back like chickens. Doors closed. He'd not gone ten feet along the hallway when a man in black with a thin and weaselshaped face stepped out and tried to take his arm. Excuse me, the man said. Excuse me.

Billy jerked his arm away. Where's Eduardo? he said.

Excuse me, the man said. He tried to take Billy's arm again. Mistake. Billy took him by the front of his shirt and slammed him against the wall. He was so light. There was nothing to him at all. He put up no resistance but seemed to be merely reaching about him as if he'd lost something and Billy turned loose of the handful of black silk knotted up in his fist just in time. The thin blade of the knife snickered past his belt and he leapt back and raised up his arms. Tiburcio crouched and feinted with the knife before him.

You little son of a bitch, said Billy. He hit the Mexican squarely in the mouth and the Mexican slammed back against the wall and sat down on the floor. The knife went spinning and clattering down the hallway. The old woman at the end of the hall was watching with her fingers in her teeth. Her eye closed and opened again in a huge and obscene wink. He turned to the pimp and was surprised to see him struggling to his feet holding a small silver penknife still fastened to the chain draped across the front of his pegged black trousers. Billy hit him in the side of the head and heard bone crack. The pimp's head spun away and he slid several feet down the hallway and lay in a twisted black pile in the floor like a dead bird. The old woman came down the hall at a tottering run crying out. He caught her as she went past and pulled her around. She threw up her hands and closed her good eye. Aiee, she cried. Aiee. He gripped her wrists and shook her. Dónde está mi compañero? he said.

Aiee, she cried. She tried to pull away to go to the pimp lying in the floor.

Dígame. Dónde está mi cuate?

No sé. No sé. Por Dios, no sé nada.

Dónde está la muchacha? Magdalena? Dónde está Magdalena?

Jesús María y José ten compasión no está. No está.

Dónde está Eduardo?

No está. No está.

Aint a damn soul está, is there?

He turned her loose and she threw herself on the fallen pimp and raised his face to her breast. Billy shook his head in disgust and went down the hall and picked up the knife and stuck the blade between the door and the jamb and snapped the blade off and slung the handle away and turned and came back. The criada cowered and held up one hand over her head but he reached down past her and snatched away the silver chain from the pimp's waistcoat and broke off the blade of the penknife also.

Has this son of a bitch got any more knives on him?

Aiee, moaned the criada, rocking back and forth with the pimp's oiled head in her bosom. The pimp had come awake and was looking up at him with one walled eye through the woman's stringy hair. One arm flailed about loosely. Billy reached down and got him by the hair and pulled his face up.

Dónde está Eduardo?

The criada was moaning and blubbering and sat trying to unclamp Billy's fingers from the pimp's hair.

En su oficina, wheezed the pimp.

He turned him loose and straightened up and wiped his oily hand on the leg of his jeans and walked down the hallway to the far end. Eduardo's foilcovered door had no doorknob to it and he stood looking at it for a minute and then raised one boot and kicked it in. It came completely off the hinges in a great splintering of wood and turned slightly sideways and fell into the room. Eduardo sat at his desk. He seemed strangely unalarmed.

Where is he? said Billy.

The mysterious friend.

His name is John Cole and if you've harmed a hair on his head you're a dead son of a bitch.

Eduardo leaned back. He opened the drawer of his desk.

You better have a shoebox full of pistols in there, said Billy.

Eduardo took a cigar from the desk drawer and closed it and took his gold cigarcutter from his pocket and held up the cigar and clipped it and put the cigar in his mouth and the cutter back in his pocket.

Why would I need a pistol?

I'm fixin to point out several reasons if I dont get some sense out of you.

The door was not locked.

What?

The door was not locked.

I aint studyin your damn door.

Eduardo nodded. He'd taken his lighter from his pocket and was wafting the flame across the end of the cigar and rotating the cigar in his mouth slowly with his fingers. He looked at Billy. Then he looked past Billy. When Billy turned the alcahuete was standing in the door, one hand on the splintered jamb, breathing slowly and evenly. One eye was swelled half shut and his mouth was puffed and bleeding and his shirt was torn. Eduardo gestured him away with a small toss of his chin.

Surely, he said, you dont believe that we are unable to protect ourselves from the riffraff and drunks that come here?

He put the lighter in his pocket and looked up. Tiburcio was still standing in the doorway. Ándale pues, he said. Tiburcio looked at Billy for a moment with no more expression than a pitviper and then turned and went back down the hall.

Your friend is being sought by the police, said Eduardo. The girl is dead. Her body was found in the river this morning.

Damn you to hell.

Eduardo studied the cigar. He looked up at Billy. You see what has come to pass.

You couldnt just cut her loose, could you.

You remember our conversation when last we met.

Yeah. I remember it.

You did not believe me.

I believed you.

You spoke to your friend?

Yeah. I spoke to him.

But your words carried no weight with him.

No. They didnt.

And now I cannot help you. You see.

I didnt come here for your help.

You might wish to consider the question of your own implication in this matter.

I got nothin to answer for.

Eduardo drew deeply on the cigar and blew the smoke slowly into the uninhabited center of the room. You present an odd picture, he said. In spite of whatever views you may hold everything that has come to pass has been the result of your friend's coveting of another man's property and his willful determination to convert that property to his own use without regard for the consequences. But of course this does not make the consequences go away. Does it? And now I find you before me breathless and half wild having wrecked my place of business and maimed my help. And having almost certainly colluded in enticing away one of the girls in my charge in a manner that has led to her death. And yet you appear to be asking me to help you to resolve your difficulties for you. Why?

Billy looked at his right hand. It was already badly swollen. He looked at the pimp seated sideways at the desk. The expensive boots crossed before him.

You think I got no recourse, dont you?

I dont know what you have or do not have.

I know this country too.

No one knows this country.

Billy turned. He stood in the doorway and looked down the corridor. Then he looked at the pimp again. Damn you to hell, he said. You and all your kind.

HE SAT IN A STEEL CHAIR in an empty room with his hat on his knee. When the door finally opened again the officer looked at him and motioned him forward with the tips of his fingers. He rose and followed the man down the corridor. A prisoner was mopping the worn linoleum and as they passed he stepped back and waited and then went to mopping again.

The officer knocked at the captain's door with one knuckle and then opened the door and gestured for Billy to enter. He stepped in and the door closed behind him. The captain sat at his desk writing. He glanced up. Then he went on writing. After a while he gestured slightly with his chin toward two chairs to his left. Please, he said. Be seated.

Billy sat in one of the chairs and set his hat in the chair beside him. Then he picked it up again and held it. The captain laid his pen aside and stood the papers and tapped and edged them square and set them aside and looked at him.

How may I help you? he said.

I come to see you about a girl that was found dead in the river this mornin. I think I can identify her.

We know who she is, the captain said. He leaned back in his chair. She was a friend of yours?

No. I seen her one time is all.

She was a prostitute.

Yessir.

The captain sat with his hands pressed together. He leaned forward and took from an oakwood tray at the corner of his desk a large and glossy photo and handed it across.

Is that the girl?

Billy took the photo and turned it and looked at it. He looked up at the captain. I dont know, he said. It's kindly hard to tell.

The girl in the photo looked made of wax. She'd been turned so as to afford the best view of her severed throat. Billy held the photo gingerly. He looked up at the captain again.

I expect that's probably her.

The captain reached and took the photo and returned it to the tray face down. You have a friend, he said.

Yessir.

What was his relationship with this girl?

He was goin to marry her.

Marry her.

Yessir.

The captain picked up his pen and unscrewed the cap. What is his name?

John Grady Cole.

The captain wrote. Where is your friend? he said.

I dont know.

You know him well?

Yes. I do.

Did he kill the girl?

No.

The captain screwed the cap back onto the pen and leaned back. All right, he said.

All right what.

You are free to go.

I was free to go when I come in here.

Did he send you?

No he didnt send me.

All right.

Is that all you got to say?

The captain put his hands together again. He tapped at his teeth with the tips of his fingers. Outside the sound of people talking in the corridor. Beyond that the traffic in the street.

How do you say your name?

Sir?

How do you say your name.

Parham. You say Parham.

Parham.

You aint goin to write it down?

No.

You've already got it writ.

Yes.

Well.

You are not going to tell me anything. Are you?

Billy looked down into his hat. He looked up at the captain. You know that pimp killed her.

The captain tapped his teeth. We would like to talk to your friend, he said.

You'd like to talk to him but not to the pimp.

The pimp we have already talked to.

Yeah. And I know what talks, too.

The captain shook his head wearily. He looked at the name on the pad. He looked up at Billy.

Mr Parham, he said. Every male in my family for three generations has been killed in defense of this republic. Grandfathers, fathers, uncles, brothers. Eleven men in all. Any beliefs they may have had now reside in me. Any hopes. This is a sobering thought to me. You understand? I pray to these men. Their blood ran in the streets and gutters and in the arroyos and among the desert stones. They are my Mexico and I pray to them and I answer to them and to them alone. I do not answer elsewhere. I do not answer to pimps.

If that's true then I take back what I said.

The captain inclined his head.

Billy nodded toward the photo in the box. What have they done with her? The body.

The captain raised one hand and let it fall again. He has already made his visit. This morning.

He saw that?

Yes. Before we knew the identity of the girl. The—how do you call him? The practicante. The practicante told my lieutenant that he spoke excellent spanish. He has a cicatriz. A scar. Here.

That dont make him a bad person.

Is he a bad person?

He's as good a boy as I ever knew. He's the best.

You dont know where he is.

No sir. I dont.

The captain sat for a moment. Then he stood up and held out his hand. I thank you for coming, he said.

Billy rose and they shook hands and Billy put on his hat. At the door he turned.

He dont own the White Lake, does he? Eduardo.

No.

I dont reckon you'd tell me who does.

It is not important. A businessman. He has nothing to do with any of this.

You dont consider him to be a pimp, I reckon.

The captain studied him. Billy waited.

Yes, the captain said. I do so consider him.

I'm glad to hear it, Billy said. I'm the same way.

The captain nodded.

I dont know what happened, Billy said. But I know why it happened.

Tell me then.

He fell in love with her.

Your friend.

No. Eduardo.

The captain drummed his fingers lightly on the edge of his desk. Yes? he said.

Yes.

The captain shook his head. I dont see how a man could run such a place if he fell in love with the girls.

I dont either.

Yes. Why this girl?

I dont know.

You told me you only saw her once.

I did.

You think your friend was not such a fool.

I told him to his face he was. I might of been wrong.

The captain nodded. I'm not a fool either, Mr Parham. I know you would not bring him to me. Even if his hands were dripping. Especially not then.

Billy nodded. You take care, he said.

He walked out up the street and went into the first bar he came to and ordered a shot of whiskey and carried it to the payphone on the back wall. Socorro answered and he told her what had happened and asked for Mac but Mac was already on the phone.

I guess you'll tell me what all this is about.

Yessir. I will. If he shows up there dont let him leave if you can help it.

Maybe you'll let me know how you propose to keep him someplace he dont want to be kept.

I'll be there quick as I can get there. I'm just goin to check a few places.

I knew there was somethin about this that didnt rattle right.

Yessir.

Do you know where he's at?

No sir. I dont.

You call me back as quick as you know somethin. You hear?

Yessir.

You call me back anyways. Dont leave me settin here all evenin.

Yessir. I will.

He hung the phone up and drank the shot and carried the empty tumbler to the bar and set it down. Otra vez, he said. The barman poured. The place was empty save for a single drunk. He drank the second shot and laid a quarter on the bar and went out. Walking up Juárez Avenue the cabdrivers kept calling out to him to go and see the show. To go and see the girls.

JOHN GRADY drank one whiskey neat at the Kentucky Club and paid and went out and nodded to the cabman standing at the corner. They got in and the cabdriver turned and looked at him.

Where are you going my friend?

The White Lake.

He turned and started the engine and they pulled away into the street. The rain had settled into a steady light drizzle but the streets were flooded and the cab moved out slowly and went up Juárez Avenue like a boat with the garish lights reflected in the black water dishing and wobbling and righting themselves again in its wake.

Eduardo's car was parked in the alley under the dark of the warehouse wall and he crossed to where it stood and tried the door. Then he raised his boot and kicked in the doorglass. The glass was laminated and it spidered whitely in the light and sagged inward. He put his boot to it again and it caved down into the seat and he reached in and laid the heel of his hand on the horn and blew it three times and stepped back. The sound echoed in the alley and died. He took off his slicker and took the knife out of the pocket and he squatted and tucked his jeans into his boottops and stuck the knife and sheath down into his left boot. Then he laid the slicker across the hood of the car and blew the horn again. The echo had barely died when the door at the rear of the building opened and Eduardo stepped out and stood back against the wall away from the light.

John Grady walked out from the side of the car. A match flared and Eduardo's face leaned in the flame with one of his little cigarillos in his teeth. The dying match arced out into the alley.

The suitor, he said.

He stepped forward into the light and leaned on the iron railing. He smoked and looked out at the night. He looked down at the boy.

You could have just knocked at my door.

John Grady had taken the slicker from the hood of the car and he stood in the alley with it folded under his arm. Eduardo smoked.

You have come to pay me the money you owe me, I suppose.

I come to kill you.

The pimp drew slowly on the cigarillo. He tilted his head slightly and blew the smoke upward in a thin stream from his thin lips.

I dont think so, he said.

He turned and slowly descended the three steps into the alley. John Grady moved out to the left and stood waiting.

I think you do not even know why you are here, Eduardo said. Which is very sad. Perhaps I can teach you. Perhaps there is still time to learn. He drew again on the cigarillo and then dropped it and twisted it out with his boot.

John Grady never even saw him reach for the knife. Perhaps he'd palmed it in his hand the while. There was a sharp little click and a wink of light off the blade. And then the wink again. As if he were turning it in his hand. John Grady drew his knife from the top of his boot and wrapped the slicker around his right forearm and caught the loose end in his fist. Eduardo walked out into the alley so as to have the light behind him. He stepped carefully to avoid the pools of rainwater. His pale silk shirt rippled in the light. He turned and looked at the boy.

Change your mind, he said. Go back. Choose life. You are young.

I come to kill you or be killed.

Ah, said Eduardo.

I didnt come to talk.

It is only a formality. Because of your youth.

You dont need to worry about my youth.

The pimp stood in the alleyway. His shirt open at the neck. His sleek oiled head blue in the light. Holding the thin switch-blade knife loosely in one hand. I wanted you to know that I was still willing to forgive you, he said.

He had come forward by steps almost imperceptible. He stood. His head slightly cocked to one side. Waiting.

I will give you every advantage. Perhaps you have not been in so many fights. I think you will find that often in a fight the last one to speak is the loser.

He put two fingers to his lips to caution silence. Then he cupped his hand and gestured the boy forward. Come, he said. We must make a beginning. It is like a first kiss.

He did. He stepped forward and feinted and passed the knife sideways at the pimp and stepped back. Eduardo arched his back like a cat and held his elbows up that the blade pass beneath them. His shadow on the wall of the warehouse looked like some dark conductor raising his baton to commence. He smiled and circled. His sleek head shone. When he moved in it was very low and from left to right and the knife passed before him three times too fast to follow and almost too fast to see. John Grady fended the blade away with his wrapped right arm and stumbled back and recovered but Eduardo was circling again, smiling.

You think we have not seen your kind before? I have seen your kind before. Many and many. You think I dont know America? I know America. How old do you think I am?

He stopped and crouched and feinted and moved on, circling. I am forty years old, he said. An old man, no? Deserving respect, no? Not this fighting in alleys with knives.

He moved in again and when he stepped back his arm was cut just below the elbow and the yellow silk shirt was dark with blood. He seemed not to notice.

Not this fighting with suitors. With farmboys. Of whom there can be no end.

He stopped in his tracks and turned and started back the other way. He looked like an actor pacing a stage. At times he hardly seemed to notice the boy.

They drift down out of your leprous paradise seeking a thing now extinct among them. A thing for which perhaps they no longer even have a name. Being farmboys of course the first place they think to look is in a whorehouse.

The blood dripped from his sleeve. The slow dark gouts vanished in the dark sand underfoot. He swung the knife back and forth before him on his slow clockwise walk. Like a man hacking randomly at weeds.

By now of course longing has clouded their minds. Such minds as they may possess. The simplest truths are obscured. They cannot seem to see that the most elementary fact concerning whores—

He was suddenly very low before John Grady. Almost kneeling. Almost like a supplicant. The boy could not say how he got there but when he stepped away and commenced his circling again the boy's thigh was laid open in a deep gash and the warm blood was running down his leg.

Is that they are whores, said Eduardo.

He crouched and feinted and circled again. Then he stepped in and with the knife backhand made another cut no more than an inch above the first.

Do you think she did not beg me to come to her? Should I tell you the things she wished me to do? Things beyond a farmboy's imagining, I can assure you.

You're a liar.

The suitor speaks.

He lunged with his knife but Eduardo stepped aside and drew himself up so small and narrow and turned his head away in disdain in the manner of toreros. They circled.

Before I name you completely to myself I will give you even yet a last chance to save yourself. I will let you walk, suitor. If walk you will.

The boy moved sideways, watching. The blood had gone cold on his leg. He passed the sleeve of his knifehand across his nose. Save yourself, he said. If you can. Save yourself, whoremaster.

He calls me names.

They circled.

He is deaf to reason. To his friends. The blind maestro. All. He wishes nothing so fondly as to throw himself into the grave of a dead whore. And he calls me names.

He had turned his face upward. He held out one hand as if to display the vanity of counsel and he seemed to address some unseen witness.

This is quite a farmboy, he said. This is some farmboy.

He feinted to the left and cut John Grady a third time across the thigh.

I will tell you what I am doing. What in fact I have already done. For even knowing you will have no power to stop it. Do you wish me to tell you?

He says nothing, the suitor. Very well. Here is my plan. A medical transplant. To put the suitor's mind inside his thigh. What do you think of that?

He circled. The knife wafted slowly back and forth. I think it may be there already. And how is such a man to think? Whose mind has undergone such a relocation. He still hopes to live. Of course. But he is becoming weaker. The sand is drinking his blood. What do you think, suitor? Will you speak?

He feinted again with the switchblade and stepped away and continued his circling.

He says nothing. Yet how many times was he warned? And then to try to buy the girl? From that moment to this all was certain as dark and day.

John Grady feinted and slashed twice with the knife. Eduardo twisted like a falling cat. They circled.

You are like the whores from the campo, farmboy. To believe that craziness is sacred. A special grace. A special touch. A partaking of the godhead.

He held the knife before him at the level of his waist and passed it slowly back and forth.

But what does this say of God?

They moved simultaneously. The boy tried to grab his arm. They grappled, hacking. The pimp pushed him away and backed, circling. His shirt was sliced open at the front and there was a red slash across his stomach. The boy stood with his hands low, the palms down, waiting. His arm was laid open and he'd dropped the knife in the sand. He did not take his eyes off the pimp. He was cut twice across his stomach and he was reeking blood. The slicker had come unraveled and hung from his forearm and he slowly wound it up again and caught the end of it in his fist and stood.

The suitor seems to have lost his knife. Not so good, eh?

He turned, he circled back. He looked down at the knife.

What are we going to do now?

The boy didnt answer.

What will you give me for the knife?

The boy watched him.

Make me an offer, said Eduardo. What would you give at this point to have the knife back?

The boy turned his head and spat. Eduardo turned and paced slowly back.

Will you give me an eye?

The boy feinted to bend and reach for the knife but Eduardo warned him away and stood on the blade with his thin black boot.

If you let me pry one eye from your head I will give you your knife, he said. Otherwise I will simply cut your throat.

The boy said nothing. He watched.

Think about it, said Eduardo. With one eye in your head you still might kill me. A careless slip. A lucky thrust. Who knows? Anything is possible. What do you say?

He paced away slightly to the left and returned. The knife lay crushed into its mold in the sand.

Nothing, eh? I'll tell you what. I'll make you a better offer. Give me one ear. What about that?

The boy lunged and grabbed for his arm. He spun away and passed the blade twice more across the boy's belly. The boy made a lunge for the fallen knife but Eduardo was already standing over it and he backed away, holding his stomach, the warm blood running between his fingers.

You are going to see your guts before you die, said Eduardo. He stepped away. Pick it up, he said.

The boy watched him.

Pick it up. Did you think I was serious? Pick it up.

He bent and picked up the knife and wiped the blade on the side of his jeans. They circled. Eduardo's blade had severed the fascia of his stomach muscles and he felt hot and sick and his hand was sticky with blood but he was afraid to turn loose holding himself. The slicker had come unwound again and he shook it free and let it fall behind him. They circled.

Lessons are hard, said Eduardo. I think you must agree. But at this point the future is not so uncertain. What do you see? As one cuchillero to another. One filero to another.

He feinted with the switchblade. He smiled. They circled.

What does he see, the suitor. Does he still hope for some miracle? Perhaps he will see the truth at last in his own intestines. As do the old brujos of the campo.

He stepped in with his knife and feinted at the boy's face and then the blade dropped in a vanishing arc of falling light and connected the three bars by a vertical cut to form the letter E in the flesh of his thigh.

He circled to the left. He flung back his oiled hair with a toss of his head.

Do you know what my name is, farmboy? Do you know my name?

He turned his back on the boy and walked slowly away. He addressed the night.

In his dying perhaps the suitor will see that it was his hunger for mysteries that has undone him. Whores. Superstition. Finally death. For that is what has brought you here. That is what you were seeking.

He turned back. He passed the blade again before him in that slow scythelike gesture and he looked questioningly at the boy. As if he might answer at last.

That is what has brought you here and what will always bring you here. Your kind cannot bear that the world be ordinary. That it contain nothing save what stands before one. But the Mexican world is a world of adornment only and underneath it is very plain indeed. While your world—he passed the blade back and forth like a shuttle through a loom—your world totters upon an unspoken labyrinth of questions. And we will devour you, my friend. You and all your pale empire.

When he moved again the boy made no effort to defend himself. He simply slashed away with his knife and when Eduardo stepped back he had fresh cuts on his arm and across his chest. He flung back his head again to clear his lank black locks from before his face. The boy stood stolidly, following him with his eyes. He was drenched in blood.

Dont be afraid, said Eduardo. It doesnt hurt so bad. It would hurt tomorrow. But there will be no tomorrow.

John Grady stood holding himself. His hand was slick with blood and he could feel something bulging through into his palm. They met again and Eduardo laid open the back of his arm but he held himself and would not move the arm. They turned. His boots made a soft sloshing sound.

For a whore, the pimp said. For a whore.

They closed again and John Grady lowered his knife arm.

He felt Eduardo's blade slip from his rib and cross his upper stomach and pass on. It took his breath away. He made no effort to step or to parry. He brought his knife up underhand from the knee and slammed it home and staggered back. He heard the clack of the Mexican's teeth as his jaw clapped shut. Eduardo's knife dropped with a light splash into the small pool of standing water at his feet and he turned away. Then he looked back. The way a man might look getting on a train. The handle of the huntingknife jutted from the underside of his jaw. He reached and touched it. His mouth was clenched in a grimace. His jaw was nailed to his upper skull and he held the handle in both hands as if he would withdraw it but he did not. He walked away and turned and leaned against the warehouse wall. Then he sat down. He drew his knees up to him and sat breathing harshly through his teeth. He put his hands down at either side of him and he looked at John Grady and then after a while he leaned slowly over and lay slumped in the alleyway against the wall of the building and he did not move again.

John Grady was leaning against the wall on the opposite side of the alley, holding himself with both hands. Dont sit down, he said. Dont sit down.

He steadied himself and blew and got his breath and looked down. His shirt hung in bloody tatters. A gray tube of gut pushed through his fingers. He gritted his teeth and took hold of it and pushed it back and put his hand over it. He walked over and picked up Eduardo's knife out of the water and he crossed the alley and still holding himself he cut away the silk shirt from his dead enemy with one hand and leaning against the wall with the knife in his teeth he tied the shirt around himself and bound it tight. Then he let the knife fall in the sand and turned and wobbled slowly down the alleyway and out into the road.

He tried to keep off the main streets. The wash of the lights from the city by which he steered his course hung over the desert like a dawn eternally to come. His boots were filling up with blood and he left bloody tracks in the sand streets of the barrios and dogs came into the street behind him to take his scent and raise their hackles and growl and slink away. He talked to himself as he went. He took to counting his steps. He could hear sirens in the distance and at every step he felt the warm blood ooze between his clutched fingers.

By the time he reached the Calle de Noche Triste he was lightheaded and his feet were reeling beneath him. He leaned against a wall and gathered himself to cross the street. No cars passed.

You didnt eat, he said. That's where you were smart.

He pushed himself off the wall. He stood at the streetcurb and felt before him with one foot and he tried to hurry in case a car should come but he was afraid he'd fall and he didnt know if he could get up again.

A little later he remembered crossing the street but it seemed a long while ago. He'd seen lights ahead. They turned out to be from a tortilla factory. A clanking of old chaindriven machinery, a few workers in flourdusted aprons talking under a yellow lightbulb. He lurched on. Past dark houses. Empty lots. Old slumped mud walls half buried in wind-driven trash. He slowed, he stood teetering. Dont sit down, he said.

But he did. What woke him was someone going through his bloodsoaked pockets. He seized a thin and bony wrist and looked up into the face of a young boy. The boy flailed and kicked and tried to pull away. He called out to his friends but they were on the run across the empty lot. They'd all thought he was dead.

He pulled the boy close. Mira, he said. Está bien. No te molestaré.

Déjame, said the boy.

Está bien. Está bien.

The boy wrenched about. He looked after his friends but they'd vanished in the darkness. Déjame, he said. He was close to tears.

John Grady talked to him the way he'd talk to a horse and after a while the boy stopped pulling and stood. He told him that he was a great filero and that he had just killed an evil man and that he needed the boy's help. He said that the police would be looking for him and that he needed to hide from them. He spoke for a long time. He told the boy of his exploits as a knifefighter and he reached with great difficulty to his hip pocket and got his billfold and gave it to the boy. He told him that the money in it was his to keep and then he told him what he must do. Then he had the boy repeat it back. Then he turned loose of the boy's wrist and waited. The boy stepped back. He stood holding the bloodstained wallet. Then he squatted and looked into the man's eyes. His arms clutching his bony knees. Puede andar? he said.

Un poquito. No mucho.

Es peligroso aquí.

Sí. Tienes razón.

The boy got him up and he leaned on that narrow shoulder while they made their way to the farther corner of the lot where behind the wall was a clubhouse made from packingcrates. The boy knelt and pulled back a drapery of sacking and helped him to crawl in. He said that there was a candle there and matches but the wounded filero said that it was safer in the dark. He'd started to bleed all over again. He could feel it under his hand. Vete, he said. Vete. The boy let drop the curtain.

The cushions he lay on were damp from the rain and they stank. He was very thirsty. He tried not to think. He heard a car pass in the street. He heard a dog bark. He lay with the yellow silk of his enemy's shirt wrapped about him like a ceremonial sash gone dark with blood and he held his bloodied claw of a hand over the severed wall of his stomach. Holding himself close that he not escape from himself for he felt it over and over, that lightness that he took for his soul and which stood so tentatively at the door of his corporeal self. Like some light-footed animal that stood testing the air at the open door of a cage. He heard the distant toll of bells from the cathedral in the city and he heard his own breath soft and uncertain in the cold and the dark of the child's playhouse in that alien land where he lay in his blood. Help me, he said. If you think I'm worth it. Amen.

WHEN HE FOUND the horse standing saddled in the bay of the barn he led it out and mounted up and rode out in the dark up the old road toward John Grady's little adobe house. He hoped the horse would tell him something. When he reached the house and saw the light in the window he put the horse forward at a trot and went splashing through the little creek and into the yard where he pulled up and dismounted and hallooed the house.

He pushed open the door. Bud? he said. Bud?

He walked into the bedroom.

Bud?

There was no one there. He went out and called and waited and called again. He went back in and opened the stove door. A fire was laid with stovechunks and kindling and newsprint. He shut the door and went out. He called but no one answered. He mounted up and gave the horse its head and kneed it forward but it only wanted to set out across the creek and back down the road again.

He turned and rode back and waited at the little house for an hour but no one came. By the time he got back to the ranch it was almost midnight.

He lay on his bunk and tried to sleep. He thought he heard the whistle of a train in the distance, thin and lost. He must have been sleeping because he had a dream in which the dead girl came to him hiding her throat with her hand. She was covered in blood and she tried to speak but she could not. He opened his eyes. Very faintly he had heard the phone ring in the house.

When he got to the kitchen Socorro was on the phone in her robe. She gestured wildly at Billy. Sí, sí, she said. Sí, joven. Espérate.

HE WOKE COLD and sweating and raging with thirst. He knew that it was the new day because he was in agony. When he moved the crusted blood in his clothes cracked about him like ice. Then he heard Billy's voice.

Bud, he said. Bud.

He opened his eyes. Billy was kneeling over him. Behind him the boy was holding back the cloth and outside the world was cold and gray. Billy turned to the boy. Ándale, he said. Rápido. Rápido.

The curtain fell. Billy struck a match and held it. You daggone fool, he said. You daggone fool.

He reached down the stub of a candle in its saucer from the shelf nailed to the crate and lit the candle and held it close. Aw shit, he said. You daggone fool. Can you walk?

Dont move me.

I got to.

You couldnt get me across the border noway.

The hell I cant.

He killed her, bud. The son of a bitch killed her.

I know.

The police are huntin me.

JC's bringin the truck. We'll run the goddamn gate if we have to.

Dont move me, bud. I aint goin.

The hell you aint.

I cant make it. I thought there for a while I could. But I cant.

Just take it easy now. I aint listenin to that shit. Hell, I've had worse scratches than that on my eyeball.

I'm cut all to pieces Billy.

We'll get you back. Dont quit on me now, goddamn it.

Billy. Listen. It's all right. I know I aint goin to make it.

I done told you.

No. Listen. Whew. You dont know what I'd give for a cool drink of water.

I'll get it.

He started to set the candle by but John Grady took hold of his arm. Dont go, he said. Maybe when the boy gets back.

All right.

He said it wouldnt hurt. The lyin son of a bitch. Whew. It's gettin daylight, aint it?

Yeah.

I seen her, bud. They had her laid out and it didnt look like her but it was. They found her in the river. He cut her throat, bud.

I know.

I just wanted him. Bud, I wanted him.

You should of told me. You didnt have no business comin down here by yourself.

I just wanted him.

Just take it easy. They'll be here directly. You just hang on.

It's okay. Hurts like a sumbitch, Billy. Whew. It's okay.

You want me to get that water?

No. Stay here. She was so goddamned pretty, bud.

Yes she was.

I worried about her all day. You know we talked about where people go when they die. I just believe you go someplace and I seen her layin there and I thought maybe she wouldnt go to heaven because, you know, I thought she wouldnt and I thought about God forgivin people and I thought about if I could ask God to forgive me for killin that son of a bitch because you and me both know I aint sorry for it and I reckon this sounds ignorant but I didnt want to be forgiven if she wasnt. I didnt want to do or be nothin that she wasnt like goin to heaven or anything like that. I know that sounds crazy. Bud when I seen her layin there I didnt care to live no more. I knew my life was over. It come almost as a relief to me.

Hush now. They aint nothin over.

She wanted to do the right thing. That's got to count for somethin dont it? It did with me.

It does with me too.

There's a pawnshop ticket in the top of my footlocker. If you wanted to you could get my gun out and keep it.

We'll get it out.

There's thirty dollars owin on it. There's some money in there too. In a brown envelope.

Dont worry about nothin now. Just take it easy.

Mac's ring is in that little tin box. You see he gets it back. Whew. Like a sumbitch, bud.

You just hang on.

We got the little house lookin good, didnt we?

Yes we did.

You reckon you could keep that pup and kindly look after him?

You'll be there. Dont you worry now.

Hurts, bud. Like a sumbitch.

I know it. You just hang on.

I think maybe I'm goin to need that sup of water.

You just hang on. I'll get it. I wont be a minute either.

He set the candlestub in its saucer of grease on the shelf and backed out and let the curtain fall. As he trotted out across the vacant lot he looked back. The square of yellow light that shone through the sacking looked like some haven of promise out there on the shore of the breaking world but his heart misgave him.

Midblock there was a small cafe just opening. The girl setting up the little tin tables started when she saw him there, wild and sleepless, the knees of his breeches red with blood where he'd knelt in the bloodsoaked mat.

Agua, he said. Necesito agua.

She made her way to the counter without taking her eyes off him. She took down a tumbler and filled it from a bottle and set it on the counter and stepped back.

No hay un vaso más grande? he said.

She stared at him dumbly.

Dame dos, he said. Dos.

She got another glass and filled it and set it out. He put a dollar bill on the counter and took the glasses and left. It was gray dawn. The stars had dimmed out and the dark shapes of the mountains stood along the sky. He carried the glasses carefully one in each hand and crossed the street.

When he got to the packingcrate the candle was still burning and he took the glasses both in one hand and pushed back the sacking and crouched on his knees.

Here you go, bud, he said.

But he had already seen. He set the waterglasses slowly down. Bud, he said. Bud?

The boy lay with his face turned away from the light. His eyes were open. Billy called to him. As if he could not have gone far. Bud, he said. Bud? Aw goddamn. Bud?

Aint that pitiful, he said. Aint that the most goddamn pitiful thing? Aint it? Oh God. Bud. Oh goddamn.

When he had him gathered in his arms he rose and turned. Goddamn whores, he said. He was crying and the tears ran on his angry face and he called out to the broken day against them all and he called out to God to see what was before his eyes. Look at this, he called. Do you see? Do you see?

The Sabbath had passed and in the gray Monday dawn a procession of schoolchildren dressed in blue uniforms all alike were being led along the gritty walkway. The woman had stepped from the curb to take them across at the intersection when she saw the man coming up the street all dark with blood bearing in his arms the dead body of his friend. She held up her hand and the children stopped and huddled with their books at their breasts. He passed. They could not take their eyes from him. The dead boy in his arms hung with his head back and those partly opened eyes beheld nothing at all out of that passing landscape of street or wall or paling sky or the figures of the children who stood blessing themselves in the gray light. This man and his burden passed on forever out of that nameless crossroads and the woman stepped once more into the street and the children followed and all continued on to their appointed places which as some believe were chosen long ago even to the beginning of the world.

EPILOGUE

HE LEFT three days later, he and the dog. A cold and windy day. The pup shivering and whining until he took it up in the bow of the saddle with him. He'd settled up with Mac the evening before. Socorro would not look at him. She set his plate before him and he sat looking at it and then rose and walked down the hallway leaving it untouched on the table. It was still there when he went out through the kitchen again ten minutes later for the last time and she was still there at the stove, bearing on her forehead in ash the thumbprint of the priest placed there that morning to remind her of her mortality. As if she had any thought other. Mac paid him and he folded the money and put it in his shirt-pocket and buttoned it.

When are you leavin?

In the mornin.

You dont have to go.

I dont have to do nothin but die.

You wont change your mind?

No sir.

Well. Nothin's forever.

Some things are.

Yeah. Some things are.

I'm sorry Mr Mac.

I am too, Billy.

I should of looked after him better.

We all should of.

Yessir.

That cousin of his got here about a hour ago. Thatcher Cole.

Called from town. He said they finally got hold of his mother.

What did she have to say?

He didnt say. He said they hadnt heard from him in three years. What do you make of that?

I dont know.

I dont either.

Are you goin to San Angelo?

No. Maybe I ought to. But I aint.

Yessir. Well.

Let it go, son.

I'd like to. I think it's goin to be a while.

I think so too.

Yessir.

Mac nodded toward his blue and swollen hand. You dont think you ought to get somebody to look at that?

It's all right.

You've always got a job here. The army's goin to take this place, but we'll find somethin to do.

I appreciate that.

What time will you be leavin?

Early of the mornin.

You told Oren?

No sir. Not yet.

I reckon you'll see him at breakfast.

Yessir.

But he didnt. He rode out in the dark long before daylight and he rode the sun up and he rode it down again. In the oncoming years a terrible drought struck west Texas. He moved on. There was no work in that country anywhere. Pasture gates stood open and sand drifted in the roads and after a few years it was rare to see stock of any kind and he rode on. Days of the world. Years of the world. Till he was old.

In the spring of the second year of the new millennium he was living in the Gardner Hotel in El Paso Texas and working as an extra in a movie. When the work came to an end he stayed in his room. There was a television set in the lobby and men his age and younger sat in the lobby in the evening in the old chairs and watched the television but he cared little for it and the men had little to say to him or he to them. His money ran out. Three weeks later he was evicted. He'd long since sold his saddle and he set forth into the street with just his AWOL bag and his blanketroll.

There was a shoe repair place a few blocks up the street and he stopped in to see if he could get his boot fixed. The shoeman looked at it and shook his head. The sole was paper thin and the stitching had pulled through the leather. He took it to the rear and sewed it on his machine and returned and stood it on the counter. He wouldnt take any money for it. He said it wouldnt hold and it didnt.

A week later he was somewhere in central Arizona. A rain had come down from the north and the weather turned cool. He sat beneath a concrete overpass and watched the gusts of rain blowing across the fields. The overland trucks passed shrouded in rain with the clearance lights burning and the big wheels spinning like turbines. The east-west traffic passed overhead with a muted rumble. He wrapped himself in his blanket and tried to sleep on the cold concrete but sleep was a long time coming. His bones hurt. He was seventy-eight years old. The heart that should have killed him long ago by what the army's recruiting doctors had said still rattled on in his chest, no will of his. He pulled the blankets about him and after a while he did sleep.

In the night he dreamt of his sister dead seventy years and buried near Fort Sumner. He saw her so clearly. Nothing had changed, nothing faded. She was walking slowly along the dirt road past the house. She wore the white dress her grandmother had sewn for her from sheeting and in her grandmother's hands the dress had taken on a shirred bodice and borders of tatting threaded with blue ribbon. That's what she wore. That and the straw hat she'd gotten for Easter. When she passed the house he knew that she would never enter there again nor would he see her ever again and in his sleep he called out to her but she did not turn or answer him but only passed on down that empty road in infinite sadness and infinite loss.

He woke and lay in the dark and the cold and he thought of her and he thought of his brother dead in Mexico. In everything that he'd ever thought about the world and about his life in it he'd been wrong.

Toward the small hours of the morning the traffic on the freeway slacked and the rain stopped. He sat up shivering and hitched the blanket about his shoulders. He'd put some crackers from a roadside diner in the pocket of his coat and he sat eating them and watching the gray light flush out the raw wet fields beyond the roadway. He thought he heard the distant cries of cranes where they would be headed north to their summering grounds in Canada and he thought of them asleep in a flooded field in Mexico in a dawn long ago, standing singlefooted in the wetlands with their bills tucked, gray figures aligned in rows like hooded monks at prayer. When he looked across the overpass to the far side of the turnpike he saw another such as he sitting also solitary and alone.

The man raised his hand in greeting. He raised his back.

Buenos días, the man called.

Buenos días.

Qué tiene de comer?

Unas galletas, nada más.

The man nodded. He looked away.

Podemos compartirlas.

Bueno, called the man. Gracias.

Allí voy.

But the man stood. I will come to you, he called.

He descended the concrete batterwall and crossed the roadway and climbed over the guardrail and crossed the median between the round concrete pillars and crossed the northbound lanes and climbed up to where Billy was sitting and squatted and looked at him.

It aint much, Billy said. He pulled the remaining few packages of crackers from his pocket and held them out.

Muy amable, the man said.

Está bien. I thought at first you might be somebody else.

The man sat and stretched out his legs before him and crossed his feet. He tore open a package of the crackers with his eyetooth and took one out and held it up and looked at it and then bit it in two and sat chewing. He wore a wispy moustache, his skin was smooth and brown. He was of no determinable age.

Who did you think I might be? he said.

Just somebody. Somebody I sort of been expectin. I thought I caught a glimpse of him once or twice these past few days. I aint never got all that good a look at him.

What does he look like?

I dont know. I guess more and more he looks like a friend.

You thought I was death.

I considered the possibility.

The man nodded. He chewed. Billy watched him.

You aint are you?

No.

They sat eating the dry crackers.

Adónde vas? Billy said.

Al sur. Y tú?

Al norte.

The man nodded. He smiled. Qué clase de hombre comparta sus galletas con la muerte?

Billy shrugged. What kind of death would eat them?

What kind indeed, said the man.

I wasnt tryin to figure anything out. De todos modos el compartir es la ley del camino, verdad?

De veras.

At least that's the way I was raised.

The man nodded. In Mexico on certain days of the calendar it is the custom to set a place at the table for death. But perhaps you know this.

Yes.

He has a big appetite.

Yes he does.

Perhaps a few crackers would be taken as an insult.

Perhaps he's got to take what he can get. Like the rest of us.

The man nodded. Yes, he said. That could be.

Traffic had picked up on the turnpike. The sun was up. The man opened the second package of crackers. He said that perhaps death took a larger view. That perhaps in his egalitarian way death weighed the gifts of men by their own lights and that in death's eyes the offerings of the poor were the equal of any.

Like God.

Yes. Like God.

Nadie puede sobornar a la muerte, Billy said.

De veras. Nadie.

Nor God.

Nor God.

Billy watched the light bring up the shapes of the water standing in the fields beyond the roadway. Where do we go when we die? he said.

I dont know, the man said. Where are we now?

The sun rose over the plain behind them. The man handed him back the last remaining packet of crackers.

You can keep em, Billy said.

No quieres más?

My mouth's too dry.

The man nodded, he pocketed the crackers. Para el camino, he said. I was born in Mexico. I have not been back for many years.

You goin back now?

No.

Billy nodded. The man studied the coming day. In the middle of my life, he said, I drew the path of it upon a map and I studied it a long time. I tried to see the pattern that it made upon the earth because I thought that if I could see that pattern and identify the form of it then I would know better how to continue. I would know what my path must be. I would see into the future of my life.

How did that work out?

Different from what I expected.

How did you know it was the middle of your life?

I had a dream. That was why I drew the map.

What did it look like?

The map?

Yes.

It was interesting. It looked like different things. There were different perspectives one could take. I was surprised.

Could you remember all the places you'd been?

Oh yes. Couldnt you?

I dont know. There's been a bunch of em. Yeah. I suppose. If I put my mind to it. If I was to set down and study about it.

Yes. Of course. That was my method. One thing leads to another. I doubt that our journey can be lost to us. For good or bad.

What sorts of things did it look like? The map.

At first I saw a face but then I turned it and looked at it other ways and when I turned it back the face was gone. Nor could I find it again.

What happened to it?

I dont know.

Did you see it or did you just think you did?

The man smiled. Qué pregunta, he said. What would be the difference?

I dont know. I think there has to be a difference.

So do I. But what is it?

Well. It wouldnt be like a real face.

No. It was a suggestion. Un bosquejo. Un borrador, quizás.

Yes.

In any case it is difficult to stand outside of one's desires and see things of their own volition.

I think you just see whatever's in front of you.

Yes. I dont think that.

What was the dream?

The dream, the man said.

You dont have to tell me.

How do you know?

You dont have to tell me anything.

Perhaps. Nevertheless there was this man who was traveling through the mountains and he came to a place in the mountains where certain pilgrims used to gather in the long ago.

Is this the dream?

Yes.

Ándale pues.

Gracias. Where pilgrims used to gather in the long ago. En tiempos antiguos.

You've told this dream before.

Yes.

Ándale.

En tiempos antiguos. It was a high pass in the mountains that he had come to and here there was a table of rock and the table of rock was very old and it had fallen in the early days of the earth from a high peñasco in the mountains and lay in the floor of the pass with its flat and cloven side to the weather and the sun. And on the face of that rock there were yet to be seen the stains of blood from those who'd been slaughtered upon it to appease the gods. The iron in the blood of these vanished beings had blackened the rock and there it could be seen. Together with the hatching of axemarks or the marks of swords upon the stone to show where the work was done.

Is there such a place?

I dont know. Yes. There are such places. But this was not one of them. This was a dream place.

Ándale.

So the traveler arrived at this place at nightfall when the mountains about were darkening and the wind in the pass was growing cold with night's onset and he put down his burden to rest himself and he removed his hat to cool his brow and then his eyes fell upon this bloodstained altarstone which the weathers of the sierra and the sierra's storms had these millennia been impotent to cleanse. And there he elected to pass the night, such is the recklessness of those whom God has been so good as to shield from their just share of adversity in this world.

Who was the traveler?

I dont know.

Was it you?

I dont think so. But then if we do not know ourselves in the waking world what chance in dreams?

I'd think I'd know if it was me.

Yes. But have you not met people in dreams you never saw before? In dreams or out?

Sure.

And who were they?

I dont know. Dream people.

You think you made them up. In your dream.

I guess. Yeah.

Could you do it waking?

Billy sat with his arms over his knees. No, he said. I guess I couldnt.

No. Anyway I think the self of you in dreams or out is only that which you elect to see. I'm guessing every man is more than he supposes.

Ándale.

So. This traveler was such a man. He laid down his burden and surveyed the darkening scene. In that high pass was naught but rock and scree and as he thought to at least raise himself above the feasible paths of serpents in the night so he came to the altar and placed his hands upon it. He paused, but he did not pause long enough. He unrolled his blanket upon the stone and weighted down the ends with rocks that it not be blown away by the wind before he could remove his boots.

Did he know what kind of stone it was?

No.

Then who knew?

The dreamer knew.

You.

Yes.

Well I reckon you and him had to of been two different people then.

How so?

Because if you were the same then one would know what the other knew.

As in the world.

Yes.

But this is not the world. This is a dream. In the world the question could not occur.

Ándale.

Remove his boots. When he had removed them he climbed onto the stone and rolled himself in his blanket and upon that cold and terrible pallet he composed himself for sleep.

I wish him luck.

Yes. Yet sleep he did.

He fell asleep in your dream.

Yes.

How do you know he was asleep?

I could see him sleeping.

Did he dream?

The man sat looking at his shoes. He uncrossed his legs and recrossed them the other way. Well, he said. I'm not sure how to answer you. Certain events occurred. Some things about them remain unclear. It is difficult to know, for instance, when it was that these events took place.

Why?

The dream I had was on a certain night. And in the dream the traveler appeared. What night was this? In the life of the traveler when was it that he came to spend the night in that rocky posada? He slept and events took place which I will tell you of, but when was this? You can see the problem. Let us say that the events which took place were a dream of this man whose own reality remains conjectural. How assess the world of that conjectural mind? And what with him is sleep and what is waking? How comes he to own a world of night at all? Things need a ground to stand upon. As every soul requires a body. A dream within a dream makes other claims than what a man might suppose.

A dream inside a dream might not be a dream.

You have to consider the possibility.

It just sounds like superstition to me.

And what is that?

Superstition?

Yes.

Well. I guess it's when you believe in things that dont exist.

Such as tomorrow? Or yesterday?

Such as the dreams of somebody you dreamt. Yesterday was here and tomorrow's comin.

Maybe. But anyway the dreams of this man were his own dreams. They were distinct from my dream. In my dream the man was lying on his stone asleep.

You still could of made them up.

En este mundo todo es posible. Vamos a ver.

It's like the picture of your life in that map.

Cómo?

Es un dibujo nada más. It aint your life. A picture aint a thing. It's just a picture.

Well said. But what is your life? Can you see it? It vanishes at its own appearance. Moment by moment. Until it vanishes to appear no more. When you look at the world is there a point in time when the seen becomes the remembered? How are they separate? It is that which we have no way to show. It is that which is missing from our map and from the picture that it makes. And yet it is all we have.

You aint said whether your map was any use to you or not.

The man tapped his lower lip with his forefinger. He looked at Billy. Yes, he said. We will come to that. For now I can only say that I had hoped for a sort of calculus that would sum the convergence of map and life when life was done. For within their limitations there must be a common shape or shared domain between the telling and the told. And if that is so then the picture also in whatever partial form must have a direction to it and if it does then whatever is to come must lie in that path. You say that the life of a man cannot be pictured. But perhaps we mean different things. The picture seeks to seize and immobilize within its own configurations what it never owned. Our map knows nothing of time. It has no power to speak even of the hours implicit in its own existence. Not of those that have passed, not of those to come. Yet in its final shape the map and the life it traces must converge for there time ends.

So if I'm right still it's for the wrong reasons.

Perhaps we should return to the dreamer and his dream.

Ándale.

You might wish to say that the traveler woke and that the events which took place were not a dream at all. But I think to view them as a dream is the wiser course. For if these events were else than a dream he would not wake at all. As you will see.

Ándale.

My own dream is another matter. My traveler sleeps a troubled dream. Shall I wake him? The proprietary claims of the dreamer upon the dreamt have their limits. I cannot rob the traveler of his own autonomy lest he vanish altogether. You see the problem.

I think I'm beginnin to see several problems.

Yes. This traveler also has a life and there is a direction to that life and if he himself did not appear in this dream the dream would be quite otherwise and there could be no talk of him at all. You may say that he has no substance and therefore no history but my view is that whatever he may be or of whatever made he cannot exist without a history. And the ground of that history is not different from yours or mine for it is the predicate life of men that assures us of our own reality and that of all about us. Our privileged view into this one night of this man's history presses upon us the realization that all knowledge is a borrowing and every fact a debt. For each event is revealed to us only at the surrender of every alternate course. For us, the whole of the traveler's life converges at this place and this hour, whatever we may know of that life or out of whatever stuff it may be made. De acuerdo?

Ándale.

So. He composed himself for sleep. And in the night there was a storm in the mountains and the lightning cracked and the wind moaned in the gap and the traveler's rest was a poor rest indeed. The barren peaks about him were hammered out of the blackness again and again by the lightning and in the flare of that lightning he was surprised to see descending down through the rocky arroyos a troupe of men bearing torches in the rain and singing some low chant or prayer as they came. He raised himself up from his stone the better to make them out. He could see little more than their heads and shoulders jostling in the torchlight but they seemed to wear a variety of adorn-ments, primitive headpieces contrived from the feathers of birds or the hides of jungle cats. The fur of marmosets. They wore necklaces of bead or stone or ocean shell and shawls of woven stuff that may have been moss. By the smoky lamps hiss-ing in the rain he could see that they carried upon their shoul-ders a litter or bier and now he could hear echoing among the rocks the floating notes of a horn and the slow beat of a drum.

When they came into the road he could see them better. In the forefront was a man in a mask made from the carved shell of a seaturtle all inlaid with agate and jasper. He carried a scep-tre on the head of which was his own likeness and the likeness carried also such a sceptre in miniature and this sceptre too in what we must imagine to be some unknown infinitude of alter-nate being and likeness.

Behind him came the drummer with his drum of saltcured rawhide stretched upon a frame of ash and this he beat with a sort of flail made of a hardwood ball tethered to a stick. The drum gave off a low note of great resonance and he struck it with an upward swing of the flail and at each beat he bent his head to listen as perhaps a man might who were tuning a drum.

There followed a man bearing a sheathed sword upon a leather cushion and after him the bearers of torches and then the litter and the men who carried it. The traveler could not tell if the person they carried were alive or if this were not perhaps some sort of funeral procession passing through the mountains in the rain and the night. At the rear of the enfilade came the horns-man bearing an instrument made of cane bound with wrappings of copper wire and hung with tassels. He played it by blowing through a length of tubing and it played three notes which hovered in the shrouded night air above them like a ponderable body itself.

How many of these people were there?

I believe eight.

Go ahead.

They advanced upon the road and the traveler sat up and swung his legs over the side of his altarstone and pulled the blanket about his shoulders and waited. They came on until they were opposite to the place where he sat and here they stopped and here they stood. The traveler watched them. If he was curious he was also afraid.

What about you?

I was only curious.

How did you know he was afraid?

The man studied the empty roadway beneath them. After a while he said: This man was not me. If he may have been some part of me that I do not recognize then so may you. I fall back upon my argument of common histories.

Where were you all this time?

Asleep in my bed.

You were not in the dream.

No.

Billy leaned and spat. Well, he said, I'm seventy-eight years old and in that time I've had a lot of dreams. And as near as I can recollect I was in ever one of em. I dont recall a time that I ever dreamt about other people but what I wasnt around some-wheres. My notion is that you pretty much dream about yourself. I even dreamt one time that I was dead. But I was standin there looking at the corpse.

I see, the man said.

What do you see?

I see you've thought a bit about dreams.

I aint thought about em at all. I've just had em.

Can we come back to this question?

You can do whatever you want.

Thank you.

You sure you aint makin all this up.

The man smiled. He looked out across the roadway and the fields and shook his head but he didnt answer.

Or did you want to come back to that?

The problem is that your question is the very question upon which the story hangs.

A tractor-trailer passed overhead and the swallows nesting in the concrete coves flew forth and circled and returned.

Bear with me, the man said. This story like all stories has its beginnings in a question. And those stories which speak to us with the greatest resonance have a way of turning upon the teller and erasing him and his motives from all memory. So the question of who is telling the story is very consiguiente.

Every story is not about some question.

Yes it is. Where all is known no narrative is possible.

Billy leaned and spat again. Ándale, he said.

He was curious and afraid this traveler and he called out to the processional some greeting which echoed among the rocks. He asked them where they were bound but never did they answer back. They stood in the old road through the pass huddled together, these mute and midnight folk with their torches and their instruments and their captive, and they waited. As if he were a mystery to them. Or as if he were expected to say some particular thing which he had yet to say.

He was really asleep.

That is my view.

And if he had of woke?

Then what he saw he would no longer see. Nor I.

Why couldnt you just say it would of vanished or disappeared?

Which?

Which what?

Desaparecer o desvanecerse.

Hay una diferencia?

Sí. Lo que se desvanece es simplemente fuera de la vista. Pero desaparecido? He shrugged. Where do things go? In a case such as that of the traveler and his adventures—where one is on uncertain ground to even say from whence they came at all—there seems little to be said as to where they might be when gone. In such a case one can come upon no footing where even to begin.

Can I say somethin?

Of course.

I think you got a habit of makin things a bit more complicated than what they need to be. Why not just tell the story?

Good advice. Let's see what can be done.

Ándale pues.

Although I should point out to you that you are the one with the questions.

No you shouldnt.

Yes. Of course.

Just get on with it.

Yes.

Mum's the word here.

Cómo?

Nothin. I'll shut up askin questions, that's all.

They were good questions.

You aint goin to tell the story, are you?

So perhaps he struggled to wake. For all that the night was cold and his bed hard stone he could not. In the meantime all was silence. The rain had ceased. The wind. The processioners consulted among themselves and then the bearers came forward and set the litter on the rocky ground. Upon the litter lay

a young girl with eyes closed and hands crossed upon her breast
as if in death. The dreamer looked at her and he looked at the
troupe standing about her. Cold as the night was and colder as
it must have been in the windswept reaches from which they
had descended they yet were thinly clothed and even the capes
and blankets that they wore over their shoulders were of
loosely woven stuff. In the light of their torches their faces and
their torsos shone with sweat. And strange as was their appearance and the mission they seemed bent upon yet they were also
oddly familiar. As if he'd seen all this somewhere before.

Like in a dream.

If you wish.

It aint up to me.

You think you know how this dream ends.

I got a notion or two.

We'll see.

Carry on.

With the troupe was a sort of chemist who carried in a belt at
his waist the nostrums of his trade and he and the leader of the
group conferred. The leader thumbed back the turtleshell to
the top of his head like a welder tipping back his mask but the
dreamer could not see his face. The outcome of their confer-
encing was that three of the halfnaked men from the company
detached themselves and approached the altarstone. They carried a flask and a cup and they set the cup upon the stone and
poured it full and offered it to the dreamer.

He better think twice.

Too late. He took it in both hands with the same gravity with
which it had been offered and raised it to his lips and drank.

What was in it?

I dont know.

What kind of cup?

A cup of horn heated in a fire and shaped so it would stand.

What did it do to him?

It caused him to forget.

What did he forget? Everthing?

He forgot the pain of his life. Nor did he understand the penalty for doing so.

Go ahead.

He drank it down and handed back the cup and almost at once all was taken from him so that he was like a child again and a great peace settled upon him and his fears abated to the point that he would become accomplice in a blood ceremony that was then and is now an affront to God.

Was that the penalty?

No. There was a greater cost even than that.

What was it?

That this too would be forgot.

Would that be such a bad idea?

Wait and see.

Go on.

He drank the cup and gave himself up to the dark mercies of these ancient serranos. And they in turn led him from the stone out into the road and they walked up and back with him. They seemed to be urging him to contemplate his surroundings, the rocks and the mountains, the stars which were belled above them against the eternal blackness of the world's nativity.

What were they sayin?

I dont know.

You couldnt hear them?

The man didnt answer. He sat pondering the forms of the concrete overhead. The nests of the swallows clung in the high corners like colonies of small mud hornos inverted there. The traffic had increased. The boxshaped shadows which the trucks shook off on entering beneath the overpass waited for them where they emerged into the sun again on the far side. He lifted one hand in a slow tossing gesture. There is no way to answer your question. It is not the case that there are small men in your head holding a conversation. There is no sound. So what language is that? In any case this was a deep dream for the dreamer and in such dreams there is a language that is older than the spoken word at all. The idiom is another specie and with it there can be no lie or no dissemblance of the truth.

I thought you said they were talkin.

In my dream of them perhaps they were talking. Or perhaps I was only putting upon it the best construction that I knew. The traveler's dream is another matter.

Go ahead.

The ancient world holds us to account. The world of our fathers . . .

It seems to me if they were talkin in your dream they'd have to be talkin in his. It's the same dream.

It's the same question.

What's the answer?

We're coming to that.

Ándale.

The world of our fathers resides within us. Ten thousand generations and more. A form without a history has no power to perpetuate itself. What has no past can have no future. At the core of our life is the history of which it is composed and in that core are no idioms but only the act of knowing and it is this we share in dreams and out. Before the first man spoke and after the last is silenced forever. Yet in the end he did speak, as we shall see.

All right.

So he walked with his captors until his mind was calm and he knew that his life was now in other hands.

There dont seem to be much fight in him.

You forget the hostage.

The girl.

Yes.

Go on.

It is important to understand that he did not give himself up willingly. The martyr who longs for the flames can be no right candidate for them. Where there is no penalty there can be no prize. You understand.

Go on.

They seemed to be waiting for him to come to some decision. To tell them something perhaps. He studied everything about him that could be studied. The stars and the rocks and the face of the sleeping girl upon her pallet. His captors. Their helmets and their costumes. The torches which they carried that were made of hollow pipes filled with oil and wicks of rope and the flames which were sheltered from the wind by panes of isinglass set into caming and roofed and flued with beaten copper sheet. He tried to see into their eyes but those eyes were dark and they had shadowed them with blacking like men called upon to traverse wastes of snow. Or sand. He tried to see their feet how they were shod but their robes fell over the rocks about them and he could not. What he saw was the strangeness of the world and how little was known and how poorly one could prepare for aught that was to come. He saw that a man's life was little more than an instant and that as time was eternal therefore every man was always and eternally in the middle of his journey, whatever be his years or whatever distance he had come. He thought he saw in the world's silence a great conspiracy and he knew that he himself must then be a part of that conspiracy and that he had already moved beyond his captors and their plans. If he had any revelation it was this: that he was repository to this knowing which he came to solely by his abandonment of every former view. And with this he turned to his captors and he said: I will tell you nothing.

I will tell you nothing. That is what he said and that is all he said. In the next moment they led him to the stone and laid him down upon it and they raised up the girl from her pallet and led her forward. Her bosom was heaving.

Her what?

Her bosom was heaving.

Go ahead.

She leaned and kissed him and stepped away and then the archatron came forward with his sword and raised it in his two hands above him and clove the traveler's head from his body.

I guess that was the end of that.

Not at all.

I suppose you're fixin to tell me he survived havin his head lopped off.

Yes. He woke from his dream and sat shivering with cold and fright. In the selfsame desolate pass. The selfsame barren range of mountains. The selfsame world.

And you?

The narrator smiled wistfully, like a man remembering his childhood. These dreams reveal the world also, he said. We wake remembering the events of which they are composed while often the narrative is fugitive and difficult to recall. Yet it is the narrative that is the life of the dream while the events themselves are often interchangeable. The events of the waking world on the other hand are forced upon us and the narrative is the unguessed axis along which they must be strung. It falls to us to weigh and sort and order these events. It is we who assemble them into the story which is us. Each man is the bard of his own existence. This is how he is joined to the world. For escaping from the world's dream of him this is at once his penalty and his reward. So. I might have woken then myself but as the world neared so did the traveler upon his rock begin to fade and as I was not yet willing to part company with him I called out to him.

Did he have a name?

No. No name.

What did you call?

I simply called upon him to stay and stay he did and so I slept on and the traveler turned to me and waited.

I guess he was surprised to see you.

A good question. He seemed indeed to be surprised and yet in dreams it is often the case that the greatest extravagances seem bereft of their power to astonish and the most improbable chimeras appear commonplace. Our waking life's desire to shape the world to our convenience invites all manner of paradox and difficulty. All in our custody seethes with an inner restlessness. But in dreams we stand in this great democracy of the possible and there we are right pilgrims indeed. There we go forth to meet what we shall meet.

I got another question.

You want to know if the traveler knew that he'd been dreaming. If indeed he had been dreaming.

Like you say, you've told the story before.

Yes.

What's the answer.

You might not like it.

That ought not to stop you.

He asked me the same question.

He wanted to know if he'd been dreaming?

Yes.

What did he say?

He asked me if I had seen them.

Them people with the robes and the candles and all.

Yes.

And.

Well. I had. Of course.

So that's what you told him.

I told him the truth.

Well it would have served as well for a lie wouldnt it?

Because?

If it caused him to believe that what he dreamt was real.

Yes. You see the difficulty.

Billy leaned and spat. He studied the landscape to the north. I better get on, he said. I got a ways to go.

You have people waiting for you?

I hope so. I sure would like to see them.

He wished me to be his witness. But in dreams there can be no witness. You said as much yourself.

It was just a dream. You dreamt him. You can make him do whatever you like.

Where was he before I dreamt him?

You tell me.

My belief is this, and I say it again: His history is the same as yours or mine. That is the stuff he is made of. What stuff other? Had I created him as God makes men how then would I not know what he would say before he ever spoke? Or how he'd move before he did so? In a dream we dont know what's coming. We are surprised.

All right.

So where is it coming from?

I dont know.

Two worlds touch here. You think men have power to call forth what they will? Evoke a world, awake or sleeping? Make it breathe and then set out upon it figures which a glass gives back or which the sun acknowledges? Quicken those figures with one's own joy and one's despair? Can a man be so hid from himself? And if so who is hid? And from whom?

You call forth the world which God has formed and that world only. Nor is this life of yours by which you set such store your doing, however you may choose to tell it. Its shape was forced in the void at the onset and all talk of what might otherwise have been is senseless for there is no otherwise. Of what could it be made? Where be hid? Or how make its appearance? The probability of the actual is absolute. That we have no power to guess it out beforehand makes it no less certain. That we may imagine alternate histories means nothing at all.

So is that the end of the story?

No. The traveler stood at the stone and on the stone visible to see were marks of axe and sword and the dark oxidations of the blood of those who'd died there and which the weathers of the world were powerless to erase. Here the traveler had lain down to sleep with no thought of death and yet when he awoke he'd no thought other. The heavens which he had been invited to scrutinize by his executioners now wore a different look. The order of his life seemed altered in midstride. Some halt-stitch in the workings of things. Those heavens in whose forms men see commensurate destinies cognate to their own now seemed to pulse with a reckless energy. As if in their turning things had come uncottered, uncalendared. He thought that there might even be some timefault in the record. That henceforth there might be no way to log new sightings. Would that matter?

You're askin me.

Yes.

I think it would matter to you. About him I got no idea. What do you think?

The narrator paused thoughtfully. I think, he said, that the dreamer imagined himself at some crossroads. Yet there are no crossroads. Our decisions do not have some alternative. We may contemplate a choice but we pursue one path only. The log of the world is composed of its entries, but it cannot be divided back into them. And at some point this log must outdistance any possible description of it and this I believe is what the dreamer saw. For as the power to speak of the world recedes from us so also must the story of the world lose its thread and therefore its authority. The world to come must be composed of what is past. No other material is at hand. And yet I think he saw the world unraveling at his feet. The procedures which he had adopted for his journey now seemed like an echo from the death of things. I think he saw a terrible darkness looming.

I need to be gettin on.

The man did not answer. He sat contemplating the roadside vegas and the barren lands beyond now shimmering in the newest sun.

This desert about us was once a vast sea, he said. Can such a thing vanish? Of what are seas made? Or I? Or you?

I dont know.

The man stood up and stretched. He stretched mightily, reaching and turning. He looked down at Billy and smiled.

And that's the end of the story, Billy said.

No.

He squatted and held up his hand, palm out.

Hold up your hand, he said. Like this.

Is this a pledge of some kind?

No. You are pledged already. You always were. Hold up your hand.

He held up his hand as the man had asked.

You see the likeness?

Yes.

Yes. It is senseless to claim that things exist in their instancing only. The template for the world and all in it was drawn long ago. Yet the story of the world, which is all the world we know, does not exist outside of the instruments of its execution. Nor can those instruments exist outside of their own history. And so on. This life of yours is not a picture of the world. It is the world itself and it is composed not of bone or dream or time but of worship. Nothing else can contain it. Nothing else be by it contained.

So what happened to the traveler?

Nothing. There is no end to the story. He woke and all was as before. He was free to go.

To other men's dreams.

Perhaps. Of such dreams and of the rituals of them there can also be no end. The thing that is sought is altogether other. However it may be construed within men's dreams or by their acts it will never make a fit. These dreams and these acts are driven by a terrible hunger. They seek to meet a need which they can never satisfy, and for that we must be grateful.

And you were still asleep.

Yes. At the end of the dream we walked out in the dawn and there was an encampment on the plains below from which no smoke rose for all that it was cold and we went down to that place but all was abandoned there. There were huts of skin staked out upon the rocky ground with slagiron pikes and within these huts were remnants of old meals untouched and cold upon cold plates of clay. There were standing stores of primitive and antique arms carved in their metal parts and inlaid with filigree of gold and there were robes sewn up from skins of northern animals and rawhide trunks with latches and corners of hammered copper and these were much scarred from their travels and the years of it and inside of them were old accounts and ledgerbooks and records of the history of that vanished folk, the path they had followed in the world and their reckonings of the cost of that journey. And in a place apart a skeleton of old sepia bones sewn up in a leather shroud.

We walked together through all that desolation and all that abandonment and I asked him if the people were away at some calling but he said that they were not. When I asked him to tell me what had happened he looked at me and he said: I have been here before. So have you. Everything is here for the taking. Touch nothing. Then I woke.

From his dream or yours?

There was only one dream to wake from. I woke from that world to this. Like the traveler, all I had forsaken I would come upon again.

What had you forsaken?

The immappable world of our journey. A pass in the mountains. A bloodstained stone. The marks of steel upon it. Names carved in the corrosible lime among stone fishes and ancient shells. Things dim and dimming. The dry sea floor. The tools of migrant hunters. The dreams enchased upon the blades of them. The peregrine bones of a prophet. The silence. The gradual extinction of rain. The coming of night.

I got to get on.

I wish you well, cuate.

And you.

I hope your friends await you.

And I.

Every man's death is a standing in for every other. And since death comes to all there is no way to abate the fear of it except to love that man who stands for us. We are not waiting for his history to be written. He passed here long ago. That man who is all men and who stands in the dock for us until our own time come and we must stand for him. Do you love him, that

man? Will you honor the path he has taken? Will you listen to
his tale?

HE SLEPT THAT NIGHT in a concrete tile by the highwayside
where a roadcrew had been working. A big yellow Euclid truck
was standing out on the mud and the pale and naked concrete
pillars of an east-west onramp stood beyond the truck, curving
away, clustered and rising without capital or pediment like the
ruins of some older order standing in the dusk. In the night a
wind blew down from the north that bore the taste of rain but
no rain fell. He could smell the wet creosote out on the desert.
He tried to sleep. After a while he got up and sat in the round
mouth of the tile like a man in a bell and looked out upon the
darkness. Out on the desert to the west stood what he took for
one of the ancient spanish missions of that country but when he
studied it again he saw that it was the round white dome of a
radar tracking station. Beyond that and partly overcast also in
the moonlight he saw a row of figures struggling and clamoring
silently in the wind. They appeared to be dressed in robes and
some among them fell down in their struggling and rose to flail
again. He thought they must be laboring toward him across the
darkened desert yet they made no progress at all. They had the
look of inmates in a madhouse palely gowned and pounding
mutely at the glass of their keeping. He called to them but his
shout was carried away on the wind and in any case they were
too far to hear him. After a while he rolled himself again in his
blanket on the floor of the tile and after a while he slept. In the
morning the storm had passed and what he saw out on the
desert in the new day's light were only rags of plastic wrapping
hanging from a fence where the wind had blown them.

He made his way east to De Baca County in New Mexico
and he looked for the grave of his sister but he could not find it.
The people of that country were kind to him and the days
warmed and he wanted for little in his life on the road. He
stopped to talk to children or to horses. Women fed him in

their kitchens and he slept rolled in his blanket under the stars and watched meteorites fall down the sky. He drank one evening from a spring beneath a cottonwood, leaning to bow his mouth and suck from the cold silk top of the water and watch the minnows drift and recover in the current beneath him. There was a tin cup on a stob and he took it down and sat holding it. He'd not seen a cup at a spring in years and he held it in both hands as had thousands before him unknown to him yet joined in sacrament. He dipped the cup into the water and raised it cool and dripping to his mouth.

In the fall of that year when the cold weather came he was taken in by a family just outside of Portales New Mexico and he slept in a shed room off the kitchen that was much like the room he'd slept in as a boy. On the hallway wall hung a framed photograph that had been printed from a glass plate broken into five pieces and in the photograph certain ancestors were puzzled back together in a study that cohered with its own slightly skewed geometry. Apportioning some third or separate meaning to each of the figures seated there. To their faces. To their forms.

The family had a girl twelve and a boy fourteen and their father had bought them a colt they kept stabled in a shed behind the house. It wasnt much of a colt but he went out in the afternoon when they came in off the schoolbus and showed them how to work the colt with rope and halter. The boy liked the colt but the girl was in love with it and she'd go out at night after supper in the cold and sit in the straw floor of the shed and talk to it.

In the evening after supper sometimes the woman would invite him to play cards with them and sometimes he and the children would sit at the kitchen table and he'd tell them about horses and cattle and the old days. Sometimes he'd tell them about Mexico.

One night he dreamt that Boyd was in the room with him but he would not speak for all that he called out to him. When he woke the woman was sitting on his bed with her hand on his shoulder.

Mr Parham are you all right?

Yes mam. I'm sorry. I was dreamin, I reckon.

You sure you okay?

Yes mam.

Did you want me to bring you a sup of water?

No mam. I appreciate it. I'll get back to sleep here directly.

You want me to leave the light on in the kitchen?

If you wouldnt mind.

All right.

I thank you.

Boyd was your brother.

Yes. He's been dead many a year.

You still miss him though.

Yes I do. All the time.

Was he the younger?

He was. By two years.

I see.

He was the best. We run off to Mexico together. When we was kids. When our folks died. We went down there to see about gettin back some horses they'd stole. We was just kids. He was awful good with horses. I always liked to watch him ride. Liked to watch him around horses. I'd give about anything to see him one more time.

You will.

I hope you're right.

You sure you dont want a glass of water?

No mam. I'm all right.

She patted his hand. Gnarled, ropescarred, speckled from the sun and the years of it. The ropy veins that bound them to his heart. There was map enough for men to read. There God's plenty of signs and wonders to make a landscape. To make a world. She rose to go.

Betty, he said.

Yes.

I'm not what you think I am. I aint nothin. I dont know why you put up with me.

Well, Mr Parham, I know who you are. And I do know why. You go to sleep now. I'll see you in the morning.

Yes mam.

DEDICATION

I will be your child to hold
And you be me when I am old
The world grows cold
The heathen rage
The story's told
Turn the page.

ABOUT THE AUTHOR

CORMAC MCCARTHY is the author of *The Orchard Keeper, Outer Dark, Child of God, Suttree, Blood Meridian*, and the novels of the Border Trilogy. *All the Pretty Horses*, the first volume of the trilogy, won the National Book Award and the National Book Critics Circle Award.

CHINUA ACHEBE
Things Fall Apart

THE ARABIAN NIGHTS
(2 vols, tr. Husain Haddawy)

MARCUS AURELIUS
Meditations

JANE AUSTEN
Emma
Mansfield Park
Northanger Abbey
Persuasion
Pride and Prejudice
Sanditon and Other Stories
Sense and Sensibility

HONORÉ DE BALZAC
Cousin Bette
Eugénie Grandet
Old Goriot

SIMONE DE BEAUVOIR
The Second Sex

SAMUEL BECKETT
Molloy, Malone Dies,
The Unnamable

SAUL BELLOW
The Adventures of Augie March

WILLIAM BLAKE
Poems and Prophecies

JORGE LUIS BORGES
Ficciones

JAMES BOSWELL
The Life of Samuel Johnson

CHARLOTTE BRONTË
Jane Eyre
Villette

EMILY BRONTË
Wuthering Heights

MIKHAIL BULGAKOV
The Master and Margarita

SAMUEL BUTLER
The Way of all Flesh

ITALO CALVINO
If on a winter's night a traveler

ALBERT CAMUS
The Stranger

WILLA CATHER
Death Comes for the Archbishop
My Ántonia

MIGUEL DE CERVANTES
Don Quixote

GEOFFREY CHAUCER
Canterbury Tales

ANTON CHEKHOV
My Life and Other Stories
The Steppe and Other Stories

KATE CHOPIN
The Awakening

CARL VON CLAUSEWITZ
On War

SAMUEL TAYLOR
COLERIDGE
Poems

WILKIE COLLINS
The Moonstone
The Woman in White

JOSEPH CONRAD
Heart of Darkness
Lord Jim
Nostromo
The Secret Agent
Typhoon and Other Stories
Under Western Eyes
Victory

DANTE ALIGHIERI
The Divine Comedy

DANIEL DEFOE
Moll Flanders
Robinson Crusoe

CHARLES DICKENS
Bleak House
David Copperfield
Dombey and Son
Great Expectations
Hard Times
Little Dorrit
Martin Chuzzlewit
Nicholas Nickleby